PETER CAREY
Jack Maggs

First published in 1997
by Faber and Faber Ltd
This edition published by The Softback Preview, 1997

Photoset by Parker Typesetting Service, Leicester
Printed in England by Clays Ltd, St Ives plc

The translation from *Du magnétisme animal* is reprinted by permission
from Adam Crabtree, *From Mesmer to Freud: Magnetic Sleep and
the Roots of Psychological Healing* (Yale University Press, 1993)

A CIP record for this book is available
from the British Library

2 4 6 8 10 9 7 5 3 1

For Alison

Think of yourself as a magnet, with your arms and especially your hands as the two poles. Touch the patient by placing one hand on his back and the other, in opposition, on his stomach. Then imagine magnetic fluid circulating from one hand to the other . . .

Question: Should one vary this position?

Answer: Yes, you can place one hand on the head without moving the other, always continuing to maintain the same attention and having the same will to do good . . .

Question: What is an indication that a patient is susceptible to somnambulism?

Answer: When, during magnetisation of a patient, one notices that he experiences a numbness or light spasms accompanied by nervous shaking. Then if the eyes close, you should lightly rub them and the two eyebrows with your thumbs to prevent blinking . . .

Question: Are there different degrees of somnambulism?

Answer: Yes. Sometimes you can only produce drowsiness in a patient. Sometimes the effect of magnetism is to cause the eyes to close so the patient cannot open them; if he is aware of everything around him he is not completely in the magnetic state . . .

Question: How does one bring a patient out of a magnetic state?

Answer: . . . it is by an act of your will that you awaken him.

Question: You mean you only need to will him to open his eyes in order to awaken him?

Answer: This is the principal operation. After that, in order to connect your idea to its object, you might lightly rub his eyes, while willing that he open them; and the effect never fails to occur.

Du magnétisme animal (1820)
by Armand Marie Jacques de Chastenet, Marquis de Puységur.

It was a Saturday night when the man with the red waistcoat arrived in London. It was, to be precise, six of the clock on the fifteenth of April in the year of 1837 that those hooded eyes looked out the window of the Dover coach and beheld, in the bright aura of gas light, a golden bull and an overgrown mouth opening to devour him – the sign of his inn, the Golden Ox.

The *Rocket* (as his coach was aptly named) rattled in through the archway to the inn's yard and the passengers, who had hitherto found the stranger so taciturn, now noted the silver-capped cane – which had begun to tap the floor at Westminster Bridge – commence a veritable tattoo.

He was a tall man in his forties, so big in the chest and broad in the shoulder that his fellows on the bench seat had felt the strain of his presence, but what his occupation was, or what he planned to do in London, they had not the least idea. One privately imagined him a book-maker, another a gentleman farmer and a third, seeing the excellent quality of his waistcoat, imagined him an upper servant wearing his master's cast-off clothing.

His face did not deny the possibility of any of these occupations; indeed he would have been a singular example of any one of them. His brows pushed down hard upon the eyes, and his cheeks shone as if life had scrubbed at him and rubbed until the very bones beneath his flesh had been burnished in the process. His nose was large, hawkish, and high-bridged. His eyes were dark, inquiring, and yet there was a bruised, even belligerent quality which had kept his fellow passengers at their distance all through that long journey up from Dover.

No sooner had they heard the coachman's *Whoa-up* than he had the door open and was out into the night without having said a single word.

The first of the passengers to alight after him saw the stranger take the porter, a famously insolent individual, firmly by the shoulder blade. He held him there for a good moment, and it was obvious from the look which appeared on that sandy-haired individual's face, that he held him very hard indeed.

'Now pay attention to me, Sir Reverence.'

The porter was roughly escorted to the side of the coach.

'You comprennay-voo?' The stranger pointed with his cane to a large trunk on the roof. 'The blue item. If it would not inconvenience your Lordship.'

The porter made it clear that it would not inconvenience him in the least. Then some money changed hands and the man with the red waistcoat set off into the night, his cane tapping on the cobblestones, and straight up into the Haymarket, his chin up and the orbs of his eyes everywhere reflecting an unearthly flare and glare.

This light had shone all the way from the Elephant and Castle: gas light, blazing and streaming like great torches; sausages illuminated, fish and ice gleaming, chemist shops aglow like caves with their variegated vases illuminated from within. The city had become a fairground, and as the coach crossed the river at Westminster the stranger saw that even the bridges of the Thames were illuminated.

The entire Haymarket was like a grand ball. Not just the gas, the music, the dense, tight crowds. A man from the last century would not have recognized it; a man from even fifteen years before would have been confused. Dram shops had become gin palaces with their high great plate-glass windows, their engraved messages: 'Gin at Threepence – Generous Wines – Hot Spiced'. This one here – it was like a temple, damned if it was not, the door surrounded by stained panes of rich dye: rosettes, bunches of grapes. The big man pushed his way up to the bar and got himself a dram of brandy which he drank in a gulp. When he turned, his face revealed a momentary confusion.

Two children were now tugging around his sleeves but he seemed so little aware of their presence that he walked out into the street without once looking down at them.

All around him was uproar, din, the deafening rush, the smell of horse shit, soot, that old yellow smell of London Town.

'Come on, Guv, come with me.'

'Come on, Sir.'

A young woman with a feathered hat had placed her hand on his elbow: such a handsome face, such short legs. He tugged himself free, walked on a yard or so, and blew his great hawk's nose like a mighty trumpet. As he carefully refolded his handkerchief – a bright green Kingsman of an earlier time – he inadvertently revealed the stumps of the two middle fingers on his left hand, a sight which had already excited curiosity aboard the *Rocket*.

His Kingsman safely put away for the moment, he started along the Strand, then seemed to change his mind, for a moment later he was heading up Agar Street, then cutting up to Maiden Lane.

In Floral Street, he paused before the now illuminated window of McClusky's Pudding Shop. He blew his nose again, whether from soot or sentiment the face gave no indication, and then, having entered that famously lopsided little shop, emerged with a syrup dumpling sprinkled liberally with confectioner's sugar. He ate the dumpling in the street, still walking. What he began in Floral Street he finished back on St Martin's Lane. Here, just a little south of Seven Dials, the stranger stood on a quiet dark corner, alone, free from the blaze of gas.

It was Cecil Street he had come to, a very short street linking Cross Street to St Martin's Lane. He dusted down his face carefully with his kerchief, and then set off into the darkness, peering to find what street numbers he could see – none.

He had almost arrived at the great river of Cross Street, with its noise and congestion of gigs and post-chaises, hackney cabs and dog-carts, when he came upon a single phaeton stopped in the street. It was a most expensive equipage, that much was clear even in the dark, and indeed, once he had crossed the street, there was sufficient light to make out a gold coronet emblazoned on the shining black door. From inside he could hear the sound of a young woman weeping.

A moment later, he would have been in Cross Street. However, the door of the carriage opened and a matron in a long dress descended from the coach and addressed the person still seated inside. 'Good night, Mum,' she said.

3

Hearing this voice, the stranger stopped abruptly in his tracks.

The phaeton drove off but the stranger stayed very still in the shadow of a doorway whilst the matron opened the gate leading to a high narrow house directly opposite him. A feeble yellow light showed through the fan light above the front door.

Then he spoke: 'Excuse me, Missus, but is this Number Four?'

'If you've come for tablets, come back tomorrow.'

'Mary Britten,' he said.

He could hear her rattling a big bunch of keys.

'You come back tomorrow,' she said.

The stranger stepped into the middle of the street.

'Get a lamp, Mary.'

'Who's that?'

'Someone you should recognize, Mary Britten.'

She remained with her back to him, still busy with her bunch of keys. 'It's dark. Come back tomorrow.'

'Someone you should recognize covered with soot.'

Finally, she found the right key. The door swung open, and the feeble yellow light – there was an oil lamp burning in the hallway of the house – revealed a tall, handsome woman in a long dress: blue or green, very fancy-looking, shimmering like silk. She hesitated a moment, an old lady, all of seventy years, but such was her carriage and her bearing that she would pass, in this light anyway, for fifty.

'So this is Cecil Street,' he said. 'I thought it would be posher.'

She hesitated, peering into the night, one hand ready on the door handle. 'What you doing here?' she whispered. 'You're a dead man if they find you.'

'That's a nice home-coming.'

'Don't bring your trouble here,' she said.

'You got respectable.'

'You come to put the bite?'

'I'm doing well myself,' the stranger said. 'You going to ask me in?'

She made no move to offer an invitation, but her tone did become more solicitous. 'They treat you bad?'

'Bad enough.'

'How'd you know I was here?'

'I saw your puff in the newspaper.'

'And now you've come home to play the old dart, you varmint.'

'No, Ma. I'm retired. I come here for the culture.'

She laughed harshly. 'The operah?'

'Oh yes,' said the stranger seriously. 'The opera, the theatre, I got a lot of time to make up for.'

'Well, I must go to bed, Jack. So you must forgive me not inviting you in to have a chat.'

'Perhaps I'll look up Tom.'

'Oh Jesus, Jack. '

'What?'

'You bastard,' she cried with real emotion. 'You know he's dead.'

'No! No, I never.'

'God help me, Jack, God save me. I ain't so green as that. I know who you paid. I know how it were arranged and all.'

'I didn't pay no one nothing, I swear.'

'What do you want, Jack?' said the old woman, and this time her voice quavered. 'What're you doing here in London?'

'It's my home,' Jack said, raising his voice and revealing the fiercer character which the porter at the Golden Ox had briefly glimpsed. 'That's what I want. My home.'

'I still got my Bilboa, so don't think I wouldn't use it.'

The stranger shook his head, and laughed. 'You worried I might have a bone to pick with you, Ma?'

'Aren't you worried someone's going to hang you, Jack?' Having made this bitter speech, she stepped inside the house and closed the door behind her.

'I'm coming back, Ma.'

There was no retort from inside the house, merely the heavy clanking of some chains which seemed to amuse the visitor.

'I'll be back tomorrow morning. We'll have a proper chat when I come back.'

There is no doubt that Jack Maggs planned to keep his promise, but the morrow held events he could not foresee. Three weeks would pass before he would call at Cecil Street again.

5

Great Queen Street had once been home to the pugnacious Lord Herbert of Cherbury. Lord Bristol had lived there. Also Lord Chancellor Finch, and the Conway and Paulett families. But on that damp Sunday morning when Jack Maggs came marching up from Long Acre with his silver-capped cane tucked under his arm, all that remained of the Golden Age were some pilasters and other ornaments still clinging to the façades of a few houses on the west.

There was now a tobacconist in Great Queen Street, a laundry, and a narrow little workroom where glass eyes were made for dolls and injured gentlemen. Actors lived in rooms at Number 30. A retired grocer from Clerkenwell now had the leasehold to Number 29.

But it was Number 27 which seemed to take Jack Maggs's close attention, and he stood across the street and stared at it very hard. It was a handsome house – four storeys, a high iron fence, a pretty gate leading down to the servants' entrance. It had a bright front door, a brass door knocker, a fan light, and such was his excitement to behold this property that the left side of his firmly sculpted face was soon visibly quivering.

A dog cart came travelling pell mell down the street towards Long Acre with its driver, a young man no more than twenty years, standing upright in the seat. All the visitor's attention was on the house, until the moment the driver cracked his whip.

Then Jack Maggs jumped out of his skin. He stepped out into the road, and raised his stick as if he intended to chase the offender and punish him, but a moment later he was a perfect gent, presenting himself on the doorstep of 27 Great Queen Street with his distress reduced to a small flickering on his left cheek.

Jack Maggs Esquire removed his hat and grasped that brass knocker. He knocked quickly, firmly, but politely.

When there was no immediate answer, he knocked again. And then, a minute later – Rap-rap-rap.

It was not possible that there was no one home. The caller was well-informed about the residents of 27 Great Queen Street. There was a butler in this house, a housekeeper, a cook.

He stepped back onto the edge of the roadside so he might look up at the high windows. He observed their dark and curtained aspect with agitated eyes, then, turning impulsively, he opened the little gate leading down to the servants' entrance.

It was at this moment that Mercy Larkin came to the parlour window of the house next door. Mercy was the kitchen maid, by title, but being the *only* maid in that confusing household, was presently arranging her employer's small library of books where he liked them set – upon the little cedar dresser with the oilcloth square atop it.

She saw the man she would soon know as Jack Maggs descending the steps to the servants' entrance of Number 27. He had come, so she imagined, to take Mrs Halfstairs's examination for the post of footman. The moment she saw him, she knew he was the one. He had the right size, the right legs, but was at the wrong address.

Then Jack Maggs turned and caught her eye. It was not really a footman's face, or no footman she had ever seen. She stood at the parlour window, her duster in her hand, and shivered.

Jack Maggs had not the least knowledge of Mercy Larkin, Mrs Halfstairs or the rest of Mr Buckle's chaotic household, but as he shut the area gate behind him he saw the maid was still staring at him. He saw her pale skin, her pretty ringlets spilling out from under her cap. Had you asked him his impression of her appearance, he would not have heard your question. He had been spotted. He felt the rough rope of Newgate round his neck.

He descended the last steps, escaping her gaze. With his broad back pressed against the wall, he could look into the kitchen. It was his profession to recognize an empty house when he saw one, and this house was like a grave. And yet he knocked, tapping and scratching against the pane.

'Excuse me down there.'

He resisted the urge to flatten himself further against the wall, but rather stepped out where the maid could inspect him.

'All's well,' he smiled. It was an easy smile, and his teeth were very good and regular. 'I'm expected.'

'They've gone,' the maid said, staring at him very hard. 'No one home but draughts and mice.'

'Gone?' he said hoarsely.

'You've come to see about the footman's position, am I right now?' The stranger smiled.

'It's Mr Buckle's residence you were wanting,' she suggested.

'Gone where? Where have they gone? I am expected.' He ascended the stairs to the street.

'Gone to Calais,' she said. 'The Spanish Main. How would I know? The gentleman didn't have the manners to inform me of his destination.'

The stranger was now at the top of the area steps, and Mercy could see that he had a twitching palsy in his cheek. He put his hand to it.

'Sometimes,' Mercy continued, 'they send a servant in a coach, but no one stays for long.'

'So they are not gone totally?' he asked.

'As I said, they come and go.' She paused. 'I really thought you were come to be our footman. Mrs Halfstairs is most particular about the height of our second footman. She is sitting in there with her ruler.'

'Footman?'

'You're the height, and all. It's a right shame you're not a footman. You're not a footman?' she repeated.

He watched her say it, like you watch an auctioneer raise a hammer, but in truth he had already decided what he was to do.

'I'm *their* footman,' he said. 'I'm Mr Phipps's new footman.'

'So you *are* a footman,' she said, smiling. 'I knew you was a footman.'

'Of course I am the footman, girl. I am a footman to young Mr Phipps who has all my papers,' Jack Maggs said to the maid. 'My letters of recommendation, all locked inside. What is a man to do now?'

'Perhaps you were late.'

'Late?' he cried, thumping his stick on the footpath. 'I am never late. I was first footman to Lord Logan who perished in the fire in Glasgow.'

8

'Mercy Larkin,' said a female voice from downstairs at Number 29. 'Come down from there immediately.'

'It is a footman,' the maid explained, 'most tragically positioned.'

3

Mr Percy Buckle was the owner of a gentleman's residence at 29 Great Queen Street, but he was no more a gentleman than the man who was presently entering his household in disguise.

A year before he had been a humble grocer in Clerkenwell, and for years before that time he had been well known, around the tap rooms and penny gaffs of Limehouse, as a seller of fried fish.

Then, on a brisk autumn morning in 1836, Percy Buckle had 'my little visit from the solicitor', as a result of which good fortune he became, in two short months, the master of a household in Great Queen Street and the owner of the Lyceum Theatre on Holborn Hill.

Having spent a lifetime laboriously elevating himself from fried-fish man to grocer, this inheritance came as a great shock. He was at first rather feverish and dizzy, and could take nothing stronger than the toast and broth brought to him by the daughter of the mad woman he employed to scrub his stairs. For days he tried to follow the dark and slippery lines of blood and law that had led from the body of a deceased stranger to his door in Clerkenwell. He lay in his newly pressed night shirt, in his freshly laundered sheets, and looked at the small square of neat sunshine as it passed across his bedroom wall.

Then on the third morning – Guy Fawkes Day, in fact – the fever lifted. Percy Buckle looked around his little room and knew he never had to weigh a pound of flour again in his life.

I can read all day.

Even as a grocer he had been a bookish fellow. All his life it had been the same – even when he was too tired to manage more than half a page of *Ivanhoe* in a night, even when he smelt inescapably of sprats and mackerel, he had been a member of a lending library, and a regular attendant at the Workingman's Institute.

9

He sat up in bed and smoothed his neat little moustache, and those mild blue eyes began to show a heat that could normally only be induced by learned men discussing anaesthesia or mechanics in a draughty hall.

Within a week he had given the contents of his grocer's shop to the Parish. He had found a tailor. He had been to Fletcher's Bookshop in Piccadilly and purchased the complete set of Gibbon's *Decline and Fall*. He had moved to Great Queen Street where he was pleased to employ his charwoman's daughter as a kitchen maid. Indeed, he was already exceedingly fond of Mercy Larkin and would have made her housekeeper had not he discovered the household overrun with servants who were still waiting to have their wages – not paid on the last quarter day – settled by the Estate.

It took a week or so for Mr Buckle to understand that he had inherited not only a house, but a bibulous and senile butler named Spinks, two footmen, a cook, and a housekeeper who had made herself queen over the butler. Sometimes it seemed to Mr Buckle that it was too small a house to have ever held so many servants, but his benefactor, it seemed, had been as fond of them as of his cats, and Mr Buckle was prepared to be fond of them as well.

He allowed the cats – there were five of them – to come and go through the open window of the drawing room. He saw no harm in them. Indeed he was soon accustomed to having both a marmalade and a tabby asleep on his chest, purring.

He also saw no harm in letting the red-nosed butler snore in front of the silver plate, although – to be quite clear on this matter – he lacked the nerve to tell the pompous old man to stop his tippling. He was a little frightened of the housekeeper, but as she bought her bacon at sixpence the pound he comforted himself that she was capable. There is, he told himself, no point in having a dog and barking too. By which he meant that it was best to leave the running of his domestic affairs to those who were most experienced in that field. He ate kippers for his breakfast and spent his days away from the house, at the library, the museum, and the theatre.

It was into this household that Jack Maggs was brought by Mercy Larkin. The newcomer found the smell of cats to be rather strong at first, but the claret which he was shortly sharing with the butler pushed that matter from his mind. He lunched on cold roast beef with the upstairs and downstairs servants, and was then brought into the presence of the housekeeper, a Mrs Halfstairs.

Mrs Halfstairs had herself seated in her Office, a peculiarly placed room, neither of the basement nor the ground floor, but located like a hunter's hide in the branches of a tree, reached either by ladder from the cellar, or a set of steep little stairs from the kitchen. Here she sat in state, surrounded by all manner of mementos relating to her brother, a Captain in the 57th Foot Regiment who had fought in those long-ago battles of Vittoria and Nive. Here, she had opened her housekeeper's journal and set about interviewing the latest candidate.

Jack Maggs was not a footman. He could not produce a letter of reference. But he was the right height, and he stood before Mrs Halfstairs with his legs astride, his hands behind his back, the scarred stumps of the two middle fingers hidden in his folded hand.

Mrs Halfstairs was a bully and a tyrant to all who came under her rule. Jack Maggs saw that and did not care. He explained to Mrs Halfstairs how it was that his references had been locked away by Mr Henry Phipps, and when he saw how ready she was to believe him, the last of his agitation left him and he began to feel a little sleepy.

Part of this drowsiness was produced by the reprieve from immediate danger, but the greatest soporific – one he had been prone to since his earliest years – was the distinctive aromas of plenty: hanging hams, barrels of apples, beeswax, even the smell of turpentine.

Mrs Halfstairs was a round-faced little woman with tightly wound grey hair. She was not quite fat but was solid and clumpish with thick wrists and narrow, distinctively pointed fingers which she now extended to pick up a rather ill-used looking quill.

'Height?' she demanded.

Jack Maggs woke himself enough to reply that he was a little under six foot.

The little soldier beetle made a fast, irritable entry in the back pages of her journal.

'A little under?' she said. 'With respect, that is exactly what I would expect from someone in Mr Phipps's employ. A little under!'

'An inch,' the applicant submitted.

'So I must do my own subtraction. But can you swear to an inch, or is it really an inch and a quarter?'

'I'm afraid I couldn't say, Ma'am.'

'Did Mr Phipps's housekeeper not measure you?'

'No, Ma'am, she did not.'

'I think Mr Phipps's first footman is rather stunted,' she frowned. 'I really can't imagine what he had in mind. I'm sure he did not have a *prank* in mind. A tall one and a short one, eh? That would be like him, from what I have heard. Japes and high-jinks. Do you think that was his plan?'

'I would not imagine so, Ma'am.'

'But who would?' said Mrs Halfstairs. 'Who would imagine what the gentleman ever had in his mind?'

Jack Maggs sensed, even before Mrs Halfstairs pulled the bell, that he was to be employed. She put down her quill, clasped her little hands, and gazed at his sturdy legs with undisguised satisfaction.

'Maggs,' she murmured to herself.

When Mercy Larkin answered the bell Mrs Halfstairs did not allow herself be distracted from her contemplation of the applicant's anatomy.

'Fetch Constable,' she said.

'I think Mr Constable is still indisposed.'

'Fetch him,' said Mrs Halfstairs, 'immediately.' Then, returning to Jack Maggs, offered the following appraisal: 'My impression is, you are five foot eleven and a half inches tall, and with your hair soaped and powdered, it will raise you to six feet.. There is nothing more calculated to ruin a carriage or a dinner table than mismatched footmen. Where is that fellow?'

No sooner had the question been asked than the low door opened and a man of most un-footman-like appearance entered the room. His hair was wild, his eyes red, his wide high cheekbones coloured with what appeared to be ashes. He was dressed in breeches and braces and a white shirt which – being unbuttoned at the neck, and flowing at the tail – gave him a wretched and tormented appearance. When he saw Jack Maggs he bestowed upon him a look of intense malevolence.

'Back to back,' said Mrs Halfstairs.

It was not clear to the applicant what the little woman meant, but the wild man with the blackened face seemed to understand for, with an obedience that belied his wild expression, he turned his back and stood erect.

'Bookends,' said Mrs Halfstairs. 'Bookends, if you please Mr Maggs.'

It took a moment to get her meaning, but then he saw it: he was to stand back-to-back with Constable.

When the humiliating little act was duly performed, it produced in Mrs Halfstairs an almost touching degree of satisfaction.

'Oh my goodness,' she said as she surveyed them. 'Oh my goodness dearie me.'

Her round, small face was stretched tight by a smile which displayed, for the first time, very short lower teeth of quite remarkable regularity.

Behind his back, Jack heard Constable sniff.

'Very good,' said Mrs Halfstairs. 'Very good indeed. Mr Spinks will indeed be pleased, as will our master.' She took up the quill and, dipping it in the ink-well, composed a few lines. Having blotted them carefully, and sealed them in a long thin envelope with all the formality one might expect in issuing an invitation to a ball, she instructed the applicant to deliver the missive to the butler, Mr Spinks, and to remind that gentleman that the new man would need to be 'kitted out' for the dinner that evening.

Jack Maggs ascended the tight little stairs to the kitchen, knowing himself to be hired without the bother of having forged a reference. As for what transpired between Mrs Halfstairs and Mr Constable in his absence, he heard only the very beginning of their conversation.

'Enough, Edward. We cannot have another day of this.'

This was followed by the sound of Mr Constable weeping.

4

That evening Miss Mott must cook dinner for seven gentlemen. When Mr Quentin had been master, this would have seemed a trifle. Then it had been ten courses every night, pheasant and guinea fowl, three different puddings to choose from. But Mr Buckle, although he had acted kindly towards his household, had not been conscious of his social obligations. He was a bachelor of an oddly private disposition, and often wanted no more than a little cheese and pickle for his tea. He hid upstairs in his snuggery with his book, his glass of porter, his round of Cheshire, and whether the housekeeper was housekeeping or the butler awake, he did not seem inclined to either notice or inquire, so long as he could have the cheeky little maid to wait on him.

Now there was finally to be a Grand Occasion, the fruits of his poor leadership were everywhere: one inebriated butler, one footman mad with grief, one untrained kitchen maid who was grating the suet so slowly that the cook could not bear to look at her.

Miss Mott worked on her apple pie. She prayed to God to speed the maid, to force Mrs Halfstairs to put her tiresome ruler away and engage a new footman. When Jack Maggs returned to the kitchen, she did not lift her head, but she had that capacity, commonly found in the short and shy, for peering up whilst seeming to look down.

When she saw no tell-tale envelope (the object of her curiosity being already in the inside pocket of Jack's waistcoat) she assumed the worst – it was a well-known fault with her – and the little woman shivered like a dog with an itch that cannot be scratched.

Miss Mott was lean and sinewy and there was nowhere much for such a violent shiver to hide itself. Consequently it went right up her spine and disappeared inside her little white cap and then, just when it seemed lost, it came out the other side and pulled up the ends of her thin mouth in a grimace.

'I'm done for,' sighed Peggy Mott, but to no one she imagined would care or listen.

She gave the fellow a slice of short-bread and poured him a cup of tea.

Jack Maggs added four heaped spoons of sugar to the tea and stirred. He sipped. He seemed to close his eyes, but all the while he was assessing his new home. He watched the cook's agitated little face as she sucked and blew and pursed her lips continually. She had the appearance of a sad and sorry bird, and he wondered about the nature of the cage that had made her so.

At the same time, Mercy Larkin watched Jack Maggs. She had no idea that she was observing an oyster working on a pearl, nor could she guess at the size of the upset contained inside the shell. Indeed, there was more than a little in Jack Maggs's manner to suggest a man used to being well-treated at the table. He sat himself comfortably with his big legs apart, his hands resting loosely on his belly. He yawned.

'Very good,' he said to no one in particular.

He rested his chin upon his chest and closed his eyes a moment. Then a moment longer.

'Cook!' said the maid. And then, when Miss Mott did not react: 'Look, ssh.'

'What is it now, Mercy?' said Peggy Mott, but she looked in the direction she was bid.

'Sssh. He's asleep.'

'These hares is not hung long enough,' said Miss Mott nervously. 'Not near long enough.'

'Come and look.' Mercy pushed her suet aside. She kneeled beside Jack Maggs's great thighs.

'Mercy Larkin!' said Peggy, turning from the stove to see the bold girl with her face so close to the stranger's. There was no doubt about it: the fellow was sound asleep.

'I don't think he's a footman at all. Don't he look ever so distinguished?'

Peggy Mott looked at the hard face for a moment and gave another little shudder. 'He looks like a murderer.'

'I think he's a butler,' said Mercy. 'Do you think we might have him instead of Mr Spinks? Do you think that might be her final plan?'

'Hush, Mercy. She has not engaged him.'

15

'Oh but she has, Mum. You are mistaken.'

Miss Mott began to rearrange the pieces of hare. 'Mercy, you were never in service before. Someone should take you in hand, my girl, before you are properly spoiled. It does not help you that your dear Mother brought our master broth when he was ill.' She turned from the stove. 'What are you doing? What are you doing?'

Mercy slid her small white hand into the sleeping man's waistcoat and pulled out the long white envelope. 'Hush, Mum. I am fetching you your heart's desire.'

Mrs Mott stared at the envelope. She blinked and sucked her lips in around her teeth.

'Oh, I do give thanks.' She held out her hand for the envelope. 'I do give thanks.' Then, quickly, her mood changed. She gave the envelope back and spoke: 'Nice and lively, Mercy. Please present Mr Maggs to Mr Spinks.'

'First we must wake him up,' said Mercy, slyly.

'Shake him, Mercy. Tap him on the shoulder.'

'I'll not touch him, Mum. It wouldn't be proper.'

The cook picked up a hand of flour and sprinkled it across the table, communicating, as she did so, a growing, almost uncontrollable tide of irritation.

'Mercy, I have seven gentlemen for eight o'clock. I have Mr Oates himself, God help me. Mercy, please be so good as to wake Mr Maggs and take him – and here, take this too, the envelope – to Mr Spinks, wherever it is that Mr Spinks is presently engaged.'

'And we know where that is, don't we, Mum?'

Cook sighed. 'Yes, Mercy, we do.'

It was as if the price was finally high enough, for now Mercy patted Jack Maggs upon the shoulder, and the new footman opened his eyes.

'We are to visit Mr Spinks,' said Mercy, 'so as you may be officially employed.'

Jack did not understand exactly what she meant, but he felt her warmth, like a plate just removed from the warming rack. He reached in his pocket for his envelope before he noticed it in the girl's hand.

'You dropped this,' she said, and handed it to him.

He knew he had not dropped it, but he took the envelope and followed her. She had a very pretty sweep to her back, and a soft white neck.

5

There was a peculiar little passageway – its ceiling low and heavy-beamed, its walls crammed with bottles of preserves – which led from the kitchen, down a step, along a chalky white wall, and then round a corner to a heavy green door which, as Mercy opened it, revealed the butler's parlour.

This was a surprisingly pleasant little room, with a window overlooking a budding old pear tree, and a big old-fashioned country fireplace in whose deep niches and sooty crannies Mr Spinks was in the habit of hiding his claret bottles. Along one wall was a mammoth oaken dresser in which was stored the household's treasury of silver plate and before which the butler now sat. He was sound asleep with his heavy brass poker across his knee, his cadaverous old skull thrown backwards, and his little mouth wide open. The pages of the *Morning Chronicle* lay scattered on the floor beside his stockinged feet.

The new footman showed no interest in this spectacle, but turned his eyes on Mercy instead.

'You picked my pocket,' he said very quietly. As he spoke he laid his hand against his quivering cheek.

'Sir?'

'You had your hand in Jack Maggs's pocket. That was very brave of you.'

She could not tell if he were pleased with her or angry.

'I'm not so brave,' she said.

As she knelt to gather up the newspaper she felt his presence all around her. She had a fancy – more, a kind of vision, a picture of herself laying her head against his manly chest. However, when she looked at him she found him staring at old Spinks.

Mercy did not like Mr Spinks – he was a bully and a snob – but when she saw the dried white spittle in the corner of his mouth, she was sorry that he should have lived so long as to let himself be seen like this. She folded the pages of the *Chronicle* and placed them carefully by the sleeping man's feet.

'Our master is a good man,' she said. 'He does not judge a human weakness.'

'Not even pick-pocketing?'

'Please don't be angry with me. I done it just to stop poor Mottle fretting.'

'Oh, so you done it for her, did you? That were generous of you.'

'Well, yes, it was. I knew you were employed, because I saw your paper in your pocket, see. But Miss Mott, she didn't see, and she was in a state on account of us being a footman short of what we should have. Tonight we have Mr Oates – Mr Tobias Oates – coming to our house to dine.' She looked at him as she said the famous name, but his features did not soften. 'It is Mr *Oates*,' she said. 'Mr *Tobias* Oates. You'd pick a pocket for Tobias Oates, I know you would.'

'I'm afraid,' he said, stiffly, 'I don't know no Tobias Oates.'

'Oh Lor.' She did not mean to laugh. 'Where have you been?'

'I was with Lord Logan,' said Jack Maggs, a little gruffly, 'in Glasgow.'

'You have surely heard mention of Captain Crumley?'

'Captain Crumley, perhaps I did.'

'Or poor Mrs Morefallen.'

'I've heard her mentioned.'

'It is all Mrs Halfstairs lives for – to see what Captain Crumley does about his son in prison. And now it is he who is to be our guest. This is a great day for Mr Buckle.'

'Mr Buckle – he is a friend of Captain Crumley?'

Mercy began to laugh, but something in the other's eyes made her stop herself.

'Mr Buckle is your new master,' she said very seriously. 'He has a famous author to come to dine with him tonight. It is because of this he has been in bed these last three days.'

'Your master is ill?'

18

'He could not bear to become ill at such a time.'

'He is sleeping?'

'He would like to sleep, but it is everything he can do to keep his poor brain from boiling over. No, he stays abed so as he don't fall sick. He would not miss Tobias Oates for the world.'

'So do tell me, Miss . . .'

'My name is Mercy Larkin.'

'Did your master also make a friend of Henry Phipps?'

'The gentleman next door? Oh, Sir, you must forget *him*.' Her almond eyes were almost grey and very still. 'Now you're going to stay with us.'

He held her gaze. Even when there was a great crashing in the kitchen, he did not look away.

'That's how she calls for me,' she said. She thought his eyes angry. 'She drops things.'

'Then you should go to her,' he said.

Mercy did not move.

'You should be more careful, girlie,' he said.

'It's for you to be careful,' said Mercy. 'If I was you I would be very careful indeed.'

'What do you mean by that?'

She did not exactly know, but she felt passionate and irritated. 'They will be likely to have you dusting, and it was the dusting that so upset he who came before you.'

'He gave his notice?'

'Aye, with a gentleman's duelling pistol. He blew his brains out.'

'On account of dusting?'

She was not sure she liked his features anymore. 'He could not tolerate it,' she said.

He raised an eyebrow.

'Beg your pardon?' she inquired crossly.

'My pardon?'

'Beg pardon, Sir,' she said, 'but I thought you was making a comment.'

'No,' he said, 'nothing.'

'Oh yes,' she insisted, 'something.'

19

She saw him hesitate.

'Did you ever *see* Mr Phipps?' he asked at last. 'How was he? What sort of man was he?'

Mercy turned to face him. She was in a funny kind of passion she could not explain and Jack Maggs, seeing her face, somehow understood that she had become his opponent. He stretched to grab her wrist, but he was too slow. She giggled, turned, flipped the brass poker out of Mr Spinks's lap so that it spun and clattered onto the tiled floor.

Mr Spinks sprang to his feet and found, before him, a stranger holding a long white envelope.

6

At five o'clock on Saturday Jack Maggs had been a man of substance, speeding towards London on the Dover *Rocket*. Now, at five o'clock on Sunday, he entered a stuffy attic which was, it seemed, to be his home awhile. It was not three paces from the squeaking door to the soot-stained dormer window, and he was across them in a trice, heaving up the stiff sash and thrusting his big head inquiringly out above Great Queen Street. Here he found no more interesting view than the melancholy apartments across the way and, in the immediate foreground, the slate tiles of the house next door to Mr Buckle's. The latter, however, was obviously of particular interest to him, and had he been a master tradesman, sent to inspect their condition, he could not have examined the tiles more closely. They were grey Devon slate, with almost half of their visible surface covered with a thin coating of yellowish moss. They seemed to be, for the most part, well secured, although he noted a loose piece of lead flashing and a dormer window carelessly left open to the weather.

So intent was his inspection that he became only slowly aware of a distant percussion. It was not until he had squeezed himself back into his room that he discovered someone was hammering on his door and crying, 'Open up!'

He stood before the door a moment with his brow quite markedly contracted. It was not at all clear that he would 'open up'. Indeed he soon retreated to the window and looked out at the narrow strip of roof that might have afforded an escape. But finally he did as he was bid.

In the open doorway he was accosted by a being with hard white sculpted hair, a creature so resplendent in his yellow velvet jacket and soft doeskin trousers, that it took a full minute – during which time the impatient visitor entered the room and got himself deep into a large oak wardrobe – for Jack to realize that he was in the presence of the very same wild-haired Tom O'Bedlam with whom he had, less than an hour before, played bookends.

Edward Constable was of a lighter build than Maggs. He had fine wrists and large expressive hands which he had, in his recent dementia, been prone to wring. He had been a good-looking youth, and it was all still there: the high cheekbones, the well-shaped red lips; even the slight ridge on his aquiline nose did his case no damage. Of his recent madness there was, if one excepted the rather dangerous aroma of his master's cognac, no remaining sign.

Now, without offering an explanation, he withdrew from the darkness of the wardrobe various items which he then laid out, with a somewhat theatrical tenderness, upon the little crib. Here he set a pair of doeskin breeches from which he picked a little smut. There a white shirt, just so. Beside it a lace cravat which he must move, an inch, no more, to accommodate a yellow velvet coat, the mirror image of his own, and from whose lapel he removed a single long blue thread. To this magnificent arrangement he added two long silk stockings and a pair of black shoes with silver buckles.

The two men stood side by side regarding the objects so assembled.

'I am to try these for size?' suggested Maggs.

'Tsk,' said Constable.

'I'll take that as yes,' Maggs said, undressing with as much modesty as the cramped space permitted, aware all the time that he was the subject of the other's censure.

'Now look here,' said Maggs, finally gaining the security of the

21

breeches, 'I know this was your mate's kit, and he was your good friend and you miss him worse than air itself. I am sorry' – Maggs paused to tuck in the shirt, but did this in such a way that his witness raised a thin, sarcastic eyebrow – 'I am sorry to remind you of the good comrade you have lost. I wish it was otherwise, but you see there is naught else I can do, in the circumstances, but wear his clobber.'

In response to which explanation, the footman hissed.

'No, good fellow. I really do not think it fair for you to hiss at me. For as I said, none of this business is my fault and I would rather, just like you would, that they would send me to a tailor and have the business done fair and square. But here we are.' Maggs slipped the jacket on. 'The shoes are tight, but the coat fits well enough, and I am sure I can limp as far as pudding if you'll be of some assistance to me.'

'Assistance. Is that so?'

'It is so, my fellow,' said Maggs, moving his bulk closer to the footman, who immediately began to back away. 'And if I might start with what comes first – you can assist me with my hair.'

From the recesses of the commode the footman produced a saucer with a bar of white soap, a round box, and a large powder puff. These were duly offered, and declined.

'Still, old fellow,' said Maggs, 'a cove needs more in the way of assistance than a saucer and a box.'

'Oh, a *cove* does, does he?'

'He does, yes,' insisted Maggs.

'You must excuse me,' shrugged Constable, 'for it is quarter past the hour, and with Mrs Halfstairs it is eat when she says or never.'

'Mr Constable, I am asking you to render me assistance.'

The footman laid his hand upon the wooden door knob. 'Mr Maggs, I am refusing it.'

Maggs's hand snapped around the other's wrist. Thus, even as the footman's silver-buckled shoes scuttled out the open door, the upper part of his body was yanked smartly inwards. Maggs leaned across his prisoner's flailing arms and drove the bolt home in the door.

'Now Thingstable,' he said. 'You are about to place us both in peril.'

22

'Oh fie . . .' said Constable in a tight, disdainful voice. He held his free hand to his neck. 'I tremble-Kemble. You'll kill me? Is that what you have in mind? By God, I think it is. He wants to kill me.'

Softly, softly, thought Jack Maggs.

'Please, Sir, go ahead. No, no really, I do beg you, it would be a pleasure to be done away with by someone so nicely fitted out.'

'Fellow,' said Jack Maggs calmly, 'you mistake me.'

'But this is rich, Mr Maggs. This is too rich for you to understand, but my friend, Mr Pope, with whom I stood and served for fifteen years – we were boys together in Lineham Hall – has done himself in. In this very room. Here, where we would chat after our day's labours. And she, the meddling duchess, has me dress you in his very clothes, and now you say you wish to kill me . . . oh, please, you really have no notion what a pleasure it would be.'

'No one said anything about killing, my dear fellow.'

'I am no one's dear anything,' said Constable, and burst into tears.

'Well, I must say then, I am sorry.'

'Sorry you wish to kill me? Or sorry to know such a thing has happened?'

'Don't never try to beat me in the game of sorrow.'

'You think to match me?'

'I will sink you,' said Maggs gravely.

The pair of them stood opposite each other like two horses at a fence.

'All I require is that you assist me with my hair.'

'Assist?'

'I do not know how to achieve the correct effect with the hair.'

'Ha-ha,' said Constable, pushing his long finger against Maggs's chest. 'What are you? A toffee-twister, a dimber-damber?'

Jack Maggs took the finger, and held it hard inside his fist. Then he pulled the finger's owner closer to him. 'Listen carefully, fool. You do not have the devil's notion who you're dealing with.'

The pale blue eyes wandered over Maggs's face.

'Who am I dealing with?' he asked at last.

'If you are very lucky, you are dealing with a footman.'

23

'A footman?'

'Hurry up, man. Before I change my mind.'

The stranger's left cheek twitched violently.

'I'll fetch the water,' Edward Constable said. 'You'll want it warm.'

When he was gone, Jack Maggs sat heavily on the crib, pushing his hand hard against the place on his cheek where the tic was centred. This tic pulled long cords of pain which ran from his left eye down to his back teeth, a pain now so intense that not even the thought that the footman might be on his way to call the police could rouse him from his seat.

Some time later, when the attack had finally begun to subside, Edward Constable returned. He brought a steaming copper kettle to the wash-stand.

'Now soak it,' he said.

Maggs looked up bleakly.

'Hair,' Edward Constable said. 'You must remove your shirt and soak your hair.'

The big man bent slowly over the basin in his woollen singlet.

'Singlet off.'

'Singlet stays on.'

Constable put two fingers against Jack Maggs's scalp and pushed his head into the bowl. The water was hot. Maggs cried out.

'Hotter the better,' said Constable. 'Let it soak one minute by the clock.'

Then Constable cried, 'Towel,' and Maggs was subjected to his first lesson in the footman's trade as Constable, standing behind him, lathered his hair with soft soap and then applied the oddly perfumed powder with a puff. Sleepy Jack regarded the process in the mirror.

Constable combed the white sticky mess backwards with a comb, and then, like a baker icing a birthday cake, scraped off the edges with a wooden spatula.

'Just look at you,' he said. 'It's enough to make a cat speak.'

7

Some time after midnight Jack Maggs would begin to record the events of his first evening as a servant.

By six o'clock that evening, he had been transformed into a footman good and proper. He ate his tea sitting at a long deal table in the company of the other servants. At half past seven he was ready to make his first entry to the dining room, and he picked up a scalding hot tureen of eel soup and prepared himself for the steep ascent to the ground floor.

His shoes pinched him. The plaster-hard white hair felt like a steel clamp on his brow.

In the upstairs hallway mirror he saw his private anger showing plainly in his eyes, but by the time he entered the dining room his manner was more that of a publican than a footman, and he came amongst the gentlemen smiling in a very jolly way, until, that is, the powdered Constable hissed instruction in his ear.

'No smile.'

Edward Constable then ushered the novice towards the table, forcing him, with the subtle insistence of his shoulder, to walk around the table towards the chair where the person known as Tobias Oates was already seated at his place as guest of honour.

Constable removed the lid from the tureen.

'Stay,' he whispered. He took the lid and placed it on the sideboard. Jack Maggs watched the guests. He saw that the visitor was no more than twenty-five years of age. He was short – they all were short – but Oates was also slight and his face, were it not for his lopsided smile, might have been described as cherubic.

'Up,' hissed Constable.

'Up?'

'Soup up. Hold up.'

Jack Maggs held up the tureen. There was something very queer about this gathering: old fellows with bald heads, red beards streaked with grey, men whose noses showed too much attachment to the brandy bottle, the host with his poor man's teeth and hair combed thinly over his white pate, every one of them giving his full attention to Mr Oates, a young gent decidedly undistinguished in manner.

Tobias Oates did not seem, to Jack's mind, to warrant any of the excitement his name had stirred in Mercy Larkin's imagination. He was sharp, like a jockey. He wore a waistcoat like a common busker, or a book-maker, bright green and shot through with lines of blue and yellow. He was edgy, almost pugnacious, with eyes and hands everywhere about him as if he were constantly confirming his position in the world, a navigator measuring his distance from the chair, the wall, the table.

So unsettling was this character to Jack Maggs that he later devoted almost one hundred words to describing him: *Oates watched close as his eel soup was ladled into his plate. Straightened his silver. Stared at me. Stared at me again. Then told a strange tale of a 'Thief-taker' by name of Partridge who he claimed could find any man in England. In the case in point he did track a house-breaker from Gloucester all the way to the Borough, at which pt he made a citizen's arrest in v. touchy circumstances.*

Jack Maggs circled the table with Constable, holding the tureen while Constable ladled. He watched everything, but he watched Tobias Oates most of all. When the writer was assured of the table's complete attention, his jerky limbs stilled, and he bestowed upon his audience a singular stroking kind of charm, relating his unlikely tale with the air of a man who is accustomed to not being interrupted.

Three times Mr Buckle put his spoon down and opened his mouth to speak. Three times he seemed to lose his courage. When he did finally talk his guests immediately turned their heads in his direction.

'The fact is' – Mr Buckle paused to acknowledge his guest's interest with a small nod of the head – 'the fact you have left out – am I right, Mr Oates? – is how this Thief-taker got this intelligence which evaded the police. That is the point of your tale, or am I wrong?'

'It is I who am wrong,' replied Tobias Oates. 'I began the story and then realized I could not politely tell it in the company of Mr Hawthorne here.'

The bald-headed, black-bearded man named Henry Hawthorne was, as Jack Maggs knew from Mercy Larkin, the chief actor in Mr Buckle's Lyceum Theatre. It was through his good graces (and doubtless for his personal advantage) that all these strangers had been brought to sit at Mr Buckle's table. He was a barrel-chested gentleman with a deep, resonant voice.

'Oh Lor,' said Henry Hawthorne, buttering his bread, shaking his head, generally affecting to be much put out. 'Are you not weary of your Hob-bee Hor-ss?'

'Sideboard,' whispered Constable. 'Put tureen.'

Maggs placed the tureen on the sideboard, and took the claret bottle which Constable placed in his hand.

'No drips.'

'It is Animal Magnetism,' the author was explaining to the gentlemen, who all leaned most earnestly towards him, 'which my friend is calling the Hobby Horse.'

'Get thee to a knackery,' cried Henry Hawthorne, pushing out his wine glass so Maggs might more easily find it.

'The Thief-taker,' said Tobias Oates, 'is not some rogue like Jonathan Wild but an educated, modern man who obtained his information by making mesmeric *passes*' – here he waved his hands mechanically up and down in front of Hawthorne's unblinking eyes – 'by making mesmeric *passes* over the four witnesses the police had already interviewed he put each into a condition of Magnetic Somnambulism. This Thief-taker, whose name is Wilfred Partridge, obtained by this method a full description of the suspect from those who *imagined* they had not seen him clearly.'

'Yes,' said the host. He spoke, this time, very quietly, as if to himself.

'The Cerebrum,' said Tobias Oates, looking from one to the other of his listeners, 'is a vessel that never leaks. It holds everything, remembers everything. And if Mr Hawthorne likes to think of Animal Magnetism as a scurrilous parlour game, it is only because he has not read his Villiers or Puységur.'

'Did you read about the Russian gentlemen in the *Morning Chronicle*?' Hawthorne asked. 'Come all the way from Sebastopol to learn Magnetism in London? You read it? No? Write for it, but don't read it. Pity. They plan to use your noble art to seduce young ladies.'

'Sideboard,' whispered Constable. 'Bookends.'

Jack Maggs stood at one end of the sideboard, his hands behind his back. Constable stood to the other.

'It is pretty clear by now,' said Oates, 'that no mesmeric act on earth will have anyone perform an act against their moral temper.'

'The report of King Philippe,' cried Mr Buckle suddenly, 'well, I have to say – it was of a different opinion.'

'You are a student of the Royal Commission?'

'My word yes,' said Percy Buckle.

Mr Buckle looked down at his own place, a red spot showing on each pale cheek.

'I must caution our host,' said Henry Hawthorne, showing a glimmer of a smile beneath his large moustache. 'My friend Oates has become such a secret Magnetist that I heard him – *I heard you, Oates* – try to persuade a King's Counsel that he should be magnetizing criminals in the dock.'

'But Hawthorne, my old fellow, you have not taken my point.'

'You have more points than a fork, Oates,' said Henry Hawthorne, and turned back to his bread and butter.

'The Criminal Mind is as susceptible to magnetism as any other,' said Oates, his pale blue eyes now showing bright little flecks of brown.

The new footman listened to this most intently.

'Now come, Oates,' said the fellow with the quivering chin. 'No hard-hearted villain is going to give his secrets up in a court of law.'

'Even the lowest type of renegade,' said Tobias Oates, 'has an inner need to give up the truth. Look at those gallows confessions they are still selling on Holborn. It is what our fathers called 'conscience'. We all have it. For the criminal, it is like a passion to throw himself off a high place.'

The footman's down-turned mouth betrayed his opinion of the matter, and so obvious was the expression on his face that it would soon have been observed, had his passions not stimulated the grizzling little palsy in his cheek to its fullest fury.

As usual, he had no warning of the attack.

The pain slapped his face like a clawed cat. It flooded like spilled lemon juice behind his eyes. It hit so hard that he could not help himself but cry out, and the bottle of claret which he had been in the process of bringing to the table fell from his hand and lay spewing its contents onto the oriental rug.

Typically, it was Tobias Oates who was first to help the fallen man. While the other guests held back, he kneeled beside Jack Maggs's contorted face and gently, firmly, pried his large, hard hand away from his cheek.

'I see it.' With the cool handle of the spoon he touched the victim's contorted face. As the spoon touched the flesh a tic, fast as a pulse, darted beneath the surface of the skin.

'Tic douloureux,' said Toby Oates, offering his ink-stained hand and pulling the heavy footman upwards. With Henry Hawthorne's help, he got Jack Maggs into a dining chair. 'Have you heard that name before? Tic douloureux?'

But the new footman was barely aware of anything except the pain and the horror that always accompanied these crises. It was not a horror of anything, or about anything, but a horror so profound that a certain time elapsed during which he hardly knew where on earth he stood.

'Look at me,' said Tobias Oates insistently. 'Look into my eyes – I can take away this pain.'

Maggs peered at Oates as if through a heavy veil. The little gent began to wave his hands. He passed them down, up, down.

'Watch me,' said Tobias Oates, and Jack Maggs, for once, did exactly as he was told.

8

Jack Maggs woke to find himself still seated in the doorway on a straight-backed chair. Opposite him Tobias Oates was also seated, so close that Maggs could smell the eel soup upon his breath and feel his neat little knees brushing lightly against his own silk stockings.

'So,' said the young man, 'where is your pain gone, Mr Maggs?' In his manner he was solicitous and kindly, and about as trustworthy as a Newgate Bird.

'Come, Jack.' He reached his finger out and touched Jack Maggs softly upon the knee. He smiled. He had long lashes and soft speckled eyes.

Jack Maggs moved his knee away.

'Come, Jack, you really are obliged to speak to me.'

Someone sighed, and the footman's shoulders rose an inch.

'One moment the fellow is making speeches,' said a man behind his back, 'and now he is silent as the grave.'

'Eh, Jack,' the writer-cove said softly. 'What say you now, Jack?'

'Excuse me, Sir, what speeches have I made?'

Tobias Oates grinned broadly, and looked away and over Maggs's shoulder. Maggs followed the direction of the other's gaze, and found himself, like someone waking from a dream, in a familiar place he could not quite explain. The dinner was now abandoned. The unsmiling guests crowded behind him, peering down at him as though he were a prisoner in the dock.

'You have been asleep,' Tobias Oates explained. 'I asked you questions and you answered them.'

'Did I answer loudly, then?'

'Well, very *clearly*,' smiled the young man. 'But come, Jack, is your pain gone or no? That is what the gentlemen are waiting to hear you say.'

But Jack Maggs had more serious things than pain to concern him. 'I was asleep?' He stood. 'I said my name was Jack?'

Tobias Oates stayed seated, his legs crossed, smiling that queer lopsided smile.

'Asleep but not asleep.'

'I was talking in my sleep then, is it?'

'Mr Oates cured you,' said the duck-legged master, now placing himself between the mesmerist and the subject. 'And now it is time for you to help cure my guests of hunger.'

The footman did not even look at him.

'Please,' continued Percy Buckle, who was, as usual, uncomfortable about giving clear orders to a servant. 'I must ask you to at least temporarily be a footman.'

In saying 'temporarily' he meant only to soften his directive, to suggest that the man must labour for the present, but that shortly he might have his rest.

Jack Maggs heard *temporarily*. He thought he was soon to be dismissed, or worse. When the master put a hand upon his arm, he felt himself in danger.

'Speed,' hissed Constable, the master's dog, who now came to shepherd him away. 'Out. Down.'

The two footmen walked shoulder by shoulder out into the hall and down the narrow stairs.

'For Jesus' sake. What did I say?'

'You were a great turn, Mr Maggs. You were a great thrill for the gentlemen, but by God neither the rug nor the flounder will forgive you for it.'

'What did I say? Tell me, cod's-head.'

'Oh, go back to Borough, why don't you.'

Maggs's face darkened dangerously. 'I spoke of Borough? What else?'

'Here he is,' cried Constable gaily to the kitchen. 'The right height, and no question about it.'

The little cook looked up at Maggs and clicked her tongue. Then she shook her head and looked away. 'Mercy, take the skin off the sauce and then warm it. We will sauce the fish in the kitchen.'

'Miss Mott!' protested Constable.

'There is no choice,' cried the little red-nosed Mott. 'The poor dear flounder is all dried. There is nothing else to do. We will serve it by the plate and you will carry the plates up to the gentlemen already sauced. Please, Mr Constable, would you be so good as to fetch the Trafalgar Doulton. We will have to warm them with water from the kettle.'

In another place, Jack Maggs's presence would have brought a hush of respect, but here, in this steamy little room, they rushed about him, ignorant of who he was. Indeed, Maggs himself moved to one side as Constable rushed past and Mercy stirred a light pink sauce.

31

'What did I say?' he repeated when Constable finally returned with the plates.

'How on earth would I know?' cried Constable carelessly. 'I was cleaning the blessed rug.'

'Then how did you learn of my connection with Borough?'

'Oh Larry,' cried Constable. 'Where else would you be from? Edinburgh?'

Maggs did not even have the space to be angered by these people. It was the man upstairs who was the focus of his animus. He was burgled, plundered, and he would not tolerate it.

9

As the two footmen carried the remnants of the puddings down the staircase to the kitchen, Jack Maggs asked if Mr Oates was in the habit of calling on Mr Buckle, but what with the clatter of their heels and the rattle of the china, the question seemed to go unheard. It was not until his fellow footman had rested his burden upon the kitchen table that Jack Maggs saw the snob had heard his question very well.

'Mr Maggs was just inquiring,' declared the Knight of the Rainbow, 'does Mr Oates come calling regularly?'

This produced a great squeal of laughter from the scullery.

'Regular?' cried Mercy Larkin, poking her white-capped head around the curtain. 'Oh no. We usually have the King on Tuesdays.'

Jack Maggs stood in the middle of the kitchen, red-faced, glowering. 'For Jesus' sake,' said he. 'You don't know what you're mucking with.'

'Language!' cried Miss Mott, but even her pinched little face was smiling at his question.

'Beg pardon, Ma'am.' The big man spoke very quietly. 'All I am endeavouring to get clear is . . . will the writing cove likely call again?'

'Oh, we are a *most* fashionable household,' said Constable, splashing a little of his master's brandy into a tea cup. 'There is not a coster or a crossing sweeper who is not laying plots to dine with our Mr Buckle. As for authors, why they are forever knocking down our door.'

'You'll mind your manners,' said Maggs in that whispering little voice which had always, in rougher places, had such chilling effect.

'Mr Maggs is such a theatrical type of gent,' said Constable blithely. 'I can't decide if he should play a footman,' and here he patted the newcomer upon his plastered head, 'or a footpad.'

There were at least two men still living in London who had reason to remember that Jack Maggs did not like his head touched, and Edward Constable might then have learned a similar lesson – but the bell from upstairs began ringing for Jack Maggs's services.

He limped up the breakneck stairs to discover all the gentlemen (Tobias Oates amongst them) were standing at the open doorway exclaiming over the rain which had just begun to fall.

'Topcoats,' hissed Constable as he passed out into the rain to call the coachman from his room in the mews.

Maggs did make some effort to do this duty as it were normally done, but he was preoccupied with Tobias Oates whom he feared would escape at any moment. When each guest had been roughly reunited with his garment, Maggs positioned himself by the open door, and here he remained with the rain blowing in his frowning face.

Oates stood out of the weather, vigorously shaking Percy Buckle's hand.

'It has been an honour, Sir,' said Percy Buckle, his cheeks showing their red-hot spots once again. 'Quite inconceivable to me, unimaginable. A year before last Christmas, I would not have dreamed that I would ever shake so illustrious a hand.'

Oates looked very pleased to be so dubbed. 'I smell a mystery.'

'Oh, you are being polite, Sir. You know my good friend Mr Hawthorne and so it follows that my life can be no mystery to you. You know I had my little shop in Clerkenwell, right on Coppice Row. A most humble business, Sir, as I'm sure you've heard. I made it no secret from your friend. All the actors are aware of my beginnings.'

'A wonderful story,' agreed Oates, smiling. 'A scholar and a grocer.'

'A very poor type of scholar, I'm afraid.'

'With a set of German scales on the counter and the cheese in a glass case labelled "Pastry".'

'Dear Lord,' said Percy Buckle. 'Who told you that?'

'My secret,' said Oates, continuing to shake Percy Buckle's hand, 'is that I once bought cheese from you, never imagining we would meet in these circumstances. It has been a wonderful evening for me, Mr Buckle, to see you so comfortably ensconced here with your servants and your Gibbon.'

'Bless me. I hope you found satisfaction in the cheese.'

'Indeed,' said Tobias Oates, his hand still held but now retired from shaking. 'Great satisfaction, for I went straight across the road to the baker's window . . . he had a sort of serving hatch with . . .'

'Mr Freepole . . .'

'Mr Freepole's is it?'

'Dead now,' offered Percy Buckle.

'Indeed, dead. And bought a little loaf of bread and made myself a small picnic in that old church yard in Cutter's Close off Saffron Hill.'

'We remember everything, eh, Mr Oates!'

'Indeed,' said Tobias Oates, finally excusing himself the handhold. 'It has been,' he said, using his free hand to indicate his host, the grim footman, the open door, 'a night to remember . . . and goodnight to you, Jack Maggs Esquire.'

'Goodnight, Sir,' said Jack. And had no choice but to stand like a fool as the man who had robbed him walked away undamaged.

But then Jack Maggs had the good fortune to be dismissed to bed.

He rushed up the stairs into his attic and, upon entering, extinguished his candle. He rushed to the dormer window. He opened it, and poked his coiffed head out into the rain.

'By Jove,' he heard a familiar voice float upwards. 'I'll tell you this, Hawthorne. You are mistaken, most grievously mistaken.'

Jack Maggs lifted his window sash as high as it would go, and when it jammed half-way he would not be stopped but squeezed himself like a python through the opening, his shiny buckled feet first, then his stomach, then (painfully) his shoulders, until he was standing on the steep and mossy slates three giddy storeys above the street.

Keeping his hand on the window ledge, he looked down over a thin line of guttering and confirmed with his eyes that which his ears had already told him: there, forty feet below, was little Tobias Oates, standing in the rain.

'I may be mistaken about what has occurred in private,' said Hawthorne. (He had his foot on the steps of Mr Buckle's coach, but did not seem inclined to enter.) 'But I am not mistaken about the Unholy Passion in the air.'

'I am sure you are mistaken.'

'I have ob-served,' said Hawthorne, 'how the two parties are *besotted*.'

Jack Maggs released his hold of Mr Buckle's window ledge and then edged his way across the slick roof tiles until he reached the partly open window of Mr Henry Phipps's dormer.

As he hooked his fingers under the sash, he heard the noise of steel rolling along cobblestones. He looked down and saw the carriage moving away with Edward Constable standing ramrod straight on the footplate at the rear of it.

Tobias Oates, however, was walking. He was crossing Great Queen Street diagonally, heading east.

Mr Phipps's dormer window yielded, opening sweetly to its full extent.

Jack Maggs entered. He bumped into a wash-stand and sent the water jug crashing. He cursed and, in a sudden fit of temper, kicked at the pieces. He found the door and then the stairs. He ran down two flights in total blackness but on the first-floor landing fell over an abandoned trunk from which silver sugar bowls and tea pots rolled, together with the intruder, all the way down to the hall below, where they lay about him on the carpet, their round forms hidden in the dark.

He stood slowly, feeling the pains in his back and ribs.

For this he laboured? To stand in Henry's hallway like a thief, his breeches smeared with London soot?

He unlocked the front door slowly and set off after Tobias Oates, hobbling north along Great Queen Street in his pinching shoes.

35

10

'I may be mistaken about what has occurred in private,' Henry Hawthorne said in his great booming voice. 'But I am not mistaken about the Unholy Passion in the air.'

'You are mistaken .'

'I have ob-served,' said the actor, grasping Tobias Oates's shoulder and squeezing it very painfully, 'I have ob-served how the two parties are *be-sotted*.'

'My hat is off to your nightmare fancy, Nuncle.'

Tobias could not walk away for fear this would cause Hawthorne to speak even louder. He could only hope that the other guests, impatiently waiting inside Mr Buckle's coach, might imagine that the 'passion' so discussed somehow related to the dinner just ended.

'Really, Hawthorne, you do not give either of the parties any credit.'

'My dear Tobias,' the actor said fondly, swinging from the coach with one arm. ' I give *you* every credit.'

'Good.' Oates tipped his hat abruptly. 'Then you will see me tomorrow at Rules.'

And then he fled, or so it felt, into the wet night with his coat drawn around him tightly, whispering to himself as he scurried round the corner from Great Queen Street, 'Good God. Great good God.'

Tobias Oates was twenty-four years old, and for twelve months past he had been the head of a family which now consisted of his wife, Mary, his son, John, and his wife's younger sister, Elizabeth. Having come from no proper family himself, or none that he could remember without great bitterness, he had for all his short, determined life carried with him a mighty passion to create that safe warm world he had been denied.

So it was that he was now the husband of a rosy-cheeked and broad-hipped wife who in no way resembled that pinched and worried woman who had brought him so resentfully into the world. He was the father of a babe just three months old, a boy, whom he doted on as his father had never doted on him. And if he had no more than a florin in his pocket, he was also still the master of a substantial house, a place of books and laughter, of colourful rugs, of mirrors, these last being desired for their light: he would not have his son grow up in dreariness, or darkness. He had a long dining table that could welcome his wife's aunts and uncles, and there was a splendid alcove in the parlour big enough to accommodate a twelve-foot high fir tree at Christmas. It was towards this pleasant house in Lamb's Conduit Street that he now walked briskly, but not quite directly. He could not arrive there yet. He was too agitated by this conversation which had set his heart beating wildly in his chest. Instead he set off down to Lincoln's Inn Fields – the long way home – to calm himself.

His secret had been seen.

This secret pressed at him all day long, and as he set out through the dark streets towards the place where the secret had its nest, it was with the most perplexing mixture of feelings. He walked briskly – some would say fiercely – with his shoulders back, a fast sort of duck-toed march as if he were intent on Moscow, as if he could escape his secret, which was that he was in love with his wife's sister.

This had never been his intention, and had begun through no other enthusiasm than their mutual concern for his wife, who had been confined to bed in the last months of her term. This confinement, coinciding with their moving into Lamb's Conduit Street, brought Tobias and Lizzie intimately together, necessitating the shouldering of small domestic offices which a husband and wife might more properly have performed together. The final act of their tragedy had been completed by no other agency than a heavy counterpane which they had folded together, halving, quartering, until they were, by reason of their honest household labour, brought into temptation.

No one who knew Tobias, not even the old actor who thought he saw the 'thunder', had any understanding of his unholy thirst for love. He had not known it himself. He did not know the curse or gift his ma and pa had given him: he would not be loved enough, not ever.

37

He never really knew this truth about himself, not even when the fame he craved was finally, briefly, granted him and he travelled from city to city like a one-man carnival act, feeding off the applause of his readers. Even when it was thrown in his face, so to speak, he did not see it.

In 1837 he had even less idea of his own character. She was eighteen years old, he defiled her. *Toby, Toby*. He had been at church an hour before he did so. Now he would have abandoned all hope of Paradise for her.

Afterwards, they knelt side by side and made solemn vows to God, which vows they soon broke, once, then twice, and again, in the little garden, in the rain, in his study at three in the morning. She was a child and he was a fool, worse than a fool. He was worse than the father whom he would never forgive and only minutes after having escaped the wine-stained Henry Hawthorne, he was thinking of her again. He gave his florin to a beggar in Lincoln's Inn Fields.

11

Jack Maggs was famously fast upon his feet, but now he was half-crippled by his dead man's shoes. God damn, but they cut him. They squeezed his toes in their vice. They cut his heel with their hooks. He took them off, but then suffered another wound on account of this: so he had no choice but to stop and put them on once more. With all this fuss, he almost lost sight of Tobias Oates, and had the writer not begun to sing so free and careless, he might have disappeared into the fog. But then, by Jesus, there came that fine tenor voice, not twenty yards ahead. 'Sally in our Alley'. It was a filthy song.

He had the bastard. He had him easy-peasy. He limped along behind him to Lincoln's Inn Fields with his shoes torturing him at every step. It was only pain, or so he told himself. He had suffered worse.

As the song arrived at that place where 'Nature's soft stream was

38

flowing' they came to coal-dark Carey Street. By then they were but fifteen feet apart.

In Chancery Lane a great lurching galoot of a link boy came rushing up the pavement holding his blazing faggot high into the night. The link boy, all of fifty if he were a day, was providing light for two young gentlemen, who were, in turn, attempting to escort a little whore, and all three of them as drunk as Captain Harry's horse.

As Tobias Oates turned to look at the link boy, Jack Maggs stepped back into the doorway of the Great High Court where he found a second whore busy at her trade and not pleased to have the interruption. A moment later Jack Maggs was out in the street again, making himself one of the party with the puffing link boy, boldly sharing the smoky light as far as Theobald's Road. He was just in time to see Tobias Oates turn off into the darkness.

Jack Maggs hobbled across the path of a hackney cab, then hip-hopped along Lamb's Conduit Street. For reward he saw Tobias Oates step up onto the front step of a house. He arrived outside this door in time to hear a heavy bolt slid home into its hasp.

Then a sudden light flooded through the fog behind him, throwing his own massive shadow on the door.

'So,' said the man with the lamp. 'What's up here?'

At first Maggs thought it was a soldier behind the lamp, but it was a bobby, an esclop, a frigging peeler with a fancy coat. Jack Maggs had not seen this type of coat before.

'You would not want to swap your uniform with mine, for all the tea in China,' said he cheekily. 'They give me shoes, the shoes don't fit. They send me out to walk behind my master, and not even a topcoat to bless myself with.'

The peeler was a big strong fellow with a face like a potato. The look in his eye, as he held up his lantern, was the same one you see in a policeman who would like to harm you badly, if only he could do it at no risk to himself.

'Where's your master?' he demanded.

'Just went in.'

'Went in where? I didn't see no one.'

The peeler ran his lantern over Jack Maggs again and there

revealed the damage done by the journey across the roof, the tumble down the stairs, the subsequent excursion through the drizzle. The Knight of the Rainbow was in a sodden, speckled state.

'Just went in,' Jack Maggs said, suddenly very sharp indeed. 'Right here. Mr Tobias Oates. The author of the tale of Captain Crumley.'

The esclop pushed his hot lantern a little closer to Jack's nose.

'Captain Crumley?'

'That's the one.'

The bobby paused. 'Get on home,' he said at last.

There was no choice. Jack Maggs opened the gate, walked down the steps into the area. There, below street level, he pressed himself flat against the kitchen door, but Mr Peel's man was not so green. He held up his lantern and peered down after him.

It was Despair made Jack Maggs try the kitchen door handle, and Fortune decreed it be left carelessly unlocked. He entered Tobias Oates's house and slid the bolt behind him. Through the kitchen window he could see the bobby's legs as they walked back towards the front door.

The village pony was not satisfied – it seemed he was going to knock up Tobias Oates and ask him questions about his footman. Jack Maggs therefore crept up the dark stairs into the hallway, ready to flee out the back if the policeman knocked.

At first he stood hard and still as a log of wood, but when it was clear that the policeman had walked on, he relaxed. Still he did not move, but stayed exactly where he was, breathing deeply.

Elsewhere in the household he heard a flurry of whispering and the fast shuffle of bare feet, and then, not too much time after, the old familiar music of a squeaking bed.

12

In the place Jack Maggs had most recently come from, the houses had been, for the most part, built from wood. They strained and groaned in the long hot nights, crying out against their nails, contracting, expanding, tugging at their bindings as if they would pull themselves apart.

Tobias Oates's house in Lamb's Conduit Street was built from London brick. It was newly painted, newly furnished. Everything in it glistened and was strong and bright and solid. This was a house that would never scream in the dark, nor did it reek of sap or creosote. Its smells were English smells – polished oak, coal dust, Devon apples. The intruder breathed these strange yet familiar odours for as long as it took the master to get himself to bed.

Then he crept up the stairs and, on the upper landing, drew his long arms around his chest. It was an action such as the Devil might make when surrounding himself with his cape. It might also have been by a mortal man wishing to cloak himself in Night, and if the latter were the case, Jack Maggs might be said to have succeeded, for a moment later he appeared, a slow and smudgy phantom, in a small room off the landing. Here he stooped over the small wooden crib in which lay Tobias Oates's first-born son.

Maggs's inky shadow flooded the crib. He leaned very close, so close indeed he might have bitten the child. Instead, he brought his wide nostrils almost up against that soapy skin and, with his arms clenched behind his back, inhaled John Marshall Oates's breath. This act he repeated three times, and when he was done he straightened himself and placed his hands deep in his pockets. In the next room, the child's father turned in his bed and coughed a most wide-awake cough. The intruder removed his hands from his pockets and moved slowly back into the shadow by the tall cupboard, and there his breathing became very slow and deep.

In other circumstances, Maggs had been known to act violently, but in Tobias Oates's house he was a sloth. His heavy limbs bled into the darkness and as the clock ticked loudly in the downstairs hallway, he seemed to flow from room to room as slow as a moon-made shadow.

He stood above the bed of a young spinster. The vigour of her dreams had served to push her night cap from her head. Her hair was loose, floating like seaweed around her sleeping face. One bare white arm was flung out across the sheet, the other held between her

41

knees beneath the covers. Beside her bed was a dresser where the intruder found a piece of jewellery, a necklace. He picked it up and ran it through his three fingers, before quietly laying it down again.

Two o'clock found him in another room, his severe hawk-nosed face an inch away from Mary Oates's small down-turned mouth. He stood over Tobias Oates who was sleeping on his stomach in a perfect imitation of his son.

As the hall clock struck the quarter-hour, he reluctantly retreated to the kitchen. There he took a draught of cold water, and splashed a little on his face. The extreme agitation which had hitherto marked his face and body was no longer to be seen.

He sat himself at the kitchen table with his glass of water, and rested his eyes.

He woke with a great start to find a woman, an older big-bellied woman with strong forearms and large hands, standing over him.

She had the oil lamps lit. She was in cap and apron. 'Did he tell you to wait?' she said.

'He did, Ma'am,' said Jack Maggs, automatically smiling and showing her his strong straight teeth.

'Said he was going to fetch you a shilling? Said you were to tell him your story, is that so?'

He stood and stretched. 'So he said, Ma'am.'

The cook – for he assumed her to be so – shook her head and went about readying the kitchen for breakfast, riddling the grate, throwing in the coal, getting the great kettle back in its place on the cold black top.

'He cannot help himself. He saw your livery, and thought: there's a chap with dirty livery. Just what you would think or I would think, but Mr Oates, he can't stop there – he's thinking, how did that fatty-spot get on his shoulder? He's wondering, in what circumstances were the stockings torn? He's looking at you like a blessed butterfly he has to pin down on his board. It is not that he hasn't got a heart. Indeed, I'm like as not cold-hearted in comparison. But he is an author, as I'm sure you don't need telling, and he must know your whole life story or he will die of it. There's a boy from Tetley's with a porcelain eye, he left the poor little mite waiting half the day. Miss

Lizzie found the little tyke crying on the doorstep when she was going walking with the missus.'

'Well, I'll be on my way then,' said sleepy Jack, noticing for the first time his torn stockings. 'For to tell you the truth, Ma'am, I must be explaining myself to my own master.'

'Sit up all night and not get your shilling? No, no. You must go up.'

'I've a long way to travel, Ma'am, and a household to attend to.'

'You can't leave now. He's left you sitting for hours. You go up and tell him. He's a fine man, a good man. You won't find a better one.'

'Just the same,' said Maggs.

'Just the same, my aunt. You go, Sir, or I'll bring him down myself.'

'But surely he's asleep.'

'Asleep? He never sleeps. It's half past five and he's in his room. Come, I'll show you where it is. If he's writing in his book, don't mind. Just say, here I am and John's my name and I am here for to get the tip you left me all night waiting for.'

So Maggs ascended the stairs a second time. It was just as well, he thought. *If 'twere done, 'twere best done quickly . . .*

13

Tobias Oates had an obsession with the Criminal Mind. He found evidence of its presence in signs as small as the bumps upon a pick-pocket's cranium, or as large as La Place's *Théorie analytique* which showed the murder rate in Paris unchanged from one year to the next.

There was a little shop in Whitechapel, the province of a certain Mr Nevus, where Tobias was in the habit of purchasing what he called 'Evidence'. Here he had recently paid a very hefty sum for the hand of a thief. With the exception of the tell-tale little finger, which was malformed, the fingers of the hand were long, thin, very delicate; sadly in opposition to the skirt of skin which trailed back from the harshly butchered wrist. This hand floated in a large wide-throated jar of formaldehyde identified by a brown discoloured label, on which was inscribed a legend in Arabic the meaning of which was not, as yet, available.

He had many such secrets hidden in his study. There, in that cubby hole labelled 'M', were the notes he had made on his visit to the Morgue in Paris. There, on that very high shelf up against the ceiling, was a parcel wrapped in tissue paper and tied with black ribbon – the death mask of John Sheppard, hanged at Tyburn in 1724.

There was much of the scientist about Tobias Oates. The study, with its circular window and its neat varnished systems of shelves and pigeon holes, was ordered as methodically as a laboratory. There was not a loose piece of anything here, not a nightingale feather or an unbound sheet of paper: everything was secured in its own place, tied up with ribbon, or tucked away in labelled envelopes. In these corners Tobias Oates stored not only his Evidence, but also experiments, sketches, notes, his workings-up of the characters who he hoped would one day make his name, not just as the author of comic adventures, but as a novelist who might topple Thackeray himself. And it was this ambition, always burning bright within him, which brought him to his desk before dawn on that day when Jack Maggs came knocking on his door.

The sharp, demanding nature of these knocks announced a visitor who was unfamiliar with his household. Tobias swiftly slid the jar into the corner of his desk. He placed an open encyclopedia in front of it, and picked up his quill. He opened his chap book. He appeared, as he turned his head towards the door, rather as he does in the portrait Samuel Laurence painted of him in 1838. That is, he looked towards his visitor as at a bailiff, or some other person with the power to knock him off his perch.

'Enter.'

The door swung open to reveal Percy Buckle's footman.

Tobias Oates took in the splashed stockings, sooty knees, damage to the powdered hair.

'Is this bad news?' he asked.

The dark eyes stared back at him balefully.

The writer reached for the golden cord which tied his gown, pulled it loose, tied it once again.

'The pain returned?' he guessed, but he was very confused by such a visitor at such an hour.

The fellow took a half-step into the room.

'What happened to your stockings?'

'I fell,' the footman said curtly, blinking and looking hard around him.

'For heaven's sake, man, it is five in the morning.'

'The hours are hard, Sir.'

'You were dragged out from your bed? Does that mild man really send his servants out at such hours?'

For answer the visitor clenched his two hands and held them out strangely from his sides. This gesture was queer and unexpected, suggesting more power than any servant had a right to assume. It was then Tobias began to feel afraid.

'Some wrong has been done you?'

'I've been waiting all the night, since you finished your pudding.'

The footman took a further step into the room. Toby picked up the only weapon available, his paperweight. It was a two-pound weight belonging to the kitchen scales.

'But where, dear God? All night?'

'In the street.' Jack Maggs closed the door behind him.

'This street? Outside my house?'

'And then most recently, I was conveniently inside your kitchen.'

'Man, you're shivering.'

'I know it.'

Tobias did not relinquish his two-pound weight, but he offered the chair he had been sitting on. 'And what is your true purpose, old fellow?'

Jack Maggs had sat himself in the chair but immediately stood up again, folding his great arms across his chest. 'What was it you did to me at dinner time? To be blunt, Sir, that's what's on my mind.'

'Ah, so that's it. The pain has come back!'

'Tell me what you did to me.'

45

For answer Tobias attempted to lay his hand against the servant's cheek, but Jack Maggs jerked back his head, curled his lips and showed his gums.

'You pried into my secrets.'

'No.'

'That's why those gentlemen were looking at me so strange when I woke up.'

'You deserve an explanation,' said Tobias carefully, 'but you'll not get it by glowering at me. Here, I'll take this stool, and you have my chair again. No one wishes you ill, you have my word. What you call "strange" was human sympathy. They are gentlemen, perhaps, and you are a footman, but they were moved by you. You are filled with Phantoms, Master Maggs. It is these Phantoms who cause you such distress. Did you know that? Do you know what hobgoblins live inside your head like beetles in a fallen log?'

'But how did you make me speak?' cried the visitor, sitting forward again in the chair, his hands upon his spattered knees. 'In all my life I never have spoke in my sleep, not never.'

'Last night you were a Somnambulist.'

'Whatever it is called, it is a terrible thing, Sir, for a man to feel his insides all exposed to public view, a thousand times worse than to come before you with my stockings in this state.'

'Would you rather keep the pain?'

'I would have it back ten times over, if my secrets came with it.'

There was a long silence

'Do you read?' Tobias asked at last.

'I am not an ignorant man, if that is what you're thinking.'

'You might like to read that little chap book by your elbow. There, that's the one. Turn to the third last page. The date is the sixteenth of April. There you may read exactly what secrets you have given me.'

Jack Maggs stared at the book but did not touch it. 'Oh Sir,' he said, very quietly. 'I do really wonder whether that were wise of you.'

'Open it. Read.'

The footman shivered so violently that Tobias Oates was reminded of *Pharaoh*, a race-horse belonging to his father whose

46

freckled flanks would twitch and shiver at the onset of the saddle. Then, as Jack Maggs slowly and carefully read the two pages of handwriting, Tobias Oates hatched his scheme.

'This is all I said? Naught else besides?'

'That is all.'

'Then I was drunk, Sir, if you'll forgive my French.'

'But this Phantom lives within you,' said Oates earnestly. 'You have a creature who wishes you harm, who lives within you like a worm lives in the belly of a pig. It is the Phantom who hurts your face.'

'I ain't acquainted with any Phantom, Sir. I never heard his name before.'

'I believe that I can remove this pain of yours for ever.'

'Oh, I have had the pain for many years, Sir. It is an old friend by now.'

'Was it friendly to be so attacked in public?'

Jack Maggs closed the little chap book and placed it carefully back upon the desk. 'I am happy as I am, Sir.'

'But what if I should take the demons from your heart where they are causing you pain? What if I write them on paper and then place the pages in this box here? When we are done, we can go to this fireplace, Jack Maggs, and we can burn them together.'

'But what is it to you, Sir? It is my pain after all.'

'I am a naturalist.'

'I heard you was an author.'

'Yes, an author. I wish to sketch the beast within you. If you were to continue with this experiment I would not only attempt the cure, I would pay you wages.'

'I do not want money, Sir.'

Tobias laughed suddenly, bitterly. 'Good. What other inducement might I offer you? Not to cure your pain? You are fond of your pain.'

'I don't need nothing.'

'An introduction?'

The footman hesitated. Oates felt that hesitation, like the dull pressure of an eel on the end of a baited line.

'What mean you by introduction?'

47

'I was imagining you might like an introduction to a superior household . . .'

The footman waved this away.

'It was some other type of introduction that you sought? Speak up.'

'Well, I had planned to ask you, Sir, if you had visited the house again. It took my attention when you spoke of it.'

'Ask now.'

'There are still Thief-takers in business,' the footman began. 'Is that what I understood you to have said?'

'You were robbed?'

'You mentioned a Thief-taker at dinner. Partridge. Him who can find any man in England.'

'There is someone you want found?'

'It's a family matter, Sir.'

'So that could be our bargain?' Tobias Oates leaned forward on his stool and put out his small square hand to shake on it.

'I never said I wanted it.' Jack Maggs folded his arms across his chest. There was a pause. 'But if I were inclined that way, when would you deliver him?'

'Directly.'

'Today?'

'No, no. Good heavens. There would have to be value in the bargain for me. Four weeks, three.'

'No, no,' the footman stood, shaking his head and knocking his knuckles together. 'I could not wait four weeks.'

'Three,' said Tobias Oates, also standing.

'Two,' said Jack Maggs. 'Two or nothing.'

'Two then. Can't say fairer than that.'

The footman put out his hand to shake and Tobias Oates imagined he could feel an equal but opposite enthusiasm in the other's violent grasp.

14

'Then this is how we will proceed,' said Tobias Oates, turning his back so that his great excitement could be hidden from the subject. 'I will send a note to your Mr Buckle, explaining the present circumstances.'

'He'll dismiss me from his service.'

'On my word, he will *not* dismiss you.'

'He will.'

'By the Lord above!' Tobias turned. 'Mr Buckle will do exactly as I wish him to.'

'If I am dismissed, where will I have my crib?'

'Your master is a student of Mesmerism. He will be pleased to make you available for science.'

Jack Maggs's eyes narrowed, his hawk-nosed face turned hard and shiny, just like, Tobias thought, a peasant with a pig to sell.

'I never said I were available to science.'

'Nonsense. You made a bargain.'

'No. You will get me to the Thief-taker. That is the bargain.'

'Yes, I undertake to introduce you to Mr Partridge and do everything in my power to make that meeting a productive one for you. You, for your part, will do what I ask of you.'

But the fellow was now staring down mulishly at his hands.

'You never said nothing about science.'

'For God's sake, man,' cried Tobias Oates irritably.

'Don't shout at me, Mr Oates. I know what I heard.'

'What is there to be unsure about?'

Jack Maggs opened his hands so that the stumps of his fingers lay plainly displayed upon his knee. 'I won't have nothing written down.'

Tobias feared he was about to lose his subject. He had played his hand too obviously. The man had seen his need.

'That's a pity, Master Maggs, because the deal is done and good enough to stand up in a Court of Law. I am going to make these movements,' he said, keeping his voice as stern and solemn as a magistrate. 'They are called "passes".'

'No.'

'You look me in the eye,' cried Tobias Oates. He began to pass his hands before the footman's malevolent, heavy-lidded eyes. 'Watch my hands, fellow.'

Finally, Jack Maggs did watch. He watched warily, sitting a little sideways in the chair, as if the square white hands might do him a damage. And yet, by the time night had lifted from the misty little garden, his unshaven chin was resting on his chest.

'Can you hear me?' Tobias Oates asked.

'Yes, I can hear you.'

Tobias blew out his red lips in silent relief. He reached across to his desk and picked up, first his note book, then his quill.

'Are you comfortable?'

The footman shifted his backside, a little irritably. 'Yes, comfortable.'

'Is the pain there?'

'Leave me alone.'

'Now you and I, Jack Maggs, we are going to imagine a place where there is no pain. Can you find a place like that?'

'Leave me alone. The pain is always there.'

'Then we are going to make a picture, like in a fairy tale. We are going to imagine a door so thick, the pain cannot get to you. We can imagine high walls made of thick stone.'

'A prison . . .'

'Very well, a splendid prison, with its walls twenty feet thick and – '

The Somnambulist began to move his arms about violently. 'No!' he shouted. 'No, damn you!'

'Quiet,' hissed Tobias. 'Do you hear me? Quiet. If you don't like a prison you can have a blessed fortress. A castle with battlements and flying flags. It can be a house. It does not matter.'

'A house.'

'Yes. A good sturdy house with double walls of London brick, and oak shutters on the windows.'

'Morrison Brothers on the doors.'

'Very good. Indeed. The locks and latches are made by dear old Morrison Brothers. Now we are standing on its threshold. Where is the pain?'

'Damn the pain. It always follows me.'

'In a shape? Is it the same shape? Like a man? Like an animal?'

'I'm trying. I'm trying.'

'Good. Good man.'

'When I look at it, it changes. Now there are two of them.'

'A man and an animal.'

'No, no, leave off, leave off of me. Leave me alone.'

'Very well. Is the pain there?'

'Yes, of course. I told you. It is always there. I have to stop. I have to stop this now.'

'We can stop it by going inside the house and locking the pain outside.'

'Must I?'

'Yes, you must.'

A pause.

'Where are you now?'

'God help me, I have done what you told me to. I have gone inside the house.'

'Where is the Phantom?'

'You know the answer.'

'Is he inside or outside the house?'

The Somnambulist placed his hands over his ears.

'Inside or outside?'

'How can I see when you are talking to me all the time? Let me alone if you please.' The footman paused, and frowned. 'There are people everywhere. I can't see him.'

'There are people inside the house?'

'Ever so many.'

'Who are they?'

'I don't know them.'

'What sort of people?'

'Gentlemen . . . and ladies.'

'What are they doing?'

'Walking around, spying on things. They are opening the drawers and the cupboards.'

'What of the Phantom?'

'Looking in through the window, most agitated.'

'Because locked out?'

'Yes, locked out.'

'And the pain is gone?'

'No, the pain is bad. They should not be there. It is my place, not theirs.'

'Yes, it is your place. Yours alone.'

'They don't want me owning it. They'll take it from me.'

'No, it is yours, Jack Maggs. You know it is yours. You must expel everything that agitates you.'

'They won't listen to me, Sir. I am not a gentleman.'

'But have you tried?'

'Yes, yes,' Jack Maggs cried passionately. 'A hundred times over, I have told them, but they will not listen to me, and I must do what they say.'

'What shall we do? What might persuade them do you think?'

'Oh, Sir, that sort . . . that sort should pet the old double-cat.'

'The double-cat?'

'The double-cat. The thief's cat. It has a double twist in the cord.'

'You mean the cat o'nine tails?'

'The double-cat is heavier.'

Tobias Oates had been sitting with his legs crossed, writing diligently in his court reporter's shorthand, but when he heard this comment he looked up sharply. 'Perhaps we could open the door and simply ask them to leave.'

'Oh, that's a joke.' The sleeping man twisted his mouth into an ugly shape. 'A very good joke, that is.'

'Well, if you would like to try a joke, my man, see what I am doing to them now.'

'I can't see.' Jack Maggs contorted in his chair. 'I can't see you doing anything.'

'Oh yes you can. You can see exactly what I am doing. I am sending them to sleep. Can't you see that?'

'I'm not sure.'

'Of course you can. Can't you see their eyes closing? You know I have the power to do that, don't you?'

'I think they are dying.'

'Some are falling down, but it is only sleep that causes it. They are falling asleep.'

'Now what will I do with them?'

'We are going to get your Phantom to carry them out.'

'He won't do that.'

'He will do it if I tell him to. I am telling him to remove these people from your stronghold. Look at him. How is he today?'

'He has a nasty look about him, Sir. He keeps staring at me.'

'Yes, but he will do as I say, and he is strong enough to carry out the sleeping people. Some of them are quite large, aren't they? Do you see a woman with double chins?'

'No, I don't think so.'

'Surely there is a woman there in a black dress with a great deal of jewellery?'

'I think I see her now.'

'Is the Phantom dragging her?'

'No, he has picked her up. He is picking her up and carrying her out of my house.'

'You must be feeling a deal better.'

'Yes, I am.'

'Is there any pain?'

'Everything is much better. Much better, thank you, Sir. He is going to stay outside the door now, Sir?'

'When he has carried everyone out.'

'He has, Sir. He's a such a jolly old bullock, ain't he?'

'He has removed them already?'

'He's a regular dervish, Sir.'

'And outside now?'

'Yes, outside.'

'Then I am locking the door. You are in your house. You are all alone. Nothing can harm you. You are going to the window now. You are looking out of the window?'

'Yes, I am looking out of the window.'

'What do you see? Any street numbers? Shops?'

'Nothing, Sir.'

'You can't see anything?'

'Pitch black, Sir.'

'Come, Jack Maggs, there is the lamplighter, now look – it's as bright as day.'

At this, the Somnambulist became extremely agitated, rolling his eyes and striking himself upon the breast.

'I am not permitted to tell you.'

'You must.'

'No,' cried the footman and threw out his arms, one of which struck Tobias Oates a grazing blow upon his temple.

'Cease!' cried Toby. 'Be still!'

But Jack Maggs groaned and flung himself violently back in his chair.

'Be still there, that's a fellow. Down now.' In this style Tobias continued to soothe his angry subject, talking very low, as to a frightened beast.

When peace was finally established, Tobias Oates stood and gazed down at Jack Maggs. He would be the archaeologist of this mystery; he would be the surgeon of this soul.

His youthful face was flushed, and the flecks in his pale blue eyes had turned as bright as mica. He picked up the stool and moved it over to the desk, and though it was too low for such a task, he sat upon it to compose his letter.

'Dear Mr Buckle,' he began, 'one sometimes hears a servant described by this or that lady as a "treasure".'

With his prisoner's breathing whispering in his ear, he continued – three drafts before he had it exactly right.

15

It was Edward Constable who informed Mrs Halfstairs that her new footman was missing. He presented himself triumphantly in her parlour door at six o'clock on Monday morning, knocking in that brisk way – *one, two, one two* – that was at once so characteristic and so insolent.

She bade him enter.

'Yes, Constable.'

'It's your man, Ma'am . . . He's bolted.'

Her stomach tightened. She lay her quill down on the blotter.

'Which *man*, Mr Constable? If it is Mr Maggs you mean, he has likely gone on an errand for the master. Did you inquire of the master?'

'It is my belief, Ma'am, that Mr Maggs was never in his life an upper servant. He seems to be some kind of rascal.'

'You are not a parson,' said Mrs Halfstairs, 'and were not employed to have beliefs. Did you check with the master?'

'You think the master harmed?'

She had thought no such thing, but now she thought it – she saw again the dreadful death of the previous footman, his skull half blown away and all that *matter* on the oaken dresser.

'I came first to you, Ma'am,' said the footman. 'I did not think to wake the master.'

'Then go now, if you please, Mr Constable, and check the silver.'

'The silver, Ma'am?'

She caught his bright hard eye.

'Not the master, Ma'am? The *silver*?'

'Do as I have asked you,' said Mrs Halfstairs. 'And pray do not disturb Mr Spinks with this news until I tell you to.'

She climbed the stairs with a heavy heart, wishing for the old days when Mr Spinks had ruled the household. Constable would not have behaved this way then. Pope would not have dared to kill himself. As she walked heavily up the stairs – her breathing came hard to her – Mrs Halfstairs was convinced already that her master had been harmed. Her mood was therefore much elevated when she peered round Mr Buckle's partly opened door and found him safely snoring in one corner of his enormous bed.

As she returned to the ground floor a knock came on the front door, and she answered it herself, to Mr Oates's messenger.

By the time Constable came to inform her that the silver had not been stolen, she had carefully examined the contents of Tobias Oates's letter and knew that Jack Maggs was to be a source of glory not of shame.

She gave the envelope to Mr Constable so he might take it to their master.

'I heard the door bell, Ma'am.'

'Yes, Mr Constable. It was this same letter.'

'Perhaps Ma'am, could I ask, that I be permitted to answer the door, as is my duty?'

'I am always pleased for you to do your duty, Mr Constable. And your master will be pleased to receive this letter at your hand.'

That gave him pause a moment. But then he came at her from a different quarter.

'And did you notice, Mrs Halfstairs, when you was answering the door, did you happen to notice that the next-door servants were about again?'

'No, Mr Constable, I did not.'

'I also went to the door, Ma'am.'

'No need for you to have done that, Mr Constable.'

'And found them all everywhere about the street.'

'I did not notice, Mr Constable.'

'I wonder, did it occur to you, Ma'am, that perhaps Mr Maggs has run away with them?'

'Run away with them, Constable?'

'He has an interest in them, does he not? He said he was to be their footman, although I doubt he was, but he had a very fierce interest in that household, and asked us many questions about Mr Phipps himself. Seeing all this activity, Ma'am, I naturally drew it to Mr Spinks's attention, and he thought that may explain your man's departure.'

'Mr Constable, did I not request you to wait until you informed Mr Spinks?'

'Ma'am, you know it most improper for a footman to go having secrets from a butler.'

Mrs Halfstairs took a breath. 'Take this letter to the master,' she said at last. 'And when you are done with it, present yourself down here.'

And then she went to find Mr Spinks and see if she might restore some order to that poor old wandering mind.

16

At half past nine the absent footman limped in through the kitchen door. His eyes were wild and red, his hair most queerly disarrayed; a great smudge of black disfigured his smart yellow livery; and yet there was, for all his hobbling, nothing in the least apologetic in his demeanour.

'Can a cove get a cup of something?' he demanded, sitting down at the long deal table and glaring at Mercy Larkin who was busy cutting the rot from the day's potatoes.

'Yes, Sir,' said she, but no sooner had she set her knife down than Mrs Halfstairs, always alert to the creak of the kitchen door, came clattering in from her parlour on her heavy heels and – without one word about Jack Maggs's disgraceful livery – escorted him straight away upstairs to be brought before the master.

'Can a *cove* get something?' said Constable mocking Jack Maggs's hoarse voice. 'That *cove* is about to get his marching orders.'

'I never heard of such a thing,' said Miss Mott. 'It is the butler's job to dismiss him. I can't imagine what Miss Halfstairs is thinking of – taking him before the master.'

'At Lineham Hall,' said Constable, complacently stirring his third teaspoon of sugar into his tea, 'he would have his livery removed at the gate house and be sent off in his undervest.'

'Mr Constable!' cried Miss Mott.

'Or worse,' said Constable, who had a fondness for shocking the cook. 'I once saw a page boy put out in the frost with nothing but a pair of old hessians on his feet.' And he then went on to describe, in some detail, the cruel ways in which various servants had been dismissed from his previous establishment.

Constable had a long repertoire of such incidents but was cut off in his first chapter not only by the return of Mrs Halfstairs and Jack Maggs, but also by the arrival of the butler himself. Mr Spinks entered the kitchen with a long brass poker which he had, perhaps absentmindedly, carried away from Mr Buckle's snuggery. He stood with his back to the dresser, swaying slightly, seemingly unsure of why he had come. Observing the distressing confusion in those cloudy eyes, Constable turned all his attention on the miscreant.

'Oh hello Maggs,' said he conversationally. 'If you had slept the night at home you would have woken to the sight of your friends next door galloping in and out of their front door.'

Jack Maggs jerked his head towards his informant.

'A stranger would have thought them thieves,' continued Constable, as if unaware of the effect he was having on his listener. 'Sugar bowls. Tea pots. You should have seen the *plunder* they carried off.'

'Mr Phipps is returned?' asked Maggs, fixing upon Constable a gaze both fierce and hungry.

'If you had been back a half hour earlier, you might have had your old job back.'

'We have no interest in that household, Mr Constable,' interrupted Mrs Halfstairs.

'Young Mr Phipps was there?' Maggs asked again but to no effect. Mrs Halfstairs was staring malevolently at Mr Constable and so Maggs repeated the question to Mercy, who answered him gently.

'Not Mr Phipps. Just his carriage, and two of the upper servants.'

'You saying he is back?'

'No, Mr Maggs. I'm afraid he ain't returned.'

Mr Spinks banged his poker. 'Sit!'

'Sit,' echoed Mrs Halfstairs. 'What is it that you are thinking?'

Jack Maggs did not sit. 'I am thinking that if Mr Phipps is home, it is time for you and me, Miss Halfstairs, to say farewell.'

Mr Spinks cleared his throat.

'Did not Mr Buckle welcome you back into the fold?' said Mrs Halfstairs, turning incredulously to Mr Spinks. 'Did you ever hear so generous and Christian a speech? No, no, Mr Maggs, it is Mr Buckle who is your master now.'

'He's not sacked?' cried Constable, indignantly.

'You skate on very thin ice, Constable,' hissed Mrs Halfstairs. She turned back to Mr Spinks. 'It is true that he has behaved in a most improper manner, but on the other hand he has found favour with Mr Oates. That is true, is it not, Mr Spinks?'

'Oates likes him?' Constable demanded. 'Oates has an interest in him? Oates will visit? This Hopping Giles has become a social ornament? Is that what I am witnessing?'

'As any crossing sweeper would know,' said Mrs Halfstairs, 'it would be a distinction to the household to have a connection with so up-and-coming a gentleman as Mr Oates.'

'But this rascal,' cried Constable, 'he never even heard of Captain Crumley.'

Mercy saw that this last intelligence reached Mrs Halfstairs with a certain force. The housekeeper blinked her little eyes. 'Still, we will not release him to Mr Phipps,' she said at last.

Constable appealed to the butler. 'He could not do his own hair. I did it for him.'

'Mr Maggs has agreed to be the subject of Scientific Experiment. Is that not so, Mr Spinks? It is your brow?' Mrs Halfstairs suggested to Maggs. 'Mr Oates wishes to measure it?'

'Surely, Ma'am,' sneered Constable, 'you measured it already.'

'You have pushed my patience, Mr Constable.'

'It is a light enough load, Ma'am.'

Mrs Halfstairs looked hard at Mr Spinks.

'The point,' began Spinks, 'the point, Sir . . .'

'The point is about service,' said Mrs Halfstairs. 'And I cannot see that you can require Mr Constable's any longer.'

There was now a great silence in the kitchen.

'Quite so,' said Spinks at last. He tapped the brass poker on the floor between his shoes, then turned a stern unflinching gaze on his footman. 'Quite so. Not require him.'

It was obvious Constable had not expected this turn of events. He began to rise from the table, a teaspoon still in his hand. His handsome face was stricken.

'Mr Spinks . . . Sir? Mr Spinks, Sir, do you know me?'

Mr Spinks tapped the poker on the floor. 'I know you, Sir.'

Constable held himself erect, but Mercy could see – anyone could see – that his cheeks were hollowed and his eyes desolate.

'Sir . . . you are dismissing me?' His proud demeanour was contradicted by his trembling voice. 'Mr Spinks, have you forgotten?

May I remind you, Sir, about the problems with my letters . . .'

During all of this dispute Jack Maggs had seemed to be occupied with his own thoughts, but now he took two paces forward and stood beside Edward Constable.

'Mr Constable and me,' said he. 'We are a pair.'

Then, much to Mercy Larkin's surprise, he smiled at Mrs Halfstairs.

'We are bookends, ain't we, Mrs Halfstairs? Can't have one without the other.'

17

It is no easy matter to ride the footplate of a phaeton, to pose like a piece of German porcelain, to float like one of God's angels above the mud and ordure of the London streets.

Yet when the two footmen walked out to the mews the following morning – that is Tuesday, April the eighteenth – Jack Maggs did not request instruction, and he rode without anyone having shown him how to keep his knees a little loose, to hold his chin high, to alight before the coach was finally still. Even Edward Constable, who was of a habitually critical frame of mind, was impressed by the performance.

Their first appointment was the Patent Office Library on Chancery Lane, and although there was no more momentous business at hand than their master's wish to peruse the plans of the latest donkey engine, they proceeded towards this destination at desperate speed, cutting in ahead of pony carts and hackney cabs, in a style at once so reckless and arrogant that even the most belligerent of London drivers – and that was the grand majority – gave way to the handsome blue phaeton with the gold lion emblazoned on its door. Having watched Maggs survive this desperate charge it was obvious to Edward Constable that his benefactor had, not to put too fine a point on it, a 'gift'.

At the Patent Office, Constable opened the coach door, guided his master past a puddle, and watched him scurry up the steps. The very sight of Percy Buckle Esq., with his sunken cheeks and bandy little duck-legged walk, would normally have been enough to put him in an irritable sort of mood, and indeed it was a constant trial to him to wait in attendance on so low-bred a master, but on this particular morning, Edward Constable had almost no interest in Mr Buckle. It was his fellow footman who preoccupied him, and in this regard his skill on the footplate was a very small item indeed.

The two servants stood side by side on the footpath of Chancery Lane. Only inches separated them, but the newcomer affected a distance which Constable, much burdened with his own feelings of guilt and gratitude, soon found intolerable.

'You are a puzzle of a fellow,' he began.

Maggs turned, briefly presenting him with the blank wall of his face.

'If I was unfriendly to you,' Constable persisted, ' – and it is not even "if" for I know I was . . . '

'It's past, mate. Forget it.'

'My friend is dead. It makes me bitter, and when I'm feeling bitter I say things I regret.'

'Say no more then.'

'But I must say more,' cried Constable. 'So help me, Mr Maggs, I must do more. I am a man that always pays his debt.'

'The old dame was whipping you, and I took a great personal pleasure in stopping her. But if you want to thank me . . . do you know that fellow driving our coach?'

'Foster.'

'You know him a good while, no doubt?'

'He was with Mr Quentin when we were at Bath.'

'You've done him some favour in your time?'

'We know each other, Mr Maggs. What do you want? Say the word.'

'Tell him that Jack Maggs begs the use of the titty he is sucking on.'

'Mr Maggs, I want to oblige you.'

'Then here's the answer. Ask him.'

'But Mr Maggs, you ask the one thing I cannot do.'

61

'Your wooden leg ain't broken, is it? Go tell that dozy old farmer that his brother the footman wants to dance with his sister Miss Flask.'

'I enjoy a gin myself, Mr Maggs, but a footman in his livery cannot be seen drinking from a flask.'

'You said yourself – I am a scoundrel, not a footman. A Knight of the Rainbow may not get a thirst, but a scoundrel . . . Come, Mr Thingstable, I have the pain back in my face. Would you rather I went into that little dram shop yonder? I do not doubt they would be pleased enough to have my money. It is a funny thing about a dram shop, they have a great fondness for we rascals. We are patron saints to them.'

'I'll speak to Foster, Mr Maggs.'

The lanky coachman, a West Country man, stayed in his seat with a rug around his knees, and from this high throne engaged Constable in a long and dogged negotiation. Finally terms were agreed on, and he handed across his 'drop of the doings'.

'You had to pay him?' Maggs inquired.

'It is my pleasure.' Constable looked up and down the street which was, at that moment, free of servants. 'Now. Drink it now.'

Alas, it was at that very moment, as Maggs tipped the flask up to his lips, that Percy Buckle came skipping down the steps of the Patent Office.

'Where to now, Sir?' shouted the coachman, but not before Percy Buckle saw what he was not meant to. He frowned and clapped his gloved hands together. 'Well, do you know,' he said, looking from Maggs to Foster very suddenly. 'Well, do you know, today I'm going to try a new one.'

'A new patent, Sir?' cried Foster, perhaps worried he would lose his silver flask for ever.

'A new book shop,' said Percy Buckle. 'The largest shop in London.'

Constable opened the door for his master. 'That would be Bowes & Bowes, Sir,' he said nervously.

'Now there you are wrong, my man,' said Mr Buckle, fetching an addressed letter from his side pocket. 'It ain't. It's Lackington's Temple of the Muses.'

'Never heard of it, Sir,' said Constable.

'Well you don't know London like I do,' said Percy Buckle. 'It's in Finsbury Square.'

'Up Holborn Hill?' The coachman groaned.

''Fraid so,' said Percy Buckle. ''Fraid it is precisely up the good old Holborn Hill.'

At the foot of Holborn Hill, Maggs and Constable were dispatched to run alongside while the groom applied the whip to the horses' backs. Thus it was a hot and weary Maggs who finally helped Percy Buckle dismount at Finsbury Square.

'Give it,' said his master.

'Pardon, Sir?'

'The flask,' said Percy Buckle, thereby causing one red spot to appear on each of his cheeks.

Constable watched Maggs. He saw how fiercely he looked into Percy Buckle's eyes, and how his master twitched and jerked in the gaze of his servant's attention. But then, to his great relief, he saw Jack Maggs take the coachman's silver flask from his back pocket and put it into his master's hand.

18

A footman caught drinking in the street might consider himself fortunate to keep his job, but to Jack Maggs, who was not a footman, the confiscation of the coachman's flask brought – *Jod's Blood* – a most ungrateful passion rushing along the capillaries of his face.

When he returned to the house he was still out of sorts, and it took everything in him to accept the polishing rags and beeswax which Mrs Halfstairs now presented to him. She put him in a dark little cubby at the back of the house. And there, with no view of the street at all, he was compelled to polish the bindings of Mr Buckle's books. *Frig me for a blind man.* He had not come to London for this indignity. *Damn me for a horse.* He had come to meet with Henry Phipps. That gentleman might be arriving this very minute and he would not know.

At supper time he took the chair with the best view of the street, and never once took his eye off it. He drank his pint before the grace was said. He repulsed Mrs Halfstairs's questions about the mysteries of Mr Oates's experiments, bolted his shepherd's pie, refused his bread and butter pudding, and – without being dismissed or excused his labour – went up the gloomy staircase leaving the silent servants sitting, rather fearfully, in his wake.

Once in his room, he drove the bolt home in the lock and changed from the doeskins and white stockings into the darker, sturdier garments he had arrived in.

He had had little sleep the previous night and his heavy-lidded eyes were now sunken and red-rimmed, and his hair was speckled with London smuts, but he had no mind for his powder puff. He opened the tight little window, pushed his body out, and stared down into the street. Once or twice he sighed, and once it seemed that he might climb out the window, but he remained in this tight, uncomfortable pose for over an hour, listening to the carriages and voices in the street.

Then, suddenly, he heaved his bulky body out through the window.

He had one hand on the sill and began to edge his great leg out in the direction of Henry Phipps's house, and there he was – splayed out like a spider – when he heard, above the noise of carriage wheels on the street below, a sound more alarming and more intimate: 'Hsst.'

Under the moonless sky he moved, sloth-like, back in the direction from which he had come.

'Hssst.'

He got his hand back on his window sill. Then he allowed himself to turn, and look back along the roof line. He was not sure what he could see, but there was an uncertain dark shape at the third dormer window of Mr Buckle's house.

'Constable?'

There was no answer, but he watched in horror as a shadow poured from the window, sliding, then crawling across the slates towards him.

He saw the hair, the skirt, the maid.

'Go back, for God's sake.'

For answer she gave a startled cry, and slipped. He leaned out towards her but the stupid biddy skittered towards the guttering, her skirt ballooning out like a spill of ink, her pale hands flapping fish-like against the tiles.

Jack Maggs did not save her, but something did, for here she was alive, and crawling up towards him.

'Get to the blazes,' he hissed. 'Go back.'

'Cor,' she said. 'Those tiles is slippery as a Christmas pig.'

He took hold of her sleeve for she was still being most careless of her safety. She hooked her hand into his belt. 'What you up to?' she inquired. 'What's a footman doing crawling round the roof at night?'

'None of your damned business, Judy.'

'My name is Mercy, Mr Maggs, as you very well know.' She brought her face close to his. He had suspected her drunk but now he discovered that her breath was sweet with sugared tea.

'Get back inside.'

'I may,' said she, 'or I may not.'

'If you don't want nothing bad to happen, Judy, you'll go, and quick and lively and forget you ever saw me here.'

She considered this threat. 'Then may I please go in through your window?'

'No.'

'It is an awful way back into my own. I'm afraid I'll fall.'

'Christ!'

'You're not very polite, are you.'

'I'll give you polite.' He helped her through into his room, and then climbed in himself and locked the door behind her. And then, with his heart pounding uncomfortably in his ears, he returned to the roof. A minute later he entered Henry Phipps's house through its unlatched dormer window.

Once inside he calmed considerably. He went carefully down the stairs, gathering blankets from the bedrooms as he went. In the gloomy drawing room he dropped the blankets on a settle and then emptied the contents of his jacket onto a pale yellow walnut bureau – a sheaf of paper, twine, a bone-handled clasp knife, a fat creamy tallow candle, a long yellow quill, a little apothecary's vial which would later reveal itself to be filled with a queer kind of ink. Lastly from his trouser pocket he removed a small silver-framed enamel portrait. He was about to place this on the desk but then changed his mind and returned the miniature to his pocket.

He next dragged the desk across the room so it stood beneath the windows. He removed his shoes. He picked up a blanket, then stood on the desk top. With the advantage of this height he was able to hang the blankets across the curtains. He used the knife to cut the twine, the twine to tie the blankets to the rods. He worked swiftly but neatly, and when he was finished there was – for all the makeshift quality of the arrangement – a workmanlike symmetry to it.

He came down from the desk, restored it to its previous position, then lit the candle, which first sputtered, then gathered strength as it revealed the sparkling nests of gilt everywhere adorning the handsome room: chairs, mirrors, picture frames, even on ceiling mouldings far above his head.

Here he settled himself, a massive man in the centre of a jewel box, carefully arranging his quill and his paper. He picked up the blue apothecary's bottle, and was about to remove its ground glass stopper when he heard a footstep on the upper stairs.

He snuffed the candle, standing quietly in the smoky dark, his heart beating very slow. He knew it was the man he sought. He knew without seeing him, without being told of his return, and when the footsteps came down into the hall he coughed first to give a decent warning.

'It's me,' he said. 'Jack Maggs.'

'I know it's you,' said Mercy. 'Who else would it be?'

19

Mercy Larkin's father had been a mechanic at the Woodwell pickle factory in Wapping, and had provided for his family handsomely. Mercy's mother had done a little of the lace work in the summers, and Mercy had for a while attended Mrs McFarlane's School where – if you put aside the blots and smudges – she did not disgrace herself as a scholar.

But one balmy night in May when Mercy – aged thirteen – was sitting on her front step cutting the patches of rot from the taters, she saw a strange procession of men walking down the steep and narrow street. There was a crowd of them on either side of a dray which was drawn by a pair of skittish chestnut mares. The men were whoaing and shouting for fear, it seemed, that the beasts would slip and fall. At first she thought the men actors in a theatre troupe but when they stopped silently before her she looked into the back of the dray and saw her pale-faced father laying on a bed of straw, with his bloody bandaged arm across his pale blue smock. It were no one's fault, the men said, for Horace had been clowning and had fallen backwards into the main drive. It was only a broken bone, but it flopped like an empty sock when the foreman himself lifted Horace Larkin and carried him inside to his bed. It was only a broken bone, yet what woe it brought, all so quickly: gangrene and death, penury and eviction, and on a hot May day in 1829 there were no crowds of men, only one workmate to help move the widow and her daughter from their little cottage in Finsbury. Their departure was early so no one would be awake to see their shame. They walked up the cobbled street on foot, then rode a dog cart to a damp and crumbling slum at the back of Fetter Lane. There Mercy and her mother attempted to set up a little business as the bakers and street vendors of plum duff.

This occupation proved taxing, and only erratically rewarding: more than once her mother came home with signs of damage on her clothes or person. Marjorie Larkin had always been quiet, but then, her husband had been noisy. He had taken up all the space and so her quietness was a relief, or at least could pass unnoticed. Now, in widowhood, her quietness seemed darker, deeper, more alarming, and when she cut her black hair so queerly short, she had nothing but silence to answer the questions of her weeping daughter. She sawed at the hair with the same knife they used to cut the plum duff into ha'penny slices.

During the day Mercy was imprisoned in their steamy little room with the foul smells of the fried-fish sellers drifting up in the hot air of the court below. Her mother would not say where she went or what she did or how much money she had. Her eyes seemed to sink back into her head and no one would guess that she was a young woman and had once been beautiful.

Then she began to take the duff out at night, loading her little cane basket and covering it with a cloth. Then she locked Mercy in the room with chains and a great black padlock. She was sometimes gone only a short time, but at other times she would be gone so long that Mercy began to fear her mother dead, and that she herself would die before anyone would find her.

They were dreary nights and days spent locked away above the gin-soaked little court. Mercy was not by nature a passive girl and she would never forget that hellish summer when she passed the hours pacing up and down the dreary room, praying to God to prevent her nibbling at the precious supply of duff-flour, to stop her dipping her wetted finger one more time.

Then one Sunday, without explanation, her mother began to work upon a pretty dress for her, sewing blue ribbon on its bodice, and adding layers of crêpe de chine which she hung from the waist. It was not a usual kind of dress but no one could deny that it was very gay, and although the girl was alarmed by its want of fashion, she was most encouraged by the fact that it was not black. Despite the fact she did not ask, she clearly understood that the mourning was now over.

No plum duff was cooked upon this long day, and the room was cooler and dryer on account of it. Finally mother and daughter set out, just as the bells began to ring for evensong. Neither of them had eaten all day long, but Mercy, although a little light-headed, was far too excited to think of food.

They walked down into Fleet Street, the mother in severe black, the daughter like a bird of paradise. They paraded, their heads high, amongst the quality along the Strand, and from thence on into Haymarket, at which jolly scene they arrived just on nine o'clock. There was a grandfatherly old fellow with a dented stove-pipe hat who had set himself up a coffee stall, and it was here, with the charcoal smoke blowing in their eyes, and the appetizing odours of coffee and chicory in their nostrils, that the two women finally paused.

The young girl's dress certainly drew attention, and there was nothing in the eyes of those who looked at her to suggest that it was – as she had been most certain – out of the fashion. It was the hottest part of summer and the crowds were heavy everywhere.

They had not been standing on their pitch more than a minute when a tall gentleman with a red set of whiskers doffed his hat to her mama, and talked to her with such solemn familiarity that Mercy supposed him to be an old employer of her father's. When, minutes later, her mother pushed her towards the man, and said, 'Go with him,' she went willingly.

That was when the storm started, not in the still, humid street that was their destination, but in Mercy's mind; years later, the confusion of her memory still blew dust and soot across that street and curled up into the evening sky.

She had set off in innocent expectation of being bought an ice, or tea; and indeed her stomach gave a most unladylike growl when they passed Reilly's Chop House. Instead, she and her companion went to the back of a casino, and stopped beside a door from behind which there emanated a great clattering of crockery, and the smell of onions cooking in butter.

The gentleman had barely spoken to her, and when he took her arm, she still thought him shy. He then called her 'Lettie' or 'Lassie'. His diction was not clear, and it occurred to her later that he had been the worse for drink. He helped her into the doorway, and she took the door knob, expecting it to open. When she found it locked, she did not have time to turn before she felt the stranger's arms around her waist, and then he was squashed against her back with all his great weight, holding her clamped, talking to her all the while he lifted the back of her dress.

She felt the air upon her skin. She did not know what to do.

What happened then happened, and like a broken plate was soon all pieces, most of them missing in the dark – the pain, the onions cooking in the butter, the smell of pipe tobacco on his whiskers, the wetness on her legs.

When he put some money in her hand, the coins dropped and rolled out into the lane and he – red-faced now – stopped and chased them, and brought them back to her, and doffed his hat.

'Thank you, Miss.' He looked as if he might cry.

'Thank you, Sir,' she said.

He hesitated, then turned back towards the coffee stand. She stepped down from the doorway and walked away from him. She sought out the dark corners of the lane, places where the wetness she could feel would not show up in the light.

She walked back through those boisterous crowds. Men sometimes spoke to her. She did not know how long she walked, or where she went. A tall severe woman, eyes glaring beneath her hat, handed her a small square of white paper: REPENT FOR THE KINGDOM OF HEAVEN IS AT HAND. She was still holding the paper when she found, at last, the coffee stand. Her mother, upon seeing her, slapped her daughter across the face, then immediately began to weep.

When the little fried-fish seller introduced himself, the mother stopped her tears and turned all her powerful upset on the stranger. She called him 'coarse' and 'vulgar'. She said he had a 'low understanding' of their situation.

'You don't recognize me, Ma'am?' said Percy Buckle, who had emerged from the confusion of Haymarket with the smell of fried fish heavy about his person. He was not 'vulgar' as Marjorie Larkin said, but had, in fact, 'a betterly appearance' with his brown surtout jauntily buttoned up to his black satin smock. He had his tray of fish slung by a leather strap about his slender neck.

'You scram. You skedaddle,' cried Marjorie Larkin, so loudly that a small crowd began to gather round them, and the owner of the coffee stall began to shout at them to move away.

'I am your neighbour, Ma'am,' said the earnest little man. 'And I am this girl's neighbour too, and with your permission I am going to take her to her home.'

But the mother did not understand his offer, imagined in fact that he was making the very offer that she had already solicited, and now the poor wretch turned – her eyes so dark and haunted – to the owner of the coffee stall, and asked him please to chase the fish seller away.

The coffee-stall holder, a large coarse man with a big voice, then began to shout. He called Marjorie Larkin a hoo-oor and other things, and splashed the slops from a cup across the cobbles at her.

'I am your neighbour,' the fried-fish man said quietly to the young girl.

'You are the Devil,' cried Marjorie Larkin.

Percy Buckle ignored the jeering crowd and repeated: 'I am your neighbour.'

Only when he opened his fishy little purse and put a silver florin in her hand, did Mercy's mother deign to notice him, and then she followed him, as he indicated she should – he did not touch her in any way – out of the Haymarket and back down along the Strand.

The sad little party made its way back into the unnamed court at the back of Fetter Lane where, the Larkins soon discovered, it was their benefactor who was responsible for the bad fish smell which daily filled their little room, his accommodation being just one floor below theirs.

That night the earnest little man cooked them a fish and potato soup, and then, having made them promise not to leave their room until they saw him again, he returned with freshly fried fish for their breakfast.

And that was the start of Mercy's long friendship with Percy Buckle who, even when he had ten fried-fish men working for him, always had time to sit and read the girl a bed-time story.

He was, as Mercy often said, the kindest, most decent man in all the world, and she would – as she later told Jack Maggs – as soon cut off her own arm as lose his kind opinion.

71

20

'I know it's you,' said Mercy, emerging from the dark of the stair, her glistening eyes holding the pin-point reflection of his candle. 'Who else would it be?'

Jack Maggs was thus exposed at his secret work: he had a dark blue apothecary's bottle in his hand, a tartan blanket wrapped around his broad shoulders.

'Christ, Judy, you have a taste for trouble.'

A half-wit would have known it wise to pretend no curiosity, but here she was making obvious note of all the clues to the mystery before her: the quill, the paper, the blankets he had tied up so neatly across the curtain rails.

He had begun to hide the bottle in his jacket pocket, but what was the point?

'Ain't you afraid of me?'

She raised her eyebrows mockingly. 'Oh, I know you would not harm me.'

He snorted. 'You is just a little mite, Judy. Your ma should be reading you fairy tales in bed.'

'My ma is a mad woman.'

It would be a lie to say the answer did not shock Jack Maggs but he continued speaking as if he had not heard her.

'Now,' he said, 'why don't I give you one more shy at the coconut? Why don't you go back to your bed, and mum's the word.'

'If you are such a fiercesome villain,' said she, 'how come you saved Eddie?'

'I don't know no Eddie.'

'Mr Constable, the footman. Him you had sworn to murder in his bed.'

He sat wearily on one of the gilded chairs which were arranged in a ring in the centre of the splendid room. He rubbed his face, smearing smuts amongst his stubble.

'I am an old dog,' he said, 'who has been treated bad, and has learned all sort of tricks he wishes he never had to know. You are a young woman with all her life ahead of her, Judy.'

'Mercy,' she insisted.

'Mercy then.'

Said she, 'I am an old dog too.'

'Mercy, I am too old a cove for you to fancy . . .'

She put her hand over her mouth but could not stop her laughter. 'Fancy? Lor, oh dear, Mr Maggs . . .'

He folded his arms angrily across his chest but said nothing.

'What are you planning?' she asked him.

'What am I planning?'

'Aye, what are you planning in Mr Phipps's house?'

'What I am planning . . .' He walked to the desk and began to shuffle through his pile of papers. 'What I am planning, little Miss Muffet, is to find my letters of recommendation which was left in this household.'

'But you don't have no letters. Eddie swears you don't.'

'Is that so?'

'He had to learn you how to fix your hair.'

Jack Maggs began to answer her, but – *Christ* – she held up her hand to quieten him. 'Shush. Listen.'

Now he, too, heard – a carriage. His first and only thought was Henry Phipps. He limped to the windows and peeked cautiously between the deep folds of blankets.

'It's only Buckle,' he said, 'come home from his Correspondence Society.'

'Oh Lor.' Mercy leaped to her feet. 'Dear Jesus – home so early.'

'He cannot need you now, at this hour.'

'No, no, I have to go. Oh dear God save me.'

And she turned and ran off up the stairs.

Maggs followed, but at a more leisurely pace. By the time he arrived at the dormer window, she was already outside, slipping and sliding her way across the mossy tiles in her stockinged feet. He did not doubt her ma had been a mad woman.

73

21

In the early morning, by the light of four bright candles, Jack Maggs finally dipped the great albatross quill into the apothecary's bottle.

He wrote, *Dear Henry Phipps*, in violet-coloured ink.

He did not write these words from left to right, but thus: sqqiɥd ʎɹuǝH ɹɐǝᗡ. He wrote fluidly, as if long accustomed to that distrustful art.

He paused, staring up at the gilded ceiling while the ink faded to a pale, pale lilac. Then he continued:

I did arrive on the date of which I had advised you and found you absent from these premises.

He watched these fresh lines fade, first to lilac, then to white; until, that is, they became invisible.

He continued:

I had hopes you might return tonight, perhaps having mistook my hastily written 23 for a 28, but I have waited these long hours on the settle, and now at your very handsome walnut desk in vain.

It is a most melancholy business to be solitary in the place in which I did invest such High Hopes, but I do trust my disappointment will be brief. I have a messenger who will soon fetch you. If you now read this letter it can only be because you have met up with him, the Thief-taker, and he has told you how to make these words visible. I hope he has remembered to tell you that you must BURN EVERYTHING when it is read. Many of the events I tell you are from a long time ago, but I fear they may still be used against me by my Enemies.

The Thief-taker has given you the mirror. If it be any cheap mirror, know that this is not the same as I gave him, for I am a wealthy man, and it was my pleasure to send the best mirror that can be obtained in London. If you are acquainted with the hallmarks of the great silversmiths, you will read a distinguished story on the mirror's handle.

Well, Henry Phipps, you will read a different type of story in the glass, by which I mean – mine own.

You will forgive me for being too much the bull at the gate in my previous correspondence. It was written in a great rush in a Dover Inn, soon after landing. I dare say that my words were not as well chosen as they might have been and that I revealed things that made you fear a Criminal coming to harm you.

Henry Phipps, you were raised to have a tender heart and to obey the laws. This was always so clear in your loving letters, and it is no stretch to imagine that you were frightened to hear Jack Maggs was finally on his way into your polite and educated life.

I had many years to prepare you, and I did not. But what is done is done and you now give me no choice but to put my life before you all at once, to make you privy to information that could, in the wrong hands, have me dancing the Newgate Jig.

You have known for many years that my name is Jack Maggs, although Maggs was not my father's name, but a name given to me by my foster mother who believed I talked too much. What my father's name was I cannot tell, for when I was just three days old I was discovered lying in the mud flats 'neath London Bridge.

I was picked up by Mudlarks. I do not recall this, but have so oft been told of my Good Fortune that for many years I saw them in my dreams: wraiths pulled up from the stinking mud of the Thames. These half-starved scroungers found the strength to fight for my shawl and bonnet with such a passion that it was always said by Silas Smith – my Benefactor – that it was a wonder I was not torn in two like the child divided thus by Solomon.

Now pay attention to this Silas Smith, for he will come into the History later. It was he, that lanky thief with the long face and claret nose – a parson's son – who paid the Mudlarks a ha'penny each for my naked body and then another ha'penny to carry me to a place where I might have the stinking mud washed off me.

He asked the moochers, did they know the whereabouts of a midwife, but they were slow of wit, and begged his pardon for never having heard of such a thing. Silas then asked them who it was attended when the babies were to be born. But the Mudlarks never lived inside a house and never saw a baby born and could not think how to get the money until the oldest of them thought that Mary Britten might answer the description.

– Then take me to her, Silas said.

He followed the shivering little river rats up Pepper Alley Stairs. He walked through that stinking rubbish strewn street – no longer there, so I have been told. He ducked under a rotting trellis, came into a court strung high and low with drying washing, its gutters spilling over with soap suds. He was always one to play the left-handed fiddle, but he could never have imagined that he would finally prosper from this adventure.

As the party came into the court, the baby was crying and the Mudlarks were growing most reluctant to proceed. The one holding me nodded his sharp little head down a passageway that opened in the furthest wall of the court, but Silas would not give the ha'penny until his guides had walked before him through the shadowed portal.

He held the ha'penny. The Mudlark still held the child. There was but one doorway at the end of the dark passageway and Silas knocked with his cane until the door was opened by a big-boned woman with wild red hair. Her shoulders were bare and her skin glowed white in the gloom.

– Madam, said Silas Smith.

Mary Britten did not even note the shining red nose. She told me, often enough, that her only observations were of me, and she did not want me. She heard the weak cry of a starving babe, the stink of cold & unwashed skin. She began to threaten with the bricks she had for the purposes of discouraging the rats.

– You take your rubbish somewhere else, she said. Take it to the foundlings hospital, she said, imagining Silas Smith a clergyman.

But then Silas did what was, for him, a most peculiar thing – he opened up his sovereign case.

Was it his heart he opened thus? I cannot say for sure, only that he was a thief, and receiver, what we called a 'Family Man' and normally very cagey with his money.

– I'll not see you disadvantaged, he told Mary Britten.

He gave her his calling card. Mary Britten curtsied to him and placed her brick bat on the floor.

Said she – I'm sorry, Sir, for how I spoke, but that is what becomes of us down here in Hell's Doorway. Sitting here, said she, looking at the Devil's thieving ways etc. etc.

Silas threw the boys a ha'penny and removed his tall black hat.

Mary opened wide her door, and invited me and Silas into her life.

I grew up being told these stories, and I never liked them even as a child. I heard a hundred times how I was starved and thin and wrinkled like a rag etcetera, how she washed me, wrapped me in a piece of clean grey blanket and persuaded me to take a little barley water.

And meat, always talk about meat. Mary Britten could not tell a story without a little meat in it.

– It's meat he'll be needing, she said. It's the lack of meat that makes them slow. In that we have been blessed, she said, for my boy Tom Britten is a finder down at Smithfield. There is always meat in my house, she said, and always has been.

– Now lookee here, said Silas Smith, you are a poor woman, but you will soon be richer for your kindness.

And then, bless him, he gave her the sovereign. He, who had more schemes than knaves in a Magsman's deck, gave away a sovereign to a poor woman.

As for Mary, this was the first sovereign she had ever touched in all her life.

– It's the meat he'll be needing, she said. Neck, scrag end, belly – that's what's missing.

And here the first entry ends.

22

At a quarter before the hour of eight the following morning, there was a boy knocking on the door at Great Queen Street with a long letter in Oates's hand wherein he apologized for the early hour, but begged Percy Buckle to be sponsor to an event which will 'satisfy your humane and inquisitive nature'.

Percy Buckle, as was his eccentric habit, was waited on at

breakfast only by the maid, and thus, his footmen being absent, he had to ring for Jack Maggs in order that he might read aloud to him the letter requesting his attendance at a Magnetic Experiment.

Jack Maggs listened only fitfully, for he was more concerned with Mercy Larkin, and the mischief he imagined in those sleepy eyes.

'He wants us now,' cried Percy Buckle, pushing away his buttered toast.

'I cannot go now, Sir.'

'Yes you can, Sir,' winked Mr Buckle. 'I would not miss this for the world.'

'You're coming with me, Sir?'

Mr Buckle stood, slurping down his tea. 'Wild horses couldn't stop me.' Mercy Larkin made a hand signal Jack Maggs did not understand.

'Your kippers are done, Sir,' he said.

But there was no time for kippers. No time for horses either. Down the hallway Buckle marched, his confused footman hard behind him. On the front step, the master paused to issue, sotto voce, the following instructions.

'Now Maggs, I'm sure you've been a footman longer'n I've been a master, but seeing as how your legs are so long and mine, well, call a spade a spade – I'm duck-legged – then I'd ask you to watch your step and stay back a little as we walk, not come down upon my heels. If ruffians call out, and they do, they do, you turn a deaf'n to them and don't feel you have to stand up for my honour. Doubtless it is some mistake yet in my wardrobe, and that will be attended to directly. But for now, old fellow, it is off we go. Three paces behind, if you could be good enough to manage it.'

Thus Percy Buckle, a passionate Chartist in his private life, emerged as a high Tory on Holborn. He marched east along that great thoroughfare in a top hat and waterproof travelling cloak that reached almost to the pavement and which he had, from time to time, to raise above the mud. His footman followed him three paces behind, coiffed, powdered, gloved, in bright yellow livery and smart doeskin breeches.

Who can say exactly what it was that made passers-by smile to see them? – the slight roll to the fart-catcher's walk, the anxious perambulation of the little master, the hundred little clues, perceived by the brain but not so easily named, to the counterfeit they were so earnestly enacting.

At Lamb's Conduit Street, Percy Buckle's inquiring knocks were answered by the master of the house. They felt the enthusiasm of his approach before they saw him and then Tobias Oates was standing before them – flash as a sharper in a bright green waistcoat.

'Splendid! Capital!' the writer said, reaching out his bony little hands to prod Jack Maggs – a finger point against each shoulder. 'Come in, come in. We have a splendid fire, carefully guarded.'

Thus Jack entered Tobias Oates's home a second time. He was guided into the front room which had, indeed, a crackling fire, and was now set up as for a lecture, with its bowl of apples gone, its large red chaise pushed back against the wall, a straight-backed chair upholstered in green velvet set up in the middle and some four or five assorted dining chairs arranged like pawns in the defence of a beleaguered king.

It was in this upholstered chair that Jack was left while Buckle and Oates whispered together in the hall. He was most apprehensive and was not calmed when he heard female voices in the hallway. He inhabited the chair as if it were a place of execution.

Then Mr Buckle entered, followed by tricky little Oates and two young women.

The first of the women was Mrs Oates, who was plump and plain with a slightly injured cast to her features, or perhaps she was merely tired by the babe she now carried at her breast. The other was a fresher daisy altogether, not merely in that she was a good five years younger, but that her manner was less put-upon. Neither were great beauties, but this younger one – Maggs heard her called Lizzie – had a hungry little mouth and big inquisitive eyes.

While Mrs Oates hovered indecisively by the doorway, this girl sat straight away in the chair closest to the footman.

Are all of them to spy on me?

Oates did not start the Magnetism immediately but fussed with the firescreen instead, touching it in that peculiar way he had earlier touched Jack's shoulders. So busy was he with this operation that he left the other three not much else to do except stare at the victim in the chair.

Maggs stood this well enough at first, but as the staring went on and on it became pretty near intolerable. He had no wish to be impertinent but what was his choice?

'So, Sir,' he called to Tobias Oates, 'it is my good fortune, Sir, to have an audience. Have I become a fellow in a penny gaff?'

'Mark my words, Jack Maggs,' said Oates, still staring at the firescreen, 'there never was a penny gaff of such importance.' He then spun suddenly, and all eyes in the room turned to him. 'Look at what we have today.'

Tobias Oates tossed two shining discs of metal in the air and caught them behind his back.

'What's that?' said Jack, now thoroughly alarmed. 'We never spoke of that.'

'Conjuring,' exclaimed Percy Buckle. 'Very good, Sir.'

'Magnets,' said Oates, holding out his open palms so that Mr Buckle could examine the discs. 'We'll drag the demons out of Master Maggs with these.'

'In front of everyone?' said Jack Maggs. 'You never said it were to be in public, Sir.'

'Old chap,' said Oates, widening his eyes to look at him. 'Do not do this to me now.'

Maggs was chilled to perceive the hard eyes behind those pretty lashes.

'You will get your introduction to the Thief-taker . . .'

'I need to talk to him, Sir.'

'Yes, we will talk to him. As we agreed. Thirteen days from now. It seems to me, Mr Maggs, that this bargain is all in your favour.'

'It was never to be in public.'

'This is not *public*. This is my wife, her sister Miss Warriner, my little son, who is the soul of discretion I assure you. Now, shall we proceed? Or shall we abandon the bargain? You tell me, but tell me now, for all time.'

'We shall proceed.'

80

'Good man.'

Oates pulled over a small piano stool and, having spun it until he had the height right, sat himself close against his subject. Then he began to pass the magnets around the other's worried brow.

'With these little magnets we shall cure you. Look.' He showed how he had secured a magnet between each finger. 'Look carefully.'

He began to make slow passes in front of that hard resistant face.

Maggs for his part felt himself a monkey in a sailor's cage. He looked at the young lady who quickly averted her eyes.

'Keep your eye on me, Sir.'

He watched the slow pass of the hands. He watched the glint of silver caught between the fingers.

He had made himself immune to the magnets, or so he thought. When Oates asked him, 'How is the pain today?', he imagined himself quite normally awake.

23

Toby had always had a great affection for Characters, reflected Lizzie Warriner: dustmen, jugglers, costers, pick-pockets. He thought nothing of engaging the most gruesome types in Shepherd Market and writing down their histories in his chap book. The subject of this Mesmeric Exhibition did not know it, but he was likely to appear, much modified, in Toby's next novel. There he would be Jack Muck, or Jock Crestfallen – a footman with a coster's voice and a chest like a strong man in a circus.

Since Lizzie had experienced a very unhappy morning so far, she sat herself down with the expectation of forgetting all those fearful apprehensions that had so bedevilled her recent days.

Mary Oates was also present at the Exhibition, although it was obvious to her sister that she would really rather not be there. Poor Mary came in order to please her husband, then succeeded only in providing further evidence that they were tragically ill-suited. She had grown up, as Lizzie had, in a house of books, but unlike her sister she had never pretended any interest in their contents. Mary

81

would rather sew than read, and it had been embarrassingly revealed, on more than one occasion, that she had never grasped the point of *Captain Crumley*.

Now, with this grizzling baby on her hip, it was clear just how little patience she had for either science or literature. She called the Exhibition 'an entertainment', asked blunt questions about the noise that would be made, and how soon the business might be over. If she had any intimation of her husband's genius, she was careless of revealing that genius was a quality she did not value highly.

While her older sister gave all her attention to the baby on her lap, Lizzie shyly observed the subject of the demonstration. He leaned backwards in his chair and patted his hands upon his stockinged legs. He looked for all the world, she thought, like a Cockney King settling down to watch a dance.

Then his gaze settled on her and she glimpsed his dark and hostile spirit. She turned her head away, only to see her dear fine Toby step forward to engage the fellow.

'Watch me, man,' said Toby.

As he held up his hands, Lizzie felt a chill of fear grip her womb; they seemed very delicate instruments with which to master such a beast.

Yet the footman must have recognized some greater power, for as he considered the writer's hands, a strange criss-crossed frown erupted on his brow. He jerked his head sharply away, across the room, then stared fiercely at Mary and her baby.

'Keep your eye on me, Sir,' said Toby.

But the footman now rested his frightening eyes on Lizzie Warriner, who shuddered.

Then Toby spoke again: 'Jack Maggs, I command you.'

The fellow subjected his reluctant attention to the other's gaze. Once he closed his eyes, but soon after he opened them again, and before too many moments had passed, the footman's head began first to nod, and then to loll. As that alien body finally surrendered, Lizzie Warriner felt an unexpected stirring of her own blood.

'Can you see our Phantom, Mr Maggs?'

The answer was very clearly spoken. 'He stays mostly behind me.'

82

He raised his head. His eyes were open. If Lizzie had not known the footman was mesmerized, she would have judged him to be fully awake.

'We are going to chase him away. What do you think frightens him?'

'I don't think my Phantom is frightened, Sir.'

Toby now put his hand into his jacket and produced a shortish horsewhip which he had had, all that time, concealed upon his person. He dangled it in the air, so its end waved inches above the Somnambulist's head. This was very good, Lizzie thought, very good indeed. Toby was a fine actor. He had played Sir Spencer Spence at the Lyceum, and loved to amuse his friends and family with skits based upon that pompous old sawbones. Indeed, he had a great talent for all kinds of dialects and voices, tricks, conjuring, disappearing cards, pantomime performances.

Now, as he raised the whip, Lizzie patted Mary's arm consolingly, for Mary was, as usual, fearful, squeezing tight her eyes, clutching her poor babe tightly to her.

'Do you imagine our Phantom might fear the double-cat?'

'No, Sir.'

For reply, Tobias swung the whip. It brushed the ceiling, and slapped against the settee. He brought it back again and down, producing a loud thwacking noise. A brass candle-stick leaped off the mantel and rolled across the floor towards the window.

The babe woke, bawling. Mary stood up, holding her hand protectively around the soft little skull. Now, too, the footman was rising. He pulled himself up slowly from his chair as if constrained by invisible chains. His face contorted pitifully.

'Oh no, not flog him!' he cried. 'You mustn't do that, Sir.'

'Toby, dear . . .' Mary whispered timidly.

'Remain seated, Sir,' said Toby. He waved at his wife, making pushing motions with his hands towards the door.

When the creaking door was finally closed behind the bawling babe, Toby silently indicated, for the benefit of the others, the footman's physical distress. He pointed at his restless limbs, his twisted mouth.

'Yes, perhaps we should flog the Phantom?' he said loudly.

'Oh God no, please . . .'

'Do you think he would like that?'

'No. Let me wake up.'

Toby mouthed to his audience: *Watch*. Then, adopting a jolly, kindly tone, he spoke again to his subject: 'Why are you so agitated, Jack? No one will harm you. It is your enemy we are to deal with today. He who is causing you pain. Can you see the place where we are going to deal with him?'

'I am used to the pain, Sir. It is an old friend.'

'I asked you another question. Did you not hear it?'

Jack Maggs began to beat his fists upon his chest. He was truly like a wild animal, and Toby his expert trainer.

'Can you see the place where we are going to deal with him?'

'Leave him alone, I beg you.'

'You are attached to your torturer, Mr Maggs. Can you see the place?'

This last question was accented by one more crack of the whip.

'Yes, yes,' said Maggs, visibly cowed. 'I can see it.'

Mr Buckle stood, his arm raised as if to protest.

'Please, everyone be calm,' said Toby. 'Master Maggs, we must see where it is he is going to be taken.'

'Please, Sir, I can't bear to watch a flogging.'

'What would you watch instead?'

'The sea, the river.'

Toby now approached his subject very close. He brought his hands up to the fellow's mouth and it seemed as if he were about to draw the poor man's demon from him, dragging it back in his splayed fingers. 'Now you are going to tell me. What is the river like? Do you know birds, Jack? Can you see birds?'

'Oh yes, Sir, hatfuls of birds.'

'Pelicans, no doubt.'

'Pelicans, Sir. Oh yes.'

'You can give me a pelican? Good old Jack.'

'I can, Sir. By golly there's a handsome fellow.'

'Paint him for me, Jack. Give me a picture.'

'Oh he's a big one.'

'Do me a sketch.'

'It has a great chest, and a great scoop of a beak. It comes in like a man o' war. It is a beautiful thing, Sir, the pelican.'

'Any other birds?'

'Is the Phantom to be whipped, Sir?'

'Tell me about the birds. Are there parrots?'

'I can't look for parrots. How can I look for parrots when you have that damn triangle set up like that?'

'Tell me about the parrots, man.'

'I'll not watch it, God damn you. I'll not watch it. You can't make me. You don't know what you're dealing with.'

'Is the pain still there?'

'Yes, yes, damn your eyes, the pain is always there. God damn it.'

'You will be calm, Jack, and keep a decent tongue in your mouth. There are ladies present.'

'Then damn you for bringing them to so damned a spot.'

'Old Sir, do please rest your mind. No one will be flogged today.'

'No flogging?'

'None.'

'Oh God, Sir. Thank you, Sir. I could not have borne it.'

'Don't cry, old chap, it is too beautiful a day. Can't you feel the lovely sun on your face?'

'That sun could kill you, take my word.'

'Indeed, Jack, it is fearsome hot.'

'Blistering, Sir.'

Percy Buckle leaned forward and patted Lizzie Warriner on the elbow. He pointed over Jack's shoulder, out the window where cold rain had begun falling once again.

'I'm so thirsty, Sir.'

'Remove your jacket if you wish, your shirt.'

'But the ladies . . .'

'The ladies are gone.'

Lizzie, confronted by a man about to undress, found herself most seriously discomfited. She stood. But her brother-in-law fiercely shook his head, and she sat down again, her eyes averted.

'I can't take my shirt off.'

'You must.'

'Captain Logan won't allow it.'

'There are no regulations here,' said Tobias.

Jack Maggs shed his jacket, then his silk ruff and shirt, then the coarse wool singlet, and stood before them, naked to the waist.

Lizzie Warriner sat in her seat, her eyes lowered.

'Turn,' said Tobias.

The footman turned. As Lizzie Warriner raised her eyes, she gasped at the sea of pain etched upon the footman's back, a brooding sea of scars, of ripped and tortured skin.

'You will stand,' said Tobias. 'You will stand perfectly still. You will not go anywhere. Do you understand?'

'I am too hot.'

'Here it is shady,' said Oates. 'You are comfortable.'

And then he quickly escorted Lizzie Warriner and Mr Buckle from the room.

24

Tobias Oates locked the door to the front parlour. Then he looked from Miss Warriner to Mr Buckle, his mouth twisted in a peculiar smile.

'I got the rascal.'

'Dear Brother, what are we to do?'

Tobias Oates waved Miss Warriner and Mr Buckle towards the staircase with little motions, like an old woman driving chickens into a coop. He ushered them upstairs and into a small cabin which, Percy Buckle realized, must be the sanctum sanctorum. The little grocer was consequently unable to refrain from touching the desk, from running his curious hand over the smoothly varnished surface of a pigeon hole. Here, he reflected, the prodigy wrote his novels. Here was the birth-place of Captain Crumley and Mrs Morefallen.

'Mr Buckle, you could have been murdered in your bed.'

Mr Buckle took his hand away from the desk at once. Tobias turned his attention to his sister-in-law.

'Did you not wonder at my intuition, Lizzie? I guessed he was a bolter from New South Wales.'

Miss Warriner took him by the sleeve of his jacket. 'Dear Brother, what will he do to us when he finds himself exposed? He is a singularly large man, Tobias, and I do not doubt he will be very angry.'

'He is mesmerized,' the young man said impatiently. 'I doubt he will remember anything.'

The young woman drew her shawl tightly around herself.

'It was when he described the pelicans, Lizzie, I knew the theorem was proved. Do you see what I have now? Do you see what I have been given?'

'I see, Toby, that you have brought a very dangerous man into your family's presence.'

'He will not wake up until I release him, Lizzie. Don't you see what I now possess? A memory I can enter, and leave. Leave, and then return to. My goodness, my gracious. What a treasure house, eh, Buckle? You can hear the cant in his talk. He has it cloaked in livery but he wears the hallmarks of New South Wales.'

'You cannot keep him here,' cried Lizzie. 'He is not some nasty hand you can store in a bottle.'

'I will visit him in prison.'

'With respect, young Sir,' said Percy Buckle.

'Yes, Mr Buckle?'

'I am very aware, Sir, that it is a privilege for me to be . . .'

'Now, Mr Buckle, come, come.'

'I don't mean to embarrass you, Sir, and I am grateful to have been called to witness such an unusual experiment.'

'Mr Buckle . . .'

'But in my opinion, Sir, and it seems that I differ from you here . . .'

'Please continue.'

'We do ourselves no credit in judging him.'

Oates snorted. 'Did you not see his *back*, man? He is a scoundrel.'

'Well, we saw a page of his history,' said the little grocer stubbornly. 'Whatever his offence, anyone with half a heart can see that he has paid the bill. I could not send him back for more.'

'I'm sure you don't wish to return with him to *your* household?'

Mr Buckle became silent.

'To be robbed? Or murdered in your bed?'

Percy Buckle brought his mild eyes up to meet those of the young host's.

'He has not hurt me yet.'

'Mr Buckle,' said Tobias Oates, laying his hand upon the other's bony little shoulder. 'I fancy that a grocer, who is every day concerned with serving honest citizens, does not see the things a journalist sees.'

'With respect, Sir, I think you forget something of my history.'

'I forget nothing,' said Tobias proudly. 'I can name the flowers growing beside the path on my fifth birthday.'

'I was one of those poor beggars you see selling fried fish in Seven Dials. I was witness to things there, Sir. You and I might trade cruelty for cruelty, but we would know it best not to frighten Miss Warriner with that which we would rather forget ourselves.'

'No one forgets. It is all in there, Buckle. This Australian of ours holds his life in his cerebrum. He carries pelicans and parrots, fish and phantoms, things the Royal Botanist would give a sov or two to hold. When he mentioned the double-cat . . .'

'God love me, Sir. The name itself.'

'When he mentioned the double-cat on our previous encounter, that was the clue to his secret. It is a punishment invented in New South Wales.'

'Did you never imagine yourself in his position? I *felt* that damned thing. Forgive me Miss Warriner, but damned is the right word for it.'

'Buckle, dear Buckle. It is my business to imagine everything.'

Percy Buckle's mouth had become small, his cheeks pale and sunken. He stared hard at Tobias Oates before he answered.

'Is it, Sir? I suppose it is. As for me, I had an older sister who suffered transportation to that same cursed place. I had the honour of standing in Newgate and seeing the Judge pronounce the words. I held my mother, Sir, when the poor old lady fell away. Excuse me crying, Sir. My sister was not an angel either. Lord knows what became of her.'

'Surely you heard eventually.'

'How could I have heard?' said Percy Buckle tersely. 'She had no letters. How could I have heard? Put yourself in her place – how could she get word to those who loved her? She was a plucky thing, our Jenny. She thought me such a sad item with my fried fish, but I never did forget that day, God help us all, that Mother England would do such a thing to one of her own.'

'I think you a fine man, Mr Buckle. A Christian.'

'I do hate to keep disagreeing with you,' said Percy Buckle, looking down at the floor, and speaking in such a low voice it was difficult for his listeners to make him out, 'but I am not a believer.'

'But surely you would not wish this fellow back inside your household.'

'I do not see I have a choice.'

'But what of your safety? The safety of your other servants?'

'I would like a better choice, and that's a fact, but I can't rightly see any. Shouldn't we, Sir, not stand here talking when he is left there by himself all alone and who knows what terrors he is going through, imagining himself still alone in that dreadful place?'

Tobias Oates smiled. 'You are a brave man, to take a lion into your home.'

'Not brave. Ask anyone. I am as timid as a dormouse. I wish I were brave, for it would make this business easier.'

Tobias Oates measured his distance from the wall. He ran his hand through his hair. He produced a tortoise-shell comb and rapidly combed himself. 'Then I will maintain my interest in the case,' he declared. 'I will not give him up.'

Percy Buckle cocked his head. 'You were about to give him up to the Law.'

'Ah yes, but seeing that you insist we keep him – '

'That *I* keep him,' corrected Percy Buckle.

'But Toby,' Lizzie said, 'we cannot let him go free.'

Tobias ignored her. 'At night, Mr Buckle, I walk the city. I walk down past your old shop in Clerkenwell, down into Limehouse, back up through your dreadful Seven Dials. Wally Duke's. The Hopping Toad. The Sheaf of Barley. I have them all here inside my cranium. But what you have brought me here is a world as rich as London itself. What a puzzle of life exists in the dark little lane-ways of this wretch's soul, what stolen gold lies hidden in the vaults beneath his filthy streets.'

'I don't follow you, Sir?'

'It's the Criminal Mind,' said Tobias Oates, 'awaiting its first cartographer.'

25

Each night, behind the double curtains, Jack Maggs impatiently roamed Henry Phipps's rooms, inquiring deftly into drawers and dressers, running his large square-fingered hands over damask and lace. Here he slept fitfully on the settle, alert to every noise that might signal the return of the man he had come to meet. Here in these rooms he continued the letter which he intended the Thief-taker to present to the house's absent tenant.

Each morning, by dawn, he was back in Mr Buckle's house, and as the clock at St George's rang for Morning Prayer, he would wearily present himself at Tobias Oates's front door. On being admitted by the taciturn house-keeper, he would carry a cup of tea up to Mr Oates's study where he would, at eight fifteen precisely, be mesmerized.

By *mesmerized* he understood that he was made the subject of magnets, and that these magnets in some way tugged at his Mesmeric Fluid, a substance in his soul he could not see. He understood that, under the effect of magnets, he was able to describe the demons that swam in this fluid, and that Tobias Oates would not only battle with these beings – named Behemoth and Dabareiel, Azazel and Samsaweel – but also, like a botanist, describe them in a journal where their host might later see them.

At first the convict had been astonished to read Dabareiel's flowery speech – he could not believe that such an educated being might exist within him – but he accepted it soon enough, and with all the various explanations Oates constructed, it never once occurred to Jack Maggs that these 'transcriptions' had been fabricated by the writer to hide the true nature of his exploration.

There were, as in all crooked businesses, two sets of books, and had Jack Maggs seen the second set he might have recognized scenes (or fragments) more familiar to him: a corner of a house by London Bridge, a trampled body in a penal colony. But even here the scenes were never very clear. For the writer was stumbling through the dark of the convict's past, groping in the shadows, describing what was often a mirror held up to his own turbulent and fearful soul.

This second set of notes was entered in a red leather volume, Tobias's daily work book. This journal contained many notes for novels, essays, and rough drafts of sketches for the *Morning Chronicle*, but from the twenty-first of April, 1837, six days after Jack Maggs's arrival in London, it was almost exclusively devoted to his hidden history.

During lunch at The Sergeant's Inn on April the twenty-third, Henry Hawthorne found the writer pale but very lively and voluble. He polished his knife and fork with his napkin and drank three glasses of claret before his soup was done. He asked nothing about Hawthorne's *Lear*, which had opened to hostile reviews the night before. He blithely likened himself to Thackeray. He said he was like an archaeologist inside an ancient tomb. He invited Henry Hawthorne to secretly observe one session, and witness him pushing into the musty corridors of the Criminal Mind.

Alarmed by his young friend's mania, Hawthorne did indeed visit on the next day, and was astonished to see the seated footman, in full livery, cry out and curse so murderously. Perhaps it was the role of Lear that made him think so, but Hawthorne was convinced that he would find the footman gone mad on wakening. Indeed, Hawthorne did not leave the house when he said farewell, but hid in the nursery with a brass poker in his hand. Here he waited until the criminal had been escorted from the house, only then revealing himself to his astonished friend.

26

On the night of Tuesday the twenty-fifth of April, having started awake from a troubled sleep, Jack Maggs took himself once more to the walnut desk in Henry Phipps's drawing room, dipped his quill into the apothecary's bottle, and penned the following:

Look, Henry, whether you like the sight or no, read these words and imagine what it was to have, not your life, surrounded by a ring of golden chairs, but mine.

Come, please, and meet *my* great Benefactor – Silas Smith. This is what passes for a Kind Man in my history. He has a long red nose, and an old-fashioned turned-up collar, and he comes into the gloomy court where I am playing at some boyish game of bones.

– Now Jack, says he, you and I are going to do your lessons.

And there is Mary Britten (whom I called a mother) and her big red-boned son – Tom with his long jaw and his lonely little eyes. He had such big hands, did Tom, but never held a pen. When Silas Smith came knocking on the door to take me to my lessons, it was me he came for, not Tom.

Tom felt this very keen. He sat on the floor in the corner with his cheek resting on his bony knees, and sulked. As for me, I would have given up all lessons if I could have had Mary Britten love me, and call me Son.

Mary was young and handsome then. She had had her Tom when still a girl and could not have been more than twenty-three when she first took me in. She was a very dervish of a woman, always scrubbing and cleaning, and angry too, never at peace, never able to sit down and have a moment free of agitation, but if I could have chosen, she is the one I would have wished to claim me as her own. She was a force of nature, the Ma – her long arms, her wild hair, her skin always smelling of snakeroot and tansy. She could fill a space. She could stand her ground. She was the Queen of England in that little whitewashed room, delivering our neighbours' babies, serving soups, examining the bones and offal on the rickety pine table.

If she was gruff and fierce with me, if she would clip my chilblained ears as soon as look at me, she also did her duty by me in those early years. She grew me up.

When I was four years old I would walk beside her great skirts, across London Bridge and up to Smithfield – an hour's walk, never once was carried – to where nine-year-old Tom was working as a 'finder', which is a polite way of saying that he were a thief. He worked the filthy slippery floors amongst the sawdust darting like a rat, a cat, and here a breast bone, there an end of chop fat, there a kick up the keyhole for his trouble. It was not till he had been scoured in the cold bath that we saw which was his blood and which blood was that of beasts.

She had such a belief in the virtues of meat, the Ma. Had you seen her on market days, coming home from Smithfield with her lads pale and close around her great grey skirts, you might not have guessed how we regarded that bounty on her back. It was our future she saw in those stolen scraps. It was lack of meat she believed made all of those children in Pepper Alley so slow and listless. She liked to point them out to us as if they were strangers to our eyes – Billy Hagen, Scrapper Jones, sitting there by the lime-green musty wall playing with the bones. They never knew the name of the country that they lived in, never knew anything but the names of the Hagens and the Smiths.

Yet I do fancy that Tom, himself, was a little slow of wit. But that, as she would say, is not the question of discussion.

Each market night, Ma Britten carried the bag of bones back to our little home. This was not as simple as it sounds, for all the poor streets we passed through were somebody's territory. On our side of the bridge it were the Hagens and the Smiths. They and their friends and allies were in a state of war. It was a dangerous matter to be unaffiliated.

But Mary Britten was her own person. She carried a great military sword, disguised from official eyes with old newspaper and hat ribbon, and more than once she drew it. One summer's evening on

London Bridge itself, she cut a slice down a young man's arm so you could see the shining blue white of bone from his elbow to his wrist.

She liked me 'be-in' useful' and I therefore urgently made myself a useful little chap, as if my life depended on it. At five I was a scavenger for the coal which was often washed up on the river bank. Sometimes I lost this coal in fights, but if I could bring it home to her, she would pick me up and hug me, and I did so like the feel of her strong arms, that grassy herby smell which hung about her, I would have done anything to get it.

At five years old I could scrub a floor as good as any char. By six I could wash and sort the bones and offal, placing them upon the table in the manner she liked – a gruesome sight to your gentle eyes I'm sure – but it was nothing for me to arrange the innards in the way she found them most useful, and I fancy I had the knowledge of a slaughterman when it came to identifying the otherworldly shapes and colours of the organs of dead beasts.

Some she selected for soup, some were sold, and others she mixed with tansy, savin, snakeroot, to make her 'Belly-ache' sausages which she hung from the ceiling and for which women paid her a tanner. At that age I had no knowledge of the great upset they caused inside their wombs.

I was, as I said, in no way her favourite, and yet I was the younger, and it was me she took with her when she went down to Kent for the hop-picking in the summer. Tom got left behind, he cried to be so abandoned, but she would not bend no matter how he pleaded. Tom felt his feelings very deep, and when we returned at the end of August he ran around the kitchen roaring and breaking her windows with a broom.

It was after this last adventure that Silas first came to fetch me for my lessons. It was to mark a new stage in his association with our household which had, until now, been most irregular.

He arrived with a suit of clothes, and he and the Ma watched closely while I dressed in them. These clothes were so filthy, they stuck to me like they were made from treacle and smelt so foul you would think I had been rolling in the river mud.

– Very good, said Silas, just the trick.

The Ma was a demon for being clean, and I never thought she would allow me to dress like that. But she nodded her head, and turned back to her stove. As she lifted the lid, the snout of a pig rose slowly to the edge of the battered old black pot.

Said she – You bring him back.

Said Silas – Don't you fret. We ain't travelling far.

But as I found out, this was not so, for we began by going onto London Bridge.

When we were standing in the middle of that mighty thoroughfare, Silas turns to me and says – Now lookee here whipper-snapper, you cannot walk aside me. I must use the footpath and you must run along the street. You must follow me, see, and not be run over. And do not lose me because we shall be going at a fair old clip. If the runners stop you, you are to say you are on an errand for Mr Parkes, the chimney sweep.

Said I – I don't know no Mr Parkes.

Said he – Oh yes you do. And he gave my ear a twist to help me understand him. Said he – Mr Charley Parkes of Ludgate Street who has called for you to help him on a particular job in Kensington.

I asked was that place far away?

– Not so far, said he. You'll follow me and when you see me walk into a stables, you'll walk down the alleyway beside and wait outside the door and in a moment, why, then your Uncle Silas will come and let you in.

I asked him what would happen then.

– Then you'll begin your lessons.

Thus all the time I followed him along the busy streets, dodging the hooves of horses and the wheels of mighty drays, I was imagining I was about to go to school.

Silas had told me about school before. He was an educated man, and once walked beside the sea with Mr Coleridge, or so he claimed. In any case, he could recite whole scenes from Shakespeare, and often did, sitting in our room at Pepper Alley Stairs.

It was by now September but the weather was still warm, and the sky blue. The rush of vehicles along the bridge was fearsome. Four-horse coaches, great omnibuses from which elegant cads cried

'Kensington! Chelsea! Bank! Bank! Bank!' I trotted amongst the starved old horses of the hackney cabs, trying all the time to keep my eyes on Silas, who strode along amongst the quality, taking me further and further from the London that I knew.

I thought I was tasting what my future would be, and I was most pleased with what I saw about me.

The footpaths were filled with men and women in fine clothes. The houses were often very grand indeed. I saw footmen in plush breeches and neat white stockings riding on coaches, and men in grand livery waiting outside great doors with brass knockers on them, and I puzzled at why Silas should have put me in such filthy clothes, and rehearsed me in this cock and bull story about the chimney sweep.

Yet I was, as I recall, most light of heart and happy to follow. It was only when we came into the Mall that I, feeling myself very small, nearly lost my nerve. Such a fine wide space ahead and, at the very end, gates that might have been the ones that Peter guarded, so brightly did they seem to shine, even at that distance.

Yet even as I approached Buckingham Palace, no one inquired as to my purpose. They saw a Climbing Boy and understood, better than I did, what my business was meant to be.

I walked beside the King's south wall. No one stopped me. I ran my hand along the bricks and as I did so my mind flooded with dazzling pictures of the school that Silas had selected for me. I wondered whether there would be a place to sleep or if I would have to take this journey every day.

It was dusk as we neared our final destination, walking along a street of very grand white houses, then down a lane filled with shining black coaches and carriages, and men busy with harnesses and reins. Here was the stable yard of which Silas had spoken, and now walked boldly into, stepping daintily in his shining shoes while I, dressed in my rags, followed down the mews until I found a small odd-smelling alleyway. There I found a door with many silver horseshoes nailed onto its bright black surface.

In a moment this strange door opened and I passed inside.

I waited to see where my desk would be, for Silas had often

described to me the school at Westminster Abbey where he had learned his Latin, but there was no desk here, rather a tall gloomy room with the strong smell of leather and linseed oil, and many different sets of harness hanging on the walls.

There was a ladder on the wall which led up to a kind of loft. Up this ladder Silas went, nimble as a spider in the dark.

I followed, and soon found him at a window looking out at the night. He had taken off his coat, and when he saw me beside him, he climbed out onto the roof of the house next door.

He held out his arms to me. Said he – Go very careful, and keep your head down.

It was only then, as I followed him across the roof tops, that I understood I was not to go to school. Yet when he presented me, fair square, with a chimney, I did not fully understand my situation.

Silas carefully lifted off a chimney pot and placed it on the roof. Said he – All right, young whipper-snapper, down you go.

Said I – What for?

– What for? He brought up his eyebrows in a show of great surprise. What for? She didn't tell you?

– If you mean Ma, said I, the answer is no, she did not.

– How forgetful of her, said he, but it is no matter, it is a simple enough errand. Slip down this here chimney and unlock the back door of the house. That's all there is to it.

I asked what would happen then.

Said he – I will come into the house.

I said that I would likely fall and break my bones.

– Nonsense, said Silas. Get in.

I said I was too frightened to.

– Nothing to be frightened of, said Silas, grimacing as he picked me up. You'll find it easy enough. It's like walking down the stairs.

And so saying, he picked me up, and slid me in, as simple as dropping shot into a cannon.

I soon had reason to doubt that Silas had ever seen the inside of a chimney. First it was tight as a pipe, and the walls were caked with soot so many inches deep that I was held by soot, swaddled by soot, and had I not got given a great push on the crown of my head, I would not have fit at all. But push I got, and there I was jammed in like a cork in a grog bottle, some foot below the top, coughing and wailing and choking myself with fear.

Then there came another great push on my shoulder – a boot most likely – and I was edged down further still, and there the cork was stuck fast in darkness. I was very afraid, and imagined I would die.

When death did not come, I kicked with my boots, and squirmed my shoulders and, in trying to climb back up towards the sky, slid even further into the pit.

I have no idea how far down the chimney I was stuck, but in any case I was caught there a long time.

Then a great sheet of soot gave way, a thick lump of it, and I shrieked out in fright as I fell. The chimney was widening. In my alarm, I scratched at the walls, thus bringing down more filth into my panicked lungs. I coughed. I choked. I might have fallen to the grate below had I not, like a babe, jerked out my arms and legs and thus gained purchase on those protuberances which Silas had doubtless referred to when he said the inside was like a staircase.

By this stage I must have been about half way through my descent, and while surprised to be still alive, I was also very frightened, for it was dark in there, and I was forever coughing and choking on the falling soot, sure that the chimney must soon become too wide for me to hold onto in just this way.

I looked up towards the sky, but could make out nothing but the faint colour of the night. I had thought to see Silas looking over me, but although I called out his name I never had a reply except the constant dropping of soot.

I began to cry. I fancy that I cried a good long time, and that Silas must have already become most impatient waiting for me to appear at the back door, and even when I did begin to move again it was with great timidity, and I might have been a good hour in my descent had I not slipped and fallen.

I landed in the hearth with the wind knocked out of me, and I lay there on the cold hard grate gasping like a mullet brought up onto the dock.

When I had my breath back, I found, to my great surprise, that I was not dead. My legs hurt a little, and there was a large bump on my head, but nothing to stop me stepping out of the high fireplace and peering around the room I had so abruptly entered. My eyes were used to darkness by now and thus I could see better than you might think.

And what a place it was I had arrived at.

It was the smells that first of all impressed themselves, the smell of apples and oranges, and what may have been cinnamon, but in any case something sweet and strange. There were no smells of drains either, and it was this I'm sure that made the other smells the sweeter and gave me a feeling of almighty comfort.

It was a long double room with great glass doors which, I soon discovered, could be shut across the middle to make it into two separate rooms, but for now the doors were open, and the resulting space was bigger than Mary Britten's quarters. In that damp, low-ceilinged little place, we shared one bed and two chairs between the three of us. Here there was enough upholstered seating to accommodate half the population of our little court. All around the room there were arm-chairs, sofas, chaises, love-seats – none of which I could have named for you, never having seen such things before. In my enchantment, I sat on each of them, each one, and it is only now, all these years later, that I reflect on the sooty mess I must have left behind.

But the door – I had Silas waiting for me at the door.

It is easy enough to say, open the back door, but he had not told me where the back door was. He did not know himself, of course, not from the inside – it was half a flight down from the kitchen, which was itself down a long and narrow staircase off another hallway.

Finally I found my way there in the dark, guided by Silas's nervous whistle. But even having found the door, my work was not done. I was six years old, no locksmith, and I was at the chains and catches some five minutes with no other instruction than Silas's curses on the other side of the door until the last chain fell away. Then the door swung in, and the knob knocked me in the middle of my forehead, and I was momentarily made insensible.

I woke to discover Silas slapping me around the head and pulling my ears, asking did I want him sent to America? I said I did not, and that I had done as well as I could, and that I had nearly died inside the chimney. Such was my upset that he soon was quite civil, even giving me a handkerchief to dry my tears. Then he lighted a little dip he had carried in his pocket, and told me to follow him and I would learn something which I would thank him for.

By now he had several workmates with him and they, having rushed in while I was insensible, were busy elsewhere in the house. Silas took me down beside the kitchen to a grand room which he said was the butler's and there he held his dip in the air and whistled.

In the spluttering light I saw first his enormous grin, and then the reason for it: three grand dressers as massive as galleons all bursting with silver plate, like so many moons – tureens, salvers, candlesticks, great trays as big as shields – all glittering behind their locked glass doors.

– There, said Silas, speaking very gently. There you are my little darling.

I thought he spoke in this affectionate tone to me, and it was a moment before I saw that it was the silver he was addressing.

Said he – There you are my fine cold little beauty.

He approached that plate like a man coming up towards an altar.

– It is Uncle Silas, come to take you dancing up the City Road.

He kept on talking, ever so gently, as from his sleeve he withdrew a long steel jemmy which he must have had up his sleeve all the way along the Mall.

– My lovely little bitch, said he. And set upon the dresser in a most brutal fashion, jemmying and levering and cursing between his crooked teeth, until the first dresser gave up its secrets with a terrible screech as the brass hasp separated from the oak.

– Hold the dip, said he, hold it high.

The dip was a little thing, just a bit of wick dipped into tallow, and it burnt my finger and splashed hot wax down my arm. I held it gingerly as Silas swung the door of the dresser open.

Above my head in another room, I heard glass breaking.

– Hold it here, over here.

I held the dip closer as he took out a great silver salver.

When I turned to look at him, he made me gasp. He had fitted a monocle on his left eye, and now it grew and swam before me like a fish.

He saw my face, and chortled.

Said Silas – Now lookee here, you coal-faced rascal, and I will show you a set of hallmarks that you will remember when you are an old man with children of your own. *Selvit Arbus est*, said he, *Servus et Cuccina erbe wit*, or words to that effect.

Of course I came close to see so wonderful a thing but Silas already had the plate wrapped up in a rag, and was adding to the contents of the sack which I had carried all the way from London Bridge.

This sack now turned out to contain nothing more valuable than soot, but amidst this acrid substance he now carefully packed those pieces of silver which took his fancy. Many a fine-looking piece of plate he lay aside, and more than once picked up an object – a plain-looking little cruet, say – that I, with my child's eye, would have imagined of no value.

Thus, most slow and careful, he filled the sack, and when he had washed his long white arms and spent one last moment inquiring of the contents of the dresser drawers, he lifted the entire load onto my bony shoulders and had me follow him out into the summer's night.

Thus we returned the way that we had come, with me staggering along the roadway amongst the shit and carriage wheels, and Silas striding with the quality on the footpath of the Mall.

The sack sawed at the flesh on my shoulder, and at times the pain was so v. bad I had no choice but stop and shift my load, though I dared not tarry for fear of losing sight of Silas.

Of course the old dodger must have kept a nervous eye upon his precious goods but he gave nary a sign of that to me, and once we were in the West End I had the dickins of a time making out his green coat bobbing and ducking through the crowds. And although I now say 'the West End', at the time I had no idea of where on earth I was, and I imagined myself at risk of being forever lost to Mary Britten and Poor Tom, who now seemed to me the dearest people in the world.

The journey was all the worse for me not knowing where it might end. Even when we finally reached a cat-infested lane-way beside a net-maker's – it must have been in Wapping – and Silas took the heavy sack away from me, I could not be sure that I was permanently excused my burden.

I followed him up a rickety wooden staircase, although I would rather not have – it was attached to the crumbling brickwork as precariously as a beanstalk tied onto a cane. At the top, Silas stooped and carefully unlocked some heavy chains, and there we entered a small, low-ceilinged room which my nose told me had, not so long before, been used for drying fish.

This, it soon turned out, was where my patron did rest his head, and I was most surprised to find it a more humble place than my own.

He laid the sooty sack inside the doorway, and when he had lit one more of his stubby little candles, I saw a movement amidst a pile of rags in the far corner. At first I imagined rats, but then saw a thin white arm, and then a pair of large dark eyes, as the creature – it was a little girl, about my own age – gazed sleepily up at us.

– Papa.

She extended her arm from her dark nest, and Silas, answering to this most unlikely title, knelt beside her and stroked her head. I was – I can still remember – most astonished by the tenderness exhibited by the man who had made me carry this cruel weight; now he was fussing amongst the tangle of bedding and dragging out a rag doll with long dark hair just like the little girl's.

The girl, however, was looking not at the doll, but at me.

– Is that Jack?

Silas admitted that it was.

– Poor Jack.

She held out her hand to me, and I, having looked to Silas for his approval, offered my own sooty paw. Thus she returned to sleep, still holding my hand with a determined grip.

Silas left me there, holding the girl's hand, and took his candle over to another corner where I heard him lifting floor-boards.

– Come here, young 'un.

I freed myself from the little hand, and went to where Silas was kneeling over the floor cavity, his stooped form silhouetted in the light of the sputtering candle. What I expected, as I crossed towards him, was to be shown some treasure he had hoarded away, and I was not mistaken. It was a small black volume with words stamped on it in silver letters, and when Silas gave it to me it was with such reverence that I imagined it must be the Shakespeare he so often liked to quote. But when I asked if it was poetry, he laughed and said it was, after a sense, and that I should memorize a line or two and it would improve my prospects no end. And then, saying he would be back in a minute, he left me alone, and as I heard his light, slippery feet descend the wooden staircase, I tried to take my mind off the fact that I was left in a very strange place, and turned my attention to the book.

I soon deduced that it was not poetry, but a peculiar collection of odd signs, thus,

with handwritten annotations attached to almost every one.

There were many pages of this type of thing, row after row of little punched shapes: squares, escutcheons, trefoils, bifoils, and inside these shapes were lions and chalices and crowns and the likeness of a man I took to be a King. I gazed long at these mysteries, trying to establish what they might mean, and when I heard Silas's foot upon the stair, I imagined myself on the brink of being admitted to an important fellowship.

Yet when Silas returned, he seemed to have lost all interest in my education. Indeed, rather than explain the marks to me, he took the book from me and returned it to its place in the floor. Whatever it was he had gone to fetch, he did not tell me, although I could smell fried fish and see a bulge in his jacket where he had a little parcel hidden.

If he intended to share his fish, it was not with me. Instead he produced a handsome little silver spoon from his pocket and said I was to give it to my mother. – Tell her I am coming tomorrow so she can cook my sausage in her pan.

I was too afraid to ask him to tell me the way home, and so I set out, running along the dark rough streets, trying as best I could to follow the route that had brought us here. Walking along the crooked lanes, trying to keep the evil-smelling river to my right, I was often lost and always frightened. Once I was chased by a drunken man who promised to cut off my ear and eat it, but I was also befriended by a man I took to be a sailor who walked me all the way to London Bridge and gave me a penny to go home with.

And how pleased I was to be home. Mary Britten, who was, for all her excitements and passions, normally a distant sort of mother, came rushing up and hugged me to her, soot and all. When I produced the penny and the silver spoon, her green eyes lit up and she took me by the hand and led me to the table, and placed a great bowl of soup beside me, while Tom sat on the bed whittling a wooden fish hook with his clasp knife.

– He stinks, he said.

Ma Britten turned that spoon over in her hands.

– He's been *use-ful*, said she, and to my nose it's a *use-ful* sort of smell.

I ate the soup hungrily. She had dished me a good-sized bowl and put the ladle deeper into the pot than was usually her wont, so the broth was thick with meat and barley, a fact not lost on Tom when he came to the table to watch me eat.

104

– He looks like a nigger.

– Aye, black as a nigger but carrying the King's silver.

She had the silver teaspoon sitting on the table, and she turned it over and over with her finger in a way that made me think of a cat playing with old knucklebones.

– Did he show you his book? asked she.

She peered down at the spoon with her handsome head cocked to one side.

I said he had.

– Did he learn you the marks?

– No, Ma'am.

– He will learn you the marks. She turned the spoon through another ninety degrees. Said she – You will be able to read a tea pot better than a vicar reads a Bible. And you will do very nicely on account of it.

It was then Tom leaned over to take the spoon, but as he got his hand to it, Mary saw him. She tried to snatch it back with the result that the precious object was knocked flying across the room and landed with a clatter beside the bed.

Ma Britten rose screeching to her feet.

– He did not mean it, I cried. Tom was already cowering with his raw hands around his ears.

Mary said he did not have to mean it, and kicked him in the backside. He did it, said she, and that's as good as meaning.

By now she had the poor fellow by his ear and was dragging him towards the bed – Where is it? Where is it?

– It's there, it's there.

Mary Britten saw the spoon and picked it up. She began to polish it upon her apron.

– Why can't I learn the marks too? Tom cried. I want to do nicely. I should do nicely. I'm not the mud rat. I'm the son.

His long pale face was now an unusual shade of red and I realized with a shock that he was crying. I think it surprised his mother too, for she softened in a way I rarely saw her do, and she clasped the bawling boy to her breast and stroked his hair.

– You are the man, said she. You are the man that gets the meat.

105

This stopped the tears and I soon found Tom staring at me from the comfort of his mother's stomach.

– I hate him, said he.

I looked at his eyes and somehow understood not only that he was jealous, which was a surprise to me, but that he was also frightened. When his mother tried to disentangle herself from his grasp he did not want her to let go.

– I'll kill him, said Tom. I'll drown him.

Mary Britten did not attempt to contradict her son's passion. She was now standing on tip-toe on a chair, hiding the stolen teaspoon up above a rafter.

– He does hate you, she said to me. It is true, and natural enough in its way, just as it is natural that you be feared of him, but I must tell you both, you are each lost without the other.

Then she turned to Tom and said – You may kill him, but you may as well cut off your arm, for it is this sooty fellow who is going to take you out of this pit. It was what he was raised to be. It was what you carried home his meat for.

It is only now I write this down for you, I allow myself to feel what I must have known all those many years ago. At the time I felt a buzz or hurt, but I was tired, and full of soup, and once I saw I was not to be murdered, I wanted nothing more than sleep.

It is only now I feel the fury in my furnace: that the bitch would make this speech before a little nipper, letting him know that he had been raised for a base purpose like a hog or a hen.

28

The clock at St Giles had long ago struck midnight, and still Jack Maggs remained at his desk, his heavy lids lowered so his eyes might better see the little whitewashed room in Pepper Alley Stairs as it had been so long ago. So deep was he in this reverie that when he heard the footsteps above his head, he imagined them – for the merest moment – to belong to Ma Britten.

But when he heard the fast patter on the last landing, he knew that it was the mad woman's daughter once again.

He frowned and laid the quill down.

It had been four days since her first passage across the slippery roof, and by now he was familiar with her habit of staring at him when she thought him unaware of her. He had thought her pretty on first sighting, but now he was concerned only with the dangerous consequences of her spying. She was a chatterbox, a gossip. She and Miss Molly Constable were for ever whispering and raising eyebrows at each other.

Now she entered his drawing room, as urgently as any heroine onto a stage. She wore no shoes, no cap. Her dark curls spilled down her shoulders.

'Mr Maggs,' she said, 'your secret is known.'

This gave him a fearful jolt, though he did not show it. He dipped his quill once more in the ink and began another sentence. His visitor, in no way discouraged by his coldness, came to stand beside his shoulder, and he quickly realized that she was trying to read what he had written. He caught her at it, but like a cat snaffling scraps from off the table, her appetite was greater than her shame. She read until the last lines of the letter faded from lilac to white.

'Very clever,' she said.

Jack Maggs then spoke in that quiet voice he used when most severely agitated. 'I'm pleased it meets with your approval, Madam.'

'But if it is intended to hide a secret, it is no longer worth such trouble.'

'Someone has been talking to Mr Phipps. Where did they see him?'

'Now whoever made you imagine such a thing?' She spoke in cadences more suitable for addressing a small child. 'Whatever did I say to make you think of Mr Phipps? What I said was, *your secret is known.*'

What the girl meant, Jack Maggs did not know, but he stood and tidied his papers. He rolled his letter up and tucked it inside his coat. In short, he prepared himself for flight.

'You are a plucky girl,' he said severely. 'And you are a pretty one, as well you know, and I dare say the young drakes is very forgiving when you tease them, but I am past these games, comprenay voo? It is bad manners for you to come talking to your footman like this.'

'Bad manners!' she exclaimed angrily. 'I took a great risk to bring you this news.'

'Then give it.'

'My master, Mr Oates, his wife, they know your secret.'

'That I am here in this house?'

'Not that.'

He reached for her arm and she, misunderstanding him, gave him her hand. This he held with a pressure so firm as to be almost cruel.

'You heard them say that my soul is full of ghosts and goblins?'

'Yes.'

He snorted and released her. 'They are my guests in their curiosity for six more days.'

'They say,' she murmured, pulling her shawl around herself, 'that you are a convict from New South Wales.'

'Damned if they did!'

'They say you told them so.'

'When?'

'I did hear it this very hour, although when *he* heard it I cannot say.'

'Him?'

'The master. He reads to me. He would be reading to me now but I said I was ill and must go back to my bed. I'm for it if he finds me gone.'

Jack Maggs fetched his boots which he had left standing by the hearth. They were not the dead man's shoes, but his own comfortable hessians, which had been made by an old hunch-backed cobbler in Paramatta.

'Are you going to bolt?'

She was a nosy little mite. He tied the green-hide laces tight and double-knotted them. Then he turned so he might privately slip his dagger into its nesting place beside his right ankle.

'Don't bolt,' she said. 'You are safer here with us.'

Jack Maggs took the little creature by her wagging chin. He held her hard, his thumb and forefinger clamping her around her jaw bone. 'They sent you here to delay me while they fetched the peelers.'

Now she saw what sort of man he was. He had her in his clamp, and her eyes were urgent in their plea.

'Think clearly, Sir. Why would I delay you when I knew you would delay yourself, when I knew you would sit up here all night dreaming in this very chair?'

He let her go, but not happily. He stoppered his ink bottle and dropped it in his pocket. He picked up the quill then threw it down. He was in no way certain about how he should proceed.

'Mr Buckle had a sister,' she said, 'who he loved most dearly. This sister was transported to Botany Bay.'

On hearing this, the quality of his attention changed. She seemed to see this. 'He wept to see your injuries. And he wept again when he told me. He could not read me another word of his *Ivanhoe*. He was so upset by what you had suffered.'

Jack Maggs then sat down behind his desk. Mercy Larkin sat simultaneously, in a gilt chair whose seat was embroidered with a hunting scene.

'We wept together,' she said.

'Did you, girlie?'

'Your secret is safe,' she insisted.

'Being known only,' he said bitterly, 'to the master and the household staff?'

'I am not the household staff. They call me a maid, but that is not my true position in the household. I have known Mr Buckle since I was a child. He has read to me for ever so long a time.'

'You are shivering.'

'It isn't right that you frighten me.'

'I ain't going to hurt you.' He offered her a blanket – the grey one under which he sometimes slept. 'But you must tell me the truth. What is it that the gentlemen have said about me?'

'Mr Oates used the Magnetism,' she said. 'He has little magnets the size of pennies.'

'That much I know.'

'The magnets are attached to your soul. They are like a poultice . . .'

'This I know.'

'And with the magnets he dragged your soul to the other side of the world and persuaded you that it was summer and so you took off your shirt in the presence of a lady and cried out to see a fellow who was to be flogged. You described a foreign bird. You were often angry and cursed God. You gave yourself away and now they know you are a convict escaped from New South Wales.'

'The bastard.'

'You are wrong. He is as decent a master as you could ever find.'

'Not him, the other. The smarmy bastard hid this from me.'

'They dared not tell you,' cried Mercy. 'They thought they would be murdered in their beds. Mr Oates has a wife and a child, and now it seems that if you have escaped they also have broke the law for arboring you.'

'Harbouring.'

'Yes. It is a very dark secret. Mr Buckle himself could be sent to Newgate.'

He did not know what he should do with her. She seemed aware of this, for when she spoke again she leaned out and touched his sleeve.

'You can depend your life on us,' she said. 'We are your friends.'

He was sick at heart but he let her go without damage or threat. He escorted her up the stairs, and locked the dormer window closed behind her.

29

Outside the house, there was a great wind storm. In the dim drawing room of Jack Maggs's dream, a man in uniform was sitting in the shadows.

Is it you?

It is I, answered the Phantom.

Maggs rolled himself tight inside his tartan rug while his dreaming eyes attempted to make out the fellow's regiment. The

110

Phantom, as if sensing his intention, lit a gas lamp which flared so brightly that the sleeper brought up his hand to cover his eyes.

It was a uniform made to protect the King himself. The jacket was ultramarine, the trousers black, and underneath his arm he held a bell-topped shako.

I am in the 15th Hussies, said the Phantom.

Hussars, said Jack.

Hussies, insisted the Phantom, opening a great-coat to reveal a naked female form, a soft bush of hair and such sweet little breasts with soft rosy nipples.

Very funny, said Jack, smiling in his sleep. He knew it was a dream. He knew the breasts would not be there if he reached for them, but might remain if he were still. He was very warm and comfortable. The bright light of the gas warmed his cheek.

That gas is a bleeding marvel.

No gas here, said the Phantom.

Jack looked to the lamp. It was still burning bright. Behind it were trays of fishes, their scales gleaming in the artificial glare.

I thought it was gas.

No gas here.

It then became very dark. Something was brushed lightly over Jack's face. He could smell the leather. He knew what it was: a horse's bridle.

You like to ride, Jack?

The bridle crossed his face again.

Yes, Sir.

I'm heading up towards Mount Irwin. You can use a theodolite, I think?

Is that Captain Logan?

In his dream, Jack Maggs saw himself still smiling. When he stepped forward to look at the Phantom's face, he saw he was the spitting image of Captain Logan.

I thought you was dead.

Not me, said the Phantom, who no longer looked like Logan. His hair was fair. He was much younger. But the uniform was the 57th Foot Regiment and the bridle was not a bridle.

We're going to do a spot of mapping, Sir?

But Jack felt the cold empty terror in his gut. There would be no mapping. This was not a bridle.

One hundred lashes, cried Captain Logan, and lay them on until I see the bone.

Maggs was standing, then he was falling. He could not bear to be seen in such a state. He walked past Parker's Hut. Ahead, at the archway of the prisoners' barracks where the cursed triangle stood, Rudder, the flogger, was standing at attention.

Weeping, Jack Maggs turned to the Phantom, and begged him to show mercy. Then the Phantom turned away, leading his horse by its bridle along a path, and Jack picked up a great round rock and brought it down upon the Phantom's head. The Phantom fell and the dreaming man lifted the rock high and flung it down onto the head so it split like rotten fruit. This action he repeated a good long while.

In London, the wind shook the windows in their frames.

30

Percy Buckle did truly wish he had a better choice than to give shelter to the convict. This is not to say that his resolve to harbour Jack Maggs weakened, but that it was a resolve bought at the cost of the peace which had finally come to him with his inheritance.

Now Mr Buckle could no longer sleep and, sadly, it had become normal that, one hour after midnight, he should still be needful of the company of her whom he called My Good Companion.

Mercy, still wearing her maid's apron but not her bonnet, sat herself at her master's feet. He was distracted, fretful, forever putting down one volume to pick up another. Tonight it had been *Ivanhoe* first, then that long piece of Hazlitt's, the one about the young lady which brought him such discredit at the time, and then – for the Hazlitt made Mercy most impatient – the French novel by Madame Valli which was called, by its English publisher, *Imogene*.

It was at that point, when he had finally arrived at the French novel and thereby gained his Good Companion's rapt attention, that he imagined he heard the footsteps on the stair.

'Hark,' he cried, and leapt up, his hand at his ear.

''Twas nothing,' said Mercy. 'Read on.'

'It's him,' he said, and laid aside the book.

'Lord,' cried Mercy, 'do you fancy he roams the house all night plotting ways to murder us? If that is so then he must be very feeble-witted because he has had a whole week and neither of us has suffered so much as a scratch.'

'Shush, there he goes.'

'This is even worse than Hasluck.'

'Hazlitt!' said Percy Buckle. He set down the gaudy blue novel and strapped on the short sword which had been part of the general jumble of his inheritance.

Mercy stared helplessly at the open pages of the discarded book. After a short while she managed to unlock the mysteries of the word *ballroom*.

''Tis the wind,' she said.

'Not the wind,' said the little man, retying his smoking jacket and drawing the short sword. 'Snuff the candle.'

Mercy, most reluctantly, did as she was bid.

Ever so slowly, Percy Buckle opened his bedroom door, and stood silently in the dark, trying to make out the noises of the house.

He was a man of small stature, no more than five foot and two inches tall. He had a weak chest and some arthritis in his hands, but in his occupation as a seller of fried fish, he had known no choice except to stand up to those who would rob, steal and otherwise bully him. Now, with his heart beating so hard he could barely hear another thing, he descended the stairs in the night with his sword drawn.

'Who's there?' he cried.

No answer.

The night was not completely dark. The clouds scudding over London sometimes revealed the moon and it was by this erratic illumination that Mr Buckle found his way into his hallway, and then down the little breakneck stairs into the kitchen.

It was darker now and yet he was aware, half-way down those stairs, of the presence of another.

'Who's there?' he cried.

He heard a small sound – not the wind or the window – which produced, in his mind, the picture of a dagger handle knocking against a dresser.

He stared down into the darkness towards a place where the blackness was knotted hard together, like ink poured into ink. It shifted as he stared at it.

'I see you,' said Mr Buckle. 'Defend yourself, for my sword is drawn.'

'Begging your pardon,' said a familiar voice.

'Maggs?'

'Yes, Mr Buckle. It is I.'

This answer did not appease Mr Buckle in the slightest. The hairs on his neck straightened themselves once more, and he felt that deathly prickling sensation all the way down his spine. 'Maggs, what are you doing in my kitchen?'

'I am eating a cheese sandwich,' said the voice. 'For I am very hungry to have missed my dinner. I had no meaning to frighten you, but your Mrs Halfstairs had me deliver your parcel to Mr Hawthorne at the Adelphi Theatre. I had to wait for him an hour, and when I was back the dinner was all done.'

'But we would feed you, man,' cried Percy Buckle. 'Good grief, we do not mean to starve you. But we do not like you to creep around the house like a thief.'

'Now I am like a thief?'

'Why did you not light a candle?'

'I can see in the dark.'

Mr Buckle said nothing.

'Because I was a thief. Did you know that?'

'No, Maggs, I did not.'

'Are you sure?' inquired the other, in a very low voice that made Mr Buckle's skin creep.

'Yes, very sure. I swear I did not.'

'In any case, I would not have broke your lock, Mr Buckle.'

'Thank you, Maggs, that's very decent.'

'I would not have broke your lock on account of – it would not have been worth my while.'

'Well, yes, I'm sure,' said Mr Buckle, quickly. 'But a thief could not know such a thing from the street.'

'He would need only look into your kitchen window.'

'My kitchen window? And what would he see there?'

'The Trafalgar Doulton.'

'The Trafalgar Doulton?'

'Trafalgar Doulton in the kitchen dresser. I would know that I would not find valuable silver plate and Trafalgar Doulton in the same household. But I can see I have frightened you. I am sorry. I can make a light now. Would you like me to light a candle now?'

'You know that about the Doulton?'

'Oh yes, Sir. It would be a rule.'

'And they have those . . . rules, in that line of work?'

'Would you like me to find a candle for you?'

'I have dined in houses, with most distinguished gentlemen,' said Percy Buckle, 'amongst the most wealthy type, and they are all for the Trafalgar Doulton.'

'Perhaps things have changed in my absence. I was abroad, Sir, as you may have been told.'

A long silence.

'A chap might guess it, Maggs, that you had been abroad.' Percy Buckle stared into the blackness. The denser part of it was moving. 'What are you doing?' he cried.

'I am putting the cheese away.'

'Yes, good,' said Percy Buckle. 'We can talk about your travels at another time. But for now, get you to your bed quickly, Maggs, for tomorrow we will need your good strong arm around the household.'

And thus he made his rapid way up into his sanctuary and there he bolted fast the door.

The room was now in darkness. He found his way into his bed, and into the sleepy arms of his Good Companion.

'Was it him?'

115

'Hush, talk in my ear. Yes, it was he.'

'He did not murder you?'

'He may not be a murderer, but he admits he is a thief. He told me, as bold as brass. He said, I am a thief and a very good thief too. He told me all the business of thieves, what they steal and what they will not.'

'Then he is an honest man.'

'He was drunk. I have been too soft with him.'

'And what great crime was he committing?'

'Hush, Mercy. He was making a cheese sandwich.'

'Do you wish your own sandwich?'

'You are a dear girl,' said Percy Buckle, and was mostly quiet for a minute or so. Then he gave a little sigh.

'Like so?' said she.

'Turn over,' said he.

'You should say, *Turn over, my pretty one.*'

'Yes,' said Percy Buckle, busying his face in all that coal-black hair. 'Turn over my pretty one, and raise your sweet white bottom in the air.'

And thus for some little while the master did manage to take his mind off the Trafalgar Doulton, and the possibility that a creature other than a cat could see in the dark.

31

Said Mary Oates: 'Your father says you are snubbing your old friends in Fleet Street.'

Her husband was surprised to hear her say such a thing, not least because he had entered the dark bedroom imagining that she was finally asleep.

'He says you imagine that the Press is now beneath you.'

'Mary,' he whispered, 'it is after midnight.'

'He says that you never reply to the *Chronicle* when they telegram you.'

'For God's sake. My father is a fool.'

'So you often say, dear.'

Toby turned to the rattling window and looked down into Lamb's Conduit Street. The wind, which had been blowing from the east in the earlier part of the night, had now changed quarter to come howling down from the north, driving an empty barrel right down the centre of the road.

'When did you talk to my father?'

'He came this afternoon to take the painting.'

'What painting?'

'The Maclise.'

'Good Lord,' he cried.

'Shush. You'll wake John.'

'Mary, you did not let my father steal our painting?'

'No, no,' she said, sitting up in the bed. 'He is to have it cleaned by an old fellow down in Whitechapel. It is all the smoke from the fireplace at Furnival's Inn. He has spoken to you about it.'

'Oh dear God.'

'Toby, don't go on so. I'm sure he'll bring it back again.'

'Then you know better than I,' said Toby, much irritated. He had been counting on being able to sell it himself. 'My father will tell any untruth to get his hands on money.'

'But it is not untrue that the *Chronicle* has been asking for you, Toby.'

Tobias was not happy to hear mention of the *Chronicle*. On two occasions, in the first weeks of their marriage, Mary had offered opinions about his business dealings, and he had very firmly insisted that a husband's work was his own affair.

'The *Chronicle* is very eager that you write for them.'

'And I am too busy to oblige them.'

There was a silence then. He felt her hardening in the dark. This capacity for hostility had shown itself repeatedly of late. Indeed, as she now turned violently in the bed, he felt he must revise his understanding of the maternal character he had presumed to know so well.

'Too busy playing knucklebones,' she muttered.

'My dearest,' he began. In spite of all the irritation that had seized

117

him, Tobias put his hand gently upon her plump shoulder. 'My dearest, I did not play knucklebones. Is that what you imagined? That I was playing games with Jack Maggs?'

'You told me yourself.'

'Then you misunderstood me, dearest. It was a game of knucklebones played in the last century, in Pepper Alley Stairs. I found it in my Somnambulist's memory. He could play the bones and describe the very floor he played it on. I have just finished recording all this in my notebook. Money will come of it, you must believe me. Entwhistle will pay me good money for this serial.'

Still she persisted. 'But you said yourself you do not have a story.'

'That is so, Mary, but the story will come.'

At last, she took his hand. 'You never needed magnets before. You used an ink and pen. You made it up, Toby. Lord, look at the people you made. Mrs Morefallen. Did you need magnets to dream her up?'

'Has not the money always come, Mary? Have I not looked after you? Do you not like your new home?'

'Lizzie likes it.'

'And you?'

'I dare not like it.'

'Why not?'

'I know we will have to leave it.'

'What nonsense, my darling. Do not say that. If we leave it, it will be to a better home still.'

'But what am I to say when the butcher will not even give us tripe until something is paid off the account?'

'Oh please, dearest, it is after midnight.'

'And the grocer, Heaven help me, they will not see me in the shop. Please Toby, will you go to Brighton?'

'Brighton?'

'Yes, for the *Chronicle*.'

'Lord help me. How did my father know this?'

'It is five pounds and expenses, and it will only take the day. Please, Toby. You could write in the coach as you did coming back from Leeds.'

'Mary, you have been reading my telegram.'

'It was lying open on your desk. What am I to do? Surely you could abandon your magnets for one day.'

'You think I have no idea of money?'

'No, my dear, I know you have a very good idea of money. You are very clever with money, but we have none.'

While it did not please Tobias that his wife should talk to him like this, he liked it even less that she was right. He could not possibly tell her that he would do as she had asked and so, even as he went to his office to pack his yellow attaché case for Brighton, she did not have any idea that he had capitulated; the young woman stayed in the dark room with her eyes wide open wondering what meal could be made from sago and potatoes.

32

Jack Maggs opened his eyes and saw, as he did every morning, the mortal stains which the attic's previous inhabitant had left upon its melancholy walls.

The late Mr Pope's room was a depressing little hole, and so far removed from the mansion Jack had left behind in Snail's Bay that he was angry and insulted before he was properly awake.

He stirred his bellicose bulk inside the bed, but when he finally swung his heavy stockinged legs free of the blankets, he was rewarded with the sound of an empty grog bottle crashing to the floor. BLACK SEAL SPECIAL SCOTCH WHISKY, courtesy of Mr Buckle's cellar. He sat with his head in his hands and watched it roll beneath the wash-stand.

Late the previous night he had gone in search of a second of the same, and had been caught by the master of the house. Drunk, he had insulted his host's Trafalgar Doulton. Belligerent, he had as good as confessed himself a crook.

Now he rose from bed, seeing clearly to what degree his safety depended on the other's good will. Thus, very wearily, he managed to make himself a footman once again. He shaved with cold water in the chipped pudding bowl provided. He sponged his livery as best he could, that is to say, not well at all. He wet his hair and tried to make a new order of it, finally resorting to a great deal of powder which did little to hide the damage to its architecture. All this time it was on his mind that he must smooth things over with his benefactor, and so he limped off down the stairs wishing with all his heart to make himself agreeable.

As he came down the back stairs he saw Mercy Larkin leave the dining room. He crept along the hallway a little, then hesitated.

'Jack Maggs? Is that you, Jack Maggs?'

It was the master calling from the dining room.

'Yes, Sir,' he answered. 'Coming, Sir.' But when he came into Percy Buckle's presence, he was dismayed to find him now very icy in his manner.

'Stand over there,' said Percy Buckle imperiously. 'Against the wall.'

This, no matter what the stakes, was a very hard sort of order for Jack Maggs to take.

'I was on my way down to the kitchen.'

'I dare say you were. Against the wall.'

Jack Maggs moved back, but he could not make himself go all the way to the wall.

'What else, Sir?'

Percy Buckle chose not to notice the resistance. 'You will see I am eating,' he said. He did not address Maggs directly; and indeed, had he not raised his papery voice a little, he might have given the impression that he was speaking to himself. 'You will see I am eating my kipper from the poor old Trafalgar Doulton.'

There was then an exceptionally long silence during which it became clear just how insulted Mr Buckle felt himself. He should not have been insulted, Jack thought: the silver on the breakfast table accurately fulfilled his prediction of the night before. That is, it was not worth the trouble stealing. Of this low quality, however, Percy Buckle seemed to remain as ignorant as ever. He sat at his table sipping milky tea, occasionally feeding a pinch of kipper to the marmalade cat which whined round his legs.

At length he announced, 'You will not be visiting Mr Oates this morning.'

'Oh. Why's that, Sir?'

'That ain't your affair, Jack Maggs.'

Now Jack Maggs did not wish to argue again. He wished only to be agreeable, but just the same he was rattled to find his mesmerism cancelled. He could not waste a day.

'With respect, Sir,' he began.

'Respect, Jack Maggs, now there's a thing.'

'Aye, it is. It is a great thing, Sir.' If his smile was strange, it was not his intention that it be so. He wished only to demonstrate good will. 'But I have a bargain with Mr Oates and I had hoped he would respect it. Here I am, aren't I? I am waiting for him.'

'A gentleman of leisure.'

'Oh, I know I ain't a gentleman, Sir. I am a servant and I don't have no leisure as it were, but I exchanged him two weeks of my life, Sir. That was my bargain with him. If the gentleman is not to call me for two days, it must be at his own cost. I am going to count those days as taken.'

'But what of your bargain with me?'

'I got no quarrel with you, Sir. You are as fine a master as ever were. My bargain was with Mr Tobias Oates.'

Percy Buckle then made a great show of adding sugar to his tea and stirring it. When this was completed to his satisfaction he solemnly laid his spoon upon his saucer.

'Jack Maggs, you wear my livery.'

'Yes, I do, Sir. Proudly, Sir, and that's a fact.'

Percy Buckle patted at his moustache with his napkin. 'Then I would require the respect a man in your position should show to one in mine.'

'A good point, Sir, but what exactly do you mean?'

'A man in your position,' began the master.

'That's it,' interrupted Jack Maggs. 'What mean you by that part? Let's call a spade a spade, Sir. Let's admit it: you saw my back.'

But Mr Buckle could not admit any such thing. Indeed, it now appeared that he could not say anything at all. Instead he began to spread butter on his previously abandoned crusts. He devoted a great deal of attention to this task and when he finally spoke he was still at it, laying on the butter like wet mortar on a brick. 'Our *bargain* is that you are my footman. And for my part, I would like your respect, Jack Maggs.'

'Yes, Sir.'

'That is satisfactory to you?'

'Oh yes, Sir. It is.'

'And seeing as how you now have free time today, I would like you to clean my silver.'

'Yes, Sir.'

'You will find all the necessary rags in Mr Spinks's little parlour. Mrs Halfstairs will direct you.'

'Meanwhile, Mr Buckle, you have what I might call my little *secret*.'

But Mr Buckle would not tangle with that question.

'Everything is kept where it should be, Maggs. You need not fear.'

'What do you mean by that?'

Percy Buckle finally looked up and, for the first time in their entire transaction, held his footman's gaze.

'I mean,' said he, 'you need not fear.'

And on the uncertain strength of that assurance, Jack Maggs departed.

Two hours later, Constable found him in the back parlour, with all the tarnished plate set out in front of him but not a piece yet touched.

'Good day,' said Constable, sitting himself down.

The other nodded sullenly, and began to brush some Oakey's on a very dumpy looking Georgian tea pot.

Constable rested his sharp elbows conversationally upon the table.

'You are not a servant, Mr Maggs,' he said. 'You make yourself miserable in acting like one.'

Jack Maggs listened carefully.

'You came to Great Queen Street with an "attachment" to Henry Phipps. When he was not here, you decided to stay and watch for him.'

Still Jack Maggs stayed silent.

'I can find your man, if you should like me to.'

'*You* can find Henry Phipps?'

'Dear Mr Maggs, it is not something I would recommend.'

This was said very gently, with the utmost consideration, but it had the most obvious effect of offending Jack Maggs.

Said Constable, 'May I inquire about the nature of your "attachment" to the gentleman?'

'Personal,' said the other coldly.

'Then I would abandon that attachment.'

'Oh, you would, would you, mate?'

Constable did not quite sigh, but his shoulders dropped a fraction and he lapsed into a rather melancholy silence which was not without a certain power.

'You know him well?' Maggs finally asked.

'I know friends of his, yes.'

'They can take me to him?'

'One would not just *drop in* on the gentleman, Mr Maggs.'

'Then you can deliver a letter to him?'

'It is quite probable.'

'Your friends would bring me Mr Phipps's reply, or take me to him?'

'If my friends can find him, they'll deliver your note. I can't say more than that.'

'It is more than a note. Tell your friends to say that Jack is waiting. Tell him that I continue to wait. No, not that. Say only that they have certain papers for him – I'll give them the papers before they set off – and that they will wait while he reads them. Would they wait an hour, your friends? I'd pay them well.'

Constable smiled wanly. 'My friends are my friends. They will not require payment, Mr Maggs.'

'You are in touch with them directly?'

'I shall meet with them on Monday.' The footman rose wearily. 'On my day off.'

But Monday was three days away. It was impossible that Jack Maggs should stay three days.

33

Typically, Mercy had managed to overhear a great deal of the conversation between Mr Buckle and Jack Maggs, and although she had not re-entered the dining room until the latter had been abruptly dispatched to clean the silver, she knew that Jack Maggs had carelessly disclosed the information she had passed on: that is, that the scars on his back had been seen.

As she set a fresh tea pot upon the cluttered breakfast table she knew that the master could be in no doubt as to the identity of the gossip. He was a generous man, but very spiteful when crossed, and as she took his empty cup from him she feared she was in danger of being cast out of the house.

She was a proud young woman, and extremely particular about who she waited upon and why. Yet when it came to retaining her benefactor's good opinion, she was prepared to jettison self-respect completely.

Her only hope in the present instance was that Mr Buckle might show the full blaze of his temper, and plainly charge her with her crime. Then she might, if not deny it, at least beg his pardon. She would lick his boots, and like the taste of it. She would make herself a worm and crawl into his ear. She would slide along his very veins and curl up inside the red wash of his angry little heart. But when she set the cup of tea before him, the master brought his cold, strange cat eyes to bear on her, and then she saw he would not lose his temper. He would not even name her misdemeanour.

He said it was a very nice sort of day.

It was not a nice day at all. It was grey and drizzling.

He said he had had quite enough to eat. He pushed his chair back and, having given her another thin-lipped smile, left the room. The wretched condition of the kipper on his abandoned plate confirmed the severity of his upset.

Mercy had always loved this dining room with its great round table and its amber and violet stained-glass windows. Sometimes, when she waited on the master, she liked to fancy that the day had come when she was finally Mrs Buckle. When the world outside was very wet or windy, there was a particularly deep pleasure to be had simply in standing behind that unbending little back and, with her hands hidden behind her, making a firm circle where her wedding ring might one day be.

Now, as she stacked the cutlery and china on her tray, she remembered the slum she had inhabited in Fetter Lane. The thought of being destined for such a place once more produced a dreadful feeling in her bowels. She would rather die than return to that life, and while she could not undo her indiscretion, she knew she must straight away explain her personal situation to Jack Maggs. He must never place her so at risk again.

In the scullery Miss Mott was cutting up the liver, but Mercy barely noticed her. She began to wash the dirty dishes, then abandoned them. She could think of only one thing: she must tell Jack Maggs to keep his mouth shut. If he revealed her visits across the roof, she would be undone for ever.

She therefore hurried off down the passageway to the room where she knew he was engaged. She came around a dog-leg and found the moon-faced housekeeper counting the preserve bottles in the passageway.

'Yes, Mercy?'

'I've come for lemon skins. For the brass in the dining room, Mum.'

Mrs Halfstairs gave her two very mouldy halves of lemon rind. Mercy could not think of a story which would get her round the housekeeper, and now she was a victim of the story she had already invented. She must return to the dining room and do the brass.

In the dining room, she discovered that Mr Makepeace was now set up with the master at the table. Mr Makepeace was the lawyer who had brought Mr Buckle his Great Good Fortune, and now it seemed it had been Mr Makepeace's Great Good Fortune too, for his accounts were constantly being dropped through the letter box by his hobble-legged boy. He himself was a young man, in his twenties. As to what his features were, it is hard to say, for the distinctive quality of mouth and chin and nose were swallowed in the sea of his great corpulence. Even his voice seemed affected, for all that escaped the gravity of the body was an exhausted high-pitched whisper which made him rather hard to hear. Mercy set the lemon skins aside, and moved closer to the conversation.

'Luck or fortune,' said Mr Makepeace, 'but in either case, it seems I have found your felon in the very first volume.'

There were crumbs on the floor below the table, and Mercy, having no whisk or pan, now counterfeited those implements with her hands.

'It is Maggs with two *g*s,' whispered Mr Makepeace. 'There is a Mags with one *g* in 1813, but he is a forger from Sheffield.'

Good Jesus, thought Mercy.

'I do not know about the *g*s,' said Mr Buckle, 'but he is a Londoner, no doubt about it.'

'Then I have the rascal,' said Mr Makepeace.

Mercy looked up across the top of the table to see him place a large leather-bound volume on the reading stand.

To discuss Jack Maggs with a man of law seemed, to Mercy, a very dangerous thing. To her, a lawyer was of the same species as a judge, and the judge the same genus as a policeman, and a policeman the same thing exactly as Harold Hoban, the hangman at Newgate Prison. So agitated was she by this conversation that she quickly withdrew into the hallway. Here there were a great many small engravings, each of which she now vigorously dusted and straightened, until this upsetting intercourse had finished and the visitor departed.

When Mr Makepeace had gone, Mr Buckle did not call for her. This confirmed her fears: he was very angry with her.

She therefore began slowly to edge her way back into his presence, as though compelled by the requirements of her labour. She arrived finally at the hall-side door, and there she was, attacking the brass door knobs, when the cause of all her trouble came thundering up the stairs and burst into the dining room.

'This is wrong!' cried Jack Maggs, waving a tin of Oakey's silver polish in the air.

It was only at this moment that she saw clearly what a dreadful liability he had become. She watched her master take the can of Oakey's and peer down at the label.

'If it is silver . . .' began Percy Buckle.

'Who gives a frig for silver? You have not been straight with me.'

The master then produced his icy smile. '*I* not straight with *you*?'

'Now I hear my history is known to Mr Constable.'

Dear Jesus, here's trouble.

'Do you have *him* in the room when I am naked? And her?' He pointed a finger to the doorway where Mercy was rubbing the lemon round and round, feeling the blood fill her neck and ears whilst the brass shone bright and yellow.

'Do you invite *her* in to see my shame?'

'Sit down, Maggs.'

'Stand or sit, you'll get me hanged.'

'Hanged? Ah, there you are wrong, Sir.'

Jack Maggs sat, not on the chair indicated by Mr Buckle, but on the table. He rubbed his face with both his hands.

The master did not respond to this impudence, but sat himself in his chair and opened the hefty volume that Mr Makepeace had brought him. 'I took the liberty of engaging my friend Mr Makepeace of Lincoln's Inn.'

Oh Lord, this is worse.

Mr Buckle calmly placed his reading glasses on the end of his sharp nose and began to peer very closely at the pages of his book. 'We have this morning, together, examined your sentencing and Mr Makepeace has made himself well acquainted with the law as it pertains to your situation . . .'

'My situation is my own damn business.'

'There is a Jack Maggs of London transported for life in 1813 Might that be your situation, Sir?'

It was heart-wrenching to witness the effect this announcement had upon this manly man. His shoulders slumped. He shook his great head slowly.

'I'm a vermin, ain't I?' he nodded towards the book.

'A vermin?'

127

He stood up from the table, his jaw a little slack, his eyes dull. 'Don't it say so?'

'No it does not.'

'I am a cockroach, isn't that so? It was very clear what would happen to me if I were to ever set foot in England again. I was transported for the term of my natural life. Weren't those the words? Did not his lordship wish to crush me with his heel?'

'There are no cockroaches here,' said Percy Buckle, speaking very rapidly. 'But it does say that one Jack Maggs received a conditional pardon in Morton Bay in 1820. And we have concluded that if only you were to remove yourself again to New South Wales you would be, to all purposes . . . well, no one would wish to hang you.'

'I *know*. God damn. I do know, Sir. But you see, I am a fucking *Englishman*, and I have English things to settle. I am not to live my life with all that vermin. I am here in London where I belong.'

'Respect,' said Percy Buckle, now obviously angry.

Jack Maggs paused.

'You give me respect, Jack Maggs, and I'll give respect to you. I'm the one that saved your skin. Now I am prepared to be your agent, to sell your property.'

'How do you know about my property?'

Dear Jesus, he is staring at me.

'It was I,' said Percy Buckle, 'who yesterday discovered that Jack Maggs is the owner of a freehold . . .'

'Who was it gave you the idea to look that up?'

Again he looked at Mercy.

'How could it be me?' she cried. 'You never told me nothing.' And to the master she insisted, 'He never told me nothing, Sir, I swear it.'

'I will shelter you, Jack Maggs, and then convey you to where you will be safe.'

'But God help me, Mr Buckle, I have just arrived. I came into the country with the most careful plans. I had a man at Dover in my pay, and when my papers were presented, he turned the other eye. Everything was as it should be. Everything was on the wink, but now there is a household full of busy-bodies all wanting to talk about my life.'

128

'It was you who came to us, not we to you.'

Jack Maggs shook his head slowly. It was true. It was not, looked at that way, their fault, and he looked from Mercy to Buckle with a countenance that was infinitely sad.

'What am I to do with you all?' he said. 'That is the question.'

34

Mary Oates was most surprised to hear her husband's footsteps on the stair, and learn that he was off to Brighton to write about the recent fire. She should not have been surprised. Money was a subject always on his mind. One can see the evidence on all his manuscripts – their margins marked with calculations headed £–s–d.

Tobias Oates knew exactly the price of pork and bacon. He knew how much they owed the butcher, the grocer, the tailor. When he caught the Mail Coach at St Martin Le Grand, he had planned his costs and revenues as carefully as the owner of a factory. On his return from Brighton he intended to sit inside and write through the night with candles burning, but as the coach rattled out of London, he was alone atop – tuppence ha'penny the mile, half the cost of being inside.

By Clapham Common, there was a light drizzle. Toby wrapped himself inside his Petersham coat, turned up his velvet collar and stared ahead into the wet dark, adding and subtracting, multiplying and dividing. The horses' hooves rang. The harnesses rattled. He added the unpaid accounts from the plumber, the boot-makers, the stationer. Glimpsing the terrifying size of the totals, he then hid certain larger debts from himself, either setting them aside or putting them against possible windfalls.

On the credit side he entered the value of the painting his father had stolen: ten guineas. To this, he added a further sum of fifty pounds, this being payment for the unwritten story of Jack Maggs.

While it was true that he had never been paid so large a sum for any piece of writing, and that as yet he had no actual drama for his Magsman to act out, he was emboldened by the hard ache behind his eyes. He knew this pain of old. It was the exact same sensation he had when he first glimpsed the comic figure of old Captain Crumley. It was the distinct twinge behind the eyes, the tension in the tendons of the hands. When he entered the soul of Jack Maggs, it was as if he had entered the guts of a huge and haunted engine. He might not yet know where he was, or what he knew, but he felt the power of that troubled mind like a great wind rushing through a broken window pane.

Dawn found his eyes resting on the soft green of the Sussex Downs, but his thoughts were still inward. So immersed was he in this hidden landscape that by the time the coach horses were changed at the Half Moon, his eyes, despite the early hour, were bright and hard and alive with calculation.

In this way he continued all the way down to Brighton, and when he finally arrived at the Old Ship Inn he was inhabiting a kind of a trance which he could not totally abandon. He took a cab directly to Hawke & Sons, the undertakers in Gibbons Lane.

While other writers might have begun to report the tragedy from the site of the fire, or from the bed-sides of surviving children, Tobias chose to begin his inquiries in a mortuary. As to why this was, he could not have told you, although it was doubtless anchored somewhere in his habit of confronting the things he feared the most, which pigeon-hole would, by the by, accommodate his fascination with Jack Maggs.

The death of children had always had a profound effect on him. When the young victims were also the children of poverty, it produced in him a considerable rage, which the editor of the *Chronicle* had reason to expect would be much to the newspaper's benefit. For Tobias had been a poor child too, and he was fiercely protective of abused children, famously earnest in defence of the child victims of mill and factory owners.

In Brighton, where a cheap-jack builder had laid a gas line to murderous effect, it now took no more than a touch of the undertaker's hand to bring all his passions to the surface.

'You wish to view the deceased?' asked the younger Mr Hawke. He was a tall sandy-haired fellow whose turned-down mouth expressed his habitual disapproval of the living. 'You wish to physically inspect them?'

'Yes. I will leave it to *The Times* to describe the damage to the hospital,' said Tobias Oates. 'I am sure their man is already kicking round the ashes as we speak. *The Times* has not been here, I warrant.'

'No, Sir.'

'The *Observer*?'

'You are the first to think of such a thing.'

'I have come to write about the children, Mr Hawke. I warrant I will be the only one.'

Mr Hawke turned his back and opened a chapel-like doorway through which he poked his beakish nose. 'Mr Threadle,' he called. 'Corporation key!'

An elderly gentleman shuffled out holding a large brass key which Mr Hawke took from him. Without speaking a word to Tobias, Mr Hawke then walked out of the office. It took a moment for the writer to realize that he was being invited on an expedition. He therefore followed Hawke's high stooped back out into a lane-way, and thence into a smaller lane, and thence into an alley. He could smell a peculiar sweet smoke in the air but, the dull red walls about him being high, he had no way of knowing if it was the hospital he could smell or something far more innocent. Finally, they entered a narrow cul-de-sac and addressed a heavy door which, after some jerking, answered to the brass key. They proceeded immediately down some worn stone steps where the light was poor, and the air damp and very earthy.

They came to a small wooden vestibule and from thence passed into a very large and vaulted basement. Tobias was to learn later that it was the basement underneath the Town Hall, but at the time it felt as if he were in a catacomb. His emotions were stirred by what he saw – achingly small coffins, spaced at regular intervals on the uneven brick floor.

Mr Hawke bent over the first coffin. 'There,' was all he said, but when he turned towards the writer his face revealed considerable feeling.

Tobias kneeled beside the coffin. It was a little girl, no more than eight, with a small posy of bluebells clasped in her hands.

'Suffocated,' said the undertaker.

Her eyes were closed, but even so, Mr Hawke had managed to give the dead girl an alert and very grown-up manner.

'You would not recognize them,' he said angrily. 'They ain't nothing like what they was when first I got them.'

The coroner's report said her name was Mavis Crofts, an orphan, and she lay there in her little box with all the solemnity of a matron at the communion rail. Tobias felt a burning behind his eyes. As he steeled himself to describe this determined little face, all the fierce subterranean passion which had accompanied his journey to Brighton suddenly found a home in the mortuary.

'This is murder,' he declared.

Mr Hawke nodded fiercely, and then turned to a single coffin which, unlike the others, was covered with a white muslin cloth.

'We may best pass over Thomas Griff, Sir.'

Tobias stared down at the muslin, the same material as Lizzie's night gown.

'It weren't just the smoke, Sir.'

'Lift the cloth, Mr Hawke.'

'You don't need to see it, Mr Oates.' Mr Hawke folded his hands across his chest.

Tobias reached out his hand towards the cloth. The muslin felt exactly as it did when it clothed his sister-in-law's young body. He pulled it aside, and thereby confronted a sight so unnatural that he did not at first comprehend what it was that he was looking at. It was a human being, wet, bubbled, like meat, the blue-white bones broken through the charred and blistered skin.

'Oh my dear Lord!' He turned away, distressed, his hand across his mouth.

'Thomas Griff,' said Mr Hawke. 'Carpenter's apprentice. He was a father to his young brother.'

'Dear God,' said Tobias Oates, resting his forehead against the cold damp brick of the nearest wall. 'Dear Lord forgive them all.'

Mr Hawke replaced the muslin cloth. He walked past the writer and opened the door to the street.

'You'd do better to see the correspondence at the corporation,' he said when Tobias had joined him in the lane-way.

'Correspondence?'

'The matron wrote many letters about the gas. You might look back to the second of January.'

Tobias wrote *January 2, 1837* in his notebook, but in his mind's eye he still saw poor Thomas Griff – the black skin, the horrid blue-white of the bone. He bid the undertaker good-bye and walked directly to the site of the fire. There, in the company of a young constable, he spent an hour tracing the path of the gas line. He went next to the offices of the corporation, and inspected the matron's correspondence. By three o'clock he had returned to the site, this time in the company of the head of the building firm responsible for the leaking gas line. Thomas Griff's body was before him all the time, and he interrogated the builder in the smoking ruin until both their shoes were smouldering.

He interviewed the weary red-eyed nurses. He collected stories about the children who had died. He brought boiled sweets to the survivors who had been evacuated to St Stephen's church hall. Here he produced pennies from behind ears and made a scarf appear inside a patient's sling. He was a good magician, and would have entertained them longer had his attention not been distracted by a weary young resident who was obviously waiting for him to finish. This was Dr McAlpine, a Scot. He had been sent to ask the writer if he would please be the guest of the hospital doctors at dinner.

Tobias did not hear him. He stared at the distressed young resident, but it was poor Thomas Griff's face he saw.

God save him, *this* was how Jack Maggs would end. He did not know how he knew this, or why this appalling spectre forced itself into his mind.

'Doubtless it's been a hard day for you, too,' said the doctor. He placed his hand comfortingly on Tobias's shoulder, and a fire exploded in the writer's mind. 'Unless you have another obligation?'

Tobias's freckled eyes stared back at his questioner, but he saw instead this horrifying vision: Jack Maggs trapped inside his burning house, a whirl of fire blazing all about him.

'No, no,' he stammered. 'Not at all.'

He turned away and watched the disturbed beetles and spiders running away across the burning floor. He had glimpsed the ending of his book.

35

The reader of Tobias Oates's novels will be well aware of the role of doctors in his work: how time and time again they betray his heroes, abandon them, act snobbishly and capriciously towards the poor. None of this can prepare us for the fact that when Tobias finally realized he was being invited to dine with surgeons, and that these distinguished men not only knew his name but were professed admirers of his comic novel, he immediately decided that he was too exhausted to travel back to London until the morrow.

Of course this meant that he would lose a good four hours of labour, but while this would have been unthinkable only that morning, it did not seem to matter to him now. He would take the dawn mail. He would lodge at the Ship Inn. He sponged his own shirt collar so he would not have to tip the maid.

It was spring, the evening fine and clear. He might have breathed in the ozone on the esplanade, but instead he lazed inside his hotel room, hands clasped in his lap. He gazed out of the window at the lane-way, occupied with no other labour than a vague and pleasant daydream of his ultimate success.

At five minutes past the appointed hour, he presented himself at the imposing doors of the Hippocratic Institute. He was greeted by a butler and then relegated to a footman. As he followed this ornate fellow up the wide marble staircase he caught his own reflection in a mirror and wondered if he had been mistaken in accepting the invitation. He was bright, but rumpled, sponged, but damp. The left side of his jacket sagged with the weight of his notebook.

A door opened before him. He entered a grand room whose high-arched windows afforded a view of the grey silky sea. Here he discovered eight elegantly dressed gentlemen waiting for him.

Those with knighthoods wore the ribbons of their rank.

They were taller than he was. They had been to Oxford and Cambridge, had grown up with Greek and Latin, with Plato and Aristotle. And if they had admired their guest's novel, they were obviously having great difficulty accepting that this was the same chap who used the English language like a lyre. He felt their disappointment even as he shook their hands.

Sir Stephen Wall later wrote a memoir in which he recalled the evening, particularly how the 'red-lipped Cockney' had sat at table and cleaned his cutlery with his napkin. Sir Stephen describes how Tobias repeatedly rearranged his wine glass, his water glass, every single piece of cutlery, 'thereby presenting himself to Medicine as a sufferer from neurasthenic agitation'.

Yet if Tobias felt momentarily disadvantaged, he would not be cowed. He solemnly gazed upon the surgeons, one by one, as if he had been appointed to sit in judgment on them. There had been a long tense moment when first he took his place at table but then, without preamble, he began to tell the story of a chance meeting with Mr Thackeray. The tale went against him quite considerably, though it soon had his audience laughing very merrily.

Next he introduced them to Percy Buckle. He gave them the fried fish, the 'Great Good Fortune', the mewling cats twining round the dinner guests' legs, the pair of footmen with their yellow livery. He gave them, in the rough, a draft of that piece which was later so often anthologized: 'A Grocer in Great Queen Street'.

By then the wine had done its work, and they became, altogether, as rowdy a group as students on the last day of term. Tobias ate roast beef pooled in blood. It was very tasty. He said so. *Tasty* was too low a word. He feared it revealed too much of his childhood, of his mother's bread and dripping sandwiches. But when he saw his hosts were charmed completely, he glowed within the enclosure of their love.

As the custard boat was passed around, Dr McAlpine revealed to the company that, last winter at the Orpheum in London, he had seen Tobias Oates play the part of that preposterous saw-bones Sir Spencer Spence. The resident was able to recall several of his lines.

In fact he chose the only lines which Toby himself had not written. But this was not exactly literature in any case, merely a sketch in which he had parodied the manners of the Regency Surgeon Sir Herbert Catswaler.

Now, in Brighton, at the end of this long disturbing day, he was pleased to put all of his energy into 'doing' the entire part for the assembled doctors.

He began, at first, with the voice alone, using no more props than a pudding spoon and a glass of port, but soon the pompous old wind-bag had a life of his own, and he was waddling up and down the room, grilling the surgeons, abusing them as 'damned wretches' and 'dunderheads'.

My God he made them laugh and roll about in their seats, and even the most proper of them, a very tall and sallow gentleman named Pepperidge, laughed so much that his beard was soon wet with tears.

For three hours Tobias felt prosperous, wise, celebrated. Then, a little before midnight, the surgeons rode off into the night, and all the writer's well-being evaporated.

He stood on the footpath outside the Hippocratic Institute and suddenly saw that he had not behaved like a man of letters but like a common conjurer, a street magician. Would Thackeray have acted thus? Never. *Never*. He had been Jeremiah Stitchem, Billy Button, taking sixpences from the footmen on Blackfriars Road. He was Toby Oates, son of John Oates, a well-known scoundrel.

He walked first along the promenade and felt the clean salt air in his face, but then he took himself back to the Ship Inn and, with an unseasonable fire built for him in the little room, he set out to cleanse himself completely, to make himself everything that he had so far failed to be. He closed his eyes, contorted his face. He was not vulgar; he was not a buffoon. He took his quill once more unto the well.

36

Tobias arrived back at Lamb's Conduit Street with a full and detailed expectation of how the morning would proceed. As it was a Saturday, he knew his wife and child would have already departed for her mother's house where they would stay until after the child's mid-day sleep. Mrs Jones would already have her large kettle boiling on the stove and he would, within ten minutes of returning home, wash all the grime and smoke from his travel-weary body. By half past ten he would be towelling himself dry. At a quarter to the hour, he would perform his callisthenics. He would then don his long silk gown and, as the hall clock struck eleven, he would watch from the sitting-room window as Mrs Jones walked up the area steps with her marketing basket under her arm. He would then walk down the back stairs and bolt the kitchen door, upstairs again, and bolt the front door. The house would then be empty of people, with the exception of Lizzie Warriner in her room.

He turned the key of 44 Lamb's Conduit Street, thinking of his sister-in-law, and most particularly of that little clasp which must be undone to remove her precious necklace.

Imagine, then, his chagrin to step into his hallway and see, through the open doorway of the sitting room, the retired grocer he had described so humorously the night before, sitting bolt upright on the red sofa by the fireplace.

The traveller dropped his case beside the hall-stand, and picked up what mail had accumulated in his short absence. He advanced towards the visitor, flicking through the letters in order to hide his irritation, although he achieved, of course, the opposite effect.

'You'll excuse me, Sir,' said Percy Buckle, rising from the sofa. 'But I felt I should tell you before I acted.'

'What is it, Mr Buckle?'

'I'm sure it is my own fault, Sir, and no one else's.'

'Mr Buckle, what on earth has happened?'

'I am talking,' said Mr Buckle, whose cheeks were now bearing the badges of his great emotion – florin-sized red spots, one on each cheek – 'I am talking about our Jack Maggs. Not to put too fine a point on it, Sir, he has gone mad.'

'Sit down, Mr Buckle. If he is mad I'm sure it is not you who made him so.'

'He knows.'

'Sit. There, I'll sit too. You'll excuse me, Mr Buckle, but I have a most pressing engagement. We will need to deal with this matter of yours rather quickly.'

'Now, Sir?'

'Now.'

Mr Buckle then spoke in a voice so low that Tobias Oates had to strain to hear him above the thunder of a passing dray. 'He knows we saw his scars.'

'Very well,' said Tobias Oates. 'This is not so bad.'

'He is certainly a bolter, Sir, and therefore he thinks it *very* bad. He reckons himself to be in mortal danger.'

'He has my word: I will keep mum. Tell him that.'

'Yes, Sir,' said Percy Buckle worrying at the brim of the sealskin hat which was balanced on his knees.

'So,' Tobias said briskly, 'that is that.'

'Well, Sir, it is and it isn't. There is also the kitchen maid. She is also a party to his secret.'

'The *maid* knows he is a bolter?'

Percy Buckle squeezed his hands together.

'You told the maid?'

'Not a great deal, Mr Oates.'

'And she told him,' asked Tobias, his voice rising, 'that you and I had been staring at him with his shirt off?'

'She meant well,' whispered Percy Buckle.

'Very well,' said Tobias Oates. 'Your Jack Maggs is concerned . . .'

'Oh, I would not say *concerned*,' interrupted Mr Buckle.

'What would you say?'

'I would say, he was in a rage.'

'With me. Is that it?'

'He has the maid held hostage, Sir.'

'The *maid*?'

138

'He has her locked up in my snuggery. He says it is to stop her gossiping to the servants, but God knows what depravity he practises on her there.'

Tobias Oates looked up, at that moment, and saw the figure of his sister-in-law standing in the open doorway in a long white muslin dress. She smiled at him.

'You are home, Mr Oates.'

'Indeed, Miss Warriner.' He half-rose.

'You will be attending to that clock?'

'Indeed, indeed yes. Very soon.'

She retreated, smiling.

'Now, Mr Buckle.'

'He has taken my sword, Sir,' said Percy Buckle. 'He held it against my throat.' And here the little fellow pulled his collar down to show a red bruise on his chicken neck.

Tobias Oates looked at the little grocer and despised him for his broken teeth, his dirty little smile. 'Mr Buckle,' he rose, 'we should discuss this at greater length this afternoon.'

'He believes that the maid has gossiped to the other servants – Mr Spinks, Mrs Halfstairs, Miss Mott. He ordered me to instruct them to stay indoors.'

Tobias sighed, and sat again. 'And you did as you were bid?'

'Mrs Halfstairs is to go to her brother's tomorrow, and it would cause a great upset if she were stopped. I tried to point this out to Mr Maggs. I cannot cage her. But when I told him this he flew into a rage, and that was when he did the damage to my throat. As for the maid, he will not let her out of his sight. She must sit locked in the snuggery, from dawn to . . .' He stopped, and turned away.

'For God's sake, man, please don't cry.'

'I'm sorry, Sir. I did not wish to trouble you, but I thought it best I tell you before I went to Bow Street.'

'Bow Street? But you have been harbouring a felon. You cannot go to Bow Street. Are you mad?'

'Well, you was going to call the police yourself.'

'No, no, Mr Buckle. It is too late for that.'

Percy Buckle then began to shake his head like a horse refusing the bridle.

'Then take him, Sir,' he cried. 'Please come and take him. Bring him to your house.'

'You undertook to keep him,' said Tobias sternly.

'You can't make me,' said Percy Buckle.

'Tell me,' Toby smiled, 'did you ever have a book dedicated to you, Mr Buckle?'

'What's that got to do with the price of eggs?'

'Mr Buckle, please be calm – if you will return to Mr Maggs and tell him I will personally undertake to keep his secret within four walls.'

'He won't believe me.'

'Tell him I will quarantine the household. Tell him no one will leave or enter. Won't that make him happy?'

'You'll lock up my housekeeper? My butler? Sir, with respect, you're going to make things worse.'

Tobias had no idea how he would do what he was suggesting, but he had unlimited confidence in his ability to do it.

'If you will deliver this message to him, then this book I'm now writing will one day bear your name.'

Mr Buckle paused. 'Bear my name?'

'Yes.'

'Where?'

'Where?' cried Tobias incredulously. 'Are you *bargaining* with me, Sir?'

'Why shouldn't I bargain with you?' cried the tearful grocer. 'You have made me break the law.'

'It would be at the front of the book, before the title,' said Tobias Oates more quietly. 'It would say *To my friend Percy Buckle, a Man of Letters and a Patron of the Arts, without whom this book could not have been written*. How is that? Is that not handsome?'

'I was christened Percival.'

'Yes, yes, Percival.' Tobias put his hand on the grocer's bony elbow. 'I will come to your house by evening. You tell him that. As for the dedication, I will write it out for you so you may study it.

We may discuss the choice of words together.'

Percy Buckle permitted himself to be escorted to the door, then he found himself gently guided out into the street.

Tobias Oates quietly bolted the door after him. Then he walked downstairs to the kitchen and, having confirmed that Mrs Jones had left for market, locked the area door, and hurried up the stairs to Lizzie.

37

Mr Buckle had a shop-keeper's manners. That is, he usually appeared timid, almost obsequious, yet when he discovered that Jack Maggs, in addition to holding his Good Companion prisoner, had also taken possession of his bureau, he was filled with a fury that was all the more intense for being incommunicable.

He looked down at Mercy, examining her closely for signs of damage, yet, finding none, he was not mollified.

'You take the ottoman,' she said.

'I'll stand, thank you very much.'

She laid aside her knitting. 'I ain't tired.'

'Sit,' Mr Buckle ordered.

And then, his raw hands folded in front of him, he leaned against the wall and waited for Tobias Oates to make his promised visit.

Soon enough, thank the Lord, the bell did ring. There was a murmur of voices followed by the distant tread of Constable's feet upon the stairs. As they arrived outside the snuggery, Percy Buckle moved impatiently towards the door but was pushed violently aside by Jack Maggs, who proceeded to interview the footman, while he, the master of the household, was left to stare at his assailant's sweat-stained back.

Upon hearing that the visitor was a doctor, Maggs, let out a curse, then returned to the bureau, a delicate piece of furniture which he nevertheless proceeded to *punch* with his bare hands.

Mr Buckle felt he had no choice but to pretend this act of violence was not occurring.

'Is it Dr Krone?' he asked his footman.

'No, Sir,' said Constable, and it was to his professional credit that he also displayed not the least reaction to the explosive situation in the snuggery. 'It is not Dr Krone. But the gentleman speaks oddly and I did not catch the name.'

'Then I'm not at home to . . .'

'See him,' interrupted Jack Maggs. 'We don't want no one thinking anything is up.'

'See him?' Mr Buckle's voice had risen almost to a screech. 'You are in such a panic lest anybody talks to anybody. Why should I see him?'

The convict ignored Mr Buckle and addressed Constable instead. 'You go with him. See no one gives the game away.'

Said Mr Buckle, 'Constable is to stay here with Mercy.'

'Go with your master,' Maggs continued. 'See there's nothing said about Jack Maggs.'

To this vexing exchange, Mercy Larkin pretended not to listen. Mr Buckle, however, saw through his Good Companion's counterfeit, and when he saw how she affected such great concentration on her pearl and plain, he understood she was ashamed for him. He left the room with Constable, feeling angry and humiliated.

His visitor turned out to be a very strange one: a portly gentleman in a Regency frock-coat who stood with his back to the empty fireplace, his legs apart, holding a great leather bag against his stomach.

The master of the household advanced with his hand outstretched. 'Percy Buckle Esquire at your service.'

'Send him out.'

' I beg pardon, Sir?'

'The servant. Out.'

'Perhaps I might be . . .'

'Out, out,' the doctor cried, making shushing movements with his hands while Constable took long careful steps backwards like an odd and long-legged marsh bird.

'Now look here,' cried Percy Buckle, who was by now tired of being pushed about by others. 'I take this very ill.'

'Ill?' The doctor poked him in the ribs with a short square finger. 'I'll give you *ill*, Sir. There is Contagion in Great Queen Street and I am here to have you act with the greatest expediency to avert a catastrophe for all concerned.'

38

A short time later, Edward Constable was recalled to the sitting room. Now only two candles were burning where before there had been six. These candles being at the far end of the room, by the curtained window, the room was now so very gloomy that the footman could barely see the visitor at all. Then, from the murky shadows of the master's wing-back chair, came a foreign wheeze.

'Ah there you are, fellow. Now bring me a nice wedge of Cheshire and a glass of port.'

'I'm not sure we have Cheshire, Sir.' The candle light made the peculiar visitor's skin look smooth and waxy, like an effigy. 'We do have a very good double Gloucester.'

'Is this fellow your only footman, Mr Belt?'

'Buckle, Sir.' The master rose from the gloom of his own adjacent chair.

Oh please, Sir, do not stand for him.

'Mr Buckle, is this the only footman?'

Sit. Sit, Mr Buckle.

'No. I have a pair.'

'Then send me the other,' cried the doctor. 'I don't like this one at all.'

'Oh no. We don't need to push it quite so hard.'

'Send him to me. I'll have to see them all in any case.'

Constable had already stood for a quarter of an hour with his ear pressed very tight upon the drawing-room door, but all to no avail. So although he now did what he was bid, and called Mr Maggs to stand attendance in the sitting room, he could not explain the nature of the doctor's business.

143

'It smells fishy,' said Mercy. 'When he has you there, Eddie, why would he want Mr Maggs?'

'He is what they call "eccentric": meaning he is rich and has no manners.'

Maggs turned to Constable. 'Go look in the street.'

'What would I look for?'

'Go look in the damned street. See who's lurking.'

'Would it be too much of an imposition,' asked Constable, feeling his voice tight inside his nervous throat, 'for you to say *please*?'

The convict turned his hard and private eyes upon him.

'Please,' he said.

Constable looked for evidence of mockery. Satisfied there was none, he went out into the drizzling night where he discovered nothing more than a passing whore with a cane basket and a boy with a lantern holding a horse. He returned to the house, and tiptoed past the drawing room. On the stairs he found Jack Maggs in the process of hiding a rough-looking dagger in his boot.

While Constable described what he had seen outside, Jack Maggs listened intently, his jaw set hard, his eyes hidden in the shadow of his brow.

'Very well,' said he abruptly. He returned to the snuggery, where he took the sheaf of papers from his master's desk, rolled them up and tied them with a ribbon. He slid these papers into an inside pocket.

'If 'twere done,' he said, ''twere best done quickly.'

Mercy began to plead not to be locked up again. She spat in her palm and crossed her heart; she swore she would die before she betrayed him.

Consequently the two footmen came down the stairs two steps at a time, leaving Mercy Larkin in the unlocked snuggery. As they entered the gloomy sitting room, Constable's heart was beating very fast. He recognized a tangled skein of shadow – the doctor – rise out of the wing-back chair. The doctor held his hand out to Jack Maggs. There was a flash of silver.

'Come, man, put out your tongue.'

'Why would I do a thing like that, Sir?'

The doctor held a silver instrument high in the air. 'Because,' he cried, 'there is Contagion in the house.'

Maggs took the doctor's wrist, and thereby wrung from him a high and sudden cry of pain. A metal instrument clattered to the floor.

'Jack Maggs,' cried Buckle, fluttering around the two men. 'Jack Maggs, I order you.'

But what he 'ordered' he did not say, and now Jack Maggs was dragging the doctor, squirming and flapping like a great fat-bellied moth, into the far corner of the drawing room.

'God save me!' cried the visitor.

Jack Maggs manacled both the surgeon's wrists with his left hand, thus freeing his right hand to pick up one of the two remaining candles. He then forced the visitor down to the floor.

'You bleeding dromedary! I'll rip your bleeding throat out.'

'Stop at once,' wailed Percy Buckle. 'It is Mr Oates.'

Constable turned expectantly towards the doorway but was puzzled to find it empty.

Maggs held the candle close upon the fellow's upturned face and there revealed: grease and powder, a kneeling Tobias Oates staring wide-eyed at the light. 'I know the dog,' he snarled.

'Listen to me, man,' cried Percy Buckle urgently, and while the big man maintained his hold of the terrified doctor, the master whispered into his ear.

39

Jack Maggs followed the doctor to the kitchen, where he watched him conduct a lesson in the correct way to wash the hands. One after another Sir Spencer Spence made the servants and their master follow his example; no one was pardoned from this exercise. When Mr Spinks claimed exemption, the doctor lashed him with such irascibility that the old man began to tremble.

Finally, when the butler's hands were washed and dried to the doctor's satisfaction, the latter set a large black bag upon the deal table. Opening it, he took out a long object which, when its wrapping of black velvet was removed, turned out to be a cruel serrated knife.

'Oh dearie,' said Miss Mott.

The doctor then produced a second instrument with a long curling tail like a corkscrew. He toyed with this while he spoke of the 'organ of secretion' and how it changed its colour when weakened by Contagion. The organ, he said, as a consequence, became large and flatulent like a great blue balloon, and he held the corkscrew as if intending to puncture everybody immediately. Finally, to the relief of all, both implements were put away.

But the ordeal was by no means over, as the doctor now announced that he would examine the members of the household individually, inside the scullery.

Although the scullery curtain was drawn, those who waited in the kitchen could hear every scrape and rustle. Mrs Halfstairs was first. Next was Mr Spinks. One by one, the victims coughed, gagged, and spat into a little silver bowl. They walked out of the scullery with hot cheeks and downcast eyes.

Jack Maggs was last of all. Entering the tight little alcove, he knew the power of Tobias Oates to be greater than he had suspected. This doctor, with his twisted red mouth and wild bright eyes, was incredible, ridiculous, and yet he *existed*, given life by some violent magic in his creator's heart. The jerky little writer was thus made invisible. A glaring demon had taken his place, and this being took Jack's jaw in its dry square hands and made as if to thrust a metal spatula down his throat.

When Jack Maggs grasped its wrist, the creature did not yield. Rather it raised its coal-black eyebrows, and brought its soft little mouth to whisper mockingly in Jack's ear.

'You wish to hang?'

Peering around the curtain, Jack Maggs saw what he was meant to see: that herd of dangerous gossips gathered in the kitchen, staring back at him.

'Sputum,' cried the doctor, and thrust the spatula down his throat.

Five minutes later, the house was declared to be in a state of

146

Quarantine. Thus, for the cost of a sore throat, Jack Maggs had precisely what he had wished: the dike was plugged; the gossips were contained. But as he set out to secure his territory, the convict's heart fell prey to a new anxiety – a blood-dark feeling in his gut – that he had become the captive of someone whose powers were greater than he had the wit to ever understand.

40

The minute Sir Spencer Spence had left the house, Maggs took himself down into the cellar where he found a rusty hammer and a paper bag of nails.

He drove in the first nail, two inches above the lock of the front door. He hammered it in on a good angle and felt it bite into the oaken frame. Each hammer blow helped ease the knotting in his gut.

'My house,' cried Mr Buckle, appearing suddenly behind him.

Maggs drove in the second nail, three inches below the lock. 'It's what your doctor ordered.'

'He said nothing of the sort. Stop! I order it. You must not hurt my house.'

Maggs stood on tip-toes to place a third nail at the top of the door. 'You're splitting it.'

Maggs drove the nail home. He turned the handle of the door and tugged on it.

'That's what I call a Quarantine.'

'Look what you are doing. Look at how it splits. Please stop this, now. I order you. This is not a Quarantine. This is not what Mr Oates meant at all.'

But Maggs was already half-way across the drawing room. He tied back the heavy maroon curtains and stood, briefly exposing himself to the night while he drove in nine more nails in fast succession.

'You misunderstand the meaning of the word,' said the master of the house. 'I'll fetch the dictionary. Hold off my windows while I get the book. I order you!'

But Jack Maggs would be no one's servant any longer. He retrieved a chair from the dining room, and, with a spray of six-inch nails poking from his mouth, moved across the three windows – bang, bang, bang.

'Here – ' Percy Buckle re-entered the room, the dictionary open in his hands. 'There's no hammering mentioned under Quarantine.'

But the drawing room was done, the curtains drawn, the windows already pinned at top and bottom. Maggs replaced the chair in the dining room, and lit the candles.

Percy Buckle laid the heavy book upon the dining-room table. 'This is my house,' he said.

But Jack Maggs was already on his way to the next floor.

41

When the house was finally snug, Jack returned the nails and hammer to the cellar. This room, being beyond Mrs Halfstairs's territory, was a rancid labyrinth of passage-ways formed by high piles of coiled rope, abandoned scenery, and hanging costumes which must have begun their life in the late Mr Quentin's theatre. Jack had not been in the cellar a moment when he heard the upstairs door open and saw candle-light shadows moving down the stairs. The maid's soft voice called out for him.

'Here,' he said gruffly, lifting his oil lamp.

They met, not without some confusion, in a corridor of ancient costumes: long ballgowns with mildew creeping up their ruffled sleeves.

'You nailed my bedroom window shut,' she said. Her voice seemed slow and sleepy.

He admitted that he had been into her room and quarantined it.

'Why not Mrs Halfstairs's, then?'

Had she been crying? In the gloom, he glimpsed her slightly swollen upper lip.

'You think she might be scampering out across the roof?' he asked sarcastically.

'As I'm sure you know, she's come down with Contagion.'

Jack knew of no such thing. The odours of dark and dirt had always had libidinous associations for him; now this smell surrounded him and for a moment he knew of precious little else.

'Of course,' Mercy said. 'It ain't really Contagion, no matter what the doctor says. It's that Metzmetric Fluid, as you know yourself. The poor old cow has got the fluid in her chest.'

Maggs raised an eyebrow.

'Oh, so you think me ignorant?' she said.

'No.'

'Then for your information, Sir, I went with Mr Constable to a Metzmetric Concert in Great Windmill Street at Christmas. That was an education I can tell you. There was a lady they made dance and sing and then she shook all over. It was done by using magnets on her Fluid. That's what he done to you with all that waving of his hands. It were the same, exactly. It's how he stopped your face hurting. You think I don't know what's going on?'

'What's *that* got to do with Mrs Halfstairs?'

'You think I don't know that weren't no doctor? It was Mr Oates with all that powder on his head.'

Quietly he asked, 'The others know it was Mr Oates?'

She snuffed her candle and dropped it in her pinny pocket. 'They wouldn't know their nose if it sneezed at them.'

'But you set them straight?'

'Not yet, no.'

'Then come with me,' said Jack, taking her by the arm.

'No! Let me be!' She pulled away.

'God damn,' he exclaimed, grabbing her by the waist so suddenly her cap fell off. Her hair brushed his face, releasing the faint scent of soot into the air.

'I'll not be locked.'

'God damn me, you will.'

She was fast and lithe, but he pinned her, took her, her feet kicking six inches above the floor, carried her up the stone stairs to the ground floor while the ancient oil lamp, which he had kept hooked in his bad hand, swayed dangerously against her skirts.

149

At this hour the ground floor was empty . He set her down and the pair of them regarded each other, breathing heavily.

'Lock me,' she burst out. 'I don't care.'

'Yes.'

She shook her hair and brushed it from her eyes. 'I don't mind.'

'Good.'

'Lock me up all night.'

In silent agreement they proceeded upstairs. A light was showing underneath the master's door. They crossed to the back stairs, and thence upwards to the attic. Three times Mercy's black skirts brushed against Jack's knees. He felt this so acutely it seemed to him she must also know his knee through the medium of the fabric. When she entered her room, he was hard behind her.

It was a very pretty little home she had made for herself, with many embroidered cushions and a framed painting of a young girl sitting below a windmill with a rag doll on her knee.

'How old are you?'

'A lady don't reveal her age.'

He passed her the lamp, which she stood on tip-toes to hang carefully from a hook at the apex of the attic ceiling. While she was so occupied, he removed the key from the door. Hearing the metal scrape in the lock, she spun around.

'No!'

But he had already stepped outside the door.

'Good night,' he said, and locked her in before he could change his mind.

A minute later, he climbed across the roof, carrying all his turbulent emotions with him to the abandoned house next door. Here he wrote page after page, pouring all his feelings into that secret history. He slept two hours on the settle, and when he woke he began again: . . . Dear Boy,

At six o'clock, he recrossed the slippery roof to Mr Buckle's house. When he unlocked the maid's door, she was dressed and waiting for him.

150

42

Mercy Larkin applied her 'nurse-maid's rouge', pinching her cheeks, tweaking them spitefully, all the time contorting her face and letting out small cries of *ooh* and *ouch*. This cosmetic recipe she had learned from her mother, who had applied it enthusiastically before launching her daughter out into the Haymarket.

Now, waiting for her door to be unlocked, Mercy set to work on her upper lip. She had no mirror with which to appraise her handiwork but when the tingling in her lips and cheeks told her the effect had been achieved, she sat upon her three-legged stool with her hands resting in her lap. The face she turned towards the door now showed those swollen, slightly bruised features that always produced so amorous a response in Mr Buckle.

Waiting for Jack Maggs, she considered her own recklessness. She had not forgotten how Mr Buckle loved to read her *Pamela*. Nor did she over-look her own deep pleasure in the tale. Neither servant nor master ever discussed their attachment to the novel, but it was as clear as day to her that she, like Pamela, might one day be mistress of the house wherein she had been called to serve.

When the door at last swung open, she should have recoiled from him who stood before her: Jack Maggs with red-rimmed eyes, unshaven cheeks, his hair spectacularly disarrayed.

'You going to put me in the snuggery?' she said.

For answer he held open the door so she might pass before him. As they walked together past the master's partly open door, Mercy's lips began to itch – an omen, as she was well aware, that they would soon be kissed.

They descended the stairs together to the kitchen, where she saw Mrs Halfstairs's small blue eyes appraising her features. Had she pinched too hard? The housekeeper opened her mouth as if to reprimand her but then, most unexpectedly, sighed and lowered her braided head into her hands.

In the sudden quiet that followed, Mercy donned her apron, then took the pan of kippers from Miss Mott, turning her face so the cook might not see her lips.

A moment later Miss Mott was sitting at the table. This was unusual: Miss Mott never sat down, not even to drink a cup of tea. Yet it took a good long moment for Mercy to realize that no one was thinking of her lips, that her amorous expectations were not an issue with the other servants. They were sick: Miss Mott, Mrs Halfstairs, Mr Spinks.

As Mercy buttered their toast she heard the butler cough. She listened to the gummy Magnetic Fluid bubbling in his chest. It was Contagion, no doubt about it.

She ate quickly then went, as usual, to set the table for the master's breakfast.

She had not been at this task a minute when Jack Maggs arrived at the doorway of the dining room; she felt his eyes upon her back. Knowing the master might arrive at any moment, she prayed to God to not let nothing happen here. She finished setting the table hurriedly, and allowed Jack Maggs to escort her back to the room they had occupied all day yesterday.

Inside the snuggery, she turned urgently to face him. Her mouth was dry, her heart agitated.

She saw his dark eyes hesitate. She thought he was going to smile, but then he walked past her to the bureau. Disappointed, she watched him select one of the new goose-feathers in the master's drawer.

'He won't like you doing that,' she said.

Jack Maggs winked at her. He cut three inches off the feather's top, cleared the barrel of its scurf, and made six fast cuts. Having thus manufactured a new quill, he set back to writing.

'It must be most important.'

'It is.'

'A good friend, no doubt.'

'I hope so, yes.'

Thus, to all intents and purposes, he abandoned her on the ottoman. There was nothing to do but knit and wait, and see what might happen. From time to time she secretly freshened her complexion, but with less hope as to the consequences.

The entire morning passed without further conversation, and she had naught to do but wonder at the passion which drove that strange hand. Some time in the early afternoon, however, Maggs stopped abruptly. A floorboard creaked outside in the hallway. Then he put a finger to his lips and carefully laid the quill down. He rose, moving towards the door.

Then she saw it: a *dagger*. She had never seen one in a man's hand before. It was at once deadly strange, and quite familiar – an ugly black blade with a hook at its pointy end. It should have made him repulsive to her, but it did not, and instead she watched how very graceful was his movement toward the door.

There was a low moan out on the landing, then a great crash as Jack wrenched the door open. She rushed to see.

'Jod's blood,' cried Jack Maggs, and pushed her roughly back into the snuggery, but not before she had seen the heaving prostrate body of Mr Spinks.

The key was then turned in the lock; she was left alone listening to Maggs's heavy tread ascend the stairs to the servants' floor.

It was only then she realized he had left his secret letter sitting on the desk.

43

Silas and Ma Britten – Jack wrote – had a very original ambition: to do a series of clever burglaries without never laying fingers on the goods. And once they got Sophina and me properly trained-up to the art, it was, so Silas said, like having ferrets, except that he was excused the bother of carrying the cages.

Looked at from his way, it was a very pretty little dart. First Yours Truly would climb down the chimney – a journey I now made as easy as jumping out of bed – and then I would light my candle and inspect the locks on the dressers and cabinets. If need be, I would then unlock the kitchen door and whistle for the lever man, a great half-wit pugilist called Wexall whose brain had been jolted in its box one time too many. Wexall had nothing more to do than break the locks and then scarper, a service for which he was pleased to receive a silver sixpence. Then Sophina would enter, always carrying a little posy of flowers – I know not why this was – and wearing her good hat. It was she who was trusted to select the most valuable pieces of silver plate, and I, her black-faced companion, who would pack the treasures in the sack of soot. We went about our work as happy as eight-year-olds, magging to each other all the while.

Silas, meanwhile, had arranged for an old dustman by the name of Mr Figgs to come to pick up the sacks which I placed outside the door. Silas told me that Mr Figgs thought himself to be carrying naught but dust and ashes, and was happy to deliver the sacks to his net loft in Wapping for a penny each. This must have been a lie, but I believed it then.

In the summer of 1801 we did over twenty of these 'errands'. We did so well that before the fireplaces of London were hot again, we had abandoned the rotten little court by London Bridge and moved, with Silas and Sophina, to Islington. We took a whole floor above a tobacconist's in Upper Street and from this address Ma Britten kept herself as busy as ever, making her sausages and ministering to her female visitors. Whereas once she had received her callers in a curtained little area beside the stove, now she saw them in a small room above the yard at the back.

It was a very proper part of Islington we moved to, or so it seemed to us, with its lace curtains in the windows and the men all wearing suits to church, and we was all pleased to be coming up in the world.

Tom was sent into apprenticeship. He bellowed and begged to remain in his former occupation and said he would happily walk the miles to and from Smithfield markets, but the Ma was determined that he would be a carpenter. He was soon indentured to a master in Notting Hill, and from this household he was permitted to come home to us every Sunday.

No one went to Smithfield any more. Ma Britten would send me with a note and half a crown to a proper butcher's shop where a number of red-faced men, all named Mr Ayres, would wrap me up some lamb chops or a piece of liver.

Thus my life improved all at once. Tom was rarely there to twist my wrist or otherwise hurt me. I ate great meals of roast meat and roast potatoes. And if we were forbidden to play with the respectable children, Sophina and I had each other for company. Silas, to give him credit, often took us to the park, where we played hide and seek, and hoop-a-penny and blind man in a sack.

Alas, life was not so merry for Tom, who suffered much from home-sickness. Each Sunday he left his master's house in darkness, arriving in Islington before the church bells had begun to ring. I would wake to the sound of his big heavy boots upon the stairs. Once inside our door he would run to our mother's room, climb up into her bed and cry.

Tom did not like Silas or Sophina either. This was to my advantage because he seemed to lose his old dislike of me. Indeed I was now his ally, and on these Sunday visits he took to walking out with me, sharing confidences about his hopes and plans.

One September morning, before it had become properly cold, he took me all the way down into St James's Park. He bought me a glass of milk from the stalls where they had the cows. There were a great many servant girls drinking the milk, which was said to be good for their complexion, but Tom paid the girls no mind at all.

It was me he watched. He was always watching me. His long bony face was alert and slightly angry.

– Does Silas buy you milk?

In fact, he bought us milk on many occasions, but I knew enough to say he never had.

– The brute has you all tied up in the harness, said Tom. He is riding on your back. He is taking all the money and won't even buy you milk.

I ventured that Silas had taught me a great deal.

– We have no need of strangers sleeping in our house, said he.

I thought, at first, that he was referring to one of Ma Britten's female customers who had recently spent the night vomiting and groaning in the small room at the back. I agreed that I did not like it.

– We should kick him down the stairs, he said, and take his clever Latin with him.

155

– Who?

– Silas, you little mutt, who did you think we were talking of?

I reminded Tom that it was Silas who had orchestrated our good fortune, that if not for him we would still be living in that room by Pepper Alley Stairs.

– We was happy there, said Tom. Before he came and stuck his big red nose in. You and me and Ma, we had good days. We didn't have no porker snoring in the night.

– Still and all, Tom . . .

– Still and all, we must get rid of him.

– Sophina is my friend.

– I never said nothing about her, said Tom. You want my opinion, she's a giddy goat, but I ain't got no quarrel with her. It's him we must get rid of.

– How would we do that, Tom?

– I ain't talking of hows just at the moment. All I'm talking of is the fact of the matter and all I am telling you is – and here he pushed his raw face close to mine – Silas is a cheat and a liar and he is not a part of our family.

Tom frightened me that day. As we walked back up Haymarket I thought I had liked him better when we were enemies.

He walked so close. He was forever bumping into me, and as he walked, he talked, his mouth pushed close over towards my ear. He told me that we could get a great deal of money and run away to Bristol. He told me that his master had a steel closet with gold bars in it, and that I should come with him and climb down the chimney and unlock the door.

As I write this now, I see what I did not see then: Tom was not right in his mind. Perhaps he was ever thus. Or perhaps it was the strain of being forbid his mother's company that finally unhinged him. Certainly that day I could make no sense of him but thought it was my own fault, that perhaps I was as slow and stupid as he said. When I pointed out that he was already in his master's house and did not need me to come down the chimney, he flew into a rage and did not quiet until I had agreed to come with him to Bristol. This promise, fortunately, he soon forgot.

156

He came back in the middle of that week. I do not know how he got into the house, only that I woke to find him shaking me. He told me I must get dressed quickly without a sound. His big mouth was close to me again, his breath smelled bad.

I slipped out of the bed which I shared with my play mate, and he led me out into the back yard. And there we stood, in the shadow of a pear tree, with his hard hand shackling my wrist, shivering, saying nothing.

I asked him what it was we were waiting for.

For answer he clipped me round the ears, then put his finger to his lips. After we had stood there a good half-hour, I heard a great loud knocking and much shouting, and then a candle was lit, and soon I saw, at the window, all manner of men with lanterns and candles. It was the police.

– That'll teach the smarmy clack-box, he said.

We then returned to our rooms, wherein we found Silas gone and Ma Britten pale and quiet. She looked at Tom very thoughtful like, and asked him how it was he was here so early of a morning.

I went in to comfort poor Sophina who was crying most piteously.

– Jack, Jack, she said, Jack, they took my da. Who will take care of me now my da is gone?

44

It was hot and close in the snuggery, and whenever he stretched Jack Maggs released a great manly smell like bed linen in the warmth of early morning. Sometimes Mercy thought she could not bear another moment of it, being confined so close with him.

For his part though, he hardly seemed to notice her, and yet she had felt his keen interest on other days, feeling his stare when he thought her ignorant of his attention.

If she was now unattractive to him, he had heard the gossip in the kitchen. He knew she was a chipped and mended cup in a rich man's dresser. It was clear to him, clear to anyone who looked into her eyes, that she was stained brown from use.

157

He was also rather stained and used, but this did not make him the least unattractive to her. Indeed, it was the knowledge of his ill-usage that stirred her heart so painfully. Why then could he not extend the same charity to her?

She had imagined his scars most vividly. She had thought of his back with particular clarity. She would have dressed it with unguents and lotions, but he was busy writing letters to his beloved and did not care for her anyhow.

The bureau had always fitted the master very well, but it was not made for Jack Maggs. She watched how those immense thighs jammed beneath the dainty little desk and, when his feelings ran away with him, how they lifted the desk clear off the floor so that the cedar top tilted like the deck of a ship at sea. Throughout all this turbulence he would keep on writing, back to front like a Chinaman, until Mercy thought she saw a kind of glow, from behind his neck and shoulders, like the light from a furnace door. As he wrote his thick lips moved, and his eyes screwed almost shut.

It was not until the middle of the second long day, as he left to carry Mr Spinks up to his bed, that she had her chance to look: *Tom did not like Silas or Sophina either*, but then the whole page vanished, and although she peered very close at the paper and held it up to the light, it kept its secrets to itself. So it was with each and every page.

She heard his tread on the stair and immediately sat down upon the ottoman.

He entered without glancing at her, but stared down at his papers for so long that she began to fear that she had somehow marked them. He had been carrying some items in his arms, though she could not make them out until he laid them down: three lemons, some twine and rough brown paper, and a splendid silver mirror.

'How is Mr Spinks?' She tried to sound conversational, but her voice quavered.

He looked at her, severely.

'Ailing.' He held out the mirror for her to take. At first she thought it a gift and her hand trembled when she took it.

'It's ever so pretty,' she said.

'He was a clever old cove what made it. Dead now.'

He held out his hand and she understood she was to give the mirror back. He began to wrap it in brown paper.

'It's a gift?' She smiled to hide the sickness in her heart.

He continued folding his brown paper.

'Here, let me do it. She'll think you've bought her a flounder if you wrap it up like that.'

She smoothed out the paper, and carefully wrapped the mirror. She felt him watching her; she imagined his breath upon her neck.

'You want me to wrap the lemons, too?' she said lightly.

Unsmiling, he placed the lemons in front of her.

He was standing next to her very close, and she felt his attention on her while she made a neat little parcel of the lemons. After she had completed this task, she wrapped the letters themselves. Finally, when the three parcels had received their kiss of sealing wax, she placed them, one atop the other, in the centre of the desk. She felt all her hair to be on end. She had to speak, no matter what it made him think of her.

'I don't mind you lock me,' she began.

There was an odd agitation showing in his eyes.

'I never did tell a soul about you,' she said.

Then he leaned down and kissed her. Upon the forehead, like a bishop or an uncle.

'How did little Buckle nab you? It don't make sense, the pair of you.'

'It makes sense.'

'Did you lose your papa?'

'What?'

'Did you lose your papa?'

His eyes were soft and brown, all their hardness gone, just as they had been last night in the cellar. She looked at him, trying to understand what it was he felt, and then he lifted his poor misshapen hand and stroked her hair.

'Lost your da?' he said roughly. 'The poor thing lost the da.'

Then she wept against his musky shirt and she felt how he pitied her. He did not embrace her, but he continued gently to stroke her hair, and she might have stayed there for ever, so she felt, had not the inevitable knock come, so soon, upon the door.

He stepped away from her.

'It is Constable,' he said. 'Come to collect the parcels.'

It was not only Constable but also, alas, the master; and this latter person now rushed into the room looking intently at her from under his raised eyebrows. The poor frightened man had strapped his sword around his dressing gown and it clanged against the doorway as he entered.

'Everyone still well?' he asked, staring all the time at Mercy.

Jack Maggs did not seem to notice him. 'Now listen here, Eddie, you reckon your mates can find this Henry Phipps.' And so saying he thrust the three parcels into Constable's arms.

Mercy thought: *not love letters.*

'Tell them Mr Phipps must squeeze the lemons in a bowl, and then brush the juice across the paper. Then he is to use the mirror. They should tell him it is a good mirror as he will find mentioned in the first letter. They should tell him there is more to the story, but he better come and hear it from my lips, soon, for I cannot stay here in this house a great deal longer. Can you remember all of this?'

Mercy blew her nose.

'Lemons, brush, mirror,' said Constable. 'More to tell.'

'They should tell him – to suggest a place where we can meet in private. He can write me a note' – Maggs turned to Mr Buckle – 'and then you will be free of me. I will be gone from your life.'

'No, no,' said his host, but Mr Buckle's earnest little ferret face was obviously relieved and Mercy saw him as she had never seen him before. She wished it were not so, but her saviour had begun to cut a pathetic figure in her eyes.

45

In foul-smelling Floral Street, Edward Constable alighted from a hackney cab and carried his three parcels to the door of *Mafooz & Son, Importers of Dates and Coffees*, this drab business being distinguished by a small lantern which had been left to burn, carelessly it seemed, throughout the night.

It was a little after dawn as he pulled on the bell, but in far less time than might have been expected at such an hour, the peep-hole in the door was opened, and his business was demanded of him.

The answer being satisfactory, he was admitted into a dim, smoke-stained corridor where a faded individual with rouged cheeks and pouchy eyes was pleased to take his hat and gloves.

This was Magnus, as much a landmark for a certain caste of Londoner as the new column in Trafalgar Square. Magnus was the subject of many anecdotes, most of which devolved from the extremely handsome figure he had cut early in the reign of George III, the period from which his present wig most certainly dated.

This club was an institution in Covent Garden at that time. It was certainly well known to the costers that a certain type of gentleman (known in their parlance as Foreman's Friends) frequented these rooms above Mafooz's shop. The costers themselves, when they were finished with their brandy at the Dog and Whistle, had been known to beg admittance, and then there would be all sorts of fun and dancing into the small hours, particularly on Saturday night and often continuing well into Sunday morning, sometimes even at the hour when Edward Constable arrived to inquire after Mr Henry Phipps.

Neither by word nor by manner did Magnus allow that Mr Phipps might be presently upon the premises, but he did not deny the possibility either. Rather, he ushered Constable into a small room with its title *Lord Strutwell* blazoned boldly on its door. The room was decorated in most masculine style, with various flags and battle standards, and armchairs upholstered in Moroccan leathers.

Here, Constable sat himself down and waited with his parcels on his lap. He displayed no appetite for the bound engravings which filled the book cases, engravings which, in a happier time, might have produced in him a state of almost damnable desire. He waited half an hour with his back turned to the book case, and when the door behind him opened, he stood.

It was apparent from the moment Henry Phipps entered the room

161

that he was drunk. He sat himself down heavily with his long legs stretched out and the contours of his manhood immodestly displayed beneath his doeskins.

He was a tall, well-made young man of conventionally handsome appearance. He had straight fair hair, long side whiskers, a good straight nose, and clear blue eyes, but it was the mouth which was the most expressive aspect of his physiognomy: being one moment utterly persuasive of its charm, and the next distinguished by its churlishness.

Now he squinted up at Constable. 'Are you not that fellow from Great Queen Street?'

'I think you know me well enough, Sir.'

'The racehorse, eh?'

Edward Constable's mouth tightened.

Henry Phipps was not too drunk to note the expression.

'Oh Christ,' he closed his eyes, 'please, don't play the footman with me.'

'I am a footman, Sir, as you might have reason to recall.'

Henry Phipps opened his eyes sufficiently to consider Constable.

'My name is Edward Constable. It was my friend who died . . .'

Phipps then leaned forward, speaking more quietly than he had hitherto. 'As I told you before, I will have no more discussions relating to that affair.' He made as if to rise.

'Stay, Sir. It is some other business.'

Mr Phipps sighed. 'Perhaps you wish to blame me for the rain last night. I am, Sir, a tall fellow. Perhaps I caused it.'

'That is not my purpose.'

'For the sky does love me, eh, and then the rain does fall, and poetry being poetry, why – ' he lay back heavily in his arm chair ' – then I am to blame.'

'Mr Phipps, it is not that business, it is another . . .'

'Not involving my supposed obligation to you?'

'No, Sir, to another.'

'Oh Lord, this is very boring.'

'I am here on a message from Mr Jack Maggs.'

'The Devil you are!'

'I am, Sir.'

Henry Phipps's manner now changed completely. He removed himself to the arm of the club chair, folding his large hands upon his lap, and regarded Constable with earnest attention.

'And how is he? How is Jack Maggs?'

'I would say that he was pining for you, Sir.'

'Pining for me, you say? How odd. But sit down, Edward. Tell me, what is he like? A ruffian, I warrant.'

'He is very comely, as a matter of fact.'

'Oh he is, is he? A racehorse?'

'A little grim at times, but the ladies are most taken with him.'

'The *ladies*?'

'There is a certain aspect to his manner which does betray his past, and yet you would not know the tortures he has passed through if you did not witness the scars.'

'He has scars?'

'He has been flogged, Sir. Yet for a man so abused, I think you will find him of a very decent disposition.'

'The thing is this, Eddie, old chap, I really do not think I will have an opportunity to "find" him at all. I am called away.'

'You were "called away" once already, were you not, Sir? Mr Maggs believes it was his imminent arrival that was the cause of your departure.'

'Now I am called away, let us say, further.'

'Abroad?'

'Further than it is your damned business to inquire.'

'In any case, Sir, he has asked me to deliver these little packages to you.'

And here Constable offered the three parcels to Henry Phipps.

The gentleman did not immediately reach for the gifts but rather peered at them.

'What's this?'

'I believe one of the objects to be a mirror.'

'A mirror? Is he sarcastic then? What in the deuce does he mean by giving me a mirror?'

'And this one on the top contains three lemons.'

163

'Lemons?'

'And the largest of the three, so I understand, is a certain document which Mr Maggs would have you read.'

Constable then held out all three parcels.

'A legal document?' asked Henry Phipps, unable to hide his growing excitement.

'No, I think not.'

'Not the title to a house, for instance?'

'I imagine it is a sort of letter.'

'A letter?' cried Henry Phipps, suddenly angry. 'Do you think I could correspond with such a one as he? And do you not consider the doubtful position you place yourself in? You are breaking the law to know his whereabouts without disclosing it. He is a dangerous man, Mr Racehorse, a man condemned to banishment, for ever. If you wish to reveal my presence to him, I swear I will make you wish that you were never born.'

'Sir, my information is that he sits up half the night writing in order to explain himself to you.'

'He said this?'

'Please, Sir, he thinks only of you. If ever he did you harm, I am very sure that he is sorry.'

For the third time, Constable attempted to deliver Jack Maggs's gifts.

'He says it is necessary to squeeze a little lemon juice upon the pages. And then to read them through the mirror image.' There was a pause. 'He is very fond of you.'

'But I am not fond of him. Tell him that I find the very notion of him vile.'

'Can I give him no comfort?'

'Yes: you may tell him that I am well aware of the obligation he has placed me under, and that he can therefore rely upon my silence for the moment.'

And with that the interview ended, and Henry Phipps strode from the room.

46

Constable, searching the house high and low, found Jack Maggs in Mr Spinks's bedroom, at which doorway he remained unannounced.

The Australian sat aside the butler's sick-bed. His back was to the door, and he was offering a spoon of broth to the old man.

'You should never look a pooka in the eye. The eye is the strong point of all these dark magicians.'

He moved the spoon closer. The butler turned his head aside. The spoon withdrew a little.

'Every creature has its strong point,' continued the big man. 'With a pooka it is in the eyes entirely. Were it not for the eyes they would be helpless as a new-hatched chicken.'

Mr Spinks knocked the spoon aside, and some liquid fell upon his counterpane.

Jack Maggs patiently set the soup bowl and spoon upon the side table. The feverish butler withdrew as far as he was able, until he was sitting up straight and hard against the bed-head, far too preoccupied to notice the footman standing in the doorway.

'Don't look at me like that, old chap,' said Jack Maggs. 'I'm not the pooka who put the spell on you.'

Mr Spinks folded his arms across his chest.

'His name is Oates.'

'Pooka!' croaked Mr Spinks sarcastically.

'So you can open your gob when you want.'

He offered another spoon of broth, but the butler's mouth stayed firmly closed.

'Very well then.' Maggs took the old man's unshaven chin and dug his thumb and second finger in at the hinge, between the gums. 'This is how I drench my sheep in New South Wales.'

'Mmmph,' cried Spinks.

As he struggled to avoid the broth, the butler's rheumy eyes alighted on Constable. The footman smiled encouragingly. Spinks began to speak, but as his mouth opened, so the soup slid in and

Maggs clamped his horny hand over the old chap's mouth and nose. There was no choice but to swallow.

'Fight fluid with fluid.'

In his distress, Mr Spinks pointed to the door.

Jack Maggs, seeing Constable, immediately set down the bowl upon the side table. 'He squeezed the lemons? He understood the mirror?'

While Mr Spinks escaped back beneath his covers, Mr Constable held up the unopened packages, then watched as the other inspected them, checking each and every untied knot along the way.

'Apparently he is not known of.'

At this point, Mr Spinks began to snore. Jack Maggs busied himself covering the old fellow's withered shanks; when he finally showed his face again, his eyes were completely expressionless.

'If the man will not be found,' said Constable sympathetically, 'he will not be found. There is no better place to hide than London.'

Jack Maggs showed no further interest in the topic.

'Mercy is doing for the women,' he said. 'I said I would do for the Bishop here.'

'You have new linen,' Constable offered. 'If you lift Mr Spinks I'll do the changing.'

Constable then removed his jacket, and draped it carefully across a chair. While Jack Maggs lifted the butler, he swiftly stripped the bed and laid a cool clean sheet upon the old man's ancient mattress. In all this, he was as efficient as a guardsman, but the effect of seeing Spinks's ruined body cradled in this way by his companion was to make the winds blow stronger, to flood his mind with Christian images of the type celebrated in the stained-glass windows of the little church of St Mary Le Bow. From here he was carried, in a great swirl, to turbulent visions of Maggs's scarred body, his massive strength, producing in him such a mighty want, not to nurse bullying old Spinks, but to *be* nursed himself, to have Jack Maggs take his head and lay it in his lap, to stroke him with that hand.

He now felt a dangerously strong desire to confess that he had indeed discovered the whereabouts of Henry Phipps, that he had thereby foolishly revealed Maggs's whereabouts to a man who did not wish him well.

He knew it unwise, but he had a passion to unburden himself, to disclose that he too had known Henry Phipps, known him in the most personal and private sense. He had been flattered and led astray by that gentleman.

He had gone next door to deliver an invitation to tea with Mr Buckle. There he was engaged by the young master in talk of the West Country and its charms. He was taken upstairs to see a small oil painting of a storm off Bristol which, as it turned out, was not hanging where its owner had advertised it. He was then persuaded to stay to wash the young master's hair, to towel him dry, to hold his head against his breast. He heard his soft promises; he had heard himself called Angel; he had taken his manhood deep inside of him.

And thought himself, for cursed truth, a princess.

For two weeks in 1836, Edward Constable had been drunk with Henry Phipps, dreamed of Henry Phipps, had been reamed, rogered, ploughed by Henry Phipps so he could barely walk straight to the table. He had been invited to take a tour of Italy with Henry Phipps, and upon acceptance, he had confessed the circumstances of the invitation to dear Albert Pope, who had been his honest friend and intimate companion during fifteen years of service.

The next day Albert blew his brains out with that horrid little pistol.

He could have told Jack Maggs how badly Henry Phipps had behaved after Albert's death, but he held his secrets tight, like a fistful of gravel against his heart.

He tried to cover Spinks but the old man again became agitated and thrashed around, kicking the coverlet away and pulling at the neck of his fresh night shirt as if he meant to tear it from his body.

Constable picked up the old man's dirty linen from the floor and tied it into a bundle. Though still dressed in his Sunday best, he hoisted the bundle onto his shoulder and carried it from the room. In the passage way he was surprised to find Jack Maggs still close upon his heels.

47

The May sunshine fell in a steep bright mote upon the household linen, which was now bubbling and ballooning from the top of the wash-house copper.

There was, for the moment, no other labour demanded of Edward Constable and, although he had at first anticipated stealing a moment in the sunshine, he now began to notice how closely Jack Maggs continued to cleave to his side. The dark and steamy wash-house began to seem a great deal more appealing than the sunshine.

While his companion leaned carelessly against the ancient wall, engaged in no more productive activity than puffing on a corn-cob pipe – the fragrant smoke of which acted as a potent tonic on the footman – Constable stirred the sheets and pillow-cases. He breathed deep of that singular blend of soapy steam and dark tobacco.

'Pear's in blossom,' he offered.

'Yes. Pear.'

After which no more words were spoken. Constable felt a slight tingling in his neck and a general tension, by no means disagreeable, of the type a chap might feel whilst dawdling beside another chap, as yet unknown.

'I lived a long time with secrets,' said Jack Maggs at last.

Constable's heart thumped in his chest.

Said Jack Maggs: 'You know where I come from?'

'No.'

'Doubtless you were told already by our little Miss.' Maggs puffed a little harder on his pipe. 'It is New South Wales I come from. There. Now you hear it from my own lips.'

Constable looked down into the confusion of the steam.

'Why do you tell me this, Mr Maggs?'

'Three years of that time I had the misfortune to be in a hell called Morton Bay. There a man might be killed on account of knowing another man's secret.'

'Killed?' Constable thought of men with secrets like his own:

Ensign John Hepburn, the drummer Thomas White, all those other jolly fellows who had been prosecuted and convicted and 'launched into eternity' outside the Newgate walls. 'You mean hanged?'

'No, no,' said Maggs impatiently. 'Listen to me: had you known anything as dangerous as what you know of me now, why, you'd be a risk to me.'

'You can speak plainly with me, Jack.'

'I am trying to, Eddie. Listen: in Morton Bay, every man would be a spy on every other man. It was how they kept us down. If you and I were lads together in that place, then you must give me a secret of yours, should you chance to stumble over one of mine. That way we were in balance.'

'Jack, are you confessing to me?'

'No. I am going to trade with you. I am going to tell you a secret.'

'But you already gave me a secret.'

'I need one of yours. I'll pay you double.'

'I have no secrets,' said Constable carefully. 'What secret?'

'The one I saw on your face when you walked into Mr Spinks's room.'

'You think you saw my secret written on my face?'

'Aye.'

'It was in my manner? How I spoke?'

'On your face.'

'That clear?'

'That clear.'

'But what would you tell *me*?'

'That Henry Phipps is my son.'

'Your son?' Constable hesitated. 'You do mean, *son*? A type of son, being like a son?'

'It is a clear enough word.'

'But do you mean he is your *petit fils*? Or do you mean that you are, an older man, like a father to the younger . . . in many ways?'

'Whatever it is called, it is clear enough,' Maggs said and Constable felt himself forced to hold that dark excited gaze.

'Henry's afraid of me, ain't that it?' demanded Maggs. 'Your friends saw him, didn't they?'

169

Constable hesitated.

'Then he must be told he has nothing to fear from Jack. I am his father. I would rather die than hurt him.'

'What of his mother?' Constable asked carefully. 'Where is she?'

'We never did meet.'

'Then you do not mean *son*.'

'Don't be so thick, man,' said Jack Maggs. 'I have said it plain. Now, come, come, I want your secret, laddie.'

There followed then a long silence, and Constable, much confused, began to hoist the first sheet high out of the copper and lead it towards the mangle.

'My secret may not please,' he said at last.

'Please or not please.' Maggs came to the handle and began, slowly, to turn it. Both men watched thoughtfully as the sheet, squashed and steaming, uncoiled itself from the mangle and lay in the stone trough.

'My secret?'

'Yes.'

'I am fond of you,' said Constable.

The roller stopped.

'You are *fond* of me?' Maggs asked perplexedly.

'I am, yes.'

'And it was that which was on your mind when you walked in. You are *fond* of me?'

'It was.'

And it was at that delicate point that their conversation was interrupted by the sound of a most piteous wailing. The two men ran out onto the little yard, and looked up to whence the sounds came. There they saw Mercy Larkin, framed in Mr Spinks's high window.

'Oh Lor,' she cried, 'come quick, come quick. Mr Spinks is taken bad.'

Jack took Constable's shoulder: 'Tell me – your friends saw my Henry? He did not want to know me? That was your secret?'

Constable was not by nature a liar, and when he looked into those hooded hungry eyes he wanted, more than anything, to tell the truth. But Constable feared that if Henry Phipps were found, then Jack Maggs would be lost.

And so he lied.

'No,' he said, looking him straight in the eye. 'I swear. They could not find him anywhere.'

48

At three o'clock on this first afternoon of May, Jack Maggs found the little grocer hidden far from the spring sunlight, in front of a sad and smoky fire in his bedroom. The curtains had been drawn and the candles lit, and Mr Buckle, dressed in an embroidered silk smoking jacket, had his pointed nose deep in a book. The unsavoury smell of cheese was strong about the room, and this smell, Jack Maggs soon saw, had its source in a yellow wedge of Stilton which, together with a glass of wine, was set up on a tray beside his elbow. When Mr Buckle finally became sensible of Maggs's presence in the room, he leapt up so quickly he almost sent this tray flying.

'Whoa there,' cried the footman.

As he fled towards the fireplace, Mr Buckle's slippers flashed beneath the turn-ups of his trousers, like the prow of an oriental boat. They were queer and sparkly, and nearly distracted Maggs's attention from the war-like poker which Percy Buckle had picked up and was holding secretly behind his leg.

'Do not fear me, Mr Buckle.'

'Fear!' scoffed Mr Buckle, backing himself up against the mantel.

'Please sit down, your Lordship.'

Mr Buckle brought the poker out of hiding and, by way of justifying his attachment, poked the fire with it.

'Sit.'

Mr Buckle sat abruptly down. 'Yes?'

'It is Mr Spinks's rattle, Sir.'

'Rattle?'

Maggs was surprised to see the fearful eyes became more distant, his manner harden. 'You mean a cough?'

171

'A rattle is a rattle. There ain't no doubting what it is. We had best get a doctor to him very quickly.'

'What else beside the cough?'

As Jack Maggs told the symptoms, Mr Buckle listened, his head a little to one side, his hands clasped in his lap. He appeared most sympathetic in his demeanour but it was soon clear that, contrary to all his earlier fright and agitation, the master had little anxiety on Mr Spinks's behalf.

When Jack Maggs offered to drag him to his butler's bed where he might inspect the patient for himself, Mr Buckle responded by pushing his bony little backside deeper into his chair.

'Then what of Mr Oates?' he cried. 'What do we do there?'

'In what respect?'

'I would be a very foolish man to go running to a doctor without asking Mr Oates's permission.'

'Why's that?'

'It is Mr Oates who should call the doctor,' continued Mr Buckle. 'He's the one responsible for the injury.'

'He laid the spell?'

'He laid the spell. That's it exactly.'

'Very well,' Jack Maggs granted. 'Then let me run the message to Mr Oates.'

'But it was only a prank, see,' said Percy Buckle, rattling the poker on the hearth. 'That's what alters it. That's where you should watch your Ps and Qs. What will Oates think if I say my man is dying of his prank? He will think me trying to blame him for something which I have no right to blame him. You may not know this, but I am a student of the Law. Oates could sue me for a slander. And if he could, he would. I hear he is a fierce gent about his reputation.'

'You tell him that Mr Spinks has the Mesmeric Fluid on his lung, and he will die of it unless Mr Oates be so nice as to take it away.'

'No, no.'

'Damn you! I'll fetch him myself.'

'He may not be at home,' cried Percy Buckle.

But Jack Maggs was already checking his fob pocket to find a shilling for a cab. 'One more thing, your Lordship.'

'I am listening,' said the other, beginning to preen his moustache again.

'You will hear me drawing nails from the front door.'

'Very good, Master Maggs.'

'But I would have to kill anyone who left your house.'

'Yes, yes,' said Percy Buckle, so distractedly that Jack Maggs would later wonder whether he could possibly have been understood.

Mr Buckle, however, had heard very well indeed, and as the criminal ran down the stairs of his house, he sat looking into the fire, watching Goats and Demons dancing in the flames above the coals.

49

Mr Buckle loved his house, and he celebrated his Great Good Fortune, not merely on the fourteenth day of each month (when he retired to the snuggery to re-read the will) but at almost every moment of almost every day.

He had been often observed to stand and stare off into space, in what his servants imagined was a kind of rapture. It was, as Miss Mott said, as if the master could see an angel in his hallway, but Mr Buckle saw no angels, it was his house he worshipped, and what a miracle it was that he should own that dark-green wall-paper, the stained-glass fanlight, the gloss of polish on the oaken floor.

You could have fed him rancid bacon and he might not have complained. You could leave the sheets unlaundered for two weeks at a stretch. But heaven help you if the floors weren't polished, if the mantelpiece wasn't dusted every day. He liked his inheritance to shine. Consequently, to see the fresh injury which Jack Maggs's departure had caused to his front door was more disturbing to the owner than even he – who had seen the rusty nails first breach that lustrous black surface – might have anticipated.

He knelt before the door as if winded. The nails had been ripped out roughly. In their place were jagged wounds: gouges, dents, raw splinters. Tenderly, he laid back the splinters inside the wounds, but the hurt was too savage for such ministrations.

Back in his sitting room, he repeatedly pulled the bell for Constable. When he was not answered, he returned to the front door and picked up the horrid nails himself. He dropped them into his jacket pocket, and hurried down the breakneck stairs into his kitchen. Here he found the fire dead and a queer pink-grey mouse eating a crust of bread on the table. The three thin lines between Mr Buckle's eyebrows deepened. At first it seemed that he might strike the mouse, but then all his energy emerged in a violent shiver. He went quickly back up to the ground floor and then up the back stairs.

And there, in the snuggery, he discovered Mercy and Constable sitting side by side on the ottoman, chatting contentedly like dowagers at a ball.

He spoke to them politely. They were lazy and familiar in return.

He requested them to come downstairs to sweep up the mess of nails and splinters. He did not wait to see how this order was received, but descended straight away to the drawing room and picked up – he could have chosen anything – a recent pamphlet from the Workingman's Association. Although he made a convincing show of reading, he was far too upset to study anything. All his attention was focused upon his servants who, even as they came down the stairs, were chatting as familiarly as before.

When they had swept up the dust and splinters, they were cool enough to enter the drawing room without an invitation.

Mercy *sat* in the embrasure of the window. Constable stood. And there they stayed, busy at *waiting*, he realized, for the return of the criminal whom they seemed to expect at any moment.

'I've got to tell him, Mercy,' whispered Constable. 'It ain't right for me to keep this secret from him.'

'Don't be so hard on yourself, Eddie. It's not fair you have to decide.'

Mr Buckle did not know what secret they meant, nor did he care. He turned the page of his pamphlet.

'Who else could decide?' asked Constable. 'I'm the one what knows.'

Behind the pamphlet the master's face was as drained of blood as their shining countenances were hot with it. Mercy whispered something. He could not make it out. In reply Constable said, with uncharacteristic passion: 'Whatever Henry Phipps has sworn, it ain't worth spit.'

Mr Buckle put aside his pamphlet.

'Mr Constable,' said he, 'you'll not speak of a gentleman in that tone.'

Mercy then presumed to raise an eyebrow.

'What mean you by *that*, Miss?'

'I was surprised, Sir,' said she, just as saucy as if it were midnight and the door were locked.

'Why would you be surprised?'

'No reason, Sir.'

'Answer!' he cried, and she realized, at last, how angry he was. Her tone became more sober.

'I recall you did not think much of that gentleman next door.'

'You value your position, girl?' hissed Percy Buckle.

She stood up straight, putting her hands behind her back. 'I'm sorry, Sir.'

There was a silence then, for a while.

'I do beg your pardon, Sir,' said Mercy.

'I also beg your pardon, Mr Buckle,' said Constable. 'I forgot myself.'

Percy Buckle looked at the maid with his eyes narrow and his mouth now exceeding small. She had, finally, a frightened look about the eyes. He stroked his moustache and then folded his pale dry hands carefully upon his lap. 'Did you attend to my bathroom yet?' he asked.

'Yes, Sir. I did it the moment you first asked me.'

Someone in the street cried *Whoa-up*.

'Is it him?'

'No, Sir.'

'What is that you have there in your apron, Mercy? What is it that you're playing with?'

'Nothing, Sir.'

'Then bring your "nothing" here.'

175

The girl came a little closer and Percy Buckle suddenly took her wrist and wrenched her violently towards him.

'Why,' he said, prying her hand open, 'it is a little lock of children's hair.'

'Two locks.'

'Two locks,' he agreed. The wool around the hair was old and faded.

'They was in his jacket pocket, Sir.'

'So our convict is a family man,' he said, looking into her agitated eyes. 'How got you to have such a personal item, my girl?'

'Why, Sir,' she said quickly. 'It was very clever of me as you'll see. He had taken his jacket off to write his letters. Then Mr Spinks was took. Then Mr Maggs left me to help with Mr Spinks. They were in a little envelope in the breast pocket. It *is* baby hair, Sir, ain't it?'

'Perhaps,' Constable suggested, 'it is Mr Phipps's hair.'

'Don't be daft,' said Mercy. 'How could it be Phipps? These babes have dark hair.'

The footman abandoned his post at the window, and asked if he might be permitted to touch the two locks of baby hair.

Mr Buckle could not decide if this was impertinent or not, proper or not. He stayed in his chair, watching uneasily as his footman held the locks of hair in his nimble long-fingered hands. This was how they were grouped, three of them clustered around these sad remains, when there came a sudden knocking on the front door.

50

Tobias dutifully began his report for the *Morning Chronicle*. He wrote a headline: 'A Fire in Brighton'. He underlined this twice and then laboured on a small distinctive flourish beneath the underline.

The ink on the flourish was still wet when his first interruption arrived: a rather chatty little bailiff with muddy boots and three promissory notes signed by John Oates on the strength of his son's good name.

Toby exchanged these three notes for one of his own, in which he promised to pay seventy-eight pounds twenty days hence.

Then he took out a sheet of fresh paper and wrote a painful letter informing his father that he could be no longer responsible for his debts. This took less than five minutes, but he then spent almost half an hour composing a more cautious public announcement to the same effect. He planned to deliver this advertisement to the newspapers when he handed in his report to the *Chronicle*, and when he had composed the announcement to his satisfaction, he made three fair copies which he placed in individual envelopes addressed to *The Times*, the *Observer* and the *Morning Chronicle*. The unexpected expense of these advertisements then led him to take a fresh sheet of paper on which he made a revised estimate of his expenditures and incomes for the following quarter. These totals were very bleak indeed, so he put aside his Brighton Fire and set out to produce a quick Character Sketch for the *Observer*. This newspaper now paid five pounds for such pieces, and he was soon standing on his chair, looking for his notes for the 'Canary Woman of Islington', 'Old Tom Wicks of Camden Town', and other *Types* and *Characters* which he had collected for this very purpose. He finally settled on a Crossing Sweeper and sat himself at his desk where, on one more clean sheet, he began:

Those readers familiar with McKenzie's Chop House in Fetter Lane have doubtless had the benefit of the broom of Titchy Tate, without ever imagining that he who wields this instrument with such violent effect, believes himself to be the luckiest little boy in all of London.

He would have executed both 'Titchy Tate' and 'A Fire in Brighton' by lunch time, except that he was pushed into a furtive conference with Lizzie (although what that conference was to be about he could not determine, for she had fled the room before it had half begun).

Next came his wife in a state of great distress on account of an angry red pustule which had emerged on their baby's breast. Toby was considerably alarmed by what he saw, but when he suggested bathing the infection in salty water his wife seemed to think this very wise advice indeed, and he was able to return to his study, and once more take up the quill.

177

Whereupon Jack Maggs appeared at his doorway, demanding a doctor for a sick butler. He had no choice. He pushed 'Titchy Tate' aside and took a fresh sheet of paper on which he composed a note to Dr Grieves of Gray's Inn Road, requesting him to please be so kind as to attend to a butler at 29 Great Queen Street. This letter he gave into the care of Mrs Jones, asking the sturdy old lady to put on her shawl and take it up to an Inn in Chancery Lane where he knew the doctor ate his lunch.

He doubted the butler's condition was dangerous, but he was a cautious man and, given his little joke about the quarantine, he thought it politic to be present at Great Queen Street to introduce the patient to his doctor. Thus he went to dress, and all the while he went about this business he had to endure the sound of the criminal's hectoring footsteps pacing in the hall below.

Some minutes later, as he followed Jack Maggs back down through the drizzling streets to Holborn, he reflected that the man had as good as stolen five pounds from his pocket. He therefore, consciously, recompensed himself.

Tit for tat, he memorized the hard shine to Jack Maggs's skin as it cleaved close to the bones of his cheek and jaw. He would use those bones, perhaps tomorrow. On the following day he would return for those deeper, more painful items which must still be cut free from the softer tissue of Jack Maggs's memory.

He was developing, with every passing hour, giddy ambitions for this novel. *Captain Crumley* had been a comedy, a pantomime, broad strokes, great larks, a rowdy tale of old London that had Mr Davidson the butcher in a fever while he waited for the next instalment. But in all of English literature there was nothing like the dark journey he now planned to take inside the Criminal Mind. He began, as he walked, to chisel away at its plot. He charted a course by abstract reasoning, almost algebraically. From Birth to Death, from Light to Dark, from Water to Fire. It was with some irritation that he found the walk had ended, and he must abandon this activity in favour of the real world.

In Percy Buckle's drawing room, he found the physician had already arrived, and was standing with his back to Mr Buckle's fireplace. Dr Grieves was a neat, well tailored man and in spite of being nearly fifty, of a markedly athletic appearance. He had always seemed a quiet fellow, almost excessively polite in his manners, so when Tobias saw the doctor's stern face, his compressed mouth, he began immediately to apologize for dragging him from his luncheon.

'It were better you had dragged me from my breakfast.'

'The patient is very ill?'

'Very dead. To put it bluntly.'

In the silence that followed this announcement, Oates could hear the most piteous chorus of wailing descending from the upper floors.

'Oh dear,' said Toby.

No response from the doctor.

'A nice old chap,' offered Toby.

Mr Buckle nodded his head vigorously in agreement.

'He came down quickly?' Toby inquired of Percy Buckle.

Before the master of the house could supply this intelligence, the doctor turned to him and asked the privilege of a moment alone with Mr Oates.

Once Mr Buckle had departed, the doctor sat himself down in a wing-back armchair by the fire. There he put his hands upon his knees, and gazed long and hard at the black and smoky logs.

'Your shirt is showing, Sir.'

Tobias Oates followed the motion of the doctor's head and saw a three-inch twist of bright green shirt sticking out from his flies. He coloured furiously. Dr Grieves continued as the writer attended to his shirt.

'As to the other business, I am damned if I know what to say to you.'

'Who else was I to send for, if not my own doctor?'

'Oh, dear God, Mr Oates, you cannot go around killing people.'

'I assure you – '

'You cannot come into this household, Sir, impersonating a member of the College of Surgeons. How do you think it would be, for you to be charged? What would the judge say, upon hearing that

179

you had convinced the deceased that you were a surgeon?'

'It was a prank, a joke.'

'Mr Oates, the old fellow is dead.'

'But not of my prank.'

'Mr Oates, it is not as if you were a Balliol undergraduate . . .'

This, to Toby's ear, was only another way of saying that he was not a gentleman.

'And on account of this lack,' he smiled bitterly, 'I am a murderer?'

'I will write pneumonia on his death certificate, but if you really want my true opinion, it is that you bewitched him.'

'Sir, you are a man of science.'

'A man is known by his deeds, Sir. And you bewitched him. Just, Sir, as you bewitched the cook and the housekeeper who – although you have not asked after their health – are, whilst upset to learn of their companion's death, not in any present danger themselves.'

'But surely, he was an old man. A pneumonia might have arrived in any case.'

'Do not, please, tell me my business, Mr Oates. I was pleased to have you a guest in my house. I enjoyed our evenings together.'

'As did I.'

'But I cannot thank you for having me commit a perjury on this death certificate.'

'Perhaps, Doctor, it is not a perjury. I do not say that I was not remiss, but – '

'A perjury. I cannot forgive you for it.'

Tobias put his head in his hands.

'I beg your forgiveness,' he said at last. When he looked up, his face showed his grief.

'But it is your God who will forgive you,' said the doctor, severely. 'It is with Him that you have your business to settle. I have no thirst for ruining you.'

This last sentence was not without its effect.

The young man looked up at the physician, curly hair dishevelled, eyes swimming with tears. 'I would do anything to undo this.'

The doctor stood up. 'Then you must pray. In the meantime, you may know that the death certificate protects your reputation at the same time as it threatens mine: you will understand me, I am sure, when I say that I cannot serve your family any longer.'

'But what if my babe is ill?'

'Then you will take your babe to a doctor, and the doctor will cure your babe, and you will be a lucky man.'

'But I know no other doctor. He had, this morning, a kind of pustule . . .'

'Mr Oates, London is a big city . . .'

'I know London, Sir. I know it perhaps better than even you do. It is an exceedingly big city, and if my babe is ill . . .'

'A big city, in which you will find many excellent doctors.'

'You will give me an introduction?'

'Please, Mr Oates, how could I do that? I have already played loose with my good name.'

'You are casting me out?'

For answer, the doctor stood and pulled on the bell.

'Who else would I turn to?'

It was the criminal, in all his wild and slovenly dishabille, who answered the call. Toby, in the midst of his own distress, noticed the doctor's astonishment as he asked the soiled and spotted man to fetch his coat and bag.

'If my wife is ill, who would I call?'

For answer, the doctor made a small formal bow, then walked out into the hall where Jack Maggs had his great-coat ready. He slowly donned the coat and buttoned it, then, without a word to anyone, he left the house.

The criminal closed the door behind him, then stood in front of it.

'Thank you,' said Toby, meaning that he would also take his leave, but the criminal did not move. He stood unnaturally straight, with his eyes straight ahead.

'Mr Oates,' said he. 'I need a word with you.'

'I can't think of that now . . .' said Tobias Oates.

The criminal then stepped so close to him that Tobias could smell the rum on his breath. Then the novelist found himself being lifted from the floor and shaken so his teeth rattled in his head.

181

He was next replaced carefully on the floor, but still held very hard by the shoulders. The smell of alcohol was very strong again. He could see the pores of his tormentor's nose, the iron whiskers, the twitch in his cheek, the black fury in his eye.

Tobias Oates's life was unravelling.

51

Tobias had spent a dreadful year, his fourth, in a home for orphaned boys in Shropshire, where he had been bullied continually. Thereafter he lived one year in Devon, with a mother who was most loudly inconvenienced by his presence. Brought by her to London at the tender age of five, he was soon put in the care of his father, although it was a very hard kind of care he got from that gentleman, and he was pretty much forced to make his own way from there, to find his feet in a city that would as soon have trampled him into the mud.

He had been cast off but he would not be flotsam.

He had been denied a proper school but he had learned to read and write and he had made himself, by will, a sorcerer of that great city.

Now, each day in the *Morning Chronicle*, each fortnight in the *Observer*, it was Tobias Oates who 'made' the City of London. With a passion he barely understood himself, he named it, mapped it, widened its great streets, narrowed its dingy lanes, framed its scenes with the melancholy windows of his childhood. In this way, he invented a respectable life for himself: a wife, a babe, a household. He had gained a name for comic tales. He had got himself, along the way, a little belly, a friend who was a titled lady, a second friend who was a celebrated actor, a third friend who was a Knight of the Realm, a fourth friend who was an author and tutor to the young Princess Victoria. He did not dare look down, so far had he come.

Until this morning, when his fun and games had killed a man.

Then the doctor had cast him out, and this *criminal*, this outcast, had felt himself free to pick him up and shake him as though he were nothing but a rabbit.

182

'You would best be very calm, Sir,' he told Jack Maggs, although it was he, Tobias Oates, who was, by some trick of Fate, suddenly the criminal. 'If you want this to end safely,' he cried fearfully, 'you had best watch yourself.'

He disengaged himself and sought to button the jacket which had been torn off in the scuffle.

'Here's the button, Sir. Give me your coat. The maid will attend to it.'

'Be *still*,' said Tobias.

'Yes, Sir, I'll be still.'

And the scoundrel was still a moment, although his contemptuous dark eyes stayed on the writer.

'You have pulled off my *button*,' Tobias said incredulously. 'Are you not a *footman*, Jack Maggs? Are you not a *servant*, man?'

For answer Jack Maggs sat insolently in the master's wing-back chair and crossed one massive leg over the other.

'I'm bogged here,' he said. 'Two weeks, and stuck up to my axles in the mud.' He rubbed his hand over his dark cheek and Toby saw the tic moving once again. 'You are bogged with me, and I am bogged with you. And every day that passes, why it gets a little worse for everyone. It was on my behalf you came up with your Contagion. You could not know it would prove a wee bit fatal.'

'I can hardly be responsible for pneumonia!'

'As I said, you could not know.'

In the silence that followed Tobias began to believe that he was being threatened.

'I am most eager,' the convict continued, 'to get along the track, but I cannot do it until I find Mr Henry Phipps. When I have him, then I'll go. It was not what I had planned, but such is life.' He paused. 'And as for what you done to Mr Spinks's magnetic fluid . . .'

Tobias Oates looked at the convict's face – the coarse black brows, the dry cracked lips – and found it vile.

'Do you imagine you can *blackmail* me?'

'I want what is owing – the name of the Thief-taker.'

'To hell with you, you tinker.'

183

That made his tic leap good and strong. Tobias saw it.

'You gave your word!'

Tobias looked into his adversary's belligerent eyes, and knew that he could not afford to lose him. 'You sold me fourteen days, Jack Maggs. I have used no more than eleven of them.'

'But it is two weeks from the day we agreed.'

'Only eleven days have you sat for me.'

The criminal raised his misshapen hand and pressed it hard against his cheek.

'Two days,' Tobias explained, 'I was travelling to Brighton and back.'

Maggs would never beg. It was written in his body that he would not bend, that he must stand straight and hold his head high. But now he was – Tobias saw it – inexplicably, at breaking point.

'I have money.' The convict tried to smile, but the tic rippled down his face again. 'Twenty guineas. How's that? I'll pay you for the man's address. If you have expenses besides, I am your man.'

The sheer quantity of money shocked Tobias. He gave a sharp incredulous laugh.

'You name the figure.' The other man was now sitting forward on the edge of his seat. The palsy had changed the texture of his skin; it was oddly pale and crêpy. 'Thirty if you must. Then I'll be out of everybody's life.'

'I'm sorry, old chap,' Toby said coldly, 'but you must give me the three days you owe me.'

'For Christ's sake, have mercy. I cannot wait three days. I cannot bear it any more.'

'You are still my subject, no matter what booty you are carrying.'

But Maggs barely heard him. His eyes rolled backwards in his head. He gave a groan and clutched his face in both his hands.

Tobias Oates watched his adversary as he slowly fell back into the cushions of the wing-back chair. To the maid who rushed forth from the shadows, he said:

'You may send him to my house at nine tomorrow morning. I'll treat him then.'

52

When Tobias Oates returned home it was already dark and he found the entire household – his wife, his sister-in-law, the housekeeper – all gathered in a circle in the kitchen, bathing his wailing baby boy in a metal tub.

'What is it? What's the matter?'

The women did not turn, and this alone made his pulse run the faster.

'What is it?' he cried and forced himself into the circle. There he saw his infant son, his face quite pale and his little chest now hugely inflamed. What this morning had been a pustule now seemed to look more like a growth. It was red and very hard, and when his papa touched it with his fingers, the little fellow emitted a thin weak wail.

'What ails him, for God's sake? What is it?'

'It is witch's milk,' said the housekeeper, laying her large broad finger tips gently on the swelling. 'Set hard as rock.'

'He has a fever,' his wife said. 'I sent for Dr Grieves. I sent the grocer's boy, but the boy has somehow upset the doctor, for he was sent away with no message.'

'That boy!' exclaimed the old housekeeper, continuing to sponge the whimpering child. 'He would be better back in Ireland praying to the French. He should not be here, nor neither should his mother.'

'Damn Grieves,' cried Oates. The three women looked at him with such alarm, that he immediately began to smile, and coo, and pat his hands in the air.

'Grieves . . . ah, Grieves,' he said. 'Poor old Grieves.'

'What is wrong with Dr Grieves?'

He could not think what to answer them, and, saying only that he would fetch the doctor himself, he fled back out into Lamb's Conduit Street just as a hackney cab came trotting by. He hailed it before he knew quite what he was to do with it.

He looked up at the mulish driver who, in turn, glowered down from his bench, with his many-skirted coat wrapped tight around him. He was a thug-like fellow with heavy brows and great yellow teeth like tombstones in his mouth.

'So what's your pleasure, Sir?'

'I need a doctor nearby. Do you know of a doctor?'

'Doctor, Sir. Yes, Sir. Straight away.'

And off they set up Lamb's Conduit Street, along Gray's Inn Road, down across to the other side of Saffron Hill, passing on the way a number of buildings with lanterns advertising doctors.

'Now listen, fellow . . .'

'Yes, Sir.'

'I only have a shilling or two about me. Where were you going to take me?'

'Why to Merton Street, to Dr Hardwick's.'

'What sort of doctor is he?'

'Blessed if I know, Sir,' shouted the cabby, 'but he is a doctor, and well thought of, I do know that.'

Tobias Oates wondered what class of person thought well of this doctor, and for what reason. But he had no choice: 'Very well,' he said, 'to Dr Hardwick's.'

Soon enough they rolled into a dismal little street in Clerkenwell. The cabby pulled up before a high narrow house, distinguished by the smoke-blackened lantern burning faintly by its door. Had it not been for the evidence of this miserable lamp, Tobias would have thought the building abandoned.

'If this is only for the shilling,' said the cabby, 'you best move smartly, Sir.'

'Very well,' said Tobias. He alighted, approaching the dark deserted pile with some uncertainty. The front gate was crooked on its hinges, and the stone stairs leading up from the street smelled as if a herd of cats had been encamped there.

He knocked on the door once, twice.

Very soon he heard a distant shuffling and then a cry of, 'Who's there?'

'I have a sick baby. I need a doctor.'

A male voice replied – a single word – but Tobias could not distinguish it. He knocked louder. 'I need a doctor.'

There followed a loud noise of chains being dropped onto a floor. Then the tall door opened a fraction, and in the darkness – for there did not seem to be so much as a candle lit inside – he saw the shadow of an old man's face, or rather, what he took to be the face of an old man, for the voice that came out of it seemed very old indeed.

'Who's there?'

'Excuse me. Are you Dr Hardwick?'

'I am, Sir, have been, and will be a good while yet. And may I have the pleasure of knowing who comes knocking on my door while I am in communion with my herrings?'

'My name is Oates, and my babe is sick.'

'How old is your babe?'

'Three months.'

'Then you must know it for a fact – babes are always sick. It is their nature. How is he sick?'

'He has a fever. There is a great red lump upon his chest.'

'If you want to ride for a shilling,' called the cabby from the street, 'I cannot wait for you to sign the Peace.'

'Who's that?' inquired the doctor.

'The hackney cab.'

'Do you owe him money?'

'Sir, will you come with me?'

'Can you pay me?' asked the doctor. 'That is always a question worth asking.'

'Yes, yes, I can pay you,' said Tobias Oates.

'My fee is five shillings, and has been since Waterloo.'

'Please, Sir . . .'

'But I have been known to accept chinaware in its stead. More than once, a little Delft. Do you know Delft? I don't press for it, but I make it known.'

'I thank you,' said Tobias Oates, who had neither Delft nor dosh to pay any bill.

'I only make it known.'

'And I thank you for giving me that possibility to consider.' With these assurances the anguished father was able to get the doctor into the cab without actually lying about his financial situation.

The journey was conducted in almost total silence, and later Tobias could recall little else of it but the strong smell of fish, which he took to be herring, upon which the doctor had obviously been making an enthusiastic attack. It was not until they reached Lamb's Conduit Street that he had a good chance to look at his companion, and there, by the light of the candle his wife held high at the front door, he saw that Dr Hardwick was a man of perhaps sixty years of age, balding on his top, but with a great shock of ginger hair much streaked with grey. His eyebrows, upon theger-coloured, were a very powerful feature of his face, pressing powerfully over his cloudy eyes. His clothing was old, his great cloak actually ragged around the hem and sleeves. Mary Oates, who saw all this at the same moment as her husband, turned as pale as the wax of her candle.

'This is Dr Hardwick, my dear,' said Toby.

His wife burst into tears and ran down to the kitchen where they found her, a moment later, holding the whimpering babe fiercely to her bosom.

The ragged old doctor entered the kitchen as though it were his own, dropped his scuffed old satchel upon the table, and called for water with which to wash.

When he had scrubbed his large freckled hands, he turned to Mrs Oates, who had removed herself as far away as the scullery. She was rocking her babe and talking to him in small and private whispers.

'Now, Ma'am,' said he, 'please give the patient to me.'

Mary Oates looked to her husband who, not without serious trepidation, echoed the doctor's request. The young author then watched his son passed to the old man, recalling at the same time the case of Dr Snipes of Wapping who had killed three of his spinster patients and fed their remains to his fox terrier. He wanted only to cry out, stop! enough! But he watched as the stranger removed the swaddling from his precious son and squeezed his stomach with his knobbly jointed hands.

'Hold him. Not you, Ma'am. You, Sir.'

Tobias Oates did as he was ordered. He held his son down on the table while the doctor removed a small spirit lamp from his bag and

lit it. Toby looked away a fraction. When he looked back, the old
man was passing a surgeon's knife back and forwards under the
bright blue flame of the lamp.

'Hold him tight, Sir. Ma'am, look away.'

Tobias Oates looked at the three women who were bunched, his
wife at the centre, over by the scullery. The two sisters had a similar
expression on their faces, their eyes wide, their lips parted.

Tobias Oates turned away from them.

'Papa's here,' he said, feeling himself a liar and a fool. 'Papa's
here, my darling.'

But as the knife approached the dear little boy's chest, the tears
began to well up in his father's eyes, and as the blade came down
across the swelling on the red protrusion, as the child's face
contorted in outrage, as the little fellow shrieked, as the great river
of pus flowed forth from the lanced boil, Tobias Oates cried
shamelessly, or so it appeared to all who saw him. In truth, however,
the shame was very deep, and when he saw the evidence of
infection pour forth from his son's innocent body, he felt the poison
to be all his own.

53

When the wound had been stitched and the old doctor had liberally
swabbed the entire of little John's chest with a violently coloured
purple tincture, when the patient's cries had begun at last to become
less fierce, and he had been dispatched with the womenfolk to the
nursery, the doctor packed away his knife and spirit lamp and
snapped shut his enormous bag. Then he turned his rheumy eyes
and tobacco eyebrows towards Tobias Oates.

'Now . . .' he began.

He did not have to venture any further – Tobias knew what was to
come next, and he came dancing out from the crease to meet it.

'I look forward to your account.'

At this, everything which had been solicitous in the old man's
manner, that which had given the suppleness to his old fingers, and

drawn the steel so kindly across the child's infection, was now withdrawn, and Tobias Oates saw the old man's head pulled down into the neck, the shoulders up towards the ears, his very flesh contract around his bones.

Dr Hardwick folded his forearms across his pale, discoloured waistcoat. His great hairy brows came down upon his eyes.

'I keep no accounts,' he said coldly. 'I am not an inn keeper. I need the five shillings, Sir, and I made that very clear when you dragged me from my dinner.'

'Pray do not embarrass me,' began the young man.

'Pray do not anger me,' said the doctor, now very quiet indeed.

He closed his bag briskly, shrugged on his ragged cloak. Tobias, relieved to imagine the painful scene to be in its final act, followed the tattered garment up the stairs to the hallway. There he found that the stranger, far from departing, was intent on pushing his way deeper into the family's life.

Dr Hardwick took a candle from the wall sconce and walked into the front room where he began a close perusal of the objects on its walls and tables. 'You are just newly established here?' he asked in a manner more like that of a customer in an auction house than a visitor in a private home.

Tobias was disinclined to answer so impertinent a question, and yet he was weakened by his impecunious position. 'Some few months,' he answered.

'What is your profession, Sir?'

'I am a man of letters, Sir.'

The doctor picked up a small porcelain ornament on the mantel-piece, turned it over, then dismissed it.

'You would be wiser to have waited a little longer before you married. Until you had a little capital.'

Tobias tried to laugh. 'What do you know about my capital?'

The doctor held the Bluebell plate which Mary had displayed proudly in the centre of the mantelpiece. 'Only what I see. But the evidence does point all one way.'

Only later, when the fellow had gone, could Tobias Oates admit how boorish and ill-mannered Dr Hardwick had been, but at the time, during the moments he was being so brazenly insulted, he was like a man who sees at some distance a human form falling from Waterloo Bridge – he did not quite believe what it was he witnessed. When, at the end of the doctor's stock-taking, Lizzie came down the stairs to announce that the babe was finally asleep, there was nothing in Tobias's manner to suggest to her that anything improper was taking place. Indeed, he laboured to give the impression that all was well.

'I was just telling Dr Hardwick,' he said, 'that we were newly arrived in Lamb's Conduit Street.'

'Oh yes,' she said brightly. 'We were previously at Furnival's Inn.'

The doctor held the sputtering candle high. 'And was it in Furnival's Inn that you received the gift of that necklace?'

'Oh – ' Lizzie's hand rose to touch the necklace, an old-fashioned little confection of silver and small blue stones. 'Well, yes, indeed, it was at Furnival's Inn, although it was a rather sad kind of a gift for it was bequeathed to me by my grandmother, a dear old lady of whom I was exceedingly fond.'

'Give it to me,' said the doctor.

Lizzie hesitated.

'No need to remove it,' said Tobias quickly, holding out his hand for the candle. 'I will hold the light so Dr Hardwick can see.'

'No, no.' The doctor fixed his eyes upon the young woman. 'Please be so good as to take it off.'

'No,' cried Tobias. 'You must not.'

He knew full well what the doctor intended, but when Lizzie, having silently reproached her brother-in-law, raised her pretty little hands to the clasp, he did not trust himself enough to forbid her once again. He watched in dismay as she delivered the precious article – that adornment of which she was, in all the world, most fond – into those alien freckled hands.

Dr Hardwick gazed down upon his treasure, his head tilted a little sideways, looking for all the world, so Tobias thought, like a crow upon a dust mound. When he looked up again, his eyes seemed to have cleared.

'This is very beautiful,' he said.

191

'Thank you,' said Lizzie, colouring with pleasure. 'I don't think my brother-in-law has ever really noticed it before.'

'Elizabeth!'

'It is worth a great deal more than the five shillings,' said the doctor.

'Oh yes,' said Lizzie. 'The Jew on High Holborn offered me two guineas without my even asking his opinion.'

'Then it is worth four,' said the doctor. 'Would you let me, if I promised to be very careful with it, would you let me borrow it a day or two?'

Lizzie looked at the untidy old man in confusion. He smiled at her; she coloured and looked to her brother-in-law, who gave her – so she later complained – no help at all.

'I'm sure that I could have it back to the young lady by Wednesday. Would you not say so, Mr Oates?'

'Tobias . . .'

The old man continued. 'You will be needing me back again. I should say, by Wednesday. Or Tuesday if the fever has not abated. In any case, you will be pleased to see me, I am sure of it.'

'You will give us a receipt, of course,' said the writer.

'If you have the pen and paper,' said the doctor to Lizzie. 'And if you will be nice enough to give the article some clear description, then I'll sign it.'

'I would describe it only as my grandmother's necklace, Sir, but what do you want with it?'

'I am a student,' the old man said, dropping the necklace into the deep pocket of his filthy cloak, 'a student of the human body, of the human nature, and of objets d'art of all descriptions.'

'Tobias?' inquired his sister-in-law.

But Tobias Oates again affected not to hear. He busied himself at the little table by the window, engaged in making a minute architectural description of the necklace and its fastening. As he wrote these hundred words, his dancing mind was once more occupied with the question of money, with how to get it and get it quickly, so that he might get this necklace safely home again.

54

As her brother-in-law escorted the peculiar old doctor from the front room, Elizabeth Warriner stayed by the lace curtains looking out into the bright moon-lit street.

While the loss of her necklace had disturbed her, this disturbance was a very small rain-drop in the storm of emotion contained within her slender frame. She watched the shadow of the peculiar old doctor passing the window, and she turned to find him who occupied her every waking thought standing before her, his dear face clearly visible in the moonlight.

'Best light a candle,' he whispered.

'She is gone to bed by now.'

'There is still Mrs Jones. She would think it very odd were she to find us in the dark.'

'Mrs Jones is sleeping in the nursery with little John.' Lizzie took the unlit candle from Toby's hand and waited for him to embrace her. 'She is asleep,' she insisted.

She saw his mouth quiver, his chin ripple. 'I am so very sorry,' he said.

She put a finger on his lips.

'Oh Toby, you silly man.'

She embraced him then, but his body was stiff and unyielding with preoccupation, and when he heard a creak of the floor boards above their heads, he sprang away from her.

'We must light a candle,' he insisted.

She took his hand, he held hers fiercely.

'I'm so sorry about the necklace,' he said. 'You will have it back tomorrow.'

'Tobias, I don't give a fig for the silly necklace.'

'Dear sweet Elizabeth.' This time he embraced her completely, holding her passionately around the waist, pressing himself hard against her, so hard, you would imagine, he must feel everything that was agitating her heart.

'Dear sweet Elizabeth, it is your only ornament. What did I hear you tell Closter's wife about the stones? Did you not say what happiness it gave you, just to gaze upon them in their little case?'

'Now it is less important.'

'It is less important because I was foolish enough to let them be stolen from you?'

'Toby, you do not mean stolen.'

'You will have them back by lunch, I promise you.'

'Even if they had been stolen, it would mean nothing to me. Other events have put it in a better perspective.'

'Yes, little John will soon be quite well again, it seems.'

She looked at his face, and saw that he had not the faintest notion of the emotions agitating her. 'He was a brave little man,' she said cautiously. 'It is of that general subject that I wished to speak with you, dear Toby.'

He faced her solemnly.

'Say it, dearest.'

'Say what, dear Brother.'

'Say it.'

'Husband,' she said, and he, hearing that forbidden word, embraced her once again, smothering her in kisses.

'Do you love me, Husband?'

'You know I do. You know it so.'

'And love all that is mine?'

'The parings from your lovely fingernails.'

'And . . .'

'Here, I give you a kiss for your thoughts.'

She disengaged. 'I am afraid that my thoughts will not be acceptable to you, my dearest.'

'Oh Lizzie,' he chided. 'How can you say such a thing to me?'

'For my thoughts are of our child . . .'

'Sweetness, that cannot be.'

'But Toby, it can, and is.'

He stepped back from her.

'My God, Lizzie, what are you saying?'

'I knew you would not like my thoughts. You should not have inquired after them.'

194

'Lizzie, do not tease me.'

'I am not teasing, Husband.'

'What are you imagining?'

'Imagining?' Her voice rose. 'Nothing. Nothing in the least imagined. Nothing, at least, you could not have imagined on the day you helped me fold the counterpane.'

They were talking thus, in low, agitated voices, when they became aware of a sputtering light making its way down the staircase. The light came towards them, like a spirit, washing over the floor outside the door, then announced a plump figure in a white night gown.

Mary stood in the doorway. The light from her candle revealed her sister still standing in the darkness by the window. Tobias was leaning against the mantel, but as his wife came further into the room, he offered his own unlit candle to her flame.

'Tobias? Are you squabbling with Lizzie?'

'It's nothing, my dear.'

'But Lizzie, you're crying.'

And indeed, as Lizzie saw her good dull sister come towards her, her round little face all drawn with concern, she knew she could not stem the tide of her own very great upset. Huge hot tears washed down her cheeks.

Mary put her plump arm around her shoulder. 'What is it, dear little Lizzie?'

'My necklace,' cried Lizzie.

'What happened to her necklace, Tobias?'

'He let the filthy doctor steal it. He let the dirty old man put it in his pocket. He did not stop him. He did not care.'

'I did care,' said Tobias, hotly. 'I cared most dreadfully.'

'He did not care,' cried Lizzie. 'He cares only for his own pleasure.'

This last remark produced a long and peculiar silence. 'Tobias, is this true?' asked Mary, finally.

'The doctor did take the necklace, but only as security against the fee.'

'He was a horrible old man,' said Mary. 'I shall take it very hard with Grieves when next I see him, that we should put our little boy in the hands of such a . . . such a *pawnbroker*. Tobias, you must get Lizzie her necklace back.'

Lizzie looked to Tobias, who was resting his elbow, rather unnaturally, on the mantelpiece. He had always appeared to her as fierce and fatherly, but now she saw how the mantel was too tall for him, and how he stretched to accommodate himself to its demands. It was a vision most profoundly discouraging, and one she wished to God she had not seen.

55

When Tobias Oates was five years old, his father was charged with killing a man named Judd in a tavern brawl in Wardour Street. John Oates was tried at the Old Bailey and condemned to death by hanging.

Toby's earliest memories of London were still locked in that fetid little death cell where his father sat writing, day and night, getting up petitions for his pardon.

The Newgate turnkeys were fond of 'John the Cock' and brought him pie and beer aplenty, so it happened that Toby, on being admitted to his company, would often find him in an emotional state. Sometimes the emotion was up, and sometimes it was down, and when it was down he would fall upon his estranged wife and son, crying to them that he did not wish to die.

All this, naturally enough, made its impressions on the little boy.

Finally his father won his pardon which, as his wife said, 'did his character no good', and from that time he settled in Soho, where he became a kind of celebrity amongst the jockeys and book-makers of the town.

In later years, Tobias came to believe that his father had most likely been guilty of Judd's murder. In the popular newspapers much had been made of the bulk and brutality of the deceased man and the diminutive size of the accused, and yet this disparity in strength was, as Toby knew, a prescription for aggressive action on his father's part.

John Oates believed that you must meet with what was frightening you. If it was a dark corner, you entered it. If it was a bucking horse, you mounted it. If it was a storm, you walked through it. And Tobias, who was almost exactly his father's height, also inherited his habit of confronting what he feared.

He feared poverty; he wrote passionately about the poor. He had nightmares about hanging; he sought out executions, reporting them with a magistrate's detachment. And on that dreadful day when Mr Spinks had died, when he learned that the beautiful child with whom he was besotted was herself with child, as bruised and violent clouds began to rise above the pacific horizon of his life, his strongest impulse was to go where he most feared the deluge would sweep him.

That night he slept in a low lodging house in Fox Court, very close by his home. He had been there previously to report its desperate condition for the *Chronicle*, but never had he laid his body down on one of those stinking palliasses. It was an exceedingly low sort of place, with a nest of rambling dormitories, and smaller rooms arranged around a central court which was slippery with the effluent of a drain. Here a raspy-voiced old fellow in an apron demanded a penny ha'penny, and showed Tobias to a large kind of cupboard – it had no windows – where a pair of ruffians lay amidst the smell of ale and onions.

Here the author of *Captain Crumley* feigned sleep while his room mates searched his clothes looking for valuables. They were brutish types, with heavy brows and thick wide noses, and he was therefore shocked to feel the gentle intimacy of their fingers as they searched under his pillow and beneath the thin coverlet. He felt their fingers move like rats across his body.

Then they left him alone and soon they were whispering and then, a little later, he realized they were enacting some foul business between them, groaning and cursing as they did so.

Finally they slept, and Tobias Oates crept out. This scene, or rather the specifics of its setting, reappears not only in *The Death of Maggs* and *Michael Adams*, but in almost everything Tobias Oates ever wrote. There is always the court with its *vile green skirt of slime*, the little room *like a stifling cupboard, stinking of spilt ale and raw onions.* You can find the peeling wallpaper, the porter's egg-stained singlet, time and time again throughout his serials, and if that is the good he got from it, it was the only good. For Tobias Oates emerged into High Holborn with his fears not beaten, but magnified, and a great certainty that he would rather drown himself than take his family down into such purgatory.

Yet once it was known that he had betrayed his wife and ruined her young sister, who would ever wish to touch a book with his name upon its spine? As he wandered down to the Thames, then through Borough, he was, in his imagination, already that reviled creature who could never hold his head up again; he would be poor, and hated. He walked the echoing streets thinking of money like that famous miser he would one day create in *French Street*. The miser is more like his creator than his readers ever guessed. True, Tobias did not have Scotty Meggitt's wealth, but he now walked the same streets Scotty Meggitt walked in the first chapter of *French Street*, adding and subtracting, subtracting and adding, *just like another man might say his prayers.*

Yet no matter how he did his sums Tobias could not get a total above eight pounds and sixpence. It was *not enough. Not nearly enough.*

Dawn found him still abroad on new London Bridge and, as the poisonous old ink received its first wash of red from the sun, he realized that the new bridge had been built atop the warren of streets where the Somnambulist spent his early years.

Pepper Alley Stairs were gone. The remaining roof tops were all grey and pink and shining in the morning drizzle. It was beneath his feet that the venomous creatures of Jack Maggs's memories lived. Here Tom dragged his bloody scraps up those grey glistening steps which still existed in the subterranean passages of that Criminal Mind. Seeing these visions, he also glimpsed the greatness of his book. That is: he had a premonition of the true majesty of the work that he would one day write. And how did he value this portent? Why, like a pawnbroker. He examined this great novel with his jeweller's glass. He might contrive to sell the copyright of such a work, and sell it entire, today, with not a word yet written.

It was not yet six in the morning – too early to do business with a publisher – but the prospect of this radical transaction now brought some colour to his cheeks. He set off, walking briskly, anxious to snaffle every pound that might be due him. As he crossed London Bridge again, the barges of the vegetable men were moving against the tide up to Covent Garden. Yes, it was too early to call on Cheery Entwhistle, but not too early to present himself to the man who had yesterday offered a fortune for a Thief-taker's address.

Like old man Meggitt, Tobias did not yet know exactly how his money might protect him, where he might flee, what bulwark he might build against the storm, but at seven o'clock he knocked at Mr Buckle's door keen to do business with Jack Maggs.

He was received by the kitchen maid, now dressed in mourning for Mr Spinks.

'There you are, Sir,' cried she, in a manner unpleasantly familiar. 'I was about to come and fetch you.'

And with no other explanation she led him, not to the drawing room, but up an empty gloomy staircase which, in a better regulated household, would have been illuminated by a decent lamp.

The little maid was, to judge from her voice, soon an entire floor ahead of him. 'This way, Sir. It's very bad, very bad indeed.'

Tobias Oates, now much confused, grasped the banister and set off to catch her up. He would simply have increased his pace but he was prevented from so doing by the treacherous irregularity of the treads.

The house was queerly empty and lifeless. It was also taller than he had imagined, and so poorly served by windows that when he arrived on the second landing, he did not see the footman until the latter had thrust a paper into his hand. Tobias started, and cried out.

'I beg your pardon,' whispered Edward Constable. 'I don't know what to tell Mr Maggs, Sir. I don't know what is right.'

Toby peered at the paper in his hand, but could make out nothing in the gloom.

199

'Up here, Sir,' called the maid.

Tobias turned to the footman, but found him gone. He pocketed the paper and set off again to the top floor, only knowing it to be such by the exceedingly low ceiling on which he bumped his head. Hearing a whisper ahead of him, he followed it glumly towards its source.

Dear God, another servant dead!

A door opened, and a feeble grey sort of daylight came out onto the landing. Negotiating around what appeared to be a great many rolled-up rugs, he stepped into a stuffy attic room.

He had feared to find Mrs Halfstairs or Miss Mott, but now he recognized the great lumpy body of the man he had come to get his fifty pounds from. Tobias immediately noted the queer waxy skin upon his cheek. It was that damned *tic douloureux*.

He peeled the grey rug slowly back. There, stripped of his only comfort, Jack Maggs whimpered like a child.

'Good morning, Jack Maggs.'

On hearing his voice, Maggs tried to raise himself. He appeared to be fully dressed, even to the hessian boots still on his feet, but he was very sick indeed. He peered at his visitor through swollen eyelids.

'It's you, Sir?'

'It is Mr Oates.'

'You'll find me Henry Phipps after all?' he asked pathetically. 'That's all I need, and then I'm off.'

'Fifty pounds, that's what's agreed? I'll get you to the Thief-taker.'

'That's the man.' He clutched at Toby's sleeve. 'Then I'm away. I'll trouble you no more. Cash in your hand, and leave you in peace. God, this damned thing hurts, Sir. It's this bleeding Phantom that you talk of.'

'You can get the fifty pounds today?'

The sick man tried to raise himself again, but failed. He lay back down upon his mattress with his hand across his eyes. 'Give me a moment, give me a moment.'

'Very well. Let us drive out the Phantom first.'

Tobias was exceptionally tired himself, but he leaned across the bed and began the long process of Magnetizing the patient. It was awkward to have a prone subject but they were both well-practised in the dance. Tobias made the passes artfully and Jack Maggs's head soon fell back onto the pillow.

Tobias dragged up a three-legged stool and arranged himself, knees up, like a passenger on a wherry. His stomach rumbled. He drew breath, closed his eyes. When he spoke his voice was flat, without enthusiasm.

'What can you see?'

'Nothing. Darkness.'

'You can see the Phantom.'

'Can't see through a bleeding brick wall, can I.'

Tobias allowed himself a weary smile. With Jack Maggs, there was always an obstacle – a wall, a moat, a bridge – some impediment which must be crossed to enter the castle of the Criminal Mind.

'Then we'll take a brick out, Jack. We'll wear away the mortar and see what we can see.'

'Not worth the trouble, mate. You take my word for it.'

'Don't lie to me, man. You know where it is. You know what is on one side and on the other.'

Jack Maggs curled his lip, but did not answer.

'Take out the brick.'

'Take my word, Sir, it can't be done.'

'Jack Maggs, I order you. Take out the brick.'

'Damn you,' cried the sick man, struggling in his bed. 'Do not make me see what has been done.'

Tobias leaned forward on his stool. 'Show it to me,' he demanded.

No answer. Then, suddenly: 'Sophina. She is heart-broken.'

This was not what the Magnetist was looking for. He already had some forty pages of copperplate, all of them concerned with Jack Maggs's love of Sophina Smith, and he did not, at this moment when he was dirty and weary and waiting for his fifty pounds, want to hear any more.

'Then Sophina will remove the brick from the wall.'

'There is no wall.'

'There is a brick wall right behind Sophina. Remove a brick.'

But the Somnambulist was deep in his rut.

'Look how she takes Tom's hand. Look how he pretends to comfort her.'

'Jack, the Phantom is lurking on the other side of that brick wall.'

'I will not look. I couldn't bear it.'

'Here's Tom. He has a chisel, he is scraping away at the mortar.'

'He will make me look, the bastard. I'll shut my eyes.'

'The brick is out.'

The large man on the bed began to whimper, and bring his hand up to his face.

'Move your hands back from your eyes. Is it not the Phantom?'

And, indeed, Jack did reluctantly remove his hands, and open his eyes and stare hard at the dull rain-speckled window of the room. What he saw there, he did not say, but released a wail, so long and dreadful, that the writer, listening to it, bowed his head and shut his eyes.

56

The convict writhed against his magnetic chains. He sat up, straining forward, his dark eyes glaring bright as gin. Tobias had entered this transaction only to collect his fifty pieces, but now all thought of gain was put aside.

'Hold,' he cried, and stood pluckily before Jack Maggs, his legs astride, his hand thrust forward as if to parry or to bless.

Jack Maggs seemed to look at him, but who could say what world he saw with those wild eyes?

'Hold now, Jack. Hold.' The writer brought his soft palms to press down on the air between himself and his subject. As he pushed out his hands, Jack Maggs partially reclined upon his crib. Determined to insist on his mastery, Tobias came a half-step closer. Jack Maggs would not surrender entirely but lay propped on his elbow, like a great loaded spring. He was held, magnetized, though Tobias lacked confidence in the strength of this instrument.

The next moment made him fear the battle lost. Jack Maggs opened his wide mouth and cried not in pain, but in horror at some unseen thing. As a great '*No!*' burst from deep in his chest, he stood, not quickly, but as Gulliver might have, had he been better able to resist the ropes of the Lilliputians. When erect, his great high forehead touched the ceiling. He seemed to fill the room, blocking the light: it took every reserve of courage for Tobias to stand his ground against him.

'Down,' cried Tobias Oates. 'I command you.'

He feared he had done something against the natural order, had unleashed demons he had no understanding of, disturbed some dark and dreadful nest of vermin. He tried to see, without removing his eyes from the subject, if there were some stave or poker with which to arm himself.

'In the name of Jesus Christ, I command you be still.'

Jack Maggs paused, blinked.

'Quiet,' Tobias cried. 'You will be quiet.'

The patient swayed, stooped over, in the middle of the attic, rubbing at his unshaven cheek.

'Now, you will lie down on your bed. And not raise yourself once more unless my voice commands it.'

Jack Maggs then sat on the crib. He tugged off his boots and dropped them heavily onto the floor.

'Christ,' he exclaimed, and then lay down, his hands still playing with his face.

Tobias reflected on how he was to lay this Phantom to rest for ever. He had by now long forgotten, if he ever knew, that this wraith was his own invention, a personification of pain that he had planted in the other's mind. He commanded the Somnambulist to describe the figure that haunted him. He could, of course, have himself described the ice-blue eyes, the cruel straight nose, the cornfield-coloured hair; but his purpose was to make his subject concentrate upon the phantom, and then, by some violent strategy he had not yet imagined, to cast him for ever, like swine, into the sea.

Thus he pointed at the stain on the attic wall. 'There he is, Jack, there he is.'

Jack Maggs, for his part, resisted. He tossed his head and squeezed shut his eyes. He plucked at his cheek, digging into it with his straightened fingers as if his hand were a trencher and his flesh mere clay to dig into.

'Is he dark then, Jack?' asked Tobias, who knew Jack Maggs liked an argument. 'Is he a black man?'

'Ah no,' the convict sighed. 'He is fair. Very fair.'

'His skin is white?'

'He has my babe.'

Tobias, weary and dirty, wished he could lie down, but he proceeded, calmly, to overcome this latest obstacle.

'Then take back the babe,' said he. 'Walk towards the Phantom. Stretch out your hands. He does not want the babe. He will return the babe into your arms.'

'He is on the other side of the wall.'

Tobias imagined that the subject was referring to the Phantom. 'You have removed one brick,' he said irritably. 'You will now remove one more. If needs be you will demolish the whole wall in order to reach him.'

There followed more childish banging of the subject's head, pulling at the cheek, etcetera. Tobias folded his hands on his lap and waited. When Jack Maggs was once more quiet, he asked, 'Have you removed the brick now?'

The other man grimaced sadly. 'It is a cess pit they throw him in.'

'The Phantom is cast out?'

'My *babe*. My babe is dead.'

'Where is your Phantom, Jack? Tell me again: how does he look?'

'Oh, he is a soldier of the King,' the convict said bitterly. 'He is a regular frigging beetle, but my poor dear little boy is laying in a ditch.' Much to Tobias Oates's consternation, his subject began to weep uncontrollably. 'Dear Lord, dear Lord. His sweet little cheek is cut open.'

And there Jack Maggs lay, sobbing, his mighty legs drawn up to his knees as though he were a babe himself.

'Do not make me see it,' he wailed, clutching at his own cheek, and dragging down on the flesh with his broad square nails. 'Oh God, I wish I were dead, and that's the truth.'

'Attend, Sir.'

'Leave me, leave, let me be.'

'I will repair your son.'

'You cannot repair him. He is dead.'

'We will close his wound. Please.'

'Leave him alone, you meddling bastard of a man.'

But Tobias Oates had received an insight. 'Look, Jack, look, the wound is healed. When his wound is healed, yours will be too. It is the same wound.'

'I want it.'

'No, look and see the wound is healed. Your pain is gone.'

'I want it,' cried Jack Maggs, raising himself on his elbow and staring at Tobias Oates with such alertness that it was hard to believe he was still mesmerized.

'I want it, fool. It is all I have left of him.'

57

The *tic douloureux* had been by no means vanquished, but the magnets had given Jack Maggs sufficient relief to enable him to scrabble under the mattress where, he now revealed, a great portion of his wealth was hidden.

He turned his back on Toby and hunched his broad shoulders so the writer might not see the extent of his treasure.

'On faith I give you ten,' he called.

When he looked back his skin was still pasty, but some of his old rascality was again shining in his eyes. He spoke gruffly. 'It's a hard bargain you've made.'

Then he seized Toby's hand. 'But, Jod's blood, you'll see me keep my word, mate.'

He drew the startled writer very close, so close Tobias could not escape the stench of his sick breath. Toby's hand was clenched into a fist but Jack Maggs pried the fist open with the hooked fingers of his mutilated hand.

'On the morrow,' said he, 'we will meet the gent himself.'

'He lives in Gloucester.'

'Then to Gloucester we will go, mate. And when I have him, then forty more of these golden beauties shall be delivered to your hand.'

And with that, he solemnly counted ten warm gold sovereigns into Tobias Oates's open palm.

Later, as his hackney cab trotted up Great Queen Street, the writer's fingers began to worry at these coins in his pocket. In the restless, ever-changing landscape of his mind's eye, he saw the circumstances whereby they might have found their way to him. As always, he believed in the scenes made by his imagination, thought them as real as anything in Great Queen Street. He saw a cabin in moonlight, a thrusting dagger, a fallen lantern, a fire blazing suddenly in the antipodean dark. These scenes led him, by and by, back to the novel of *Jack Maggs*. He began to rehearse the ways he might describe it to old Cheery Entwhistle.

He soon had himself immersed deep in the details of Jack Maggs's birth. He had learned, by medium of his magnets, that the infant Maggs had been thrown off London Bridge. Now he began to play with the notion that the convict was, like Richard Savage, a bastard son of noble parents. It was here he would start to tell the tale to Cheery Entwhistle. He saw himself pacing up and down the publisher's comfortable office while the old man sat with his hands folded contentedly across his waistcoated belly.

He came back from the depths of this fancy to discover that his cab had been a long time halted. He looked out the window and saw his cabby and the driver of an omnibus standing with fists raised in the middle of the street.

There was two guineas to be made here. He could write it in an hour. 'An Altercation in High Holborn'.

Add his sweeper boy (two guineas).

Add his canary woman (two guineas).

If he did not pay the grocer's or the butcher's bill, he might amass four hundred pounds by the time the deluge arrived.

The cab set off again, at speed. He took out his chap book and began to write, thereby achieving two hundred words by the time he closed the book again at Merton Street. Here he instructed the driver to wait, and ran up the cat-sour path to Dr Hardwick's door.

The doctor answered the door with a grey and unsanitary napkin in his hand.

'Dr Hardwick,' said Tobias. 'I have your fee, as I promised.'

This information seemed to confuse the doctor.

'I am Tobias Oates.'

'You are, are you?' said Dr Hardwick, and then wandered back up the hallway, leaving his front door ajar behind him. Not being invited to follow, Toby had no choice but to wait in the doorway, wondering all the while what sort of doctor would open his own door. On the evidence of the shadows, the old man was in the front room, walking hither and fro in the manner of someone conducting a search.

Some ten minutes passed, but when he finally returned to the front door, he still did not have the necklace in his hand.

'Here is a sovereign,' said Tobias urgently. 'I believe I am your debtor to the extent of five shillings.'

Dr Hardwick looked with some surprise at the coin thus proffered. 'How goes my patient?'

'The babe is well. I hope you can give me change, Sir.'

This matter the doctor attended to readily enough, but he did not proffer any jewellery in return.

'I believe you have something of mine,' Tobias said at last.

Dr Hardwick frowned. 'Of yours?'

'Well then, of my wife's sister.'

'Oh, you wish the girl's necklace?' The old man then began fumbling around his jacket pocket.

'It is not lost, I hope.'

At this the doctor slowly drew the necklace from the fob pocket of his waistcoat.

'You show too much of yourself,' he said to Tobias Oates, as he held the jewellery in the air in front of him.

'Sir?' said Tobias, blushing brightly.

Dr Hardwick lowered the necklace into Tobias's impatient hand.

'I trust you are as careful of your sister-in-law as I am with her necklace,' he said.

Tobias could not believe what he had heard. He looked into the stranger's yellowish eyes, and saw the eyes staring boldly back at him. Beneath the man's discoloured whiskers he thought he saw the mouth move in some benign amusement. And, for a brief moment, he was tempted to unburden himself of all his woes, to seek a medical solution to that crisis which was presently threatening to destroy his entire world.

But then he observed a curl in the old man's lip, a steeliness in the eyes. He turned on his heels and returned to his cab.

58

Dear Henry, I imagine you waiting and watching. I imagine you beyond the door, outside on the street, peering through the cracks in the curtains. I fancy that you are waiting to see what sort of cove your Da is. You are careful.

I also was a watchful lad. I watched Tom most particular, and I was not wrong to do so. Tom, at eighteen, had got tall and almost handsome. His hair had grown wild and curling, and thus did him the great service of hiding his ugly ears. All his spleen had concentrated in his ripe red mouth, where its meaning had become mixed up with appetite. This was a boy who liked to kiss, but there was also a conspirator's air to him, and a hardness, a fierceness in his eye.

– We are brothers, Jack, he would say, leaning over the famous carved oak table at the Swan with Two Necks. We don't need no outsiders to do our work.

By 'outsiders' he meant Silas who, even whilst locked away in jail, still continued to control much of our activity and to take, according to Tom, the lion's share of the profits. He was not permitted to complain of this to Mary Britten, so to me he poured out all the bitter feelings in his heart. He would take me by the wrist and hold me hard. – You are not blood, but you are family. I would die for you, Jack, etc. etc.

This passion of his made me ill at ease, and even if I learned to counterfeit its equal – for he was very prickly and needful of my doing so – in truth I pitied him. And so, in looking down on him, I did not watch him as closely as I should have.

When I tried to have Sophina join with me in joking about Tom, she reproached me severely. – You should be shamed, she said, to have a brother who would die for you, and to make a muck of it.

In Tom, to her great cost, she heard and saw only what she wished were true. She did not understand the great animus he bore her Papa.

Tom was both secretive in his habits and careful with his tools, and this lucky combination gave him a great talent for house-breaking. He had become, now that he had stopped trying to escape the bonds of his apprenticeship, his master's great pet. This master had no idea that Tom Britten was a thief. Indeed, he boasted that there was no one in all the West of London who could make a dovetail so neat and fast. I do not doubt his claim was true. Tom told me once there was a way that lumber gave before him which felt like a beast surrendered. He made it sound a dirty thing.

Tom might well have gone on to have a useful, honest sort of life, but he was his mother's son and they were set on bigger things.

By 1806 we ate best brisket, chump chops, rolled roast beef from the butcher's shop in Upper Street, and Mrs Britten was the owner of two freehold titles, and her rooms were now attended by a better class of female who – if nervous to venture into Islington – were presumably relieved that they would see no one there they knew.

Now the Ma dressed in a get-up she had invented for herself, all in white with a queer white cap upon her head. She sold her belly-ache sausages no more. Instead she advertised her Dr Britten's Cock's Spur Pills for Female Disorders. These pills she compounded from Ergot, a substance which gave all our hands an unpleasant fishy smell. Sophina and I spent many a morning counting the rough purple lumps into small brown bottles.

At fourteen, I had grown too big to fit into a chimney, but both Sophina and I had got a mighty knowledge of old silver. Together with Tom, who had all the skills of his apprenticeship, we had elevated our thievery to a higher state than any Silas could have imagined.

Sometimes Tom might pick the lock, yet often a simple cut of his fret saw would make the key a cuckold to his finger. Sophina and I were not present when the entry was effected, though it is easy to see Tom feeling his way into the house with tarred string and wire ticklers and saw-blades fine as a human hair. He made less mess than a death-watch beetle, and when he was done the house would sit waiting for us, as easily opened as the pages of a book.

When he met us in our rendezvous to instruct us how we were to go about our entry, he would have his colour high. His movements would be quick but soft, and there was about him at once a great excitement and a heightened shyness. I saw how he cast looks at Sophina from beneath his long lashes, and how, in telling the story of his entry, he would seek to emphasize the risk. He wished to appear the real dog in the doublet. He did not speak to Sophina, or about her, but I was not blind to his strong feelings.

When he came to see us in the house in Islington, he would ignore us both. He would stay up late conferring with his mother, hunching with her over the dining-room table where they spent endless hours going through their 'papers'. What these were I could not say, although I do believe they included a sworn deposition relating to Silas's innocence, and the title of her two properties, although I never did see the other property – which she described as a 'commodious gentleman's residence' in Notting Hill.

On Sunday afternoons the pair of them sat at the table drinking gin from yellow Venetian glasses, while they added up rows of figures and hissed secrets at each other. What these secrets were, I still have no idea. I cannot tell you if she knew that he had betrayed Silas, or if the whole thing had been done on her instruction. Anything you might imagine about that pair, you could not call impossible.

Sometimes Tom left early after some upset, but more often he was there long after Sophina and I had gone to sleep in our little room.

We were, for most of the time, exhausted, and not because we were walking half of London several nights a week – or not that only – but because we were charged with the care and cleaning of the household, and never was a downstairs maid worked harder than we were.

It was not so much the upstairs quarters which exhausted us, but that entire ground floor which Ma Britten had now devoted to what she called 'my ladies'. These rooms, where none might eat or sleep, where one could be thrashed for introducing a slice of bread and dripping, she decorated after her idea of a ladies' room.

Mary Britten was not an educated woman, and there was about her tall raw frame a great rude energy which might remind you more of a coster than a nurse, and yet she had a passion to be genteel, to walk St James's, to be admitted without question at Ranelagh, and she made this front room an altar to her passion, filling it with expensive flounces, and ruffles, with jardinieres, with doilies, and statues of dusky maidens whose outstretched hands could accommodate a lighted candle. And it is curious that I, who had certainly been in far more gentlefolk's houses than she had, did not think to quarrel with either her knowledge or her taste.

Sophina and I, of course, spent a great deal of time considering the very particular nature of that taste, for it was our task to clean both rooms, the pretty room and the plain room, as we called them.

The pretty room was a nightmare of oak floors (which must be waxed) and heavy rugs (which must be beaten). Lord help us if we did not have the skirting board shining, if insufficient elbow grease had been applied to the mantelpiece, if there were a residue of silver polish left upon the silver vase I had stolen from a farmer's house in Hampstead.

The plain room was at once easier and more difficult – easier in that it was free of flounces and curlicues, difficult in that we might here find blood in quantities enough to frighten any child, and discover things in muslin-covered basins that haunt me to this day. We said nothing about the plain room to each other, but emptied the contents of the basins into the cess pit at the back of the garden. We cleaned the plain room with soap and scrubbing brush, quickly, holding our breath.

To walk from these rooms up the stairs was like stepping behind the scenes at the theatre. Here was where we lived, and in quite a different style than previously. There was the large 'cupboard' – in fact a small room with a window – where Ma ground up her Ergot and made her little pills: a painstaking process, for she moulded each small pill by hand, and one that made her tired and bad-tempered. There was the small kitchen with its fierce black stove on which we were forever burning ourselves. There was the room where Ma slept and in which, in a series of large boxes, she stored all the peculiar goods which had, before Silas's arrest, been kept in the net loft in Wapping.

There was a small 'dining room' which also served as Ma's office, and here she kept, in the tin box, the titles, and mysterious other Certificates and Orders which she was forever checking.

We were both, Sophina and I, instructed to call her Ma, but did so knowing that we would be often reminded that we were not her children. When Tom came to visit, they would somehow team against us and, as they huddled over their papers, we did not think to calculate how much of the household income was produced by us, but believed instead that we had a roof over our heads only as a result of their whimsical charity.

When he came to the house, Tom did not look at Silas's daughter directly. And yet I was aware, even then, of the fierceness with which he did not look.

You would think it incredible that I, who knew his ways so well, would ever leave my pretty treasure undefended. But if I often did so it was because, my dear boy, I had already become Silas's son-in-law. Not, of course, that Sophina and I were married in a church, though we often talked of that, and longed for the day when we might suggest such a thing and not be beaten on account of it.

> *Amo, Amas*
> *I love a lass*
> *She is so sweet and tender*

We were then, as far as I can reckon, fourteen years old. And we lay under our counterpane at night, asleep in each other's arms, imagining ourselves safe, at least, in our heartfelt feelings for each other.

59

Henry, had you been able to hear Judge Denman make his ignorant speech to the jury about what a poisonous line of blood ran through my vermin veins, had you heard the phlegmy old lambskin list my misdemeanours, you might have imagined me so devoted to burglary that I had not a moment to spare between cock crow and midnight.

Sophina and I were worked hard, it's true, but more often as chars than burglars. When the Ma's floors were scrubbed and her banisters polished, time was often heavy on our hands and many is the fine summer's day we spent confined to the upstairs floor with no other amusement than to lie on the bare floorboards with a tumbler against our ears, trying to overhear the sad little dramas enacted in the room below our kitchen.

Silas in his penitentiary had more freedom than we did. He was permitted often times to stand at the open door of the prison in his fine grey tailored coat, and there, puffing on an Indian cheroot, pass the day with whomsoever passed by. But Sophina and I were forbid the little lane that ran down beside our home. Even hopscotch was denied us.

It is not so queer then that we looked forward to our burglary more than we feared its consequences. It was not our blood-line, or our criminal craniums, but our natural human desire for something other than the tedium of close confinement. Thus we waited to be called to risk, waited while the ground-floor voices murmured, while the blacksmith across the way set up his steady cling-cling-cling, while a housefly died noisily, buzzing against the green window glass.

The front-door bell rang frequently, but these were ladies for the Ma, and no business of ours. If there were a call for us, it would most likely come after supper when we were scrubbing down the kitchen tables.

– Come, my lovelies.

We would look up from our grey soap and our hard brushes, and see a cabby standing at the kitchen door.

– I am Uncle Dick, and I am here to take you for a little trot.

And in three minutes we would be dressed for the street and clattering down the stairs, leaving the bowl of soapy water on the table for the Ma – for she would never hinder us on our way to do our business.

Every Joe knows that the brotherhood of hackney drivers has a calling in the criminal professions, but our Uncle Dicks and Handsome Micks were innocent, at least temporarily. No matter that Silas himself had engaged them, no matter what skivers and magsmen they might be on a Monday morning, on those sweet summer evenings they had nothing more criminal to do than to get us to an inn.

They were, as Silas told us, base links in a chain of gold.

Likewise, Tom would break the door of the house, but never enter it. Likewise, my pretty sweetheart and I would select the silver and pack it in the hessian sacks, but take the sacks no further than the kitchen door.

– You ain't breaking the law, Silas told us. You did not break no lock, and you did not remove nothing from the premises.

It was a scheme, in all its very definite Divisions of Labour, which would have met with the approval of Mr Adam Smith, but I do not think that this was an author I ever heard Silas mention, although he was a well-respected scholar and able to recite long passages from the Bible and from Shakespeare.

Even in Newgate, he kept his books about him, and complained often about favourites he could not accommodate in his cell. Alas, he needed sufficient shelving for his port wine and his claret, for he could not be without them either. Silas did not go short of comforts. He always had a ham and two or three different pies, all nicely covered with muslin to keep the flies away. All this drove Tom into a great frenzy, but I don't think I ever really believed that Silas's comfortable way of life was paid for by my labours. Indeed, I had come to think of these labours as being for my own amusement. And as the cab began, as it most-times did, to head towards the West wherein the faint glow of the departed sun could still be seen, my heart would be already pounding hard in my chest. My hand would soon go out across the seat and find my sweetheart's. All around us, the drivers of coaches, carriages, dog carts, phaetons, roared and raced their mighty race, while we two children were like insects brought to fervent life by a summer thunder storm.

As I had grown tall, Sophina had kept her own pace beside me, and when we sat opposite each other in the soft London light, our eyes were level, and each as hungry and curious about its opposite as our tangled hands. I sought those grey eyes in the gloom. What a heady blend of sagacity and recklessness I found there.

And hurt, also. There was much hurt my Sophina carried with her silently, hurt you would never guess unless you heard, as I often did, her crying by herself at night, and there was a certain wariness about her affections which had to be won over just when you imagined there was no more winning-over to be done.

But I said she was a beauty, so let me prove it to you: Sophina had dark luxurious curls and an oval face with such wise and gentle grey eyes and a wide, well-shaped mouth whose naturally serious expression was forever breaking in a most glorious smile. Her lips were soft – so soft I break my sentence to close my eyes and mourn them. And when we met with Tom at the inn, I was all impatience to get to the house, to get to the job, where I might kiss them.

Was this safe? For the most part, yes. It is much to Silas's credit that we were rarely called to any house where the danger of discovery was very great. Of course this was not necessarily on account of kindness, and one has only to think him like a fellow with a pair of good fighting cocks he does not want to lose too easily, to understand why he took great care in the gathering of his Information.

Twice there were slip-ups. Once we found a master by his fire when we expected no one home. Once we had a party return from Sussex when they had not been expected, but it is one of the wonders of great houses that their owners are forever closing them down, and these were the houses we were sent to do our 'little spot of shopping'.

Had we such a house – as Sophina and I said to each other – we would never sleep in any other, and it was our great fancy that the houses where we exercised our craft belonged to us, and thus, even in the selection of the silver plate we were to steal, we acted the parts of a lady and gentleman choosing which items to send to their country estate.

We were fast at our work, faster than those who depended on us could ever guess, and when we had filled our sack, and I had placed it carefully beside the kitchen door, I would mount the stairs and set off, in all that great house, to find my 'wife' who had gone on ahead of me.

And who was in bed, of course, and waiting for me.

My dear boy, I pray I do not shock you with this tale or that you, in imagining us wild animals, will doubt me when I say, what innocents we were. Sophina was not one of those girls who bloom suddenly into womanhood. She ripened slowly in the London mist, and when I embraced her, I was a boy embracing a girl.

But a man too, for the man now who writes this embraces her still, and longs, thirty years later, for the smooth whiteness of her skin and all that great house around us.

'Twere the sweetest thing in all my life, to go burgling with Sophina and to flirt with the great dangerous web of sleep which came down to claim us afterwards.

60

On the twenty-eighth of July 1807 we were dispatched to a large gentleman's residence in Montpelier Square, an easy mark because of the lane-way entrance to its stables at the rear. We first met with Tom at the Golden Sheaf, a little inn in one of the smaller streets which lead into the square.

There we watched Tom fill his face with cold boiled beef and pickled walnuts. Finally, when he had washed all this down with ale, he pointed out the open window and showed us the house that had been selected for us. It was a tall, thin, four-storey beauty, straight and tall as a guardsman with all its iron work blacked and its brass work shining in the soft green summer light.

We waited for the dark to fall, and then left Tom sitting drinking his second tankard and playing solitaire.

A half an hour or so after we had gone inside, Tom heard a commotion down below and, kneeling on his settle, he looked out and saw a team of Bow Street runners 'fair galloping' across the square, shouting at each other as they went. It seemed to him that they were heading towards the lane-way at the back of our house.

This alarmed him at first, but after he had watched the house a while and seen its windows remain dark, he went back to his solitaire. He had performed this vigil many times and was now accustomed to the long time it took us to select our merchandise. But when the clock struck midnight and the landlord wished to know would he like a room to sleep in, Tom paid his bill and went on out into the night.

He had a Mr Steelshank waiting in another inn nearby, and when the bag was ready he would call on Steelshank and tip him the wink. But now he began to imagine that the Robin Redbreasts had nabbed us in the kitchen, or the butler's pantry where – naturally enough – no light would have showed. If that was the case, they might be waiting in there now, and he could not send in Steelshank but neither could he make up his mind what he should do. He walked around the square two or three times until his activity was noted by a watchman who wanted to know what it was he was looking for. As the fellow raised his lantern, a hackney cab came into the square and Tom straight way hailed it and set off, not to Steelshank, but up to Islington where he set about the dangerous task of raising Ma Britten from her bed.

The Ma was a restless body who oft-times needed a dram or two of French Cream to get her to her sleep. Once that precious land was won, she did not gracefully surrender it, and when she was finally drawn up from the depths towards the light of Tom's lantern, she brought a foul mouth and an evil temper with her.

Now I was not, I am pleased to say, a witness to this event, but I spent enough years with the pair of them to now offer an honest sketch.

– You better not have lost them little varmints, said she, or by

God, Silas will have the Push come looking for you.

– I ain't lost nothing, Ma, said he, I just did my job, and then the runners went into the house and now they ain't come back.

– You dunghill, said she.

– Ma, said he, don't call me that. I ain't a coward.

– Dung, she hollered.

She liked to call him that, call him anything that would make him red in the face and even more needful of her affections. So even though he were a big fellow now, and handy with his raw red fists, he was, as they journeyed out into the night, a whining little mutt around her great black skirts.

– You lose those little Nokes, said she, and I'll cut your bleeding ears off. Etc., etc.

She might call us Nokes, and worse, but the truth was she feared she was at risk of losing her golden geese, and although she was normally a very careful woman with a penny, she did not hesitate to pay for another hack to get her as far as Montpelier Square.

When they arrived at the back lane by the stables, Tom, being convinced that the runners were waiting there to trap him, gave his mother one more reason to call him a dunghill. She pushed her way ahead of him and walked into the house.

There, in the face of Tom's pleas that she do otherwise, Ma Britten lit a candle, located the kitchen, and there discovered the bag of silver Sophina and I had packed so carefully. That this valuable booty was still in its place was, to the Ma's mind, proof positive that the Robin Redbreasts had not been near the place. She jubilantly administered one or two fast clips across Tom's ears, and (having thereby calmed herself a little) set off to search the house.

Tom, however, had an awful terror of transportation. He tried to lag behind, and the Ma was forced to escort him by his ear up the stairs, and she did not let him go until, on a landing, she heard Yours Truly snoring.

God knows what Tom thought the sound was, but it did serve to send him into a dreadful panic.

The Ma demanded – Draw the curtains! But he had slipped away from her into the darkness, and she had to run the risk herself – as she was not slow to remind him later – of standing in front of the open window in a public square while she quickly drew the curtains. When this was done, she held the candle high.

– Nokes, she cried.

I woke to see her there, her hair all wild as if for bed, but dressed in the long dark skirts she favours to this day. She tilted the candle and a drop of hot wax spilled onto my bare stomach, then onto poor Sophina who leapt startled from her bed and stood in the corner, trying to cover herself.

– Out! Ma cried at Tom, who now was standing at the doorway, staring at our nakedness.

– Out! she cried again. Tom had gone, but I pretended not to know what she meant.

– Get out, idjeet! she cried, never once taking her eyes off poor Sophina.

It is to my eternal shame that I then deserted Sophina, and stood like a shivering child outside the door where Tom, having glared at me and shaken his head, was temporarily restrained from any more physical attack upon my person by his intense curiosity about what was being said inside.

– Stand! we heard the Ma say. Hands by your sides!

But then she dropped her voice, and the conversation inside the door began to sound like the conversations we heard through the floor boards of the kitchen. The questions, the answers, the tears. Only in its conclusion did this interview show Ma Britten's different relationship with the person whom she now interviewed.

– Five months! she cried. You stupid little bitch.

She had discovered, so I imagined, the length of time we had been man and wife.

61

Toby had been abroad a day and night. He had slept in a flop house, magnetized a criminal, retrieved a necklace, and drunk first claret and then brandy with Cheery Entwhistle.

219

He had sold the copyright to *Jack Maggs*. He had signed a contract for sixty pounds, and now, as he stood outside his house in Lamb's Conduit Street, he could feel the sticky dirt of London on his skin and taste its sulphurous corruption in his mouth.

A light rain was falling, scarcely more than mist, and it gathered on the outside of his curling hair like dew on a spider web. It ran down his unclean cheeks and thereby helped produce, in concert with a swollen mouth and shadowed eyes, a picture at once demonic and pathetic. He stood awhile in the shadows and watched his own household with a kind of dread.

As he gained the footpath he was able to look down into the kitchen and see Mrs Jones busy scrubbing down her table in readiness for the morrow. How he envied the old biddy the dull certainty of her day.

He let himself in the front door very quietly, only to be rewarded with her whom he wished most to avoid.

The girl was seated on the bench seat by the hat stand, clad only in dressing gown and slippers. Her hair was loose and falling on her shoulders, but still she came and recklessly embraced him, pushing against him with that darkest and most womanly part of her anatomy.

'Where is my wife?'

He drew her into the dark drawing room and sat her down opposite him at a small card table. Then, in the interests of propriety, he lit a candle.

'I have been waiting for you, dearest.'

'Where is Mary?'

'In the nursery, but listen to what your Lizzie has been waiting all day long to tell you.'

She then stretched out her free hand and touched his face. He could not help but flinch from her.

'Lizzie,' he explained, 'my face is dirty.'

In reply she leaned across the table to kiss him once again. He saw then, quite clearly, the full curve of her breast.

'Toby – I plan to go away, by myself, to France.'

'For Heaven's sake, do up your nightgown.'

She did as he requested but in a teasing manner inappropriate to their situation.

She continued. 'My French is really very good, as you have said yourself.'

To France? He would not know how to effect such an adventure himself. She was but eighteen years old, and scarcely knew her way to the Royal Academy.

'Whom have you been speaking to?'

'I would be away but half a year.'

The floorboards creaked upstairs.

'I would stay in a good Protestant house in Paris.'

'Which house?' he whispered. 'How could you find such a thing? Who would be with you?'

'I would be back by Christmas with the baby.'

'No!'

'Oh, silly dear Tobias. I would not say that he was our own.'

He looked at her with such alarm that she, in her madness, began to laugh. 'I have already told Mary that I wish to adopt a foundling.'

'You must do no such thing, do you hear me? My wife is one hundred times sharper than you imagine.'

'No, poor Toby, she is one thousand times less sharp than you imagine. In any case, I told her this morning that I was resigned to being an old maid, but that I would adopt a babe of my own.'

'You are treading on thin ice, girl.'

'Do not be so cold with me, Toby.'

'I am not cold. I am shocked that you should discuss this with anybody. What did my wife reply?'

'Well, you can imagine the scene, I'm sure. First she must drink her tea. Then she must contemplate the matter as if it were a frightful conundrum. In this case she was silent an awfully long time, but at last she said that she was sure that it was forbidden by the English foundling hospitals – to give their charges out to spinsters.'

'She is correct.'

'Of course she is correct, dear. She had considered it, don't you see? That is why she considers things. She has a terror of being wrong, especially in your company. I then asked her, did she think the French foundling hospitals would have the same proscription, and she said that she did not know, but that foreigners did the most peculiar things.'

'Dear Lizzie, I will not give you up.'

Lizzie frowned. 'Of course. We will none of us give up the other.'

'Mary would be the first to know it was your flesh and blood. Can you not see how we would insult the very foundation of her life?'

Whether Lizzie heard this or no, was not clear, for something he had said had obviously angered her, and now she stared at him so malevolently that he chose this moment to return her necklace. He laid it on the table, as evidence.

'I have been busy on your behalf,' said he.

'On my behalf?'

She raised an eyebrow, then draped the necklace over her wrist. For a moment she twisted it to and fro, seeming to admire the way the stones reflected the candle light.

'So what would you have me do, Tobias?'

'It is a dark hour.'

Lizzie was silent.

'That is all you have to offer?' She laid the necklace back upon the table. 'It is a dark hour?'

'No,' said Toby. 'It is not all I have to offer. I have a plan but first I must speak with Mary.'

'You cannot discuss it with *me*?' she cried suddenly, a great temper erupting in her eyes.

'Please, Elizabeth. Please be a little quieter.'

'And when might you have the time, Sir, to make the nature of your thoughts available to the mother of your child?'

He had no plan, of course. He had accrued one hundred and eighteen pounds and sixpence but no clear plan had come to him.

'I have a *wife*,' he pleaded, 'and tomorrow I must earn my necklace money by being a servant to the convict.'

'But when will you reveal your plan to me?' She spoke loudly, carelessly. 'How long do you plan to leave me alone with my mind spinning round and round?'

When Tobias stood, Lizzie remained in her chair, her shoulders rounded in despair.

'I will take care of this matter,' he said. 'You can rely on me.'

And then he turned and walked up the stairs, where he discovered his wife standing on the landing, a peculiar expression upon her face.

'I go to Gloucester,' he said.

62

Tobias took no change of linen with him on his journey to Gloucester. Instead he had brought his faithful yellow case, and in it he had carefully packed his cut-throat razor, his toothbrush, a quill, his work book and an ink bottle. Even before the coach had escaped the congestion at the turnpike, he had opened this ingenious portmanteau upon his knees, and made his travelling desk.

He uncorked his ink, set the bottle in the cavity made for this purpose, and there, in what de Quincey called 'the great Mediterranean' of Oxford Street, he began the first chapter of *Jack Maggs*. He wrote in an ornate but graceful hand: not a wavering stroke to indicate that he was sitting in a coach, not a smudge or blot to suggest that this was a young man in despair, someone who felt himself to be moving only just ahead of the tide of his own disgrace.

He was not unaware that the subject of his tale was seated staring at him. Although Jack Maggs was in the far right-hand corner with his back towards the horses, as far away as he might be, the *True Briton*, as the coach was named, was no bigger than any other mail coach. That is, it was made exactly as the Post Office insisted, with the same cursed three feet and four inches from seat to ceiling, six feet and six inches on the horizontal diagonal.

Tobias wrote 'Chapter One', and underlined it twice. Then he began:

It was a dismal January day in the year of 1818, and the yellow fog which had lain low all morning lifted a moment in the afternoon and then, as if the desolate pile of rock and stone thereby revealed was far too melancholy a sight to be endured, it descended again like a shroud around the walls of Newgate Prison.

'How do you do that, Sir?'

This from a clergyman, seated on his right. Tobias smiled, and dipped his quill again.

'I could not read with all this motion,' said the clergyman. 'But to write, Sir, that is certainly an accomplishment.'

These walls, being made from Welsh blue stone, had not been easily broken by the quarryman . . .

'I did once see a lass at Amersham Fair who could knit a scarf whilst cantering a pony around a field.'

This from a farmer who had squeezed in opposite Tobias. He was a big square-headed fellow who could not get his knees anywhere they did not touch another passenger and who had seemed, until this moment, rather irritated on account of it. 'Now that were something,' he insisted to Jack Maggs, who responded by folding his arms across his red waistcoat.

The farmer then turned to the clergyman. 'That were worth the penny, that lass.'

'Indeed,' said the clergyman. 'But our companion produces an even greater entertainment, Sir.'

'Oh, it were a *very* fine show,' said the farmer. 'That lass were no more than ten years old.'

. . . and yet the fog, by virtue of its persistence, had been able slowly to penetrate the stone's dark, inhuman heart . . .

'I do not doubt it, Sir,' said the clergyman, 'but I suspect the young lass is being over-shadowed, as it were.'

'You'll not persuade me so easy, your Reverence . . .'

The clergyman had seemed at first to be a man with no big range of emotions, but now his mouth was very straight and his face exceeding red. Said he, 'To tell the tale of Captain Crumley and Mrs Morefallen: why that must be a performance of some great difficulty.'

Between the farmer and Jack Maggs there sat an old lady in a white cloak and faded red bonnet who had been quietly pecking from a pannikin of roasted wheat. Now hearing Mrs Morefallen's name, she looked sharply up.

'Mr Oates?' she said. 'It is not Mr Tobias Oates?'

The farmer was then suddenly, and most noticeably, silent.

This occurrence was by no means usual, and Tobias, although puzzled to know how he was recognized, was inordinately pleased to feel himself esteemed by these strangers. Yet so deep was his certainty of his own imminent disgrace that he could not savour their love without calculating how soon, and how brutally, it was to be torn from him. He therefore took no bow, engaged in no conversation, and in this manner gave his fellow travellers the impression of a cold and arrogant young man.

The attention of the other passengers turned soon enough to the signs of May – bluebells, the plum blossom by the church at Hammersmith, the hare fleeing across the turnpike. Toby's eyes were on grimmer territory altogether.

There were a great number of women inside Newgate that year. They had been brought from all over the British Isles: petty thieves, murderers, all manner of wickedness crammed into that grim pile on Newgate Street.

He was still at that same address when the coach passed the great Park of Lord Dingley. Here, the clergyman and the farmer got into an argument about the virtues of the fir tree, a matter which would not be easily or simply settled. The farmer began to shout, the clergyman to laugh in a high and unpleasant manner. Tobias hardly heard this and yet there was another, more silent element, which really did distract him. That is: Jack Maggs's gaze upon him.

He continued to write diligently, but now he was over-conscious of the other's stare. It was like a ray from an eye-glass, warm at first, but soon too hot to be comfortable. He brought his own hard stare up to match the convict's.

Time passed. One minute, two. It was a silent exchange yet such was its force that the conversation of their fellow passengers died away, and it was in the face of their attention that the convict finally retreated.

A moment later, it was as if nothing peculiar had occurred. Tobias returned to his labours, Jack Maggs looked out the window. Soon after they arrived in Hounslow, and the two travellers found themselves left alone in the coach for the next stage.

'What is it that you write about me?'

Tobias felt the colour rising up from beneath his shirt. 'These notes do not concern you, Jack.'

'I know you've been writing about me.'

The convict then held out his hand toward the chap book.

'Dear fellow, this is not your business.'

'Give me,' insisted the other.

'No, Sir.'

'Deliver.'

Tobias hesitated and then, desperately, began to read out loud an item in his work book he had written late the night before.

In the region of Camden Town there were once to be found many famous old eccentrics, but lately it seems that they have 'passed on' whilst we have slept, and now even 'John The Happy Hooper' is said by local people to have gone to Sweden to amuse the family of the King and Queen. But the Inquirer did find, in Shaky Row, she who is known in those parts as The Canary Woman.

'Deliver!' insisted Jack Maggs, and Tobias had no choice but to give up his work book, his finger indicating the passage he had read from.

He watched with his heart racing, as Jack held the pages to his hard-boned face.

'You see,' said Toby. 'It is as I said.' But Jack Maggs doggedly read all six hundred words.

'It is an old woman.' He did not smile, as the writer had rather hoped he would, nor did he relinquish the book, but held it stubbornly clasped in his lap.

'As I said, not you.'

'You get a good laugh out of the old biddy, I must say.' The convict opened the book again.

'She is a comic figure, Jack.'

'I reckoned it were *me* that were the comic figure.' He was turning the pages slowly now, and then he paused. He was staring down at the annotated plan of the Newgate cell in which Tobias planned to

226

accommodate Sophina. On the right-hand page was the start of the chapter he had so recently composed.

'Come, Jack Maggs. My book, if you please.'

Jack Maggs frowned, as if dimly perceiving the unhappy fate before him on the page. Then, as if brushing off a spider web, he pushed back his long black hair from his forehead, closed the book, and returned it to its relieved owner.

'To the Gods we are all comic figures,' Tobias said.

'As flies to wanton boys are we.'

Toby's heart was beating very fast as he tied up the red leather covers of his notebook. 'If you could look at my life from on high you would split your sides to see the muddle I am making of it.'

He tucked the book back in its place inside the attaché. He screwed the top on his inkwell, wiped his quill clean, and returned these items to their respective places, and when he had secured one with a ribbon, and the other with a leather strap, he snapped the case shut.

'You are a chap what plans,' said Jack.

'How plans?' asked Toby, although he was apprehensive about where any new conversation might take him.

'You have the one place for your pen, the other for your ink. I should have planned this better,' said Jack. 'I was famous for planning in the Colony.'

It was the first time, outside of a trance, that he had acknowledged his past to the writer.

'Even before my pardon, I was known to be a chap what planned. I provisioned parties for exploration. I could make a list twenty pages long and not leave out an item. I thought nothing of provisioning that house in Great Queen Street from half the world away.'

'What house, Sir?'

'Go on with you. You knew the house was mine.'

'Buckle's house?'

'He didn't tell you? I am Buckle's neighbour, or should have been.'

'You have the lease?'

227

'It is freehold, mate.'

To say this shocked Tobias is to understate it. To think this criminal should own a lease while he should be forced to waste his time on Comic Romps and Brighton Fires!

'As I said, I provisioned it from far away. I had a bachelor, a solicitor in Gray's Inn. He sent me five score squares of wallpaper until I found the one I wanted.'

'This house you let to Henry Phipps? The fellow we are seeking – he is your tenant then?'

Jack Maggs frowned. 'My point is that I should have taken as much care with Mr Phipps as I did with the house in which he lived. But I put it off, see. I was a busy man in Sydney town, busy with my bricks from one day to the next.'

'You were a brick-maker?'

'At the time of my conditional pardon, I was given a small grant to encourage me in my new honest life. It was a very poor bit of land, about twenty acres, all of them covered with vines and poisonous scrub. Beneath the scrub were solid clay.'

'It did not serve?'

'You could not grow a cabbage, but you could, if you had the nous' – and here he tapped the side of his considerable nose – 'make a brick as good as anything in London. That clay made my fortune, Mr Oates. It gave me a mansion in Sydney. It gave me the dosh to buy the freehold of the house in Great Queen Street. And then, as I said, I provisioned it. I bought the wallpaper, the china, the finest Oriental rugs.'

'Oh, to stumble on such a landlord!'

'Mr Phipps wrote me very frank and respectable letters. I only regret I never took the time to be so frank with him.'

'Because?'

'Because, mate, I cannot bear him to think me a common criminal.'

He turned and looked out the window, leaving Toby surprised that so hard a man should give a fig for the good opinion of his tenant.

'I'm not your comic figure, Mr Oates.'

228

'In what way do you mean?'

'This old soul with her canaries – do you have a tin box for her?'

'Tin box, Jack?'

'Like you made a tin box for me. The tin box in which you locked all the demons you extracted with your magnets.'

'I have Behemoth and Dabareiel locked up safe and sound. I am not carrying them out on the high road.'

'But do you have a tin box for your Canary Lady? That was my question. For if you do, you must have more tin boxes than a pawn-broker.'

'I keep the canaries here.' Toby tapped his own forehead and smiled. 'In this tin box.'

Maggs turned and looked out at the fields to the north. After a little while the turnpike became narrow, almost like a lane, and the hedgerows pressed in close upon the coach.

'All this,' Maggs said at last, 'I keep in *my* tin box.'

'The country, Jack?'

'Aye,' said the other wistfully. And then he shifted in his seat and sighed.

They rode thus for a while longer, the convict turning more and more toward the window.

'By this *country* you mean Buckinghamshire?'

'Look how the blackthorn grows,' the other cried, as the untrimmed hedgerow lashed the coach.

'I took you for a London sparrow.'

'And so I am, but look, damn me: hedge bells, ground ivy. You smell that smell.'

'Is that violets?'

'Besides the violets, there's another baddish kind of smell.'

'Can I smell Herb Robert?'

For answer, the convict bestowed on the writer a rare and candid grin. 'My ma called it Jack in the Hedge,' he said.

'The bad smell?'

He shrugged. 'She were a strange woman, my ma.'

Now Toby had already glimpsed this ma magnetically. He knew the pattern of her sword, but could not have yet drawn her hawk's eye, her handsome red hair, her startling white shoulder. She was shadow, passion, hurt, an inky malignancy in Jack Maggs's dreams, and now he sought to tease more winkle from the shell. 'That could not have been so cosy, to have your mother name a bad smell after you.'

Maggs turned away again, but when he turned back his eyes were bright, and it was not hard to see the boy in him, to imagine the orphan's hunger for affection.

'I don't believe she named me after nothing,' he said. 'She was from Bucks and that's what they call Herb Robert in these parts. But even if what you say were so, Sir, I'll tell you the truth: I'd rather be a bad smell here than a frigging rose in New South Wales.'

And he was thereafter silent and sulky all the way to Maidenhead.

63

In Maidenhead, the *True Briton* filled up with a family of Harris, all of whom were set on going to the fair in Abingdon. There were five in total, the most senior of them being a grand old fellow with a white beard and a silver fob watch, which instrument the children got much amusement from finding and consulting. There was also a very comely Mrs Harris who sat with straight back and square shoulders, and sang hymns and ballads with her eldest girl. Lastly there was her husband Mr Harris, whose beard was more than equal to his father's, its fine growth covering the greater part of his broad chest.

From time to time, Mr Harris would amuse his children by undoing his broad leather belt and strapping the beard down upon his stomach. For some reason, mysterious to Tobias, this was regarded by all of the Harrises as a great joke, and the pater was entreated to repeat it constantly.

The effect of this family on Jack Maggs was not clear, for he had got himself in hard upon the window and, with his back to all the company, was either sleeping or looking at the passing scenery. But for Tobias, who had a tendency to exaggerate the goodness of people he did not know, the Harrises were a living reproach to his own miserable cupidity. He felt himself judged by their very Christian ordinariness.

What would they think of him to know how he had so shamed his own family?

In his misery, he also turned to the window as the coach, straining up a long slow hill, came through a grove of ancient lime trees. Behind the trees he spied a mossy Norman church, a vicarage, a garden, and the parson himself standing in the middle of his field of wheat. There was a breeze, enough to bend the wheat, enough to make the crab-apple blossom fall from the trees on the vicarage lawn.

He opened his chap book. He crossed out his entire first chapter. He wrote:

Many of M–'s companions could not stand the torture of banishment, and went mad on the voyage out. Sinners they may have been, but English sinners in their hearts. Whether plucked from village or the festering heart of the great Wen, they could not bear the prospect of never more seeing their beloved Motherland.

M– would not go mad, but only because he carried with him the strong conviction that he would, no matter what Judge Denman read to him, walk once more in England's green and pleasant land.

He was by now convinced that this was the last novel he would ever publish. He wrote full-steam, brazenly, daring Jack Maggs to turn around and snatch his book again.

At the crossroads at Wallingford he wrote the famous line with which, thirty years later, *The Death of Maggs* would finally begin: *As certain birds do declare themselves unto their intended, so the Murderer returned to court his beloved England, bold as cock robin in his bright red waistcoat.*

He then began to describe a storm at sea which he then imagined as the heart of Chapter Two. On the edge of his own disgrace, he wrote about his belligerent subject with a sympathy he would never find again. In the dark face of the waves, in the cold foul air of the convicts' hold, he made a place beyond the reach of God Himself. There M– was pinned to the deck, his left wrist broken. Beside him

231

lay a man named Harris with a sodden grey beard upon his cold and lifeless chest.

The coach stopped in Abingdon, which pleasant town he barely saw. It was not until the Harrises had departed the coach, when the shadows were lengthening and the *True Briton* was already labouring up the hills towards Farringdon, that he looked up from his own toils and saw himself again the focus of Jack Maggs's malevolent attention. Reluctantly he locked his book away, and engaged the fellow in conversation.

'Penny for your thoughts, Jack Maggs.'

'Well, you already got my thoughts, mate,' the other whispered in return, glancing at the other passenger: a straw-haired young gentleman who smelt strongly of both the tap room and the stables. Ascertaining that his neighbour was sound asleep, Maggs raised his voice to normal – normal, that is, with regard to volume, although not to tone, which was less respectful than before.

'Penny for my thoughts,' said he. 'That's awful rich, mate.'

Then, with no explanation, he grabbed Toby's head and held it hard. He began slowly to pull the writer's face towards his own as if he meant to kiss him.

'How am I to get those thoughts back out?'

It is difficult to converse normally while having one's head pulled like a melon from the vine. Toby edged a little forward on his seat to ease the pressure. 'I did not know you cared so much for them, Jack Maggs. You never took the time to read the minutes of our meetings. But when we return to London I'll give you the tin box and all my notes. And we will burn them together. Now kindly release me. You are hurting my ear.'

Jack Maggs held him grimly. 'Your notes are lies, mate. Your notes say nothing about me taking off my shirt. The truth is: you have had me reveal secret information in my sleep.'

'All your secrets will be returned to you. Please let me go.'

'Shut your gob.'

Tobias suddenly understood how easily his life could be snuffed out.

'When I read you making fun of that Canary Woman,' said Jack

232

Maggs, with a quietness that in no way contradicted the violence of his dark eyes, 'why, then it was clear as gin – you'd do the same with me. You'd tell my frigging secrets to the world.'

Toby could not think how he should answer.

'How much will they pay you for a bit of fun like you have with that poor old biddy? One quid? Two? How much does it take to put her secrets in the gutter?'

'I told none of her secrets, Jack.'

This Maggs answered by tightening his massive grip. 'This is where my secrets are,' he whispered. 'Inside *this* box. The brain box. This is what we must break into.'

Who knows what might have happened next, had not the guard sounded his bugle and the sleeping gentleman begun to stir. Then they were entering the yard of a village inn and the burly hostlers were shouting up at the coachman. Jack Maggs sat back in his corner like a wrestler between rounds, his arms folded across his bright red vest.

As they stepped down into the yard, Toby's heart was beating fast. He began to walk out into the High Street, but found Jack Maggs strolling close at his side. When he turned one way, Jack turned with him; and when he turned the other, he was beside him there also. At the end of five minutes of this perambulation, he had no choice but to return to the coach and hope there might be another honest citizen inside. It was not to be: the snoring gentleman had departed. No one had taken his place.

The coach returned to the turnpike. Maggs put his hands pacifically on his knees but continued to stare at his companion. This went on for some miles until Tobias could bear it no more.

'Well damn it, I am very sorry I have your blasted secret, Jack Maggs. I have no use for it. I wish I had never got it from you.'

'If you had a very bad secret of your own,' said Maggs, 'it would take you out of danger.'

'So now you threaten me.'

'I do.'

'Do you really think that wise?'

'I am not a wise man. I am a varmint.'

233

'I have no "bad" secrets, Jack Maggs.'

'Well, that's a shame for you.'

'You imagine I would give you the power to blackmail me?'

'That's the one I want,' said Jack, in a much lighter tone. 'By Jove, if you have a one like that, you can sleep like a babe all the way to Gloucester and know no harm will come to you.'

Tobias wondered how he could be in danger when he was about to introduce Jack Maggs to his Thief-taker. And yet he was by no means certain of his companion's rationality. In Magnetic Sleep he had witnessed his torments and his rages, and it was not difficult to imagine Jack Maggs strangling him and throwing him from the coach. Indeed, as the darkness approached, he began to imagine himself stabbed, cudgelled, suffocated. He saw his broken, bloodied body in a ditch. He saw his work book torn, left to moulder beside the road. These visions remained in his mind's eye as vivid prophecies.

The road went over a stone bridge and entered a dark wood.

'You think me such a proper citizen, I'm sure.'

'I don't know nothing about you, mate. I never formed an opinion.'

'Then let me tell you, Jack Maggs, I have a secret twenty times as bad as yours.' And then, as his heart thundered inside his chest, he found himself unburdening himself to his companion.

It was, in truth, a huge relief to do so.

64

'Lizzie,' said Mary Oates, 'could you help me a moment with this little jacket?'

Lizzie Warriner looked up from *Castle Rackrent* and saw her sister struggling to dress her child. Mary, she decided, had no natural sense for how to clothe a body, even her own. It was not merely that her sense of colour had always been a little awry. Of that short-coming she was, at least, aware, and had developed a palette of grey and white and black in order to avoid the worst embarrassments, but poor Mary, no matter how she laboured, could not present herself to the world without a ruck or a rumple, and she could do no better with her child. She had lain little John out on the sofa and now, as she sat awkwardly beside him, was attempting to clothe him in a very beautiful embroidered jacket while holding his head clumsily with one hand. It was hard, so very hard, for Lizzie to look at this and not feel irritated. This was 'Good Mary' and 'Sweet Mary' whom everybody loved?

'Don't you think it still too big for him?' she asked at length.

'It is Aunt Bet's gift,' said her sister simply.

'But what will Aunt Bet feel to see the arms rucked up so and the collar out around the poor chap's shoulders?'

'Aunt Bet has raised ten children on a clerk's income. I'm sure she will be pleased to see how much more use we will have from her thoughtfulness.'

'I'm sure Aunt Bet can wait until little John is three months older. It will be a very handsome jacket then.'

'Lizzie,' said Mary, crossly. 'Do you have other business to attend to?'

Lizzie put her book down and went to her sister's side. She put her arm around her shoulders. 'Mary, dear good Mary, I am sorry. I know not the first thing about babies or their clothing. Besides, I am a horrid little beast as everyone has always known.'

'You are not a horrid beast at all, dear Lizzie, but I do think you have been very sad all day.'

Mary fussed further with the embroidered jacket and then lifted her son up for Lizzie to admire. 'There darling, see, you like Aunt Lizzie. You will make Aunt Lizzie happy. There is nothing like a little one to make you happy in your heart, Lizzie. So often I am out of sorts or worried about one thing or another, and then I pick up little John and hold him to me and really, I swear . . . well, it is the best thing in all the world.'

Lizzie took the baby from her sister and put her nose against the babe's soft downy little neck and breathed his milky soapy smell.

Mary sat on the sofa with her hands folded simply in her wide lap. 'Why are you so sad, dear Lizzie?'

'Sad?' Lizzie brushed her eyes against the little fellow's short fair hair. 'I am not sad, Mary.'

'Yes,' persisted her sister. 'I think you are very sad. At first I thought it was because the doctor took your necklace, but then I thought it was because you fought with Toby. Did he speak to you of money? You know his father has been writing cheques again?'

'Where has he gone, Mary? I heard him leave the house very early.'

'You should not be upset by what he says. He went to Gloucester with the convict.'

'He has left *London* with him?' said Lizzie, very much astonished.

'You know how he loves to rush about.'

'But how long is he gone?'

'Only two days.'

'Two days!'

'Lizzie, you make it sound a life-time.'

'Well it may be so,' said Lizzie darkly.

'Whatever do you mean?'

'He is your husband, Mary.'

'And whatever does *that* mean?'

'If he were the father of my child I would not permit him to travel so recklessly with a murderer. Why, poor little John, if something should happen . . .'

'Lizzie, nothing will happen. He is brewing up a story so he may sell it. We should not be too angry with him. Lizzie, you are crying.'

'I am crying to think of poor little John,' said Lizzie. 'I am crying that anyone could be so careless of his happiness.'

Mary was quiet then for a moment, and Lizzie saw the good slow soul was thinking.

'You are not thinking of our own papa, Lizzie?'

No, Lizzie had not been thinking of their papa. Their papa had never cared for her. It was Mary whom their papa had loved so.

'No,' she said, walking up and down before the window with little John sucking on her neck. 'No, I am thinking of Toby.' She was so very angry. She stood at the window looking out at the beautiful spring day and the urchins from the stables playing cricket in the middle of the street.

'It would be a dreadful thing for anyone to lose their papa,' said Mary. 'Or their husband, for that matter.'

Lizzie turned to look at Mary's sentimental little eyes.

'I am sad, Mary, I confess it. I really do think I should adopt a child. I think it would be very good for me. I'm sure it may be very hard to do in London, but why might I not go away? I could sell my necklace, Mary.'

'Is it something in your novel that is making you talk of this? Do you remember when Mama forbade you to read any more on account of all the notions you were getting from your novels? You will have your own husband in good time.'

'Can you see my future, Mary?' said Lizzie.

'Oh yes,' said Mary blithely. 'You will have ever so many children and you will have your own handsome husband and a splendid house and live next door and our children will all be friends and we will have Christmases together around a great oval table and Toby will perform his magic tricks.'

'And my husband?'

'Perhaps he will perform tricks too. We don't know who he is as yet.'

'I don't like him,' said Lizzie. 'I really do not see why I should not adopt a child.'

Mary frowned. 'Dear Lizzie.' She patted the sofa. 'Come, bring John and we will all sit together, and you can tell me the story of your book.'

And so, indeed, Lizzie did, and spent a very strange, and oddly exhilarating, hour as she invented a variation on *Castle Rackrent*.

But when the hour was finished, her condition was not altered and there was no one who could tell her what it was that she should do.

65

Dear Henry,

I write this with the borrowed quill of Tobias Oates, the author of *Captain Crumley*. The paper inside the yellow envelope contains facts most damaging to that individual.

Henry, even if you presently abominate me, remember what you had from me, and in honour of my generosity, do the following: If I am arrested and charged on that man's Information, make a copy of the paper and take it to his wife at Lamb's Conduit Street which is just north of the Inns of Court. I don't know where his Pater lives, but believe he goes by the moniker of the *Fighting Bantam* and *John the Cock*. Find him too, and whatever members of his family or associates you can learn of. Then go to Fleet Street, go to whichever Tap Room is preferred by those Gentlemen of the Pen. Buy these gents whatever takes their fancy and Mr John Plasse at the Temple will make up your expense one thousand-fold.

If I am not arrested, let Justice prevail – burn the letter.

Me and this Oates are on our way to Gloucester, but where we are at this moment, I do not know. It is a case of Jack-be-nimble, for the night is dark, the coach hard as a rough dray and my dreams are troubled by a Phantom who stares at me and makes threats against me. This creature has been recently introduced into my sleep by Magical Arts. Perhaps you, with your education, will know how he can be drawn out again.

We are promised Gloucester by dawn. There we seek the famous Thief-taker who can find any man between London and Cardiff – all this on your account. I blame myself for the way I withheld my true history from you. I left a blank map for you and you have doubtless filled it with your worst imaginings.

This letter I will entrust the Thief-taker, and in it you will find the end of the tale regarding myself and Sophina. Much relief I hope you may find in the truth. Then you may lay these pages aside and say – Ah, is this the monster I was so afraid of?

I previously related how Sophina and I did fall asleep and were discovered by the Ma, and although a great deal were made of the *five months* etc., I had no idea that she was with child. I wrote this? I think so.

Sophina and I were hurried from the house as if in close arrest, and Tom felt himself obliged to carry the great hessian bag of silver plate upon his back. The Ma told him to give it up, but he was a good son and a foolish thief, and struggled with it through the dark streets until, by Piccadilly, we managed to wake up the driver of a lonely cab. Once we were, all four of us, squashed in together with the stolen goods, all of the Ma's poison was turned on me.

She told me that I was to be punished and was kind enough to describe my treatment in advance of its execution. It was a new punishment, and now she drew the picture exactly: Tom was to pull my arms through a ladder and keep me pinned there so she could wield the strop.

It was an hour before dawn when we arrived back in Islington. The sky was still dark but I could hear the cocks crowing, as they will, before there was any need to do so.

Ma had me carry Silas's heavy ladder upstairs from the hallway. Then Tom helped me lay it on a slant against my bedroom wall, and then Ma made me lie against it while great hulking Tom – having sat himself obligingly on the floor beneath the ladder – pulled down on my arms so hard I feared they would be wrenched from my shoulders. I imagined I was being punished for being a filthy swine, but no one told me that I was to be assaulted for being the father of an unborn babe.

Ma, as I see now, was more concerned with business than our morals. She did not wish to lose her little girl-thief to motherhood, or me to Sophina. She needed both as servants to her cause. Thus she dealt with me in a manner very fierce.

Once she had me on the ladder, she hitched her skirts up in a style that revealed her white and muscled calves. She then retreated into the kitchen from whence she presently came running, and laid the strop down hard on me with an ugly grunt. Twenty times she did this, and though she were huffing and puffing at the end of it, there was not a stroke where she did not admonish Sophina to keep her

239

eyes upon my humiliation, or to take her hands off her ears so she might hear my cowardly cries.

Then it was done, and Tom let go my arms. So caught up was I with my own shame that I did not notice Ma take Sophina from my room, had no inkling of what fate there was for her, but the moment I heard her cry to me – *Jack, Jack* – I sprang up from my rack with the intention of coming to her aid.

I have gone over this moment all my life, and in my waking dreams I have oft seen myself reach my beloved on the stair, and there I have imagined myself to punch the Ma – yes, by God, I did say punch, and sometimes stab and sometimes slash with that great sword. I have dreamed, over and over, the happiness of saving Sophina, of running out into the dawn street – our babe alive – into our fresh young lives.

In the half-light before that dreary dawn, I got only part way across the kitchen before Tom settled me. He came down on top of me with all his might and held me hard against the floor with my arm jerked up behind my back. I was a big boy, fifteen years old, but he was all of twenty and he sat atop my bleeding bum heedless of whatever pain he caused me.

– You dirty little scrub, he said to me. You rag-tag, etcetera. He pushed my head down against the boards and I can, to this day, feel that splintered surface against my cheek, hear Sophina's tearful voice in the hateful little room below. Much of the Ma's speech I did not hear exactly, but the following I did.

You want me to fetch Tom so he can hold you still?

Now I am going to tell you something which you may think unlikely – I imagined Sophina being beaten much as I had been.

You want Tom to come and look at you like this?

I did not see my beloved until the bright light of day came to the kitchen, and then she appeared, standing at the open door, and I – recently released by Tom and now sitting at the table drinking tea – looked up at her.

Her face was wan. Her hand was resting on her pinny. When she caught my eyes, she turned away and walked into our room.

I leaped up but Tom laid his hand on my shoulder.

– Now leave her be, you dirty little swine.

Still I would have gone to her, but he took me by the arm and, by virtue of his superior strength, was able to detain me at his pleasure.

– You come with me, Mr Mutt-sucker, said Tom, and thereupon did take me down through the house, down through the horrid little plain room, out towards the privy and the thistles to the brick wall, then along the little dirt track beside the wall, up and over a collapsing drain, and round the end of the wall. And here the smell was very bad – all kinds of excrement and rottenness.

Here Tom forced me to stoop and kneel beside the little drain as it pushed its way under the cheese shop. He kept me pinned, jerking my arm back a little now and then to remind me of the pain, and all the while he poked into the filth with a stick.

– Look here, he said.

I feared he meant to push me into the cess pit, and so was undefended against the real assault.

Thus, I looked.

– See, said Tom, it looks like a toad.

There lay our son – the poor dead mite was such a tiny thing. I could have held him in my hand. And on his queerly familiar little face, a cruel and dreadful cut.

Cannot write more at this time.

P.S. Went to sleep and woke to find Oates with hand familiarly on my knee. Says he, were you dreaming, Jack Maggs?

I told him, no, I weren't.

That were a lie – the Phantom above-mentioned had appeared to me. I saw *It* sitting opposite me in the coach. Yellow hair, long side whiskers, blue frock coat with gold buttons.

I said to *It*, is it you?

It replied, yes it was. Then *It* lay its hand upon my head and the hand so cold it burned me. I cried out, and woke to find the coach filled with strangers.

We gallop through the endless night, eleven miles the hour and candles sputtering.

66

It was barely sun-up when they came to the crown of Burlip Hill, and all of Gloucester could be seen rising above a light low mist in the great dish of the Vale. The coach stopped, and the guard and driver entered into earnest consultation, at the conclusion of which it was suggested that the ladies and gentlemen might like to view the road ahead. If you yourself have viewed Burlip Hill, you will understand why, at half past five of a spring morning, Jack and Tobias and their fellow passengers decided to abandon the comfort of the coach and walk in ankle-deep mud down the road while the *True Briton* descended with all its locked brakes screaming against the wheels.

The slippery surface of Burlip Hill muddied the backside of more than one passenger, but Maggs impatiently galloped the slope towards his promised Thief-taker. It was, he observed, as pretty a scene as you would see in all of England – the land divided by hedges into fields and orchards, and the whole picture, with the Cathedral in the middle and the Morvan Hills of Wales in the distance, 'was worth the price of twice the mud'.

Of course, the ruffian was excited. His eyes were bright and everywhere about him. Twice he sneezed, loudly, and blew his nose like a trumpet at the dawn. Even as he loped down the hill he carried his three wrapped parcels – mirror, lemons, paper – as though the Thief-taker were ready to receive him at the bottom of the hill.

The writer, now contemplating his imminent disgrace, was in a darker mood entirely. He had in truth never met this Thief-taker. He had no address for him, only Dr Eliotson's assurance that messages left at the Bull would reach him. Eliotson, although perfectly respectable, was also given to both vagueness and naivety. It was a foolish and dangerous position he had placed himself in.

When the coach arrived in Southgate Street, it was Jack who found out where the Bull Inn was. He set off towards the Cross, carrying his parcels before him. Tobias – known for his brisk and energetic walk – was forced to skip to keep the pace.

Maggs's unbuttoned oil-skin, that garment he referred to as his Great Joseph, floated behind him like a cape as he strode the streets of Gloucester, past Mercer's Entry, and down into Bull Lane where they found a very decent-looking little inn with a sign proclaiming *Entertainment for Horse and Man*. It being so early in the morning, the tap room was empty, and there were chairs on tables, and the smell of soap fighting with the stale odours of the pipe and brandy bottle. The sound of pouring liquid, however, gave away the whereabouts of the landlord who was down behind the bar, seated on a three-legged stool, filling a line of bottles from a cask.

He was a narrow man of less than middle age, with a long hard face and a little slit of a mouth that was not hidden by his beard. He had the poached-egg eyes of a man who enjoyed the stuff he sold, and these eyes, blood-shot and a little yellow in the whites, considered Jack Maggs with some considerable astonishment.

'Jod's blood,' said he.

'Now ain't this a treat!' said Maggs in a tone that seemed very jovial.

'I don't owe you nothing, Jack.'

'I never said you did, George Conklin.'

George Conklin looked sharply and briefly at Tobias, and returned his attention to Jack Maggs. 'I'm Herbert Holt.' He hesitated. 'We are settled on that business. I don't owe you nothing.'

'Aye, we're square, mate,' said Maggs who now turned to survey the tap room: and a very neat and prosperous tap room it was, decorated with all manner of brass gew-gaws, and Toby jugs. It was the sort of house, Tobias felt, in which one would see solicitors and merchants gather to discuss their affairs, where you might expect to see a judge, still gowned and wigged, come to sit by the fire with his cheese and claret.

'If we're square, why're you looking for me?'

'I ain't.'

The landlord, having accepted this with obvious scepticism, now transferred his attention to Jack's three parcels. 'If you been talking

243

to the silver again, I retired. I'm sorry, Jack. Don't take it personal. I sell nothing here but what is up and up.'

'We're both gentlemen then, George.'

'Herbert,' he corrected.

There was then a longish period of silence while the landlord frankly appraised his visitor's attire. 'I wouldn't wear a red waistcoat, Jack,' he said at last. 'Not in your position. A red waistcoat is going to catch the eye. It is like a rule of nature, that it is the poisonous things that got the stripe of red upon them.'

'Bullshit, George.'

'Herbert.'

'Herbert, do you know a cove named Partridge?'

The long-faced man's mouth contracted. Silence.

'You know him?'

'Aye. Wilf Partridge. He who found the missing Duke. I knew him when he were a hedge creeper in Kent.'

'They say he can find any cove in England once he sets his mind to it.'

'They?' The landlord shrugged. 'They say also he is a witch, or at least is married one.'

'But you know him?' asked Tobias. 'He is nearby?'

Herbert Holt glanced at Tobias Oates and then looked away. He bent and collected half a dozen bottles of spirits and silently stoppered them. 'I'll get you the Private Room, Jack,' he said at last. 'But you'll not be staying in the house, and you'll use the back door when you leave. No, no need to pay me.'

'Very generous, Herbert.'

'Now you and your mate, listen to me,' said Herbert. 'This Private Room was given for a meeting of the Wanderers' Society, and that won't matter for the morning, but if you're still there at noon time they'll be none too happy. They wouldn't be happy to know I gave their room to a fellow in a red waistcoat. So it's best you lock the door from the inside, and don't let them in. If Partridge comes, I'll give him a key.'

'No one's going to recognize me, Herbert.'

'I recognized you, Jack. Very nice too, very nice to see you, but that's enough. You stay in there and don't come out for nothing. I'll send the boy to put the word around for Partridge, and you can pray he ain't in Bristol again, for if he's not here by evening, you shan't stay here, Jack, and no knife is going to help you. It isn't personal.'

'Where there's no cheating, Herbert, there's no knife.'

'I've got mates here, in the lane.'

'You wouldn't shop me, George?'

'I couldn't be that civilized, Jack, if you take my meaning. I couldn't risk the association, like.'

And with that the stringy landlord shepherded his unwanted guests through the tap room, down a half-set of stairs and along a corridor to a room which was, in spite of the gold-leaf letters on the door, a charmless hole. The windows were small and uncurtained; it had bare distempered walls, and furnishings consisting of nothing more than a long table and two mucky benches that appeared to have just been brought in from some barn where they had long been banished.

Tobias loathed the room, but he sat at the wobbling bench and slowly picked the dried mud from his boots and trousers. Jack Maggs stayed at the window, peering out into the dismal yard where, presumably, the horses found their entertainment.

Time passed slowly. It began to rain. The writer opened up his attaché case but his fingers were unpleasantly dry with the mud of Burlip Hill, and he could not bring himself to unscrew the ink bottle. Out of the window he saw an old man chop the head off a rooster, and the old man and a hostler stood and laughed while the headless bird ran flapping round the yard. The convict noticed the same event and his broad and powerful figure soon occupied the embrasure of the window, thus blocking out the light. The symbolism of this was not lost on Tobias. How deep had he sunk into the slough. One sin had led him to the next. Each danger spawned a bigger danger and now he was cast down into a room with a man whom he had cheated. He closed his attaché case and locked it. He had come a long way from his God.

At noon there was a rattling on the door knob, and both men looked up expectantly.

'Oh drat,' they heard a woman's voice. 'This is very very poor, you know. Very poor indeed.'

Thus, in the space of an hour, the two men suffered the raising and dashing of their hopes by ten different visitors. The door was tried, rattled, but no one came in, not even a servant with the vittles Jack was convinced his 'previous acquaintance' would send to them. They sat with their stomachs rumbling loudly, and when the key finally entered the lock it was hard to say what Tobias wished for more: the Thief-taker or his luncheon.

In either case he was disappointed. The door opened to reveal a clergyman, a black-clad fellow, with bushy brows sitting low upon his eyes.

'I beg your pardon,' said Tobias, rising. 'The room is taken.'

Yet so confident was the visitor of his rights that he shut the door behind him. He carried a big calico parcel tied under one arm and a black and knobbly walking stick under the other.

'Wrong room,' said Jack, hurrying forward so violently that Tobias was reminded it was a fight about a private room that had his father in jail for murder. He put his hand on Jack's shoulder to restrain him.

'This room is ours,' cried Jack. He flung Toby's hand away and took the intruder by the elbow.

To this assault, the clergyman raised an eyebrow.

'Mr Maggs?'

'Who says so?' demanded Jack.

'You say so, Sir,' said the clergyman, and shook himself free. 'If you were not Mr Maggs, you would say, *I am not Mr Maggs*, and that would be that. If you say, *Who wants to know?*, you have admitted it. *Q.E.D.*'

Toby saw the tic quiver on the convict's cheek.

'Are you perchance a Wanderer, Sir?' Tobias asked.

He was answered by one more invader, a woman, who promptly took a seat at the table.

'Not us,' said she.

67

'You are Jack Maggs,' said the clergyman in a voice which evidenced a rougher calling than his collar indicated. 'And I am he whose acquaintance you were so eager to make.'

'*You* are the Thief-taker?' asked Tobias, much relieved.

'If you wish him to remain in your company, Sir,' said the woman, 'don't never call him that.' She was very plain and stocky with straight grey hair cut in a brutal fringe. Now, in her chagrin, she was giving off a strong odour of a cellar: earth, onions, something worse. 'It were a term used in ignorance.'

Toby was not pleased to be talked to in this style by one so low-bred. 'Indeed, Madam?' He looked to her husband but found – to his considerable astonishment – that Wilfred Partridge expected an apology for being called a Thief-taker.

It was then, so early in the transaction, that Tobias knew the Partridges for tyrants. *God help me if I ever fell under their power. Why, they would have me eating sawdust and picking locks for breakfast.*

But Jack Maggs seemed oblivious of Partridge's character.

'We apologize,' he said. Toby was shocked to see how that pugnacious old body did bend itself so easily. 'We had no wish to offend your Lordship.' He reached urgently into his gunny sack and brought forth the wrapped papers, the mirror, the lemons, stacking them one atop the other.

Without abandoning his injured stance, Mr Partridge now contributed his own package to the table. It was a large oblong parcel about the size of *The Times*, but three or four inches thick.

'I am not a Lord,' he corrected Maggs.

'If you truly can find any man in England,' said Jack, 'I will call you Duke or Baron.'

'Plain Mister will serve me very well.' Wilfred Partridge untied a knot and wound the string around his liver-spotted hand. Then he tied the twine with a loop and placed it on the bench. Next he peeled back several layers of wrapping: the first one calico, the next two coarse brown paper, the remainder, a yellow tissue like that often used by milliners. Finally, having tormented Jack Maggs considerably with his delay, he revealed a very learned-looking leather volume with a great deal of gold filigree on the cover and, on the spine, an artfully tooled crest. The scholarly appearance of this book reminded Toby of the company in which he had learned of Wilfred Partridge's name; this now softened him towards the fellow.

'I do believe,' he offered, 'we have a mutual acquaintance.'

Wilfred Partridge considered Tobias Oates without interest.

'My friend, Dr Eliotson.'

'There are many men of science,' said Mrs Partridge, coldly, 'who have studied my husband's powers.'

'Mr Partridge is a student of Animal Magnetism. You studied with M. Labatte,' Tobias addressed the husband. 'Dr Eliotson wrote a paper on your Magnetic techniques. He was particularly impressed with the case of . . . who was it? You interviewed the witnesses Magnetically and then made the arrest yourself?'

'Eliotson?' the other responded moodily. 'I don't recall.'

'It is published in *The Zoist*.'

'I am published everywhere,' said Wilfred Partridge, opening his book to reveal, on the first page, a yellow newspaper clipping glued to the middle of a large white sheet.

'Did I not,' Partridge brooded angrily beneath his heavy brows, 'did I not find Emily Tudball who was taken from her mother's arms?'

'He did,' cried his wife, pointing at a long glue-stained column of yellow newspaper:

EMILY TUDBALL IS FOUND.

'Did I not find the body of Lord Thompson when everyone said he was touring in the Pyrenees?'

'He did,' announced his wife, and placed a close-bitten finger nail against the item:

LORD THOMPSON IS DEAD.

They had a long litany to complete between them and it took a good five minutes, and in all that Mrs Partridge did not vary her response by so much as a word.

'And how is it, Sir, that you work your art?' asked Toby once the case histories had all been recited. 'Where do you stand on the issue of Magnetic Fluid?'

'No Magnetizer can doubt the Fluid,' said Wilfred Partridge, indicating the leather-bound reports of his success, 'but the Fluid stays in its puddle without the good faith of the subject.'

'Faith?' cried Maggs. 'By Jesus. We come from London. Ain't that faith enough to get the Fluids gushing?'

'Mr Partridge,' said his wife, 'requires a personal sign.'

'I'm here. What more personal than that?'

Mr Partridge closed the book. 'By personal,' he said, 'my missus is referring to two most personal matters.'

'Money,' said she.

'How much money?' asked Tobias.

'Fifteen on the table.'

'Shillings?'

'Pounds.'

Toby drew in his breath loudly, but the Partridges both kept their eyes on Jack Maggs, whose manner remained uncharacteristically amicable. 'What was the second matter?'

'The second matter,' said Wilfred Partridge, beginning to re-wrap his parcel, 'would be an item, any item at all, however small, that is personal to the object of our quest.'

'How *personal*?' asked Jack.

'Something that the party has laid his hand upon, Mr Maggs. Something that the surface of his skin has brushed across. A toy, a hairbrush.'

Jack Maggs put his hand deep inside his Great Joseph, and brought into the light an extravagantly framed enamel miniature which he had kept hidden, mostly, in his trouser pocket. Now he revealed to the company an exceedingly well-bred young man in a blue coat, a white cravat. The character thus portrayed was most familiar to Toby, although he could not immediately place him. The young man seemed at once proud and companionable; although his light blue eyes were averted, his countenance was animated. The oval frame was silver and decorated, exotically, with stars.

249

'That's my son,' said Jack Maggs proudly. 'Mr Henry Phipps, Esquire.'

This was the first time Toby had any intimation of Jack Maggs's very personal relationship with the tenant of the house in Great Queen Street. In the midst of his astonishment he was struck by the father's proud bright eyes as he offered the enamel portrait of his son to Wilfred Partridge.

He is waiting to have the lad admired, thought Toby.

If it was so, Partridge must have disappointed him. He did not look at the portrait at all but, having closely scrutinized the hallmarks on the gorgeous frame, handed the object to his wife.

'They all do leave a little of themselves,' said she. Toby noted that she also looked carefully at the hallmarks. 'They brush against it, they leave themselves behind.'

'It is a good likeness.'

'The question is, Sir, did he touch it recently? Was it in his possession?'

'The point is, Mum, I'm looking for my son.'

Mrs Partridge slid the little portrait away from her. 'If he hasn't touched it, it is of no use to Mr Partridge. We don't wants what he looks like. We wants where he is.'

Tobias saw, or thought he saw, such a profound look of sadness on his companion's face that he felt compelled to take a lance against his tormentors. 'Madam, you are making very little sense.'

For thanks, his own man turned on him. 'That's enough of that,' said Jack Maggs.

'Wait,' said the wife. 'I can feel that you have something we can use.' And produced, as if from nowhere, two small locks of children's hair. 'His hair!' declared Mrs Partridge, her face now taking on a reddish sheen.

'Get out of my pocket,' Jack Maggs cried, snatching the hair away from her. 'That's private.'

'That's the boy's hair,' insisted the woman. 'That's our man, Wilf. It's the son's hair. I won't be contradicted.'

This was all uttered in a fierce and certain sort of way. Tobias was surprised to see that Maggs was, in some sense, cowed by it. There was a furtive, shame-faced air about him when he spoke again.

'Damn you. It ain't the one I want.'

Tobias had no time to wonder at this information, for now the clergyman was rising like a warrior in his seat.

'You'll not *damn* my wife, Sir,' said he.

The convict hesitated. Then he sighed, and sat slowly down, his head resting in his hands. 'The hair don't belong to Henry Phipps,' he said.

The clergyman now picked up the portrait from the table and carefully appraised it as closely as a jeweller. He passed it to his wife, who then placed the portrait against her ear, as if it were a seashell.

It was obvious to Tobias – indeed, it would have been obvious to a sensible child – that the Partridges were charlatans, but as the blunt-nosed little pick-pocket lowered the portrait from her ear, Jack Maggs waited humbly for her verdict. Tobias was touched, against all his expectation, by the eager way he leaned towards the woman. How sad, Tobias thought, the Somnambulist had become.

When the two Partridges begged that they might be excused to consult further in private, Jack Maggs suggested that he and Tobias Oates leave the room.

68

Toby drew his companion down into the dark end of the passage where someone had stacked some wooden saddle frames and then left them rotting on the floor.

'So, Master Maggs,' he whispered, 'what is your opinion?'

The convict's face had, on the whole, a rather frozen quality but his eyes were now glistening with excitement.

'They know their onions, that's for sure. The only thing against us – my Henry never touched his own portrait.'

'Did you note the way they looked at it?'

'It weren't what they wanted.'

'They each read the hallmarks first. Is the frame valuable?'

'I would not frame his portrait with rubbish, that's a fact.'

251

'Jack, we are being swindled.'

'It is not Partridge?'

'It is Partridge, yes.'

'How swindled? No, I don't believe you. Trust me, mate, I know the game.'

'And trust me, Master Maggs. This is mumbo jumbo. He cannot find anyone by placing a silver frame against his ear.'

'It don't work?'

'It cannot.'

Jack looked down at Tobias Oates, looked at him very hard. 'But this is the same cove you vouched for.'

'Now, Jack, that ain't quite it. He was vouched for by Dr Eliotson. And I am sure he performed the act my friend attributed to him.'

Maggs's face contorted, a whole ugly spasm that passed from his eye down to his mouth. 'You promised me I would find my son,' he said coldly. His brows were down hard on his eyes. 'That was our understanding. It was for this, and only this, I wasted all my frigging time? Why would I make myself a fart-catcher? Why would I be a lackey to that ugly little wretch?'

Toby was afraid, but he stood very still and held the convict's eye.

'I'm sorry, Jack, from the bottom of my heart. I also have a son. It is not hard for me to understand your feelings.'

This did nothing to calm Jack Maggs at all. Indeed it had the opposite effect. He began to drum a foot upon the boards. Toby took a half-step backwards.

'You understand nothing,' cried the other, brushing roughly past him and coming back up into the passageway. 'You can hoodwink me into taking off my shirt, but you don't know a rat's fart about me.' A great flood of colour had risen in Jack Maggs's face. 'You steal my Fluid but you can't imagine who I am, you little fribble. What was that noise?'

'I do believe,' said Toby, whose heart was pounding very hard, 'that they've locked us out.'

Uttering a curse, the convict literally *spun* upon his heel. In two strides he was at the door to which he administered such a mighty kick that it was brought screeching off its hinges and thus revealed, like a stage curtain raised through misadventure, the two actors in a state of some embarrassment.

That is, the Partridges had the window open, and Mrs Partridge already had one leg out into the court, and one blue-veined ham-bone showing to the room. Mr Partridge was by her side, his wide-brimmed hat back upon his head, the partially wrapped portrait still in his hand.

Jack's three parcels were still on the table, but the Partridges' bound volume was nowhere in sight.

Jack Maggs came across the room, moving with a grace his bulk had hitherto concealed. He moved like an acrobat, or a dancer whose steps, being much practised, appear more natural than they are. To be particular: he crossed the bleak little room crouched queerly low but with his stride undiminished, a contortion demanded by his need to withdraw a knife from inside his boot.

There was then a very loud explosion, and Tobias was confused about its cause until he saw a pistol fall onto the floor and smelled the distinctive odour of gunpowder. But even when the pistol lay revealed, he still did not understand that Wilfred Partridge had fired it at Jack Maggs.

Mr Partridge was sitting on the sill. Then Maggs stepped back from him, and Toby saw the blood on the Thief-taker's shirt and imagined he had been wounded by this pistol. Then he saw: Wilfred Partridge's throat was cut. His hand was holding the wound. Bright red blood streamed through his fingers, down his arm, across the face of the miniature portrait which Jack Maggs was now brutally prying from his hand.

Wilfred Partridge fell into the room. His head hit the floor very hard.

The convict turned, the bloody portrait in one hand, a rough black blade in the other. He looked Tobias Oates threateningly in the eye and thus they stood the two of them, the one with the power to take away life, breathing heavily, the other hardly daring to draw breath.

Toby thought: I am a dead man now.

It was then, facing the warrant he imagined in those dark brown eyes, that he spoke the words: 'Come, Jack. Quickly. We must run.'

69

Jack Maggs had bolted, she knew not where. He had departed as he had first come in, in mufti. He had not spoken, not even waved. She had looked up from the kitchen window and seen him walk up Great Queen Street with his kit-bag across his shoulder. That night, after midnight, she went across the roof again, but the house was cold and frightening. She knew then: he had gone for good.

If the master knew his whereabouts, he was not saying. Indeed it seemed that Jack Maggs's departure had allowed all Percy Buckle's bottled feelings to spill out in a stinking rage. Mercy knew what her offence had been, and yet it could not be spoken of.

The master had seemed, in the shadow of Jack Maggs, a plain little thing, but in the quiet that followed the latter's departure she saw what a false perception that had been. Mr Buckle was her life, her safety. Her association with Jack Maggs had humiliated him to a degree she had been too intoxicated to see at the time.

Now he would not permit her to so much as pour his tea for him. Thrice she went to him unbidden; thrice he ordered her back to the kitchen.

She was ill. She could not eat. She assisted Miss Mott as she was ordered, working with her back towards the light so the cook might not see the hot tears falling onto the liver she was preparing for dinner.

'Wherever he has gone to, dearie,' said she, 'it's better off for you.'

'I don't know what you mean, I'm sure.'

'If I was you I'd be running up stairs and taking the master a plate of that toast and cinnamon he is so partial to.'

'He don't want no truck with me today.'

'You get up there and get back in the master's good books or God knows what sort of life you're going to have.'

She knew what sort of life. She knew it exactly. She saw the stinking little room in Fetter Lane. She saw the Haymarket, the vile dress with its gaudy ribbons.

'Go on, git.' Miss Mott took forcible possession of her three-legged stool, and pushed its sniffling occupant aside. She took the knife from the maid's hand. 'That other is a hard man. You can see it in his beak. He's not the man for you, girl. Go, wash your hands now. Make the master his toast, there's a good miss.'

Miss Mott then took charge of the liver, lowering her little wire spectacles so she could see the veins the better. 'Do what I say, and one day I might have the pleasure of calling you Madam. Fetch me the flour, that's a girl.'

Mercy walked slowly down into the pantry. Her legs felt weak and wobbly, her bowels loose. She returned with a cup of flour. She watched as Miss Mott spread it across the table and dredged the slices of liver in it.

'Now bring me the loaf, Mercy, and I will cut it thin the way he likes it.'

Thus Mercy called on Mr Buckle a fourth time. She knocked hesitantly on the snuggery door, and entered. He was at his precious bureau, quill in hand, but it was his eyes she noticed first, how naked they were: his hurt was plain to her now.

'A little bit of something,' she offered. It was a way of speaking she was accustomed to use in their more personal moments together, and it was certainly a risk to use it now. But he did not immediately reject her, and she carefully set a small lace doily close by his ink bottle, then lay the toast in front of him.

'Shall I make a nice pot of Orange Pekoe for you, Sir?'

Percy Buckle stared mutely at the toast. The four slices were soaked with butter, sprinkled with ground cinnamon. They were laid one atop the other and sliced into lady-fingers.

'Is he gone for good?' he muttered angrily.

'I do not know, Sir. He did not say so, Sir.'

She watched him nibble cautiously at his toast. Then she gave him her treasure. She had no other currency to offer: it was everything she had.

'If he ain't gone, Sir, I know how we could make him go. I have discovered where his Henry Phipps is hidden.'

Mr Buckle finished his lady-finger and took a second. His appetite appeared to be returning.

255

'You did not tell him you had this information?'

'Oh no, Sir. I wouldn't do that, Sir.'

'But how do you know such a secret, Mercy?'

'Well, it seems that Mr Constable visited Mr Phipps at the gentleman's club. He discovered that Mr Phipps is no friend to Jack Maggs, and so he did not inform Jack Maggs that Mr Phipps was found, not wishing to make him angry, Sir.'

'Are you sure you did not tell Jack Maggs?'

'Oh no, Sir. Never. I would not want to make him angry either, him being a convict and all. He would be ever so upset to know he was hated by his son.'

'His son!'

'He told Mr Constable that Mr Phipps was his son.'

'But Mr Phipps is a gentleman!'

Mr Buckle's astonishment was so great that he seemed, for this moment anyway, to forget his umbrage.

'Good Lord,' said he. 'And hated by him? I do not wonder. A son, and hated. Hated by his own son. Son? It is beyond belief. The convict owns the house next door? Pretends to be my footman, but owns the freehold? So, Mr Phipps . . . his son. Why, I'd wager his fortune all comes from our Jack Maggs. It's convict gold, that's what it is.'

'I couldn't say, Sir.'

'And now this Mr Phipps, he doesn't like Jack Maggs?'

'No, Sir. He hides from him.'

'Well, who can blame the gentleman? Dirty money. Thievery. Murder. Of course he would hide. He don't want Jack Maggs trampling through his life. But what if the rascal cuts off all his funds? Disinheritance: it may be on the cards, Mercy. It must be on the cards, by gosh.'

'It's true that Henry Phipps hoped that Mr Constable was bringing him the title of a property.'

'Then there you are,' said Mr Buckle. 'Then there you are exactly. That's his worry. That's a very big worry for a gentleman to have. Disinheritance. He fears he will lose his house, poor devil.'

Mr Buckle then set upon his toast most hungrily.

'This Mr Phipps,' he said, 'could turn out to be a very dangerous person for our Master Maggs.'

And with that he smiled at Mercy. She was back. She was safe. She would never be so foolish ever again.

70

Tobias could never have seriously imagined himself running away with Wilfred Partridge's murderer. Yet once the two men had passed a policeman in Bull Lane, no further moment presented itself when he could easily extricate himself, and so he continued to accompany Jack Maggs in the direction indicated by the other's elbow. No word passed between them.

Tobias did not look at his companion. However, he was almost neurasthenically aware of his force, his heat, his potential for further violence.

As they came down to the place where Westgate Street runs into the quay, they found themselves amongst a mob of foreign sailors who, crowding urgently around a seated officer, made a dense and rum-sour knot upon the cobblestones. Here was Tobias's chance, and he took it, slipping back amongst the sailors, pushing through them towards the peelers.

Yet at the very moment the bobbies came into view, he saw this was no freedom at all. It was in his interests to keep Jack Maggs out of the dock. If Jack were guilty of murder, Toby was guilty of being his accessory; if Jack were a bolter, it was Toby who had knowingly, criminally, harboured him. Of course he was a man of letters but he had been a Fleet Street hack himself and knew that, once he was in the dock, the Press would feast no less greedily on one of their own. He did not need to consider the explosive secrets Jack Maggs might add to this conflagration.

And so he turned his back on Robert Peel's men and quickly found Jack Maggs again. Reunited, they walked calmly down towards the Severn. There they leaned casually over an iron rail and peered down into the mist-shrouded river.

'Tide,' said his fellow conspirator, very casual in his manner. 'Ebbing,' he said, pointing down at a willow branch drifting slowly to the south.

Tobias watched those light green leaves drag in the current, and felt an unexpected sensation, like cool water, running along his neck. He looked at Jack Maggs, who winked at him. Tobias watched the willow branch and, as it was swallowed by the mist, thought that he too might have his freedom, and a larger freedom than anything he had imagined when he had fretted at his pennies and his pounds on London Bridge.

He would flee!

He would flee wherever Jack Maggs fled. It was not his fault he had to flee. He had no choice but flee. He would flee anywhere he damn well chose. He might invent himself again, as Simon Winchester in Jamaica, or Cecil Gunnerson in Cape Town, or Phineas O'Brien in Boston.

Once he had glimpsed this possibility, a wild, conscienceless beast rose in his breast and turned his cheeks pink and his lips an extraordinary red. 'We can take ship here, in Gloucester? If you buy my ticket now, I'll make the money later. You have my word – I can make the money.'

The convict looked narrowly at the excited young man. Then, without further response, he hoisted his kit-bag onto his shoulder and walked slowly towards the end of the quay where a lock-keeper's cottage was perched between the basin and the river. Here, without explanation, he climbed its garden fence.

Maggs's hessian boots trampled lettuces, broke carrot stalks. Tobias took the same course. He put one hand in his pocket and jiggled his change while he strolled though a wicket labelled *Private*, and then along a pretty cobbled path (which was, on this fifth day of May, bordered with primroses) and thence to a steep set of steps leading down to the river.

From that giddy precipice, Tobias looked down on the sorry-looking little punt which was tied up at the landing. This was not the sort of ship he had had in mind. He looked across the silky surface of the Severn, and remembered that it was a famously

258

difficult river with fierce tides and the dreadful Severn Bore which came rushing up from the sea on a crest six feet high.

He halted.

The convict gave a small blackbird whistle from the water's edge.

There was now a considerable distance between the two men, thirty steps. Jack Maggs came to the bottom of the wall and squinted anxiously up, as if seeing, for the first time, just how easily he now might be betrayed. To judge from the pinched look upon his worn-out face, he might have been staring at the gallows themselves, but Tobias had moved past betrayal, beyond the point where a small and sorry-looking punt could make him hesitate for long, and he was soon running down the mossy steps to the landing. Here he undid the rope, and stepped aboard.

'Now sit on the mid-thwart,' said Jack Maggs.

The mist closed mercifully around them. The river sucked them slowly, inexorably, down towards the sea.

71

At first the journey was sluggish and malodorous. The mist stank of the tannery but it was also a good opaque yellow and hid their escape. In any case, they had not been travelling ten minutes before it became obvious that their pace was quickening, and soon the little punt was rushing forward through the waters at a speed its builder would never have anticipated. The broad square-nosed craft handled well enough, and Jack soon lay his pole down and allowed himself to squat near the aft-thwart and give his fellow traveller a wink. This period of rest lasted all of a minute, then the big fellow was on his feet again and squinting down-stream into the mist.

'What's that?' he asked.

'Is there a ship?'

'Listen.'

Toby slowly became aware of a distant roaring.

'There may be factories along the shore.'

259

'That ain't no factory.' Maggs leaned forward, took his kit-bag and set it firm between his knees.

'There are tanneries. That's what the smell is.'

'Get aft. Jod's blood, move your arse, man.'

Toby reluctantly did as he was ordered. He sat on the aft-thwart beside Jack Maggs. The noise of rushing water – for such was clearly what it was – now filled his ears. Following Maggs's example he placed his yellow attaché between his legs and gripped it with his heels.

'Dear Lord – is this the Severn Bore?'

'Hang on, mate.'

It was not the Severn Bore but it was the weir, and they were on the lip of it before the danger was apparent. Then the convict did something which later, in recollection, would touch Tobias's heart: that is, he put one strong arm around the writer's narrow shoulders and held him tight.

The punt was catapulted out into the air.

Maggs cried: 'God save us!'

To hear such a cry, from one such as he, was enough to convince Tobias that his end was near.

He too cried out: 'God save us!'

The drop was nearly three feet at that hour, and when the little punt smacked down, its nose bit into the foaming river and the waters engulfed the craft completely.

'Swim!' cried Toby.

But the older man held him tight until the punt emerged, still afloat, but with less than three inches of gunnel showing above the water.

'We're sinking.'

'Bail! Give that to me!' Jack Maggs grabbed for the yellow case. 'It's all we have to bail with.'

The river was still turbulent and fast, and the square nose, being so low, seemed to invite the incursion of more water every passing second. Tobias therefore opened his lovely case, removed his soggy notebook and, having sadly consigned his quill and ink bottle to the river, offered the case to Maggs.

'You wish *me* to do the bailing?' Tobias was shocked to see the temper burning in his eyes. 'I ain't your fart-catcher now, mate.'

Tobias silently slid his wet notebook into his jacket pocket, and got busy with the bailing.

Thus they proceeded down-stream: Maggs standing guard with his pole and keeping the punt away from the shoals and banks, Tobias ruining his expensive attaché case with river water.

The mist stayed low but their noses soon told them that they had left the region of water meadows and that they were passing between new-mown fields. Tobias – having, by dint of much labour, reduced the water to ankle level – trailed his cramped hand in the silky cold water.

Maggs set down his pole and watched with satisfaction as the punt sat itself mid-stream and drifted. He observed the craft's progress for a moment, and when he was satisfied that it could find its own way a while, he took from his coat the enamel miniature which had cost the Thief-taker his life. This gore-stained object he laid on the aft-thwart of the boat while he carefully removed his great-coat, and then turned its bloodied pocket inside out. Drawing his dagger, he then cut out the pocket, and dropped it into the Severn like so much offal. Having carefully washed the dagger's dark blade, he dipped the portrait over the side and washed it also.

After a little time they drifted close by the bank, where they were confronted by the sight of a young woman and her old mother fishing for eels. When Tobias saw how they stared into the mist towards the silent punt, he raised a hand, and called, 'Good evening'. The girl waved back, but then the woman said something and the daughter's hand abruptly dropped.

Soon they were alone again in the mist, and Maggs, dipping his precious portrait in the Severn one last time, handed it across to Toby.

'Were it my purse he would have been welcome to it, but not my boy.'

The frame was slippery from the river water, and it was difficult for the writer not to think of the blood that had so recently washed over it. The light was now rather poor, and yet when Tobias held the enamel up very close to him he saw what he had not noticed when examining it in the Bull Inn. The likeness had seemed familiar, he realized now, because it was George IV dressed as a commoner. The Order of the Garter was absent. He wore a plain blue jacket, not the uniform of the Prince of Wales Light Dragoons, but this little miniature was, to all intents and purposes, a copy of Richard Cosway's portrait which Tobias had viewed, only last year, at the Royal Academy.

'Were he to have stolen my gold watch, he would not have suffered so,' said Jack Maggs, standing and picking up the pole which he then dove vigorously into the water. 'But he were a foolish man to steal my son.'

As the punt came forward he began to wield the pole regularly, bending his strong body effortlessly to the purpose.

'You have not seen your son in a goodly while?' Tobias asked carefully.

'To answer your question,' said Maggs, jutting his chin, and gazing at Tobias a moment, 'he ain't my son by way of having lain with his ma, but he is my son in every other way.'

The little craft drifted around a rather sharp bend by a cottage, and for a moment Maggs was busy navigating with his pole, but even when he had piloted the craft into the next long stretch, he did not pick up the conversation and Toby, curious as he was, thought it wisest to remain silent. In any case, he judged it kindest to let the fraud remain.

'It were a rainy autumn day,' Maggs said at last. 'A cold miserable sort of day, with a bitter wind blowing low and hard across the marshes, and the off-side lead horse of my coach threw its shoe.

'That is how I met Henry. He were sitting in the smithy's forge, looking for that place by the vice where he could feel a little of the warmth and not suffer any of the rain. When our coach drew up, there he were. He were all of four years old.'

It was almost dark now, although Tobias could still make out the outline of the smallish elms. If there was anyone on the banks with an interest in the fugitives, they were careful to keep their presence concealed.

'It were an honest everyday coach, with honest everyday citizens inside, but outside two wretches were held hard in chains. The first wretch was a poor mad forger from Hull who was trying to hurt himself by ripping at his arms with his bare teeth. The second wretch was me. We were, this mad man and I, in the care of two soldiers who took it in turns to be outside with us. They had spent all their food allowance on ale, and had no means to feed either us or themselves no more.

'My Henry had a pig's trotter. That was how I noticed him. And, oh, how I wanted that pig's trotter, Toby. I wanted it every bit as bad as you want your Lizzie. And I stared at him, doubtless, most fierce and wild. And what did he do? Why, first he ran away. But then, two shakes later, his little head appeared up amongst the baggage on the coach and he held out the very thing I might have stolen from him. When he saw my chains would not allow me to eat it without assistance, he did the holding for me, so I could gnaw each morsel off that bone.'

'Very kind,' said Toby.

'I'm much of your opinion,' agreed the convict, 'and brave. For all the time he fed me, the poor mad cove from Hull did gnash and moan enough to make a soldier nervous. Henry watched him, wary like, but he did not flinch from feeding me.

'When I had done eating, I asked the little chap where his daddy was, for I wished to pay him a compliment. Then Henry pointed over across the road where there was a small church yard and gave me to understand that his ma and pa both resided at that place.'

'They were dead?'

'Passed away.'

'Oh dear,' said Toby. 'Poor little mite.'

' "I am an orphing, Sir," said he. That is how he spoke it: *orphing*. "And I am tomorrow bound to live outside of Harrismith with the other orphings there."

'I was in a emotional condition, Toby. I had, the month before, been betrayed by my brother Tom. I had seen my childhood sweetheart sentenced to be hanged. I had heard her cries and seen her struggle and kick as the turnkeys carried her away. I also was to be cast out of my dear England, not in a year or two as was the custom, but on *the very next tide*. I was feeling very bitter about my lot.

'Then I see this little boy just starting out on the journey of his life, a very kind boy, with all his God-given goodness still undamaged. And I thought, so must *you* have been, Jack, before you were trained to be a varmint. I was much affected by this, Toby. It made a great impression. So when I finished my meal, I made this solemn promise to the little boy. I knew exactly what I said. I spoke it out loud: and promised anyone who would listen that I would come back from my exile and take him from his orphanage, that I would spin him a cocoon of gold and jewels, that I would weave him a nest so strong that no one would ever hurt his goodness. I would clad him in a scholar's robe and learn him his numbers and his letters, not only English, but Greek and Latin too, and I went on so long with my speech that soon even the mad man stopped his twirling and wrenching and sat still beside me.

'"There's mad," he said to me. "There's mad as anyone can find in a butcher's shop."

'He never lived to see me get my pardon for he was stabbed with a bone knife that very night aboard the *Enterprise,* and all the clothes and leather shoes stolen from his body before his last breath was gone.

'But this boy' – Maggs retrieved the framed portrait from the writer's hand – 'this boy has kept me alive these last twenty-four· years, and I will not have him taken from me. Nor will I permit him to be placed in harm's way. I am his da. He is my son. I will not abandon him.'

Tobias Oates leaned back in the craft and looked upwards. He realized only then that the mist had cleared: the sky was black and bright with stars, and he inhaled the acrid sweet perfume of hawthorn blossom. The little punt slid through the velvet water towards Newnham. The writer sat hunched over, staring into the blackness, remembering the horrid sound of the blood bubbling from Wilfred Partridge's throat, wondering about those two locks of human hair that must be, even now, inside the murderer's pocket.

It had been Jack Maggs's plan that they should continue down the Severn until they arrived at Bristol, and there was an unspoken understanding, or so Tobias imagined, that they would find a ship in that great port. But there are many sand shoals in the Severn below Gloucester and at around ten o'clock, still not having passed Newnham, they came into a stretch of water where the mist lay very dense and thick. Here they got themselves so badly stranded by the sands that Maggs announced he was frigged if he would go any further. As there was still a good two inches of water in the bottom of the craft, and neither of them had any wish to lie there, they tried to sleep leaning forward on their haunches.

It was very damp and cold. Tobias could hear water rats nearby, and it gave him no peace to imagine those wet grey furry bodies climbing aboard the punt and sniffing around his sleeping head. Somewhere nearby was a cow with a bell. He listened to it come close, then recede. He slept, only to be immediately awoken.

'Toby?'

'Yes.'

'Are you awake, Toby?'

'Yes, Jack.'

The boat tipped, and remained listing on the sand. Toby felt something on his knee. Imagining a rat, he struck out against it and barked his knuckles on something hard and cold.

'Careful,' said Maggs. 'That's good brandy I'm giving you, mate.'

'Good man, Jack.'

'Something to make the Phantom doze.'

Tobias allowed his hand to be taken and fitted around a cool silver flask.

'Paint me a picture of him who tortures me, Toby?'

'I wrote down what you told me in your sleep, Jack. One day you will read every word of it. Every dream and memory in your head, I'll give them to you, I promise. You have had a hard life, my friend, and more than your fair share of woe. I would never make light of your misfortune.'

'Yes, yes, very Christian of you, Toby. But what is his appearance?'

'Tall and fair-complexioned. He has long side-whiskers.'

265

There was a long silence on the aft-thwart.

'But you have never seen this Phantom yourself, Toby?'

'Of course not. He lives within you.'

'Then here's a strange thing. I never heard of this Phantom until I met you. I never saw him, asleep or waking.'

'You lived with the pain the Phantom caused.'

'What would you say if I said you planted him inside me?'

'How could I do such a thing?'

'I'm damned if I know. But he was not there before.'

'Your Phantom is as real to your eighth sense as Silas and Sophina, and I did not put *her* there.' Toby smiled. 'I can vouch for that.'

A moment later he was crushed. His head was banged. His breath pushed out of him. He lay pinned, half-winded, with the great weight of the convict's body on his chest, the deck and thwart pressing painfully against his spine.

'Don't never say that name again.'

As Jack Maggs's heavy body shifted painfully upon his own, Toby felt the heat of his breath.

'You say her name, I'll . . . You must not do it.'

Maggs's hand moved in the direction of his boot. Imagining himself about to be stabbed, Toby twisted his shoulders and bucked his hips.

'Help!' he cried. 'Help!'

Jack Maggs then began to laugh. Indeed, he laughed so raucously that he not only released his captive but fell back rather heavily into the bow.

'*Help*,' he cried in a weak, affected voice. Then he righted himself and came back once more to sit himself beside Tobias.

'*Help*,' he whispered in the writer's ear, but not so unkindly, and soon Tobias began to laugh too, if rather cautiously.

'Do you take it as an insult that I was afraid of you?'

'Oh no, Tobias, I take it as very sensible indeed.'

Tobias could feel the rough unshaven face lean towards him in the dark.

'I am with you, Jack.'

266

There was a long pause during which there was no noise but the jangle of the cow bell in the dark.

'We are together till I find my boy.'

So saying, the big man laughed and put his arm around the writer, and squashed him affectionately against his chest.

72

Three weeks earlier, Henry Phipps had been safe in his own dear house, breakfasting on salmon, and when he had opened the letter with the Dover postmark he had, naturally, not the faintest inkling that the rather common little envelope with its formal script would be such a harbinger of destruction.

Now his house was abandoned, his spring flowers uncared for, his most cherished valuables stored in a dank cellar on Blackfriars Road.

He stood at the window of his rooms in the club. He looked out at the bedraggled pigeons huddling on his window ledge, and beyond that at the dirty green roof of Covent Garden, and beyond that at what appeared to be a hawk circling slowly in the poisonous yellow sky.

He was, he thought, like a rabbit hiding in its hole.

As holes went, it was quite adequate, but he would never have suspected that the club to which he had been hitherto so attached, where he had enjoyed so many adventures and amusements, could be such a very depressing place to live.

There was nothing *wrong* with the rooms exactly, but in the morning light the green carpet was thread-bare and spotted, and the dark burgundy wallpaper was peeling at the joins, and the oval mirror was split on its frame. As he had, once again, made the mistake of breakfasting in, he had to endure that awful curry smell which seemed to affect everything that was cooked here.

In Great Queen Street, he had employed a splendid cook, an austere and handsome Cornish woman whom he had, of course, sent away. He had sent all the servants on leave, just on the quarter day –

so he had paid them up until the end of June; and this meant overlooking several pressing debts, and required a meeting with the bank to discuss the account which was then overdrawn a hundred guineas. Whether this account would ever be 'topped up' again was by no means certain. Today was the fifth, the day 'topping up' would normally occur, but he was reluctant to call on his bankers for fear of discovering the procedure had been abandoned by his benefactor.

And thus he was sitting by his gloomy little window, with its forlorn prospect of the roofs of Covent Garden, when a knock came on the door. It was Magnus announcing that there was a gentleman to see him. As he was, to all intents and purposes, in hiding, this news produced a very queasy feeling in his stomach.

'What gentleman, Magnus?'

'I really could not say,' said Magnus, exhibiting the closed and shiny countenance of a freshly tipped servant.

'Did he state his name, his business?' asked Henry Phipps, who had, after three weeks of close acquaintance, grown weary of Magnus.

'Yes, I would say it was definitely business,' said Magnus. And waited, his eyebrows raised, as if he were a witty subject in charades.

'Inasmuch, Magnus?'

'Inasmuch as it could not be *pleasure*, Sir.'

'What are you telling me?' asked Henry Phipps impatiently. 'Is he rough?'

'Oh no, Sir.'

'Is he a large man?'

'Oh no, Sir.'

Henry Phipps placed his tea cup heavily upon the dresser.

'He's a wee chap,' Magnus obliged quickly. 'He would not worry you, Sir, if that's your meaning. He's just a wee wee chap, with his wee little legs and his wee little hands.'

'Very well then,' said Henry. 'Thank you, Magnus.'

'You never asked me his name, Sir?'

Henry sighed. A great surge of temper pressed up into his sinuses, and he bent his head, his hands pressing down beside his long straight nose.

268

'Very well then. What is his name?' he asked at last.

'His name is Buckle, Sir.'

'Thank you, Magnus. I will be down directly.'

Now Percy Buckle and Henry Phipps had been neighbours a good year, and on one or two occasions they had acknowledged each other whilst dismounting from their carriages, but that was all of the contact they had so far had. When Henry heard his neighbour's name today, it meant nothing in particular to him, and when he had brushed his hair one more time and buttoned his fourth button, he descended the narrow little staircase to the *Lord Strutwell*, hoping that the volumes of engravings had been locked away in their glass case. Indeed, when he entered the room, his eye went first to that case. It was safely locked.

Then, turning his attention to the visitor, he beheld this most peculiar little gent with his short legs and his expensive spats and his tailored coat and his thinning hair. Henry Phipps did not like ugliness. Did not like it in any form, in any thing. Now, as he looked at Percy Buckle, some small signs in his handsome face betrayed his feelings.

'I'm much obliged,' said Percy Buckle, extending his hand.

Henry Phipps heard his accent and thought: *debt collector*.

'I don't think you recognize me,' said Percy Buckle.

'No,' said Henry Phipps, releasing the clammy hand. 'Have we met?'

'We have a brick wall in common,' joked Percy Buckle, then added, 'and also an interest in a fellow named Jack Maggs.'

Henry Phipps felt his breath stop.

'You are his friend?' he asked at last. He sat himself carefully in the leather armchair. 'He sends you here?' His heart was beating very hard and all the old uncertainties of his troubled life came bubbling to the fore. His pulse was racing as it had raced the day he had been delivered at the door of Mrs Gummerson's orphanage.

'Oh no,' said Percy Buckle, also sitting – or rather perching, for his legs were so short he thought it best to stay well forward – on the very edge of the armchair. 'No, I fancy he would be very angry to see me here. As' – he paused delicately while his cheeks betrayed his

269

anxiety with a most distinctive patch of colour – 'as I believe *you* would be displeased to see Mr Maggs sitting where I sit.'

Henry Phipps had so absorbed the notion that Mr Buckle was Jack Maggs's messenger, that it took him some time to understand that he was not: that, although his visitor knew Jack Maggs, he did not come to further Jack Maggs's interest in the matter. By the time he had reached this conclusion, Henry Phipps's shirt was soaked with perspiration, and he had more than once brushed at his fair hair with his hands, and more than once wiped his hands with his handkerchief. He now attempted to wrest some order from the chaos of his feelings.

'Let me ask you a question.'

'No,' said Percy Buckle, 'let me ask you a question.'

Henry Phipps blinked. 'Very well,' he said, surprised by the hardness in the other's tone. 'If you wish.'

'What have you done to protect your assets?'

'Sir!' Henry Phipps stood up. 'That's damned impertinent.' And he began to pace around the room. He did not know what was happening.

'Sit down,' said Percy Buckle, 'and quit the prancing.'

Henry Phipps could not obey such a creature completely, but he did stand still.

'Your house is not your own,' insisted Percy Buckle. 'It is the property of Jack Maggs. I have seen the title again this morning, and as far as I can tell it is still in his name.'

Henry Phipps had never inquired about this title, but once he heard this information, his worst fears were realized. Now this too would be taken from him.

'And if Mr Maggs is to get himself arrested, do you know what will happen to that title?'

'No,' admitted Henry Phipps, and sat down in the chair.

'Why, it would be subsumed *nullus contredris*,' said Mr Buckle, mumbling to obscure the fraudulence of his Latin. 'It would be taken from him, as a felon, and auctioned by His Majesty – or Her Majesty as soon it will be. Were you not aware of this?'

'You are sure?'

270

'You were not aware,' said Mr Buckle. 'But now that you are, I assume you would do anything in your power to prevent him being arrested.'

'Has he been arrested?'

'No, nor do you wish it. Nor do I, for reasons you need not know of. But, on the other hand, Sir, I see that you do not wish to play the part that he has written for you. You do not wish to sit around his fire eating cakes and drinking brown ale.'

An involuntary shudder passed over Henry Phipps.

'You know he is attached to you?'

Henry Phipps slumped in his chair. He knew, in this instant, that his leisured life would soon be over. He had known this time would come ever since the day sixteen years ago when Victor Littlehales, his beloved tutor, had rescued him from the orphanage. Now this privileged tenure was ended and he must leave his house, his silver, his rugs, his paintings. He must be a soldier.

'I would imagine,' continued the hateful little creature, 'that there is a Last Will and Testament . . .'

'I understand I am his heir, yes.'

'Well,' said Mr Buckle, 'then the news is not all bad.' He took Henry Phipps's cup of tea, though it must have been luke-warm by now, sugared it enthusiastically and drank it with gusto. 'Not all bad by any means.'

Henry Phipps looked into the fellow's excited eyes and was made to feel most uncomfortable

'May I ask, Mr Buckle, what is your interest in Mr Maggs?'

'It is a matter of the heart, Sir.'

'Jack Maggs is your *rival*?' asked the other incredulously.

'He is.'

'You would not mourn him, Mr Buckle?'

'He has betrayed my trust, which was very foolish of him.' The little man looked him straight in the eye, and Henry Phipps was surprised to find himself pinned by the gaze. 'There are people like Jack Maggs who see me, Sir, and they pity me, or make mock of me – well, I don't mind that, you know, I can see that point of view – but it is just a skip from pity to abuse, so I have found. And I will not be

271

abused, Sir, not by anyone. And if I am to be humiliated in my own home, well then, that person will be punished.'

'My, my!' Henry Phipps raised his eyebrows.

'You be careful, Sir. Do you hear me?'

This was a very different creature from the one whom the young man had first cast eyes upon. 'Yes,' he said. 'I hear you.'

'Jack Maggs has gone up to Gloucester, without informing me, but I found out. Yes, he has gone to Gloucester, trying to find you. I have not the foggiest where he sleeps in Gloucester. But I know, Sir, I have learned, the secret place he lays his head in London. And that's the point for you.'

'And what would you have me do with that information?'

'Why,' cried Mr Buckle, rising from his chair in a very energetic style, 'I leave that to you, Sir. It is none of my business, but I do believe it is yours, for the house he sleeps in might easily be your own.'

And with that he took his tall beaverskin hat, and carefully brushed it with the back of his hand.

Henry Phipps shook his hand once more, and when Mr Buckle had departed the club, he sat down in the chair alone, feeling rather cold and shivery.

73

Having heard Sophina's name on Tobias Oates's lips, having finally begun to understand the extent to which his secrets had been burgled, Jack Maggs became, by degrees, severely agitated.

He could not sleep, and as his mind tried to understand what had been done to him, a familiar dread slowly took possession of his being. As the punt lifted slowly off the sand, as the intensity of this feeling grew, he took his son's framed portrait from his coat and pressed it to his stomach with both his hands. And there he stayed, hunched over on the mid-thwart, hugging the image as he had on many nights before. Now he could feel the Phantom pulling with his strings inside his face, long lines of cat-gut knotted to his flesh. He felt the demon stirring in his belly and everywhere about him. He imagined that horrid half-smile upon his patrician face.

He did not know what was done to him, or how it was achieved. He rocked back and forth, stubbornly alone, waiting for the light.

When, at last, the yellowish light of dawn penetrated the mist, he found they were bumping around the shore of a 'pill', or cove. His companion was still asleep, sitting sideways on the aft-thwart, his forehead resting on his drawn-up knees. Maggs leaned towards him. At first it seemed that he intended to shake him awake, but instead he executed the plan he had carried with him through the dark. Half-rising in his seat, he twisted his body and – with a thin, hard smile upon his face – inserted his three-fingered hand into the writer's jacket pocket; then, very slowly, he withdrew the notebook. Once it was well clear of its owner, he sat down again and set the sodden treasure ever-so gently upon his knee. There he sought that which was his.

The pages were very wet, and the ink in some places washed away, but he began his search from the beginning of the note book and very soon, on page three, he was rewarded: *M– would not go mad.*

His brows came down upon his eyes.

M– would not go mad, but only because he carried with him the strong conviction that he would, no matter what Judge Denman read to him, walk once more in England's green and pleasant land.

The hairs on his neck stood on end.

He had had that feeling in his gut before, that cold terror associated with the triangle. He knew his life and death were not his own. His forehead creased in a grid of criss-crossed frown marks. He turned the page.

Jack Maggs is a criminal who presumes to come home from Banishment, who, having accrued great wealth, buys the great mansion in which he will finally be burned alive.

He turned the page and found: *Chapter One*. Before the title, and afterwards: the sign of the Cross. All the following pages were vigorously crossed out.

74

Chapter One

It was a dismal January day in the year of 1818, and the yellow fog which had lain low all morning lifted a moment in the afternoon and then, as if the desolate pile of rock and stone thereby revealed was far too melancholy a sight to be endured, it descended again like a shroud around the walls of Newgate Prison.

These walls, being made from Welsh blue stone, had not been easily broken by the quarryman, and yet the fog, by virtue of its persistence, had been able slowly to penetrate the stone's dark inhuman heart and touch the skin of a young woman prisoner who had fallen asleep with her face against her cell wall.

There were a great number of women inside Newgate that year. They had been brought from all over the British Isles: petty thieves, murderers, all manner of wickedness crammed into that grim pile on Newgate Street. Here, in a small cell on the second floor, eight women waited for the Majesty of the Law to turn its weary eye on every one of them by turn.

There was a good thick palliasse of straw in the corner of the cell. This, however, had already been claimed for the sole use of a ham-legged female servant 'without situation' who was said to have robbed and murdered travellers on the Turnpike at Bayswater. The rest of the women – one of them a mother suckling a new babe – made use of what straw had spilled from the palliasse in the battle for its possession. They did not speak to each other, though when the name 'Sophina Smith' was called through the spy-hole they looked at each other to see who 'Sophina Smith' might be.

She who had rested her cheek against the wall now stood, revealing the bloody injury which had made her seek that cold comfort: four deep scratch marks on her face.

When the door opened she stepped out. Chains were put around her wrists and ankles and she was led off.

This Sophina Smith was a very comely young woman. She had exceptionally fair skin, and coal-black hair which hung in pretty ringlets around her face. She was tall and stood erect. Although slender, she had a most womanly figure. It was this very comeliness which had so affronted the ham-legged servant who had scratched her face.

Being brought out of the side door of the prison, the young woman blinked, then lowered her head, walked ten paces, then was admitted through a second door. Thus she passed from Internment to Judgment, for she was now inside the Old Bailey.

She was brought first into a dark and dingy room, illuminated by a single soot-stained lamp. Here, in company with other women similarly shackled, she waited for an hour. Then she was called into court to stand before the Judge.

The court had heard many charges that morning: a mother had tried to drown her babe, a woman had pushed a red-hot poker into her husband's eye, but the charge against this prisoner brought a new gravity to the room.

Sophina Smith, it was now said, had used hammer and chisel to break into a house in Frith Street, Soho, the property of Gilbert Gunn, a solicitor, and therein she had stolen silver plate valued at one hundred and fifty pounds.

It was a figure high enough to have her hanged three times over.

'So,' said the Judge, 'what plead you to this charge?' He was a benign-looking man in spite of his lambskin, and although his mouth turned down at the edges, an honest citizen might easily imagine him as an umpire at a county cricket match, holding the bowler's jersey draped around his shoulders. When his question went unanswered, he bore it with good grace, repeating himself in a tone that made the recording clerk smile slightly.

Yet the young woman could not be teased into speech. She stared up at the high, panelled bench, her pretty face contorted by a rather mulish scowl.

The Judge inquired about her injury. She turned her head abruptly so it was hidden from him.

After one or two more questions, the Judge finally lost patience. He slapped his hand loudly down upon the Bench. The prisoner flinched.

Everyone who sat in the court could see her fright. Now, finally, her eyes were bright with tears. She addressed the Judge in a whisper.

'Again. I cannot hear you.'

275

The young woman spoke in a louder voice. She said that there could be no value in her testimony because she was a thief.

'Do you mean that you are a thief by nature or a thief as evidenced by these charges? If you are a thief by nature, that is not the concern of this court today. But if you are guilty of these charges then you must plead "guilty". If not, you must plead "not guilty". How do you plead?'

There were forty or fifty people in that court and every one of them understood that this comely young woman might be hanged for this offence. Thus her continued silence had a great effect on all of them; none more than upon a certain young man who had witnessed the proceedings with impatience from the very start. He was a tall youth, dressed in a flash style, with a green kerchief around his neck and a bright red waistcoat covering his chest. This wardrobe, in accompaniment with his rather bellicose expression, might cause one to suppose that he had been up to no good, and had profited from his wrong-doing. His hair was cut short and he was closely shaven, and there was nothing therefore to mask his raw emotion, to distract one from the restless anger of his eyes. Yet had his head been covered by a leather hood, he would have given himself away, for he continually twisted in his seat, leaning forward and then back, and when the young woman finally whispered that she was guilty, he leaped up to his feet and cried out that she was innocent.

Immediately the constabulary were after him, trampling over a little boy in their attempts to reach the heckler. He was big-boned, but he was nimble, and he leaped onto the bench behind. With one boot on the back of the bench and another between a parson's legs, he called to the Judge that it was he, Jack Maggs, who had done the crime.

By this time he was surrounded, and he stepped down to the floor, still very hot and passionate, trembling like a horse.

'Bring that ruffian to the Bench,' said the Judge. Three constables, all of them shorter than their prisoner, brought the young man to stand before the Judge, who immediately declared him in contempt of court, and thereupon, without recourse to any other authority, began the young man's interrogation himself.

'Do you know this woman?' asked the Judge, and although the young man did not answer, the answer was obvious to all: he was hissing at the young woman and she was shaking her head back at him.

276

'She is my brother's wife.'

'Ah,' said the Judge, 'you can speak. The malady does not run in the family?'

'Yes, I can speak,' said the young man. 'And I was also in that house in Soho and I can tell Your Honour that this young woman did not do nothing. It was her husband, Tom England, who broke the lock.'

'And you, I suppose, are an innocent by-stander?'

'How can I be? It was I who packed the silver.'

'Very well,' said the Judge. 'Then I will swear you as a witness.'

At this, the woman in the dock began to rock back and forth. There issued from her a high and desolate keening that continued even as she was taken from her place and sat in the front row with a policeman each side of her. Then the young man, still trembling but straight-backed, did formally reveal his name and place of lodging, swearing upon the Bible that he would tell the truth. Then he grasped the top rail of the dock and looked down at the court. He looked pale, stunned by what he had done; his belligerence had faded.

'You entered these premises in Frith Street, Mr Maggs?'

'I did.'

'You saw the silver taken from the chest?'

'I did.'

'Who took that silver?'

'I did.'

'Did anyone assist you?'

'Only so far as the door was broken. This was done, as I said, by Tom England, a carpenter of Pottery Lane in Notting Hill.'

The clerk stood to whisper in the Judge's ear.

'Please explain to the court,' said the Judge, very irritably, 'why someone would break a door down and then call the police himself.'

'Damn him,' cried the witness, although whom he meant to damn was not made clear.

'Silence!' roared the Judge.

'Tom's interest is elsewhere.'

'I fail to understand you. Who is Tom? How does this answer the question I have just asked you?'

'Tom England. His eye is taken.'

'Jack Maggs, you will make yourself clear to the court.'

'He has another Jill who takes his fancy.'

'He has another woman, you mean?'

'He is tired of Sophina. He wishes to be quit of her, but she cannot afford to leave him and so he bent the twig.'

'Bent the twig?'

'Set the trap, Your Honour. He put her in the house, then called the police, Sir. He wants her off his hands.'

'Then you went ahead and stole the silver anyway.'

'Yes, Sir.'

'Do you know you can be hanged, Jack Maggs?'

'I do not care.'

'You do not care?'

'It is over in a minute.'

'You have sworn on the Bible, Jack Maggs. Do you not care what might happen to you when you stand before your God? Eternity is not over in a minute.'

The young man seemed as hard as the streets he lived by, but not so hard that this did not give him pause. 'Sir, I swear by God, I'm telling the truth.'

'Do you imagine,' said the Judge, 'this court is like some street fair that you can work your wickedness and profligacy upon? Do you imagine you can shout and lie before me and line your own pockets when it is obvious to anyone who hears your testimony that you and this young woman were partners in crime on that day? You, Sophina Smith, were unlucky enough to be caught. You, Sir, were impudent enough to imagine you could alter the course of justice. You shall be taken from this place henceforth and charged with the crimes of perjury and burglary.'

'I'm telling the truth.'

'Then you have confessed before these witnesses that you stole silver from Mr Gunn of Frith Street. But that will be dealt with at another time. Now,' he said, 'the prisoner will stand.'

And then, on that foggy Wednesday afternoon whilst children played with hoops, and their nursery maids flirted with soldiers in St James's Park, the young woman named Sophina Smith was sentenced to death by hanging and he who had tried to save her wept openly in the dock.

75

Jack Maggs sat on the mid-thwart of the lock-keeper's punt with the notebook on his lap, and from his bent bulk there now emerged a very peculiar series of sounds such as you might have imagined to be made by an injured animal: a hedgehog or a mole.

Jack Maggs was weeping. He bent his body into a hard, tight ball. He grasped his stomach and rocked to and fro. Then came the sound of a squeaky wheel, very close by. The convict stopped weeping immediately. He sat bolt upright, staring with his red eyes into the wet mist. The shadows of some elms were visible, nothing else. Chains clinked together. Jack Maggs reached for the dagger in his boot. He withdrew it with his right hand, while his high hawk's nose followed the progress of the ghostly vehicle.

The cart (if that is what it was) passed by slowly, but even when it could be heard no more, Maggs showed no intention of sheathing his weapon. Rather he turned its cruel hooked tip toward the author of the note book.

Tobias Oates continued to sleep with his forehead resting on his knees. Jack Maggs waved the knife across him. Then he paused, placing the weapon between his teeth, and kneeled upon the thwart. Without troubling to remove his great-coat, he lowered himself into the Severn.

The river at this point was some three feet deep, and it was therefore a simple enough matter to spin the punt around so that the sleeping author was presented to him back first. Maggs took the dagger in his right hand and he placed his left arm tight around the other's chest.

'You are a thief,' said he quietly. 'A damned little thief.'

Tobias Oates woke up, struggling and splashing his heels amongst the bilge-water, but when he felt the blade up against his throat, he stopped. He lay as still as a fox caught in a snare, his speckled eyes staring straight ahead.

'Don't kill me, Jack.'

'Shut your hole.'

'You're cutting me!'

Maggs's coat floated out around him, like the skirt of some great antipodean squid. 'You'll know when I'm bloody well cutting you.' He turned the boat in the water so the frightened passenger was facing him.

'Why should I not kill you now?'

Tobias Oates glanced quickly towards the bank. If he'd had thoughts of running, he abandoned them for now. He remained huddled up on the aft-thwart, waiting for what would happen next.

'You stole my Sophina, you bastard.'

Tobias felt in his jacket, but his note book was gone. 'No, no. She cannot be stolen . . .'

'It were a very low scheming thieving thing you did, Toby.'

'You read my note book, Jack? You read my chapter, is that it?'

'Oh, you wrote a chapter did you? With my name in it?'

'It is a memorial I am making. Your Sophina will live for ever.'

'Don't say her name.'

'I write that name, Jack, like a stone mason makes the name upon a headstone, so her memory may live for ever. In all the Empire, Jack, you could not have employed a better carver.'

Jack Maggs did not answer, but some lessening of agitation on his part encouraged the writer to continue. 'Your painful life . . .'

'You are planning to kill me, I know that. Is that what you mean by painful? To burn me alive?'

'Not you, Jack, a character who bears your name. I will change the name sooner or later.'

'You are just a character to me too, Toby.'

'Very funny, Jack.'

'Funny? I have no reason not to kill you also, Toby.'

'Except that I am flesh and blood.'

'Did you ever see a man lashed, Toby? Did you ever see the parts of his back splashed across the soldier's uniform?'

'You would not be wise to kill me, Jack. Not now.'

'But I am not a wise man, Toby. I am a vermin who made ten thousand pounds from mucky clay. I have a grand house in Sydney town. There is a street named for me, or was when I sailed. I keep a

280

coach, and two footmen. I am Mr Jack Maggs Esquire, and I left all that so I might end up here today. You have cheated me, Toby, as bad as I was ever cheated.'

And here he began, very slowly, to turn the boat around, with the intention, it seemed, of bringing the young man's neck once more within his reach. Tobias waited, staring all the while into Jack Maggs's unstable eyes.

'Spare me,' he cried at last.

'Why would I spare you?' asked the other.

'Forgive me, Jack, but I know where your son is. I knew when I left London.'

There was a long silence. Then Maggs spoke. 'Oh, you are a very brave little chap, Toby.'

'I am a wretched creature, Jack.'

'Why in God's name did you bring me here?'

'The money.'

'Are you not a clever man? Is not that the dart with you? Did it not enter that big brain box of yours that I would have paid you twice the price for you to take me to my son in London? Where is he?'

'I will arrange to take you to him.'

'He has been in London all this while?'

'It does seem so, yes. I had a communication from your fellow footman. He has been so tormented by this secret, he knew not what to do.'

'Why tormented? Why did he not tell me?'

'It was on the eve of our departure. It was only because of my desperation I hid it from you.'

'What in God's name do you have to be desperate of? What would make you act so cruel as this?'

'I told you of my situation.'

'Your wife's sister? Are you serious? Here you are writing the story of the death of Maggs, and you do not know how to take care of her condition? Take me to my boy, and I will give the pills to you.'

'And my fifty pounds.'

'To hell with your fifty pounds. I will give you what you need,

281

which is more than you deserve. We'll stop off and get the medicine on our way into London. But let me tell you, if you do not find my boy, that is the end of you. Can you make a bargain like that? You are wagering me your very life.'

'I can.'

'Very well. Hand me your note book.'

'You have it, I believe.'

'It is on the thwart, beside you.'

Toby picked up the book.

'Give it to me.'

It was given.

'I forbid you now to write Sophina's name, now or ever. Do you understand?'

'Yes.'

'Do you have your magnets with you?'

'No.'

'You will not use your magnets. You will not write my name in your book. You will not write the Phantom's name.'

'Yes.'

Jack then hurled the book high out above the Severn. As it flew up into the mist, its pages opened like a pair of wings. At this moment a horn was blown very loud and there was a great thundering of hooves and wheels.

Tobias looked towards Jack Maggs, his face white with fright.

'Coach,' said Maggs.

'Coach?'

'Stay!'

But Tobias had already jumped. He plunged down to his waist in water. Then, before Maggs had even let go of the punt, he was scrambling helter-skelter up onto the bank towards the road, wet sand clinging to his trouser legs.

76

If Tobias had not jumped into a rocky hole, his leg would not have twisted, and if his leg had not been twisted he might conceivably have made it to Newnham village before the convict caught him.

But his leg *was* injured, and thus he *was* easily felled, pinned down with his face pressed amongst the bluebells. And there he lay: winded, bruised, crushed beneath the convict's weight, as a wagon-load of hay rolled down the road, passing not six feet from where they lay.

Two young men in bright red smocks walked beside the load. One carried a long stave or quarter-staff across his shoulders. The other was unarmed, but he walked with such an easy yeoman gait that Toby never doubted he would fight in the defence of an honest stranger. Still, Jack Maggs's dagger kept him quiet and, like the hero of *Michael Adams*, he watched his liberators pass him by while all the time berating himself for his own cowardice: *He was crippled by that vision of the cut throat, the horrid mortal gurgling of the windpipe, the knowledge that his very Life could be drained as easily as from the bung hole of a keg.*

When the wagon had passed, Maggs squatted beside him, the black blade ready in his hand.

'Turn turtle,' said the convict grimly.

Toby rolled onto his back and watched from the corner of his apprehensive eye as his captor cut a length of cord from his kit-bag.

'What are you doing, Jack?'

'Hands on your head.'

'All I wished was to hail the coach.'

Maggs brought the blade up to his bare neck, and Toby pressed his head hard back into the bluebells.

'Put your blasted hands on your head.'

Toby did as he was bid.

But when he felt the other's fingers at his trouser belt, he brought his hands down to protect his privates.

'Please, Jack . . . No.'

For answer he received a sharp sting on his thumb. He cried out with pain. Tears flooded his eyes. He felt the Australian undo his waist button.

Then the horrid hands were on the buttons of his flies. Numb with horror, he stared through his tears at the sky, the over-hanging trees. He felt the murder weapon slicing at his trousers.

'Now, put your hands into your pockets.'

Toby imagined the cruellest consequences, but when he spoke his voice was level.

'You want your son,' he said. 'You would be wise to recognize that I am your only chance.'

'Put your hands in your pockets, Toby.'

This Tobias did, very slowly. He found the bottoms of his pockets cut away.

'Don't you move,' said Maggs, dragging the right hand through the pocket and trussing it rapidly with cord. A moment later he had trussed the left.

'Don't pull on them,' Maggs said.

Tobias did pull on them, and found his wrists to be manacled.

'Don't pull on them, if you don't want to get green rot.'

And then, with the blade once again gripped between his teeth, he did up the buttons of the writer's trousers and helped him to his feet.

Toby looked at the brigand's face and saw that he was grinning around his blade. This obstacle to his mirth he very soon removed and laughed at Toby freely.

'Look at you. You thought I was going to cut off your gooseberries.'

Tobias stood with his trussed hands deep in his pockets and was aware of being a very sad and sorry figure.

'See now,' said Maggs, 'you count your change, Toby. Make sure you've got your penny and two farthings.' With that he hugged him, wrapping his arm tight around his shoulders and pulling Toby's face into his breast, thus forcing him to inhale what would always thereafter be *the prisoner's smell* – the odour of cold sour sweat.

284

'Come, Your Lordship,' said Jack Maggs, 'you can count your treasure all the way to London.'

The two men then walked through the wildflowers to the road. The big man was still laughing, the smaller man was rather red-faced and grim-looking. He walked with his hands deep into his pockets, hobbling back towards everything he had hoped to escape from.

77

As her manacled husband was being helped aboard a coach in Gloucestershire, Mary Oates came down into the drawing room and was unpleasantly surprised to discover Lizzie, who usually liked to lie in bed till breakfast time, sitting at the window like a sea captain's wife, her placid hands atop her stomach.

'That little boy from Jones's shop will get himself run over,' said Lizzie.

Mary did not comment. She settled herself in the low chair in which she liked to feed her baby, and in a moment she and little John had reached their usual accommodation.

'He is running his hoop across the street under the very hooves of the horses.'

'Lizzie, are you waiting for Toby to return?'

The light was behind her sister, rendering her face in shadow, but there was no mistaking the false note in her voice. 'Oh, is it today he comes, Mary?'

Mary did not deign to answer.

'It is today, Mary?'

This disingenuousness was so repugnant to her that Mary could pretend no longer. 'You know as much as I do, Lizzie.'

'Oh, I think you know much more, Mary. Look at how you have dressed.'

Mary had already noted how her sister was dressed that morning – in her bright blue poplin, with her best lace shawl around her shoulders.

'I think that you have had word from him,' Lizzie continued heedlessly. 'Because you are wearing your velvet.'

The notion that she should have to wear her best dress to win her husband's good opinion was so insulting to Mary that it was a moment before she could answer calmly.

'Perhaps *you* have heard from my husband, Lizzie.'

'Oh Mary, you say the queerest things.'

'Not near as queer as you,' said Mary darkly.

She laid a white napkin on her lap and then laid the infant on it and gently paddled his back before setting him on the other breast.

'Mary, are you angry with me?'

'No, dear.'

'What queer things were you referring to? Have I been babbling again? I know I do babble. I think perhaps I really should give up my novels. They give me very peculiar dreams.'

'I was referring to no particular thing,' said Mary, but those extraordinary conversations about adoption still burned bright in her memory. Had Lizzie not come back to this theme so repeatedly, Mary might never have noticed the way her sister sat with her hands resting complacently on her belly, or the way her bosom lately pressed against the bodice of her gown. These two symptoms had gnawed at her daily while every aspect of her sister's behaviour gave further indication of the true nature of her disease.

It was as if someone had died, but there was no death, just a horrible agitation she could reveal to no one. If she felt rage, it showed only on the itchy rash across her back. If she had tears, they were contained within the water blisters which had risen in the middle of these red weals.

She was a blunt woman, in many ways, but what she now knew, she would not name. What she was about to do, she would not look at.

She had carried the little newspaper advertisement for nearly a week, but even as she cut it out with her sewing scissors she did not admit to herself where it might lead her. This morning she had put on her best dress so that whoever she must now encounter would know she was, in spite of the circumstances, a respectable woman.

286

She finished feeding little John, and buttoned her bodice. She carried her child towards the door.

'Will you come back and sit with me, Mary?'

'No, dear. I have an errand to run.'

'If you don't mind, I'll stay and read.'

'Yes, dear.'

She took little John to Mrs Jones and, with no proper explanation of the formality of her attire or the nature of her errand, she walked out of the house.

She might have taken a hackney cab – her husband would never have hesitated to do so – and yet Mary Oates, ever mindful of the economic stress under which Tobias suffered, walked.

Mary Oates was from Amersham, in Buckinghamshire, and had lived in London only since her marriage a year before. On her husband's arm she had travelled to places as various as Limehouse and the Guildhall, but unless thus escorted, had been content to stay pretty much within the confines of her rooms. Thus to find her way to Cecil Street was no small expedition for her, and she had not got so far as Holborn without inquiring the direction of three different shop-keepers.

The day was clear and fine, although it was perhaps too hot for such a heavy velvet dress, or too warm to wear such a dress and walk so fast. In any case, the plump young woman finally arrived in the Haymarket very red in the face and out of breath, and allowed herself to be charged a penny for a glass of water by the owner of the coffee stand.

From the coffee stand to Cecil Street is no more than two hundred yards, yet Mary stopped twice more for directions before she came to that corner where the convict had stood on his first night back in London. From this point onwards their paths were so close that she must, from time to time, have brought her stout little heel down on the same spot of pavement where Jack Maggs's hessian boot had trod. As for attaining her destination, she was more successful than her precursor, for she not only got through the gate of 4 Cecil Street but to the brass knocker on its door.

Her knock was answered almost immediately, and Mary was

287

confused to discover that the person who stood before her appeared to be both respectable and friendly.

'These are Mrs Britten's rooms?' Mary inquired.

'Indeed they are, Mum,' said the maid politely. 'You come on in. You come on in and rest your feet, Mum.'

The young woman ushered her into a small room, decorated rather excessively with lace and flounces, and an almost violent looking wallpaper. There was a single window, large and arched, which was covered with two layers of white muslin. There was very little light from that source, but there were various lamps burning, and several ornate mirrors, and it was, as a result, a bright and determinedly happy little room. Three women were already seated here, though none looked up when Mary Oates entered. This collective expression of shame went hard against the intention of the decorations, emphasizing the dishonour the latter were presumably intended to disguise.

Mary Oates sat in the chair she was offered and accepted a cup of tea. It was very good tea and Mary sipped it carefully. When she looked up her glance was not towards the other women but in the direction of the handsome marble fireplace and, above it, a rather troubling engraving which depicted Napoleon's army in grotesque and bloody disarray.

No more than ten minutes later, she was escorted along a hallway into a small plain room containing little more than a high leather couch and a straight-backed wooden chair. Here she was met by a tall, rather severe old woman in a starched white dress. The woman had a strong nose and chin, and piercing, angry eyes. She wore an extravagant tall white head-dress that reminded Mary of a painting she had once seen of a Dutch nun.

'And how may I assist you, dearie?' she inquired, raising her hands in a peculiar little greeting which might, in a church, have been taken for a blessing.

Mary felt very hot and itchy across her blistered back. She hesitated.

'What do you want of Mrs Britten, dearie?'

For an answer, Mary Oates held out the frayed little advertise-

288

ment. Mrs Britten took it from her, and Mary, seeing how the fierce old lady held it between thumb and forefinger, was reminded of the way in which her grandfather had squashed caterpillars in his garden.

'These pills,' said Mrs Britten, indicating the illustration in her puff, 'are from a recipe given me by a Swedish doctor. Very good pills they are.' She had a decidedly rougher voice than her initial appearance suggested, and although her features were handsome there was something of the fish wife about her hands, which were large and swollen at the knuckles.

'Very good pills,' she continued seriously. 'Except for just one wee shortcoming.'

And here she winked, much to Mary Oates's distress.

'And the shortcoming is as follows: should you be so unfortunate as to take them when you was with child, then, oh dear . . .' She dropped the crumpled advertisement into the waste-paper basket. 'Know what I mean?'

'I think so, yes.'

'We are married women. We can be plain between us: you would lose the baby. You understand the shortcoming now?'

'I do.'

A long silence followed while the old woman stared at her so hard, Mary could only look away.

'How far along are you?'

'I beg your pardon,' protested Mary.

Before Mary could say anything further, the old woman had reached out and felt her stomach. It was a fast invasion, over before it had begun. Mary said nothing. What could a lady possibly say? She stood there like a goose, itching unbearably, blushing to the very roots of her hair.

'You come here for another lady?' Mrs Britten produced a yellow printed sheet. 'Never mind. I have writ it all down, but the long and short of it is she must never, never, take these pills of mine if she is gestational.'

From her pocket she produced a small porcelain jar which she placed in Mary's gloved hand. 'Of course, she'd need to be taking one every morning and night for that to happen. Unless she did that, there'd be no danger.'

'Every morning and every night?'

'Every morning and every night.'

Mary felt another urge to scratch her back.

'As to payment . . .'

'Five guineas.'

Mary looked up and found the old eyes staring at her implacably.

'The advertisement said three.'

Mrs Britten shrugged. 'Five is the price. Take it or leave it. Makes no diff to me.'

'I've got no more than four,' Mary fretted. 'The advertisement said three guineas.'

'Four will do.' Mary Britten held out a weathered hand, thus revealing the name SILAS tattooed into the underside of her broad wrist.

Two minutes later Mary Oates was standing outside again. She set off back down Cecil Street holding the jar of pills tightly in her gloved hand. She arrived home without recalling the direction she had come.

78

As dark cumulus clouds spilled through the dirty air, stacking themselves high above St Paul's, Tobias Oates crossed the River Thames. It was seven o'clock on a May night, and the two men, having arrived in Borough at The Swan with Two Necks, were now passing over London Bridge in a hack. After thirty hours of travel, Toby's hands were still deep in his pockets, his wrists still bound together.

As their vehicle came into the West End, Jack Maggs leaned out the window whilst drumming his right foot upon the floor.

Tobias, meanwhile, was deeply troubled. He feared the poison they were about to buy. He feared Lizzie, and could not imagine how he would persuade her to take such a potion. There were many other strands of apprehension in the matted tangle of his mood, and they were knotted harder by the persistent pain in his wrists and the unholy pressure on his bladder, which pride had forbidden him mentioning to his companion.

The London they left behind had been a sunny place where daffodils grew in the window boxes. The London they returned to seemed hellish – broken cotton bales, cracking whips, an omnibus alight on St Martin's Lane – all the streets awash with a weary sulphurous kind of evening light that seeped into his very thoughts, and finally surrounded the image of the family he had come so close to abandoning.

His captor then brought his big unshaven face close, and Tobias could smell the cheap brandy on his breath.

'Soon be there, eh, mate?'

'Indeed.' Tobias quickly turned his head away.

'All our trials will soon be ended.'

'Indeed, yes.'

'Miss Lizzie's troubles mended.'

Toby shuddered at the damnable state to which he had descended: his very respectability depended upon enduring this insolent familiarity.

'We will visit Henry Phipps in the morning,' he told the convict firmly. And once more looked away, praying to God that the footman had spoken true, for if Constable did not really have Henry Phipps's address, then Tobias was a dead man.

'It is a dream come true, mate. An old varmint's dream come true.'

In spite of his previous vow to murder Toby, Jack Maggs had been unusually friendly to him throughout the journey, and now, as the convict leaned towards him, Tobias feared another embrace. But Maggs wished only to gaze up at the great sky, which was now, in the north, so very black and swollen.

'Isn't that a queer thing to go out of a cove's head?' said the convict. 'When I was imagining my lovely English summers – and I did meditate on this subject an awful lot, my word – I would be suffering the mosquitoes and the skin-rot, to mention two of the least of my discomforts, but I would oft-times make a picture of me and Henry puffing our pipes comfortably in the long evenings. Do you ever make a picture like that, Toby?'

'On occasion.'

'Sophina and me, it was the storms we loved to watch. Do you think the Day of Judgment might look like this, Toby?'

Tobias pushed himself harder against the wall of the coach.

'My Sophina always thought so. Look, she would say, how all our troubles are little things beneath that mighty storm.'

Toby smiled weakly, sickened by this puerile philosophizing.

'See yonder clouds above Holborn,' continued his companion. 'Look at all the old men's faces in the sky. They'll rattle the windows, Toby. There'll be some fireworks with this one. But we'll survive it, you and me. Perhaps you may visit me and Henry when you've forgotten the pain in your wrists. Are they paining badly?'

'I can bear it.'

'See, I'm as good as my word, for here we are almost in Cecil Street where Mrs Britten sells her famous pills. I'm surprised you never read her puffs. Well, I will be a moment collecting these items and I am sure you won't scarper, for if you should, I would have a very sad story to deliver to your wife.'

The carriage stopped, and Jack jumped down. He was soon hammering on a black door with his silver-topped stick.

There was some brief dispute with a person inside, then Jack was admitted. Not three minutes passed before he was clambering back aboard to sit opposite Tobias once more, and the cabby was plying the whip *con gusto*. As they pushed violently into Cross Street, the convict's face was clearly very strange: the cheeks hard and hatchet-like, the eyes awash with such violent emotion that Toby began to fear that the potion had been refused him.

'All in order, Jack?'

Maggs delved deep into the pocket of his Great Joseph and produced a small white jar.

Tobias looked at his companion's trembling hands with some apprehension, but whatever drama had transpired behind that door he was never to know. Jack Maggs returned the jar into his pocket.

292

'I cannot produce your son tonight, you know that.'

'But you *will* produce him, Toby.'

'Yes.'

'What time in the morning would that be, Toby?'

'Ten o'clock,' said Toby decisively.

'Could you deliver my papers to Henry beforehand? It would be useful for him to read a little before we sit to have our yarn.'

'I could not deliver anything before ten.'

Said Maggs: 'You know too much to lie to me again.'

'I know the forfeit.'

They travelled in silence until they had entered Lamb's Conduit Street and Tobias realized that Jack Maggs intended to disembark with him.

'Jack, I do think this matter with the lady is my own affair. It is not something to be done in company.'

'I have business in your house, Toby.'

'It is private business, Jack. You must trust me. Cut my bonds, I will not run away.'

'First, we are to burn the contents of the tin box. Second . . .' Jack Maggs removed the cork from the porcelain jar and held it out so its contents might finally be examined.

Before they disembarked, Tobias had time to look inside the jar and see, not the clean white pills he had hitherto imagined, but some strange unsanitary little lumps of matter the colour of Virginia tobacco.

79

Henry Phipps had always been excessively afraid of thunder; so much so, that in those long-ago days of his wardship, his tutor had built the most fanciful fortifications against it.

This tutor, V. P. Littlehales by name (the same individual named in that famous case with Dr Wollaston), had conceived a most elaborate series of towers and trenches on the quarter-acre of meadow attached to their cottage at Great Missenden. To the extent that this maze had been pedagogical in intention, it had failed: Henry learned nothing useful of the nature of the elements. To the extent that it had been magical, its power was insufficient: lightning had twice struck the old oak tree at its centre.

Victor Littlehales had been a gentle but troubled soul and, if truth be told, very superstitious about lightning. No matter what lectures he delivered on Natural Law, the great sum of his instruction was that they were base beasts, naked before a vengeful, all-seeing God. The only comfort he could offer his pupil was the mortal cradle of his freckled arms, and even that he finally withdrew: Victor Littlehales abruptly and inexplicably disappeared from Henry Phipps's life on the eve of the young man's twenty-first birthday.

On the same humid afternoon on which Jack Maggs returned to London, Mr Buckle paid a second visit to Henry Phipps. His host on this occasion looked neither like a boy abandoned nor like a man afraid of thunder. He received the ex-grocer and his whispering lawyer in the uniform of a subaltern of the 57th Foot Regiment. He stood before them stiffly, his hands behind his back, and, in looking down at them along the barrel of his straight thin nose, gave the impression of being both impatient and sarcastic.

When the thunder first sounded in the distance, Henry Phipps squinted slightly, but otherwise showed no emotion.

Mr Buckle did not hear the thunder, being too preoccupied with his own agenda to notice very much else at all. Not even the military uniform surprised him, and it certainly would never have occurred to him that this commission had been purchased in a great panic not three days previous.

Mr Buckle and Mr Makepeace seated themselves side by side on the Chesterfield. Henry Phipps remained standing with his back to the windows, flexing his knees a little strangely.

'May I ask you your business, Mr Buckle?'

'I have come,' said Mr Buckle, 'to inquire as to your decision about your benefactor.' He was about to introduce his companion, but Mr Phipps turned his back and abruptly drew the curtains shut. This disconcerted Mr Buckle, who felt himself somehow reprimanded. 'Of course it is not my affair.'

294

'True.' Henry Phipps struck a match, and spent some moments fiddling with a lamp. 'It is in no manner your business, and yet I would have thought it obvious I have a new benefactor.'

'I have told no one, I assure you.'

'No, you mistake my meaning. His Majesty has become my benefactor, Mr Buckle. As you see, I am now a soldier.'

Now Mr Buckle appraised the uniform. Though no great student of the military, he knew enough to realize that the regiment was unfashionable, the rank lowly.

'No,' he said. 'This won't do.'

Outside, the lightning flashed. Henry Phipps sat down quickly, and rested his chin in his cupped hand. 'I am not going to be a dancing boy for a criminal.'

'No, Sir. Indeed not. That is not what I wished, Sir. The opposite. Did you forget our conversation?'

'You seemed to imagine that I was corrupted by my comfortable life and would do anything to sustain it. But I would not lower myself to that, Sir.'

'Nor should you, Sir. That was not my idea at all. It is for this very reason I have brought with me Mr Makepeace. Perhaps you have heard his name, Sir: he is a distinguished solicitor. Mr Makepeace has, at my request, studied the appropriate precedents.'

'Precedents,' Mr Makepeace whispered in agreement.

'Precedents which by their very nature must affect yourself. It is not too late, Sir. You are too good a man to be a subaltern.'

'It is the case of the Crown *versus* Forsythe,' continued Mr Makepeace in his distinctive whisper.

'What?' said Henry Phipps.

'In the best of weather, he is hard to hear,' admitted Mr Buckle. 'But always worth the effort.'

'In the case of Mrs Forsythe,' continued Mr Makepeace implacably, 'who did kill her son. The Crown *versus* Forsythe. It is a case well known in the Inns of Court. It has that immediate advantage – you may mention it to anyone and be saved the time and expense of their going to look it up.'

'I cannot hear you.'

'It is Mr Makepeace's affliction,' interrupted Mr Buckle, 'that his voice box was damaged as a child. But it is to your advantage, Sir, for he comes the cheaper on account of it.'

'It is of the Crown *versus* Forsythe that I speak,' said Makepeace.

'Then speak, for God's sake,' snapped Henry Phipps. The rain was now coming down very hard against the window pane, and Henry Phipps leaned forward in his chair and held his elbows in his cupped hands.

'The Crown charged that Mrs Forsythe had murdered her son in order to reclaim the ancestral home from which she had been cast out on the occasion of her husband's death. She was a very proud woman, and much attached to entertaining. Her son, as the heir to the property, was expected to take up residence in the Hall, and the mother to live in a dowager cottage on the estate. Nothing wrong with that. All quite in order. Then one wet night the son, it was alleged, broke into the dowager cottage with an axe, and his mother, allegedly mistaking him for a violent burglar, shot him through the heart.'

'I do not have time for this,' said Henry Phipps abruptly. He peered around the curtains, then sat immediately down again.

'Ask me the verdict,' Mr Makepeace demanded.

Henry Phipps pointedly ignored him, and turned up the lamp.

'What was the verdict, Mr Makepeace?' asked Percy Buckle.

'English law has always held that you cannot profit from your own crime. A chap cannot inherit the estate of a person he has unlawfully killed.'

'Unlawfully. That is your point, I warrant.'

'Indeed it is,' said Mr Makepeace. 'The law has always held that reasonable force may be used in defending one's own home. Mrs Forsythe was found not guilty.'

'It is too late for this,' said Henry Phipps, but his manner was very sad, and when Mr Buckle advanced upon him, he seemed to have lost all will to resist.

'In a short while,' announced Mr Buckle, 'a criminal will break into your house.' He then produced, from the depths of his tweed jacket, a large pistol. 'You will shoot him through the heart.'

Henry Phipps stared with horror upon this weapon.

'For God's sake, man. Are you mad?'

Mr Buckle continued to hold him with his eyes. There was a fixed sort of grimace, almost a rictus, on his face.

'You have a very nice house,' said Mr Buckle, laying the weapon on a nearby table. 'It is natural that you would wish to keep your hands on it, so to speak. If Jack Maggs breaks in your door with an axe, you are allowed to shoot him.'

'Why would you think he would carry an axe?'

'What I know, I know,' said Percy Buckle.

'You are certain he will come?'

'I have spoken to his travelling companion's wife. They are expected in London today or tomorrow. You should wait upon his arrival.'

'I do not know the man.'

'When you are a soldier, Sir, you will be called upon to fight many men you do not know, and for less reason than this.'

'But he has done nothing to me that I should harm him.'

The oil lamp sputtered, and went out. Mr Buckle could see the huddled dark shape of Henry Phipps not three feet from him in the gloom. He was all bent over himself, like a great round boulder that must be somehow levered off the hillside and sent plummeting onto the enemy below.

80

The rain had been heavy this last half-hour, but as Mercy let herself in through the kitchen door, it began falling in sheets, flooding the street and cascading down into the area. She leaned her dripping umbrella beside the door, and a small yellow rivulet began to invade the gloomy kitchen. It crossed the floor, making directly for Miss Mott, who was standing at the deal table not more than a yard away.

'I'm very sorry, Cook.'

Miss Mott continued to sprinkle flour, and roll out pastry.

'I was running a message for the master.'

There was a mighty clap of thunder. At this, Miss Mott raised her tightly braided head like a turtle.

'I was on an errand, Miss. It ain't my fault.'

Mercy now cut her path wide around the cook.

'And where might you be off to now?'

Mercy hesitated. Then, as lightning flashed through the window, she set off briskly up the stairs.

'You come back here.'

'I'll be back in a moment.'

Whereupon Mercy ran. She left tracks of mud in all six ground-floor rooms without finding the object of her search. The house was unusually cold and dark. She took one of the small wax dips Mr Constable kept in a china bowl in the hallway, but did not light it as yet. She ascended the stairs to the second floor which was queerly deserted. The door to the snuggery was shut.

Please God, let Jack Maggs be returned.

She opened the door. Though it was very dark inside, she had the feeling of someone present. There was a small sound, clear above the sound of the storm: *tap, tap, tap*. She lit the dip and held it up.

A single sad sheet of paper lay upon the bureau. It was from here that the *tap* was emanating, like a whispering ghost. She touched the paper, then felt a sharp shock as a drip of water hit the back of her hand.

The roof was leaking. This is what she tried to explain to Miss Mott when the angry cook came to fetch her back to work. The box gutter was blocked again. It was what she told the master when he arrived, soaking wet, a moment behind Miss Mott. Indeed, she stood on his chair and held her finger up to the drooping fabric canopy. She showed them: the drip became a trickle running down her arm.

Then Mr Buckle sent Miss Mott back to her kitchen. He held out his wet hand so he might help Mercy down off the chair.

'He's back, ain't he?' he asked Mercy.

'Is he?'

She watched him as he brushed away the mud her shoes had left upon his chair.

298

'What are you doing skulking round here?'

'The roof's leaking, ain't it.'

Mr Buckle took an altar candle from the bureau drawer; it burned with a smoky yellow flame which gave his face, wet from the rain, a strange and ghoulish appearance.

'You tell me where Jack Maggs is hiding or by God I'll make you sorry, Missy.'

Although rain was now pouring through the ceiling, Mr Buckle did not seem to notice.

'I don't wish him harm,' he said.

Mercy laughed incredulously.

For answer, he hit her. She did not see his hand but felt the jolt, saw the explosion of sparks inside the darkness of her skull.

She fell back, steadying herself against the paisley drapery. He knelt down with her, bringing the candle so he might peer into her eyes. She saw molten wax spilling onto her apron; she felt the snuggery curtains as wet as sheets upon the clothesline. Resting her cheek against them, she began to cry.

He was sitting upon the little ottoman from which she herself had watched Jack Maggs write his history. Mr Buckle's moustache was sodden, and his brown eyes glistened with tears. As the water cascaded through the paisley he patted down his side burns, as if to still whatever beastliness had been awakened in his heart.

'I'm sorry, Missy, very sorry. I can't bear the damage he has done to us. I swear to God I will never hit you again, only tell me: is he hiding in the house next door?'

The water had plastered his hair dark close upon his head, and she could see, through the wet poplin of his shirt sleeves, his dreadful ropy wrists. He made as if to touch her knee. She drew back into herself. He was vile.

'You must not leave me, Mercy.'

'How could I leave you?'

She had a vision of the filthy water sliding behind the wallpaper, creeping down into the dining room below. She pictured all the house below her to be wet, spongy, beyond repair.

'Where would I go? You've ruined me.'

'You will always be my Good Companion,' said Percy Buckle with much emotion. 'I have taken care of you, have I not? When you have been naughty, have I not forgiven you?'

'I was *not* naughty,' said Mercy angrily. 'And I never would have been alone with him if you had stayed with me in the snuggery. It was not my fault what happened.'

'What happened?'

'Nothing happened.'

'I'll kill him,' said Percy Buckle quietly.

Mercy rose to her feet. 'I know where you was just now,' she said. 'I know what you was up to. You went sneaking down to Covent Garden to talk to Mr Phipps.'

Mr Buckle remained seated upon the ottoman. He placed his large hands on his bony knees. 'Say you didn't follow me. That's all. Say that to me.'

'I didn't need to follow you. I heard your wicked scheming before you put a step outside. You were plotting with that lard-bag from the Inns of Court again.'

Percy Buckle cocked his head on one side. 'My, my.' He made a small round O with his mouth and then covered it with his hand. 'You seem to have lost all of your respect.'

'I heard what harm you wish to cause that man.'

'You can have no idea what I intend. I never said what I intended.'

'You just said it, then. You're going to murder him.'

Mr Buckle did not deny this. 'So, something did occur between you?'

'I kissed him,' she responded fiercely.

'In my house?'

'Aye, I kissed him, and he held me here inside this very room. When you left me like the coward you are, I kissed him. And I am not sorry that I did.'

'You are a very brave little miss,' said Percy Buckle with a dangerous smile.

'Hit me again.'

'No, Miss, I will not hit you.'

'Then what will you do?'

Percy Buckle removed the key to the snuggery from his pocket, and held it out to her. 'Why, I will present you with this key.'

The water had eased off and was just dribbling down onto the desk. Mercy looked at the key lying in the master's hand.

'What is this?' she asked. 'What would I do with this?'

'It's the key to the city,' said Percy Buckle sarcastically.

'What do you mean?'

He dropped the key back in his jacket pocket. 'You are dismissed,' he said, and remained staring at her with his horrid smirking face until Mercy turned and left the room. She had nowhere to go. As she trod the dark staircase to her attic, she reflected that she was now worse off than when she first arrived.

She bolted the door behind her. She opened the window and climbed out onto the roof.

81

At the moment the two travellers entered that deep green drawing room, Elizabeth Warriner was sitting in a straight-backed chair by the window. She was wearing a dress which was very bright and luminous, like the whites in Henry Bone's enamel portraits. There was light also in her eyes and this, combined with the angle of her head, immediately bespoke a very intense kind of interest in her visitors, as if she knew that her fate was to be decided by the pair of them.

She placed her tea cup carefully on the sill and rose to meet them. Tobias then came to the fore. He approached her, his hands still manacled inside his pockets.

'Hullo.'

'Hullo.'

She was exceptionally agitated, and for a moment it seemed to Jack Maggs that she would rush into her lover's arms, but then he saw her gather herself in. She stretched out a hand to tug at the arm of her brother-in-law's travel-stained coat.

'Something is the matter with your hands, Toby?'

301

'No, no.' His red lips twisted into a lopsided smile. 'A little prank of Master Maggs. Where is my wife, Lizzie?'

'I rather think she will sit with Grandma Warriner until the storm is over.'

'Yes,' said Tobias Oates, staring at her expectantly.

'It will be a big storm,' she said. 'The sky is extremely dark. I have been watching it.'

'You are not frightened?'

'Of the storm? Oh no.'

'There is a spot of business I must transact with Master Maggs.'

The girl looked briefly at Jack Maggs, but quickly returned her frank gaze. 'Tobias, we really must discuss my trip to France.'

'Yes, I will drink a cup of tea with you the moment this business is concluded. Is the pot fresh?'

'It is rather bitter, as a matter of fact. Mary insisted on making it herself. I tell her she is poisoning me, but she says it is from Rajasthan.'

'Mr Maggs, come up to my office, and we will deal with the contents of the tin box.'

While Jack Maggs judged the gentleman very hard for this off-hand behaviour with his beloved, he obligingly followed him up the stairs. It was not until they were both inside the writer's office that he took Tobias Oates roughly by the arm.

'Go back downstairs,' he demanded. '*Kiss* her.'

Tobias attempted unsuccessfully to shake himself free.

'She is still a girl,' said Jack. 'She is in a terror. Tell her you have the pills, and you will take care of the situation.'

'Then release my hands, Sir.'

'Do not give me orders, mutt.'

'If you do not release my hands I cannot do as you wish, for I do not have hands to give her the pills.'

Jack Maggs took out his dagger, and did that which was required. He cut roughly and watched while Tobias did up his buttons.

'Give her two pills, and when you have done that come back to me. If you run away or leave the house, I will have to hurt her.'

Petulantly, Tobias rubbed the red marks on his wrists. Jack

Maggs despised him for a sissy. 'Go,' he said. 'Do it now.'

'Why would you have me tread this path?'

'You would be a very stupid lad to argue with me.'

'But is this not the very path that brought you and Sophina so much pain and anguish? Is this not what I hear you howling about each time the magnets touch you?'

Jack Maggs put his mangled claw upon his face, clamped his nose, his chin, his jaw, as if he were a dog whose life could be shaken from him. The convict's rage was very great, and he brought his vile cracked lips very close into the other's face.

'What else can she do? If she has your baby her life is ruined. This is the only path she has available.'

'I cannot take it.'

'It is not for you, Nokes. It is for her.' And with that he pushed Tobias out the door. Halfway down, the reluctant writer turned and saw Jack Maggs's massive shadow on the landing.

He made a venomous, impatient sound, which Tobias would remember later as a kind of hiss.

82

It had always been Tobias's method to approach his subject by way of the body. When he had set himself the task of writing about Jack Maggs, he had first produced a short essay on his hands, pondering not merely the fate of the hidden tendons, the bones, the phalanges, the intercarpals which would one day be liberated by the worms, but also their history: what other hands they had caressed, what lives they had taken in anger. He began by picturing the newborn hand resting briefly on its mother's breast, and then he sketched, in the space of four pages, the whole long story leading towards and away from that 'hideously misshapen claw'. This essay he knew to be a jewel, and he had hoarded it like a clock-maker, setting it aside for its small part in his grand machine. Now, with his wrists raw and red from bondage, he had, to put it very mildly, lost interest in his subject: the Criminal Mind had become repulsive to his own imagination.

Yet it was the Criminal Mind which now controlled Tobias. It was at its directive that he must now, this instant, hold his sister-in-law in his arms. Under its orders he placed two pills in that tender white hand and spoke as confidently, nay, as reverently, as if they had been communion wafers. Yet even as he calmed Lizzie's fears he saw, in the pills' brown misshapen form, not the salvation he promised, but the excrement of something abominable and verminous.

Then came three loud thumps on the floor above his head. Returning to his office, he found the murderer, legs wide apart, demanding to be presented with his 'secrets'. He showed the writer no particular respect; indeed, he occupied his office wholly, the rank oil-skin odour of his coat possessing every corner of the room.

Later Tobias mourned the manuscripts he then so readily destroyed, for he very soon forgot how badly he had wanted Jack Maggs gone from his life. He might have contrived to hold back the best of his treasures, but no, he jumped up and down on chairs and ladders, divesting himself of everything related to Jack Maggs. Here – pigeon-holed at 'H' – was the essay on the hands. Beside it, folded in four, were another two pages labelled 'Hair'. This Jack Maggs received incredulously.

'This is my hair? All this about my bloody hair?'

'Yes.'

'But nothing else?'

'That only.'

There had been eight magnetic sessions in all, and the record of each one was tied and bundled in good neat order as you see the clerks do at the Inns of Court. Toby had to stand on his desk top, on tip-toes, to reach, and then he threw them at their subject.

'All this is me?'

'One way or another.'

Jack Maggs, for his part, untied each bundle and, although he did not read everything, he did read a good deal, enough to cause a very great embarrassment to show upon his face.

'My boy must not read this,' he said.

'We burn it,' agreed Tobias Oates. 'We burn it now.'

The thunder echoed in the streets. Wind and rain rushed round and round the little garden.

83

Lizzie sat in her chair. She sat with her novel open on her lap while she endured her terrible thoughts. Sometimes she read a line or two, but there was not a word in *Castle Rackrent* that could not in some way lead her back to her situation, to that homunculus which, being a creature of her own heart and blood, must be at least dimly aware of its fate. Did it not then, as she did, wait in dread, knowing that its last small hope had been taken from it?

She could not feel the poor creature any more than she could feel the presence of God or His angels, and yet she knew every moment of her life to be ruled by its presence, and even as the storm descended upon them and a mighty wind rushed down Lamb's Conduit Street, pushing an empty wooden barrel before it, Lizzie sat with her hands resting over her belly.

When she heard Toby's footsteps on the stairs, she felt no great expectation of comfort from that quarter. He had talked; she had listened. She did not blame him. She had done as he said.

But then she saw he brought that wretched convict back with him, and that the pair of them were carrying all manner of scrolls and piles of manuscript which they dropped, carelessly, before the fireplace. They did not look at Lizzie, or acknowledge her. Thus there was, in their general busyness, a kind of heartlessness.

Toby removed the fire-screen which she and he had bought together, one happy morning on Holborn in the early spring. Toby had always been afraid of fire, as if it would be the thing which would dash in and steal everything from him. How often, she thought, we defend ourselves against the wrong thing.

It was quite hot and close in the room, with the windows closed against the storm, but the two men were tearing up Toby's manuscripts, as if they planned to begin a fire. Now her brother-in-law knelt before the grate and Lizzie caught, in the cast of his mouth, a glimpse of his great stubbornness, his will. Why he was about to destroy his own creation was beyond her, but how she wished she might have a will like that, and not be sitting here now when she might have gone away on a ship to France.

The rattling of the window pane brought her attention back to the street, and there she presently spied a small bent woman attempting to cross the busy road. She was not an old woman, but clearly destitute. Her clothes were ragged, her legs bowed, and she had the panicky motion of a small creature that knows itself the prey of many larger ones. She was carrying some treasure in her pinafore, and there she was, like a beetle or an ant, determined to cross whatever obstacle chance put in her path. The rain was very heavy but the wagons were no smaller or slower on account of it. Lizzie watched the woman take a step forward, then one back, then forward and then, finally, the poor soul made a fast and desperate foray out into the centre of the road.

Here, with a brewery dray almost on top of her, she slipped and fell.

She had been carrying onions in her apron and now all these treasures went rolling out across the coal-black road. The Clydesdale's soup-plate hooves scattered the onions. The wheel of a brewer's dray passed by the woman's head. She rose hastily and began to gather up her onions.

Lizzie began quietly to cry.

On hearing the striking of a match, she turned. Toby was holding a match to the papers in the grate. She watched the fire catch. She watched the papers burn.

Then she saw that Toby had closed his eyes, and in that moment his face was so forlorn that she could easily see what great damage was being done to him as well. As the flames illuminated his familiar face, Lizzie saw, not stubbornness any longer, but a death mask, like the one he had always kept in his office.

It was then she understood that her life had always been travelling towards this point. There was always to be this storm. The poor woman was always going to fall. This moment had lain there waiting since the day when Tobias had first come to court her sister at her father's house at Amersham.

Now the wind rushed down the chimney, blowing smoke into the room. Toby and the convict were arguing. Toby wished the convict to go to his home. The convict said that he would 'damned well' stay all night. She did not pay them much attention. She was thinking that she had been a very selfish girl indeed. She had always known the hurt she risked doing to her sister, and of that she had been careless enough, but she had never considered the harm possible to that luminous young man who had appeared before her family's window one Sunday morning, dressed-up as a sailor, dancing a hornpipe. He had a boy's face, and sweet needful lips, but he had been, although the world had not yet seen it, a giant amongst men.

And she, Lizzie, had almost ruined him, and she could not bear that that be so. She laid her hand again upon that little mound, that soft roundness of her stomach.

The men's voices were softer now. It seemed the convict would indeed depart for his own establishment, and return here in the morning. A threat was made, a last match lit. She watched the final sheaf of papers flare, and saw the shrouds of blue and yellow as Toby stirred them with the poker. In the flames she saw ghostly figures, fictions rising amidst the skirts of flame.

When this last blaze had died away, the grate was filled with mourning: all those lines of gorgeous copperplate had become sheets of black crêpe which he now struck at with a poker. Whether they were struck in anger or merely from a desire to make them burn more efficiently, she could not tell; but if the latter, this intention was soon thwarted by the wind, which once again blew fiercely down the chimney and this time carried the black and broken paper out into the room. The men leapt back, coughing and waving their hands. The burnt papers rose, like black moths, as high as the ceiling.

Elizabeth Warriner, Tobias Oates, Jack Maggs – they all stood as the black ash fell around them.

84

'Like I said, mate,' said Jack Maggs, opening the door and stepping into Lamb's Conduit Street, 'I'll be at your door at ten o'clock tomorrow morning.'

'You trust me now, Jack?'

Jack Maggs shrugged. The pills Lizzie Warriner had now ingested would soon begin their work. Then Tobias Oates would be so fully occupied, his hands might as well be tied.

'Are you not the least concerned that I might run?'

The other smiled grimly. 'You tried that once already.'

'Still, I might betray you.'

'You're in too deep, mate. You'd get no benefit, no benefit at all.'

For all this, Jack Maggs was by no means complacent. When he once again approached his property in Great Queen Street he in no way resembled the fellow who had got down off the Dover *Rocket*. Like a rat along the wainscot, he moved very quietly, melting with the shadows. He spied on his own house for a full hour before he crossed the street and unlocked its front door with a set of 'ticklers'.

While the storm had long since abated, the windows were heavily curtained and so, although it was only nine o'clock, the house was very dark.

As Jack Maggs closed the door behind him, he felt the presence. There was no unexpected sound, no foreign odour: the ground floor gave off that same satisfying beeswax smell as hitherto. Yet there was someone here, no doubt about it. And now Jack allowed himself to acknowledge that he had hoped it would be thus. Indeed it was this very prospect which had drawn him away from Lamb's Conduit Street when prudence should have kept him there all night. The hairs on the back of his neck prickled.

Cautiously, he stooped for his knife. He felt the rough sure grip of the handle which he himself had made with twine and tar. A convict's knife, it dated from before the time when he could have afforded the finest steel and ivory for the handle. He crouched now, a powerful shadow in the doorway of his own living room, drawing the blade in wide circles through the night.

Noiseless as a shade, he then moved forward towards the settle. He heard a small sniffle.

'Henry?'

There was a second sniffle.

'Henry, is that you?'

He struck a match, thus revealing a sad and sorry Mercy Larkin, huddled in a tartan cocoon upon the settle.

'Christ, that was a foolish thing to do.'

He sat heavily on a gilded chair, well apart from her.

'I'm sorry.'

'I told you, don't stick your nose where it ain't wanted.'

'I'm sorry.'

'I told you long ago it were dangerous.'

'You thought I were Mr Phipps.' Mercy sat up and blew her nose. 'I'm sorry if I frightened you.'

'You could not frighten me, girlie. It would take more than you to frighten me.' But he felt sick and sour with disappointment and he did not bother to hide his great displeasure.

'You was expecting your Henry?'

He slid his knife back in his boot. 'None of your business.'

'If that's what's got you in a snot, I can take you to him now.'

'*You*?'

'Why do you look at me like that?' She folded up the tartan rug as if her departure were imminent. 'Do you think I am such an idiot I couldn't find my way to Covent Garden?'

85

In Jack Maggs's dark and empty house, Mercy Larkin had prayed, *Dear God forgive me for not visiting my mother. Dear God, grant me a position.*

Around herself she had assembled those few possessions which were her own: the cushions she had embroidered for her room, and the picture her grandma had painted of her poor mama, sitting below a Dutch windmill with a rag doll on her knee.

On and on she prayed, curled up inside Jack Maggs's tartan rug.

Dear God, please soften the Master's heart. Have him write me my references. Dear God, if that ain't possible, let Jack Maggs come back and let me find favour with him. God send him to me.

Then she fell asleep, and when she awoke, she felt the dark air moving across her cheek and heard, 'Henry? Henry, is that you?'

A match exploded in the air above her head.

Lo: Jack Maggs.

He was wild and shabby. His eyes were red, his hair lank and greasy, unwashed and sprinkled throughout with ashes. The lining of his coat was torn, and there appeared to be a dark brown stain upon its hem. There was about him that bitter unwashed smell of a man weary from long labour.

'Christ!' he cried. 'By Jesus, that was a silly thing to do.'

Dear God, forgive his words.

He sat on a chair against the wall, rubbing at his cheek, gathering its flesh and pushing it up towards his temple. His bright red waistcoat was all speckled with mud. He was ever so cross, glaring at her from his red-rimmed eyes. And she was sorry, and sorry again, and sorry one more time, until she realized it was in her power to bestow on him his wish.

Dear God, I thank you.

'Why do you look at me like that?' she said, placing the folded tartan rug neatly on top of her embroidered cushions. 'Do you think I am such an idiot I couldn't find my way to Covent Garden?'

'Henry Phipps is in Covent Garden?'

'He is.'

His belligerence then washed away, and left in its place a kind of soft confusion. She felt a powerful urge to take his wild and knotted head and wash it in warm water.

'How came you by this information, Mercy?'

Mercy could not admit how long she had known this secret, but neither did she wish to begin to tell untruths again.

'Constable told me Mr Phipps was your son.'

310

'It's true,' he sighed. 'But I ain't seen him since he was a nipper.'

'Then he carries a picture in his heart of the last day he saw you.'

'He was but four years of age.'

'I too can remember when I lost my da, Jack Maggs. I remember the very day, and were he to come back to me, why I know my heart would burst. Sometimes I still dream he is alive. And in those few precious moments when I wake, I am happy beyond anything you could imagine. Surely it is going to be the same with him when he looks up . . . and there you will be.'

Even as she drew this happy picture, she had that unclean feeling that always accompanies deception. She knew that she was sending Jack Maggs to break his heart, and yet she could not help herself, when she saw how benevolently he began to look upon her. It was what she had craved, dear God forgive her.

Jack Maggs lit the candles and gazed rather forlornly at a place above his mantelpiece. Mercy followed his gaze and found, inside that elaborate circle of gilt which framed a massive mirror, the prodigal father's soiled and care-worn image.

'You cannot go calling in those clothes,' she said. 'Here, give them to me. You don't want to frighten the boy.'

He gave a long sigh, then divested himself as she indicated: first surrendering the long great-coat, then the four-button jacket beneath it, then the red waistcoat. Finally, he stood before her, his white shirt stained with sweat, wet on the back.

'You rest yourself now,' she said.

Jack Maggs lay down as commanded, curling up his legs on the settle. At that moment she truly did love him.

There were shutters on the kitchen windows, and these Mercy closed. She lit the fire and stoked it high. She put on the kettle. She also set two flat irons on the hottest part, near the fire box. When the kettle was boiling she steamed the mud spots on the waistcoat. These ran in a fine spray, like the tail of a peacock across the breast, but by dint of careful sponging and judicious use of soap jelly, she soon had this first garment restored to its best crimson.

Her cheeks were flushed from the hot steam. She pressed the waistcoat, then hung it on the door knob. Miss Mott would not have recognized her diligence. Without so much as a teaspoon of sugar to refresh herself, Mercy laid out the oilskin coat across the kitchen table and ministered to it with a stout scrubbing brush. It had been a handsome coat, with three wide capes on its shoulder, and she was pleased to make it seem so once again. One pocket had been ripped clean away, and although this damage was not obvious on the surface of the coat, there was some dark brown sticky substance below the pocket flap. This she sponged away. The other pocket was undamaged and housed the selfsame locks of hair she had found on an earlier occasion.

With these two mysteries in her hands again, she sat on a three-legged stool before the fire box and carefully interrogated them. She sniffed, but there was no smell to them. She picked at the woollen yarn with her nail, but could judge nothing from it.

'Mercy, what are you up to?'

She jumped. He held out his hand and she returned the locks of hair to him.

'I didn't mean nothing by it,' she said. 'I was just helping you.'

'Is it not too dangerous for you to help me?'

'You refer to the Master? He has dispensed with me.'

'Dispensed, Mercy?'

'I have been dismissed, Sir.'

She was surprised to find how easily she could say it, and then she saw his brow erupt in a frown of such concern that it brought a sudden well of tears into her eyes.

'I don't mind,' she reassured him. 'I don't mind at all.'

'What was your crime?'

'Go home to your babies,' she said.

It was not what she had intended to say.

He blinked at her.

But it was obvious to her now. She saw it. Perhaps she had always known. 'You have babies in the place where you have come from.'

His mouth tightened in denial.

'My son is an Englishman.'

'I meant your real children.'

'I am not of that race.'

312

'What race?'

'The Australian race,' he said. 'The race of Australians.'

'But what of your babes?'

'Damn you, don't look at me like that. I am an Englishman.'

'You are their da, Jack. They walk along the street, they think they see your face in the clouds.'

'I made my promise to Henry before they were born.'

'He looks at no clouds for you.'

'He what?'

'He don't see your face.'

At this, he shook her till her teeth rattled in her head.

'What do you know?' he roared, his face turning a dark russet red. 'What . . . do . . . you . . . know?'

At which Mercy burst into tears and threw her head upon his broad chest. 'I know what it is to lose a da.'

He stood still and hard as a post a moment, but then he put his arms around her waist. The kettle began to boil. The pair of them swayed to and fro like a couple in a dance.

86

The spasm had passed, and Lizzie Warriner, now exhausted and putty-skinned, curled herself up amongst the discoloured sheets of the bed wherein she had suffered these last five hours.

Mary sought to push back the damp hair from her sister's brow, although this brought the sufferer no peace. Lizzie thrust the hand away, then pulled irritably at the tangled rope of sheet between her knees.

'I have been poisoned.'

In response, Mary tucked her plump chin into her neck and looked sternly at her sister. Then she picked up and folded a yellow shawl that had fallen to the floor. She placed the shawl on the dresser beside a chipped brown basin which had been fetched with such urgency from the nursery. Now she covered the basin with a beaded cloth and placed it beneath the bed. 'Come, come.' She put her arm beneath the girl's slender back. 'We will change the sheets again.'

'No, Mary. You will only ruin your best linen.'

At this Mary's face crumpled, and she fell upon her sister's neck. 'Oh Lizzie, Lizzie, I do love you.'

'Ssh, Mary. Please save your tears for someone better.'

'There is no one in the world better. It is I who should be better. For it is I who have caused you such suffering.'

'Rest easy in your mind, poor dear girl. The blame is hardly yours.'

'I did not do it maliciously, I swear. But I have guessed your secret these last two weeks.'

This revelation produced a most noticeable silence, broken only when the next spasm shook the girl on the bed and produced a loud high cry of pain. When the convulsion had passed, she tugged at her sister's sleeve.

'You knew of my condition?' she whispered. 'How could you know? Who could tell you such a thing?'

'You will be well again soon. When the medicine has finished its work.'

'What medicine do you mean?'

'Tablets, dearest. You remember the tea you complained of. You said it was so bitter . . .'

'Oh Mary, Mary,' cried Lizzie despairingly.

'It is for the best, you will see,' said Mary, beginning to fuss once more with her sister's hair. 'Your secret will trouble you no more, my darling.'

In answer Lizzie thrust her hand angrily away and looked out into the lamp light with the wild and angry eyes of an animal that her sister did not recognize. 'You really should have told me what it was you planned.'

In her mind's eye Mary Oates suddenly saw the horrid rouged face of Mrs Britten. She saw the drooping eyes, the great pitted nose, the manly hand with the name SILAS tattooed on its wrist.

This vision was disturbed by her husband, inquiring anxiously from outside the locked door. She opened it a crack to tell him there was nothing new to report. Although she barely recognized the fact yet, she had begun to hate Tobias. Later the roots of this emotion would penetrate the deepest reaches of her soul and make her into the slow and famously dim-witted creature who was commonly thought not to understand half of what her famous husband said, but for now the hate was only a small sharp seed, a pin prick in the corner of her heart, and she was far too worried to concern herself with it. Meanwhile Tobias paced outside the bedroom door, a model of 'brotherly concern' and 'propriety'.

'Put your arm around my shoulder and I will slip the bottom sheet from under you.'

'No.'

'It will make you more comfortable.'

'No, damn you!'

'Lizzie!'

Lizzie grasped her older sister by the wrist. 'Listen to me, Mary.' She stared so fiercely and frankly that Mary was ashamed. 'Promise me,' Lizzie demanded.

'Yes, dear. What shall I promise you?'

Lizzie's dark hair had long ago become unpinned, and now it formed a great tangled frame around her damp white face. 'You must swear.'

'Dear Lizzie, tell me and I will swear it to you.'

'When I am gone . . .'

'Don't! You must not say such things.'

'When I am gone, you will roll up my sheets. You will not look at them. You will burn them on the fire.'

Mary looked at the vast amount of blood which was soaking into the mattress on which her younger sister lay, and was suddenly afraid.

'I will call the doctor.'

'No,' said the girl, lying back on her pillows. 'It is too late for doctors.'

'Tobias will fetch Dr Grieves now,' said Mary. She would surely go to prison once the doctor discovered the sorry deed that had been accomplished that night. Soon all of England would know how she had put poison in her sister's tea.

'Promise me, Mary.'

Mary called urgently for her husband. 'Tobias!'

There was no answer. She flung open the door and found the landing empty. She ran downstairs but he was nowhere to be seen. Back in the sick room, Lizzie was writhing convulsively upon the bed. Mary held the basin ready for her sister to release the green fluid from her stomach. What was spilled into the bowl was laced around with red. When the spasm was done, Mary placed the beaded cloth on the top of the bowl, and wiped her sister's brow.

87

Mercy would have preferred to cut his hair in the kitchen, but no, His Majesty must sit in his grand room on his throne, dressed up once more in his cock robin waistcoat and his nice sponged jacket. You could see him as the Lord of his Manor, dogs at his feet, a fire blazing in the grate.

She tucked a sheet around his newly shaven chin and began to snip at his wet hair while he sat upright, formal in his living room. She had, cross her heart, no plan to be in the least bold with him. She would cut his hair and make him look nice for his visit. As God was her witness, she had no other plan, unless it was to be granted a position in his household.

'Keep still.'

'I'm thinking.' He blew out his cheeks. 'I've got such bloody marvellous thoughts inside my head.'

'What would you be thinking?'

'Could I ask you to run a message for me early?'

She put her hands upon the top of his head to hold it firm. 'Well, I ain't employed by no one else.'

'You could be employed by me?'

He caught her eye in the mirror. Once, in the cellar, he had looked at her like that. That time she had misunderstood him. She would not misunderstand him so readily again. She held his gaze a moment before returning to her work.

'Yes, Sir. It would be a great relief.'

'I have certain papers that I want my son . . .' and at this word he glanced up to the mirror and smiled shyly at her. 'I want my son to study these papers before we meet.'

Never having observed this sweetness on his countenance before, she pitied him the cruel disappointment that awaited him on the morrow. She knew, God forgive her, what had happened when Constable had visited Mr Phipps. All Jack Maggs's great passions were to be dashed upon the cobbles of Covent Garden.

'I'd be happy to take your papers to Mr Phipps.'

'Is he in the habit of rising early?'

'I know nothing of the gentleman.'

She avoided his glance and applied the scissors to his hair. It was dense and strong like the hair of an animal; alien, yet somehow intimate. She pondered the question of whether she need confess her moment of indiscretion with Mr Buckle. She had told him Henry Phipps's whereabouts at a time when she imagined Jack Maggs had gone for ever. He was staring at her again. She felt her deception guessed at, and could not bear it.

'Is your wife a tall woman?'

He withdrew his gaze. Combing the hair down round his ears Mercy discovered that the top of the left ear was missing. It was not a clean cut, such as might be made with a knife, but a rougher, crueller kind of tear.

'You would not say *wife* if you knew the truth. You don't know nothing about what it was to be in that place. You would not be judging me. You would shoot a man you saw treat a dog as we were treated. You might blow his brains out and not think yourself a bad'un for having done the business. As for me, Miss, I had no more wife than a dog has a wife. A girl like you cannot imagine what it was, to live in such darkness.'

'You have no wife anymore?'

'You're a right little terrier, ain't you?'

She did not reply, but as the scissors flashed around him, he answered her.

'No, I ain't.'

'Beg your pardon?'

'Ain't got a wife.'

She knew she would do well to leave this subject alone, and yet she could not. It was not the wife particularly concerned her: it was those little children.

'Are your children with their mother now?'

'Oh ain't you ever the Miss Quizzical! There is two boys and two mothers. The boys are lodged with a mate of mine, a carpenter, and his wife, a good honest woman named Penny Sanders. It is a home they have known all their life.'

'You left them alone?'

'No, not alone.'

'But you were their *da*,' she insisted. 'You were their da, but you had an aim to find a better class of son.'

'Jesus save me.'

She snipped and cut. God make me calm, she prayed. God, stop this dreadful temper.

'Yes,' said he. 'I do hope I have found a better class of son. Yes, I most sincerely do. For his education, which is one thousand times as much as ever went into my brain box, cost me fifty pounds each year. I don't know why you look so angry, Miss. It is what every father wants – his son to be the better man.'

'I ain't angry. What have I got to be angry about?'

She came now to the short coarse wet hair around his neck. His collar was loose, and as she snipped the hair close to the bare skin, the long, cruel fingers of the lash were visible. It was a shocking thing, to see those scars glistening like torture in the candlelight.

'I am not a hard man, Missy.'

'Who lashed you, Mr Maggs?'

'He were a cockney named Rudder. A soldier of the King.'

'Then it were the King who lashed you,' she insisted.

'We were beyond the King's sight. Not even God Himself could see into that pit.'

She cut the hair, staring down into the deep shadow inside his shirt.

'If I were your da, I would not leave you, Mercy.'

318

'You ain't me da, though.'

'No, I ain't.'

'What are their names?'

'None of your business.' He paused. 'Richard,' he said.

'Richard?'

'I call him Dick.'

'How old is Dick?'

'John is six. Dick is ten.'

'And while these little boys wait for you to come home, you prance round England trying to find someone who does not love you at all.'

'You cannot know that, girl.'

'I can,' she confessed. 'And I do.'

88

Henry Phipps left his club with neither raincoat nor umbrella to protect his new subaltern's uniform from further rain. On the whim of Mr Buckle's lawyer, the self-appointed navigator of their little party, they set course for Great Queen Street by way of Russell Street and Drury Lane. It was not the sensible course, nor the most direct, but Henry Phipps followed, and said nothing which might question lawyer's choice of route.

He was, as Edward Constable might have told him, a wilful and inhibiting man, but like many such individuals, Henry Phipps feared that he was weak of will, and as he followed Mr Makepeace, he brooded about that quality of character which allowed him to accept the direction of so poor a leader.

He walked down Russell Street with hands clasped behind his back, all the time looking with particular resentment at Mr Makepeace's posterior as it pushed against the confines of his mackintosh. In those ample haunches he saw evidence enough to confirm his fear that he would follow any damn fool rather than the dictates of his own common sense.

What that common sense dictated was that he bid his house goodbye and report on the morrow to his regiment. But the fact was, Henry Phipps had long neglected the call of common sense, and it was a stronger force, his passionate desire to ensure his own comfort, which held him in the company of a man who wished him to commit a murder.

In this turmoil of mind, he turned the corner into Drury Lane and, before he knew it, had set his new boots deep into foul yellow clay. The mud was past his ankles and up around the bottoms of his trousers.

'This was a damned fool way to come,' cried he, staring down at the mucky ruin of his uniform.

'It is excavated for the sewer,' whispered Mr Makepeace.

'I am perfectly well aware that it is the sewer.' He withdrew his boots from the deep sticky clay and climbed up to the vantage of a broken brick. 'Why would you come here when you could perfectly well walk up Long Acre? What possessed you?'

'I am more accustomed to Drury Lane,' whispered Mr Make-peace.

'We'll clean you up, Sir, don't worry. You come to my house first. My housekeeper will call her troops out for you.'

'Quiet.' Henry Phipps's face in the gas light now clearly revealed that spleen which Edward Constable claimed to be so much a feature of his character. 'I will lead the way.'

'Very good, Sir – please.' Mr Makepeace stepped back and, perching himself like a wet black biddy upon a pile of rotting lumber, gestured that Henry Phipps should move ahead of him.

Henry Phipps, however, did not move. He gazed instead down into that long pit the engineers had dug in the centre of the street. The trench was criss-crossed with new black pipes, and below this grid of iron was a further shadowy world of excavated arches leading to God knows what place. The sight induced in him a vertiginous unease which so paralleled the general anxiety about his life that he feared, even though he was some six feet from the edge, he might tumble into it.

He looked at Percy Buckle and found that gent nodding at him.

He looked back along Drury Lane, but it was a wild and

unexpected landscape in no way like the Drury Lane he knew. Great wooden beams criss-crossed the street, like intrusions in a nightmare. Others had been propped against the walls of shops. These beams were joined together like inverted, lopsided *A*'s, and something in their rude design brought to mind the gallows. A kind of fog now rose from the excavation, and in the penumbra of the gas light Henry Phipps imagined he saw a man's body hanging from a beam, suspended above the pit.

'You go,' he said, much frightened. 'You first.'

He let the grocer squeeze past him, feeling, as he did so, the hard edge of the pistol case Mr Buckle carried concealed beneath his cloak. Then he followed suit, keeping close against the walls of the houses, avoiding the crumbling edges of the pit.

89

The yard at Morton Bay had distinctive odours: of dry clay dust, of fetid tidal mud, of some antipodean plant which gave off an oozing stink like blackberry mixed with sweat. And although it is sometimes said that the experience of smell itself cannot be remembered any more than the experience of pain, Jack Maggs could remember these smells as well as he could the carolling of those so-called 'magpies', and the squeaking wheels of the carpenter's dray and the bloody red colour of its timber planks which would, in the course of one wet summer, be devoured by white ants.

He could still see the small red button at the apex of the flogger's forage cap, the worn supple thongs which bound his wrists and ankles to the triangle.

There was a most particular smell hanging like bad meat around that cursed place, and small iridescent blue flies which crawled upon his face and nose. As the flies began to tease his skin, the wretched man would begin to build London in his mind. He would build it brick by brick as the horrid double-cat smote the air, eddying forth like a storm from Hell itself.

Underneath the scalding sun, which burned his flesh as soon as it was mangled, Jack Maggs would imagine the long mellow light of English summer.

The flies might feast on his spattered back; the double-cat might carry away the third and fourth fingers of his hand; but his mind crawled forward, always, constructing piece by piece the place wherein his eyes had first opened, the home to which he would one day return, not the mudflats of the Thames, nor Mary Britten's meat-rich room at Pepper Alley Stairs, but rather a house in Kensington whose kind and beautiful interior he had entered by tumbling down a chimney, like a babe falling from the outer darkness into light. Clearing the soot from his eyes he had seen that which he later knew was meant by authors when they wrote of England, and of Englishmen.

Now, all these long years later, Jack Maggs had become such an Englishman. Dressed in his red waistcoat and his tailored tweed jacket, he stood before what Tobias Oates might have called 'a cheerful fire'.

The face he turned towards Mercy Larkin was hardened by its time in New South Wales – it had been rubbed at by pain until it shone – yet there was in his dark eyes a bright and glittering excitement which even he, with all his schooling in the art of secrecy, could not hide.

When he had suffered pain, pain so intense he had begged for death, he had seen this woman with her dark tangle of hair, sitting with hands folded thus upon her lap.

Now he took the brandy bottle from the mantel and refilled her tumbler. He watched with approval as she drank, not daintily, but as one suffering from a deep and persistent thirst.

'To you, Miss.'

'To you, Sir.' She continued to toy with those locks of children's hair upon her lap. While he had insisted that the hair was not her business, it did not displease him that she was so stubborn. Tenacity was a quality he had good reason to value highly.

'What say you, girl? You will keep house for me?'

She drained the last drops of brandy, then looked him straight in the eye.

'I will keep house for your babes.'

She stood up. Thinking that she intended to give him back the locks, he held out his hand to receive his property.

'They are in another country,' he said.

But she gave him her left hand, retaining the locks of children's hair in the right, and so they remained, hand in hand, at once at cross-purposes and yet not.

'They are waiting for you,' she smiled.

'Hark.'

He withdrew his hand abruptly.

'It is the street door,' she whispered.

In an instant he had the candles snuffed, but there was nothing he could do to staunch the fire which continued to burn brightly, throwing their two fretful shadows up onto the walls and ceiling.

Jack's hair bristled on his naked neck and, as the door swung open, he reached for the tarred twine handle of his dagger. A spectral figure entered the room, holding the candle high.

There, in the firelight, he beheld his nightmare: long straight nose, fair hair, brutal dreadful uniform of the 57th Foot Regiment. The Phantom had broken the locks and entered his life.

The apparition held a heavy pistol. Jack Maggs saw this instrument very clearly, yet he stayed rooted to the spot, his gaze fixed upon the spectre's uniform. The firelight flickered on that line of horrid buttons, each one embossed with the number 57. He smelt the bad meat smell of the yard at Morton Bay, felt the soft supple leather bind his wrists and ankles again. He could see the great dull gape of the pistol's barrel, and the fire light twinkling on the bright brass hammer which was fully cocked. *I am to die before I meet my son.*

Then, suddenly, inexplicably, there appeared from the darkness of the hallway none other than Percy Buckle Esquire. He pushed violently at the Phantom's back so the creature lurched even closer to Jack Maggs, who was still staring, his mouth agape. 'Take back your house, Sir. Defend your life against this burglar.'

The dagger was ready in his hand, and still Jack Maggs made no move.

323

'Fire!' Mr Buckle stamped his foot repeatedly upon on the floor. 'Fire, for God's sake, fire.'

At this confusing juncture, just as the pistol was raised and pointed at Jack Maggs's heart, Mercy rose quietly from the shadows.

Jack Maggs watched paralysed as she walked softly towards the Phantom in her stockinged feet. In her right hand she still held those two precious locks of hair, but it was her left hand that he watched as she raised it, palm outwards, towards the barrel of the gun, as if by so doing she might catch the deadly ball; as if she were in truth a spirit, a force of nature equal but opposite to the malevolent being who now threatened to snuff out Jack Maggs's life.

90

Henry Phipps was ushered into his own hallway which seemed narrower and longer than he had remembered it. He did not feel himself a murderer, but an animal at Smithfield, hemmed in and hounded at all sides, with all his confusion magnified a hundred times by Percy Buckle, who was now pushing at his back with the point of his umbrella.

Gone was the mild apologetic little grocer who had first walked into his rooms at Covent Garden. In his place was this hissing, dark-shelled incubus whose alien and agitated presence strained the young man's already over-stretched emotions. Percy Buckle, without being aware of it, had already twice placed himself in mortal danger.

It was Mr Buckle who flung the door open to the living room.

'Fire,' he cried, while the lawyer hovered somewhere behind them in the darkness.

'Fire!' – and pushed him forward into the room.

For Henry Phipps, everything in this present nightmare seemed to be happening very slow. He had all the time he required to look at the man who had written to him for most of his young life. He had always known Jack Maggs to be a convict, known him transported for 'the term of his natural life', and Victor Littlehales, his Oxford tutor, had taught him how to gratify the needs of him who signed his letters 'Father'. They had laboured together on the replies until young Henry finally found his voice, and thereafter the role came to him easily enough. If the letters could be called 'lies' they could also be called 'comfort'.

Henry Phipps had sung to Jack Maggs, sung for his supper. He had sung without understanding it was a siren song, without ever dreaming that this tortured beast might demand of him that which had been conceived only as a flight of fancy.

'Defend your house,' cried Percy Buckle.

Henry Phipps had no choice. He raised the gun.

From the shadow by the fire, a young woman came towards him. Her feet were bare. She raised her hand raised towards the barrel.

91

At the instant Henry Phipps discharged the pistol, Lizzie Warriner died in her bed. Even though her pain ended, there was in that wracked body no suggestion of repose, but everywhere tension, angularity, distress. She lay in the midst of the rucked and tangled carmine sheets, her hand thrust into her mouth as if she were still biting it.

Tobias was not yet the bearded eminence he would finally become. On the night Lizzie died, he was a frightened, ambitious young man. His eyes were bloodshot, his red mouth contorted by spasms of grief. He wept upon his dead lover's pillow, and then on the skirts of his wife, although this lady, uncharacteristically, made no move to comfort him. Instead she sat upon the death bed, expressionless, heavy-jowled, the corpse's cooling hand in hers.

'Light the fire,' she said.

'I will call the doctor.'

Mary Oates bestowed on her husband a look of passionate antagonism. 'You will light the fire, you foolish man.'

'You are wrong,' he said, although what exactly she was wrong about he did not say. It was clearly not the fire he was speaking of, for he soon took himself downstairs and managed to make a vigorous blaze of coals and faggots. Then he obediently performed that service which the dead girl had beseeched of her sister. That is, he made a pyre of her linen. Given that the fireplace was not large and the sheets were still, in some places, wet, it was not an easily accomplished task, but he persevered.

Throughout all this, he wept unashamedly. Mary, by contrast, sat woodenly in a straight-backed chair, the same chair in which Jack Maggs had first been mesmerized. When Mary did look finally at Tobias Oates it was with a gaze of such coldness that her husband quailed before it.

'You do me a great wrong,' said he.

'We have both done great wrong,' she said.

Later Tobias would think he had imagined this reply, but now he sat on his heels and watched Lizzie's very life blood burning upon the flames. In those flames he saw, as he would throughout his life, the figures and faces of his fancy dancing before him. He saw the wraith of their dead child folding and unfolding in the skirts of fire. He saw Lizzie herself, her face smiling and folding into the horrible figure of decay.

He could not bear it. Would not carry it.

He poked at the blackened linen and found in it one abhorrent face, that of the man who had led him to Mrs Britten's door, who had placed those dung-coloured pills where they would poison that precious life.

It was Jack Maggs, the murderer, who now grew in the flames. Jack Maggs on fire. Jack Maggs flowering, threatening, poisoning. Tobias saw him hop like a devil. Saw him limp, as if his fiery limbs still carried the weight of convict iron. He saw his head transmogrify until it was bald, tattooed with deep wrinkles that broke apart and floated glowing out into the room.

It was Jack Maggs who had done this, and in his grief Tobias began to heap up all his blame upon him. It was now, on the seventh of May, in the darkest night of his life, that Jack Maggs began to take the form the world would later know. This Jack Maggs was, of course, a fiction, and so it may not matter that Tobias never

326

witnessed the final act of the real convict's search: never observed Henry Phipps raise that pistol with his trembling hand, never heard the deafening explosion, nor smelled the dark and murderous scent of gunpowder.

It would not have been lost on him that Mercy Larkin's wedding finger was blown away, and that when Jack Maggs came to her side, the pair were finally matched in their deformity. But the forces that made that famously 'abhorrent' face inside the fire were different from those that drove the real Jack Maggs, who escaped London with Mercy Larkin that very night on the Portsmouth Mail. There is no character like Mercy in *The Death of Maggs*, no young woman to help the convict recognize the claims of Richard and John to have a father kiss them good night.

Dick Maggs was eleven years of age when Jack returned from England. He had twice been up before the magistrate, and little John, who was four years younger, had the same hard belligerent face, the same dark and needful eyes. It was not an easy role for Mercy Larkin, yet she applied herself to being their mother with a passion. She who had always been so impatient of the 'rules' now became a disciplinarian. She brushed their hair and wiped their faces. She walked with them to school and saw they stayed there. It was she who moved the family away from the bad influence of Sydney. And in the new town of Wingham where they shortly settled she not only civilized these first two children, but very quickly gave birth to five further members of 'That Race'.

Jack Maggs sold the brickworks in Sydney. In Wingham he set up a saw mill and, when that prospered, a hardware store, and when that prospered, a pub. He was twice president of the shire and was still the president of the Cricket Club when Dick hit the cover off a new ball in the match against Taree.

The Maggs family were known to be both clannish and hospitable, at once civic-minded and capable of acts of picturesque irresponsibility, and it is only natural that they left many stories scattered in their wake. Yet amongst the succeeding generations of Maggs who still live on those fertile river flats, it is Mercy who is now remembered best, not only for the story of how she lost her wedding finger, not only for the grand mansion on Supper Creek Road whose construction she so pugnaciously oversaw and whose servants she so meticulously supervised, but also for the very particular library she collected in her middle age.

The Death of Maggs, having been abandoned by its grief-stricken author in 1837, was not begun again until 1859. The first chapters did not appear until 1860, that is, three years after the real Jack Maggs had died, not in the blaze of fire Tobias had always planned for him, but in a musty high-ceilinged bedroom above the flood-brown Manning River. Here, with his weeping sons and daughters crowded round his bed, the old convict met death without ever having read 'That Book'.

For this lack, Mercy compensated. She read *The Death of Maggs*, first as it appeared in serial, then again when the parts were gathered in a handsome volume, then again when the author amended it in 1861. Finally, she owned no fewer than seven copies of the last edition, and each of these is now (together with Jack Maggs's letters to Henry Phipps) in the collection of the Mitchell Library in Sydney. Of the seven volumes, six are cloth, one is leatherbound, and this last is signed: *To Mercy from Captain E. Constable, Clapham 1870.*

The Mitchell's librarian has noted on each index card the 'v. rough excision' of that page which reads:

Affectionately Inscribed

to

PERCIVAL CLARENCE BUCKLE

A Man of Letters, a Patron of the Arts

INTO THE BLUE

Robert Goddard

CORGI BOOKS

INTO THE BLUE
A CORGI BOOK : 0 552 13561 5

Originally published in Great Britain by Bantam Press,
a division of Transworld Publishers Ltd.

PRINTING HISTORY
Bantam Press edition published 1990
Corgi edition published 1991
Corgi edition reprinted 1991 (twice)
Corgi edition reprinted 1992 (twice)
Corgi edition reprinted 1993
Corgi edition reprinted 1994
Corgi edition reprinted 1995
Corgi edition reprinted 1996 (twice)
Corgi edition reprinted 1997

A CIP catalogue record for this book is available from
the British Library

This book is set in 10/11pt Plantin by
Falcon Typographic Art Ltd, Wallington and Edinburgh.

Corgi Books are published by Transworld Publishers Ltd,
61–63 Uxbridge Road, London W5 5SA,
in Australia by Transworld Publishers (Australia) Pty Ltd,
15–25 Helles Avenue, Moorebank, NSW 2170
and in New Zealand by Transworld Publishers (NZ) Ltd,
3 William Pickering Drive, Albany, Auckland.

Printed and bound in Great Britain by
Cox & Wyman Ltd, Reading, Berkshire.

For Phil Dwerryhouse

Acknowledgements

I am grateful to Tina Maskell-Feidi for guidance on the use of Greek in this book and to the Commanding Officer and staff of Britannia Royal Naval College, Dartmouth, for information on life at the College in the 1960s.

1

If she should return now, of course, or even five minutes from now, it would still be all right. The thought that he might never see her again could then be dismissed as a delusion, an absurd over-reaction to an excess of solitude and silence. And from the notion that, at any second, she would return, calling to him as she came down the track, part of his mind could not be dislodged: the orderly, housetrained, rational part. It was only in the chaotic realm of instinct and sensation that a contrary suspicion had taken root, only, as it were, in the part of himself that he did not care to acknowledge.

Besides, Harry had every justification for blaming his anxious state on the position in which he found himself. To spend three-quarters of an hour sitting on a fallen tree trunk halfway up a pine-forested mountainside, whilst the warm glow of the afternoon sun faded towards a dusky chill and silence – absolute, windless, pitiless silence – quarried at the nerves, was enough to test anyone's self-control. He wished now that he had gone with her to the summit, or stayed in the car and listened to the radio. Either way, he really should have known better than to wait where he was.

He stubbed out the fourth cigarette of his vigil and took a deep breath. It was growing cold now in the shadow of the mountain, yet the coastal plain below was still bathed in warm, golden sunlight. Only here, on the thickly conifered slope, or out there, invisible but palpable in the

9

clear, frozen air, could the waning of the day no longer be ignored.

Why had she not returned? She could scarcely be lost, not with the guidebook *and* a compass. After all, she had been to Profitis Ilias before, which Harry never had. Nor, if the truth be told, did he ever want to again. Two hours ago, he had been basking in the sun at a terrace table of a *psarotaverna* just down the coast, lighting the first cigarette in this packet at the leisurely conclusion of a relishable meal and wondering how jealous the waiter might be of an overweight, middle-aged Englishman for finding such an attractive girl to lunch with him. Now even visualizing the scene was difficult, for Profitis Ilias possessed the power to consign every memory and perception beyond its own domain to half-forgotten remoteness. And Profitis Ilias had been Heather's choice.

'We could drive up there in half an hour from here,' she had said. 'It's a fantastic place. Deserted, crumbling old villas left over from the Italian occupation. And stupendous views. You *must* see it.'

Harry had felt no such obligation, preferring the décor of a dozen bars he could think of, suitably refracted by a well-filled glass, to any vista of nature, however supposedly breathtaking. Nevertheless, he had raised no objection.

And so they had come, driving up the winding road through the village of Salakos towards the wooded mountaintop, climbing slowly but relentlessly till all other traffic was left behind and only the limitless ranks of pine and fir stood witness to their progress. At first Harry had detected nothing amiss in their growing isolation. It was not until they had reached the hotel that the road served and found it, as expected, closed for the winter, that the character of Profitis Ilias had made itself known.

Silence, he rather thought, was the bedrock of its mood. Silence that had waited for them to climb from the car and slam the doors, then pounced from the very heart of the forest to awe them into whispered exchanges. Silence that the empty hotel and the ruined villas in the woods around

10

seemed merely to magnify, as if abandoned habitations were worse than no habitations at all. And silence, moreover, that even nature respected, for here no wind stirred the trees, no bird sang among the branches, no squirrel scurried along the boughs. On Profitis Ilias, all was still, but all was not at rest.

Two months ago, the hotel would still have been open for the season, the children of its guests playing in the grounds, perhaps even climbing on the very tree trunk where Harry sat. Noise, movement, laughter, company: at other times they might be irritants; now he craved them from the depth of his soul. It was surprising to discover how uncomfortable he found it to be alone. If, that is, he was alone. For he could not help remembering that, when they had first left the car and strolled down to admire the view that the hotel commanded, he had glanced up at the wooden balconies and red-painted shutters that gave the building its stolid, Alpine quality – and seen a figure withdraw abruptly from one of the unshuttered first floor windows. At the time, he had dismissed it as a trick of the light, but now the memory added its weight to all the other anxieties by which he was beset.

Why had she not returned? She had seemed so confident, so reassuringly certain that she would be back before he had had a chance to miss her. It had been a stiff climb from the hotel up the uneven, overgrown path towards the summit, and Heather had set a sharp pace. Out of breath and far from his normal stamping grounds, Harry had been willing enough, in the circumstances, to stop at the point where a fallen tree blocked their route, while she went on to the top. 'Take the keys,' she had said, 'in case you want to go back to the car.' Then she had added, noticing his frown: 'Don't worry. I'll keep to the path. And I won't be long. It's just that I can't turn back now, can I?' And so saying, she had scrambled up round the tree, smiled back at him once, and then gone on.

Nearly an hour ago, and seemingly a world away, that last smile beckoned to Harry from up the wooded slope.

Peace of mind, he reckoned now, had lasted no longer than the first cigarette. Since then, his thoughts had ranged over many subjects, but always they had returned to what in his surroundings adamantly refused to be ignored: silence so total that the ear invented a half-heard chorus of whispering voices in the trees around, silence so complete that his straining senses insisted that somewhere, above or about him, something must be watching him.

Harry looked at his watch. It was nearly four o'clock, which meant there was little more than an hour's daylight left, a meagre, bone-chilling hour at this altitude and time of year. With an effort, he forced his mind to confront a series of practical choices. He could return to the car, in case Heather had done so herself by a different route. Yet, if she had, she would surely have come looking for him by now. He could stay where he was, on the grounds that that was where she would expect to find him. But one glance around reminded him that he could bear to remain there no longer. Or he could follow the path to the top, in case she was in some difficulty or had simply lost track of time. That, he concluded, was really the only choice open to him.

He raised his legs, swivelled round on the tree trunk and dropped down on the higher side. There was the path, still marked by a border of flints, for all the years of its abandonment, curving away ahead of him up the slope. He started along it, feeling at once the relief that action brings after the suspense of indecision.

Soon, the trees began to thin and the summit ridge came into sight. Once it had done so, it struck Harry as ludicrous that he had not insisted on accompanying Heather all the way, for it was neither as far nor as steep as he had supposed. He could not help wondering if she had deliberately encouraged their separation, though why she should have done so he could not imagine. And he was also aware that the thought itself might be a delusion, an investment of her words and actions with meanings they did not bear.

12

Emerging into a patch of sunlight just short of the ridge, Harry paused to catch his breath. Ahead of him, to the right, a towering red and white radio aerial crowned the summit, with a small building at its base: an army observation post by the look of it, apparently unoccupied. Not that he had any intention of checking the point. Nine years on Rhodes had taught him to give the Greek military a wide berth. But would Heather have been equally cautious? Yes, surely she would. Besides, the path curved away to the left and she had promised she would keep to it.

He walked up onto the ridge and swung round to look back the way he had come. As he did so, the exposed nature of his position conjured up a threat more ominous in its way than the unease which had oppressed him in the forest. He suddenly wondered whether this was what he had been intended to do, whether this was another step closer to the trap that had been prepared for him. Rebuking himself for entertaining such thoughts, he forced his eyes to follow the line of the coast far below where it curved away to the west. That crumpled inlet, he told himself, must be Kamiros Skala, those whale-backed islands out to sea Alymnia and Halki. They were reference points which proved that a reality beyond Profitis Ilias still existed and that he might soon return to it.

But first he had to find Heather. Dismayed by how reluctant he felt to shout her name aloud – an act which the prevailing silence seemed irresistibly to forbid – he began to follow the path, still faithfully bordered with flints, as it twisted along the ridge between outcrops of rock and gnarled, wind-carved cedars. If she had kept to the path, he could not fail to find her. But if she had not . . . .

Then he saw it. Snagged on a lower branch of one of the cedars, hanging limp and forlorn in the motionless air. Four equal stripes of pink and white. Cerise and silver, he remembered her correcting him. It was Heather's scarf, the long woollen scarf she had been wearing when she left him by the fallen tree. He could recollect, quite distinctly, seeing her toss one end of it over her shoulder as she

13

disappeared up the slope. And now it was here, where she was not.

Harry pulled the scarf loose, then stood with it clutched in his hands, struggling to comprehend the significance of its discovery. Had she left it there by accident? Had it been blown from her neck as she ran along the path? If so, what had she been running from? He gazed around at the stunted cedars and the harsh white boulders standing up like fangs on the grassy ridge, but they held no other clue, no other token of her fate. By their very emptiness, they defied him.

Looping the scarf round his neck, Harry strode on along the path. It topped a bluff, then swooped down into a dale and up again to a farther peak. A view of the island's interior opened up to the south, bathed in sunlight. Could Heather have become disorientated, he wondered, and gone down the wrong side of the mountain? Pausing to lean against a rock and recover his breath, he considered the point. No, it was inconceivable. The path was clear, the route an easy one to follow. She could only have left it out of choice or dire necessity. And the touch of the scarf against his chin prompted him to fear the latter. He hurried on.

By the time Harry had traversed the dale and ascended to the next peak, the rational part of his mind had reasserted much of its former control. His ignorance of local geography, he reminded himself, was as good as total. Even were it not, he could scarcely search the area single-handed. If Heather had met with a mishap, of whatever kind, the best way to help her would be to raise the alarm in Salakos, and to do so before nightfall. He glanced at his watch. To follow that course, he would have to return to the car at once. Though to leave now seemed premature, leave he clearly must.

But not, his instincts told him, without making one last effort to locate Heather on his own. The obvious method was the one he had, till now, drawn back from, but he knew he could not depart without resorting to it. He must shout her name as loudly as he could, in case she was near enough

14

to hear. From the bluff on which he was standing, his voice would carry well: there was no excuse. Determined to give his nerve no chance to falter, he climbed onto an adjacent rock, took a deep breath and cupped his hands to his mouth. But then, in the second before Heather's name formed on his lips, Profitis Ilias found its own voice with which to strike him dumb.

One long, shrill, unwavering blast on a whistle. It came to Harry's ears from no direction and every direction, from above him and below him, from close at hand and far away. And then it stopped. And Harry's arms dropped slowly to his sides and he began to tremble in every limb and to breathe in rapid, shallow gulps of air. What did it mean? Where had it come from? Was it a signal? A message? A warning? To him or to another?

Suddenly, like a cliff face that is undermined for years by the sea before abruptly subsiding, his self-control disintegrated. He had been manipulated every step of the way. The face at the window, the abandoned scarf, the disembodied whistle: all were part of the trap into which he had been led. Logic and reason were beyond him now, headlong flight his only recourse.

The path began to descend from this point, zig-zagging down the steep, boulder-strewn slope. But Harry did not follow it. Instead he plunged straight down from one bend of the path to the next, stumbling over rocks, scrambling down stretches of loose, shingly earth. The spines of a stout little shrub slashed at his cheek. He skinned his knuckles on a sharp outcrop of flint. But he did not care. All pretence had vanished now. He only wanted to be off the mountain, away from the corroding fear that its air had refined to a pure, unhinging essence.

Bursting through a thicket of bracken and slithering down the flank of a huge, half-buried boulder, Harry suddenly found himself on a wide, earthen track, rutted by the wheels of a heavy vehicle. Forcing his mind to concentrate, he recollected that the road had forked just beyond where they had parked, the left fork signposted to

Eleousa, the right leading up blindly into the forest. What he was standing on must surely be that unmarked track. If so, he had only to follow it down to reach the car.

He began to run along the centre of the track, ignoring the tightening pain in his chest. Rounding a bend, he saw the white shape of the car and the red-tiled roof of the hotel beyond. He was nearly there. Then, almost at once, his pace slackened. Within twenty yards, he had come to a halt. For with the sight of the hotel had come also the memory of a face snatched back from one of its windows and the dreadful, slowly-forming thought that he might still be following a route prepared for him, a series of false turnings promising escape but leading only to deeper entrapment.

He stood where he was, panting for air, struggling to think clearly. Clutching at his neck, he noticed that he had lost the scarf. It must have fallen off, or been dragged off by one of the bushes he had blundered through. Was that, he wondered, how Heather had herself come to lose it – in desperate flight from the same, intangible horror? Was he merely retracing her earlier, unavailing steps? No, the rational compartment of his mind insisted. She was still up there on the mountaintop somewhere, lost and helpless, relying on him to fetch assistance. For her sake, he must remain master of himself.

He began to walk slowly ahead, looking neither to right nor left, concentrating his attention on the car as it grew ever larger in his field of vision. By this method, he found it possible to ignore all that his mind suggested might be following or, worse still, awaiting him. He counted each step as he took it, reciting the numbers to hold his imagination in check. He passed the junction of the track and the Eleousa road. Then the signpost proclaiming the name he had come to dread. ΠΡΟΦΗΤΗΣ ΗΛΙΑΣ: Profitis Ilias. He reached the car.

Sensing that haste might yet be as fatal as hesitation, Harry took the keys carefully from his pocket, opened the door and climbed in. To his unutterable relief, the engine

16

started at the first turn of the ignition. The burst of sound – and the promise of mobility it conveyed – repaired his shattered confidence. He jerked the car into gear, slewed it across the road, reversed, completed the turn and accelerated down the hill.

With every yard that the car carried Harry away from Profitis Ilias, the influence that it had exerted on his mind faded. Soon it became easy to reason away what had happened. His brain, deprived of its normal stimuli, had begun to play tricks on him: that was all. Heather had lost her way and faced the dismal prospect of a night in the open. With help from Salakos, however, he might be able to spare her that. Even if the worst did come to the worst, she should be able to shelter till morning. Twelve uncomfortable hours lay ahead of her, twelve anxious ones ahead of Harry. Then normality would resume.

Not until the very last moment did Harry see the goat standing directly in his path. It had wandered into the middle of the road just beyond a hairpin bend and almost seemed to be lying in wait for him, so difficult was it to make out in the deep shadow of the overhanging trees. With his foot hard down on the accelerator as he emerged from the bend, Harry wrenched instinctively at the wheel as soon as he saw the creature and succeeded in narrowly avoiding it. But his relief lasted no more than a second. As the car skidded across the road, he realized he was heading straight for a sheer drop on the other side. It was too late to brake and the roadside fence looked too frail to hold him back. All he could do was aim for one of the stout concrete fenceposts and hope for the best. An instant later, there was a great, jolting thump, an explosion of steam from the bonnet and a blare of the horn as Harry hit the steering wheel.

For a minute or so, he was too dazed to move. Then he pushed the door open and stumbled out. The goat had fled – he could hear its bell clanking away frantically into the forest – but it was obvious that the car was going nowhere.

17

The front was staved in and the offside wheel was twisted round at an angle. Harry leaned against the roof, swearing under his breath. His head hurt and his ribs ached. He felt in need of a stiff drink, but he was a long way from getting one. This latest misjudgement had only worsened his plight – and Heather's as well.

Weary and self-pitying though he felt, Harry knew he could not afford to indulge the mood. With a last reproachful kick at the distorted wheel of the car, he turned and began to trudge down the road.

2

Inspector Miltiades stared at Harry for some time from the doorway. Then he walked slowly across to the table and sat down opposite him. Harry had waited six hours for him to return, six hours that had seemed like as many days, yet he felt reluctant to ask what the Inspector had found, deterred by the slowly stirring conviction that the truth was bound to be worse than the worst he had imagined.

All day he had been kept in this bare and sparsely furnished room at Rhodes Police Headquarters, with only the clock on the wall, the blank face of the constable guarding the door and his own limitless thoughts to scan for clues as to what Profitis Ilias might have yielded to its searchers. More than twenty-four hours had passed since his last sight of Heather and now, as the failing light beyond the half-shuttered window signalled, night was once more about to draw its veil across her whereabouts. Unless, of course, Miltiades already knew them.

But Miltiades' expression communicated nothing. A thin, ascetic-looking man with his well-pressed uniform and sleek black hair, he carefully removed his spectacles, massaged the sore patches on his nose, then replaced them, all the while keeping his solemn unblinking stare fixed on Harry.

Harry's lips parted in readiness to speak, but an upward twitch of the other man's eyebrows at once dissuaded him. Then, struggling to order his thoughts, he said: 'What have you to tell me, Inspector?'

Miltiades did not reply. Instead, he drew a small tape recorder from the briefcase beside him, placed it on the table between them and switched it on.

'I think I've a right to be told something.'

Miltiades leant forward onto his elbows. When he spoke, it was in Greek, and his remarks were addressed to the machine. '*To Savato thotheka Noembriou chilia enniakasia ogthonta okto, exinta treis ores.*' Then he looked straight at Harry and said, 'What would you expect to be told, Mr Barnett?'

'Whether you've found Miss Mallender, of course. Whether she's all right.' Harry could hear the rising note of impatience in his voice, but could not suppress it. What business had the man prolonging his agony like this? 'You've had all day to search Profitis Ilias. What have you found?'

'We shall assume, for the purposes of this interview, that we have found nothing.'

'What the hell does that mean?'

'It means that you will answer my questions before I answer yours.'

So that was it. The suspicion that had been growing on him all day was finally confirmed: they did not believe him. That was why he had not been allowed to remain on the scene when the search began. And that was why Miltiades was telling him nothing: because he hoped protracted uncertainty would lead Harry to betray himself. What did they think? he wondered. That he had murdered Heather? That he had buried her up there on the mountain? Why should they think such a thing – unless they had found something to plant the idea in their mind? Her body, perhaps? Good God, it was too awful to contemplate.

'You have lived on Rhodes since March 1979, Mr Barnett?'

'What?'

'You have lived here for nine years, I believe.'

Harry could not concentrate in the face of all he now

20

envisaged. He could only appeal to Miltiades' mercy. 'For God's sake, Inspector, just tell me: is she dead?'

Miltiades' expression did not alter. 'We shall assume, for the purposes of this interview, that we do not know.'

'You callous—' Harry closed his eyes, willing himself to repel the vision that had just formed in his mind: Heather's white, naked body supine on a mortuary slab . . . . When he opened his eyes, Miltiades' searching stare was still fixed upon him.

'*Endaksi*. We will begin at the beginning. You have lived here since March 1979 as caretaker of a house in Lindos – the *Villa ton Navarkhon* – owned by a fellow-countryman of yours. Is that correct?'

The vision had gone. In its place was this blank, sterile room where his interrogation was about to commence. He thought of the *psarotaverna* where they had lunched, of how warm it had been at their table beneath the rubber tree, of how softly the shafts of sunlight had fallen upon her hair. He felt tears start in his eyes and, swallowing hard, he said: 'That is correct.'

'Your full name is Harold Mosley Barnett.'

'Yes.'

'Mosley is an unusual Christian name is it not?'

Was this what the fellow meant by beginning at the beginning? 'Oswald Mosley was a British politician of the inter-war years, Inspector. My father approved of his views.'

'Which were?'

'He was a fascist. *Enas fasistis*.'

Miltiades nodded. 'A pity for you.'

'I don't let it worry me.' It was strange to be reminded of his father by, of all people, a Greek policeman. He had not thought of him in years, that blurred, remote figure from his past whom he knew only from photographs and his mother's unsentimental memories. 'How did—'

'You were born on the twenty-second of May 1935.'

'Yes. But—'

'At Swindon in Wiltshire.'

'How do you know all this?'

'It is in your passport.'

'My passport?'

'I have it here.'

For a moment, Harry could not speak. They had been to Lindos and searched his belongings. And all the while he had sat here believing them to be combing Profitis Ilias inch by inch.

'It was Miss Mallender's passport that I was looking for,' Miltiades continued. 'Do you know where it is?'

'In her handbag, I suppose. But you had no right—'

'We telephoned the owner of the house, Mr Barnett. When we explained the circumstances, he readily gave his consent.'

So. They had spoken to Dysart. And what had they told him? God alone knew. 'Why are you so curious about Heather's passport?' For the first time, Miltiades smiled. 'Now it is "Heather", not "Miss Mallender". Did she object to you addressing her by her Christian name?'

'Don't be so bloody— Why should she?'

'Because she was staying in Mr Dysart's house as his guest – and you were there as his employee.'

'I'm not his employee.'

'Then what?'

What indeed? The difference was a fine one, as Harry would have to admit. 'I look after the house for him in exchange for free accommodation.'

'His tenant, then?'

'In a sense.'

'That sense is something I am curious about, Mr Barnett. You should have told us sooner what an eminent person Mr Dysart is. A Member of Parliament. A minister in the British government.'

'A *junior* minister.'

'How is it that such a person entrusts his holiday home on Rhodes to your care?'

'Why shouldn't he?'

22

For answer, Miltiades surveyed Harry with barely disguised contempt. 'How did you first meet Mr Dysart?'

'He worked for me once when he was a student. A long time ago. But what has this to do—'

'With Miss Mallender? I hoped you would tell me, Mr Barnett. Her brother is flying here from England tonight. He and his parents were astonished to learn that you and Miss Mallender were . . . friends. I believe you worked for Miss Mallender's father before you came to Rhodes.'

'Yes. I did.'

'And that you were dismissed as a result of a financial irregularity.'

'An *alleged* financial irregularity.'

'The point is, Mr Barnett, that you are not the companion Miss Mallender's father would have chosen for his daughter. You might still bear him a grudge. You might want to hurt him – or somebody close to him.'

'I don't give a damn what . . . .' His voice trailed away into silence. This was indeed worse than he had imagined. All he wanted to know was whether they had found Heather. If they had, she must be dead, for she would never have permitted this nonsense to be perpetrated in her name. But if not . . . .

'You are fifty-three years old, Mr Barnett. Have you ever been married?'

'No.'

'Have you any children?'

'No.'

'A man alone in the world, then.'

'You could say that.'

'What do you do to satisfy your . . . sexual needs?'

Harry felt his jaw drop. Did their suspicions have to weevil their way back to this last and grubbiest of resorts? He had liked Heather. He had liked her very much. But, strangely, lust had never tainted that liking. Somewhere else, with somebody else, it could easily have done. But not with Heather. 'I drink too much, Inspector. What do you do?'

23

'I have read the statement you made in Salakos last night very carefully, Mr Barnett. You remember what you said?'

'Of course.'

'I will refresh your memory.' He reached down to the briefcase and lifted out a sheaf of papers. 'Your description of Miss Mallender: "Approximately five feet six inches tall. Twenty-seven years old. Shoulder-length flaxen hair." Flaxen is an interesting word, Mr Barnett. I am a student of words. I pride myself on my knowledge of the English language.'

'Justifiably.'

'But flaxen I did not know. It is a very particular word. It suggests that the person you were describing made a great impression on you.'

'It's just a colour.'

'But the colour of what? The colour of desire, perhaps? You did not say whether Miss Mallender had a good figure.'

Harry felt the blood rush to his face. Say nothing, he told himself. Don't let this man provoke you. He thinks he's very clever. Prove he isn't.

'Is she fat? Is she thin?'

'Neither.'

'Perfectly proportioned, then. A veritable Aphrodite.'

'Go to hell.'

Miltiades smiled. 'Let me return to your statement. You described the clothes she was wearing. "A pink and white scarf." Which you later found, of course. And later still lost. "Black corduroy jacket. Red sweater. Navy blue woollen gloves. Pleated tartan skirt, knee-length. Black walking shoes. Black stockings." That is what you said?'

'Yes.'

'Stockings, not tights.'

'Yes. Stockings, not tights.'

'How do you know?'

'Know what?'

'Which she was wearing?'

24

'I don't.'

'Then why specify stockings? Are you saying now that you cannot be sure?'

'Of course I can't. It was just a word.'

'Another very particular word, Mr Barnett.'

'Meaning what?'

'Meaning that you may be in a position to know whether she was wearing stockings or tights.'

Rage was gnawing at Harry's resolution. What had they found? Anything or nothing? Whichever it was, Miltiades was not about to tell him.

'We found the car, at the point you described. In your statement, you said it was empty.'

A trap-door seemed to open beneath Harry's feet. The car. Surely Miltiades did not mean . . . . He had not checked the boot. He should have done, but he had not thought to. 'Are you saying it wasn't empty?'

'Not quite. There was something in the glove compartment.'

The relief must have been visible on Harry's face 'What was it?'

'Two unused postcards. I have them here.' He laid one of them on the table. 'Recognize it?'

It was a photograph of the Aphrodite of Rhodes, the famous statue of the goddess drying her hair in the sun after emerging from the sea. 'Yes, Inspector, of course I recognize it. There must be hundreds of these postcards for sale on Rhodes, for Christ's sake.'

'You did not buy this card, though?'

'No. Heather must have.'

'And this?' He placed the second card alongside the first. It was another photograph of a statue: the satyr-god Silenus, half-goat, half-man, flaunting, in this representation, a hugely erect phallus.

Harry said nothing. There was nothing he could say. He had seen both these pictures before, of course, on postcard-racks the length and breadth of the island. And he could guess why Heather had bought them. The one as an object of beauty she would characteristically have admired. The other in preparation for a joke she had no doubt planned to play on him later. 'Who's Silenus?' she had asked him, on discovering his association with the *Taverna Silenou*. 'Better that you shouldn't know,' he had teasingly replied. But now the tease had rebounded on him.

He looked up and found Miltiades' eyes ready to engage his own. There was no longer any doubt what the Inspector thought. A beautiful young woman carved in soft white marble; a debauched old man cast in harsh, green bronze: the parallels were too striking to resist.

'Heather must have bought both of them,' Harry said at last. 'To send to friends in England, I suppose. I didn't know they were there.'

Miltiades took a deep breath. 'Would Miss Mallender have thought it amusing to send such a card as this' – he pointed at the obscene depiction of Silenus – 'to "friends in England"?'

Harry hesitated. How honest to be, or how dishonest, with this shrewd and patient man was a riddle beyond his solving. 'No,' he said, subsiding into honesty. 'She wouldn't have thought it amusing. She would have bought it for another reason.'

'What reason?'

'During the season, I wait at table and wash-up at a *taverna* in Lindos. The *Taverna Silenou*.'

Miltiades nodded. 'I know, Mr Barnett. The proprietor is Konstantinos Dimitratos. We have spoken to him. He has been most . . . informative.'

'You've spoken to Kostas?'

'Certainly.'

'Why? He hardly knows Heather.'

'But he knows you, Mr Barnett. For the moment, that is more useful to me. What he told me was most valuable.'

'What did he tell you?' Harry knew Kostas would not deliberately have blackened his character, but the poor man's instinctive response to uniformed authority could still have been damaging.

'Many things. For example, I gather you had some difficulty with one of his customers last summer. A Danish girl . . . of about Miss Mallender's age. Pretty, was she?'

Harry could almost hear Kostas blurting the story out. He would have said anything to appease Miltiades. For Harry, however, there was no hope of doing the same. 'A misunderstanding, Inspector. That was all.'

'Of course. Did *she* have flaxen hair?'

'No. Nor was she "a veritable Aphrodite".'

Miltiades gazed at him for some moments in silence. Then he said: 'Had you ever met Miss Mallender prior to her arrival in Rhodes on the seventeenth of October?'

'No. That is . . . . I don't think so.' But he *had* met her before. The occasion recurred to his mind as he spoke. Two girls straight from school, still in their uniforms, climbing from their mother's car on the forecourt of Mallender Marine, come to pay their father a visit. Their father. His boss. Grey weather. The season? That he could not recall. Perhaps autumn. Perhaps this very same, ever-darkening time of year. Portland Harbour a dull, flat, neutral backdrop. And two girls, one a little haughty, a little aware of herself, preparing for womanhood, whilst the other, with socks round her ankles and a gap-toothed grin, must surely have been . . . Heather, unawarely glimpsed by a bored, slightly hung-over, fourteen years or so younger Harold Mosley Barnett.

'You don't think so? So much uncertainty. It will not do, Mr Barnett. It really will not do.'

'I *may* have met her, when she was a child. I did work for her father, after all.'

'Of course. I must not forget that. But, when she came to Lindos, it was as a stranger to you?'

'Yes.'

'Had Mr Dysart warned you to expect her?'

'No.'

'Was that unusual?'

'No. I'm completely self-contained in the gatehouse flat.

27

There's no need for me to know if he's coming – or if a friend of his is either.'

'She came for what – a holiday?'

'Yes.'

'Nothing more?'

'Recuperation, I suppose you'd say.'

'Recuperation from what? Had she been ill?'

'She told me she'd been suffering from depression. Her sister died in tragic circumstances last year. Her psychiatrist recommended—'

'Ah! She had a psychiatrist?'

'I believe so.'

'We may therefore assume her depression was not . . . trivial?'

'I never said it was.'

'No. You did not. So, Miss Mallender came to Rhodes to recuperate, courtesy of Mr Dysart. And you made her acquaintance?'

'Yes.'

'Befriended her, in fact?'

'I'd like to think so.'

'You remained in the gatehouse flat. She stayed in the villa.'

'Yes.'

'And you offered to show her the island?'

'No. That was her own idea. She'd hired a car soon after her arrival and spent a few days seeing the sights. On Wednesday, she hired a car again, for a farewell tour of the island. She was going home next week. She invited me along for the ride.'

'And you thought the opportunity was too good to miss. You thought that out in the car, away from prying eyes in Lindos, you would have her all to yourself.'

In a sense, he had thought precisely that, but it was a sense which Miltiades was clearly unable or unwilling to envisage. 'I accepted her invitation. That's all.'

'Very well. Miss Mallender hired the car here in Rhodes Town on Wednesday afternoon, according to the rental

28

company's records. Were you with her when she did so?'

'No. I didn't even know then what she was planning. The first I heard of it was when she got back to the villa that evening. That's when she asked me along.'

'And when did the "farewell tour" commence?'

'The following day.'

'Where did you go?'

'Katavia and Monolithos.'

'And yesterday?'

'We visited Ancient Kamiros in the morning. After lunch—'

'You went to Profitis Ilias.'

'Yes.'

'Why?'

'Heather had been there before, but hadn't had time to climb to the summit. She wanted to put that right.'

'No other reason?'

'She said the atmosphere appealed to her.'

'Did it appeal to you?'

'No.'

'Why not?'

'The hotel was closed, all the villas shut up. There wasn't a soul anywhere. And the silence was . . . unsettling.'

'But Miss Mallender did not find it so?'

'No.'

'Not even when you thought you saw somebody in the hotel?'

'I didn't mention it to her.'

'Why not?'

'Because I couldn't be sure they were really there.'

'In that case, you will be interested to know that we could find no sign of anybody having been on the premises.'

'Perhaps I did imagine it, then.'

'Perhaps you did.' Miltiades paused, then went on: 'You both started to climb to the summit, then you stopped and Miss Mallender went on alone. Why?'

'I was tired. Heather wasn't.'

'And that was the last you saw of her?'

'Yes.'

'You merely sat on a tree trunk waiting – for nearly an hour – until you became concerned for her safety.'

'That's right.'

Suddenly, Miltiades brought the flat of his right hand down hard on the tabletop. The impact made Harry jump; even the constable at the door looked startled. 'You are lying, Mr Barnett,' Miltiades said, in a harshly raised voice, 'lying with every word.'

For a moment, Harry was too shocked to respond. His numbed brain told him to cling to one thought: that this abrupt change of tempo was merely an interrogator's device, a show of aggression designed to unsettle him after the subdued exchange of question and answer.

'You made sexual advances to Miss Mallender, which she resisted. Then you tried to rape her. But something went wrong and you ended by strangling her with her own scarf.'

'No.'

'You then staged the car crash so as to give yourself an excuse for not raising the alarm before nightfall.'

'No.'

'You murdered her and left her half-naked body on the mountainside for us to discover.'

There it was again. The picture his mind could not keep at bay. Heather's bruised, gashed, lifeless body, sightless eyes staring, speechless mouth sagging . . . . They had found her. There was no hope left anymore. She was dead and they had found her.

'Tell me the truth, Harry.' Miltiades' voice had struck a different note now: a gentle, insistent note of invitation. Unburden your conscience, it urged him, share the load with me. 'You did not mean to kill her, I know. It was her fault as much as yours. Is that not right? Is that not how it was?'

'Where did you find her?'

'Where you left her, Harry. Where else? Have a cigarette and tell me all about it.'

Miltiades was holding a packet open for him and Harry reached out automatically to take one. It was when he noticed the brand – *Karelia Sertika*, the brand he had himself been smoking on Profitis Ilias – that he hesitated. Miltiades' smile was too broad, his sympathy too blatant. Harry looked down at the tape recorder. It was no longer running. In some moment when his attention had been diverted, the machine had been switched off. But why? There could only be one reason: because Miltiades did not want the lie he had just told preserved on tape. They had not found Heather. They had not found anything, except four cigarette butts by a fallen tree trunk. 'I've already told you all I know,' Harry said slowly. 'And I don't know any more.'

Miltiades leaned back in his chair and sighed. Then he stretched out his hand and switched the tape recorder back on. He said nothing, but his expression conveyed the message clearly enough: the game of bluff was at an end.

'Do you know where Heather is, Inspector?'

'No, Mr Barnett, I do not. Our search of Profitis Ilias yielded many traces of your presence – but none of hers. Not even the scarf you claim to have chanced upon.'

Harry did not know whether to feel glad or sorry. Glad she might still be alive, or sorry they had not found her at all. 'What happens next?' he said eventually, certain of little but that something always did happen next.

'The search will resume at dawn tomorrow. This time, you will participate in it.'

'Good.'

'Until then you will be held here.'

'On what charge?'

'None. But one can be devised if you insist. Dangerous driving, perhaps. You may, however, prefer to seem to be cooperating with us, in which case . . . .'

'I'll stay – voluntarily.'

'I felt sure you would.' Miltiades leaned forward and

switched off the tape recorder. He gave Harry one last, scornful stare, then said: 'Is there anybody you wish to telephone?'

'No.'

'A lawyer perhaps?'

'I don't have one.'

'Very well.' Miltiades rose from his chair. 'This interview, Mr Barnett, is at an end.'

But there was no end. No end, through the long, sleepless night that followed, to the futile convolutions of his thoughts. No end, in all his conjectures, to the fear of what her continued absence meant. Why had she not returned? He was no nearer an answer now than when he had first started up the slope after her.

With his paltry breakfast in the morning, they gave him a newspaper and he found on its front page the headline he had dreaded. Η ΕΞΑΦΑΝΙΣΗ ΤΟΥ ΧΕΔΕΡ ΜΑΛΛΕΝΤΕΡ: the Disappearance of Heather Mallender. Η ΑΣΤΥΝΟΜΙΑ ΔΙΕΡΩΤΑΤΑΙ: the Police are Mystified. He did not read on. He did not need to. For he knew more than anyone. And even he knew nothing.

3

Harry looked down the rutted track and frowned. All his senses told him what only geography said was false: this was not Profitis Ilias. Not, at any rate, the Profitis Ilias he knew and feared, the still, silent, wooded mountaintop that had terrified and entrapped him. Human voices and the yelping of bloodhounds filled the forest with sound, a helicopter droned overhead and static crackled from a nearby radio. What he had prayed for two days before – noise, movement, company – were his, but in circumstances he had prayed since to avoid.

Army conscripts had been drafted in to aid the search. Harry could see their stooped, camouflage-clad figures moving slowly through the trees bordering the track, keeping in pace with each other as they sifted the undergrowth, looking, it struck him, rather like beaters in a grouse shoot. He did not expect them to find anything. Heather's scarf had been recovered more than an hour ago – a young policeman had come rushing up to Miltiades shouting excitedly *To mantili! To mantili!*' – but it had been a false dawn. The conviction was growing stronger within Harry all the time that no other evidence of Heather's presence on the mountain was there to be found. The police had meticulously retraced every step she was known to have taken, they had followed every route that might have led her away from the summit, they had searched the woods yard by yard. And they had found nothing. True, the forest was vast, the search area ill-defined: they could go on looking for a week and still not be able to say their task was complete. But in Harry's mind it already was. He did not expect Miltiades to understand let alone believe it. He was not, for that matter, eager to believe it himself. Yet the conclusion could no longer be resisted. Not merely Heather, but every sign and circumstance of that day, had vanished with the coming of men and dogs. Their diligence and their energy had banished the secrets as well as the silence of Profitis Ilias. And, in so doing, had sealed its mystery.

'We will return to the hotel now,' said Miltiades, touching Harry on the arm. 'There is nothing more that we can accomplish here.'

Harry did not reply. They began to walk down the track, retracing his headlong flight of forty-eight hours before.

'The scarf will, of course, be subjected to forensic scrutiny. It may tell us something.' But Miltiades' voice conveyed no confidence in his words. He had expected to find more, that was clear, and, now he had not, he did not know what to think. He had suspected Harry of murder, but not of being capable of concealing the crime.

'Heather could be anywhere by now,' said Harry. 'She could be off the island altogether.' But he too lacked faith in what he was suggesting.

'Strange as it may seem,' replied Miltiades, 'I had thought of that.' He shot Harry a sarcastic glare. 'If Miss Mallender had left the country, she would have been obliged to show her passport and a record of her journey would therefore exist. None does exist. The airport and harbour authorities have been placed on the alert, however, so, if she should still attempt to leave, it will not go unnoticed. I cannot say, however, that I believe it to be any more than a remote possibility. Do you know any reason, Mr Barnett, why I should take it more seriously than that?'

'No.'

'Is there something else, perhaps, that you are not telling me?'

'What do you mean by something *else?*'

'Merely that you might have told me about the death of Miss Mallender's sister, rather than leave me to hear it from your Consulate.'

'I did tell you about it.'

'You chose not to mention that she was employed by your landlord, Mr Dysart – and that she was killed by a terrorist bomb meant for him.'

So. Miltiades had wasted no time in digging out another coincidence. But coincidence, Harry knew, was all it amounted to. He had not even been aware that Clare Mallender was Dysart's personal assistant, until the English newspapers were suddenly full of how a botched IRA attempt on Dysart's life had claimed her as its victim instead. Anyway, it was irrelevant. It had happened seventeen months ago and the whole of Europe away. 'Why should I have mentioned it?' Harry snapped. 'It has no bearing—'

'Let me be the judge of that, Mr Barnett. It at least sheds light on Miss Mallender's mental state.'

'She'd got over it long ago, for God's sake.'

'Had she? You said she came here for the purpose of recuperation.'

'So she did, but—'

'And it is more puzzling than that. Mr Dysart evidently has close links with the Mallender family, yet he asked you to act as caretaker of his holiday home here on Rhodes.'

'So?'

'Why choose for such a role a man whom his friend had recently dismissed for taking bribes?'

Old wounds, it seemed, were to be re-opened in the search for new clues. 'Because I'd been a friend of his longer than Charlie Mallender had. And because he didn't believe I had been taking bribes.' Was that the real reason? Harry wondered. Or had Dysart felt some measure of guilt for recommending him to Mallender Marine in the first place? It mattered now, he supposed, hardly at all.

'It will be interesting to hear if Miss Mallender's brother agrees with your interpretation.'

Since the interrogation, Harry had forgotten that Roy Mallender was on his way to Rhodes. Yet how could he have done? He never wanted to meet the man again under any circumstances, let alone those which now seemed to be drawing them together. It was doubtful if ten years had improved his odious character; once a swine, in Harry's experience, always a swine. 'When's he due to arrive?'

'He already has arrived, Mr Barnett. There he is, waiting for us by the hotel.'

Miltiades had planned it this way, of course. He had been alerted to Roy Mallender's arrival, but had decided that Harry should have no warning of it, no chance to prepare himself for the encounter. There, in sight already, standing with a constable and another man by a car just beyond the Profitis Ilias signpost, was his old rival. As they drew closer, Harry took stock of him. He had put on weight since their last meeting and looked older than Harry's estimate of his age. He was still loathsome, of course, if not more so, yet he was not quite the man against whom Harry had once sworn futile oaths of vengeance, the man who had taken him for a fool and proved him to be just that.

'*O yos too afenteekoo,*' murmured Miltiades.

'What?'

'The boss's son, Mr Barnett. Is that not what we see before us? An unattractive species, I think you will agree.'

Harry did agree, but he refrained from saying so. In a sense, he owed it to Heather to be as conciliatory as he could. He and Roy were both there, after all, on her account; what did an old quarrel and past disgrace matter by comparison with her safety?

As they approached, Roy stopped talking to the man beside him and turned to meet them. His eyes narrowed as he looked at Harry and his lower lip protruded in a familiar sign of looming anger. For once, Harry supposed, he could scarely blame him; he braced

36

himself for the outburst that must surely follow. But it did not follow. Instead, Miltiades stepped between them and offered Roy his hand; he smiled, introduced himself and politely proffered his sympathy. Roy did not so much as glance at him; his gaze remained fixed on Harry.

'What have you found?' he said gruffly. His voice was as brusque and impatient as ever.

'As yet,' Miltiades replied, 'only your sister's scarf has—'

'Is this man under arrest?'

'Mr Barnett is assisting our enquiries. Did Mr Osborne not explain the circumstances to you?'

The man standing beside Roy – a sandy-haired, slack-faced fellow whom Harry took to be a representative of the British Consul – signalled with his eyes that explaining anything to his companion had been, to say the least, difficult.

'He didn't have to,' barked Roy. 'You don't know this man like I do, Inspector. If my sister's come to any harm—'

'We do not yet know that she has, Mr Mallender. I am investigating a disappearance, nothing more.'

'Nothing more? How can you say that when it's obvious he's lying through his teeth?'

'I'm not lying,' Harry put in. 'I don't know where Heather is, Roy. I wish I did, but I don't. I'm sorry, but there it is.'

Roy took a step towards him. 'Are you trying to get back at us, Barnett? Is that what it is? Is this your revenge for being caught with your hand in the till ten years ago?'

'Of course it isn't. Talk sense, man. I like Heather, for God's sake. I didn't want this to happen.'

'You didn't want to be found out, you mean – then or now. Sorry? You don't know the meaning of the word. But you will. Believe me, you will.'

There was something wrong in all this, Harry felt, something false to itself. It was not that Roy's accusations were groundless – that was only to be expected. It was that they were too sudden, too all-encompassing, even for such an impetuous man.

'That you should be upset is understandable,' said Miltiades, his voice striking a calming note. 'But rancour will achieve nothing. All efforts that can be made to find your sister, Mr Mallender, are being made. I would therefore recommend that you return to Rhodes and await further developments.'

'That would probably be best,' added Osborne.

Roy glared at both of them in turn. He seemed about to protest. Then the idea palled. 'All right. I suppose there's nothing else for it. But I want to be kept in regular touch.'

'You will be,' said Miltiades.

Roy grunted. 'I'd better be.' He turned to Osborne. 'Come on. I've seen enough.' Then with a parting scowl at Harry, he climbed into the car and slammed the door. Shaking his head, apparently in self-pity, Osborne made his way round to the driver's side. Miltiades murmured something to himself in Greek, then the engine started and they moved off.

'What did you say, Inspector?' Harry asked, as the car faded from view.

'Nothing that you should hear, Mr Barnett.' He paused, then added: 'Mr Mallender does not like you, does he?'

'He never has.'

'How long have you known each other?'

'Since he joined the family firm – Mallender Marine – in 1977. That was the year before I was "caught with my hand in the till".'

'Regrettably, I am not familiar with the phrase.'

'In this case, it means I was accused of over-paying a sub-contractor and taking a share of his excess profit.'

'Justly accused?'

'Roy assembled enough evidence to convince the auditors – and his father.'

'But were you guilty?'

'Believe it or not, no. I wouldn't have had the nerve for it, or the ingenuity. I was stitched up. Framed.'

'By Mr Mallender?'

'Who else? It doesn't pay to antagonize the boss's son, Inspector. They're an unattractive species, like you said.'

'And unpredictable, Mr Barnett. I had expected Mr Mallender to be extremely worried about his sister. Instead, he seemed merely extremely angry with you. I had expected him to imply that we Greeks are incapable of mounting an efficient search operation. Instead, he seemed unconcerned about how we are conducting it. I found his attitude puzzling in every respect.'

Harry gazed down the road after the vanished car. He was less surprised than Miltiades by Roy Mallender's apparent indifference to Heather's fate. Family ties would mean more to an upright Greek than a self-centred Englishman. Roy, he suspected, had come to Rhodes either at his father's insistence or because others expected it of him. Seen in that light, his flood of accusations made perfect sense. The truth – that Heather's disappearance was a total, unfathomable mystery – would seem to Roy at best inconvenient, at worst embarrassing. To fend it off, what better fall guy could there be than Harry Barnett of the blasted reputation and tattered credentials?

'It won't happen again,' Harry muttered under his breath. 'I won't come quietly this time.'

'What was that, Mr Barnett?'

'Nothing, Inspector.' Harry smiled grimly. 'Just a promise to myself.'

4

Harry flung back the sheet, lowered his legs to the floor
and pushed himself up into a sitting position. He was
shivering, but not because he was cold. The explanation
was the empty bottle of *metaxa* he could see standing on
the table in the adjoining room. Draining it had seemed,
last night, not merely the best but the only thing to do.
Permitted at last by Miltiades to come home – brought
home indeed, by speeding police car – he had confronted
solitude for the first time since Heather's disappearance
and had found it scarcely more bearable in Lindos than
he had on Profitis Ilias. Why had she not returned? For a
while at least, alcohol had kept the question at bay.

From the bedside cabinet, Harry picked up his wristwatch and peered at the face. It had stopped in the small
hours, but not before the day-and-date panel had clicked
round to Monday the fourteenth and so prepared for him
their unnecessary reminder that a third night had passed
without news of Heather. Time's reputed qualities as a
healer did not apply in this case, he reflected: its slow,
wearing passage only wound the ratchet ever tighter on
the anticipation of a dreadful discovery.

Somewhere, on the other side of the island, beneath a
tree or a rock, in a ruined goat-pen or a dried stream-bed,
the ghastly truth was surely waiting. All the alternatives –
the bizarre, the improbable, the downright impossible –
were merely games the mind consoled itself by playing.

Rising to his feet, he paused to let the throbbing in his

head subside, then hauled on a dressing gown, stepped into a pair of espadrilles and shuffled into the bathroom. It was another sunny day, he noticed: the lattice-work shutters were casting sharp dog-toothed shadows on the white-washed walls. He ran cold water into the basin, douched some onto his face, then risked a first glance in the mirror. No worse than he had expected, though worse than he had hoped, a puffy, unshaven, grey-haired likeness of himself stared back through red-rimmed, dark-socketed eyes and pronounced its silent judgement. *'This is the worst, Harry, the least and lowest, the nadir of your never-soaring life.'*

Why had she not returned? By that one abstention, Heather had laid waste his refuge. With each of the nine years he had spent in Lindos, he had grown less and less concerned about the futility of his existence there and more and more content with the comforts and compensations it offered. Every year, every season, every day was much the same amidst the bleached sand and winding alleys of this picture-postcard town. A little money, a little laughter, a little food and drink: these had been the staples of an unashamed pointlessness. Now they had become the components of an insufferable helplessness.

Recoiling from the mirror, Harry pushed open the shutters and squinted out at the familiar, harshly lit view. A cobbled path led down from the front gate of the villa beneath his window towards the clustered white-faced houses of Lindos, whose every occupant and alleyway he knew from long proximity. The sky was a deep and cloudless blue. Only a suggestion of haze that hovered over the orange groves and softened the bare slopes of Marmari south of the town told him that he had slept later than he had thought. Leaning out, he glanced down at the harbour, empty at this season of sunbathers and pleasure craft, and felt, like a stab of pain, his own indifference to the perfection of its setting. A few days ago, he would have been appalled by the very notion of leaving this place. Now he sensed that turning his back on it would cause him not a moment's regret. It was, he supposed, the true measure of how deeply Heather's disappearance had affected him.

It was less than a month since he had ambled back from the *Taverna Silenou* for his siesta and found Heather's note wedged under the knocker on the gate, explaining that she was a friend of Alan Dysart's come to stay in the villa and that, having found nobody in, she had gone to visit the acropolis; if he should return in the interim, could he come and fetch her? Cursing this girl he did not know for forcing such an ascent on him in the heat of the afternoon, he had climbed the steps to the old castle where it loomed above the town, talked his way past the ticket barrier without paying and finally arrived, panting for breath and bathed in sweat, at the ancient ruined temple enclosed by the castle walls. Normally immune to the fabled attractions of Lindos's crowning glory, he had detected, on this occasion, something unaccountably eerie about its crumbling walls and worn columns, something windless and hushed which, reinterpreted in the light of his experience on Profitis Ilias, he was tempted now to call expectant.

He identified her at once by the paleness of her skin: a slim, solitary figure sitting on the very top step of the great staircase that led to the propylea, a little hunched, it struck him as he laboured up towards her, as if afraid of something, her face in shadow, but the sun falling brightly on her shoulder-length hair, her shoulder-length flaxen hair.

'You must be Heather,' he said breathlessly, as he reached the top, for thus had she signed the note.

'And you must be Harry,' she replied, smiling up at him. He felt absurdly abashed as they shook hands, suddenly conscious of not having shaved or put on a clean shirt that morning. 'I'm sorry to drag you up here.'

'Oh, it doesn't matter,' he said, flopping down on the step beside her and trying to admire the view of the shimmering blue bay far below, by which, in his experience, newcomers were usually enraptured.

'I didn't know whether Alan had forewarned you of my visit.'

'No, I've not heard from him recently. But don't worry. It's no problem as far as I'm concerned. Late holiday, is it?'

'More of a rest cure, actually.' Then she added, as if eager to change the subject: 'Tell me, where does Alan moor his yacht when he's here?'

The strangeness of the question should have alerted Harry, but it did not. 'Down there in the harbour. At least, he used to, but I'm not sure he's bought a replacement for the *Artemis* yet. She was a beautiful boat.'

'Was she?'

'Didn't you ever see her? I thought—'

'I've only got to know Alan recently – since he lost the *Artemis*, that is. Only, I suppose *because* he lost the *Artemis*.'

'I don't follow.'

Her chin dipped slightly as she replied: 'Clare Mallender was my sister.'

'Oh,' Harry said lamely, instantly regretting his clumsiness.

'Yes. The girl who was aboard the *Artemis* when the IRA blew it up.'

Harry stared down at the canopy of bougainvillea that trailed over the gate beneath his window and sought, in its dazzling blood-red blossom, a sanctuary from the associations every corner of Lindos seemed now to hold for him. From that inauspicious beginning on the summit of the acropolis, he and Heather had felt their way towards the kind of genuine friendship he thought he had long outlived. Now she was gone, the easy comforts of the *Villa ton Navarkhon* were merely bitter reminders of what he was in no danger of forgetting: that he could not rest until he had learned the truth.

Suddenly, some movement on the very edge of his vision caught his eye. Glancing to his left, he could see down into

43

the flagged courtyard which separated the gatehouse from the western frontage of the villa. At first, all seemed as he would have expected, the flower-urns, the lemon trees, the terracotta roof-tiles and the whitewashed walls composing their familiar pattern. Then he saw it: a mobile shadow in one of the rooms of the villa that told him he was no longer alone. It was not Wednesday, so it could scarcely be Mrs Ioanides on one of her housekeeping calls. Besides, she had no key. If not her, then . . . . He ran back into the bedroom, pulled on some clothes and raced towards the stairs, banging his knee painfully on a table in the process. Not that he cared about that. Not if there was the slightest chance . . . . Heather had a key. He kept one for visitors and Heather still had it.

He ran headlong across the courtyard, his heart pounding madly, from hope as much as exertion. The door was ajar, a window stood open. It was true, then: it must be true. She had come back: there could be no other explanation. He was almost laughing aloud as he charged into the hall and turned towards the room where he had seen the shadow.

'Hello, Harry.'

It was Alan Dysart, not Heather Mallender, who turned to greet Harry as he burst into the room. Alan Dysart, of the flashing smile and perpetually boyish good looks, of the fair almost golden hair which had so aided his political career and seemed no thinner now than when Harry had first met him. Alan Dysart, Member of Parliament, government minister and owner of the *Villa ton Navarkhon*: the one visitor Harry should have expected, but not the one he had hoped to find.

'I gather you're in a spot of bother,' Dysart said. 'I hope I can help.' It was typical of the man to minimize the gravity of the situation. A relaxed approach to crises had been his trademark, both in the Navy and in politics. It had been, indeed, the key to his success. What in others might have seemed like negligence, Dysart had always contrived to

44

present as an unflappability bordering on courage; he was, according to at least one newspaper editorial, the only hope for gallantry in an ungallant generation. 'I looked in on you when I arrived, but you were sleeping like a babe. I imagine you've had a bastard of a time. Want a drink?'

Harry, who had pulled up in the doorway, moved unsteadily across the room, telling himself to hide any disappointment he felt in the light of all he owed this man, not least an apology for inadvertently setting the Greek police on his trail. 'A drink?' he said bemusedly. 'Yes, I could do with one.'

Dysart clapped him on the shoulder and grinned. 'Well, sit down before you fall down and I'll pour us both something reviving.' Harry subsided obediently onto the couch, whilst Dysart went on talking to him from the drinks cabinet behind him. 'You seemed surprised to see me.'

'I was.'

'Didn't Heather tell you I was coming out today?'

'No.'

'That's strange.' Dysart reappeared with two glasses, handed Harry one and sat down opposite him. 'I phoned her last Tuesday and asked her to let you know.'

'You were planning to come before . . . all this happened, then?'

'Yes. Preparatory work for next month's European summit.'

'She said nothing to me about it.'

'It must have slipped her mind, then.'

They both sipped their drinks in silence for a moment, then Dysart glanced around the room and said: 'Everything here seems shipshape, I'm glad to say.'

So it did, though Harry could claim no credit for the fact. Since going into politics, and especially since losing his yacht, Dysart had visited the villa less and less often. He would, in all probability, have found the rooms poorly aired and the furniture somewhat dusty on this occasion, had it not been for Heather's long stay, during which she had made Mrs Ioanides virtually redundant by her zeal in

45

household matters. The thought was yet another reminder for Harry of a subject which Dysart seemed to be shying clear of. 'I'm sorry to have involved you in all this,' he said abruptly. 'It must be . . . embarrassing.'

'A little,' Dysart replied, smiling ruefully. 'The English papers have made more of it than they otherwise might because Heather was my guest here. But that's hardly your fault. You weren't to know she was going to vanish, were you?'

'The police think I know more than I'm telling them.'

'But you don't, of course.' The remark, as Dysart had phrased it, sounded strangely like a question. 'I imagine you know her no better than I do. I only felt obliged to try and help her because of what happened to Clare.'

'Of course.'

'Do they know you once worked for the Mallenders?'

'Yes.'

'That must strike them as odd.'

'It does.' And me too, Harry thought: me too.

'So, what exactly happened?'

Dysart was clearly entitled to an explanation and Harry embarked upon one willingly. With Miltiades, it had been question-and-answer tainted by continual suspicion. In his own thoughts, recollection had been spasmodic and disorderly. This was therefore the first time since Heather's disappearance that he had imposed a logical sequence on the events leading up to it: her arrival, his liking for her, their growing confidence in each other, her invitation to join her in a farewell tour of the island, their visit to Profitis Ilias – and the total inexplicability of what had occurred there. It came to him as freshly as it must have done to Dysart and, with it, came also the certainty that, from the very start, he had missed something, perhaps even everything, that was truly important.

As Harry spoke, Dysart left his chair and began to walk around the room, his glass cradled in his hand, pausing as he went to raise and replace the lid of a decorated pot or straighten with his toe the lie of a woven rug.

46

Mobility, Harry recalled, had always been his preferred state: at the helm of his yacht, or the wheel of a fast car. Even when confined by four walls, he lapsed into it to aid concentration. Never hurrying but never still, never evasive but never easy to know, this man had proved his staunchest ally more than once, yet Harry was not sure he could claim to understand him any better now than when he had first strolled so obligingly into his life.

It was a hot afternoon in June, 1966. Harry was at his desk in the small rear office of Barnchase Motors, Marlborough Road, Swindon, reading, though scarcely bothering to follow, a letter of complaint from a customer. He had drunk too much in the Railway Inn at lunchtime and the sun on the back of his neck was beginning to bring on a headache. He was about to get up and take a stroll round the cars on the forecourt in the hope of reviving himself when he suddenly became aware of a figure standing just inside the open door.

'Mr Barnett?'

The newcomer was a tall, slim, well-bred young man of about twenty, dressed casually, but too expensively to be the average Swindon youth. Besides, he had spoken in a cultivated accent with hints of public school about it. What he wanted Harry could not imagine. 'Yes?' he said defensively.

'Harry Barnett?'

'That's me.'

'The proprietor?'

'One of the proprietors, yes.'

'But you hire and fire?'

'I suppose you could say that.'

'Good. I'd like to apply for the temporary job you're advertising. I'm a student in need of summer employment. My name's Alan Dysart.'

Harry had finished his account. He had related every event

47

of that fateful day at Profitis Ilias and many events of the days before it, whilst Dysart had walked slowly round and round the room, concentration apparent in every detail of his expression, just as, Harry recalled, it had been during their first desultory interview in Swindon all those years ago.

'I stopped off at the Consulate on my way here,' he said, after a lengthy pause. 'They told me the police suspect foul play.'

'They do. They suspect it of me.'

'Have they any explanation for the face you saw at the window?'

'None. They're satisfied the building was empty at the time.'

'And the whistle?'

'Army manoeuvres, perhaps. Or a goatherd. The sound could have carried a long way. If there was a sound. They don't believe there was.'

'But you heard it.'

'Yes, I heard it.'

'The postcards in the glove compartment?'

'They don't believe my explanations of them either.'

'And there was nothing – absolutely nothing – Heather said or did to make you suspect she might have planned this?'

'Nothing at all.'

'So you think she was abducted – or murdered?'

'What else can I think?'

'But the villagers in Salakos saw no car heading for the mountain that afternoon apart from yours.'

'I know.'

'And nobody could have known you were going there, because you didn't decide to do so until Heather suggested it over lunch.'

'Exactly.'

'There are other routes, of course, other ways of getting there, but, even so . . . .'

'None of it makes sense.'

48

'Had anything, however apparently insignificant, happened recently to worry Heather?'

'I don't think so.'

'Strangers in Lindos paying her undue attention, perhaps?'

'There are always strangers in Lindos. I noticed nothing.'

'Nothing . . . .' Dysart abstractedly echoed the word, then crossed to the drinks cabinet and returned with a bottle to re-fill Harry's glass. 'You're in a fix, old friend. A very nasty fix.'

'I know. But that worries me less at the moment than . . . .'

'What might have happened to Heather?'

'Yes.'

Dysart glanced at his watch. 'I have to get back to Rhodes PDQ, I'm afraid. There's a lot of work to be done and I'm due home again on Wednesday.'

'You're not staying here?'

'No. The Consulate's putting me up. It saves the toing and froing.'

He smiled reassuringly. 'I'm not giving you the cold shoulder, Harry. I'll make a point of calling on Inspector Miltiades and telling him that you have my unreserved support – and that he's barking up the wrong tree.'

'That's good of you.'

'There is just one thing, though.' Dysart moved away towards the window, as if embarrassed by what he was about to say. 'I'm told you had . . . a spot of bother . . . with a Danish tourist back in the summer.'

Harry winced at the memory. 'That was just drink and stupidity.'

'Even so, it looks bad in circumstances like these. If there's any question anything similiar might have occurred . . . .'

'What are you trying to say?'

'The postcards somehow heighten the impression. Heather was – is – a pretty girl. If something happened . . . if you did something . . . to frighten her . . . it might explain . . . .'

This was only, Harry knew, what everybody would think anyway, and then the least vile version thereof. Nevertheless, the fact that Dysart could entertain the idea was somehow doubly shocking. 'I did nothing. To harm her or frighten her.'

'Is that the truth, Harry? Is that God's honest truth?' He turned from the window and looked at Harry intently.

'Yes, it is.'

Dysart smiled apologetically. 'Then I won't raise the subject . . . ever again.'

An hour later, Harry was alone once more in the gatehouse flat. Dysart had set off back to Rhodes, leaving him to lock the villa, shower, shave, put on clean clothes and assemble some kind of dignity with which to confront whatever was to follow. To remain there, inert and inactive, while the search went on elsewhere, edging ever nearer to what he bleakly took to be the truth, was a heavy penance indeed. When he looked next in the mirror, it was to see a marginally less shabby representation of himself than he had seen there on waking, but most people's image of him, as Dysart had gently implied, was unlikely to alter from that of a drunken old lecher twisting and turning to escape a crime. Unlikely, that is, unless Harry could alter it for them.

5

It was the afternoon of the following day. One of autumn's periodic downpours had come to Lindos, turning its cobbled alleys into minor watercourses, its flat roofs into miniature lakes. The sky and the sea, both usually a dazzling blue, had assumed instead a dull and uniform grey. Even the lofty castle walls had lost their proud, golden hue. Melancholy, as well as cloud, had settled upon the town.

At the open-fronted *Taverna Silenou* in the main square, the interlocking branches of a pair of fig trees formed a canopy beneath which two middle-aged men sat at a rusting metal table, staring out forlornly at the curtain of rain. Copies of Rhodes' three daily newspapers lay on the table before them, wedged beneath a well-filled ashtray and flanked by empty coffee cups, half-empty beer glasses and the crumbling remnant of a bread roll. Neither Harry Barnett nor Kostas Dimitratos had said much during the past half hour, but each had derived a modicum of comfort from the company of the other.

'How much more times can I say it?' Kostas enquired suddenly, plucking a toothpick from his mouth and flicking it towards the nearest puddle. 'I am sorry, Hari. Sorry for telling Miltiades about . . . *tee Thaneza*.' He was a short, round little man with a disproportionately large, absurdly luxuriant, walrus moustache. This, which gave him a vaguely lugubrious appearance even at the sunniest of times, now conspired with the elements to invest his words with the weight of total despondency.

Harry, who had been leaning forward on his chair, sat upright and turned to look at his companion. 'Kostas,' he said with heavy emphasis, 'not even your best friend expects you to be reticent. I should know, because I'm it. So for Christ's sake stop feeling so guilty. I was hoping you'd cheer me up.'

The other man frowned and scratched his considerable stomach. 'Ret-i-cent?' he repeated doubtfully.

'*Ligomilitos.*'

It was clear from his expression that Kostas did not know whether he had been complimented or insulted. Rather than pursue the point, he prised one of the newspapers loose, stared for the fifth or sixth time at the article reporting a complete absence of progress in the police investigation of the disappearance of Heather Mallender, then slammed it back onto the table with a grunt of disgust.

'Besides,' Harry went on, as if he had not noticed his friend's display, 'you're about the only inhabitant of Lindos who's still prepared to talk to me, so I can't afford to be choosey, can I? Do you know, when I went into the bakery this morning, it was as if I'd become invisible.'

Kostas shook his head sadly and clicked his tongue. 'I am sorry, Hari.'

'Do stop saying that.'

'It will be different when. . . .' His reassuring remark trailed into silence as both men's attention was taken by the arrival of a car in the square. It sped down the short slope from the main road and came to a halt in a cloud of spray. They could not make out the occupant through the rain-smeared windscreen, but the fact that it was a hire car seemed suggestive in itself. A few moments later, a tall thin man in an oilskin coat climbed out and ran across to them.

'Hi,' he said. 'Either of you two know Harry Barnett?'

He was an Englishman, with one of those educated but slovenly accents Harry had come to hate. Lean-faced and dark-haired, with intent, darting eyes and a suggestion of stubble about the chin, he was clearly neither tourist nor public servant, but whether Harry wanted to make his acquaintance was far less clear.

Kostas, noting his friend's failure to respond, at once assumed the role of an uncomprehending Greek. He cocked his head and frowned up at the stranger. '*Parakalo?*'

The man raised his voice. '*Harry Barnett!*'

'*Then milame Anglika.*'

'What?'

'*Then milame—*'

'He's saying we don't speak English,' Harry interrupted. 'But he's only trying to be helpful. I'm Harry Barnett. Who are you and what do you want?'

He was a journalist, as Harry might have known, had he studied the signs more carefully. He introduced himself as Jonathan Minter of *The Courier*, a new national Sunday newspaper Harry had never heard of. He ordered a pizza which Kostas departed huffily to prepare – then turned to the purpose of his visit without further ado.

'We simply think it's time you had your say. Poor little rich girl goes missing on holiday island. Friend of government minister and a looker to boot. Obviously, the tabloids have had a field day. And you've figured as the villain of the piece. But what's the truth of the matter, eh? That's what we'd like to know.'

'So would I.' Already, Harry felt sure he did not like Minter. He had encountered his type before, flaunting his girlfriend and his credit card around Lindos in the season. It was only envy, in the final analysis, that he felt, but envy of a very personal kind. It seemed like years since he had met an Englishman who was not younger and wealthier than he was. Perhaps that was why he had come to prefer the Greeks.

'Oh, come on. You know more than you're telling.'

'Do I?'

'I gather you used to work for Mallender Marine.'

'So?'

'And were sacked over a contractual irregularity.'

'What's that to do with you?'

'Nothing. But why let the Mallenders say what they like about you? Why let them have it all their own way? I'm sure you could deliver a few home truths if you wanted to.'

'What have they been saying?'

'See for yourself.' Minter took a sheet of paper from his pocket and handed it to Harry. It was a photocopy of three separate newspaper articles arranged on a single page. 'They all appeared on Sunday following a press conference Roy Mallender gave before flying out here on Saturday night. He doesn't have a very high opinion of you, does he?'

Harry did not need Minter to tell him of his standing in Roy Mallender's eyes. Nevertheless, it was a shock to have it spelt out in spare, journalists' prose:

> Mr Mallender said he was disturbed by reports that Heather had been in the company of an Englishman named Harry Barnett when she disappeared. He described Barnett as 'a man with a grudge against my family', 'A former employee of Mallender Marine who was dismissed in 1978 for taking bribes'. Mr Mallender said Barnett was 'the very last person I would have wanted my sister to associate with. Now it's been confirmed she was alone with him, it's difficult not to fear the worst.'

Minter leaned across the table and lowered his voice. 'He's virtually saying you murdered her.'

'Perhaps he believes I did.'

'But you didn't, did you?'

Kostas reappeared, placed a bottle, a glass and some cutlery in front of Minter, then withdrew.

'Well?'

'You're not getting a story out of me,' said Harry. 'Whatever I told you, you'd distort it to serve your own ends.'

'But they'd be your ends too, Harry. We're on the same side, you and I. Neither of us likes the Mallenders – or what they stand for.'

'What do they stand for?'

'Privilege. Hypocrisy. Corruption. The three pillars of their kind of life.'

This sounded personal, Harry thought, personal and infuriatingly close to what he himself believed. 'I didn't take bribes. I didn't murder Heather. What else is there to say?'

'Everything. What happened on Profitis Ilias wasn't as simple, or as inexplicable, as you seem to think. I reckon you're the weak link, Harry, in a chain of events that connects Roy Mallender, and other far more important people, with something very nasty indeed. And I reckon you know what it is.'

'I've no idea what you're talking about.'

Kostas made another lumbering entrance, this time with a plateful of unappetizing pizza and a basket of bedraggled bread. When they were alone again, Minter said: 'Ask yourself this, Harry. If Heather Mallender *was* murdered, and you didn't do it, then who did? If the motive wasn't robbery, or rape, then what was it?'

'I don't know.'

'She'd been here for a month. Long enough for you to get to know her, I'd have thought. Didn't she say anything in that time, anything at all, that might explain what's happened?'

Harry was about to reply when another car drew into the square: a police patrol car, with two uniformed officers inside. One of them climbed out and bustled towards the *taverna*. As he drew closer, Harry recognized him as a member of Miltiades' search party. He explained himself in gabbled Greek, from which Harry gathered that Miltiades wanted to see him immediately.

'What's going on?' said Minter, as Harry rose from his chair.

'They're taking me in. I think they've found something.'

'You mean Heather?'

'I don't know.'

As Harry stepped past him, Minter caught his arm and pushed a small piece of paper into his hand. 'It's the number of my hotel in Rhodes,' he whispered. 'Think about what I said. If anything comes to mind, give me a call. And Harry. . . .'

'Yes?'

'If you do come up with a link in that chain I mentioned, there could be money in it for you. A lot of money.'

As the car sped up the coast road towards Rhodes Town, the two policemen became absorbed in an argument about football. Left to brood on the back seat, Harry stared out at the stark, rain-swept scenery, and scoured his memory for the clue Minter had seemed so sure he possessed. Places he had been with Heather and snatches of conversations he had held with her recurred kaleidoscopically to his mind, reaching momentarily towards significance, then relapsing into a meaningless jumble. If only he could shrug off the enfeebling sense of loss that had gripped him since her disappearance. If only he could summon the energy and concentration needed to deduce what had become of her. Had she not once said . . . ? Had her expression not once implied . . . ? But no. The thought, the impression, the link in the chain, was gone before he could grasp it. The wipers whined mechanically across the windscreen, the rain sluiced down the glass close to his face, and meaning floated out of reach.

6

'No, Mr Barnett,' said Miltiades, his face retaining its mastery of the impassive, 'we have not found her. But you might say she has found us.'

'What the hell does that mean?'

'It means that Miss Mallender's mother received a postcard from her daughter in England this morning. It was posted here in Rhodes on the ninth of November – last Wednesday – and states her intention of flying home on the sixteenth – tomorrow. More significantly . . . . But read it yourself. The British police have telexed the contents to me.'

Miltiades slid a sheet of paper across the desk. When Harry stooped over it, he saw that it was indeed a telex, originating from New Scotland Yard. It read:

Mallender communication ran as follows, 'Rhodes, Wed. 9th. Mummy (underlined). Am flying back a week today, the 16th. Should arrive mid-afternoon. Will phone you from Heathrow. Looking forward to being home. Something not quite right here will make me glad to leave. See you soon. Lots of love, Heather.'

'Something not quite right here,' said Miltiades, stressing each word. 'What do you conclude from that?'

For Harry, the postcard was final proof that his unawareness had assumed culpable proportions. The Heather he had looked upon as a friend could not have written those

57

words. *'Something is not quite right'?* There had been nothing, he was sure of it, to imply she felt uneasy; nor had she seemed eager to leave Rhodes, quite the reverse. He looked at Miltiades and shook his head weakly. 'I don't know . . . . I don't know what to say.'

'Permit me to recommend the truth. It is much simpler, in the end.'

'It may not be what you want to hear.'

'Tell me anyway.'

Harry slumped down in the chair beside him and tried to frame the words that would describe how confused he felt. He was gripped by a powerful inclination to confide in this man. Perhaps the cause was a change of venue, from the bare, echoing interrogation room where they had first met to this comfortably furnished office with its mahogany desk, its antique print of Rhodes on one wall and its modern map on another, its air of a civilized man's study. Or perhaps the cause was Miltiades himself, in whom some spark of passion seemed to have been extinguished and replaced by a bland and patient curiosity. Whatever the reason, Harry was no longer deterred by the inadequacy of what he had to say.

'I feel sad and angry by turns. Sad I didn't understand her better. Sad I didn't put the time we spent together to better use. And angry that nobody cares about me. Angry that I'm just at best a witness, at worst a suspect. Everyone else is allowed simply to be worried about Heather. But I have to worry about myself as well. What do you all think I did? Nothing is the answer. And that, I suppose, is the worst of it. Whatever happened to her on Profitis Ilias, I could have prevented it, but I didn't. So is that what you want me to confess to? The failure to intervene – though intervene in what God alone knows.'

The outburst was over. Silence reasserted itself for just as long as it took Harry to feel ashamed of what he had said. Then Miltiades' chair creaked faintly as he leaned back in it. He put the tips of his fingers together and gazed at the ceiling like some fastidious consultant about to pronounce on the progress of a fatal disease. 'First we are bewildered. Then we enter a brief phase of hope. When that is shown to have been unwarranted, a form of grief is experienced, sometimes accompanied but always followed by an apportionment of blame, an increasingly desperate search for somebody to bear the guilt we feel.' He smiled and looked at Harry. 'Does it sound familiar, Mr Barnett? I am quoting from recent research into the consequences of disappearance. This case appears to be displaying certain classical symptoms.'

'You mean I'm the peg for others to hang their guilt on?'

'Inevitably, since you were the last to see Miss Mallender. Her brother was here earlier, demanding that I arrest you. I tried to explain to him that there was no evidence to form the basis of a charge against you and that, whilst I hold your passport, there need be no fear of you attempting to flee the country. But he was not satisfied. The reason is clear. Miss Mallender's family feel guilty about neglecting her, as they now accuse themselves of having done during her stay here. One way to assuage that guilt is to fasten it on you. Your problem is that there is nobody on whom you can fasten your guilt; it stays with you.'

It was true. Miltiades had described his plight exactly. 'Do the consequences continue?' asked Harry bleakly. 'Are there further phases we've yet to enter?'

'Oh yes. They may be interrupted at any point, of course, by the discovery of the truth. The discovery of a body, I mean, or the discovery of the missing person. One phase you have already exhibited: a tendency to blame the person who has disappeared. Secretly, you may already hope that she will be found dead rather than prolong the uncertainty. And it is probable that you will have begun to think: how could she do this to me? It is, I fear, a short step from there to the next phase.'

'Which is?'

'Indifference, Mr Barnett. A few months from now, most

of Miss Mallender's friends will have forgotten her. A year from now, they will all have forgotten her.'

'I can't believe that.'

'Then wait and see. I speak from experience. Have you ever heard of Eirene Kapsalis?'

'No.'

'Then the point is made. Eirene Kapsalis was married to the shipping magnate, Andreas Kapsalis. She disappeared without trace seven years ago. She is now a forgotten woman.'

'You remember her.'

'That is because my failure to find Mrs Kapsalis led to my being transferred here from the Athens force. In that case, you see, I was made to bear the guilt of others.' Nothing in Miltiades' voice conveyed the resentment he evidently still felt, seven years on, at his demotion. Heather's disappearance, Harry suddenly realized, must have held unpleasant reminders for him. 'Shortly before leaving Athens,' he went on, 'I saw Mr Kapsalis being driven along a street. His mistress was with him. They were laughing and drinking. I did not receive the impression that they were thinking of Eirene.'

'Perhaps not, but—'

'Miss Mallender's brother reminds me of Kapsalis. There is a physical and, I suspect, moral resemblance.' His thoughts seemed to dwell on the past for a moment, then he said: 'You will be glad to know that Mr Dysart has been here to speak on your behalf. A politician is always a valuable ally, is he not?'

'What did he say?'

'Simply that we are wrong to suspect you of murdering Miss Mallender.'

'Do you still suspect me?'

'Let us say that other possibilities have assumed greater significance.'

Be cautious, Harry told himself. This may all be an elaborate method of undermining your defences. 'What possibilities?' he asked neutrally.

'There are several. Firstly, there are the innocent explanations. Miss Mallender may have fallen, hit her head, lost her memory and wandered off the mountain in a concussed state. But, on an island as small as this, she would surely have been found by now. She could, of course, have fallen and killed herself, or been badly injured and died subsequently. But the search would, I think, have uncovered her body in that event. Secondly, we have the criminal explanations. A madman chanced upon her and murdered her, or tried to rape or rob her and, in the process, killed her. He then hid the body. But madmen are somewhat conspicuous among the villages and vineyards of the island's interior. I think we can rule that out. You may have murdered her, of course: I have not dismissed the idea. But frankly, Mr Barnett, I doubt your ability to have hidden the body effectively. If I underestimate you, you will have an apology when I arrest you. She may have been murdered by somebody else for some reason of which we have no knowledge. But that would require planning and we know that the visit to Profitis Ilias was not planned. Besides, who would this person be? There appear to be no obvious candidates. Something of the same objection applies to the theory that she was abducted. The only plausible motive for abduction would be to demand ransom. But Miss Mallender's family, though wealthy, is scarcely wealthy enough to make that likely and, besides, no demand for ransom has been forthcoming. This brings us to the possibility that Miss Mallender staged her own disappearance. Since she has recently undergone psychiatric treatment, it is at least conceivable that she was so disillusioned with her life as to want to escape from it. This too, of course, would require planning, in the way of an escape route. Islands are the most difficult of places to leave unnoticed. In her position, I would have disappeared anywhere but on Rhodes. If she acted on the spur of the moment, without prior planning, she would encounter the same difficulty. She knows nobody here who would shelter her. Yet there is no sign of her having boarded a plane or ferry. If she had hired a fisherman to take her to the Turkish coast, for instance, he would surely have come forward by now. And why, if such was her intention, should she put that tantalizing phrase in a postcard to her mother – "something not quite right"?'

Harry waited for him to continue, but he did not. Yet there had to be more. Every possibility he had listed he had convincingly excluded. 'Well? what else is there?'

Miltiades sighed. 'Ah, now we enter dangerous territory. Mr Mallender gave me some photographs of his sister. Look at one.' He reached into a drawer of the desk, took out a photograph and handed it to Harry. It was a picture of Heather, certainly, yet not the Heather Harry felt he knew. She was a few years younger when it was taken, with slightly shorter hair and a marginally fuller face, smiling conventionally at the camera with the unaffected, clear–eyed amiability of a well-balanced, unremarkable young woman. 'Do you recognize her?' said Miltiades.

'Yes, of course. Except . . . .'

'There is something wrong?'

'This is Heather, Inspector. Obviously it is. But it must pre–date her sister's death. When she arrived here a month ago, she wasn't like this. She's changed.'

'In what way?'

'In every way. Life had thrown her its first major challenge. It had shaken her, certainly, but it had also extended her. It had made her more vulnerable, of course, but also less complacent. This picture is of the girl she was, not the woman she'd become.'

Miltiades reached across the desk and retrieved the photograph. 'Would it surprise you to learn,' he said 'that thousands of people disappear all over Europe every year? Not vagrants, you understand, but respectable, financially secure, contented people: husbands, wives, sons, daughters, lovers, friends. One day' – he snapped his fingers – 'they simply vanish. Where do they go? What happens to them? A certain number die, or are murdered, and are never found. A certain number kill themselves and are

62

never identified. A certain number run away and begin a new life under a different name. But how many? How many does that account for and how many does it leave still unexplained?'

'I don't know.'

'There is a residue of all such cases, Mr Barnett, a small, stubborn fraction, for which there is no explanation. One moment they are with us, the next they are gone. It is death without a corpse. Mrs Kapsalis, it seemed to me, was one of those. Perhaps Miss Mallender is also.'

'Death without a corpse? What way is that for a policeman to be talking?'

Miltiades smiled. 'No way at all. You are correct to reproach me. The search will resume as soon as the weather permits.' He looked round at the window, where rain was still washing across the glass. 'But water, alas, is a great destroyer of evidence.' He shook his head dolefully. 'I am not optimistic.'

Harry waited for Miltiades to turn back and face him, but, for a minute or more, he continued to stare at the window. He raised his left hand to his mouth and began to tap the band of a signet ring against his teeth. Then, as if it were no more than an afterthought, he said: 'You may go now, Mr Barnett.'

'You've finished with me?'

At that, Miltiades turned to look at him with the slightly puzzled expression of a man surprised not to find himself alone. 'Yes,' he replied. 'For the moment.'

7

The rain was beginning to ease and dusk to fall when Harry
left Police Headquarters. He felt overwhelmingly reluctant
to return to Lindos, where only an empty villa and sundry
reminders of Heather awaited him. Instead he made his
way down to the harbour and walked out along the eastern
mole till he had reached its far end. It was deserted, as he
had hoped. He sat at the base of the column on which the
statue of a doe stood guard over the harbour entrance and
gazed out at the darkening blend of sea and sky, taking
comfort from the chill wind tugging at his hair and the rain
spitting at his face.

Then, when night had irrefutably closed upon the scene,
he walked slowly back towards the floodlit walls of the
medieval Old Town, tired and cold enough by now to
think that human company might be bearable. Entering
by Freedom Gate, he wandered into the Knights' Quarter
of the ancient city, letting the silence and emptiness of
the cobbled streets ease his self-pity. Halfway along Odos
Ipoton, he heard a piano being played in an upper room
and, finding the sound hauntingly beautiful, lingered for
twenty minutes or more beneath the window, listening to
the notes rise and fall against the sputtering backdrop
of water draining from roofs and gutters. He had no
ear for music, but Heather had sometimes played the
piano in the villa; he had heard her from the gatehouse flat. It was impossible, it seemed, not to think
of her at every turn, and on the whole, he did not

object, for to do so was less painful than the effort of forgetting.

At length, he found himself in the Turkish Quarter, where the shops were still open and light and music beckoned. Down a side-turning off Odos Sokratous, he spotted a bar which looked dowdy and quiet enough to deter any English tourists. There he installed himself at a corner table with a bottle of *mavro* and a packet of cigarettes and began to make determined inroads on both, slipping, as he did so, into a misanthropic mood which excused him, for a while, from confronting any failings of his own.

How long he had sat there when it happened he had no way of telling, time having ceased to seem of consequence. He had thought the alley on which the bar was located to be a cul-de-sac – certainly few passers-by had come or gone along it – and that assumption made what occurred all the more startling. He had just drained the bottle of wine into his glass and begun to consider the merits of ordering another when his eye was taken by a young woman walking past in the alley, heading down it and hence away from what he had taken to be a block end. Not that this was what took him aback when he saw her glance towards him through the open doorway. His astonished reaction had quite another origin.

It was Heather. Surely to God it was Heather. She was dressed as she had been that last day at Profitis Ilias, in a black jacket and tartan skirt. She flicked back her hair – her shoulder-length, flaxen hair – with one hand as she passed by and cast so brief and piercing a look in his direction that he could not doubt it was her, nor that she had seen and recognized him. But she did not stop. While he sat in his chair, too amazed for the moment to move, she walked steadily on and vanished from sight beyond the angle of the next building.

Breaking free of his momentary paralysis, Harry lunged for the door. He would have gained the alley at her very heels had not the barkeeper, who had been eyeing him suspiciously, adroitly intercepted. Valuable seconds were thus lost searching his pockets for enough drachmas to appease the wretched man. When he did emerge, it was to see her already turning into Odos Sokratous. A desperate fear that she might disappear among the shoppers drove his legs like pistons and left him no time to consider why she should not have stopped of her own accord.

He reached the corner. There she was, on the other side of the street, just turning into another alley. 'Dear Christ,' he almost cried aloud, 'don't let me lose her now.' He flung himself after her, only to collide with a small man built like a barrel who hurled invective after him as he plunged on towards the mouth of the alley. It swallowed him instantly in its dark, over-arched world, blanking off the commerce of the street. Within thirty yards there were two side-turnings to the left and one to the right, before the alley described a sharp right angle of its own. Why here? his racing mind thought. Why choose this maze of passages and courtyards in which to show herself? Unless . . . . No. That was unthinkable.

Each turning was the same and each was empty. Nothing but reflected light in standing water met his gaze, nothing but the distant shifting shapes of scurrying cats in the dark shadows of ancient buttresses.

He kept to what seemed the major route. It dog-legged to right and left and there, once more, halfway along a straight, uninterrupted stretch, he saw her. He shouted her name, heard it magnified and multiplied by the walls around, then judged, by some movement of her head, that she had looked back and seen him. But she did not stop. Still, as he ran towards her, feet beating a mad tattoo on the cobbled alley floor, she did not stop. Instead, without seeming to quicken her pace, she drew ahead, then vanished abruptly down a turning to the right.

His chest was heaving, his breath straining to the limit, when he swerved into the side-alley. He had almost expected another disappointment, another bewildering choice of wrong turnings. But not this time. The alley was straight, and better lit than most by the windows of habitations set high in its flanking walls. Nor was she hurrying. She had almost come to a halt indeed, moving slowly and distractedly from one pool of light to the next.

'Heather!'

She stopped, but did not turn. He saw her shoulders hunch at the sound of her name, as if in expectation of some blow or shock, but still she did not turn. He walked towards her, resisting the temptation to run, or to speak again until she had looked him in the face. As he reached out to touch her, his mind had already begun to frame the questions he would put, but his hand never made contact, because, at the last moment, she turned round to confront him in the full glare of an uncurtained window and, at that, his arm fell back to his side.

It was not Heather. The face was different, harsher, older, overly made-up. She was of similar height and weight, no doubt, but so unlike her in the indefinable sum of features and impressions as to render his mistake absurd, if not grotesque.

They stared at each other in stupefaction for a moment, then she spoke and, to crown his error, she spoke in Greek. *'Tee thelete?'*

Harry was dumbfounded. He did not know what to do or say, whether to apologize for accosting her or accuse her of misleading him. Greeks with flaxen hair were rare indeed. This, taken together with the clothes she was wearing, seemed to add a hint of deliberate deceit.

'Then sas ksero!' The tone of her voice as she protested that she did not know him suggested that she was becoming annoyed and possibly nervous. For this – if she were innocent – he could scarcely blame her.

'Lipame,' he apologized lamely. *'Ena lathos.'* A mistake? Yes, it was certainly that. But whose? He could not believe that this walking, talking simulacrum of Heather was a freak of nature, yet neither could he bring himself to put the matter to the proof.

'Poo eenai Heather?' she said with a frown. Who is

Heather? It was a question Harry could no longer answer with both honesty and certainty.

'*Then pirazi.*' Harry shook his head. He could bear their exchanges no longer. Costume and disguise or pure, outrageous chance, it made no difference: she was both too alike and too unalike for peace of mind. The suggestion of sympathy in her last remark had, moreover, revolted him in a way he could not understand. Muttering a last apology – '*Signomi*' – he turned and hurried away along the alley.

He headed back towards Odos Sokratous, trying and failing to put the experience out of his mind. It must all have been wishful thinking on his part, he supposed, a wild hope founded on a chance resemblance; perhaps she had not really looked at him as she passed the bar at all. Either way, a stiff drink in convivial surroundings might repair the damage. He entered the first bar he came to, a noisy, smokey, low-ceilinged drinking den, and ordered a brandy.

A figure who had been leaning against the counter whirled round at the sound of Harry's voice. It was Roy Mallender and the sight of his flushed, scowling face told Harry that he had just made his second mistake of the evening.

'Barnett!' The man's voice was thick with drink and animosity.

'I don't want any trouble, Roy. You were here first. I'll leave, OK?'

'No, it's not OK. I want a word with you.'

'Some other time.'

Harry moved towards the door, but Roy intercepted and grabbed him by the arm. 'If the police can't get the truth out of you, maybe I can,' he rasped. 'Why the hell should you be free to wander in and out of here when my sister's lying out there dead somewhere?'

'We don't know she's dead.'

'You know, all right. You know because you murdered her.'

'Why exactly do you think I should have done that?'

'There's no need for me to spell it out. We all know what kind of man you are.'

They were not discussing Heather. Intuitively, Harry realized that what was between them was what had always been between them: the animal loathing that two humans sometimes feel for each other without the need of a cause, even a good one. In former times, Roy had cunningly constructed pretexts for venting his hatred of Harry; now, when the opportunity was ready-made, he was not about to let it slip. 'Let go of me,' Harry said, suppressing his own instincts beneath an attempt at softly-spoken reason.

'Make me.' Roy's face was twisted in some kind of triumphant leer; drink had robbed him of every pretence. 'If you think you can.'

Harry had intended merely to shake the fellow off. Instead, he jerked his arm free so violently that Roy, caught off balance, was sent reeling into a table-load of backgammon players. Board, dice, counters, drinks and ashtrays fell in all directions as Roy crashed down between two cursing men. Harry did not wait for him to pick himself up, but rushed straight out into the street.

It was cool and damp and mercifully quiet. Behind him were raised voices and canned *bouzouki* music, ahead only the black, blanketing anonymity of the Old Town, in which he might yet contrive to lose himself. Why he did not hurry he could not clearly tell, for Roy Mallender was not the man to leave a slight unavenged, never mind a vendetta unpursued. Nevertheless, Harry merely ambled across the street and began to make his way westwards with no sense of urgency at all. He had reached the railed-off perimeter of a mosque, whose soaring, domed shape he could just make out in the gloom, and was about to turn down a flight of steps between the railings and the blank wall of the next building, when Roy caught up with him. In the circumstances, Harry should not have been surprised. Yet, strangely, he was.

'Barnett, you bastard!' Roy shouted, grasping him by

69

the shoulder and swinging him round. 'You don't get out of it that easily.'

'Out of what?'

'Out of admitting what really happened on that mountain.'

'Nothing happened.'

'You don't expect me to believe that.'

'No. As a matter of fact, I don't.'

'What did you do to her? You may as well tell me before I beat it out of you.'

Harry saw it at last. He caught and held the perception in his mind. Fear was the component he had detected in Roy at their meeting on Profitis Ilias but had not identified till now: fear that emanated from the man like an odour, that fouled his every action and debased his every word. The truth he clamoured for was merely a lie he meant to force from Harry, a lie with which he meant to bury truth.

'Well? What have you to say for yourself?'

Harry smiled. 'She did have something to run away from, didn't she?' he replied. 'She was running away from y—'

Roy hit him in the midriff before he could finish the sentence. His ribs were still sore from the car crash and the blow left him doubled up, gasping for breath. As he made to rise, he saw, through tear-blurred eyes, his opponent waiting for him, fist drawn back to strike, teeth gritted in a fury of concentration. An absurd thought flashed into his mind: did somebody not tell him once that Roy Mallender had boxed for Millfield? Then the blow struck him square on the jaw and sent him plunging backwards down the steps. This punishment was partly self-imposed, he realized, in a compartment of his brain where pain did not register. Then a harsh, blunt, metallic surface slammed into the back of his head. And impact and oblivion became one.

8

There were moments when dream and waking met. In one such ill-defined interlude, Alan Dysart seemed to be leaning over him, his hand touching his shoulder, his face creased with concern, his mouth moving as in speech – though what he was saying Harry could not tell. For the rest, confusion was all, but confusion of a strangely reassuring kind. Crisp, institutional linen and noises without context: these had already told him where he was before he had mastered collected thought.

Harry had not been in hospital since having his appendix removed in 1946. He had detested every moment of the experience and had determined to avoid a repetition. It was odd, therefore, to realize how congenial he found his new surroundings; perhaps it was a sign of growing old. Of course, in straitened post-war Swindon he had not been given a room to himself, nor the attentions of a strikingly beautiful Greek nurse; the medical resources of Rhodes seemed markedly superior to what he had always supposed.

A doctor visited him shortly after he had come to himself and informed him that he had been found unconscious the previous night at the foot of a flight of steps in the Old Town, with a badly gashed head; there was a dressing in place to confirm it. He had also suffered a bruised jaw and two broken ribs; hence the tight swathe of bandaging around his midriff. X-rays had happily established that his skull was intact, but concussion was always to be dealt

71

with cautiously, especially in a man of his age (a shaft which Harry found particularly painful): several days of bed-rest and observation were in order. Harry protested that he felt well enough to leave at once, but the doctor assured him that he would not when the pain–killers wore off. Then Harry confessed what was really troubling him: he could not afford the cost of a lengthy stay. But the cost, it transpired, was to be entirely borne by Mr Alan Dysart: he had been adamant on the point. Nor was Harry in a position to contest his generosity, since Mr Dysart had flown back to England that morning. The doctor closed with a homily on the subject of drunkenness, to which, it seemed, he attributed Harry's injuries; Harry bore the injustice in silence.

An hour or so later, the nurse woke Harry from a doze to say that Inspector Miltiades was there to see him. It was implied he could postpone the visit if he wished, but he chose not to, intent as he was on paying back Roy Mallender in any way he could.

Miltiades looked, it seemed to Harry, not quite himself. There was something vaguely apologetic about him, something almost shamefaced. He held a whispered conversation at the door with the nurse, then came forward and sat beside the bed, holding his uniform cap somewhat awkwardly in his hand.

'Good news, Inspector,' said Harry, attempting a sarcastic smile but finding that the dressing on the back of his head in some way prevented it. 'This is an open-and-shut case.'

'An open-and-shut case of what, Mr Barnett?'

'Assault and battery.'

'You wish to lodge a complaint against somebody?'

'Certainly.'

'Then you may wish to know two things before doing so. Firstly, a common symptom of concussion is an inability to remember accurately events immediately prior to the concussion being incurred.'

'I remember them perfectly.'

72

'Secondly, Mr Roy Mallender left Rhodes this morning and is not expected to return.'

'What?'

'He is no longer here, Mr Barnett. And he is not coming back. So to accuse him of anything would be a waste of time and effort.'

Harry's immediate reaction was to thump the mattress in protest, but a stab of pain from his ribs deterred him. Instead, he merely glowered at Miltiades. 'Why the . . . .' he began. Then another thought intruded. 'Just a minute. How did you know I was going to accuse Roy Mallender of doing this to me?'

Miltiades smiled. 'I fear I owe you an apology. Not for letting Mr Mallender leave Rhodes, but for practising a small deception on you last night.'

'Deception?'

'The woman resembling Miss Mallender was one of my female officers. She wore a blond wig and dressed according to the description you yourself gave us.'

Harry let out a small sigh of exasperation and surprise. So that was it. She had been neither wraith nor simulacrum, but a policewoman in disguise.

'I did warn you that I had not excluded the possibility of your having murdered Miss Mallender. It seemed to me that a murderer, confronted by the ghost of his victim, might well give himself away, whereas—'

'If I'd been telling the truth, I'd be taken in by the disguise.'

'Quite so. And you were taken in, Mr Barnett, you were. I no longer suspect you of murder. You should be pleased.'

'You had me followed when I left your office yesterday?'

'Yes. Every step of the way. Until the time seemed ripe. And afterwards as well. Not closely enough to intervene in your altercation with Mr Mallender, it is true, but at least you were not left to lie where you fell.'

'Thanks very much.'

'But you will be wondering, of course, why I allowed Mr Mallender to go free when one of my own officers had witnessed his assault on you.'

'Surprise me.'

'The answer is that *I* did not. Higher authority determined that Mr Mallender should be released. It was felt that a charge against him would make him the subject of public sympathy, especially in England, where it might also arouse some anti-Greek feeling. For all Mr Mallender knew, you were still under suspicion for murdering his sister. What he did could therefore seem to some exactly what a conscientious brother should do. I believe Mr Dysart made certain diplomatic representations on Mr Mallender's behalf which proved decisive. They left together this morning.'

Harry said nothing. He should have foreseen this, of course. He should have read it in that floating, remembered face at his bedside. The action was typical of Dysart. It captured perfectly his politician's instinct for compromise. Pay Harry's hospital bill. Escort Roy back to England. And subvert the relevant officials. It was like a prefect resolving a dispute between two schoolboys. Which was only fitting in a sense, since, but for Dysart, there would have been no dispute in the first place. But for Dysart, come to that, Harry would know nothing of the Mallender family.

It was the close of a quiet lunchtime at the Glue Pot Inn about ten days before Christmas, 1972, and Harry had just measured himself a sly double scotch. When he turned back from the optics, it was to find Alan Dysart smiling at him from the other side of the bar, looking prosperous and absurdly well-groomed in his civilian clothes.

'Christ! Alan! What are you doing here?'

'Looking up an old friend. Can I get that for you?'

'This?' Harry grinned sheepishly. 'OK. Thanks.' Harry poured a drink for Dysart as well, then suggested they adjourn to a table. The only other customer was devoting an age to half an inch of stout; he did not look in need of service.

'I went to the garage first,' said Dysart, after one sip of his scotch.

Harry felt himself flush with embarrassment. How to explain or excuse what had happened was beyond him.

'They told me you closed in August.'

'That's right.' A rueful smile. 'We did.'

'They implied . . . bankruptcy.'

Harry took a deep breath. 'It was.'

'Enforced?'

A weary nod. 'Total would be a better word. Barry saw it coming. He skipped to Spain a few weeks beforehand, taking what cash was in hand and leaving me with the debts.'

'Good God.'

'Jackie went with him.'

'She would.'

'Yes. You were right about her.'

'So what are you doing now?'

'Getting by. I've a job here till Christmas.'

'And then?'

'I don't know. Something's bound to turn up.'

Harry's optimism must have sounded as false to Dysart as it did to Harry himself. He did not, in truth, foresee anything turning up. For Dysart even to go to the trouble of seeking him out was more than he would have expected. After all, Harry had done him no conspicuous favours during those university vacations he had spent working at Barnchase Motors. Now that he was a rising young naval officer, there seemed no reason for him to be concerned about his ex-employer's present plight. But concerned, it transpired over a second drink, he nevertheless was.

'Have you ever thought of leaving Swindon, Harry?'

'Often. But where would I go?'

'Well, the skipper of the first ship I served on – who also happens to be a good friend – retired three months ago. He's set up a small marine electronics company in

Weymouth. As a matter of fact, I supplied some of the capital. The point is, he's looking for several good people on the managerial side. I could mention your name.'

'You'd do that?'

'It'd be a pleasure.'

'But an undischarged bankrupt—'

'I worked with you, Harry, remember? I wouldn't be doing this just for old time's sake. I happen to think you'd fit in rather well at Mallender Marine.'

During the days of enforced immobility and abstinence that he spent in Rhodes Hospital, Harry thought more clearly about his life than he could ever remember doing before. He found it surprisingly easy, when all his wants were catered for and all his pastimes banned, to view his fifty-three years as a continuum, in which the false hopes of the past were as significant as the predictable disappointments of the present. It was not a pretty tale, he was bound to admit, not a glorious succession of ever-outstripping achievements. Assessed objectively, indeed, it had more the appearance of a shabby march-past of dismal failures. Yet, for all that, it was his own.

In the opinion of his form master at Commonweal, Harry's academic promise was 'blighted by weakness of purpose and a tendency to self-deprecation'; the phrase from his last school report was as memorable as its author's disapproving face. His Uncle Len put matters less tendentiously but perhaps more succinctly. 'Treat life as a joke, son, and that's how it'll treat you.' Uncle Len was known to think that Harry's lack of a father was a handicap to proper character development. There had even been a time when he aspired to fill the role himself, until life decided to remove him so suddenly and ludicrously from its arena that it might almost have been trying to tell him something. It was strange that both Barnett brothers should die accidentally – Stan, Harry's father, when a wheel fell on him in the GWR locomotive erecting shop; and Uncle Len in collision with the laden bicycle of a butcher's delivery boy, whose brakes had failed on Prospect Hill. Perhaps it explained why Harry never took life quite as seriously as others thought he should.

From school, Harry passed straight, at fifteen, into the deadening maw of Swindon Borough Council, his mother deeming a steady clerk's job with the municipality infinitely preferable to any of his more fanciful notions. And there he remained – bar a two-year spell of national service – for fifteen dull, unvarying, ill-rewarded years: excellent training, he always maintained, for growing old, bored, cynical and disagreeable before one's time. But for Barry Chipchase, his spivish, scapegrace chum from national service days, he would probably still have been there twenty-three years on. As it was, Barry's invitation to open a garage business with him offered an irresistible escape route from bureaucracy. And so was born, by happy combination of their surnames, Barnchase Motors. It proved, in the long run, to be both the best and worst of Harry's decisions in life, the best because it brought him into contact with Alan Dysart, the worst because every penny he had was lost in its fall.

Dysart spent six Oxford vacations working at Barnchase, initially as cleaner-cum-pump attendant, later in a variety of administrative roles. He had originally looked for a job in Swindon simply to be near a girlfriend in Wootton Bassett. Later he made the thirty-mile journey from Oxford because he had become genuinely attached to the firm. Looking back, Harry could see just how astute many of his commercial suggestions were. That was why Harry had so often claimed the credit for them. Perhaps if Dysart had still been involved, Barnchase would not have collapsed when it had.

The last Harry had heard of Barry Chipchase, and the ruinously spendthrift wife he had insisted on making a partner in the firm, involved a car-hire business in Alicante. Only ill he wished them of it, considering that even his house had been forfeited to Barnchase's creditors. Lodged with his mother in the tiny railway worker's cottage where he had been born, contemplating through a haze of alcohol the circular nullity of his achievements, he could not afford to be scrupulous when Dysart offered to recommend him to Mallender Marine.

It had gone well at first; Harry could not say otherwise. Charlie Mallender's contacts in the Navy and the Admiralty, taken together with the proximity of the Portland Naval Base, ensured steady demand for Mallender Marine's products, whilst Harry concentrated on the private market in yachting gadgetry – not so different, in its way, from the world of car spares. Harry settled in Weymouth, found some lodgings and began to believe that the bad days really were behind him.

The awareness that they might not be started to dawn on him soon after Roy Mallender joined the business in the autumn of 1977. It was popularly believed that Roy had tried to follow his father into the Navy, but had failed to make the grade. Whatever the truth of this, he was clearly aggrieved at not enjoying as much power over others as he held to be his due. The fact that Harry declined to play the part of a fawning subordinate would therefore have been enough to make him a marked man even without the personal antipathy that sprang up between them. Just as he had failed to appreciate Barry Chipchase's duplicity until it was too late, so he failed to realize what lengths Roy Mallender would go to in order to be rid of him until the trap had already closed about him. Charlie Mallender told him at the time of his dismissal that he was lucky to be spared prosecution for fraud; little did the old man know that his own son was the real fraudster.

Once more, however, Alan Dysart came to the rescue. He had owned the *Villa ton Navarkhon* for less than a year then and was keen to have somebody reliable in Lindos to keep an eye on the place. Rent-free accommodation in the gatehouse flat in return for light caretaking duties appealed to Harry more than he could properly say. Unemployed and well nigh unemployable in Weymouth as the harsh winter of 1978/79 dragged down both his finances and his spirits, Rhodes sounded to him like the promised land: warm, inexpensive, undemanding and a long way from all his troubles.

And so, in many respects, it proved. Looking after the villa was, of course, a sinecure: Mrs Ioanides cleaned whilst Mr Ioanides painted, repaired and gardened. Harry was simply the man on the spot, the familiar English face to greet Dysart and his guests, free to earn enough during the season as barman or tour guide to sustain himself through the winter. He slipped happily into the Greek approach to life: why do yesterday what you can put off till tomorrow? Best of all, as they said and believed, *perasmena, ksehasmena*: past things are forgotten things. In Lindos, Harry was merely the overweight Englishman who pottered about the town in faded cricket flannels, shirt and sunhat, ogling the topless sunbathers and drinking too much, a figure of fun and a source of amusement. What he had been in England was a matter of no consequence; his slate was clean, his reputation spotless. Unsophisticated, indeed primitive, though a year-round existence in Lindos might be, it offered him everything he required. It was his home-from-home, his safe haven, his general amnestic, his painless admission of defeat. It was sufficient, in short, for his every purpose. Until Heather came.

On the third afternoon of his confinement, Harry was allowed to get out of bed for a few hours. This gave him a chance he had been waiting for, since it had occurred to him that Jonathan Minter might be interested in the circumstances surrounding Roy Mallender's sudden departure from Rhodes; he had, after all, spoken of a fee. Accordingly, Harry made his gingerly way to the pay-phone down the corridor and dialled the number Minter had given him.

'Astir Palace Hotel.'

'I'd like to speak to one of your guests: Mr Jonathan Minter.'

'Wait please.' A delay, then: 'Mr Minter is no longer with us, sir.'

'No longer with you?'

'He booked out yesterday.'

'Did he say where he was going?'

'Back to England, I believe, sir.'

So Minter had gone. As had Dysart. And Roy Mallender. And Heather, as well. They had all gone. They had abandoned him, he suddenly realized, to an obscurity he no longer desired. They had left him to relapse into the somnambulism of exile. But he could no longer close his eyes.

It was the following Monday before Harry was allowed to leave the hospital. Kostas came to collect him in his ramshackle van and, as they drove out of Rhodes, he tossed Harry a morning paper to read on the journey to Lindos. The headline Η ΕΞΑΦΑΝΙΣΗ ΤΟΥ ΧΕΔΕΡ ΜΑΛΛΕΝΤΕΡ – the Disappearance of Heather Mallender – was still present on the front page, but in smaller print, jostling for space in a corner with a discotheque advertisement. The sub-heading was what held, however, the bleakest tidings. Η ΑΣΤΥΝΟΜΙΑ ΕΓΚΑΤΑΛΕΙΠΕΙ ΤΙΝ ΑΝΑΖΗΤΗΣΗ : the Police Abandon the Search.

9

Opening the gate to let her in was the last Harry had hoped to see of Mrs Ioanides that day; she could, after all, let herself out easily enough. Yet within the hour she was back, banging a broom on the flat door and demanding guidance on a domestic matter. Was she or was she not to clean Miss Mallender's room and should she or should she not remove Miss Mallender's belongings?

Till now, Harry had not thought about Heather's effects. They were still there, he assumed, in the small south-facing bedroom she had occupied in preference to two other larger rooms, probably left in disorder by the police and rightfully the property, he supposed, of the Mallender family. He did not like to think of Mrs Ioanides adding her unfeeling attentions to them, so insisted on dealing with the matter himself. Inevitably, Mrs Ioanides took this amiss and accused him, in the light of his earlier complaints about painful ribs and aching head, of being *enas psevthomarteeras*. Fortunately, Harry did not know what the word meant and refrained from asking. He managed to shake the woman off in the hallway of the villa and went upstairs alone.

As soon as he entered the room, he realized why he had been reluctant to do so. Rush matting covered the floorboards and the whitewashed walls were bare save for one Lindian plate. The furniture was stolidly functional: a brass-steaded bed, a small bedside cabinet, a wardrobe, a dressing-table, one upright wooden chair. There were no lamps to supplement the central light, just a candle in a holder on the bedside cabinet. The view through the window was of the barren slopes leading up towards the acropolis and a triangular stretch of intensely blue sea. For all its plainness, this room was where Heather had slept and woken every day she had spent in Lindos. This was where her presence still seemed close at hand and where her absence was hardest to bear.

Harry walked across to the wardrobe and opened the door. There were her clothes, hanging in line on the central rail. That skirt she had been wearing when he first met her at the acropolis, that dress she had worn on the one occasion she had dined with him in the flat; he had cooked *moussaka* because it was the only thing he knew how to cook and she had pretended to enjoy it. At the bottom of the wardrobe was stowed her rucksack, in which, he supposed, he would have to pack her belongings. Perhaps the Consulate would arrange to send it on. At the very thought of undertaking this task, his emotions rebelled. He closed the door and leaned his head against it, waiting till the absurd and sudden desire to cry had abated, then turned away.

On the dressing-table stood the usual array of feminine toiletries – hair-brush, mirror, powders, lotions, creams, shampoo, perfume, mascara, lip-gloss – and all were as charged with memories of Heather as were the clothes she had worn. There were traces of flaxen hair still caught between the bristles of the brush. And when Harry absent-mindedly opened the small tub of lip-gloss, there was a fragment of her fingerprint still preserved in the waxy surface.

He moved across to the bedside table, on which a travelling alarm clock stood open beside the stump of candle. Tilting the clockface towards him, he was almost relieved to find that it had stopped. Then something caught his eye beneath the pillow on the bed. When he pushed the pillow aside to see what it was, a sudden rush of grief came upon him. It was her nightdress, lace-hemmed and patterned with tiny forget-me-nots. He slumped down on the coverlet and put his hand to his face. This was too much, too awful, too hideously reminiscent. Better to have left it to Mrs Ioanides, better to have locked this room and never entered it again.

He uncovered his face. Nothing had altered. Beyond the window sunlight still fell with stark indifference on the scrub-strewn landscape. Below him Mrs Ioanides' vacuum cleaner moaned and spluttered away. Automatically, with no sense of purpose, he reached forward and slid open the drawer of the bedside cabinet. Inside, he could see a box of matches, a Greek phrase book, a packet of tissues and a well-thumbed paperback: *The Psychopathology of Everyday Life*, by Sigmund Freud. He lifted it out, weighed it in his hand and stared at the cover, struggling to come to terms with a feeling of remoteness from his own actions, resisting as best he could the insistent notion that some overlooked significance attached itself to what he was doing. The book fell open on his palm at a selected page: the piece of paper that had marked the place fluttered to the floor.

Harry drew the book closer. The passage he was looking at must have been read by Heather shortly before, possibly the very night before, her disappearance on Profitis Ilias. It was not a chapter end, but part of some lengthy, closely argued disquisition. Harry's knowledge of Freudian theory was that of the average sceptic who had never read any and did not intend to start. His eye ranged over the paragraphs randomly, alighting on phrases with no appreciation of their context. 'The "remarkable coincidence" of meeting a person we were at that very moment thinking about is a familiar one.' 'A meeting at a particular place, which has been expected beforehand, amounts in fact to a rendez-vous.' None of this meant anything to Harry, yet he was reluctant to abandon the hope that it might hold a clue to Heather's state of mind. He would study it later, when he had more energy for the task: that seemed the obvious course to follow. He stopped to retrieve the slip of paper so that he might mark the place.

And found himself staring at a numbered receipt, on which a name and address had been stamped and date recorded. Δ. Ψαμβίκης, Φωτογράφος, Πλατ. Κύπρου, Ρόδος, 7/11/88: D. Psambikis, Photographer, Platia Kiprou, Rhodes, 7 November 1988. Suddenly his memory found a gear and lurched forward. An unredeemed photographer's receipt, dated four days prior to Heather's disappearance. That was Monday. She had gone into Rhodes on the ten-thirty bus; he could remember her asking if there was anything he wanted. And the previous day, Sunday, had been warm, sunny and lethargic. And she had cooked lunch for him. And they had eaten it in the garden. And she had taken a picture of him. And he of her. 'To use up the film,' she had said. 'I'll take it in tomorrow. I can't wait to get it back. There's ever such a lot on it. And now there's you as well.'

'Ever such a lot on it.' Two hours later, Harry was sitting on a bench near the post office in Rhodes Town. Mr Psambikis had handed over the wallet of photographs without demur and now Harry was about to look at them. Twenty-four colour photographs taken with Heather's camera. The camera and its owner had vanished. But the photographs remained. Innocent and inconsequential – or perhaps not. Harry opened the wallet.

They were not holiday snaps. Not, at any rate, just holiday snaps. They had been returned printed in reverse order and the last picture – Heather in the garden of the villa, toasting Harry with a glass of *retsina* in one hand and a coil of fried octopus in the other, smiling and aproned, slightly blurred as if already fading from existence – took him by surprise even though he had been responsible for it himself. He stared at it for a long time, trying to remember just how carefree he had felt at the moment he had opened and closed the shutter, then looked at the next. It was the same occasion, but this time Harry was the subject, caught with precision against a backdrop of pink geranium, slightly drunk to judge by the broad, crumpled grin, his own glass of *retsina* cradled against an ample stomach, his free hand half-raised in a mocking gesture. This was the idle, indulgent Harry who thought his defences impregnable: this was the Harry he no longer was and could never be again.

There followed three predictable shots of Lindian vistas. The harbour as it appeared from the front of the villa: two or three boats standing at anchor on its ultramarine surface, with the bare, rocky promontory behind. Then the villa seen from the beach, cactus blossom peeping over the white garden wall, sunlight catching an open window in Harry's flat, the terracotta tiles of the villa roof clearly visible against a background of white-faced dwellings, the rocky slope climbing behind them through stately cypresses towards the high fortress walls. Lastly the harbour, promontory and bare wrinkled coastline stretching away to the north, seen from the acropolis itself, from the top of the great staircase in fact, for its lower treads were visible in the bottom left-hand corner and the crumbling pillars arrayed in the foreground were certainly the columns of the Doric stoa. This could have been taken on Heather's first afternoon in Lindos, from the very spot where he had found her waiting for him. Indeed, as he peered closer, a figure disclosed itself to his eye, obscured by the shadow of the ruined Byzantine chapel lower down the slope, a stumbling, white-clad figure moving towards the camera who could only be Harry himself, captured on film minutes before Heather would have known who he was. This sudden perception induced in Harry a curious, queasy response. He found himself reciting dates under his breath. 'The sixth of November': when they had lunched together at the villa. 'The eighteenth of October': when they had met for the first time. The photographs had begun to assume a magnetic quality of their own, drawing him further and further into the past. Before Heather had disappeared. Before they had met. Before she had come to Lindos. Before . . . .

Profitis Ilias. The dreaded name. The still more dreaded

85

place. He knew she had been there once before, of course, yet still he was not prepared to find its familiar colours and contours awaiting him in the next picture: its summit of jagged white rocks, scantily clothed in lichen, grass and dead bracken, patched and shaded by stunted cedars, with the coast and sea below impossibly distant, out of focus and out of reach. Here he had searched for her in vain. And here she had raised the viewfinder to her eye and seized, for reasons of her own, this paper image of a place. For reasons of her own, which he could neither ask nor guess.

Then the photographs reverted to tourist type. The windmills of Mandraki Harbour. The castellated outline of the Grand Masters' Palace. The picture-postcard dullness of these scenes came as a shock after the tantalizing ambiguity of what had gone before. They were followed by more of the same, taken, Harry surmised, during Heather's two-day stopover in Athens on her way to Rhodes. He had never visited the capital – other than to change planes – but a standard view of the Parthenon and a cityscape from the summit of Lycabettos, despoiled by other visitors, were instantly recognizable. He was nearly halfway through the film and beginning to lose interest.

Suddenly, he was in England. There could be no mistaking that grey, moist, reproachful light, nor the trimmed Anglican propriety of the grave which filled the next picture. The ostentatious black marble stone was engraved in gold: FRANCIS DESMOND HOLLINRAKE. BORN 19TH SEPTEMBER 1915. DIED 14TH APRIL 1973. Francis Desmond Hollinrake. The name meant nothing to Harry, and yet . . . Hollinrake: surely he had, however long ago, heard the name before. When or why he could not say, but somewhere his memory still held a trace of its meaning.

Next came buildings of various sizes and purposes, all English, all rural, and none familiar to Harry. An elegant L-shaped slate and cob farmhouse, with what looked like stabling running away to the rear; a large turreted and gabled red-brick Victorian mansion set in well-tended grounds, with enough signposts and parked cars in sight to suggest an institution of some kind; a gloomy ivy-shanked stone house overshadowed by trees at the end of a curving drive; a typical country church dwarfed by its own pinnacled and battlemented tower in what Harry dimly recognized as the Perpendicular style; an assortment of Victorian red-brick structures climbing away up a wooded hillside, with grand steps and entrances suggestive, thanks to the distant white H of rugby goalposts, of a school or college; and a large Tudor-style country house, with too many cars on view to be a private dwelling and croquet hoops arranged rather too conspicuously on the lawn. If there was a theme running through the selection, Harry could not discern what it might be.

A country lane seemed all that the next photograph held. Tarmac shining after rain, green fields to either side, dry stone walls flanking the route, a junction with a wider road visible at the bottom of the hill down which the lane curved. It was unlocatable and indecipherable. Next came a mellow old village inn, all sun-warmed stone and bright-bloomed windowboxes. The angle of the inn sign, suspended from a bracket above the main entrance, meant that Harry could not read the name. Nor could he place the austere, grey-stone courtyard in the picture that followed it. There was an academic feel about the rows of windows looking down on the quadrangle of grass which put him in mind of Oxford or Cambridge, but he could claim no certainty on the point. The flagstones were wet with rain, as if, it occurred to him, this photograph and that of the lane, along therefore with that of the pub, had been taken on the same day. But such supposition took him nowhere. Only Heather could tell him why and when she had been to these places – and what in the scenes she had wished to preserve.

There were only four photographs left now and the first of them was of another building. It was a white-rendered, slate-roofed cottage with black shutters, set in a hedged and wooded garden, with a newer-looking garage at the rear. For all that the sun was shining brightly, there was a weather-beaten, lop-sided look about the trees that suggested a coastal setting. Once again, the place was unknown to Harry. But unfamiliarity ended with the very next photograph.

Nigel Mossop had joined Mallender Marine straight from school and Harry had originally thought him a poor choice compared with other applicants. Well-intentioned and eager to please, he was also timid, slow-witted and profoundly dull; Harry could not deny having sometimes made life hell for him. Only when Roy Mallender had begun to victimize the lad had Harry warmed to him, though his efforts to help had come to very little. Mossop must be thirty-odd now and looked more, soberly bespectacled and sombrely dressed, grinning nervously as if uncertain what pose to strike for the camera. Heather had never mentioned knowing him, yet there he unquestionably was, standing by some broad, anonymous sweep of a river estuary, the fields and woods on the farther bank looking lush enough for high summer, a sea-going yacht passing by in the stream. Harry could not say where it might be, but, as he scanned the picture for clues, a white speck that was surely a house caught his eye: it could easily be the cottage from the previous photograph, peeping out from a thicket of trees on the other side of the river. This at least, then, with Mossop's help, he should be able to locate.

The penultimate photograph was of another gravestone, or rather a memorial, for no grave as such was visible and the other stones around it were so closely packed as to suggest a garden of remembrance at a crematorium. There was, in this case, no doubt or mystery about Heather's interest in the subject: it was her own sister. CLARE THOMASINA MALLENDER, 1959-1987. That was all: no biblical text, no touching sentiment, no allusion of any kind to how she had met her death. All Harry knew of the circumstances was what he had read in the newspapers at the time. On becoming an MP, Dysart had bought a cottage in his constituency. It was beside the river Beaulieu in Hampshire and was ideal as a mooring for the *Artemis*, thus permitting him to combine business and pleasure during constituency weekends. The fact that he was something of a war hero on account of his conduct as a frigate commander in the Falklands and the fact that he had subsequently become a junior Defence minister made him, by the twisted logic of the IRA, a legitimate target. A speech he had given, confidently anticipating the IRA's military defeat, had evidently sealed the issue. But it was Clare Mallender, not Alan Dysart, who had stepped aboard the *Artemis* that fateful day and detonated the bomb. How the MP felt about his assistant's death and his own narrow escape Harry hardly knew, for Dysart's visits to Rhodes since then had been few and fleeting. How Heather felt about it he was also uncertain. She had implied that Clare's death had been the cause of her psychiatric problems and Harry had shied clear of the subject since clumsily referring to it at their first meeting.

Looking back at the two photographs that had gone before, Harry was tempted to conclude that the river behind Mossop was the Beaulieu and that the white-rendered cottage was Dysart's constituency hideaway. If so, Heather's reasons for taking these three pictures were easily imaginable. They could have been by way of commemoration, by way of coming to terms with her loss. The only puzzle they left was her choice of Mossop as a companion.

The last photograph – the first she had taken – was of Mallender Marine. At sight of it, Harry was taken aback to discover how keenly he still resented the circumstances of his departure from that low, grey, nondescript building ten years ago. There was the door through which he had stormed and there the forecourt across which he had marched in high and final dudgeon one dismal afternoon in October 1978. It had been the end of his last illusion: that he could succeed at something.

But the end, in this case, was also the beginning. As

Harry assembled the photographs in their correct chronological order and leafed through them again, he was struck by how they seemed to hint at a message concealed beneath their unconnected scenes. 'Ever such a lot on it', Heather had said, and Harry found the temptation to believe that there was irresistible. Yet how to prove it? There was no evidence worthy of the name to be derived from these pictures, unless . . . .

Profitis Ilias. As soon as he saw it again, he realized what he should have noticed at once. It was a photograph of the *summit*. Not the hotel, or the lower slopes, or even the fallen tree, but the summit. Heather had told him she had not had time to ascend it. Yet this picture proved that she had. She had not been venturing into the unknown that day. She had been retracing her own steps all the way. And had been lying when she claimed otherwise.

Suddenly, the odds had shifted. Until this moment, Heather had simply vanished. Now, for the first time, it was possible to believe that she had planned what had happened. Until his discovery of the photographs, Harry had found the mystery impenetrable. Now it seemed that there might be a solution, if he could but penetrate the meaning of the scenes she had recorded.

During the jolting bus-ride back to Lindos, Harry forced himself to consider the possibility that the photographs meant nothing, or at any rate had no bearing on Heather's disappearance. After all, if they had been important to her and if she had known what was to happen on Profitis Ilias, why would she have left the film with a photographer for Harry – or anyone else – to collect? Why not collect it first herself? Because, of course, it was not ready, in which case the pictures were either less important to her than she had implied or she had not planned to disappear at all.

An alternative to these explanations came to him about halfway through the journey. She may have had no intention of vanishing when she took the film into Rhodes on Monday the seventh, but by Wednesday the ninth, when she hired the car and first proposed the farewell tour, the plan must have been formed. If that were so, every action from then on was a charade and Harry was merely her dupe, a tame witness to be taken to Profitis Ilias so that he could report the baffling circumstances to others and thus encourage the belief that she was dead.

But why? Why should she have wanted or needed not simply to disappear but to do so in a way suggestive of foul play? And why, moreover, should this desire or need have arisen so suddenly? Reviewing in his mind the days during which Heather had presumably reached her decision, he could recall nothing abnormal, nothing which, even in hindsight, seemed to support his theory.

Back at the villa, he was glad to find that Mrs Ioanides had gone. Alone in the gatehouse flat, he laid the photographs out on the kitchen table and carefully re-examined each of them in search of clues he might have overlooked. The early pictures seemed to have been taken in the summer, yet in the last English one, that of Francis Hollinrake's grave, the brown leaves of autumn were evident, which suggested it had been taken shortly before Heather left for Rhodes. The later pictures he could date independently and the film could therefore be assumed to cover not less than three months. Without going to England himself, he really could glean no more.

Then the significance of his conclusion dawned on him. He could not turn his back on the possibilities raised by his discovery. He could not pretend he had neither found the photographs nor begun to speculate on what they meant. As far as they would take him, even if no further, he would have to go. Pride and curiosity would drive him where, till now, they had always held him back. England. Home. The last place on Earth.

10

Inspector Miltiades was not available when Harry called at Police Headquarters the following morning. But at the British Consulate it was a different story. Mr Osborne consented to a ten-minute audience and listened patiently to Harry's request, regarding him with fixed langour over the top of a miniature Union flag mounted in a cork plinth on his desk.

When Harry had finished, Osborne consumed nearly a minute in unresponsive silence, then said: 'Why are you so anxious to retrieve your passport, Mr Barnett?'

'Because I wish to leave Rhodes as soon as possible.'

'To go where, may I ask?'

'England.'

Osborne raised one eyebrow. 'A curious choice.'

'I am English.'

'When were you last there?'

'Apart from a couple of flying visits, ten years ago.'

'But this wouldn't be a flying visit?'

'I can't say.'

Osborne rubbed his chin doubtfully. 'I believe Miltiades wanted to keep you on hand in case there were any developments in the Mallender business.'

'But according to Monday's *Rhodian*, the Police have given up looking for Heather.'

'Yes. Well, strictly *entre nous*, Mr Barnett, security for next month's European Summit is probably taking up all their time now.'

'So what's the problem? After all' – Harry lowered his voice – 'you wouldn't want me making a nuisance of myself when all those reporters show up for the Summit, would you?'

Some kind of weary smile flickered around Osborne's lips, then was snuffed out. 'I'll see what I can do for you, Mr Barnett.'

'Thanks.' Harry made to rise.

'Ten years, you said?'

'Away from England? Yes, good as.'

'You'll notice lots of changes.'

'For the better?'

'I doubt you'll think so.' Now the smile was rekindled. 'I doubt it very much.'

For the rest of that day and all of the next, Harry remained at the villa, determined not to antagonize Osborne by demanding results too soon. Nobody knew why he should suddenly be so eager to leave Rhodes and he intended to keep it that way. Whether in a spirit of cautious prudence, or from some less laudable motive, he had resolved to keep the photographs as a secret between himself and Heather, as sacred ground on which nobody else could trespass.

With time hanging heavy on his hands, he fell to studying the book in which he had found the photographer's receipt. The passage Heather had been reading was about halfway through a chapter entitled *Determinism, Belief in Chance and Superstition*. At first, he made little progress, stumbling over terminology and floundering amidst case histories. At length, however, having resorted to the editor's introduction, he began to grasp the argument and found himself largely subscribing to it. Every lapse of memory, it seemed, every slip of the tongue or the pen, every error or bungled action, might reveal a psychological secret. He attempted to apply the theory to Heather's oversight in leaving the receipt where it could be found. This suggested a repressed desire on her part that it should be found. But this only held true, he realized, if she had planned her disappearance. If not, it was merely bedtime reading of no significance.

Except, of course, that it showed what she had, however distractedly, been thinking about. The section she had been reading dealt with superstition, which Freud defined as 'in large part the expectation of trouble.' Since trouble had indeed followed, the coincidence was suggestive. 'A person who has harboured frequent evil wishes against others, but has been brought up to be good and has therefore repressed such wishes into the unconscious, will be especially ready to expect punishment for his unconscious wickedness in the form of trouble threatening him from without.' Had Heather felt threatened, then? Had she referred to this passage to reassure herself that the feeling was psychologically explicable, only to find that it also implied subconscious malice on her part? If so, malice against whom?

It occurred to Harry at this point that, if Heather had followed such a line of thought, it could have been fatally misleading. It might have encouraged her to ignore certain warnings, only for the warnings to prove horribly well-founded. It was, after all, just the sort of mistake somebody uncertain of their psychological well-being might make. But what warnings? What signs could she have been prompted to disregard? None that he had noticed, that was certain.

He returned, time and again, to the actual pages she had marked. These dealt with prophetic dreams and coincidental meetings. Freud demonstrated convincingly that such experiences were generally illusory, that prophetic dreams were either unfulfilled or not recalled until they had been fulfilled, and that meeting somebody whilst thinking about them was never truly coincidental: one was prompted to think about them by already being subconsciously aware of their presence.

A dream, then, or a meeting, whose significance these pages had called into question: was that the warning which Heather had resolved to ignore? If so, it would be necessary to believe she had foreseen what would happen on Profitis Ilias but had nevertheless gone there, determined to prove it was no more than a delusion. That would explain her wish to be accompanied so far but no farther and the lie she had told to persuade Harry to let her go on alone: he had been taken there to bear witness, not to intervene. In that case, Heather was as brave and selfless as he wanted to believe; her only mistake was to think, because some Freud-soaked psychiatrist had told her so, that she had imagined the threats against her.

Harry took heart from his conclusion, for all its obvious unreliability. It was so much preferable to his other hypotheses, from which Heather had emerged as a liar and Harry as a fool, that he clung to it as would a drowning man to a raft. This, he felt sure, would carry him through. And maybe Heather too, for he had begun to entertain the hope that she might not, despite all that had happened and all that he feared, be lost to him forever.

Early on Saturday morning, Harry had a visitor. When he heard the knocking at the gate, he assumed it must be the postman with a parcel. But when he had stumbled down and opened up, it was to find Inspector Miltiades standing on the doorstep, looking as dapper and supercilious as ever.

'*Kalimera*, Mr Barnett. You look surprised to see me.'

'I am.'

'You should not be. Mr Osborne has communicated your request.'

'I could have come to Rhodes to collect my passport. There was no need to deliver it.'

'Do not assume that I am delivering it. First, I will need to be persuaded that its return is justified.'

Harry had hoped to avoid explaining himself to Miltiades, but plainly it was not to be. He invited him up to the flat, where the Inspector cast a fastidious look around before declining all offers of refreshment. Harry then embarked on a hastily prepared statement of his reasons for wishing to return to England: since Heather's disappearance, he had felt ostracized in Lindos (true); he had become homesick (false); his mother wanted to see him again before she died (true, but she enjoyed the best of health).

When Harry had finished, Miltiades regarded him calmly for a moment, then said: 'You are a liar, Mr Barnett. You are, moreover, a poor liar, which has counted in your favour in my investigation of this case. I suspect you are also a neglectful son. And it is a strange form of homesickness which only exhibits itself after nine years.'

'You don't believe me?'

'I believe you wish to return to England. The question is: why?'

'I don't have any other reasons to give you.'

'Then I will give you one. You hope to learn the truth about Miss Mallender's disappearance.'

At that, Harry decided to abandon the pretence. 'What if I do? I gather you've given the case up.'

'Our efforts have been directed elsewhere, certainly.'

'Then what's the point of holding me here?'

Miltiades smiled. 'None, Mr Barnett.' He slipped a British passport from his tunic pocket and passed it to Harry. 'You are free to go.'

Harry noticed at once that something had been slipped inside the cover of the passport. When he opened it, he found himself staring at the postcards of Aphrodite and Silenus they had found in the car.

'I have been thinking about those postcards,' Miltiades went on. 'Your explanation of why Miss Mallender should have bought them was adequate, but it did not account for them being left in the glove compartment of the car. That action suggests deliberation to my mind. It implies that they were meant to convey a message.'

Harry had thought the same himself, but it had led him nowhere. 'What message, Inspector?'

'I do not know, but you and she were together here – a pair, that is. As are the cards a pair. It is suggestive, is it not? The goddess and the satyr. Commonplace emblems, but emblems of what? I was originally inclined to interpret them as precisely what they seem. Female beauty and male desire. Youth and age. Temptation and lust.' He paused and Harry was about to speak, but he held up his hand to silence him. 'Let me continue. I visited the Archaeological Museum recently to remind myself of how fine the original Aphrodite of Rhodes is. Have you ever seen it?'

'No. I'm not much of a museum-goer.'

'As I suspected. One of the distinguishing features of the statue is that it dates from a period when anatomical accuracy was sacrificed to visual satisfaction. It is thus physically perfect, but spiritually dead. It is an object only. It tells us nothing.'

'What should it tell us?'

'Only this. That people are not statues. That what we see of them is only the outward form. Beautiful or ugly, it is irrelevant. Aphrodite or Silenus, it makes no difference. I think the message is meant for you, Mr Barnett, but I am not sure what it is. So, take the postcards with you. Maybe you will understand them in the end.'

A few minutes later, Harry was saying goodbye to Miltiades at the gate of the villa. He felt a perverse liking for this aloof and thoughtful man, born of a sudden, unaccountable suspicion that they would never meet again. 'Have you really closed your file on Heather, Inspector?' he said, as Miltiades stepped out into the alley.

'Officially no, Mr Barnett. But unofficially . . . .'

'I see.'

'One thing before I leave you. Are you familiar with the place of Silenus in Greek mythology?'

'No.'

'He was tutor to Dionysus, before Dionysus was elevated to divine status. It is something of an achievement, you might think, to train a God, yet none of the sources speak well of him. According to Euripedes, he was incapable of distinguishing between truth and falsehood. A profound handicap, would you not agree?'

97

Was that the message? Harry wondered. Was that what Heather had intended the postcards to tell him? That he was blind to what she really was and that he did not know the difference between fact and fiction? If so, it was a bleak message indeed. But to understand it was, in a sense, to disprove it.

'*Pathima, mathima*, Mr Barnett. Something suffered, something learned.' Miltiades smiled, as if he had read Harry's thoughts. 'When will you leave?'

'As soon as possible.'

'Then I wish you luck.' With that, he turned and walked away. There was no handshake, no salute, no formal farewell. Yet, for all that, Harry could not resist the feeling that Miltiades had, at the last, entrusted him with something. Both of them, it seemed to him, understood now that the investigation had not been closed at all. It had merely changed hands.

11

On Monday morning, Harry caught the workmen's bus into Rhodes, drew out the meagre balance of his account at the Commercial Bank of Greece and proceeded to spend a woundingly large proportion of it on an Olympic Airways single ticket to London. Leaving at short notice was evidently an expensive undertaking, but it could not be helped. In two days' time, he would be on his way.

A short walk took him to the OTE office, where he telephoned his mother in Swindon to warn her of his imminent homecoming. Apart from a telegram two weeks previously telling her 'not to worry', he had failed to make contact since Heather's disappearance, despite knowing full well what a dim view she would take of his silence. He had calculated that a call-box would enable him to claim lack of coinage before she could berate him overmuch, but he had forgotten that Greenwich Mean Time was two hours behind Greece, a fact which blighted their brief conversation from the outset.

'It's Harold, Mother.' (His mother had never believed in diminutives.)

'Who?'

'Your son.'

'Harold?'

'Yes.'

'What sort of time do you call this? It's not yet seven o'clock.'

'Ah . . . Sorry.'

'So you should be. All these weeks without a word, then you call at this ungodly hour.'

'I *am* sorry. But listen: I'm coming home.'

'You're what?'

'Coming home. On Wednesday.'

'Wednesday?'

'I should be with you late afternoon.'

'You mean to say—' The pips intervened.

'I've no money left, Mother. Wednesday afternoon: is that all right?'

'It'd be all the same if it wasn't, wouldn't it?'

'Don't cook any—' They were cut off.

Depressed by his own ineptitude, Harry adjourned to a nearby bar, ordered some coffee and glumly surveyed a newspaper. Heather's name had vanished from the headlines, which were now preoccupied with the forthcoming European Summit. It was as Miltiades had predicted: she had been forgotten.

But not by Harry. When the Archaeological Museum opened its doors at nine-thirty, he was its first visitor. There was only one exhibit he wanted to see: the Aphrodite of Rhodes.

It was smaller than he had expected, glass-cased and ornamental, strangely bland, as Miltiades had implied, by contrast with the rougher-hewn statues around it. They declared themselves boldly, while the Aphrodite seemed to preen and simper behind its protective barrier. Now he had seen it, he did not like it. As a picture it was beautiful; as an object distasteful. The polished marble imparted a plasticity to the flesh and the lack of definition a pliancy to the limbs that simulated too well the appeal of what it depicted. Part peep-show, part sensual display, the goddess surprised in her ablutions was both sublime and obscene, both unattainably desirable and blatantly available. What she represented was one with the priapism of Silenus. The message and the meaning were the same: image was all.

As soon as he was back in Lindos, Harry let himself into the villa, went up to Heather's room and packed her belongings in the rucksack as neatly as he could. Do it quickly but do it well, he told himself: do not pause to think what this might also symbolize. He tried to telephone Dysart to warn him of his departure, but ran into an answering machine at his London flat and decided to try again tomorrow. Then he went back to the gatehouse flat and commenced his own packing. Such were the necessary acts and practical tasks of the penultimate day of an exile he had thought might last forever.

'Why do you want to go back there, my friend?' said Kostas, when Harry told him he was returning to England.

'It's where I come from.'

'You are too old to go back, Hari.'

'You're never too old.'

At this, Kostas resorted to what he thought he knew best about England, despite never having been there: the weather. '*Vrehi poli.*'

'You get used to it.'

'*Kani krio.*'

'The question is: will you drive me to the airport tomorrow morning?'

But Kostas had not given up yet. 'This is a mistake, Hari. A grand mistake.'

Yes, Harry thought, it is precisely that: a grand mistake, perhaps the grandest he had ever made. 'Will you drive me there?'

'You will regret it. It will be too late and you will regret it.'

'That's the story of my life.'

'You will wish you listened to me.'

'I expect I will.'

'You should stay here.'

'Will you drive me to the airport or not?'

Kostas narrowed his eyes and stared into the middle distance. '*Tee ora fevgi to aeroplano?*' It was his way of saying yes.

*

Harry telephoned Dysart again and was again answered by a recorded voice. This time he left a message, a stumbling, inadequate message which can have conveyed very little.

Just as he was leaving the villa, he thought he heard a movement on the upper floor. A splash or a rustle: he could not be certain. He stood at the bottom of the stairs and listened intently. There was nothing. His ears, or his nerves, had deceived him. He turned to go.

Then he heard it again. Faint and fluid. Incontestably there, above him, inside the villa. He walked slowly up the stairs, the blood thumping in his head. The light was fading fast outside. It was that uncertain hour of grey, deceptive twilight, that interlude between day and night when nothing can quite be relied upon.

Water dripping, cascading into more water, as when a body rises from a bath. And some liquid shadow moving on the ceiling to warn him. A message, or a meeting pre-ordained. No need to go on. No need to believe it. No need, now he had reached the top of the stairs, to turn his head and look along the landing towards the open bathroom door.

Heather naked rising from the bath, running her hands through her hair, water flowing across her body, lapping every curve before retreating, dripping from elbows and knees, beading on breasts and hips. Pale flesh, offered mysteries and a smile as cold as marble.

'Don't worry. I'll keep to the path. And I won't be long. It's just that I can't turn back now, can I?'

Harry reached out and silenced the alarm. With it faded also the pattering feet of a departing dream. He did not know whether he had heard anything as he left the villa last night or not: he had not stayed to find out.

It was five a.m. and pitch dark on the last day of November. It was time to go. Time to rouse Kostas and catch a plane to England. Time to end a nine-year daydream and begin an open-ended search. With an unexpected sense of exhilaration, Harry climbed from the bed.

12

Not until he was aboard the flight from Athens to London did Harry begin to appreciate the significance of what he had done. Next to him, two Greeks argued about politics. On the other side of the aisle, two Englishmen swapped sales figures. Far below, the Alps slipped majestically by. And Harry, chain-drinking duty-free gin, stared about at the plastic upholstery of the plane and the artificial smiles of the stewardesses, whilst a bewildering sensation of unreality crept upon him. Speed was just a green digital fiction on an overhead display, movement a bird's eye cavalcade of snow-crusted scenery. He was not going anywhere, least of all home. It was too quick, too easy, too shorn of effort.

But it was true. Within a couple of hours that seemed like minutes, he was standing by a luggage carousel at Heathrow Airport, sobered by grime and noise, befuddled by the swiftness of his journey, thinking: Kostas was right, damn him; there are some exiles that should never be ended.

With Heather's rucksack on his back, his strapped-shut suitcase in one hand and a duty-free carrier bag in the other, Harry filed bemusedly through customs and traversed the synthetic wilderness of shops, escalators, snack bars and travelators, blinking at the brightly-lit signs, gaping at his fellow bustling humans. Was this really England? he wondered. How could he have forgotten what it was like? How could he have supposed that it would seem like home?

He queued to change his drachmas for pounds. Then

he queued to buy an Underground ticket to Paddington. Aboard the train, he became acutely aware that the passenger to his left was reading an Arabic newspaper, the passenger to his right a London guidebook printed in German, and that the two youths opposite him were talking to each other in what sounded like Swedish. Harry stared at the blue and red Underground symbol on the window, framed between the youths' heads, and tried to remember the England he had left nine years ago. It had been no better, he told himself, nor very much different. His reaction now was merely the disorientating effect of a sudden transition from sleepy out-of-season Lindos. He closed his eyes, wishing he could open them to see that blue unchanging sky.

He woke to the spluttering of a dying engine, a draught from an open door and sallow, unexpected daylight. Stumbling out onto the platform, he confronted the station nameboard. Cockfosters: the end of the line. Then he noticed that he was one item of luggage short. He peered back into the carriage, but to no avail. That he had fallen asleep was bad enough. That someone had stolen his duty-free litres of gin and *retsina* was altogether too much. He aimed an idle kick at a plastic bench leg and muttered under his breath: 'Welcome home, Harry.'

Eight p.... was not late afternoon, as Harry was well aware. He was also aware that, if he had devised a way of presenting himself at his mother's door that would most antagonize her, several hours late and the worse for drink was probably it. As he walked down Station Road, Swindon, trying and failing to steer a straight course along the pavement, he asked himself why he had made such an obvious mistake. All-day pub opening was to blame, he suspected, compounded by the excellence of English beer, which seemed one facet of his native land unspoilt by the passage of years. If not the only facet, as he had noisily and persistently informed several fellow-customers in the pubs where he had seen out the afternoon and seen in the evening.

At least the dark, soaring boundary wall of the railway engineering works was there, on his right, to offer some sombre consolation. His mother had spoken in a letter of the works closing, but he could see no evidence of it. There was the main entrance, locked at this hour, naturally, but apparently unaltered, and there, on the other side of the road, was the reassuring bulk of the Mechanics' Institute, where, as a child, he had screamed himself hoarse at many a pantomime witch. Crossing Emlyn Square, and resisting the idea of calling in at the Glue Pot for old times' sake, he headed for home.

Falmouth Street was empty and silent. There were lights at the windows, but not a soul abroad. Harry walked down the centre of the road, listening to the sound of his own footfalls, glancing to right and left as he went, listing in his mind the occupants of each house as they had been when he grew up there. As a schoolboy, he had composed a poem featuring every one of their surnames. It had not rhymed of course, but it had scanned pretty well.

Suddenly, he found himself standing at the door of number thirty-seven. He dropped his suitcase and fumbled in his pocket for the key. All those times, all those thousands of times, he must have performed the same action before, in school blazer, in working suit, in sports jacket on Saturdays, in RAF tunic home on leave, were instantly revived, momentarily relived. He slid the key into the lock. Home. Where one starts from, as the poet said. Another poet, that is. Back from school, with time to brew tea before Mother got in from the laundry. Back from the office, with one too many on board to escape her vigilant nose. Back from a windswept airfield in Lincolnshire, with Chipchase for riotous company. Back from wherever, whenever, he turned the key, pushed the door open – and pulled up sharply as the chain snapped taut to exclude him.

*

'I can't afford to take risks at my age, Harold. There are some queer folk about these days, and no mistake. Come to that, you look pretty queer yourself. The sun's turned your hair stark white. It makes you look, well . . . .'

'Old, Mother?'

She reached up and pinched his cheek. 'If you're old, I'm ancient. Now, take the weight off while I fetch your supper. It's been under the grill these two hours past, so don't expect cordon blue.'

'I said not to cook anything,' he called after her as she stumped off into the kitchen.

'Sit yourself down,' she called back, her voice contending now with a rattle of pans and plates. 'There's a place set.'

Harry submitted meekly and moved to the table. The same old gate-leg, the same utility chairs, the same EPNS cutlery, even the same *Cathedral Cities of England* placemats: he wondered if Rochester really looked like that anymore. The gas fire sizzled familiarly behind him. The smell of his mother's cooking – wholesome, unsophisticated and totally unique – reached him as a long forgotten memory.

He made brave inroads into the congealed stew, while his mother drank tea and watched him for signs that he had, as she would naturally assume, 'let himself go'. She made no reference to the beer on his breath, which represented a substantial concession, nor yet to what they both knew had caused him to leave Rhodes, which was her normal way of dealing with anything 'unpleasant'. Harry, for his part, was surprised how spry and alert she was looking. He had not seen her since her less than successful visit to Rhodes three summers ago, when he had detected signs of failing powers. Now he thought perhaps that had just been the effect of the heat.

Contrary to Harry's addled impression, the railway engineering works had closed. A few months ago, 'A' shop – 'where your dear father was killed' – had been demolished. The Mechanics' Institute was to make way for a luxury hotel, 'according to the *Advertiser*'. And the Council wanted to sell off the estate – 'over our heads' – to a private landlord. This last she had taken as a personal affront. She had lived in the Railway Village all her life, had been born just round the corner in Exeter Street, had moved to Falmouth Street as a young bride fifty-six years ago and had remained there ever since; now, in her dotage, 'some Rachman type' was set to turn her out. Harry tried to sound reassuring despite having no good reason to doubt her prediction.

As she carried the plates out, she noticed the bags standing in the passage. 'Is this your suitcase, Harold?'

'Yes, Mother.'

'And your rucksack?'

'Ah . . . no.'

'Then whose is that?'

He cleared his throat. 'Heather Mallender's.' She came back into the room and stared at him. 'It contains her belongings. I intend to return them to her family.'

She deposited the plates back on the table, sat down and fixed him with a flushed and purposeful glare. Recognizing the signs of an imminent 'once and once only' statement, he fell silent. 'I shall say this once and once only, Harold. I am certain, absolutely certain, that you did well by this girl and that there is no foundation, absolutely no foundation, for what some of the papers have suggested. That Korea was the worst, but never mind. I shall stand by you through thick and thin. Now there's an end of it. We shan't talk of it again.' With that, she bustled back towards the kitchen.

Korea? What the devil could she mean by . . . *The Courier*. The rag Minter had claimed to work for. He got up and pursued her into the kitchen. 'What did *The Courier* say, Mother?'

'I never buy the thing,' she replied, irrelevantly. 'You think I can afford fifty pence every Sunday for an armful of wastepaper?'

'What did it say?'

'I'd not have known if Joan Tipper hadn't made a point

107

of showing me. You may be sure she regretted trying to goad me.'

'But what did it say?'

'I can't remember.'

'Come on, Mother.'

Abandoning the sink for a moment, she turned and faced him with a tight-lipped frown of determination. 'I told you just now and I meant it: we shan't talk about this subject again. I've said my last word on it. Now, go and sit down while I serve afters.'

'Afters?'

'Treacle pudding. What else?'

What else indeed? Harry retreated.

Harry made no attempt to assist with clearing the table or washing-up after his meal; he knew better than to do that. Leaving his mother to her laborious routines, he lumbered into the front parlour, feeling tired and bloated, and switched on the television. Then he returned to the passage, stepped across to the row of pegs where his jacket was hanging and slipped the quarter bottle of scotch he had bought before leaving London from the pocket he had turned towards the wall. His mother kept only cooking sherry on the premises, a fact he had not forgotten.

Back in the front parlour, the television had warmed up. Some kind of political discussion before a studio audience was in progress, which Harry reckoned would do as well as anything. He looked for the glasses but they were not in their normal place, or rather the cabinet they were stored in was not. Casting about for its new location, Harry noticed an attaché case standing open beside his mother's armchair, with Commonweal School headed paper visible at the top of the piled contents. His curiosity aroused, he knelt down by the case and tilted the lid forward. As he had anticipated, the initials S.R.B. were embossed on the cracked leather. It was his father's old work case, the repository for as long as he could remember of valuable family documents. Harry smiled. Knowing that he was coming, his mother must have fetched this down from her bedroom in order to sift through her keepsakes of his childhood. There were his school reports, tagged together in date order. And there his certificate of baptism: St. Mark's Church, September 1935. 'You screamed from start to finish.' And there . . . .

The Evening Advertiser, Saturday 22 March 1947. Harry lifted out the yellow, crinkled newspaper, unfolded it and confronted the well-remembered record of his one obscure moment of unsullied glory:

A dramatic rescue act yesterday by a Swindon schoolboy saved the life of an abandoned baby. Harold Barnett, aged eleven, of 37 Falmouth Street, was returning home from school at about 4.15 when he stopped to do some train-spotting in St. Mark's Church yard and noticed a cardboard box standing on the down-line about half a mile from Swindon station. By the time he had made out what the box contained, a Cardiff-bound express was approaching, gathering speed rapidly as it left the station. Showing considerable presence of mind, young Harold wriggled through a gap in the churchyard fence and plucked the box and its helpless cargo from the train's path, thus narrowly averting a tragedy. The baby, only a few days old, is said to be recovering well in Victoria Hospital. The police have appealed for the mother to come forward as soon as possible. They believe the baby was either thrown from a moving train or placed deliberately on the line in an attempt to bring about its death. They praised young Harold's conduct and described him as 'a brave, quick-witted and resourceful lad who is a credit to his school and his family'.

Where did it all go wrong? Harry wondered. The quick wits, the resourcefulness, the presence of mind: when exactly did he lose them? Lost them he surely must have, for otherwise he would not have left school to become a mere Council clerk, would not have presided over the bankruptcy of Barnchase Motors, would not have allowed Roy Mallender to get the better of him. His ribs gave a sympathetic twinge at the very thought and he struggled to his feet. Suddenly, the voice of Alan Dysart cut across Harry's dismal reflections. He turned round to see Dysart pictured on the television, seated in a swivel-chair and flanked by what looked like fellow-politicians of contrasting persuasions, expounding with his customary ease and fluency the government's attitude to some issue of the moment.

'I've listened with great interest to Denis Rodway's remarks,' he was saying, in the barbed and languid tone that was so peculiarly and persuasively his, 'and I'm sure all of us who have our country's security at heart are grateful to him for reminding us so vividly of the reasons why his party must never be allowed to impose its policies on the nation. Some of us who shout less and think more than most of Denis's colleagues happen to believe that patriotism is neither outmoded nor unworthy. In fact . . . .'

Spontaneous applause from the studio audience caused Dysart to pause. He leaned back slightly in his chair and inclined his head in acknowledgement. He did not smile but he did not resist. His measured response to the judgement of the people was a perfect compromise between pride and humility. Rodway, anyway the fellow Harry took to be Rodway, squirmed with resentment and it was easy to see why. Dysart had nothing to prove or deny. War hero, terrorist target, lucid thinker, pyrotechnical debater and honest, handsome, dedicated patriot: he was all things which his opponents could least refute.

Harry slumped down in the armchair and took a swig of scotch from the bottle. Failure, he supposed, was every man's prerogative. Yet not every man had been shown the example he had of how to wrench meaning and worth from a life, how to hone a character to a fine point of high achievement. What was the secret of Dysart's success? Inherited wealth? An advantage, certainly. Luck? That

110

must come into it. Or something else? Whatever it was, Harry had either never acquired the commodity himself or had lost it somewhere along the way. Quick wits, resourcefulness and presence of mind stood contradicted by the record of his life. There remained only bravery. And to that, in the hope of it still hiding somewhere within him, he drank a silent toast.

13

Where 'A' shop had been, a plain of faintly smoking rubble stretched away into the middle distance. It seemed barely credible to Harry, as he surveyed it from the Rodbourne Road entrance on a cold grey morning, that so stark and sudden an end could have come to a building which he remembered as a vast, grimy and implacably permanent fixture in the life of the town.

On the other side of the road, the Old Tank and Boiler Shops were still in existence, but weed-choked and forlorn, as if aware what fate had been reserved for them. As for the workers whom Harry could recall holding up the traffic when they streamed through the gates on foot or bicycle, flat-capped and overalled to a man, they had vanished forever.

Depressed by the speed and scale of the changes being visited on his home town, Harry set off back towards the centre. Cars and lorries seemed everywhere about him, their noise and fumes attaining levels which he was amazed the residents were prepared to tolerate. To think how he had complained about a few motorcyclists in Lindos only proved Kostas's point: he had not known when he was well off.

The Brunel Centre offered a haven from the traffic, but only at a price. Christmas shoppers clogged the walkways, electronic carols blared above the tumult and Harry found difficulty knowing which route to follow in the shop-lined maze. A wizened old man was playing a concertina at one corner, the tune inaudible against a synthesized jingle of artificial sleigh bells. Convinced for no good reason that he was a former railway worker, Harry dropped a fifty pence piece into his hat, but the old man did not catch his sympathetic look.

Harry was aiming for the Central Library, which lay to the south, but, when he at last emerged from the pedestrianized labyrinth, he realized that he had headed east instead and there, in front of him, was an object described over breakfast by his mother, which he had found hard to envisage. *The Amazing Blondinis* was a ten-feet high bronze statue of two trapeze artists, one male, the other female. The man was poised as if on a tightrope, with the woman sitting on his shoulders and balancing a spotted parasol on her forehead. Both were adorned in pink tights and yellow leotards and had been cast, he gathered, in the railway works foundry as a final send-off before closure.

He must have been standing gape-mouthed in front of the statue for some minutes when a woman's voice reached his ears from close behind.

'Harry?'

He swung round.

'It *is* Harry. My life, it is.'

At first, he did not recognize her. She was a woman of about forty, trying, not altogether unsuccessfully, to look nearer thirty, in pin-striped suit and flounced white blouse, with artfully layered make-up and loosely curled blonde hair, every inch, it appeared, the sophisticated business-woman. But that voice? That voice was familiar – and far from sophisticated. It belonged to Jackie Fleetwood, the mini-skirted secretary who had become first Barry Chipchase's mistress, then his wife and finally little better than his partner in crime.

'I've been reading about you in the papers, Harry. Haven't *we* been a naughty boy? Why not tell me all about it over a cup of coffee?'

*

Why he was unable to resurrect the anger he had felt sixteen years ago Harry did not know. Jackie Oliver, formerly Chipchase, formerly Fleetwood, had come up smelling of Chanel perfume since she and Barry had vanished from Swindon in the summer of 1972 and Harry, left to face the creditors alone and to devise exquisite retributions for those who had deserted him, could not decide now whether to laugh or cry, whether to applaude her shamelessness or demand an apology.

Jackie sat opposite him at a tiny corner table in a garishly lit coffee shop. Her legs were extravagantly crossed, displaying several shapely inches of sheer-stockinged thigh, she was sipping *cappuccino* and smoking king-size cigarettes in such a way as to ensure he never lost sight of her diamond-encrusted engagement ring, and her overall demeanour was that of a woman who expected her fleshly charms and obvious prosperity to forbid complaint even if they did not command admiration.

'I ditched Barry soon as I realized he couldn't keep his hands off the *señoritas*. Ran a chalet franchise in Benidorm for a few years, then I came back to this country. I married Tony in '83 and, when he was looking to relocate his business, I thought of the old home town. I've branched out on my own now and opened a hair salon: Jacoranda Styling. It's just round the corner. Maybe you saw it?'

'Can't say I did.'

'Why not try us out? You could do with a trim and it'd be on the house. For old time's sake, eh?' She gave him a wide, lipsticked grin and he found himself trying to remember whether her teeth had been quite so white and regular when she had first minced into his life.

'I think I'll give it a miss. But thanks anyway.'

'Up to you. Here . . . .' She leaned closer, treating him to a vista of cleavage as the negligently buttoned blouse gaped. 'Did you see Al on the box last night?'

'Al?'

'Alan Dysart. Handsome devil, isn't he?'

'I suppose he is.'

114

'If only I'd known twenty years ago that he was going to be a power in the land . . . .' There was a hint of regret in her faraway look, regret, Harry assumed, for having chosen the wrong man at Barnchase Motors to make a set at. 'It's funny, isn't it?' she continued. 'Everybody at Barnchase went on to better things, 'cept . . . .'

'Me?'

She smiled. 'Well, you said it, Harry. Must say, though, I don't see you having done what the papers seem to think you've done. After all, you never tried it on with me, did you?'

'No, Jackie, I never did.' Despite, he refrained from adding, ample encouragement.

Her eyes played for a moment with the implication that he would not have been disappointed had he tried to exploit their working acquaintance, then she leaned back in her chair, exhaled a plume of cigarette smoke and said: 'Have *The Courier* got something against you?'

'Not as far as I know.'

'I thought they must have, the way they wrote about you the other day.'

'What did they write?'

'Haven't you seen it?'

'No.'

She arched her plucked eyebrows in surprise. 'Really?' Then she glanced at her gold-banded wristwatch. 'Christ, is that the time? I must dash.'

Harry made no move to finish his coffee, having already decided he would prefer to leave alone. As Jackie rose, however, she opened her handbag, took out a five pound note and slipped it under his saucer.

'Pay with that, Harry,' she said. 'My treat, eh?'

Harry listened to the tap of her high-heeled shoes retreating towards the door and watched the cigarette smoke disperse in her absence. It would have been better, he felt, if they had argued about the past, or simply pretended not to recognize each other. Anything would have been better than to confront his own inability to sustain a

115

justified grudge. Or to realize that even Jackie Fleetwood regarded him now as a deserving case for charity.

Harry found what everybody else seemed already to have read about him in the reference section of Swindon Central Library. Page five of *The Courier* for Sunday 20 November featured an article headed HOPES FADE FOR MISSING ENGLISH GIRL ON GREEK ISLAND, credited to none other than Jonathan Minter:

> If a week is a long time in politics, it may be an eternity in the search for a missing person. Heather Mallender, an English schoolteacher who was staying on the holiday island of Rhodes as a guest of Westminster MP and junior Defence minister Alan Dysart vanished without trace from a mountaintop in the island's interior on November 11 and already seems destined to join the ranks of those who disappear and are never found. Meanwhile the one person who might be able to shed some light on what happened to her, odd-job man Harry Barnett, is saying and doing nothing to aid the search. When I spoke to 55-year-old Barnett last week in the Rhodes bar where he spends much of his time, he gave the impression of a man more concerned to avoid incriminating himself than to help those still looking for a girl he claims to have known merely as a friend. If he is reluctant to talk about what occurred when he and Miss Mallender went for a drive on the fateful afternoon, he is even less eager to talk about his own chequered past and dubious present. Harry Barnett, in short, is a man with plenty to hide . . . .

Harry closed the newspaper. He did not need to read any more. In truth, he could not bear to read any more. The inaccuracies were not what hurt: they were only to be expected. But 'a man with plenty to hide', 'concerned to avoid incriminating himself': was that really what Minter

116

had thought of him? Harry could not believe it. Yet why, if not, should he have painted such a harsh and biased picture?

All the way from his table to the librarian's desk, and beyond that to the exit, Harry sensed that people were watching him, watching him because they knew who he was and why he had asked for *The Courier* of 20 November. It was absurd, of course, for his photograph had not been in the paper and nobody in Swindon (bar Jackie Oliver) was likely to recognize him, yet he could not rid himself of the sensation.

As he emerged from the library, reflecting gloomily on the injustice of life, he very nearly bumped into somebody who had stepped forward to meet him. Pulling up sharply, he saw, to his astonishment, that it was Alan Dysart.

'Hello Harry,' Dysart said, smiling and clapping him on the shoulder. 'I didn't think we'd meet again so soon.'

With an effort, Harry smiled back. 'Neither did I.'

'You're probably wondering how I knew where to find you.'

'Well . . . yes.'

'I've been to Falmouth Street, of course. Your mother told me how put out you were by *The Courier* article, so I reckoned you'd want to read it for yourself as soon as possible. I got here just as you were going in.' Another smile. 'Thought it best to wait.'

It never failed, Harry thought, Dysart's ability to predict the reactions of others. Perhaps that was the secret of his success he had failed to identify last night. Perhaps that was what invested his words and actions with such a relaxed and maddening certainty. 'I've booked a table at the Goddard Arms for lunch,' Dysart went on. 'Trust you'll join me?'

The Goddard Arms was the perfect if ironical choice. It was the ivy-clad Georgian inn in Old Swindon where Harry had taken Barnchase's better-heeled clients in palmier, far-off days. He would like as not have left Dysart to mind the shop on such occasions and now the wheel had

117

come full circle: Dysart was the indulgent host, Harry the indigent guest.

'My car's just round the corner. What do you say we go straight there?'

And Harry said what he always said when confronted by Dysart's irresistible generosity. He said yes.

The head waiter made a face at Harry's dishevelled appearance, but clearly recognized that Dysart was a person of importance and therefore raised no objection. A window table was swiftly arranged and, within minutes, Harry found himself sipping Chablis and picking at smoked salmon in a mannered travesty of his normal eating habits.

'I got your message,' Dysart said. 'I don't blame you for leaving Lindos. I imagine the atmosphere must have become distinctly uncomfortable.'

'Yes, it did.' Harry had no intention of revealing what had really prompted him to leave. 'But I'm sorry to have left you in the lurch.'

'Don't worry about that. I'm sure we can rely on Kostas to keep an eye on things. When are you planning to go back?'

'I'm not sure.'

'Well, there's no hurry. How does it feel to be home?'

'I'm not sure about that either. I feel . . . disorientated. As if the England I've come back to isn't the England I left.'

'It isn't, Harry. It's moved on, by rather more than nine years, I fancy. You left stodgy old post-war England. You've come back to the high-tech enterprise culture. Didn't anyone tell you?' Dysart smiled, declaring as he did so the extent to which he was guying his own description as much as Harry's confusion. 'Did you catch me on the television last night?'

'Yes. You were very impressive. As always.'

Dysart leaned across the table and lowered his voice. 'Balls. I was slick. I was witty. I was word-perfect. That's

118

just training, Harry, nothing more. All mind and no heart. Not that much mind, if it comes to it. We're all ad-men now. Didn't you realize?'

'Ad-men?'

'Image is everything, presentation is all. McLuhan had it right: the medium *is* the message.'

'Are you serious? What about patriotism? Last night, you said—'

'"Neither outmoded nor unworthy"? A nice phrase, wasn't it? The truth is, Harry, patriotism is a cage, from which the bird has long since flown. I'm not complaining – it got me into Parliament, for God's sake – but let's not . . . .' His voice trailed into silence. He relaxed back into his chair and gazed for a few moments through the window into the bustling High Street. Harry had experienced such lapses into introspection on Dysart's part before. They seemed to signal dissatisfaction with whatever he was expressing at the time, a temporary loss of faith or confidence that came as inexplicably as it went. Accordingly, Harry was content to wait patiently until his companion had recovered himself. 'Let's not talk about politics,' Dysart said at last. 'Let's talk about you. You said over the telephone that you couldn't just sit in Lindos waiting for Heather to be slowly forgotten.'

'That seemed to be what was happening.'

'I hope you don't think I was encouraging the process by hastening Roy on his way. How is the head, incidentally?'

Harry smiled shamefacedly. 'Fine. I've been meaning to say how grateful I was—'

Dysart held up his hand. 'Please don't. It was the least I could do. I felt partly to blame myself, for not foreseeing what Roy might do.' Then he fixed Harry with an enquiring stare. 'I do hope you haven't come back to even the score in some way.'

Harry shook his head. 'No. The less I see of Roy Mallender, the happier I shall be.'

'Then how *do* you intend to ensure Heather isn't forgotten?'

'By finding her, if I can. Failing that, by establishing what really happened to her.'

For an instant, Dysart looked surprised, as if he had seen in Harry something he had not expected. He plucked the bottle of Chablis from its nearby ice-bucket and recharged both their glasses, then said quietly: 'Is that why you've come home, Harry? Is that what you hope to accomplish here?'

'In part, yes.'

'But Heather vanished on Rhodes. Why look for her in England? Unless . . . .' He paused long enough to imply that he had guessed the reason. 'Unless, of course, you know something the police don't. Has some clue come your way – some piece of—'

'No, nothing like that.' Harry smiled and shrugged his shoulders, but he sensed his interruption had been counter-productive. It had been too abrupt and too emphatic. Dysart's keen-eyed gaze would not leave him now, would not cease to probe until it had found what it sought.

'Then why start here?'

It was a fair question, but, even to Harry, his answer sounded unconvincing. 'Because this is where her friends are. This is where those who know her better than I do are to be found.'

Dysart stroked his chin musingly. 'What do you hope to learn from them?'

'Her true state of mind, I suppose. It's pretty obvious I misread it.'

'Did you?'

'It seemed to me that she'd put her psychological problems behind her.'

'What makes you think she hadn't?'

'Well, it would explain her running away, wouldn't it? If that's what she did.'

'As you say, *if* that's what she did. For what it's worth, I'd agree with you: when I suggested she make use of the villa, it was because I thought she'd finally recovered from the effects of her sister's death. I suppose I felt responsible

120

in some way for what happened to Clare – still do, if it comes to that – so I was keen to help Heather come to terms with it in any way I could. She must have secretly wished I'd been the first to go aboard the *Artemis* that morning, rather than Clare, though she never said as much. At all events, as I saw it, she deserved any assistance I could give her.'

Dysart had never told Harry much about the circumstances of Clare Mallender's death. There was nothing strange in this, since he had been similarly reticent about his various brushes with death in the South Atlantic. Now, however, he seemed willing for once to break his vow of silence.

'Survivors always tend to feel guilty. Everything happens at the time in a split-second. Later, you re-run the experience slowly in your mind, calculating how you could have saved those who were killed, or prevented the incident taking place at all. It's a futile activity – but an inevitable one. Heather wanted to hear precisely how her sister had died, so I told her. Perhaps I told her too well. Perhaps that was the start of her troubles.

'It happened in the middle of the election campaign. I'd spent Sunday at Tyler's Hard, writing speeches for the following week. Clare drove down from London first thing Monday morning to go through them with me. We were due to meet my agent for lunch. Sunday had been fine and I'd worked aboard the *Artemis*. It's a weakness of mine to think best afloat. I'd left the speeches on board overnight, which I only remembered when Clare arrived at breakfast time. She went out to fetch them. I was standing in the kitchen with Mrs Diamond, the cleaning lady, when we heard the explosion. The *Artemis* was blown to pieces, and most of the pontoon with it. Clare must have been killed instantly: that's about the only blessing. The bomb had been wired up so that simply opening the cabin door detonated it: textbook stuff. If I'd remembered leaving the speeches aboard sooner, or if Clare hadn't offered to go and get them . . . . Well, life and death turn on such chances.

'The problem is that if you devote too much thought to how vulnerable we all are – how much we all owe to pure luck, be it good or bad – the mind may lose its equipoise. Heather didn't have a breakdown because of how cruel fate was to her sister, or because she was grief-stricken to lose her, or even because of the senseless way terrorists select their victims. In my opinion, she didn't have a breakdown at all. She merely ceased to observe the normal social conventions about what to say and think and what not to say and think. That the frailty of life makes our careful planning for the future ridiculous is a commonplace truth. But how many of us really believe it? How many of us really imagine we might walk under the proverbial bus at any moment? The answer is very few, and most of those who do we call insane, because to live for the present is to realize how barren the present is. I saw it happen to several good men in the South Atlantic. And I saw it happen to Heather. The road back from that state of mind is a long and difficult one. But I thought Heather had successfully made the return journey, until . . . .'

'Until she disappeared on Profitis Ilias?'

'Yes. Until then. Of course, I'm in no position to give a professional opinion on Heather's psychological condition. For that, you'd need to speak to her psychiatrist.'

'I'd thought of doing just that. But he'd be unlikely to give me confidential information about a patient and, besides, I can't see the Mallenders volunteering his name and address, can you?'

Dysart smiled. 'As it happens, you don't need to ask them. His name's Kingdom: Peter Kingdom. He has a London practice. I don't know his address, but Heather spoke of visiting his consulting rooms in Marylebone. You should be able to find him in the phone book – if you think it's worth trying.'

Harry could not suppress a flare of resentment that Heather had confided in Dysart where she had not confided in him. But he was in no position to indulge the sentiment. Once again, he found himself in Dysart's debt.

'It's worth trying all right,' he said, struggling to sound grateful. 'I'll contact him as soon as possible.'

When they left the Goddard Arms, Dysart suggested a drive into the country. Harry was surprised he had no business to attend to, but did not object. They headed south, out through Wroughton and up onto the Marlborough Downs. At the top of Barbury Hill, Dysart parked with the car facing back the way they had come. The Vale of the White Horse stretched away below them and a keen wind tugged at the tussocky, sheep-cropped grass beyond the windscreen. Harry, who would energetically have denied any affinity with nature, nonetheless felt some emotional attachment to the scene. He assumed this was because the distant towerblocks of Swindon represented, for good or ill, his point of origin in the world. Dysart, whose origins lay elsewhere, nevertheless seemed to share the mood.

'During the Falklands business,' he said, 'I used to dream of views like this: England caught in some perfect, pastel miniature. That's the worst of danger: it makes you homesick. Now that I live here all the time, I hardly every think about how beautiful the country is.' He paused for a minute or so, then resumed. 'Clare and Heather walked the Ridgeway Path together when they were both students. Did Heather ever mention that to you?'

'No.'

'Well, it must have been about the last thing they did together.' He paused for a moment. 'I think Heather felt overshadowed by her sister. Clare was older, more intelligent, more successful: superior in every way, it must have seemed. Charm, brains and beauty. Without her help, I'm not sure I'd have been elected in '83. But an all-round sportswoman with a degree from Oxford and a budding career in politics makes a timid primary school teacher look and feel drab by comparison. When Clare was killed, nobody said "What a pity it had to be the talented sister who died and the dormouse who remained", but Heather believed they thought it, which was just as bad.'

'You think that contributed to Heather's breakdown?'

'I'm sure of it. Incidentally, it may have crossed your mind, given how highly I speak of Clare, that she was rather more than just my assistant.' It had crossed Harry's mind, but he was not about to admit it. 'I wouldn't blame you for wondering. God knows, it's common enough in politics. The truth is, however, that ours was a purely professional relationship.'

A silence fell. Dysart had not made the mistake of protesting too much and Harry had no reason to doubt what he had said. It was true Mrs Dysart had seldom visited Rhodes with her husband, but a dislike of sailing explained that. As far as Harry knew, theirs was a happy marriage, in which the strains of political life had been accommodated as easily as the separations of naval command. Harry had attended their wedding, down in Devon, all of eighteen years ago, and he supposed a match which had lasted as long as that could scarcely be an unstable one. His mind wandered back to the occasion: a South Hams village church, Naval officers and Wrens in dress uniform, the county set in their buttonholed finery, a vast pink marquee in the grounds of a farm-cum-manor house, as much champagne as anybody could . . . . Suddenly, at the blurred edges of his memory, something familiar, something significant, made a vague and shifting appearance. What was it? What had he heard, or seen, that now he sensed he should recall? Just as he was about to apply greater concentration to the effort, Dysart spoke again, and whatever it was fled before his words.

'I'm glad we've been able to have this talk, Harry. I was worried I might miss you, because I'm due to fly out to the States tonight for a NATO pow-wow. Fortunately, the flight's from Brize Norton, so a stopover in Swindon was no problem. I'll be away for a week. When I get back, I'd like to hear what you make of friend Kingdom.'

It was almost, Harry thought, as if Dysart was not merely giving him what help he could, but was pushing him in a particular direction. He could not be certain now which of them had first suggested approaching Kingdom. 'Have you ever met the man?' Harry asked neutrally.

'Yes. *En passant*, that is. But I wouldn't want to slant your impression of him. We disagreed about politics, as I recall, but that doesn't necessarily invalidate his medical opinion.' Dysart smiled faintly at his own joke. 'On another track, Harry, how are you for funds?'

It did not stop at direction, then. There was even a suggestion of payment. 'I'm solvent, thanks.'

'If you need a loan, let me know.'

'There's no need—'

'It's what friends are for. I'm a wealthy man, and you're as deserving a recipient as my accountant, believe you me.'

'Even so . . . .'

Dysart held up a hand in acknowledgement of Harry's reluctance. 'I won't press you. The offer's there if you need to take it up.' He glanced at his wristwatch. 'Time to make tracks, I think.'

They drove back down the hill in silence, the Daimler purring extravagantly along the lanes towards Swindon. Returning to England, Harry realized, had clarified his relationship with Dysart. He was the younger man's mascot, his reminder of humbler days, his representation of what a man becomes without luck and money and talent. He had seen a film once in which a victorious general returning to Ancient Rome led his legion through the streets, cheered to the echo by the crowds along the route, applauded by them to the point of worship. Behind the general in his chariot, standing by his shoulder as he saluted the adoring masses, was an insignificant man in a horsehair tunic, who whispered in his ear as they went along: 'Remember, you are human; you are not immortal; you are not infallible; you are an ordinary man.' That, Harry saw clearly for the first time, was his role in Dysart's Roman triumph of a life. He symbolized for this perpetually successful man the possibility of failure.

Dysart's generosity could more accurately be called patronage and Harry's acceptance of it his consent to play the part assigned to him.

Harry stared ahead at his reflection in the windscreen as they sped down the damp, sloping lane, whilst rooks flapped up in cawing, black-winged flight from the grey-green fields to either side. What he saw, and bleakly recognized, was the face of a man he no longer was. The drunken, feckless caretaker of the *Villa ton Navarkhon* had ceased to be. And Harold Mosley Barnett had set out on the road back to whatever he was destined to become.

14

All Harry told his mother when he left Swindon the following day was that he was travelling to Weymouth in order to return Heather's belongings to her family and that he might spend a night or two down there. He did not feel free to speak of what he really hoped to gain by the journey, because he was not entirely sure himself.

He was in London by ten o'clock on a cold, wet morning. As Dysart had suggested he would, he found Dr Kingdom's address in the telephone directory. It was within walking distance of Paddington station: first-floor offices off Crawford Street, with the doctor's brass plate beside the door dwarfed by the platinum insignia of a Middle Eastern concern that conducted its business on the ground floor. The upstairs waiting room was empty, but, in an adjoining room, Harry found a secretary audio-typing at her desk.

'Excuse me. I wonder if it's possible to see Dr Kingdom.'

The secretary was a young Asian woman of elegant, disdainful bearing. After a calculated delay, she removed her headphones, gazed up at him through spectacles which made her dark eyes look haughtily immense, and said: 'You do not have an appointment.' This was not only pointedly phrased as a statement rather than a question, but accompanied by a faint twitch of the eyebrows which suggested she inferred from his shabby appearance an inability to afford the good doctor's fees.

'I realize that, but—'

'Your name?'

'Barnett. Harry Barnett. He won't—'

'You are not a patient of Dr Kingdom's.' Again she asserted, she did not enquire.

'No, I'm not. However—'

'He only accepts new patients by written referral from their general practitioner.'

'Let me explain.' With a smile intended to be disarming, Harry sat down on the edge of a nearby chair. 'I don't want to consult Dr Kingdom. I want to speak to him about one of his patients – a friend of mine – who disappeared recently. Maybe you read about her in the papers: Heather Mallender.'

The secretary's self-control faltered, he felt certain, at the mention of Heather's name, as though more than mere recognition of a patient was involved. But she said nothing, either to refute his suspicion or to confirm it.

'Have you read about her?'

The response was guarded and accompanied by a reluctant nod of the head. 'Yes.'

'Perhaps you've read about me as well, then.'

'Barnett?' A frown, then another nod. 'Yes. You were with her when she disappeared. In Greece. Last month.'

'And she *is* a patient of Dr Kingdom's?'

'Yes.'

'Then maybe he'd welcome talking to me. After all, he must be worried about—'

'Dr Kingdom is abroad at present. He will not be back until Monday.'

'Ah, I see.'

Suddenly, she seemed to remember something. 'There was an article about you in *The Courier*, Mr Barnett. Yes, I recall reading it.' Her gaze intensified, as if she were deciding for herself, now he was in front of her, whether Minter's description had been accurate. It struck Harry as typically unfair of fate to decree that everybody he met should be a *Courier* reader. 'Are you really a man with plenty to hide?' she asked, after a moment's deliberation.

'You shouldn't believe everything you read in the news-papers, Miss—'

'Labrooy. Miss Labrooy.' She smiled for the first time: a flashing, transforming smile that was unaccountably superior. 'As a matter of fact, Mr Barnett, I believe *nothing* I read in the newspapers.'

Harry was becoming aware of a curious sensation. It was as if Kingdom's secretary was subjecting him to as much analysis as might Kingdom himself. 'The truth is, Miss Labrooy, I'm very worried about Heather. Contrary to what the papers think, I've no idea where or how she is, but I'm trying every way I can devise to find out. I was hoping Dr Kingdom could tell me whether her disappearance could have a psychological explanation. She was reading this just beforehand—' He fumbled in the rucksack and pulled out *The Psychopathology of Everyday Life*.

'Dr Kingdom's dealings with his patients are completely confidential. He would not be free to tell you anything.'

'These are exceptional circumstances.'

She considered the point for a moment, then glanced at the book he was still holding up and said: 'Do you know what chapter she was reading?'

'Determinism, Belief in Chance and Superstition. Page 327.'

She jotted the information down on a pad. 'Thank you. Dr Kingdom may consider it material to his analysis.'

'Does that mean he'll see me, then?'

'I do not know.' The hint of a smile, then: 'I will ask. I can make no promises. He is a very busy man. But I *will* ask.' And the way Miss Labrooy said it suggested she would not ask in vain. Harry felt suddenly cheered by the thought that here, at least, he might have found an ally.

The offices of *The Courier* were anonymously plate-glassed and a long way from Fleet Street. Harry had read some-where of the revolution which had overtaken British journalism in his absence and this, he supposed, was a representation of it. He could, in the event, have spared himself the visit, since, as a security guard curtly informed him, Minter had the day off. And no, his telephone number was not available.

Harry retreated to the nearest pub, procured a supply of ten pence pieces and commenced dialling the numbers of every J. Minter in the book. At the fourth attempt, he found the one he wanted. True, it was only a recorded message, but the voice was unquestionably that of *The Courier*'s acerbic correspondent. Half an hour and another drink later he tried again. This time, he was in luck. Just as the answering machine commenced its routine, it was cut off by the receiver being picked up. But nobody spoke. Harry braced himself for Minter's sneering tones, only to be greeted by silence.

'Hello?' he said, as soon as he had abandoned hope of Minter speaking. 'Is that—' Then the phone went down. It had not been slammed, merely calmly replaced, as if Harry had failed to say the magic words.

Already angered by what Minter had written, Harry was now irritated as well. He made a note of the address, gleaned from the barman that it was a twenty minute walk away, swallowed another drink and headed straight round there.

London was fast assuming for Harry the character of a city he had never visited. Wapping's old warehouses, for instance, had mostly been converted into Porsche-fronted apartment blocks. Everywhere Harry went in his homeland, he was confronted by a material prosperity which he could not help resenting. The hardships of a wartime childhood and the grim years of rationing that had ensued stood emphasized in his memory by the complacency and extravagance that seemed to have followed. For this, as much as for what he had written in *The Courier*, Harry was determined to make Minter answer.

The entrance to Kempstow Wharf, where Minter lived, was security-locked, with a separate bell and speaking grille for each flat. Harry's heart sank at the thought that Minter might simply refuse to admit him. Then, just as he was considering how to announce himself, the tinted-glass door was opened from the inside and a girl in a tracksuit and training shoes, carrying a squash racket and a bag, walked out, leaving the door to slam shut behind her. As it swung back on its hinges and the girl strode away, Harry stepped inside.

Minter's flat was on the third floor. From the landing window, where Harry paused to catch his breath, there was an imposing view of the Thames winding upriver towards Tower Bridge. *The Courier*, it seemed, paid well.

The absence of a fish-eye viewing lens on the flat door was a stroke of luck, Harry felt. He knocked. There was no answer, though he thought he could detect music within. He knocked again, harder.

A moment later, the door opened. The person opening it was at first invisible; Harry merely had a glimpse of a hallway leading towards a large, picture-windowed lounge, with Tower Bridge again visible in the distance, and heard a woman's voice say: 'Sorry, Jon. I forgot I'd put the catch—'

Suddenly, she was in front of him. Tall, taller than Harry in fact, naked save for a bath towel tucked beneath her arms that only just covered her hips, with long strands of wet hair clinging to her head and neck and droplets of water standing out on her shoulders and thighs. She was neither young nor old: a mature woman confident of her looks, her face high-boned and aquiline, her expression one of pleasure transformed into horror, though her horror could, in the circumstances, scarcely eclipse Harry's: she was Alan Dysart's wife, Virginia.

'Who the hell are you?' she said, glaring at him affrontedly.

Could it be true that she did not recognize him? Harry found it hard but not impossible to believe: she had never been one to waste attention on the likes of him. Besides, they had not met in years.

'I said: who the hell are you?'

131

'I'm looking for Jonathan Minter.'

'Well he's not here. How did you get in?'

'The . . . ah . . . front door was ajar.'

'Then shut it on your way out.'

With that, the door was closed in his face. Not slammed, he noticed, remembering his telephone call, merely closed.

Harry took a boat from Tower Bridge to Charing Cross, intending to walk from there to Waterloo station. He sat on deck, gazing at the steel-grey, altered skyline of London and wondering what use to make of his latest discovery. Privilege. Hypocrisy. Corruption. They had been Minter's own words. And now they were laid at Minter's own door. It was all so wantonly predictable. Minter on leave. Dysart in America. And Virginia Dysart in Minter's bed. The seducer who had villified him. The cuckold who had befriended him. And the adultress who had forgotten him. A triangular link in the winding chain that could only lead, as Minter had predicted, to 'something very nasty indeed'.

More, and worse, occurred to Harry's mind as he sat aboard the Weymouth train, drinking canned beer and watching Surrey and Hampshire flash past him through the grey afternoon. He had taken Heather's photographs out to remind himself of what Nigel Mossop now looked like and had begun leafing through the pictures. When he came upon the unfamiliar gravestone of Francis Hollinrake, he wondered again who the man was and what he had meant to Heather. It was doubly puzzling, since not only had Heather never mentioned him, but she could only have been twelve when he died, all of fifteen years ago.

Then he remembered. Hollinrake. Of course he knew the name, from rather more than fifteen years ago. The ruddy-faced father of the bride who had crushed his hand at the entrance to the marquee. 'Glad you could be here,' he had growled amiably. 'I'm Frank Hollinrake.' Yes, that was it. Hollinrake was Virginia Dysart's maiden name. And Frank Hollinrake was her father.

15

The premature darkness of an overcast December afternoon was descending on Weymouth when Harry arrived. He followed a well-remembered route from the station to his old lodgings in Mitchell Street, through knots of sauntering, larking schoolchildren, past brightly lit, Christmas-decorated shopfronts; here too an electronic chorus of carols was ready to welcome the prodigal.

Away from the main street, fragments of a discarded life began to claim his attention. A few, late, wheeling gulls contested a sodden slice of bread. A whiff of the sea reached him from a turning that led to the bay. Then the soaring flank of a cross-Channel ferry moored at Custom House Quay loomed ahead, blocking, it seemed the very end of the street, its funnels dwarfing the tiny, jumbled terraces.

Harry turned into Mitchell Street and crossed to the other side. At this time of year, the Loves were unlikely to have a lodger. Before Harry's arrival on the scene – and after, he assumed – they had relied on holidaymakers and ferry-goers. Indeed, they had originally told Harry he must be out by Whitsun. In the event, he had stayed five years. Beryl had grown fond of him, Ernie had learned to tolerate him and Harry, even when he could have afforded better, had not bothered to seek it.

Yet there was no VACANCIES sign displayed on the door. And, when Harry rang the bell, Ernie, not Beryl, answered it. He seemed even shorter, grimmer and shabbier than Harry recalled: a shrunken, ferret-eyed man with a roll-up glued to his lower lip, wrapped in an over-sized cardigan and an air of self-imposed misery.

'Hello, Ernie. Remember me?'

For answer, Ernie tapped his forehead. 'Forgotten more'n you'll ever know. Harry bloody Barnett. What d'you want?'

'My old room for a couple of nights, if it's free. Beryl in?'

'Beryl's in Weymouth bloody Crem. Cancer. Three years ago. Don't take lodgers. Not since.'

Beryl was dead. That ever-laughing, ever-working, warm-hearted blancmange of a woman was dead. And her work-shy, gloom-devoured ingrate of a husband was still alive. It was only to be expected, of course. Harry should have known. Given a choice, life was generally unfair.

'Bugger me,' said Ernie. 'You look proper cut up.'

'I had no idea . . . .' Harry leaned against the doorpost for support, struggling to come to terms with this further sadness that fate had reserved for him.

'A couple of nights, you said?' A hint of softness had entered Ernie's expression, like a stubborn flower blooming on a granite cliff.

'Yes, but . . . .'

'Reckon you'd best come in, then. For Beryl's sake, like.' He led the way down the narrow, cluttered passage and Harry followed, noting as he went the odour of fried onions which had replaced the beeswax aroma of Beryl's day. Ernie paused as they turned into the parlour, looked back at Harry and said: 'She treated you better than she ever treated me, y'know.' It was as if he felt the trace of affection in his earlier remark required instant correction, as if this least uxorious of husbands was determined to prove he had not become a sentimental widower.

The parlour was in chaos. Dust had settled thickly on Beryl's china animals and jugs. Ash was piled in old take-away trays and scattered across the newspaper-strewn settee. The embroidered antimaccasars were torn and stained, the potted plants shrivelled and sickly. The curtains, hanging from alternate runners and half-drawn across the windows, added their filtered gloom to the soiled glumness of the scene and the contrast with what had formerly been struck Harry dumb with depression.

'Want a cup o' tea?'

'Er, no thanks.'

'Or a beer?'

'Actually, I've got to go straight on somewhere.'

'Have you, though?'

There was nowhere, it seemed then to Harry, nowhere he could go in this country he called his own, without finding the past trampled on, his memories insulted, his assumptions contradicted. Beryl dead, her home neglected, her husband in festering decline: if Harry had known, he would have walked on by.

'Why d'you come back?'

'I'm not sure.'

'Somebody in the Globe said they'd read about you in the papers. Something about—'

'Was Beryl . . . . Did she suffer a lot?'

Ernie's glare conveyed his meaning better than any words: the subject was taboo. 'I'd have to charge . . . for the accommodation, like. Fiver a night. In advance.'

Harry shrugged the rucksack off his shoulders and deposited it behind the door. Then he took a ten pound note from his wallet and pushed it into Ernie's waiting hand. He knew Ernie to be mean, yet he suspected this was not what had motivated his request. The cash was intended to distance them, to purge their relationship of anything that might smack of commiseration. Ernie required no companion in his bereavement.

'Where you off to, then?'

'Er . . . Mallender Marine.'

Ernie's perpetual frown deepened. 'They've not taken you back?'

'No. I just want to see one of the staff. It could take a couple of hours.'

135

'Then you'd best look in at the Globe when you get back. I'll be there by that time, like as not.'

Harry nodded. 'Yes. Like as not.'

It was as well, Harry reflected as he sat aboard the Portland bus ten minutes later, that Ernie Love was the least sociable of men, his interest in gossip entirely confined to form talk in the betting shops. He at least could be assumed never to have read a copy of *The Courier*.

The bus moved slowly through the rush-hour traffic, indecisive rain spitting against the windows. For all the hundreds of journeys Harry had made on this same route from Town Bridge to Mallender Marine, for all the years he had lived in Weymouth and for all the years he had believed he would remain there, he felt for it no fondness, no kinship of any kind. Nothing, he knew, but the irresistible necessity by which he was bound, could or should have drawn him back.

It was, then, with an awareness of his own reluctance as much as a consciousness of how ill-advised his behaviour might be, that Harry rose, pressed the bell and stepped off the bus at the appointed stop. He gazed after the illuminated shape of the vehicle as it headed on along the arrow-straight road towards Portland and let his sight and memory absorb the distant, neon-lit profile of the Naval Base, its lights refracted and extended in the black, unseen waters of the harbour. Then he crossed the road and re-entered with determined tread another precinct of his past. Mallender Marine was a two-storeyed office building with a car park at the front and workshop and loading bay at the rear. In its way, it was the quintessential unprepossessing workplace of every man's acquaintance: drab, utilitarian and wholly unremarkable.

But, for Harry Barnett, standing outside in the drizzle, this place was, for good or ill, the starting-point of his quest after Heather Mallender's secret: the first photograph on the film she had taken, the first intersection of their interwoven destinies. The car park was mostly empty, as he had hoped, with lights on in only half the offices. This late on a Friday evening, he had judged, none but the desperate and the dedicated would still be working. Roy Mallender, for one, would be long gone. But Nigel Mossop, timid naïve laborious Nigel, was likely, if Harry's memory served, to be found even now at his desk.

Harry began to trace a path that would lead him past all the ground-floor offices. Mercifully, the window of what had once been his was in darkness: there was no need to confront whatever alterations his successors had made. In the next, two girls he did not recognize were joking with a cleaner. It was strange to think how oblivious they were to being observed. There followed an empty room and two more darkened windows. And then, as expected, an office of four desks, only one of them occupied, but occupied by Nigel Mossop.

Grey-suited and tousle-haired, thin and hunched as if weighed down by his own inadequacy, frowning and fretting over a scatter of papers, Nigel Mossop appeared entirely faithful to Harry's recollection of him: earnest, well-intentioned and essentially good-hearted, but crippled by insecurity and obtuseness. Not a man to inspire either affection or confidence and certainly not a man to be relied upon, in or out of a crisis, he was nevertheless the one sure witness to what Heather had been about when she had taken his photograph.

Harry stepped closer to the window, so that he was no more than a yard from Mossop, though still invisible to him. He could discern every tiny symptom now of the other man's unaltered character: untidy, hesitant, inclined to panic, consumed by uncertainty. His nose had wrinkled in bafflement as he tapped the keys of a calculator, his brow had knotted itself in unavailing concentration. Harry reached out and rapped his knuckles on the glass.

Mossop reacted like a rabbit to a shotgun report. He leapt back in his chair, mouth open and eyes starting in his head. When he looked at the window, and saw Harry's face, it was clear that he did not, for a moment, believe the

137

evidence of his senses. Then Harry mouthed and motioned for him to open the window. Mossop glanced around as if afraid he was overlooked, though Harry could see that he was not. Still he hesitated. Then, at last, he reached across the desk, released the stay and gingerly pushed the window ajar.

'Harry,' he said, breathless with confusion. 'What are you . . . I mean . . . . This isn't . . . .'

'Hello, Nige. Surprised to see me?'

'Well . . . I certainly didn't . . . . What . . . what are you doing here?'

'I was hoping to have a few words with you.' Though the chances of those words being coherent, Harry thought, did not seem good.

'Oh . . . . Really? What . . . what about?'

'Heather.'

Shock now convulsed Mossop's startled expression. 'Heather? You mean H-Heather . . . M-M-M—'

'Heather Mallender,' Harry interrupted, finishing Mossop's sentence as he had always done when the young man's stammer became too much for him.

'I don't . . . didn't, that is . . . . Didn't really know . . . Heather . . . at all.'

'That isn't strictly true, Nige, now is it?'

'Yes, of course . . . . Of course . . . it is.'

Harry drew the wallet of photographs from his pocket, selected the one of Mossop and held it up for him to see. 'Remember her taking this one of you?'

Mossop's jaw sagged. 'Oh . . . . Oh yes . . . .' He reached out as if to take it, but Harry snatched it back before he could.

'Are you going to let me in?'

Again, Mossop looked anxiously over his shoulder. 'No . . . . That is . . . . I'll come out.'

Harry watched as the young man bundled some papers and an empty sandwich box into his briefcase, pulled on an anorak and headed for the door, switching the light off as he went. As he walked round towards the main entrance to meet him, Harry wondered if any significance was to be attached to the furtiveness which seemed to have compounded Mossop's natural timidity. It was understandable, he supposed, that he should not wish to be seen fraternizing with Roy Mallender's sworn enemy, but his feeble attempt to deny knowing Heather implied some deeper-seated fear.

Mossop appeared in the porch just as Harry reached it, but he did not pause or even glance in Harry's direction. Instead he hurried across to his car, unlocked the door and climbed in, then waved for Harry to join him. As soon as he had done so, Mossop started the engine and pulled out of the car park with choke roaring, attracting, Harry suspected, all the attention he had been hoping to avoid.

'Where are we going, Nige?' They had started south towards Portland, but, in Harry's day, Mossop had lived with his mother in Radipole and it was hard to imagine that he had moved.

'Well . . . . Well . . . I thought somewhere private . . . would be best.'

'Is driving without lights intended to add to the privacy?'

'Oh God.' Mossop grabbed at the headlamp switch and Harry noticed, as he did so, how much his hand was shaking. 'S-Sorry.'

'There's no need to apologize. Just tell me why you're so nervous.'

'I . . . I'm not.'

'Have it your own way.'

Clumsily, Mossop changed the subject. 'A lot . . . . A lot's altered . . . since you left the firm.'

'I'll bet it has.'

With this minimal encouragement, Mossop embarked on a gabbled and stumbling account of who had come and gone, who had prospered and who had fallen by the wayside, in the ten years since Harry's departure. None of it should have been or was surprising. Charlie Mallender had begun to take a back seat, leaving Roy to impose his own philosophy on the company. This meant more low-risk sure-profit Defence contracting and fewer speculative ventures into the private leisure market. It also meant recruiting sycophantic nose-to-the grindstone staff in preference to anybody with an ounce of flair or individuality. Not that Roy's methods had been unsuccessful. Commercially, Mallender Marine had gone from strength to strength. As for Mossop, though he evidently missed the earlier pioneering times and had gained precious little personal advancement under Roy, ingrained humility ensured he was not about to complain.

Mossop's babble finally expired where the road ended, at Portland Bill. He pulled into the empty lighthouse car park, stopped, turned off the engine and seemed at last, in this remotest and darkest of refuges from prying eyes, to grow calmer in both speech and expression.

'We all heard . . . read, that is . . . about you and Heather, of course.'

'Did you?'

'I didn't believe . . . what they suggested. Not . . . not for a moment.'

'What *who* suggested?'

'Well . . . . The papers, of course . . . and . . . .'

'Roy Mallender?'

'He never liked you, Harry . . . . You know that . . . .'

'He never liked you, either.'

'No . . . . No, he didn't . . . . But things are . . . different now.'

'Are they?'

'Oh yes . . . . Yes, of course.'

'Does he know you were going out with Heather?'

'I . . . I wasn't.'

Mossop's relative composure had ended now. A sudden spikey rush of odour told Harry that he was sweating in the deepening chill. 'Come on, Nige. The photograph, remember?'

'Where did you . . . ? How . . . ?'

'After she disappeared, I had the film in her camera

developed. Don't worry. I haven't told anybody that you're on it . . . yet.'

'What do you m-m—'

'I mean that, strictly speaking, I ought to hand the photographs over to the police. They might want to know, of course, why you're in one of them.'

'It's just . . . just a snap.'

'Taken when, may I ask?'

'Back in the, ah . . . back in the summer.'

'And taken where?'

'Oh . . . . I'm not sure. I can't—'

'Can't remember? Perhaps I can help. I think the house in the background is at Tyler's Hard. I think it's Alan Dysart's cottage in the New Forest. You *have* heard of Alan Dysart, haven't you?'

'Well . . . yes, of course.'

'So, why were you there?'

'There was . . . nothing to it. Just a . . . d-d-day t-t-trip.'

Harry felt suddenly sorry for his companion. Poor Mossop could not withstand the pressure he was under. Time had not bolstered his self-confidence. If anything, it had undermined it. But, sorry or not, Harry could scarcely afford to be squeamish. 'If Roy ever found out you and Heather were friends, it wouldn't do a lot for your career prospects, would it?'

'Oh God.' Mossop's head sagged onto his chest. 'I never thought . . . not for a moment . . . . ' His voice thickened, as if tears were not far away.

'Why not just tell me all about it, Nige, eh?' To his own ears, Harry's gentle encouraging tone sounded reminiscent of Miltiades: the same implication of sympathy, the same flavour of the confessional.

'I suppose . . . I might as well.' Mossop spoke now without the strangled note of earlier indecision. He had abandoned the unequal struggle. 'You know Heather had this . . . breakdown . . . that made her give up teaching?'

'Yes.'

141

'Well, after she'd recovered . . . she came to work at Mallender Marine . . . . Just as a temporary arrangement, of course . . . . Ease her back into everyday life . . . . I suppose that was the idea . . . . They put her in the . . . the same office as me . . . April, it must have been . . . when she arrived. Well, we got to know each other, like you do . . . when you work with somebody.' His voice was gaining strength and fluency as he spoke. 'We had a drink together on a few Friday evenings after work, that was all . . . . There was nothing to it . . . . I think she liked talking to me because I didn't, well, didn't ask her . . . about her sister, about her breakdown. Probably she liked me because I was . . . no threat, you know?'

'I know, Nige, I know.' It sounded disturbingly similar to what might have appealed to Heather in Harry himself.

'Well, last August . . . the Sunday of the bank holiday weekend . . . she asked me if I'd drive her to the New Forest. She said she wanted to see . . . to see where her sister had died . . . Tyler's Hard, like you said. She didn't want to go alone and she didn't want her family to know about it. That's why . . . she asked me.'

'What happened?'

'Nothing. We drove there . . . had lunch at Beaulieu . . . and looked at the stretch of water where . . . where the boat blew up. Then we . . . came back.'

'That was all?'

'Yes . . . of course. Wh-wh—'

'What else?' Mossop's stammer had betrayed him. 'Out with it, Nige. What else happened?'

'Well, we . . . we visited a couple of p-people. An old woman who, ah, cleaned for Dysart. Mrs D-Di—'

'Mrs Diamond?'

'Yes. Heather had her address. She . . . wanted to look her up.'

'Why?'

'I don't know. I . . . waited in the car while she went in.'

142

'Who else?'

'Oh . . . Dysart's handyman. I can't . . . can't remember his name. We found him . . . at the house. But it turned out he hadn't witnessed the explosion, so Heather didn't get much out of him.'

'What was she trying to find out?'

'I don't know. Honest, Harry, I don't. Nothing in particular . . . as far as I could tell.'

'What happened afterwards?'

'Afterwards? Nothing. Nothing . . . at all. Heather left Mallender Marine in October and . . . that was the last I saw of her.'

A silence fell and Harry stared ahead at the dark, blank windscreen. If Mossop was telling the truth, his visit to Tyler's Hard with Heather had been an end in itself, not a herald of other discoveries. But Mossop, of course, did not know what the later photographs showed. Nor was he privy to Heather's reasons for going to Tyler's Hard and seeking out witnesses to her sister's death.

'Is that . . . any help, Harry?'

'It's not enough, Nige. I'm afraid I've got to ask you a favour.'

'What f-f—'

'Drive me to Tyler's Hard. Like you did Heather. Take me wherever you took her. I want to meet Mrs Diamond . . . and the handyman. I want to see everything she saw that day.'

'But . . . why?'

'If I knew that, we wouldn't need to go.'

'Well, I can't . . . actually. I can't get away, you see. My m-mother—'

'Tomorrow or Sunday. It's your choice. But it has to be one or the other.'

Silence intruded once more. Harry did not need to remind Mossop of why he was obliged to grant him the favour he had asked. It was merely a question of waiting for him to accept the inevitable.

'S-Sunday, then. I often . . . go bird-watching along the

143

Fleet on Sundays. My mother wouldn't think it odd . . . if I was out all day.'

'Pick me up by the Jubilee Clock at half past nine.'

'All right. I'll . . . I'll be there.'

'Be sure you are. Remember: I'm counting on you.' Which was ironical, Harry thought as he said it, since his assessment of Mossop's character told him that to rely on such a man, in lesser matters as in greater, was likely to prove the starkest folly.

16

'Good of you to drive me, Ernie,' Harry said, as the gears of Love's van gave another mangled squeal.

'You'd not have got there bloody else, would you?'

'No, I suppose not.' He winced as they sped round a bend, suspension and wheel-arch grating, and wondered again if the taxi fare would not have been a sound investment.

Ernie's occupation, aside from betting, was that of a jobbing plumber, but he had freely confessed to Harry that it had 'gone by the bloody board' since Beryl's death, hence the illegibility of his name on the side of the van, the lamentable state of the vehicle's mechanics and the unserviceable appearance of the ballcocks and tap-fittings clanking around behind Harry's seat.

'We're coming into the village now,' said Harry, trying not to sound as relieved as he felt at sight of the Portesham sign. Ernie had volunteered to drive him there midway through his seventh Mackeson in the Globe the night before and, like the hard-nosed gambler he was, had insisted on honouring his pledge.

They turned off the Bridport road with a sickening tyre-screeching lurch and plunged down along the narrow main street of the village. 'Been here before, have you?' Ernie calmly enquired, oblivious to the speed he was maintaining.

'Once, yes.' It had been a dark winter's night, as Harry recalled, within a year of his joining Mallender

Marine. Charlie Mallender had invited some of the staff to a house-warming at Sabre Rise, his newly completed country residence near Portesham. Warner from Personnel had given Harry a lift. He had drunk too much and told Mrs Mallender a *risqué* joke by which she had not been amused, then given Lambert, the unctuous works manager, the benefit of his opinion. Even fifteen years later, the memory was embarrassing. Where had Heather been that night, he wondered: at boarding school – or a friend's? Perhaps she had been upstairs in her bedroom, listening to the adults prattling below. Perhaps she had even . . . . 'Pull in here, Ernie, we can ask for directions at the pub.'

Sabre Rise, it transpired, was a short walk away along the lanes. In the circumstances, Harry was happy to leave Ernie imbibing at the bar of the Half Moon, hoist Heather's rucksack onto his back and follow the landlady's directions at his own solitary pace. The day was grey and still, the straggling outskirts of Portesham reserved and cautionary in the well-bred way of a monied English village. He climbed the steep winding road slowly, preparing and rehearsing the overtures he would make, the condolences he would offer, above all the questions he would ask.

Suddenly, without warning, a large dark blue estate car burst into view round the bend Harry was approaching, consuming, it seemed, the entire width of the lane. Instinctively, Harry flattened himself against the hedge. With a rush of air and a roar of sound, the car was past him and gone, spraying water from a puddle across his legs and leaving only a glimpse of the driver's stonily indifferent face to remember. But a glimpse, Harry realized as he recovered his breath and mopped his trousers, was enough. The thornproof jacket, the tweed hat, the fat-bowled pipe, the set and veinous expression of a self-made man: they belonged to Charlie Mallender. He had not noticed Harry, which was only to be expected, since pedestrians would be one to his mind with all the lower orders, below decks, beyond consideration and beneath contempt. The golf-bag lodged in the rear of his car suggested a lengthy absence from home and that, Harry thought, augured well, for an anxious mother was always likelier to be reasonable than an outraged father.

Five minutes later, he reached the entrance to Sabre Rise. The boundary wall was of raw unpointed stone, the gate of stout, heavily varnished wood. Beyond lay broad immaculate lawns, a curving coarse-gravelled drive and the house itself, red-bricked, low-roofed and redolent of unseasoned wealth. The windows were too large, the surroundings too bare, the architecture too crudely expensive for a quiet fold of the Dorset countryside. Heather would have hated living there, he felt certain. Nothing in her gentle undemonstrative nature could have found a mirror in this bruising statement of her family's prosperity.

Harry opened the gate and started up the drive, listening to his feet crunching loudly on the gravel. At one of the ground-floor windows a dalmatian appeared and began to bark. A net curtain in one of the first floor rooms was twitched back by an unseen hand. He reached the door and pressed the chiming bell.

A young woman answered. Her jeans, apron and Dorset accent suggested hired help. Before Harry could explain himself, a figure came into view down the open stairs. Thin, sour-faced and trembling faintly like a leaf in a breeze, she nevertheless possessed some high-cheeked memento of her daughter's features and stared at Harry with instant ice-cold recognition. 'All right, Jean,' she said in a shallow, quivering voice. 'I'll deal with this.'

Jean obediently vanished. The dalmatian materialized silently in a doorway. Harry removed the rucksack and deposited it on the mat. And Marjorie Mallender walked slowly towards him.

'What do you want here, Mr Barnett? It *is* Mr Barnett, isn't it?'

'Yes.' Harry tried to smile, but the expression died on his face as she glared frigidly back. 'I . . . I thought I ought

147

to return Heather's things. Clothes, jewellery, personal effects: you know the kind of . . . . '

'They're in the rucksack?'

'Er, yes.'

'Then you may leave it there.' She said no more, but Harry felt the full force of her unspoken wish that he should go. His preference, in different circumstances, would have been to do just that, but he knew he could not. 'If you want my thanks, then you have them, Mr Barnett. Now, is that all?'

'No. That is . . . . ' Silence leapt between them like a physical entity. Why was this woman so incurious? Harry wondered. For all the lies her son might have told her about him, he was still the last man to have seen her missing daughter and she was still the distracted mother eager for news. Yet she seemed to wish neither to accuse him nor to question him. 'I thought . . . you might want to talk.'

'About what?'

'About Heather.'

She flinched at the sound of her daughter's name, then instantly composed herself. 'Why have you come here, Mr Barnett?'

'I've just told you.'

She stepped forward and clasped the door as if to close it in his face, saying as she did so: 'Please don't call again.'

'I'm looking for Heather,' he shouted in response. She froze in mid-movement and, seeing that his words had won him a temporary reprieve, he went on: 'Whatever Roy might think, Mrs Mallender, I didn't murder Heather, or kidnap her, or even frighten her. I'm just the somebody who happened to be there when she vanished. I'm just the friend who's trying his damnedest to find her.'

'To find her?'

'I'm convinced she's still alive. I'm determined to prove it the only way I can: by following every trail that might lead me to her.'

'The police believe she's dead.'

'But do you?'

'Everybody thinks . . . . ' Her voice died away but, in her eyes, a fragile hope was born. 'Do you really mean what you're saying, Mr Barnett?'

'Yes.'

She stared at him for another moment of scrutiny, then said, 'Come in', and pushed the door back to admit him.

He followed her into a large picture-windowed lounge in which the furnishings and decorations seemed, for all their lavishness, not quite to fill the available space. Logs were blazing in the wide copper-cowled fireplace, yet a chill no thermometer could register robbed the thick carpet of warmth and the plush settees of comfort. The dalmatian kept an apprehensive vigil by the door whilst its mistress crossed to a sidetable where drinks stood on a tray. She poured herself a large gin and a miniscule tonic, neglected to offer Harry the same, then turned to face him.

'We had no idea you were the friend she'd made in Rhodes,' she said, with no more than a hint of hostility in her voice.

'But you knew she *had* made a friend?'

'Yes. She spoke of it in postcards.'

'Perhaps she thought you'd worry if you knew it was me.'

'Perhaps. Alan really should have warned us you were his caretaker.'

'I'm perfectly harmless, Mrs Mallender. Surely you can see that for yourself?'

'But my husband did sack you.'

'That was ten years ago. Do you seriously think I still bear a grudge because of it, or would take it out on Heather if I did?'

'Roy tells me there was trouble before then: complaints from some of the female staff.'

So Roy had added invention to misrepresentation. Harry should not have been surprised, but he was. It explained why Marjorie Mallender had been reluctant to speak to him, let alone admit him to her home, yet it did not explain why she had relented, nor why there was such a doubtful

149

tone in her voice as she related what her son had told her. Sensing that to ignore Roy's allegations would count for more with his mother than any number of denials, Harry offered none. Instead he adhered to a line of reason. 'It seems to me, Mrs Mallender, that there are three possible explanations for Heather's disappearance. One is, forgive me for saying so, that she was murdered and her body concealed where no search could find it.'

'That is what my husband and son believe.'

'But not what you believe?'

She countered with an uncommunicative stare.

'Another possibility is that she was kidnapped and is being held somewhere against her will. It did occur to me . . . .'

'Yes?'

'There's been no ransom demand, as far as I know, but it's not unheard of for the families of kidnap victims to keep contact with the kidnappers a secret, so as not to endanger—'

'There has been no contact, Mr Barnett. You have my solemn word on that.'

'Then only one possibility remains: that she vanished of her own accord; that she ran away rather than face—'

'Rather than face what?' Marjorie Mallender was breathing heavily now, her cheeks flushed with something more than gin. Either she had detected an implication in Harry's words that he had not intended or those words had been nearer the truth than he had supposed.

'I don't know. She was due to come home in a few days. She seemed happy on Rhodes and reluctant to leave. But I didn't think that was anything more than end-of-holiday blues. Then again, I'd only known her for a few weeks. She's your daughter. You're better placed than me to say if . . . if there was anything she might have wanted to run away from.'

Marjorie Mallender moved to the settee and sat down. She took a cigarette from a gold box on the coffee-table, lit it with an oversized onyx lighter, then gazed about for a moment at her expensively unsympathetic surroundings. For the next minute or so, she seemed to forget Harry's presence, brooding on whatever memories or portents his words had brought to her mind. Then, just as he was beginning to wonder what he should do next, she looked up at him and said: 'You know about her breakdown?'

'Yes. She told me.'

'She kept apologizing about it, Mr Barnett. For the embarrassment it caused us, you understand. Quite absurd, of course: one should not need to apologize to one's own parents for something like that. But she thought she did, partly because she felt this ridiculous *pressure* on her after Clare's death. Not grief: that's to be expected. But responsibility for being left behind when Clare had been taken from us. Completely unjustified of course, but the more difficult to rid her of for that very reason. After her breakdown, when she had to give up teaching, she became dependent on us, at least for a while, and that only made matters worse in one sense. At all events, I'm sure it contributed to the relapse she suffered in October.'

'Relapse?'

'Oh yes. It's why she left Mallender Marine. Working there at all was a silly idea in my opinion. What she needed was a complete break from the family, which is why I was so pleased when she accepted Alan's invitation to visit Rhodes.'

Cautiously, Harry lowered himself into the armchair opposite her. 'Do you think it possible, then, that she was desperate to avoid returning . . . to her family?'

This time there was no flare of injured pride. 'No, I don't. I considered Heather needed a rest from us, but she would never have agreed with me. Always there was that desperate eagerness to please, you see, that longing to prove she wasn't a disappointment to us. It's inconceivable she should have run away and left us to believe the worst.' Marjorie Mallender glanced at a framed photograph standing in front of her on the coffee-table. Harry could see her eyes drift out of focus as its subject carried her thoughts away once more. She reached forward, picked it up and gazed intently at it for several moments, shaking her head slowly as she did so. Then, catching Harry's enquiring look, she turned it towards him. 'This was taken on Clare's twenty-first birthday: the twenty-fourth of August, 1980. I had two beautiful daughters then. Now . . . . ' A sigh took the place of her dismal conclusion.

More from politeness than anything else, Harry leaned forward to examine the photograph. It was the standard back garden family snapshot: Marjorie Mallender flanked by her daughters, Heather instantly recognizable, Clare scarcely less so as a sophisticated, immaculately groomed version of her sister. By Heather's left shoulder stood brother Roy. At the opposite end of the group, his arm round Clare's waist, was a relative or friend Harry did not know, or rather . . . . Suddenly, recognition dawned. It scarcely seemed credible, yet there was the photographic evidence to tell him it was so.

'Is something wrong, Mr Barnett?'

'No. That is . . . who's the fifth person in this picture?'

'Oh, Clare's boyfriend. Fiancé, I suppose I should say, because—'

'Fiancé?'

'Yes, though the engagement was broken off within a year. I was always sorry that Clare didn't marry Jonathan. He'd have made her an excellent husband. Such a charming boy.'

'This *is* Jonathan Minter, isn't it?'

'Why yes. Have you heard of him, Mr Barnett? I believe he's made quite a name for himself as a journalist since then. He and Clare met at Oxford, you know.'

Harry looked back at the photograph and confronted the prosaic grin Minter had prepared for the camera. There he was again, where he had no business being: Clare Mallender's fiancé as well as Virginia Dysart's lover.

The fawning yelps of the dalmatian and the beating of its wagging tail against the door were what first alerted Harry to the fact that they were no longer alone. When he looked up, it was to see Charlie Mallender standing in the room, his face twitching with anger.

'Why Charles,' said Marjorie, glancing round at him. 'You're back earlier than I expected.'

'Passed him in the lane,' Charlie said, pointing at Harry. 'Couldn't place his face, though, until I got to the golf club. Reckoned he must be coming here. Came back at once.' It was obvious from his voice that he was trying to control himself in his wife's presence. 'Must ask you to step out here, Barnett. Straightaway.'

'But Charles—'

'Stay out of this, woman.' The self-control had not lasted long: his tone now was harsh and peremptory. 'Barnett!'

Judging that nothing was to be gained by contesting the point, Harry rose and moved towards the door. As he passed the end of the settee, Marjorie caught his eye and conveyed, by the directness of her gaze and the faintest nod of her head, that she at least was prepared to believe he was acting in good faith.

As soon as Harry reached the hall, Charlie Mallender closed the lounge door behind them and rounded on him. 'What the hell do you mean by coming here and upsetting my wife?'

'She's not upset.'

'Well I am. Now get out.' He moved abruptly to the front door and flung it open. 'Well? What are you waiting for?'

'Listen, Charlie—'

'Not another word! Get out of my home.'

Quick to rile and slow to listen: it had been the man's way as an employer and Harry should have known it would be the same where his family was concerned. Charlie Mallender subscribed to the philosophy of being as scornful of his inferiors as he was sycophantic to his superiors; there was no doubt into which category he had placed Harry.

'Get out, damn you!'

Harry walked as far as the threshold, then turned to Charlie and said: 'I might be able to help you find

Heather. Doesn't that interest you at all? It certainly interests your wife.'

'Heather's dead and we're trying to come to terms with that fact. What my wife doesn't need is false hopes and empty promises – which is all you have to offer.'

'How can you be sure she's dead? She might simply have run away.'

'She had nothing to run away from. She had everything she could possibly want.'

Except, thought Harry, a sympathetic father. 'There's something I don't understand about your family. You and your son in particular. I almost get the impression you'd prefer Heather to be dead than—'

The sharp intake of Charlie's breath, the sudden widening of his eyes and the speed with which he swept back his right arm as if to lash out struck Harry dumb. They stared at each other in silence for a moment, each contemplating and recoiling from the possibility of violence and what it might signify. Then Charlie Mallender said, in a tone so subdued as to render it more threatening still: 'I should have handed you over to the police ten years ago, Barnett, rather than just sack you. I blame myself for being too damned reasonable.'

'Don't give me that. You must know Roy set me up.' Old quarrels and ancient grievances: why did they matter more than a straightforward concern for Heather's safety? Harry did not know, but clearly it was so.

'Are you leaving?' said Charlie levelly. 'Or do I have to phone the police as I should have done then?'

It was inevitable Harry would fare worse if the police became involved. Surrendering to the force of that threat if to no other, he stepped over the threshold. As he turned round to deliver a final goading remark, the door crashed shut in his face, setting the knocker and letterbox rattling.

Slamming doors, averted eyes, unanswered questions: each successive reverse was, in its way, a victory, Harry

154

told himself as he walked away down the drive. Evasion and discouragement greeted him wherever he went, but only reinforced his certainty: he was on truth's winding trail and his stubborn inquisitive nature would not let him abandon it.

17

Harry took his leave of Ernie Love the following morning
and presented himself at the Jubilee Clock twenty minutes early for his rendezvous with Nigel Mossop. The
Promenade was empty of people at such an hour on a
Sunday. The gulls were in good voice, however, soaring
and shrieking overhead in a fickle, shifting breeze, and
Harry was surprised how contented if not downright happy
he felt, sitting in the shelter nearest the clock and gazing
out at the white horses in the bay.

His mood was one of puzzlement mixed with hope.
Resisted and resented though he had been at every turn,
he nonetheless detected a direction to his enquiries that
promised to become an unwavering course. Nor was the
thought that he alone might hold the key to the mystery
the sole component in his strangely elated state. Two nights
under the same roof as Ernie Love had, he suspected,
sealed his condition, for Ernie represented the squalor
and futility to which his own life could so easily have
led but for the sense of purpose looking for Heather
had brought to it. Though whether purpose was the
correct description of his motivation he rather doubted.
Something more stubbornly personal, something closer to
the rot within him he was determined to stop, lay perhaps
rather nearer the mark.

Suddenly, a car horn sounded from close by. When
Harry looked round, it was to see that Mossop too was
early for their appointment.

'Didn't . . . didn't sleep very well,' Mossop confessed, as soon as Harry had climbed into the car. 'W-Worried.'

'What about?'

'Not . . . sure.' He smiled nervously. 'That made it worse.'

On the back seat was a waterproof coat, a sandwich box, an ornithological guidebook and a pair of binoculars. Evidently Mossop had done his best to deceive his mother, though Harry suspected his blinking, stammering parade of insecurity was bound to have betrayed him.

'Where . . . where to, then?'

'Wherever you went on Sunday the twenty-eighth of August, Nige. I'm in your hands.'

As confirmation of the significance Harry had detected in Heather's photographs, Mossop's retraced route of three months before could not have made a better start. He had collected Heather from the Portesham turn-off on the Bridport road, not from Sabre Rise itself, which smacked of subterfuge from the very start. They had then returned to Weymouth and diverted to the crematorium, where Heather had left the car just long enough to take a photograph.

The site of the second photograph on the film was thus their first port of call. Leaving Mossop sitting in his car, Harry took a slow, considered circuit of the red-brick chapel set amidst tended lawns and flowerbeds on a summit above the town. Hereabouts, Beryl Love's ashes must have been scattered beneath a rose bush, though he knew better than to think Ernie might have invested in a memorial plaque. Clare Mallender's commemoration was, however, a different story. Down the third row of stones he tried in the garden of remembrance, he found the spot where Heather had raised the camera to her eye and captured the second image in the sequence he was seeking to follow. CLARE THOMASINA MALLENDER, 1959-1987. It was a natural subject for a grieving sister, a fitting start to her journey – and for Harry's.

Back on the road, they headed east in silence, Harry's

mind registering with calm intensity every mile and vista of their route, as if this process alone would bring him closer to what Heather had been thinking. It was noon by the time they reached Beaulieu, a smug little New Forest village at the head of the Beaulieu estuary, but Harry was too eager for progress to permit the halt for lunch that Mossop had enjoyed with Heather. Instead, they drove south, down the western side of the estuary, to a pull-in at the end of a lane, whence Mossop and Heather had walked down to the river's edge and taken the third photograph.

The scene had been altered only by the season. The trees were bare now, the reeds forlorn, the sky a disgruntled grey. Otherwise, with Mossop standing by the river's edge, ill-at-ease and chattering furiously, Harry could envisage the previous occasion without difficulty. Tyler's Hard stood out even more clearly on the opposite bank now the trees were no longer in leaf: the jetty, the lane-end, the white-walled cottage where Dysart spent his constituency weekends. Heather had borrowed his binoculars, Mossop said, and studied the cottage through them for some time. Perhaps, Harry thought, she had been checking to see if Dysart were in residence, looking for his car or some such sign of his presence. Presumably she had seen nothing to deter her from taking a closer look.

But she had not, Mossop revealed, gone straight to Tyler's Hard. Instead, they had driven on eastwards, beyond the last heath of the New Forest as far as the housing estates fringing Fawley Oil Refinery, on one of which lived Molly Diamond, Dysart's cleaning lady.

Mossop could not remember the address and it required several false starts and wrong turnings before they located the right house, one grey-dashed end-of-terrace dwelling among the featureless many that spread like silt round the fenced-off acres of pipelines and flares. Mossop, faithful both to preference and history, remained in the car whilst Harry walked up the front path, trying to ignore the ravenous alsatian growling and tearing at the neighbour's fence.

A grease-smeared youth answered the door, accompanied by a gust of rock music and an aroma of gravy. When Harry asked if 'Mrs Molly Diamond' was at home, the youth slouched back along the passage, shouted 'Ma' once at the top of his voice, then carried on without change of pace towards a dismantled motorcycle Harry could see beyond the back door.

In response to the call, an aproned figure peered at Harry from the kitchen, then bustled towards him, wiping her hands in a towel as she came. She looked like a once proud young woman waging an unequal struggle against slatternly middle age, her hands red from labour and her face grey with exhaustion, but her eyes preserving some yet-to-be extinguished sparkle of ambition. She seemed inclined to give Harry short shrift, but at his mention of Heather's name, she relented and showed him into the front room, where a meagre measure of calm and quiet prevailed.

'I read about 'er disappearance, o'course,' she began. 'It proper upset me, I can tell you, when they said she was probably dead. Such a nice, polite, *well-bred* young woman. Are you related?'

'Er, no. A friend. The name's Barn—' Harry hesitated, then decided to risk a lie. 'Barnes. Horace Barnes.'

'What can I do for you, Mr Barnes?'

'Well, all Heather's friends and relatives have racked their brains for clues as to what might have become of her, as you can imagine, and I remembered her mentioning visiting you here a few months ago.'

'She told you 'bout that?' A doubtful look crossed Mrs Diamond's face.

'Er, yes. Yes, she did.'

'You do surprise me.'

'Really? Why?'

'I got the impression she'd not 'ave wanted anyone to know about it. She told me . . . . ' Hesitation slowly became determined silence; the line of her mouth tightened.

'Told you what?'

'I don't know as I can say.'

Harry tried to assume an appealing expression. 'Your discretion does you credit, Mrs Diamond. In normal circumstances, I wouldn't ask you to break a confidence. But these aren't normal circumstances, are they?'

A moment of frowning consideration preceded the grudging reply. 'Reckon they're not, no.'

'And doesn't it reassure you to know she told *me* about coming here when she kept it from her family?'

By now, however, Mrs Diamond was ready with a challenge of her own. 'What did she tell you, then? Why did she say she came 'ere?'

'To see where her sister had died and to speak to those who'd witnessed her death.'

'And that's all she said?'

'Yes. Do you mean there was some other reason?'

'No . . . .'

A little encouragement seemed in order. 'If it helps you make up your mind, Mrs Diamond, I should tell you that I'm a friend of Heather's rather than a friend of her family . . . if you see what I mean.'

'It's not them I'm—' She broke off, stared at him intently for a moment, then said: 'What do you know about me, Mr . . . Mr Barnes?'

'Nothing, beyond the fact that you do some housekeeping for Alan Dysart at Tyler's—'

'*Did* some 'ousekeeping. I don't anymore.'

'Oh, I didn't realize. Why, er . . . ?'

'Not since June of last year.'

'You mean not since Clare Mallender's death?'

She nodded in confirmation, but showed no inclination to expand on the fact.

'It was very upsetting, I suppose.'

'That weren't the reason,' she snapped.

All of this, it seemed to Harry, was beside the point. He was about to make an attempt to steer the conversation back to Heather's visit in August when, in a sudden rush, Mrs Diamond reached the limit of her reticence and revealed what he did not doubt she had also revealed to Heather.

'Mr Dysart paid over the odds for charring, and my Wilfrid thought I was mad to give it up, but I was glad to go, believe you me, glad to be out of that house for good and all. What 'appened there on the first of June last year weren't just a tragedy, oh no. It were also wrong, plain wrong. It weren't the way everyone said an' thought it was, you see, not by a long chalk. An' I should know, 'cos I was there. D'you remember what the papers and TV said about it, Mr Barnes?'

'Well, not exactly. I understood—'

'Beautiful Miss Clare Mallender blown up by the IRA in mistake for Mr Dysart. 'ighly thought of. Much admired. The model secretary. Well, that's not 'ow I remember 'er. 'ard little bitch she was, take my word for it. 'ard as nails an' cunning as a vixen. As for Mr Dysart finding 'er indispensible, well that's not my recollection. They 'ated each other: I could see it in their eyes. And they fought like cat and dog at times. Even that last morning. There was a terrible row between 'em just before she went out to the boat an' got blown up, God rest 'er soul. But did any of that come out at the inquest? No, it did not. Was I called as a witness? No, I was not. So, what do you make of that, Mr Barnes, eh? What do you make of that?'

'I don't know, Mrs Diamond. I suppose nobody wants to speak ill of the dead.'

'Huh! That's all you know. That Morpurgo, for one, 'e never did anything else.'

'Morpurgo?'

'Mr Dysart's caretaker, 'andyman, call 'im what you like. Lives in a room over the garage at Tyler's 'ard. 'as the place to 'imself when Mr Dysart's not there, o' course, which is most o' the time.'

Harry had never heard of the man, but his status and circumstances sounded disturbingly similar to his own. 'Was Morpurgo present when Clare Mallender was killed?'

161

"Course 'e was. Never stirred far from Tyler's 'ard in my experience. Me and Mr Dysart were in the kitchen and Morpurgo was in the garden when it 'appened. I'd seen Miss Mallender walking out along the pontoon to the boat and I'd turned away from the window over the sink to 'and Mr Dysart 'is coffee when there was this great *whoomph* outside. All the windows that side o' the 'ouse shattered and then there was just silence for 'alf a minute or so. Next thing you could 'ear bits of wood and such – bits of the boat, like – falling into the river. An' a crackling of flames, 'cos the pontoon 'ad caught fire and some o' the wreckage was ablaze as well. An' I looked at Mr Dysart an' 'e looked at me and we both knew what 'ad 'appened without going to see. A bit o' glass 'ad caught him on the fore'ead, but otherwise we 'adn't a scratch to show for it between us. Yet we knew, right enough – knew by instinct, I s'pose – that Miss Mallender was dead.'

'It must have been dreadful,' Harry said lamely. 'But what has this to do with—'

'We ran out there, o' course, but it was obvious she was beyond 'elp. There was nothing left of the boat, let alone Miss Mallender – which was a mercy in its way, I s'pose. Still, Mr Dysart went to see what 'e could do, while I went back to phone for the police. I passed Morpurgo on the way. 'E'd come running from the back garden and we nearly bumped into each other coming round the corner of the 'ouse. That's 'ow I can be so sure, you see. That's 'ow I can be so certain about the expression on 'is face. 'e was smiling, Mr Barnes, smiling like a cat who's got the cream, smiling like 'e was pleased by what 'ad 'appened. That shook me, I can tell you. That chilled me in a way I can't properly describe. I 'aven't been back to Tyler's 'ard from that day to this – I couldn't bear to. It's not because of the explosion: it's not delayed shock, or anything like that. It's because the whole thing was off kilter in some way, not what it seemed, not what people thought it was, not . . . well, just not *right*.'

Quite what Mrs Diamond meant to convey by the phrase

'not right' was as impenetrable as it was incontrovertible. Harry would have felt inclined to dismiss it as the invention of a hysterical mind but for the fact that Mrs Diamond's mind was clearly anything but hysterical. She was neither rich enough nor impressionable enough to have walked out on a well-paid job simply in order to indulge a vapourish mood. Even to Harry, then, her reaction to Clare Mallender's death seemed too sincere to be ignored. As to its effect on Heather, struggling to shake off nervous depression and come to terms with her sister's loss, that could only be imagined.

'I said a few words to Miss Mallender – Miss Heather Mallender, that is – at her sister's funeral, last year. I thought at the time she made nought of it, but back last summer, like you say, round August bank 'oliday, she came to see me and asked me to tell 'er everything I remembered 'bout the day of the explosion. Surprised me, it did, 'ow little I'd forgotten. It was all still lodged there, every moment of it, in me mind. The noise the bomb made. That 'ollow, sickening *whoomph*. And the flames all round the pontoon. And, later, the wailing of the police sirens, the flashing of their blue lights, the crackle of their radios. But all that's nothing, really, compared with Morpurgo's smile.'

'Why do you think he was smiling?'

'Why? Well, if I knew that, Mr Barnes, I'd know what it was that wasn't right that day, wouldn't I?'

'Couldn't you just have asked him?'

'I see you don't know the man. Well, as it 'appens, I did ask 'im, in a roundabout way, later that day.'

'What did he say?'

'Nothing.'

'Nothing at all?'

'He just smiled, Mr Barnes. Smiled like 'e did before, like 'e was pleased as punch about something. That's what got to me: Miss Mallender only a few hours dead – and Morpurgo smiling.'

There was no need to ask Mossop where he and Heather

163

had gone after leaving Fawley. She must have been seized, thought Harry, by the same curiosity that gripped him now. Who was Morpurgo? Why had he smiled? What had not been right that day? They drove cautiously, navigating from Mossop's memory, down the narrow lanes towards the Beaulieu estuary, past fringes of forest, paddocks, pasture and mellow creamy-red cottages.

'You're very q-quiet,' Mossop said, after they had driven in silence for a mile or so.

Harry did not reply. He hoped the young man would relapse into muteness and leave him to read the privilege and privacy imbedded in this landscape, to note the pampered thoroughbreds grazing beyond the fences and glimpse their owners' residences tucked down driveways discreetly screened by firs. There was something in the train of his thoughts, he sensed, that pointed to the answer he sought.

'It's odd . . . really, I remember Heather was . . . quite chatty . . . over lunch. But, after we'd been to see Mrs Diamond, she was like you . . . . Well, like you are now.'

Harry tried to shut Mossop's stumbling remarks out of his head, to concentrate instead on Heather's words, the last words, in fact, that she had ever spoken to him. '*I can't turn back now, can I?*' Was this the moment, he wondered, on this dank pine-shuttered road to Tyler's Hard, that she had realized, for the first time, that there truly was no turning back, that the momentum of her progress towards whatever awaited her on Profitis Ilias had become irresistible?

A Range Rover pulling a horsebox sped towards them round the next bend, straddling the middle of the lane and causing Mossop to swerve through a muddy ditch at the roadside. The splash of the water against the wheel and the splatter of it across the windscreen recalled to Harry's mind the sound of falling water that had drawn him in a dream up the stairs of the *Villa ton Navarkhon*: a dream of statues made flesh, of messages concealed in images, of meetings both expected and located, amounting to what all logic suggests they cannot be: *rendezvous* to which one has already unconsciously agreed.

Suddenly, they were there. A single-track lane had taken them down through a straggling copse to a brackish meander of the Beaulieu river and Mossop had stopped the car just short of the cottage so they could see the building, the garden, the overgrown jetty which had given it its name and the shadowed finger of the pontoon reaching out into deeper water, without themselves being seen at all.

'Did you go in with her, Nige?'

'N-No. I waited here. She didn't . . . didn't want company.'

'I daresay she didn't.'

Harry climbed from the car, closed the door as quietly as he could and began to walk along the lane. He felt a measure of guilt for visiting Tyler's Hard without Dysart's knowledge, but the impetus of his curiosity more than overcame it. Coming to the gate, he looked in at the cottage and instantly recognized the fourth photograph in Heather's collection. It could have been taken, he reckoned, from the very spot where he was standing, capturing the scene much as it now was, altered only by the onset of winter. Double gates to his right led to the garage, a modern construction complete with first-floor flat served by an external staircase and styled to resemble the cottage itself, which lay straight ahead of him, evidently well cared-for in the absence of its owner. To Harry's left, the lane petered out in a gravel track curving round past the garden hedge to serve the jetty. Peering out along the pontoon, he could see the contrasting starkness of new wood at its farther end, the only trace in all this orderly solitude of what had occurred there eighteen months before.

Harry pushed open the gate and walked in. Then he hesitated, uncertain whether to try the cottage, the garage flat or the rear garden. A curl of smoke from a bonfire behind the house clinched the issue. As he followed the path that led towards it between bare-branched shrubs and sturdy evergreens, he fancied for a moment that he would

165

come upon Morpurgo and find him a replica of himself, some *doppelgänger* of Dysart's devising planted here in England whilst he had been banished to Rhodes. When he passed through an ivy-clad trellis arch and saw the man he sought, however, raking dead leaves and twigs into an incinerator, he realized how absurd the idea was that they could somehow be twin actors of the same part who had never met on stage till this unscripted moment. Between them, he discerned at once, there could flourish no hint of fellowship.

Morpurgo – Harry did not doubt that it *was* Morpurgo – was a tall, awkward-looking figure in beret, muddied boiler suit and galoshes, feeding the incinerator with needless energy, forcing the rake-held bundles down into its smoking contents with disquieting relish, with an intensity, indeed, which warned Harry from the first that something was amiss.

He did not look up as Harry approached, but went on working with the zeal and single-mindedness of one who is totally absorbed. The smoke from the incinerator made Harry blink and cough, but Morpurgo, who was stooped over the very top of it, seemed unaffected and still he paid his visitor no heed.

'Excuse me . . . . Mr Morpurgo?'

There was no response.

'Mr Morpurgo?'

At last, there was a reaction. Holding down the latest addition to the incinerator with the prongs of his rake, Morpurgo slowly turned his head to look at Harry over his left shoulder. Harry nearly jumped back in surprise and flushed instantly in embarrassment at the distaste his flinching movement had signalled. Where Morpurgo's left eye should have been was only a sickening fold of flesh. The cheekbone too, and much of the left side of his face, had vanished into this ill-defined cleft, leaving the nose twisted and the mouth distorted. An area which was presumably more hideous still, in the vicinity of the ear and temple, was obscured by the tugged-down band of his beret. As for his right eye, this was a perfect startling blue, gazing out blankly from beneath a solitary tuft of eyebrow.

'Good . . . good afternoon.'

With a sudden lunging wrench, Morpurgo swung the rake free of the incinerator. For an instant, Harry thought he might be about to attack. Some snatch of verse from a Jacobean tragedy flashed through his mind: '*When I look into the fishponds in my garden, methinks I see a thing, armed with a rake, that seems to strike at me.*' Then his misapprehension was explained. Morpurgo slammed the instrument down on the pathway and leaned against it, breathing heavily and fixing Harry with his cyclopean stare. There was clearly some disability to add to his disfigurement, as physical as it might well be mental.

'My name's . . . . Well, it doesn't matter.' An obvious lie occurred to him. 'I'm looking for Alan Dysart.'

Morpurgo's mouth had begun to twitch in painful preparation to speak. When the words came, they were hissed and halting, each of them separately delivered and stressed and they were in answer to Harry's first remark as if those that had followed had not yet been absorbed.

'I-am-Morpurgo.'

'Ah, splendid.' Cursing himself for sounding so patronizing, Harry felt a wave of pity wash over him. Morpurgo was some harmless retarded constituent for whom Dysart had provided employment and accommodation. Or perhaps some Falklands veteran crippled in mind and body while serving on Dysart's ship. Either way, the smile Mrs Diamond had complained about was no more than a grim legacy of drastic surgery. What was 'not right' was no more sinister than the inarticulacy of a maimed human.

'Good-afternoon.'

'Good afternoon to you.' Harry grinned fatuously.

'Alan-is-not-here.'

'Oh, I see. Another time perhaps.'

'Yes.-Another-time.'

Harry made some weak farewell gesture with his arm, then turned to go. There was no point, he felt sure, in prolonging the conversation. It would prove as anti-climactic as Heather must herself have found it. He walked back along the path, rebuking himself for entertaining Mrs Diamond's lurid notions. Perhaps she had allowed a horror of Morpurgo's appearance to bias her judgement. Perhaps . . . .

Abruptly, Harry pulled up. It was when he had pictured Morpurgo in his mind's eye that it had occurred to him: such a trivial matter, yet nonetheless not right, not right at all – surely he must be mistaken. He turned round to find that Morpurgo had not moved. He was still leaning on the rake, gazing along the path towards him and, even at a distance of several yards, Harry could see that he was not mistaken. Beneath the boiler suit Morpurgo wore a shirt and tie. The shirt looked frayed and stained. But the tie was what seized his attention. Its pattern was a simple one: wide equal diagonal stripes of pink and white. Cerise and silver, Heather had corrected him. Cerise and silver, like the scarf she had lost on Profitis Ilias. '*It belonged to my sister actually*.' That phrase of Heather's, snatched from a context he could not recall, alighted in his memory.

'Was-there-something-else?' asked Morpurgo.

'No. That is . . . . Your tie: I couldn't help noticing it.'

'My-tie?'

'Yes. It's very . . . distinctive.'

Morpurgo pulled the end of the tie out from the boiler suit and stared down at it, frowning in puzzlement.

'Where did you get it? Was it a gift from somebody?'

Morpurgo looked up. 'No,' he said with heavy emphasis.

'You know: a present?'

'Not-a-present.-It's-mine.-I-earned-it.'

'You earned it?'

'Yes. At-uni-' He paused, then tried again. 'At-university.'

'Which university was that?'

'Oxford.'

Connections flashed through Harry's mind. The scarf had belonged to Clare Mallender. It had the look of a college scarf. She had been to Oxford. She had met Jonathan Minter there. Perhaps they had attended the same college: the college whose colours were cerise and silver. And Morpurgo had been there too. And Morpurgo had smiled the day Clare was killed.

As he was smiling now. Some flood of childish pride as he pushed the tie back into the boiler suit and fondled the knot made Morpurgo grin at Harry: a chilling grin of fathomless delight; the same grin, beyond question, that had frightened Mrs Diamond. 'Goodbye,' he called, as Harry hurried away.

By the time Harry reached the gate into the lane, he was certain. The lure had been too compelling for Heather to resist and he had the photographs to prove it. Morpurgo must have been wearing the same tie the day she came to Tyler's Hard. Perhaps he always wore it. At all events, there could be no doubt that the courtyard pictured in the next photograph, the fifth on the film, belonged to the Oxford college whose colours were cerise and silver and whose past bound three people to their parallel fates. According to Mossop, Heather had been tight-lipped during the drive back to Weymouth. She had told him nothing of what her interviews with Mrs Diamond and Morpurgo had yielded and he had not pressed her to do so. Instead, he had dropped her outside the Half Moon in Portesham, exchanged with her a few platitudes about the working week to come, then driven home to Radipole in time for tea with his mother. He had thought no more about their excursion until Heather's disappearance had recalled it to his mind – and been followed by Harry's visit.

None of this surprised Harry. Heather would have been as disinclined to confide in Mossop as he was himself. The young man was merely a means to an end and, in both cases, that end had now been served. Harry had Mossop drop him off at Brockenhurst station, where he commenced the journey back to Swindon, happy to find himself alone among anonymous travellers, able to concentrate at last on all the implications of what he had learned.

Morpurgo was too old to be a contemporary of Clare Mallender's: he was closer to Dysart in age. Since Dysart too had been to Oxford, it was possible that by taking Morpurgo on at Tyler's Hard he had merely been doing an old chum a favour. War service of some kind would account both for Morpurgo's disabilities and for Dysart's generosity. If theirs was the same college attended by Clare Mallender, that might be explained by Dysart recommending it to her at her father's request. So far so inconsequential, but Heather would have been quite capable of deducing as much herself. Yet the photographs proved it had not stopped her pursuing her curiosity to Oxford.

The rail journey to Swindon involved no fewer than three changes, at Southampton, Basingstoke and Reading. During the trudging to and fro along echoing subways and draughty platforms that this necessitated, Harry began to notice, for all his preoccupation, that a man who had boarded the train with him at Brockenhurst was making the same complicated series of connections. At first, he thought little of it, assuming that their parallel paths, like those of all travellers, would eventually diverge. Joining not only the same train as him but the same carriage twice could be dismissed as a coincidence. When it happened for a third time, it became remarkable enough to distract him from a rapt analysis of Heather's reasoning. At Reading, however, he felt sure that the coincidence would snap.

It did not. Less than ten yards away from Harry as he waited for the Swindon train, the same man stood examining paperbacks on a bookstall. Thin, slope-shouldered, raincoated and thoroughly inconspicuous, he could easily have been an innocent Sunday evening wayfarer, but for the fact that Harry was now convinced he was not.

The Swindon train arrived. Harry boarded it and the man followed, selecting a seat several rows distant but facing Harry down the open carriage. He seemed to make no use of this position for the purposes of observation, keeping his eyes trained instead on the pages of the paperback be had bought at Reading. It was soft-core pornography, to judge by the girl in black underwear featured on the cover, and it appeared to have riveted the man's attention. His salacious choice of reading matter somehow reassured Harry, who, deeming his nerves to be in need of calming, made his way to the buffet and bought two drinks: a scotch, which he downed at the counter, and a beer, which he bore back to his seat.

As he moved past the man's shoulder on his way back, Harry could not help glancing down at the book. The man was in the act of turning a page, and, in so doing, he momentarily exposed its front cover, which Harry had, till now, only seen at a distance. With a start, he saw that the girl in black underwear was slumped, dead, across a couch and that she had been strangled with a scarf, which was still knotted around her neck.

Harry stumbled to his seat. Why did it have to be a scarf? he wondered. Why did this man he had just begun to believe had no interest in him have to have chosen that book among the dozens of others? The coincidence was as incredible as its alternative, for if . . . . Suddenly, Harry realized that the train was slowing. Glancing out of the window, he saw they were drawing into Didcot station, the only stop before Swindon. A way out of his dilemma at once presented itself to his mind. Yielding to the impulse, he rose and hurried towards the door.

The man did not follow. As Harry stood on the platform a minute or so later, watching the train pull out, he could see him through the brightly lit window, still immersed in his paperback, oblivious, it seemed, to Harry's departure. It was foolish, he told himself, ever to have supposed anybody might be following him, yet the hour he was destined to spend on a chill damp station, awaiting the next Swindon train, was not entirely wasted. At least it proved that his suspicions were groundless. It proved it almost beyond question.

171

18

Sooner than he had expected, Harry found himself back in Swindon Central Library, this time perusing the national newspapers for 2 June 1987 in the hope of gleaning from them some clue as to what had eluded him on his visit to Tyler's Hard.

Their reports of the attempt on Alan Dysart's life were, however, as similar as they were familiar. Harry felt as if he had heard or read them all before, in one form or another, and none of them shed any light on what had struck Mrs Diamond as 'not right':

The IRA yesterday claimed responsibility for the bomb outrage at the New Forest cottage owned by Alan Dysart, Parliamentary Under-Secretary of State for . . . .

The IRA admitted yesterday that it had mistakenly killed secretary Clare Mallender instead of their intended victim, Alan Dysart, the junior Defence minister, by planting a bomb aboard Mr Dysart's yacht . . . .

The peace of a New Forest riverside was shattered yesterday by another addition to the sorry record of IRA terrorism on the British mainland . . . .

Alan Dysart, the outspoken junior Defence minister, yesterday insisted that attempts on his life would not deter him from denouncing those seeking to overthrow democracy in Northern Ireland . . . .

On inner pages, there were tributes from friends and relatives to 'Clare Mallender, the beautiful and talented girl who lost her life in an explosion meant for her employer . . . . , '"It's hard to believe such a vivacious personality is lost to us",' Dysart was quoted as saying, '"and harder still to accept that the stand I have taken against terrorism may have brought about her death."' But Charlie Mallender, fighting back tears according to one reporter, had flown to Dysart's aid: '"Grief-stricken though we are, we take comfort from the fact that Clare had always wholeheartedly supported Alan Dysart's campaign . . . . "' And the editorials were unanimous: 'This appalling act will deflect neither the government in general nor, we suspect, Mr Dysart in particular from their principled rejection of the objectives of its perpetrators . . . . ' There was no mention anywhere of Morpurgo or Mrs Diamond by name, nor hint in anything Harry read that all was not as it appeared to be.

A night's sleep and this blank trawl of the news columns had considerably undermined Harry's confidence in what he was doing. The photographs might represent a wild goose chase after the random neuroses of an insecure young woman. He had only known Heather for a few weeks, after all, and may well have been deceived by the impression she had created in Rhodes' alien environment. Suppositions built on postcards and photographs might be as ill-founded as his short-lived suspicions of being followed the night before.

It was thus in a disillusioned, self-reproachful mood that Harry walked back to Falmouth Street. Absorbed in his own thoughts, he paid no attention to the purple saloon car parked at the roadside just short of number thirty-seven until, as he made his way past it, the driver's door was pushed abruptly open to block his path.

A hard-faced young man stepped out and engaged him with a fixed stare. 'Harry Barnett?'

'Er, yes.'

'Police.' A warrant card was briefly flourished. 'Get in the back, please, sir.'

'Well, I—'

'Get in!'

Harry obeyed. The seat he climbed into was the only empty one in the car. To his left was a heavily built grey-haired man, who looked straight ahead. The driver did the same. The man in the front passenger seat turned round, however, and grinned at Harry with cold-eyed hostility. 'Lovely weather for the time of year, eh?' he said, disregarding the fact that it was depressingly grey and damp.

'What's this all—'

'You've just got back from Rhodes, we hear.'

'Yes, but—'

'Bring back anything you shouldn't?'

'What do you mean?'

'Drugs, that kind of thing.'

'Of course not.'

'We wouldn't find any suspicious substances, then, if we turned over your mother's house?'

'Of course you wouldn't. What makes you—'

'Shut up!' The grey-haired man beside Harry had spoken and now he turned his jowled and pitted face towards him. 'Listen to me, Barnett. The Greek police couldn't nail you for anything, but we're not quite so fussy over technicalities. On the other hand, we're not unreasonable. We won't feel obliged to put you under the microscope unless you force us to, but, if we do, we'll find something nasty, take if from me. So, my advice is: don't force us to.'

'How am I—'

'Shut up!' He glared at Harry for a moment in silence, then resumed. 'If the Mallender family hear from you just once more, directly or indirectly, by telephone, letter or in person, by any means whatsoever, we'll come down on you so hard you'll think a giant had stamped on your head. Drugs are only one way. Your old ma might take up shoplifting. You might try it on with a girl in the park

174

who turns out to be a policewoman in disguise. Either way, you'll find yourself in it right up to your neck, get my drift? If so, just nod.'

Harry knew he should have felt indignation at this crude evidence of Charlie and Roy Mallender pulling strings, not to mention a certain satisfaction that they thought they needed to pull them, but all he could detect within himself was a sickening clutch of fear. Hard-nosed policemen in unmarked cars belonged to a world of violence and intimidation he had no wish to enter. In his stomach there churned a disabling sense of his own vulnerability. He nodded dumbly.

'On your way, then, sir,' said the grinning occupant of the front passenger seat.

Harry climbed out onto the pavement. The door slammed behind him and the car moved off. Harry watched it until it had turned into Emlyn Square, then began walking unsteadily in the same direction. He did not turn in at the door of number thirty-seven, however. After what had happened, quite a different destination seemed appropriate.

Two hours later, full of beer and bravado, Harry contemplated a reflection of himself in the mirror behind the bar of the Glue Pot Inn and calculated that, even when sobriety had returned to drain away his courage, he would not change his mind. If Roy and Charlie Mallender had hoped to frighten him, they had succeeded. But they had also demonstrated, by their eagerness to deflect him from it, that his was no fool's errand. As a result, fear was no longer enough. It had come too late to be effective. Wherever Heather's photographs led, he was determined now to follow.

19

Though Oxford was less than thirty miles from Swindon, Harry had been there only twice before. A school visit to the Ashmolean and a business trip to Morris Motors comprised his entire experience of the city. His unfamiliarity with it was not, however, the result of indifference. He had, in fact, long cherished a secret fantasy in which he had joined the privileged ranks of Oxford undergraduates, racketed through three glorious years of academic and sexual triumphs, then gone on to lead the kind of effortlessly successful life from which working-class origins and a foreshortened education had in reality excluded him.

Alan Dysart was the model for what Harry imagined he could have been, given the advantages bestowed by an Oxford career. He too, it seemed in his more envious moments, could easily have become an officer and a gentleman, if only his father had been as wealthy as Dysart's, if only he had applied himself to his studies at Commonweal, if only . . . .

But life, as Harry had learned, did not function according to the principles of wish-fulfilment. It insisted that irrevocable decisions be made before their consequences could be appreciated. It ensured there was no turning back, no switching to alternative paths, no way of avoiding the future it had prepared. And no possibility of resisting the force which drew him on, through Oxford's Christmas-lit streets, beneath the gilded spires and haughty cupolas of a world which had denied him, towards the next link in the chain.

The window of a tailor's shop halfway along the High Street was where he found it, in an ample display of college scarves, ties and blazer crests. Harry went in, enquired and was given, with no more than an eyebrow-twitch of puzzlement, a comprehensive catalogue of Shepherd & Woodward's university wares. He did not turn to the centre-spread of college colours until he was outside again, guessing that he would need the privacy of a crowded pavement in which to confront a discovery that was as chilling as it was unsurprising.

Cerise and silver in four equal stripes, vertical for the scarf and diagonal for the tie, were the colours of Breakspear College, Oxford. Dysart's old college. And Clare Mallender's. And Minter's. And Morpurgo's. The connection was made, forged beyond the power of pure chance to explain. Dysart had referred to it often enough while working in Swindon. *'I'm at Breakspear. Why don't you look in some time during term, Harry?'* Harry never had, of course. The contrast between Dysart's carefree existence and his own would have been too much to bear. But he had remembered – the name and all that went with it. Heather had been this way before him, had seen and understood what he would shortly see and might yet understand. There was not a doubt in his mind as to where she had taken the fifth picture on the film.

Breakspear was both more venerable and less ostentatious than most colleges. Its low-arched entrance off one of the narrow lanes linking High Street and Broad Street could easily have been overlooked had Harry not been intent on locating it. Founded 1259, open to visitors during daylight hours, it proclaimed itself with the modesty of an institution whose confidence in its purposes was rock-solid. And there, in its first and oldest quadrangle, Harry found what he sought. Worn flagstones and an oblong of sodden grass surrounded by grey-stoned walls, leaded windows and the lower treads of spiral stairs glimpsed through open doorways was all that some would have seen. But Harry saw far more. He saw evidence and proof. He saw confirmation and encouragement.

He retreated to the porters' lodge and tapped on the window. A mottle-faced man with slicked-down hair slid back the glass panel and looked out at him enquiringly. He reminded Harry, in his build, expression and asthmatic wheeze, of a bulldog peering ill-humouredly from his kennel. To his apparent relief, he was able to direct Harry elsewhere.

'You'd best see the College Secretary, sir. Mrs Notley. Her office is at the bottom of K staircase.' There followed an elaborate consultation of a gold fob-watch. 'You *should* find her in.'

Mrs Notley was indeed at her post, tapping at the keys of a word processor which appeared to represent Breakspear's one concession to modernity. Harry swiftly discovered that she was impervious to charm, but a sense of duty evidently compelled her to answer his questions.

'Sixty-five to sixty-eight, you say?' (Harry had quoted Dysart's years as a starting point.) 'Morpurgo is an unusual name, so there should be no difficulty. Let me see.' She pulled down a bulky volume from the shelf beside her and thumbed through it. 'Yes, here we are. Morpurgo, W.V. Resident for the period you named. He took an unclassified degree in Modern Languages.'

'Why unclassified?'

'There could be many reasons. Illness, perhaps.'

Illness, yes: Harry supposed it could be called that. 'I wonder if you could look up somebody else. Clare Mallender, late seventies.'

Mrs Notley obliged. 'Miss C.T. Mallender. Resident 1977 to 1980. First-class degree in Philosophy, Politics and Economics.' The name began to stir her memory. 'Don't I know that—'

'And another,' Harry interrupted. 'Jonathan Minter. Same period.'

But here his deductions encountered their first contradiction. Minter had not been at Breakspear, exactly or even approximately contemporary with Clare Mallender. It was an insignificant point in its way, for Harry knew from Marjorie Mallender that Clare *had* met Minter whilst at Oxford – he must simply have been at another college – yet somehow his faith in his own reasoning was undermined. He returned to the quad, glumly debating with himself what to do next.

There were at least the photographs to fall back on. Drawing the wallet from his pocket, he separated the one of Breakspear from the rest and studied for a moment the view of the college it presented. Gazing about at the walls flanking the quad, it was possible to calculate the exact position where Heather had been standing when she took it: the extreme south-western corner. He walked across to it, turned and surveyed the scene. The angles and perspectives of what he saw were identical with those in the photograph. Yet still, stare about him as he might, they refused to yield their meaning.

As Harry stood there, lost in thought, the porter he had spoken to earlier appeared from the direction of the lodge, rattling a bunch of keys in his hand. At sight of Harry, he pulled up, frowned, then walked slowly across to him.

'Mrs Notley tell you what you wanted to know, sir?'

'Er, yes thanks.'

'You interested in the history of the college, then?'

'In a sense, yes.'

'We produce an informative guidebook on the subject.' He rattled the keys again. 'Very reasonably priced.'

'I'm sure it is, but I don't suppose it would contain the sort of history I'm interested in.'

'What sort might that be, then?' He sounded more amiable than before, more inclined to be helpful. Perhaps, it occurred to Harry, he was hoping for a tip.

'Well, tell me, how long have you worked here?'

'Twenty-six years, sir. Ever since I left the Marines.'

Harry's hopes rose: twenty-six years were sufficient for

179

his purposes. 'In that case, you'll remember the government minister, Alan Dysart, when he was a student here.'

'Of course I do, sir. A most likeable young gentleman.'

'And a contemporary of his named Morpurgo?'

'Morpurgo. Oh yes. Quite a friend of Mr Dysart's as I recall.' He shook his head. 'A sad case though, was Mr Morpurgo. Badly injured in a car accident in his final year.' Then he tapped his temple significantly. 'Never right afterwards, I'm afraid.'

'A car accident, you say?'

'Yes, sir. You know how these young gentlemen are when they get behind the wheel.' He sighed heavily.

'And in his final year?'

'Final term, as a matter of fact. Just a few weeks before the examinations. Trinity term of sixty-eight, it would have been. A sad time at Breakspear, that was.'

'Because of the car accident, you mean?'

'Not *just* because of the car accident, no, sir.'

'Then . . . what else?'

'Well, it's strange you should stand there and ask that question, sir, very strange indeed.'

'Why?'

'Because it was the same term – Trinity sixty-eight – when Mr Everett met his death in this very corner of the quad. Fell from a second-floor window smack down on the flagstones not a yard from where you're standing. He was in the same year as Mr Morpurgo – and Mr Dysart. That's why I say it was a sad time.'

But Harry was far from saddened by the porter's recollections. Heather had not chosen this corner of the quad at random. She had deliberately recorded on film the link her mind had established between her sister's death and that of a fellow-student of Morpurgo's twenty years before. Had he smiled that day too? Harry wondered. 'Which came first?' he asked, exerting himself not to sound too eager for the answer. 'The fall or the car crash?'

'Oh the fall, sir.'

'How did it happen?'

'Nobody every really knew. He was drunk, the window was open, he leant out for a breath of air, he fell: that was the general opinion.'

'And the car crash?'

'Oh, that was in a country lane somewhere. Mr Morpurgo was driving two other students back from a pub. Drunk, of course, and going like the clappers as they all do.'

'Was Mr Dysart one of the passengers?'

'Not as I recall, sir, no. They were . . . . Well, I'm pretty sure Dr Ockleton was one of them. Yes, I'm certain he was. As for the other—'

'Dr Ockleton?' Something in the porter's voice had suggested to Harry that the good doctor was particularly memorable.

'Yes, sir. He doesn't often speak of it these days, but—'

'You mean he's still here?'

'Oh yes. He was an undergraduate then, of course, but he stayed on for his doctorate, then became a fellow. A charming gentleman is Dr Ockleton. Very considerate to the staff.'

'And approachable?'

The porter smiled. 'Approachable?' he said, with a wheezing hint of ambiguity in his voice. 'Oh yes, sir. Dr Ockleton is *very* approachable.'

181

20

Early that afternoon, Harry returned to Breakspear College. He had been disappointed to find Dr Ockleton absent from his rooms in the morning, but a pretty girl in jogging kit, who had come loping down the stairs whilst he was knocking at Ockleton's door, had run on the spot long enough to tell him that the doctor lectured on Tuesday mornings and that Harry would probably have better luck after lunch.

Harry had adjourned to a small low-ceilinged pub in Broad Street to pass the interval, installed himself by the window, supped beer and watched the customers come and go: down-at-heel old soaks somewhat beyond his own position on the scale of decline; and garrulous little knots of students with faces as downily naïve as their opinions were falsely wise. Uncertain whether it was their extreme youth or their budding self-confidence which he envied more, Harry had recognized but not restrained his decline into drunken self-pity. Where was Heather? Why had she not returned? What would he not give to have her by his side, supplanting with her company all the resentment he felt now at the friendship of others? The truth, he had been morbidly inclined to conclude, was as remote as ever.

But the mood had passed by the time Harry walked once more into Breakspear College, sucking at an extra-strong mint and glad to see that a different porter was manning the lodge. He traversed the first quad, its flag-stones dented by seven centuries of learning, entered the slightly less ancient quad that lay beyond and ascended to Dr Ockleton's rooms. The outer door was open this time and a sonorous voice responded to his knock.

Cyril D.G. Ockleton, MA, PhD, looked even younger for his known age, circa forty, than Alan Dysart. Whereas Dysart had the bearing and features of an accomplished thirty-year-old, Ockleton lacked only short trousers and a catapault to pass for a skylarking schoolboy. It was as if, Harry reflected, Breakspear were some kind of Shangri-La, brief exposure to which ensured a stubborn youthfulness, prolonged exposure an accelerating regression to the cradle.

Ockleton's mop of jet black hair, his apple-cheeked face and the spectacles which had slid to the end of his nose combined with a tattered gown and a skew-knotted tie to create an impression of immaturity entirely at odds with his voice. Visually, he was a blinking caricature of arrested development, an owlish, overgrown nursling sheltered from the world. Vocally, however, he inhabited a different plane, some Olympian plateau of detached and perfect judgement whence the most trivial phrase descended as a profound statement of intellectual certitude.

'Can I help you? I don't believe we've met.' The limpid tones were those of a bishop addressing a beggar. Harry could have listened to this man for hours on end simply reading the telephone directory, yet one glance at his absurd and dishevelled appearance would instantly have broken the trance.

'My name's Harry Barnett.'

Ockleton grinned toothily. 'Regrettably, I am none the wiser.'

But Harry knew better. Wisdom was to this man as boredom was to others. And all attempts at deception would therefore be wasted. 'I'm a friend of Alan Dysart.'

Ockleton sprang from his chair, steered an unerring course through the piles of books and papers that littered his apartment and shook Harry clammily by the hand.

183

'Any friend of Alan's, Mr Barnett, etcetera, etcetera. What brings you to Oxford?'

'Heather Mallender.'

'Once more, I fear you have the advantage of me.'

'She disappeared last month, while staying in Alan's villa on Rhodes.'

'Ah, *that* Heather Mallender.' The incident had been a breakfast-time talking point in hall, his manner suggested. Without the incidental involvement of an old Breakspearean, it would not even have been that. Perhaps they did not take *The Courier* in the senior common room.

'I believe you know Heather.'

'Do you now?' Ockleton described a sweeping circuit of the room, missing all the many obstacles in his path without apparently noticing them, and finished by the window, where he peered out for a full minute or so at the view it commanded of a blank gable-end and half the dome of the Radcliffe Camera. Then he turned back and stared intently at Harry, his eyes gleaming like those of an aged eagle in his bizarrely fledgling face. 'You, of course, are Alan's *caretaker* on Rhodes.'

'Correct.'

'The last person to see Miss Mallender prior to her disappearance.'

'Yes.'

'She . . . mentioned me to you?'

'No.'

'Then—'

'She visited you here about three months ago. Late August or early September, I should guess. You told her something – something significant.'

Ockleton paused to consider a point that had apparently baffled him, then said: 'If Miss Mallender never referred to visiting me, Mr Barnett, what is there to make you think she *did* visit me?'

'I know she came to Oxford and I'm certain in my own mind that she came to Breakspear College. If she did, she won't have left without seeing you.'

'Why not?'

'Because you were a contemporary of a student named Morpurgo and were with him when he was injured in a car crash in the Trinity term of 1968. Because you were also a contemporary of a student named Everett who fell to his death from a window in the next quad a few weeks before the car crash. And because those two incidents are in some way related to the death of Heather's sister in June of last year.'

Ockleton frowned. 'Extraordinary.' Then he smiled. 'I congratulate you, Mr Barnett, on teasing out this line of reasoning. It defeats me, I must confess, but clearly there is some strand in it that you are determined to follow. As was Miss Mallender.'

'You admit she came here, then?'

'I never denied it.' He crossed to a disorderly desk, tugged out a diary from amongst the academic detritus and began leafing through it. 'Here we are. Saturday the third of September. Yes, indeed. A showery day, as I recall. Miss Mallender called at eleven. She wanted to talk to me about her sister. Clare was a student of mine, you know, and I was naturally distressed by the circumstances of her death, so I offered Heather what sympathy I could. It struck me that she was less brilliant than her sister, both mentally and physically, but also, perhaps as a consequence, less conceited. Clare had evidently mentioned my name to her. At first, especially when she divulged that she was recovering from a nervous breakdown, I assumed that she merely desired a consoling chat with her sister's old tutor.'

'But she wanted more than that?'

'You already seem to know what she wanted, Mr Barnett: information about Willy Morpurgo.'

'You know Morpurgo works for Alan Dysart?'

'I do now. Heather told me. As a matter of fact, I think I can claim unwitting credit for Alan taking Willy on.'

'Why?'

'Willy's been more or less gaga since the crash. Brain damage, as you're probably aware. Such a pity, in view of

185

the quality of his brain. But there it is: poor Willy left his intellect spattered across a dry-stone wall in the Cotswolds and, like Humpty Dumpty, can't be put back together again. They let him have his degree, of course, out of pure charity. Then I rather think his parents looked after him until they died. Left alone in the world, Willy gravitated back to Oxford, for which, be assured, I who have never been away am unlikely to blame him. He became one of the more notorious tramps of the city, begging and bawling on every street corner. I used to give him a pound whenever I met him: let no-one call me ungenerous. About five years ago, when Alan was campaigning to get into Parliament, he accepted an invitation to take part in a student debate here at Breakspear. The academic equivalent of kissing babies, I suppose. I daresay he wouldn't bother with such gestures now. At all events, I dined with him when he came up and happened to mention poor Willy's plight. Alan never said anything at the time, but Willy vanished from Oxford shortly afterwards. I concluded from what Heather told me that Alan had taken him on for old time's sake.'

There was something about Ockleton that Harry was beginning to dislike. Informative and amiable as he seemed, he yet possessed a cold inhumanity that seeped through his every witty remark. The contrast between his treatment of Morpurgo – the occasional condescending coin – and Dysart's – a roof over his head and some honest employment – was obviously lost on him. Logic he could no doubt purvey in abundance, but of true feeling he was entirely bereft.

'There you are, Mr Barnett: the life of Willy Morpurgo in a nutshell. So much I laid before Heather Mallender and so much I lay before you. The question is: what does it signify? Something – or nothing?'

The saving grace of Ockleton's cloistered and analytical mind was that he had no use for deception. Unlike Heather's family, he had nothing to hide. On his openness Harry now sought to trade. 'Is that all you told Heather?'

'Not quite. She seemed more interested in Willy's student days than his subsequent misfortunes. She wanted to know all about the Tyrrell Society, of which Willy, Alan and I were members.'

'The what?'

'The Tyrrell Society. A dining, drinking and debating club for Breakspeareans of similar persuasions, prejudices and pretensions. I believe I quote from the minutes of our inaugural meeting. The original idea was Alan's, embellished by others. It represented our rebellion against the prevailing student culture of the day. Meditation and Maoism were very much not for us. We preferred to stimulate the sensibilities with something a little more baroque, a little more aesthetically traditional. By your expression, I judge that you suspect me of pseudo-intellectual flim-flam and it is undeniable that our deliberations tended more towards the sybaritic than the Socratic. Nevertheless—'

'Who was Tyrrell?'

'Tyrrell?' Ockleton looked peeved to have his reminiscences directed along such practical lines. 'Dear me, Mr Barnett, do you not know?'

'Why should I?'

'Because you, like all of us, were a schoolboy once. Walter Tyrrell was the man alleged to have slain King William Rufus with an arrow, either deliberately or accidentally, in the New Forest on the second of August in the year 1100.' Ockleton smiled at Harry's frown of puzzlement. 'Perhaps the allusion was a trifle abstruse. The point of the episode, so far as we were concerned, was that the truth of it has never been established. Tyrrell remains an enigma. Was he an assassin or an innocent? A daring and devious regicide or merely a clumsy archer? We shall never know. It was on such ultimately unanswerable questions about the past – and, indeed, the present – that we chose to dwell. The name was Alan's suggestion, and an apt one we all thought it. Apt, as it turned out, in a way none of us could have anticipated.'

'What do you mean?'

'You referred earlier to the death of Ramsey Everett and there you have my meaning, for the exact circumstances of his death remain elusive in a truly Tyrrellian fashion.'

'I gathered he fell from a window whilst drunk.'

'Quite so. It would be absurd if it were not so unlikely. As I told Heather – But wait: you should see something that will add piquancy to a bald recital of what few facts are known.'

It was necessary for Ockleton to push an armchair out of the way to reach the cupboard he sought, set low in a corner wall. After crouching by it for several minutes, sifting through the contents, he uttered a triumphant 'Aha!' and pulled out a large framed photograph, from which he blew a cloud of dust before placing it on the desk and inviting Harry to look at it. It showed a dozen or so young men casually grouped around a bench on a sunlit lawn, wearing knife-creased flannels and striped blazers: the very antithesis of student life in the sixties. Harry recognized Dysart among the trio seated on the bench and Ockleton standing to the rear, clumsily clutching a champagne bottle.

'You've spotted Alan and me, have you?' Ockleton asked after a moment.

'Yes.'

'Willy's the one to my left.'

'Good God.' Harry could not at first believe that the tall and graceful youth beside Ockleton in the picture was the same man he had met at Tyler's Hard. If only Morpurgo had been a less thoroughbred specimen the contrast with what had subsequently overtaken him would have been easier to accept.

'What a falling-off was there, eh? That's Ramsey.' Ockleton pointed to another member of the group. Stockier than Morpurgo, with a less untroubled brow and a glare at the camera of barely bridled contempt, Ramsey Everett looked of the whole pack the one most prone to question their right to behave as they wished. 'And they, you may care to note, are Jack Cornelius and Rex Cunningham.' Ockleton pointed in turn at a broadly built man smiling conventionally towards the camera and a short, fleshy fellow beside him raising a glass as if to join in a toast.

'Who are they?'

'Patience, Mr Barnett, patience. First I have some questions for you. How did you come to meet Alan Dysart? If you will forgive me for saying so, you scarcely seem his type.'

'He worked for me during university holidays.'

'*He* worked for *you*?'

'Yes. I ran a garage business then, in Swindon.'

'Swindon? Of course. I might have known. Thus the whirligig of time, etcetera, etcetera.'

'What?'

'Never mind, Mr Barnett. I have not yet done with questioning you. How did you come to be Alan's employee, when he was initially yours?'

'Hard times. Perhaps you've never known them.'

Ockleton smiled. 'Alan is a universally charitable man, it seems.'

'Yes. I think he is.'

'And what do you hope to accomplish by retracing Heather's movements in this way?'

'I hope to find her.'

'You think she is alive, then?'

'Yes.'

'Then your motive is a laudable one. She seemed a charming girl to me. So much more *genuine* than her sister. Clare was a true Breakspearean: too subtle for her own good. But Heather? Fortunately, she had never fallen into our clutches. She remained . . . unsullied.'

They stared at each other in silence for a moment, surprised to find that they shared some fragment of a common cause: the unsolved mysteries that troubled them both, though twenty years and half a world apart, were somehow one and the same.

'Are you in a hurry to be be on your way, Mr Barnett?'

'No.'

'Then come for a drive, if you will. I will take you where I took Heather. And show you what I showed her.'

Away from the ether of Breakspear and deprived of his occupational gown, Cyril Ockleton was transmuted into a more subdued and less boyish version of himself, as if sensing that his true persona required a measure of disguise in the wider world. Piloting his tinny little car west out of Oxford with blithe disregard for the rules of the road, he declined to specify their destination – beyond the fact that it was where Morpurgo had met with his accident – and instead treated Harry to a detailed account of the death of Ramsey Everett, an account which he had previously given Heather, almost, it seemed, word for word.

'The Tyrrell Society comprised, as you might imagine, good and ostentatious patriots. St George's Day was thus red-lettered in our calendar. On the twenty-third of April each year, we held a dinner, at which, in honour of the patron saint, over-indulgence was not simply customary but mandatory. So it was on Tuesday the twenty-third of April, 1968, an occasion given a special *fin de siècle* luminosity by the knowledge that, for many of us, it was the last such event in our Oxford careers. At some late and inebriated stage of the proceedings, Ramsey Everett made his way, alone so far as could be established, into an adjacent sitting-out room. Both it and the Tyrrell Society meeting room, where the dinner was held, were on the second floor of Old Quad. The night being unseasonably warm, most of the windows were wide open. Ramsey presumably leant out for a breath of air. There was a suggestion at the inquest that he sought to relieve himself out of the window rather than trudge down to the jakes in the basement, a distressing but not unprecedented recourse for chaps well gone in their cups. However that may be, and for whatever reason, he lost his balance, the window being set hazardously close to the floor, and toppled out. Unhappily, he landed on the flagstones, not the lawn, and head-first at that, fracturing his skull and snapping his spine. Death, we were assured, was instantaneous.

'This dreadful incident was, as you may imagine, a shattering blow to the society. Ramsey, though a touch priggish at times, was well-liked. The stupidity of his death made it somehow the harder to accept. To make matters worse, the college authorities interpreted it as a reflection on the conduct and organization of the society, which they accordingly ordered to be disbanded with immediate effect.

'Formally, the Tyrrell Society came to an end the day of Ramsey's funeral. Alan, I recall, took it particularly hard. Naturally, some of us continued to meet from time to time, constituting the Tyrrell Society in all but name. It cannot be denied, however, that Ramsey's death cast a shadow over all our activities. Nothing seemed as carelessly enjoyable as before.

'Some of us hoped that, once the inquest was past, our spirits would be revived. It was scheduled to open on the twentieth of May. As the date approached, those due to give evidence became increasingly nervous and depressed. Willy exhibited these symptoms to the most marked degree, which I for one thought odd, since he and Ramsey had often clashed. A few days beforehand, Jack Cornelius suggested a jaunt into the countryside to cheer us all up. Alan's car was in dock, so Willy, the only other car owner, agreed to drive. There were five takers originally, but only four could hope to squeeze into Willy's Mini, so Alan volunteered to drop out. That left Willy, Jack, Rex Cunningham and me. On Friday the seventeenth of May – mark the date – we set off. It was a bright spring morning. Our destination – then and now – was the village of Burford.'

They were speeding along the A40 trunk road now, the landscape growing ever more undulating as the Cotswolds drew near, the pale winter sunlight falling warmly on honey-stoned farmhouses and curving boundary walls. Why Burford? And why the seventeenth of May? Harry did not even need to ask the questions before Ockleton supplied the answers.

'How are you on seventeenth century history, Mr

191

Barnett? Rusty? Or was the metal never applied in the first place? I trust you have heard of the Levellers, our homegrown *sans-culottes*. They were the most intelligent and least deferential members of the army raised by Parliament to defeat the King in the Civil War, who believed, God help them, that victory would usher in a democratic state. Needless to say, the generals, stolid landowners to a man, never had any intention of allowing such a thing to happen. Such concessions as they made were mere delaying tactics. When the time was ripe, they struck back, ordering the Leveller regiments to Ireland and withdrawing all their hard-won rights. Those who resisted were denounced as mutineers and treated accordingly. The last such mutiny was put down at Burford on the thirteenth of May, 1649, by Cromwell in person. He confined 340 mutineers in Burford Church for the next three days under general sentence of death. Then, on the seventeenth, he spared them, save for three ringleaders, whose execution in the churchyard the others were forced to watch. So ended the Burford mutiny.

'Of what interest, you may ask, was this incident to the Tyrrell Society? The answer lies in its ambiguity. Cromwell had thrown in his lot with the Levellers when it suited him two years before and so was regarded by them as no better than a mutineer himself when he turned against them. Yet at Burford, within a matter of days, he converted all the rebel officers to his cause. An air of double-dealing and deceit hangs over those negotiations, as if to suggest that the record of them is in itself a distortion. Who betrayed whom? And why? We shall never know. For that reason Burford was a singularly appropriate destination for our excursion. We were celebrating the anniversary of what we most adored: an enigma.'

At Burford, they left the main road and headed down the sloping High Street. Harry glimpsed the typical slate-roofed tea rooms and cream-stoned antique shops of a well-to-do Cotswold town, primly battened, it struck him, against all suggestions of treachery. Then Ockleton turned off along a narrow lane and, a few moments later, they pulled up by the church.

'This was naturally our first port of call,' Ockleton continued, climbing from the car and leading the way into the churchyard. 'Willy rambled on about Norman archways and Perpendicular naves, as if glad to have some arcane topic to take his mind off the inquest. Rex mooched about the graves wondering when we were going to have lunch. That left Jack and me to pay some attention to the history of the place. Jack's Irish blood made him sympathize with the Levellers – the Irish have never forgiven Cromwell for the Drogheda massacre, you know. I had a pretty open mind on the subject. Still have, if it comes to that. Couldn't have abided the Levellers' politics, of course, but betrayal always leaves a nasty taste in the mouth, don't you agree?'

They entered the church: large, high-roofed and multi-chapelled, reflecting much of Burford's past and present wealth in its vaulted tombs and grandiloquent memorials. Harry trailed along behind Ockleton, bemused as he always was by beeswaxed pews and glittering plate in what experience had taught him was an irreligious world. They came to the font and halted. Standing beside Ockleton, Harry could see centuries-old graffiti scratched on its leaden lip. Ockleton pointed to one of them and read it aloud.

'"Anthony Sedley. 1649. Prisoner." I wouldn't have noticed this if Jack hadn't drawn it to my attention. One of the Levellers carved it, in desperation I suppose, during their confinement here. Pity the poor blighter couldn't spell. Moving, what?'

Ockleton had spoken sarcastically, but Harry was genuinely moved by what he saw. Sedley had carved the Ns the wrong way round and omitted the O from 'prisoner', but these mistakes only heightened the poignancy of his message. On their way out of the church, Harry took from the rack of postcards one reproducing Sedley's inscription. He felt surprised by his own honesty in dropping the requested payment into the box and could not quite fathom his motive in lodging the card in the same envelope in his pocket where he kept those of Aphrodite and Silenus.

'There's nothing like trudging round a cold church to raise an appetite, Mr Barnett. Jack, Willy, Rex and I took ourselves off to the Lamb Inn for lunch and put away as much ale and steak and kidney pie as four young men could desire. I entertained Heather to lunch there as well. Regrettably' – he glanced at his watch – 'it will not be open at this hour. I therefore suggest—'

'I'd like to see the pub where you took Heather though, if that's possible.'

Understandably, Ockleton was puzzled by Harry's request, but he raised no objection. 'Very well. We'll drive round that way.'

The Lamb Inn lay on the other side of Burford, down a side-turning off the High Street. As soon as Harry saw it, he felt reassured. It was unquestionably the subject of the sixth photograph, as Ockleton at once confirmed.

'Strange you should want to take a look at this place. As we were leaving, Heather took a snap of it. Pretty enough, I suppose, but hardly photogenic, is it?'

'Obviously Heather thought it was.'

Ockleton frowned. 'You seem about as forthcoming as she was, Mr Barnett. I bring each of you on a guided tour of my past and you each remain tight-lipped. Why is it, then, that I have the impression you each perceive something here that I have overlooked?'

Harry did not reply and Ockleton did not press the point. The truth was that Harry's only token of significance was the set of photographs which he had resolved to show as few people as possible. He justified his secrecy to himself as a necessary precaution, but, lying somewhat deeper, there was a wish to preserve the intimacy of the link with Heather that they represented, a desire to conceal both his possession of them and his pursuit of what they meant.

They drove north out of Burford, down over the old packhorse-bridge across the river Windrush, then up into the hills beyond. After a mile or so, Ockleton turned off the main Chipping Norton road and headed east up a narrow lane that breasted the downs above the Windrush valley.

'When we came to leave the Lamb that afternoon, Mr Barnett, we were all in similar states of intoxication, but Jack had become as maudlin as only an Irishman in liquor can. He insisted that he wanted to return to the church to sample some more of the atmosphere: commune with the spirit of the Levellers – that sort of nonsense. The rest of us were all for starting back to Oxford and Jack suggested we go without him. He said he'd prefer to visit the church alone anyway and that he'd catch a bus back to Oxford when he was good and ready. Rex and I had annoyed him by belittling the Levellers over lunch and there was no reasoning with him when he got into one of his self-righteous moods, so we left him to it.

'I stretched out in the back of the Mini and Rex travelled in the front with Willy at the wheel. Willy was as drunk as any of us, if not more so. He began by taking the wrong road out of Burford, then tried this lane to get back to the A40. As you can see, it runs flat and fairly straight along the crest of the hill until it dips down suddenly, in a quarter of a mile or so, towards the valley floor. By this time, I for one was asleep. Willy was driving too fast for safety, naturally, but that didn't become apparent until we started down the hill.'

Ockleton had slowed as the lane began a sharp and winding descent. Round the next bend, Harry saw two things simultaneously: give-way lines at the foot of the hill, where the lane joined another road, and a scene with which he was already familiar – the subject of the seventh photograph. Even as recognition flashed into his mind, Ockleton pulled in by the hedge and stopped the car. Thirty yards ahead, an innocent rural road junction presented its prosaic features for inspection. The hedges suggested that, in May, they could well have obstructed vision. The dry-stone wall on the farther side looked solid and uncompromising. Twenty years on, the ingredients of a predictable accident remained intact.

'I was oblivious to the danger right up to the moment the crash happened. According to Rex, we never had a chance of negotiating the bend, let alone stopping, given how fast we were travelling. The car careered out diagonally across the lane, heading straight for the wall on the other side. Instead of ploughing into it, however, it struck a tractor and trailer coming from the left. The sound of the collision was what woke me up: a terrible grinding, smashing wrench.

'I was the lucky one, Mr Barnett: a broken arm, a couple of broken ribs, assorted cuts and bruises. The front of the car, and those in it, took the brunt of the impact. Rex was trapped by his legs and had to be cut free. Willy was propelled through the windscreen onto the wall: that's how he incurred such nasty head injuries. The tractor driver walked away without a scratch. As for the longer term consequences, Rex was paralysed from the waist down and Willy, as you know, was left with severe brain damage.

'It was all our own fault, of course. We were culpably self-indulgent and criminally irresponsible. Yet what our little coterie suffered was, I believe, disproportionate to our vices. Ramsey was dead, Willy and Rex were crippled. The rest of us were left to reproach ourselves for what had happened. Jack for one never forgave himself for encouraging the venture in the first place. I daresay we have all tried to forget about it, but I don't suppose any of us has succeeded – except Willy. And maybe not even he.'

The frail winter sunlight had faded and dusk was advancing across the silent fields to either side. Harry shivered – but not because he was cold. Here, it seemed, twenty years ago, the mystery of what had befallen Heather Mallender had begun to unfold. Its nature remained unknown, but now at least it had a name. Ockleton had unwittingly supplied it and Harry sensed that he would find, in the mark it had left on both its victims and its practitioners, the indelible trace of what he sought. Betrayal had become the name of his quarry.

21

Harry woke the following morning in a guest room of Breakspear College which Ockleton had generously made available to him. They had found too much to discuss for the last train to Swindon to remain a realistic option and Harry had gladly accepted the offer of overnight hospitality. Only when his first movement unleashed the pounding headache bequeathed to him by half a bottle of the college's specially shipped port did he begin to regret the decision.

They had returned to Oxford from Burford in the early evening. At an alcove table of the Eagle and Child, Ockleton's favourite pub, they had then debated the circumstances of Heather's disappearance on Rhodes and how they might relate to her visit to Oxford more than two months before. Ockleton, true to his academic training, had been disposed to dismiss the very idea of such a connection. Yet he had been unable to deny, especially when alcohol had begun to leech the starch from his scholarly brain, that her avid interest in the distant doings of Everett, Morpurgo and the Tyrrell Society was inexplicable, unless it constituted a cause corresponding in some way to the effect of her disappearance.

Pressed by Harry to tell what he knew of his fellow Tyrrellians' subsequent careers, Ockleton had covered familiar ground where Dysart and Morpurgo were concerned. As to Jack Cornelius, it seemed that he had returned to his roots in Ireland and become a teacher. Lately, Ockleton had heard it mentioned that he was on the staff of a Roman Catholic boarding school in the West Country. Despite confinement to a wheelchair, Rex Cunningham had evidently prospered and was now the proprietor of a country house hotel-cum-restaurant in Surrey.

'Strangely enough,' Ockleton had said, Harry having to strain to hear him amidst the noise and smoke as closing time drew near, 'Rex was the one who seemed to interest Heather the most. When I referred to this restaurant of his, the Skein of Geese, her ears pricked up. The Master dined there last term and told us all about it. He said it was done out like a brothel and that the food wasn't fit for a rabbit. But the Master, it must be said, is a man of plebeian tastes. At all events, when I mentioned it to Heather, she asked me to repeat the name of the restaurant. When I confirmed that it was called the Skein of Geese, she pulled out one of those little books of matches they give away in such places and said: "The same as this, you mean?" And there it was: an artist's impression of three geese in flight and the name and address of the restaurant, all clearly shown on the flap. Naturally, I assumed she had eaten there herself, but she denied it. Somebody had apparently given her the matchbook and she had been carrying it around with her ever since.'

Why Cunningham? Harry wondered as he climbed from the narrow guest-room bed and began to dress. Why this trail of lapsed tragedies and tantalizing trifles? Heather must have had some compelling reason to follow in the direction they led, yet what that reason might be he was no nearer discovering. To visit Tyler's Hard, even Oxford, in mourning for her sister made a kind of sense, yet the photographs proved she had not stopped there. She had gone further, far further, than bereavement alone could justify.

And, along the way, Harry had chanced upon a minor mystery that impinged on his own past. Back in Ockleton's rooms at Breakspear, seated by a roaring fire and sipping finer port than he could ever recall tasting, he had asked

Ockleton to explain his reaction earlier to Harry's revelation that Alan Dysart had once worked for him in Swindon.

'It's simply that we all thought it so unnecessary, Mr Barnett. Alan's father died during his first year at Breakspear, leaving him a very wealthy young man. A fortune from nuts, bolts and screws, as I expect you know. That being so, vacation employment was scarcely something he needed to seek. If he were simply bored, I should have thought, begging your pardon, that he could have found an occupation rather more civilized than grease-monkeying in Swindon—'

'It wasn't grease-monkeying!'

Ockleton had raised his hands in a placatory gesture. 'Forgive me, Mr Barnett, for trampling on your entrepreneurial sensibilities. You will agree, nonetheless, that it was more than a little odd. Many of us speculated as to his reasons. I personally favoured a psychological explanation. The whole arrangement seemed to me irresistibly reminiscent of T. E. Lawrence retreating from fame as an army officer to obscurity in the ranks, or of Anthony Asquith, the film director, spending his weekends behind the counter of a transport café in Yorkshire. Put bluntly: slumming. Expressed more sympathetically: hiding behind the anonymity of the common working man from a more celebrated but also more demanding life. Alan was well aware of his own gifts and of what they might lead him to become, but I am not sure he entirely welcomed his role as a leader of lesser men. I think his "Swindon vacations" were a way of forgetting what his future held.'

Harry had derided Ockleton's theory at the time. Now, as he stumbled towards the window of his room, he recognized that resentment lay behind his disbelief: resentment that his friendship with Dysart might have an origin he had never dreamed of; that, in lending him a helping hand whenever he could, Dysart had merely been slumming.

Harry tugged back the curtains and squinted out at the painful brightness of a frosty morning. Condensation was streaming down the windowpanes, so he wiped one dry with his shirt-cuff to gain a sight of the day. His room was on the first floor of the college, looking down into a narrow street that ran beside it. Straight ahead soared the blank rear wall of another college. Suddenly, as he peered out through the moisture-smeared pane, something near the base of the wall seized his attention: letters spray-painted in white on its blackened surface, forming words he could not, in that instant of recognition, quite believe. Wrenching up the sash, he leaned out for a clearer view.

ΠΡΟΦΗΤΗΣ ΗΛΙΑΣ. The unique and unmistakeable characters roared their silent greeting up at him. PROFITIS ILIAS. In Greek. In Oxford. Lying in wait for him. Placed there to confront and confound him. Profitis Ilias. Where neither chance nor accident could deflect its meaning. He was followed. Or foreseen. Tracked. Or forestalled. Profitis Ilias had stretched out its hand to find him.

A few minutes later, Harry was standing on the pavement below, staring across the road at the crudely wrought message. He could ransack his brain a dozen times, he realized, and still he would be unable to explain it. Nobody but Ockleton knew who he was or why he was in Oxford. Yet somebody had sprayed those two words on the wall, somebody who knew what they would mean to him and to no other occupant of Breakspear College.

A weary-looking man in overalls appeared from the college entrance to his right, carrying a scrubbing brush and a bucket full of acrid-smelling liquid. Catching Harry's eye, he tossed his head and said ruefully: 'These bloody students!'

'You think students wrote that?'

'Who else?'

'It's Greek, you know.'

'Oh yes? Well that proves it was students, doesn't it?'
 'Why?'

'Who else do you know who can write flaming Greek?'

Who else indeed? As the man crossed the street and started work, Harry headed back into the college. He could believe some drunken classics student had run amok with a spray-can, but not that he had chanced to write two words of no classical significance beneath the window of the room where Harry happened to be staying. Nor could he believe he had been followed to Oxford by somebody determined to leave this macabre calling-card for him to see, for to believe that opened up possibilities too sinister to be endured. There thus remained only one explanation consistent with logic and the sooner he tested its validity the calmer he would feel.

Harry found Ockleton eating breakfast in hall with three or four other fellows of the college, spaced round a vast high table beneath drab oil paintings of half a dozen dead masters. They all looked suitably taken aback by his entrance, muttering disapproval whilst he insisted that Ockleton step outside. Eventually, his face crimson with irritation and embarrassment, Ockleton agreed, only to repeat as they crossed the quad what he had maintained throughout their whispered altercation in hall.

'I suggest you pull yourself together, Mr Barnett. In the first place, I am no classicist. In the second place, if you think I crept out into the street last night and daubed some portentous graffito on the wall opposite your room, you are very much mistaken. In the third place, you may recall that I escorted you to your room at half-past twelve; but the college gates are locked at midnight, from which it follows that I would have had to rouse the duty porter in order both to be let out and to be let in again, something he will most certainly confirm I did not do. In the fourth place, I consider the levelling of groundless allegations to be a shameful response to the hospitality I have extended to you. And in the fifth place . . . . '

They had emerged into the street and looked across at the overalled figure and the patch of wall on which he was working. The cleaning fluid he was using had been remarkably effective. The letters were becoming blurred and faint. Soon, they would be erased altogether. Some of them had already run and spread in such a way as to lose their identity. Π now more nearly resembled an M and Φ a Q. The evidence was disappearing before their very eyes and, once it was gone, Harry was not sure he could convince even himself that it had ever been there.

Half an hour later, Harry left Breakspear College with scarcely a glance at what was now only a faint stain on the opposite wall. He walked swiftly westwards, eager to leave behind the scene of his humiliation. Message or mirage? From beneath the caves of ancient colleges flanking his route, gargoyles grinned down to torment him with the knowledge of his own uncertainty. Atop their pillars round the Sheldonian Theatre, the busts of Roman emperors cast classically guarded looks at his retreating figure. But Harry hurried on, consoling himself with the thought that he still retained one secret advantage over those who thought they had the better of him.

At the corner of Broad Street and Magdalen Street, he walked into a bookshop. Among the welter of aids to discerning travellers, he found exactly what he was looking for: a comprehensive guide to British hotels and restaurants, each entry accompanied by a brief description of the establishment and a small photograph. He flicked quickly through to the section covering Surrey, then proceeded a page at a time until he reached his goal.

> Skein of Geese, Haslemere, Surrey. Proprietor: Mr R. Cunningham. Rating 72%. Standing in its own attractive grounds, this haven of civilized living combines old-fashioned comfort with captivating individuality in that rarest of double acts: princely accommodation and memorable cuisine. All bedrooms are equipped with . . . .

But its picture spoke louder to Harry than any drooling prose. The small scale marred definition and the angle was not the same, but there was no doubt at all about what he was looking at. The Skein of Geese was the subject of Heather's eighth photograph.

202

22

Resolution carried Harry only so far. He reached Haslemere
in early afternoon, hired a taxi and discharged it fifteen
minutes later on the other side of the road from the Skein
of Geese Hotel and Restaurant a few miles south-east of the
town. And there the momentum of his pursuit faltered for
the first time.

It was not as if what he saw fell short of his expectations.
On the contrary, the Skein of Geese was exactly as Heather
had photographed it, save only that the trees behind it
had been stripped of their leaves and the croquet hoops
put away for the winter. A black-and-white Tudor manor
house, separated by a gravelled car park from a modern
two-storey extension mocked up to resemble stables; lawns
behind sloping away towards the wooded flanks of the
Surrey hills; the colours of St. George hanging limply from
a flagstaff; three geese in flight across a swash-lettered
nameboard; and smoke pluming vertically from slender
chimney stacks. The cold and windless afternoon made
of the mellow brick and pastel grass a perfect conspiracy
of pretension and nature, an exact depiction of everything
Harry most loved and loathed in his homeland. But this,
he knew, was not the reason for his hesitation.

Profitis Ilias was the reason. His memories of Heather,
bolstered by his possession of her photographs, had given
him courage and hope, emotions to which he had been a
stranger for more years than he cared to remember. Yet
Profitis Ilias, whether recollected in repose or recorded in

the teeth of logic on an Oxford wall, remained his undoing. There he had come to Heather's aid too late. And there, some plunging sense of his own inadequacy assured him, he would find the bitter end of his search.

He crossed the road, willing himself to suppress the significance of what he had already accepted: there was no turning back. With every step he took, innocent as it might seem, trivial though it was in itself, he made retreat the more impossible.

The reception desk was located in the modern part of the hotel. Here muted lights, soft leather, stained wood and anaesthetic chamber music prevailed. Somewhat to his own surprise, Harry found himself booking a single room, despite the exorbitant tariff, and following the prim receptionist as she led him to the door.

The room was comfortable, though scarcely as 'princely' as the guidebook had led him to expect. The view from its ground-floor window was of an empty reach of the car park. An equine print after the style of Stubbs adorned the longest wall. The key-fob was decorated with the hotel's logo, as was the complimentary book of matches to be found in an ashtray on top of the television. Harry slipped the book into his pocket, wondering as he did so which previous patron of the Skein of Geese had handed such a thing on to Heather. Then, as much in guilty reaction to the receptionist's parting look of disapproval as in the hope of ordering his thoughts, he took himself off to the bath.

An hour later, bathed, shaved and refreshed, Harry was lying on the bed, wearing nothing but a hotel dressing gown, across the breast pocket of which three ubiquitous geese were in embroidered flight. Refreshment had not brought inspiration, however, and he was beginning to despair of ever deciding what to do next when the crunching of car tyres on the gravel by his windows was followed by an exchange that instantly resolved his difficulty.

'Good meeting, Mr Cunningham?'

'Bloody awful, Ted, since you ask.'

204

'Back to your office, is it?'

'How did you guess?'

Harry was instantly upright. Through the net curtain he could see a porter assisting the driver of the car into a wheelchair. Rex Cunningham was living disproof of the youth-preserving powers Harry had imputed to Breakspear College. He looked to belong to a different generation from that of Dysart and Ockleton, his face flushed and lined beneath a mane of grey hair, his chest heaving desperately as he lowered himself into the wheelchair. It was clear that the events of 17 May 1968 had left their mark on him as indelibly as they had on Willy Morpurgo.

Harry tore the dressing gown off and flung on some clothes. Another squint through the net curtains showed Cunningham being pushed up a ramp in the direction of the reception area. Grabbing his key, Harry hurried from the room and followed the corridors round to intercept. By the time he arrived, however, the pair were nowhere to be seen. He glanced down one passage to no avail, then tried the next, just soon enough to catch the porter emerging from the third door along.

'Mr Cunningham in?' he enquired casually as they crossed.

'Yes, sir. Is he expecting you?'

'Hard to say.' He knocked and went in without waiting for an answer.

'Yes?' Cunningham looked up from his desk with a frown of irritation. At close quarters, he appeared less decrepit than dissolute, blotched and bloated like the least repentant of debauchees. This might have seemed merely the occupational hazard of the self-indulgent restaurateur, but for a manic edge contributed by the tightly-curled crop of hair, the thin cigar drooping from his wide mouth and the garishness of a turquoise tie standing out against a black suit and matching shirt.

'Hello. My name's Harry Barnett. I'm staying here tonight. You're the proprietor, I take it: Rex Cunningham?'

'Yes, but—'

205

'You don't know me, but we have a mutual friend: Alan Dysart. I expect you read about the girl who disappeared while staying in his villa in Rhodes. I was his caretaker there.'

Cunningham slowly removed the cigar from his mouth and propped it carefully in an ashtray. His lips were too large for his face, Harry noticed. When eating, they would make him look as if he were gobbling. Even now, they were irresistibly suggestive of greed. '*Was* his caretaker?'

'I'm not anymore.'

'Then what are you?'

Harry ignored the question. 'You know Heather Mallender, I believe.'

'*Know*? Don't you mean *knew*, Mr . . . . '

'Barnett. You don't deny it, then?'

'Why do you ask?'

'I'm trying to find her. I think you might be able to help.'

'How?'

'She came here about three months ago and made your acquaintance, didn't she?'

Cunningham backed his wheelchair away from the desk and stared at Harry quizzically, though whether because he was reluctant to answer or because the mere asking of the question puzzled him it was impossible to tell. 'Perhaps,' he said. 'On whose behalf are you making these enquiries, Mr Barnett?'

'My own.'

'Not Alan Dysart's?'

'No. Not Alan Dysart's.'

'And what precisely do you want to know?'

'What happened when she came here.'

'I haven't said she did.'

'You don't have to. I know she did.'

'How?'

'By putting two and two together.'

'Then you must be a better mathematician than you look.' Cunningham moved his chair round to Harry's side

206

of the desk, stopped in front of him and stared up into his face. Suspicion was apparent in every doubt-ridden defile of his expression, perhaps, it suddenly struck Harry, too apparent, as if blazoned there to conceal something else. 'Heather Mallender did dine here about three months ago, Mr Barnett, it's true, but so what? I have fifty different diners every night. The Skein of Geese is justly famed for its cuisine. I didn't even remember her until I read about her in the papers.'

'But she came here specifically to see you?'

'How should I know? I always take a turn in the restaurant to see there are no complaints. I may have had a few words with her, but that's all.'

'Was she alone?'

'No. There was an admirer in tow.'

'Who was he?'

'I've absolutely no idea.' Cunningham smiled a broad slow smile of undisguised provocation. It left Harry in no doubt that he would learn nothing from this man without offering him something in return.

'Did they stay overnight?'

'I don't think so.'

'Then why did they come so far? Haslemere's hardly an evening's drive from Weymouth.'

'Weymouth?' Cunningham's ignorance was now patently assumed.

'Where she lived, Mr Cunningham, as I think you know.'

'Do I?'

'She wanted to speak to you about her sister, didn't she? The late Clare Mallender.' It was a guess, though scarcely a wild one, and Cunningham's reaction confirmed it had hit the mark.

'Offhand, I can't think of a single good reason why I should tell you anything that passed between us, Mr Barnett.'

'How about this?' Harry tapped the foot plate of Cunningham's wheelchair with the toe of his shoe.

'What do you mean?'

'I mean the car crash twenty years ago in which you lost the use of your legs and Willy Morpurgo the use of his brain.' Cunningham's jaw sagged. He was clearly surprised. Perhaps, thought Harry, Heather had not told him of her visit to Oxford – or what she had learned there. 'Your old chum Cyril Ockleton was most—'

'Ockleton?' It was true, then: for reasons of her own, Heather had kept Cunningham in the dark.

'Yes. I've spoken to Ockleton, just as Heather did, and what he told me has led me here, just as it led her.'

Something akin to sudden understanding crossed Cunningham's face. Then he said in a voice to which composure had been restored: 'Perhaps, after all, there's some merit in discussing the matter. Why don't you join me for dinner, Mr Barnett? I'll be less busy then, better able to recollect the details of Miss Mallender's visit.'

'All right.'

'Shall we say seven-thirty – in the bar?' He smiled charmlessly.

'Seven-thirty it is.' Harry turned to go.

'Oh, Mr Barnett . . . .'

'Yes?'

'Our restaurant's very select. Do you think you could spruce yourself up a little? The way you look at present, my *maître d'* may well refuse you admittance.'

208

23

The bar of the Skein of Geese was the kind of drinking establishment Harry detested: fiddly little bowls of cashew nuts and olives littering every surface; an effeminate barman who looked as if he would not know a handpump from a cocktail umbrella; lighting so subdued a fellow could not see to count his change; and a tape of Glenn Miller standards that made him positively nostalgic for the reception area's bastardized Vivaldi.

Harry had arrived early for his appointment with Cunningham and was already regretting it. The tie he had unearthed from the neglected depths of his jacket pocket was badly creased and stained with what he strongly suspected to be taramosalata. What was worse, wearing it had obliged him to fasten the top button of his shirt, an exercise which had drawn his attention to an extra half inch of fat his neck had gained since the last such occasion. This, followed by a pint of the Skein of Geese's execrable ale and an overheard conversation between two gin-guzzling county ladies concerning the merits of shorter hemlines, had plunged him into abject misery.

He had just glanced at his wristwatch, to discover that Cunningham's arrival still lay approximately two replays of *Little Brown Jug* in the future, when a woman slid onto the next bar-stool to his and said: 'Hello, Harry,' in a tone of husky confidence which suggested they had been lifelong friends.

'I don't think I—'

'Nadine Cunningham. You met my husband earlier.' She was at least ten years Cunningham's junior, Harry judged, blonde-haired and bright-eyed with a sparkling smile; all pert vivacity and curvaceous promise in a black woollen dress that fitted where it touched, as Barry Chipchase would undoubtedly have phrased it. What the pair of county ladies thought of its mid-thigh hemline Harry could not imagine, but he for one was not about to object to the brush of her black-stockinged knees against his drab-trousered legs. 'My usual, please, Vince,' she said to the barman, 'and another of whatever Mr Barnett is drinking. Do you have a light, Harry?'

'Er, yes.' He pulled out the Skein of Geese matchbook and clumsily lit her cigarette.

'Rex might be a few minutes late. He asked me to keep you amused.' The way she smiled as she exhaled a first lungful of smoke suggested she fully intended her remark to be ambiguous. 'I gather you're trying to find Heather Mallender.' Preliminaries, it seemed clear, were not something she cared for.

'Well, yes, but—'

'My husband tells me everything, Harry. Well, *almost* everything.'

'Then you'll know Heather came here about three months ago. Cheers.' He started on the drink she had bought him.

'She dined here on Saturday the tenth of September. I checked our records, you see.' This time her smile was in open acknowledgement of her own efficiency. 'The booking was made in her name, but the bill was paid by her escort: a P.R. Kingdom, according to the credit card receipt.'

September 10th was the Saturday following Heather's visit to Oxford and thus just when Harry would have expected her to proceed to the Skein of Geese. The date did not surprise him, but the identity of her companion certainly did. 'I'm grateful, Mrs Cunningham, but what—'

'Nadine, please.'

'All right: Nadine. What made you dig this information out?'

'To be honest . . . . ' She leaned towards him and lowered her voice. 'I'm worried, Harry.'

'What about?'

'I can't explain here. Perhaps we could meet . . . later.'

'All right.'

'What room are you in?'

Harry had to take the key from his pocket to remind himself. Rooms at the Skein of Geese were given infuriatingly anserine names rather than mere utilitarian numbers. His was Covey. Nadine nodded and he put the key away again. Why he felt as if they had just agreed to an illicit liaison he did not know, unless it was the air of sexual invitation this woman wore as other women wore perfume, the practised composition of glance and gesture that she used to imply everything whilst proposing nothing.

'Rex tells me you used to work for Alan Dysart.' She had swayed back into an upright position and reverted to a tone of easy confidence. 'I've met him a couple of times. He seems just as charming in the flesh as on television. Did you find him a good employer?'

'Actually, he wasn't strictly my employer on Rhodes.'

'No?'

'No. In fact, we only know each other because *he* worked for me – when he was a student.'

'Really?' She seemed suddenly attentive. 'In Oxford, you mean?'

'No. Swindon. I ran a garage business there. I'm afraid it went bust all of . . . . ' He heard his own words peter into silence. Nadine was staring at him with a fascination entirely disproportionate to his remark, a fascination, indeed, bordering on transfixion. 'What's wrong?'

'Nothing . . . . Nothing at all . . . . ' She shook her head in unconvincing denial. That he had in some way taken her aback was as obvious to him as the reason was obscure. 'Ah!' Her eyes focused gratefully on the door. 'Here's Rex – sooner than I expected. I'll leave you to it.'

Before Harry could say another word, Nadine had slipped from the stool and moved past him to greet her husband. He could not catch what she said as she touched Cunningham's shoulder and she did not look back as she walked swiftly from the bar. Harry was still gazing after her, struggling to make sense of what had happened, when Cunningham, who had positioned himself next to him, said: 'Like a gazelle, eh?'

'Sorry?'

'My wife, Barnett. She moves well, doesn't she?'

'Er . . . yes.'

'Don't worry.' He smiled. 'I'm not the jealous type.'

Quite what type Rex Cunningham was did not become clear to Harry in the course of their meal together that evening. Generosity, affability and an overwhelming fondness for the sound of his own voice: these characteristics, founded on a ready wit and a gargantuan appetite, created a superficial impression of warmth and worldliness which Harry took to be typical of an upper crust Home Counties hotelier. He steered a middle course between intimacy and aloofness which would have endeared him to the most demanding of guests.

But not to Harry. Cunningham's chummy dropping of the 'Mr' from his name did not fool him for a moment: the withdrawn and irascible figure he had encountered in mid-afternoon was nearer the soul of this man than mine accommodating and smiling host of the Skein of Geese's oak-panelled restaurant. Through three rich courses and as many fine wines, by candlelight and hectic reminiscence, he entertained Harry to a highly plausible account of himself which yet failed to convey one ounce of conviction.

'So Ockleton's told you all about the Tyrrell Society, has he? Truth is, Barnett, we just liked our food and drink. All the rest – philosophy, history, politics – was pure hogwash. Well, perhaps not the politics. We were Tory when it was out of fashion. Not like these bumptious young boys today. 'Fraid we overstepped the mark, though. Everett taking

212

a dive in Old Quad. Morpurgo precious near writing us both off in that bloody car crash. Symptoms of the same problem, I daresay: headstrong but brain-weak. Know what I mean? Probably not. Don't take this the wrong way, Barnett, but unless you're a 'varsity man – proper 'varsity, that is, not these red-brick hell-holes – you can't imagine what it means to know you're truly and deservedly special. Elitism they call it now, but that doesn't capture the half of it. No, not the half. Have some more wine, Barnett. Like blood, isn't it? Blood for the brain – in an anaemic world.

'What did Ockleton say about the car crash, then? Whatever it was, it's unreliable. Nil powers of observation, that man: always did have. Besides, he was dead to the wide on the back seat when it happened. I was pretty far gone myself, if it comes to that, Morpurgo likewise. Six or seven too many, you know how it is. If you've been to Burford and seen the spot, there's nothing more to be said. We went straight out into the road and bang! Christ, the pain I was in while they cut me free! That's what I most remember about it: pain like you wouldn't believe.' As a demonstration, he held his fingers in the candle-flame between them. 'It makes you immune, you see: it makes you special all over again.'

Everything about Cunningham was pretence, Harry began to suspect. The whole glad-handed garrulous exhibition was intended to divert and deceive. But why? Either he had perfected the performance over the years to ward off sympathy from the able-bodied, or he was hiding something far worse than a self-destructive youth. Whichever was the case, the subject of Heather's visit to the Skein of Geese on 10 September held no terrors for him. Over the stilton and port, without need of prompting, he came to what Harry most wanted to hear.

'If you think the Mallender girl was interested in all that twenty-year-old nonsense, Barnett, you're much mistaken. Never so much as mentioned it. I went round the tables that night as usual, making everybody feel welcome, and she introduced herself as Clare's sister. I knew Clare quite well, as it happens. She used to come down here from London, sometimes just for a meal, sometimes to unwind for a few days, sometimes with some young swain or other, sometimes on her own. Pretty girl, intelligent to boot. A real asset for Dysart. Ideal for entertaining boring bigwigs on his behalf. I admired her – a lot. Can't tell you how cut up I was last year to hear those Irish madmen had killed her.

'Anyway, for some reason Heather wanted to know all about the last time Clare had been here, which, as it happened, I remembered very well, not just because it turned out to be the last I ever saw of her, but on account of something odd that had occurred. Saturday the sixteenth of May, 1987, it was. You can thank my wife for the date. She's a dab-hand at that kind of thing. The sixteenth of May, or course, was only about a fortnight before Clare's death. She was heavily involved in the election campaign at the time and Dysart brought her down here for dinner. A few hours of relaxation away from the whirl of London for both of them, I suppose.

'I used to wonder about Dysart and that girl, Barnett, don't mind telling you. Nobody could have blamed him for trying it on, could they? Not with that frigid bitch of a wife. Clare was, well, desirable to say the bloody least, and they must have spent a lot of time together writing speeches, or whatever it is politicians do. I always got the impression she wouldn't have minded slipping between the sheets with him, but I can't claim there was ever any real evidence she did. Matter of fact, as I told Heather, I stumbled on something that last evening which suggested I had completely the wrong end of the stick.

'Dysart had to take a telephone call halfway through their meal. You know these politicians – always on the hop. You'd sometimes think they stage such incidents to persuade us poor bloody electors that they work hard. Anyway, off he went to the phone, asking me *en route* to make sure Clare didn't get too bored waiting, because it might be a long call. Always keen to spend time with the gorgeous creature, I obliged.

'Clare didn't see or hear me coming. Wheels are quieter than feet, you know, which is about all I *can* say for them. She was sitting at the table with her back to me as I approached, concentrating on something in her hand. As I came up behind her, I saw what it was. Must say, it gave me a shock. Inconsequential in its way, but not to me. A photograph, that's all. Small, black-and-white, crumpled at one corner. Head and shoulders picture of a man. Smiling and informal, you understand, not some passport mug-shot. More the sort of snap a relative or friend might carry. Or a lover.

'That was my first thought. She had her handbag open on the table and had taken out a small leather wallet with several plastic pockets in it, for cheque cards and the like. I had the impression – fleeting, I grant you – that the photo had come from one of the pockets. That she'd removed it to look at, I mean. Just as some moonstruck Juliet would if it were a picture of her other-side-of-the-world Romeo. To be reminded of the distant object of her affections. Well, what's so remarkable in that? A mystery man in her life would have explained a lot. Her chastity where Dysart was concerned for a start. But that's not the point, Barnett, not the bloody point at all. I was just silently congratulating myself on tumbling her secret at last when I realized who the man in the photograph was. I recognized him, you see, and his identity took me properly aback, I don't mind admitting. Surprise isn't the word for it.'

Cunningham drew on his cigar and paused for eye-twinkling effect, but already Harry had foreseen what he would say next. Heather's film would have led him there even if intuition had not, for the next picture on it was of some kind of school or college and there was one member of the Tyrrell Society's inner circle, the circle in which Heather had been vitally interested whatever Cunningham might believe to the contrary, still unaccounted for. He was neither dead nor crippled. He had proposed the visit to Burford on 17 May 1968 but had dropped out of the ill-fated return journey. And he had been lately reported, according to Ockleton, teaching in the West Country.

'The photograph was of somebody you seem to have heard of already, Barnett. A fellow Old bloody Break-spearean of mine. Jack Cornelius.'

24

Harry returned to his room shortly before midnight, feeling less drunk than he had latterly behaved. Rex Cunningham, it had transpired, was a toper of the old school, who believed in polishing off a bottle where lesser men would merely finish a glass. Harry had realized at an early stage, however, that he would need to keep a clear head if he was to remember all he was told. Accordingly, he had restrained his own consumption just as Cunningham's had begun to accelerate out of control.

Cunningham had now been wheeled away to bed by an obliging porter, having reached that maudlin stage of inebriation which is most painful for others to bear. Harry, by contrast, had no intention of subsiding into forgetful slumber: he had far too much to occupy his mind for sleep to seem attractive. Cunningham had strengthened his belief that if he could only follow the clues for which Heather's photographs were somehow emblems he would find the truth – and Heather with it. The next step along the road was therefore all he could think of.

At first, the difficulty he had in opening the door of his room seemed no more than an irritating trifle. Forced to devote his attention to the problem, he found he had succeeded in locking it when he had thought he was unlocking it, the reason being that it had been open all the time. Only when he trawled his memory of leaving the room earlier, and found there a distinct recollection of checking that he had locked the door behind him, did irritation turn to anxiety.

But it was short-lived. When he switched on the light and went in, he found everything in order. No drawers gaped open, no cupboard doors swung free. The bed had been turned down, however, and he assumed the maid who had done that had also been responsible for leaving the room unsecured. He fetched himself a scotch from the mini-bar and dismissed the matter from his thoughts. By the time the telephone rang a few minutes later, he had forgotten it altogether.

'Nadine here, Harry. Rex is sleeping like a babe. Could we have that chat you promised me?'

'Er, yes, or course.'

'I'll come to your room straightaway.'

She was still wearing the clinging black dress and seemed to have passed a stressful evening, to judge by the dark smudges beneath her eyes and the odd loose strand in her previously immaculate hair. Somehow these hints of vulnerability seemed to make her more attractive still, more likely to accept and understand the needs and fallibilities of others. Harry poured her a drink and noticed that her hand was shaking as she accepted a light for her cigarette.

'How did you find Rex?'

'Generous, amiable: the perfect host.'

'Really?' She shot him a wild, almost desperate look. A smile was overdue, but showed no sign of coming. 'You don't have to mince your words for my benefit, Harry.'

'I wasn't.'

'It's one huge act. You must have noticed.'

'Must I?'

'You of all people.'

'Why me – of all people?'

'Because of what you are. Because of what you know.'

'Which is?'

She did not answer. Instead, she began to pace around the room, casting cryptic glances at the Stubbs and nervous

218

puffs of smoke towards the ceiling. Why she should have discarded her confident pose of earlier in the evening he could not understand. He had said nothing to disturb her, nothing, that is, that should have disturbed her. He found himself following the line of marks left in the carpet by the sharp heels of her shoes, caught himself watching the alternate bracing of her calf muscles as she moved to and fro. She had said she was worried and now he believed her. This, he felt certain, could be no act.

'I'm a nobody, Nadine, who knows next to nothing. That's the truth, take it from me.'

'It can't be.'

'Why not?'

She turned to face him, her eyes blazing where before they had sparkled. 'Why did you come here, Harry?'

'You know why. I told you. I thought your husband might be able to help me find Heather.'

'There's more to it than that, though' isn't there?'

'No, there isn't.'

'There has to be.'

'Why?'

Again there was no answer. She stubbed out her cigarette with an air of decision and sat down on the bed, leaning back against the plumped pillows.

'When I told you earlier that Alan Dysart had once worked for me, you seemed . . . surprised. Why was that?'

'Because I *was* surprised.' Nadine's voice was calmer now, subdued and contemplative as she gazed up at the ceiling. 'Alan Dysart works for no man – except himself.'

'I thought you hardly knew him.'

'You thought right. But Rex knows him – from way back. Which means I know him. Him and his like. Rex has told me all about the Tyrrell Society and their activities a dozen times if he's told me once. He still lives it, you see, all that lost frothy fecklessness of his youth. He calls it the 'varsity spirit. Says nobody who hasn't experienced it can understand it. Least of all a woman. Co-education was unheard of in his day, of course. I think he was crippled by his upbringing just as badly as he was by the car crash. I can't get near him, you know, not within touching distance. I don't mean physically, I mean . . . mentally. He's a closed book. A locked door. I've tried to fathom him, God knows. I thought I was too clever to be kept at bay by his all-pals-together manliness, but I was wrong, Harry, so wrong it's almost laughable.' But she did not laugh. Instead, she seemed close to tears.

'How long have you been married to him?'

'Seven years. I was a waitress in his previous hotel. A smaller place, in Godalming. Altogether less grand. He wanted to expand. Hence the Skein of Geese. Hence our marriage. He needed a wife for professional reasons and I was it. It got me out of clearing tables for a living, but I thought it meant more than that. Some mistake, eh?' She paused to sip her whisky. 'The truth is, Harry, Rex is obsessed by that car crash twenty years ago and what led up to it. Understandable, you might think, but the tragedy of the accident isn't what concerns him, oh no. It's the weeks beforehand. The weeks following a St George's Night dinner when—'

'Ramsey Everett was killed.'

She looked at him in mild surprise. 'You know about that? I was right then. There *is* a connection.'

'A connection with what?'

'Did you tell Rex that Alan Dysart worked for you in Swindon during university vacations?'

'No. The subject didn't crop up.'

Nadine clicked her tongue and smiled for the first time. 'Then that's one up to me. You see, Harry, Rex adored the Tyrrell Society and everything it stood for. He says now he was only interested in the food and drink, but that's a lie. Maybe he never was on the same intellectual plane as some of the others, but he still believed in their picture of the world. The Tyrrell Society was everything to him. Body and soul. Its suppression after Everett's death was a shattering blow. That comes out clearly when he's drunk enough to let it.

'It's typical of Rex really that he should blame the poor man who died for all his troubles. Ramsey Everett was never quite one of them, it seems, never quite convinced that the world *did* owe them all a living. He was the weevil in the fruit, according to Rex, the canker in their midst. His death was the beginning of the end, the ultimate cause, as Rex sees it, of his own injuries. Don't ask me to justify it for him, because I can't, but that's what he believes. He even has a name for it. He calls it the Defenestration of Ramsey Everett. His grand undoing. I had to look the word up, you know, look the word up in a dictionary to find out what it meant. He wouldn't have told me. No, not him. Do you know what it means, Harry?'

'Defenestration?' Somewhere, buried deep in his memory, Harry sensed that he had once known the word. Into his mind came a sudden vision of a classroom at Commonweal School, with motes of chalk-dust swirling in shafts of sunlight. He seemed to hear the gravelly voice of Cameron-Hyde the one-eyed history master discoursing on the origins of the Thirty Years' War. The Defenestration of Prague (yes, that was it): as significant in its way as the assassination of Franz Ferdinand at Sarajevo. But it was no good. At the vital moment of explanation, Harry must have been selecting the England cricket team on the back of his exercise book. Cameron-Hyde had discoursed in vain. 'It's beyond me, Nadine. What *does* it mean?'

'Defenestration is to be thrown from a window, Harry. Not to fall or slip, not even to throw oneself, but to *be* thrown. Or pushed. Like Ramsey Everett was.'

Ramsey Everett had been murdered? Cameron-Hyde's lesson at once recurred to him. For some reason quite beyond Harry's comprehension, somebody had been thrown from a window in Prague in the year of grace 1618 and this had provoked thirty years of bloody conflict all over Europe. A tiny spark for a vast conflagration. And so it was with Ramsey Everett. Somebody had pushed him to his death from a window in Oxford in 1968 and, twenty years later, Harry was pursuing the consequences. This was

221

the starting point, the origin of the mystery, and the end was whatever had befallen Heather on Profitis Ilias. The photographs were markers on her path to the answer. And the answer was where he would find her.

'Could you fetch me another drink, Harry?' Nadine spoke consolingly, as if she had read his thoughts.

'Sure.' He carried her glass across to the mini-bar, re-filled it and walked back with it to the bed. Their fingers brushed as she took it from him. Then he picked up his own glass and sat down on the edge of the bed beside her.

'Are you in love with her, Harry?'

'Who?'

'Heather.'

Was he? Surely not. His principal objective was to clear his name of the suspicion attached to it. Friendship finished a poor second and love . . . . But as soon as he had reminded himself of his motive, it rang as hollow to him as he felt sure it must to others. He smiled ruefully. 'I don't know,' he murmured. 'I'm not sure.'

'Did you ever make love to her?'

'No.'

'Did you ever try?'

'No.'

'Not even when you felt lonely?'

'Not even.'

'Then you don't have to be loyal to her, do you?'

He turned to look at her. Made the more appealing, perhaps, by alcohol and half-light, she was nonetheless beautiful, her elfin face crossed by a touching sadness, her brow furrowed by some longing she could not define. She cradled the whisky glass between her breasts, the amber surface of its contents trembling faintly in time to her breathing. 'Why do you ask?' said Harry, his voice thick with sudden loneliness.

'Because I don't have to be loyal either.'

What would happen if he took the glass from her hand and kissed her parted lips Harry glimpsed in that instant,

222

prefigured in the alluring darkness of her dress, darker, it seemed, than even the deepest of the shadows around them. He saw himself, as in a mirror, lifting the black cloth from her white flesh, felt, as if it had already happened, the softness of her body closing around him. Night had fallen and with it his defences. He had been alone too long.

It was Nadine, in fact, who took the glass from Harry's hand, and placed it with her own on the bedside cabinet. She smiled nervously as she looked back at him and seemed about to say something, then, instead, leaned forward to kiss him. As their lips met, the urgency of their mutual need declared itself. They were suddenly breathless, falling together onto the pillows. Her hand was loosening his tie, his was sliding up the tingling curve of her thigh. She rolled onto her side to let him pull down the zip of her dress. He opened his eyes and reached round to find the fastener.

Then he stopped. For an instant, his gaze had shifted to the bedside cabinet, where their whisky glasses stood beneath the lamp. From this angle he could see what he had not noticed before: the drawer of the cabinet, open by a few inches, and, inside, picked out clearly in the lamplight, an envelope with two words written on it in Greek. ΧΑΡΗ ΜΠΑΡΝΕΤΤ. Harry Barnett.

'What's wrong?' said Nadine. But Harry did not hear her. He reached across and pulled the drawer fully open. It was a Skein of Geese envelope, with three of the wretched birds embossed in brown on heavy cream vellum. And Harry's name, written in black anonymous ink. ΧΑΡΗ ΜΠΑΡΝΕΤΤ. Nothing else. Just his name. In Greek. In England. A violent shudder ran through him. He grabbed the envelope, felt the thickness of at least one page inside, ripped the flap open and plucked out the contents.

A single sheet of hotel writing paper, blank save for the pre-printed address. No message. No other words, in Greek or any other language. No greeting but his own accursed name and empty, watermarked derision.

'What is it, Harry? What's the matter?' Nadine was sitting upright beside him, staring at the envelope. She was a party to his deception, he felt certain. She had to be. The unlocked door. The timely phone-call. The expert seduction. Was it meant to end when it did? Had she judged the precise moment when he would make his chilling discovery?

'Who put you up to this?' he demanded.

'I don't know what you're talking about.'

'This!' He thrust the envelope towards her.

'What is it?' Her mixture of alarm and bafflement would have been utterly convincing, had Harry not already passed beyond the reach of any appeal she might care to make.

'My name. In Greek.'

'I don't understand.'

'Was it your husband, Nadine? Did he tell you to plant this here while he wined and dined me? Did he send you here tonight to make an utter bloody fool of me?'

'This is—'

'Did he?'

She made to rise, but Harry grabbed her by the wrists and she subsided back onto the bed with a sharp cry of pain. 'Let go of me!'

'Not until you tell me the truth.'

'What truth? This is insane!'

'When I came back here tonight, I found the door unlocked. I thought the maid must have left it that way. But it wasn't the maid, was it? It was you, Nadine, come here to leave this letter where you knew I'd be bound to see it. Bound to see it because you planned every move – every touch – in this tender little scene.'

'You're mad!'

'No. That's what you want me to be. But it's not going to work. Because you're going to tell me who planned this. And why.'

'Nobody planned anything.'

'Yes they did. You know they did.'

Nadine's mouth set in a firm, determined line. She was breathing heavily and, in some clinical compartment of his brain Harry pondered how that same panting note could signify three completely different emotions: the passion she had simulated, the fear she was struggling to control, the anger that bubbled beneath the surface. 'Listen to me, Harry,' she said with icy composure. 'If you don't stop this now, you'll regret it. They think you murdered Heather, don't they? They think you raped her and killed her. I don't, but they do. What happens if there's an assault on me to be taken into the reckoning? What happens then, eh? Do you think anyone will believe it wasn't just more of the same?'

Silence, and with it a circle of bewildering calm, closed about them. Nadine was right. Nobody would believe him. The Mallenders. The police. The newspapers. They would all be vindicated. Nadine's defiant glare told him what he should have realized already. She was stronger than him in every respect save the purely physical. Only greater humiliation could result from an attempt to wrench the truth from her. His grip slackened. His hands fell away from her wrists. 'Get out,' he murmured.

And she was gone. Without another word. There was a click of the door as it closed behind her. And Harry was alone. He stared at the envelope again but found there no clue to what had been enacted. A wall in Oxford. A locked room in Surrey. They were drawing closer, ever closer, whoever they were, but their purpose remained obscure. To stop him? To unnerve him? Either way, they would not succeed.

He rose from the bed and walked across to the chair where he had slung his jacket. He took the Skein of Geese matchbox from its pocket, lit one of the matches and held it to the envelope until the flame had caught. As his own name shrivelled in the heat, he dropped the envelope into the ashtray and watched it burn to a husk, then prodded it into tiny fragments with the extinguished match. With the evidence destroyed, there was some hope of pretending it had never existed. Not that it really mattered. Harry knew his own nature if he knew nothing else. He could not be deflected now.

225

25

'I'd like to check out, please,' said Harry.

'Not having breakfast?' the receptionist responded brightly.

'No.'

'Very well, sir.' Harry could see the realization dawning on her that small talk would be wasted on this guest. 'Have you made any telephone calls this morning?'

'No.'

'Or used the mini-bar?'

'No.' (Harry had decided that to pay for entertaining Nadine Cunningham would be to add insult to injury.)

'That'll be seventy-four pounds and seventy-five pence then, sir.'

Harry winced. 'I thought the room was sixty-five a night.'

'It is, sir. But there's VAT to be added.'

He sighed, took out another ten pound note and slid the money across the counter, calculating as he did so that he could have eaten adequately and drunk excessively for a fortnight in Lindos for what a night at the Skein of Geese had cost him. Not that he would have felt nearly so hard done by had only his wallet suffered by it. He pocketed his change and turned to go.

'Oh Mr Barnett—'

'Yes?'

'Mr Cunningham asked if you could spare him a few

minutes before leaving the hotel. You'll find him in his office.'

Harry's first inclination was to ignore the request. All he really wanted to do was walk away from the Skein of Geese and never return. He had no taste for further encounters with either Cunningham or his wife. Then curiosity got the better of him. At the very least, he might leave them with a few choice phrases to remember him by.

'Ah, Barnett! An early riser, I see.' Cunningham was leafing through a copy of the *Financial Times* at his desk amidst a cloud of cigar-smoke, beaming like some genial movie mogul, altogether unaffected, it seemed, by the events of the previous night. Amongst the papers before him stood an empty breakfast cup and an egg-smeared plate, suggesting that his digestion was as robust as his nerve.

'What do you want?' said Harry.

'Ah! The acid tone confirms my worst suspicions. 'Fraid I disgraced myself last night. Should know better. Inexcusable, really. Thought I'd make my peace with you before you left.'

Harry was taken aback. Surely Cunningham did not mean to pretend nothing had happened. 'Is that all?' he snapped.

'More than enough, I'd have said. Can't apologize too much. Just hope I didn't say anything to offend you.'

Was it possible, Harry wondered, was it remotely conceivable that Cunningham was an even bigger dupe than he was himself? Surely not. Yet perhaps it was at least a contingency worth testing. 'You said nothing to offend me, Mr Cunningham.'

'You mean it? That's a load off my mind, believe me.'

'But you did puzzle me. Do you remember mentioning the defenestration of Ramsey Everett?'

'Oh God.' Cunningham put a hand to his forehead. 'I treated you to that, did I?'

'You really think he was murdered?'

'Probably not, Barnett, probably not. It's just a hare-brained theory of mine. I'm given to them, you know. My wife thinks I'm paranoid. Perhaps she has a point. Somebody could have murdered Everett, of course – in the circumstances, nothing simpler – but I expect it was just an accident, don't you?'

'I don't know. You were there.'

'So were we all. Ockleton, Morpurgo, Cornelius, Dysart *and* half a dozen others too drunk to mention. But there was so much coming and going that any one of us could have slipped out, pushed Everett through the window and slipped back again without being noticed. Damn it all, we didn't even notice Everett was missing until a porter tripped over him in the quad, so anything's *theoretically* possible. Motive, means, opportunity: the classic combination, isn't it?'

'The means and opportunity you've established. But what would have been the motive?'

'Well, I daresay it's just me flying a kite, but the fact is Everett was too bloody inquisitive for his own good. Planned to be a criminologist after Oxford, you know, and started applying the craft to friends and acquaintances at Breakspear. He'd think nothing of checking up on a fellow's credentials. Did he do as well at school as he claimed? Was his father really a war hero? That kind of thing. Embarrassed several of us with his discoveries, I can tell you. It struck me he might have come up with something one day that wasn't just embarrassing but downright scandalous. He was enough of a prig to revel in disgracing any poor sod he dug up some real dirt about. That could have made him a candidate for murder, couldn't it?'

'Yes, I suppose it could.'

'And it raises all sorts of questions about the car crash, doesn't it?' Cunningham was warming to this theme now. There was a feverish blush to his cheeks, as if he had seldom found so receptive an audience for his speculations. 'Perhaps that wasn't an accident either. Three days

228

before the inquest on Everett's death makes it a suggestive coincidence, don't you think?'

'But it *was* an accident. You were all drunk. Morpurgo was driving too fast. You said so yourself.'

'Oh, Morpurgo was speeding, not a doubt of it, and he was pie-eyed, I don't deny. But he might still have been able to stop in time if he'd braked hard enough. Ockleton and I were both asleep, so neither of us can be sure he didn't slam on the brakes – only to find they weren't working. Morpurgo knows, of course, but he's incapable of telling us. And the car was such a mess nobody would have been looking for a sawn brake cable.'

'You're suggesting the car was sabotaged?'

'I'm suggesting it may have been, yes.'

'But why?'

'Suppression of evidence, Barnett. Suppression of evidence.' He sat back in his wheelchair with the self-satisfied grin of a man proud of his own ingenuity. Then he laughed and took a puff at his cigar. 'Or it could be just the over-ripe fruit of my suspicious mind. Thanks to this contraption' – he slapped the arm rest – 'I've had plenty of time to cook up an outlandish conspiracy theory. It could easily be nothing more than my way of coping with the consequences of a senseless accident. That's what my wife thinks it is. You can take your bloody pick.'

It was no accident. Half an hour later, walking slowly along the road into Haslemere through the mild grey morning, Harry described in his mind another circuit of all the barely linked half-chances that persuaded him Cunningham was right and concluded, not for the first time, that logic and probability were irrelevant. He believed Everett had been murdered for the same reason Cunningham did. He needed to.

Think it through again, he told himself: sift every grain of what you know until you find the answer. Suppose Everett was murdered to prevent him blackening the name of a fellow Breakspearean. Suppose one or more of those

229

who visited Burford three weeks later had witnessed the murder or knew what Everett had discovered. Suppose the car crash was a botched attempt to kill them. If that were so, the answer lay with one of the occupants of Morpurgo's car. The likeliest was Morpurgo himself, because, though not killed, he had been silenced, whereas both Cunningham and Ockleton could have spoken out afterwards – unless they were too frightened to do so. That left Cornelius. Was his withdrawal from the return journey good luck or self-preservation? Harry's own half-formed suspicions tended to focus on him because Clare Mallender had been seen mooning over his photograph at the Skein of Geese two weeks before her death. But an alternative explanation had also come to him which he knew he should not ignore. What if Everett's putative murderer had been the intended victim of sabotage rather than its practitioner? What if revenge had been the motive rather than the silencing of a witness? If that were so . . . .

A sleek blue BMW purred past him and halted about ten yards ahead. As Harry approached, the nearside front window wound automatically down. He glanced in to find Nadine Cunningham smiling at him from the driver's seat.

'Want a lift, Harry?'

'No thanks.'

'Where are you going?'

'The station.'

'It's a long walk.'

'I know.'

'Then jump in.' She was wearing a dark tracksuit and was smiling warmly, as if she had simply stopped on her way to the solarium to pick up a neighbour. 'There's something I want to tell you.'

Pride, Harry reminded himself, was a luxury he could not afford. He climbed in and they started off. 'Well?' he said neutrally.

'I owe you an apology.'

'True, but I don't expect one.'

'I can see why you reacted the way you did last night. It must have been a shock. The letter, I mean, addressed to you in Greek.'

'It was. As you intended.'

'No, I didn't. That's what I wanted you to understand. It was no doing of mine. I even questioned the maid. She's a reliable girl. She's sure she locked the door after her. Somebody must have picked it. If they'd had a key, they wouldn't have been so careless as to leave it open, would they?'

'You're wasting your breath.'

'But don't you see, Harry? It was nothing to do with me, or anybody else on the staff. It must have been an outsider.'

'You really don't have to make all this up on my account.'

They turned off sharply to the left and headed up a straight, sloping road between sombre stands of oak and beech. This was not the route Harry recalled from his taxi ride, but, for the moment, he did not protest.

'I spoke to your husband this morning. He pretended to know nothing about what happened between us.'

'He wasn't pretending, Harry. That was genuine. I wanted to thank you – for not enlightening him.'

'You expect me to believe that?'

'Yes. But I don't expect you to believe I was simply looking for a good time. There *was* an ulterior motive.'

'Which you're about to volunteer?'

'Yes. It's the least I owe you in the circumstances. You see, I've been offered a great deal of money for information which might discredit Alan Dysart: anything scandalous from his past or present. I knew from Rex that his work in Swindon had mystified his contemporaries, so, when you turned up, the one man who might know all about it, it seemed an opportunity too good to miss.'

She cast a brief and dazzling smile towards him, declaring without a hint of shame her duplicity as well as her frankness. Why he did not feel angrier than he did he could not understand. Perhaps it was the sheer blatancy of her confesssion. Perhaps it was the nagging awareness that he too had hoped to gain more than mere gratification from their acquaintance.

'Don't look so worried, Harry. I'm not going to try again. If things are so serious that people start picking locks and planting letters, I don't want to know anymore. That's strictly out of my league. The money would have—'

'How much money were you offered?'

'The figure was negotiable, depending on what I discovered.'

'And who made the offer?'

'Are you sure you want to know?'

'I'm sure.'

'He's a reporter from one of the Sunday scandal-sheets.'

Harry might have guessed. 'Jonathan Minter?'

'Yes. How did you know?'

So that was Minter's true objective: character assassination of a popular politician – the modern journalist's stock-in-trade. It explained his interest in Heather's disappearance as well as his offer of money to Harry if he could give him a story. Perhaps it even explained his relationship with Virginia Dysart.

'He first contacted us last year, shortly after Clare Mallender's death. Apparently he knew the girl. He said he was researching a piece on Alan Dysart and wanted to ask Rex some questions about their Oxford days. Rex refused to cooperate when he realized that what Minter was really looking for was a scandal – any scandal. Rex worships this government, you see, more than he worships money, which is saying something. So Minter went away with a flea in his ear. He came back a couple of weeks ago and this time approached me rather than Rex. I told him about the defenestration of Ramsey Everett and he gave me five hundred pounds. He called it a down-payment and said there could be a hundred times that sum on offer for the right kind of information about Alan Dysart. The trouble was I didn't have any – until you arrived.'

They topped a rise and began a slow descent towards

the town. The woodland was thinner hereabouts, with the roofs of secluded residences dotted amongst the trees in a landscape of tamed nature and Home Counties opulence. It came as a surprise to Harry that even here cheque-book journalism could make its inroads.

'I expect you're thinking: is she really that desperate for fifty thousand pounds? The answer is yes. I have no money of my own, Harry. Everything belongs to Rex. So, if I'm to leave him, I need capital. You might think it's a sordid way to raise it, but at least it's quick.'

'That's what you want to do, is it – leave him?'

'On my own terms, yes.'

'Why?'

'The usual reasons. I've never loved him, but now I've started to hate him – for making me the mercenary bitch I am. It's no excuse, but you may as well know anyway: in Rex's case, paralysis below the waist really does mean what it says.'

They had reached the centre of Haslemere now and their progress had slowed amidst a tangle of straying pedestrians and lumbering delivery vans. The electronic strains of a synthesized choir could be heard above the rumbling exhausts and Harry, gazing out at the tinsel-hung shopfronts, wondered if it was this jangling ubiquity of Christmas spirit which made his fellow men and women seem so dismally ignoble.

'It's not a pretty story, is it, Harry? I'm sorry about it, really I am. Don't think too badly of me. A girl's got to look to the future, you know.'

'As a matter of fact, Nadine, you were wasting your time all along. Minter wouldn't have paid you a penny for what you might have got out of me. You see, Alan Dysart doesn't have a secret to hide.'

'I thought everybody had at least one.'

'Well, he's the exception that proves the rule.'

For a second, it crossed Harry's mind that he could be wrong. Just because he knew and liked Dysart, the man was not necessarily above suspicion. On the other hand,

Minter had evidently found no skeleton in his cupboard, for all his efforts to do so. With Virginia Dysart as either his ally or his dupe, only sheer desperation could have made him offer bribes to the likes of Nadine Cunningham.

'Tell me,' Harry said as they neared the station, 'if I hadn't found that letter last night and thrown you out, would you have told me all this?'

'No, I wouldn't.'

'Then why now?'

'Because I'm hoping you'll agree to pass on a message for me to Minter. You will be seeing him, won't you?'

'Yes, but—'

'I thought you would. I want you to tell him I can't assist him any further and there's no point him contacting me again. Will you do that for me?'

'All right. But why so adamant?'

'Because that letter was a warning, Harry, one *I* don't intend to ignore – even if you do.'

They pulled up in the station car park. Nadine kept the engine idling but Harry made no move to climb out. 'You're frightened?' he said incredulously.

'Yes, I am. Aren't you?'

'No. Why should I be?'

'Isn't it obvious? Heather Mallender started asking the same sort of questions you're asking – and look what happened to her. I didn't take the idea seriously until last night, but, believe me, I don't need fifty thousand pounds *that* badly. To put it bluntly, Harry, I don't want to disappear. Do you?'

Watching the BMW ease out into the traffic a few minutes later and accelerate away along the road, Harry turned Nadine's words over in his mind. The point she had made was an obvious one, but, till now, he had succeeded in overlooking it. In searching for Heather, he was faithfully reproducing her movements – and quite possibly her mistakes as well. In following the same clues as her, he might well be heading for the same destination.

26

Harry thought well on trains. He found their steady, rhythmic progress an aid to concentration and the oddly oblique views of the world they offered – weed-choked farmland at the feet of embankments, gnome-dotted gardens on the edges of towns – ran somehow parallel with his own. He supposed it was due to the railways' air of resentful obsolescence, combined with their persistent insights into what was so often ignored: abandoned pastures, neglected buildings, all that was overgrown and outmoded, all that was best forgotten.

Like Harry himself. That, of course, was the source of the affinity. He was, in his way, as redundant as the steam engines whose numbers he had avidly collected as a boy in Swindon. All those roaring blurs of hissing steam and belching smoke were gone now to the breaker's yard. The very sheds where their boilers were forged had been levelled to the ground. Compared with them, however, Harry possessed one crucial advantage: the right to decide that he would not go quietly. He should have felt as tired and inadequate as his age and circumstances dictated, but he did not. He should have been cowed and compromised by fear and debt, but he was not. Instead, halfway between Guildford and Woking, he experienced a curious surge of elation. He was gaining ground on all of them, he had the beating of them yet. From Waterloo station, he phoned the offices of *The Courier* and somewhat to his surprise, found himself put straight through to Jonathan Minter. Still suffused with a sense of equality to the challenge that confronted him, he slipped deftly into the image he believed the other man would have of him.

'Is that . . . er, Jonathan Minter?'

'Speaking.'

'Ah . . . . It's, er, Harry Barnett here.'

'Hi, Harry Barnett there. What can I do for you?'

'Well, er, you said when we met on Rhodes—'

'That where you are now?' (So: Minter did not even know he had left Rhodes, far less all he had discovered since then – notably about Minter himself.)

'No. That is . . . I'm in London.'

'Really? How long have you been here?' (His curiosity on the point was transparent: he wanted to know if Harry was likely to have seen the article in which Minter had traduced him.)

'Oh, only a few days.'

'And you've got something for me?'

'I might have.' (Pause long enough to whet his appetite, Harry instructed himself, then resume – hesitantly.) 'Er, that, um, link in the chain . . . you mentioned.'

'Oh yes?' (Minter's voice was suddenly more alert.)

'Concerning Alan Dy—'

'No need to spell it out over the phone, Harry. Why don't we meet and talk about it?' (He was nervous now, as well as interested.)

'OK. But . . . where?'

'Can you get out here?'

'Yes, I should think so.'

'Great. Let's say noon. At the Grapes. It's that pub in Limehouse, down by the river. Think you can find it?'

'Yes.'

'Then I'll meet you there. Don't be late.'

'I won't be.'

Next, Harry phoned Dr Kingdom's consulting rooms in Marylebone. Quite apart from the fact that Heather's psychiatrist might know more of what was in her mind than anyone, Kingdom had accompanied Heather to the Skein of Geese on 10 September. Was that, Harry had begun to wonder, a purely professional act?

'Dr Kingdom's surgery. May I help you?' (The secretary's faintly accented voice was instantly recognizable.)

'Miss Labrooy, this is Harry Barnett. I called—'

'Ah, Mr Barnett! I remember your visit.'

'I was wondering—'

'Dr Kingdom returned on Monday and I explained the nature of your enquiry. In view of the exceptional circumstances, he is prepared to see you.' (Miss Labrooy had obviously pleaded eloquently on Harry's behalf.)

'That's great. When could—'

'He is fully committed for several weeks ahead, but he could spare you a few minutes at the end of his list one day.'

'What about today?'

'A moment please.' (There was a rustling of an appointments book.) 'His last patient is at four o'clock. If you called at five—'

'I'll be there.' (Minter and Kingdom within hours of each other: at last Harry was making progress.)

A little over an hour later, Harry felt more in control of events than he had at any time since Heather's disappearance. He and Minter were huddled at a table in the narrow bay window of the Grapes public bar, overlooked and unattended as the lunchtime rush gathered pace and noise, cocooned from the gossip and laughter that swirled about them. Twenty minutes before, Minter had arrived full of a swaggering blend of confidence and contempt. Now, as he eyed Harry warily and started his third cigarette, he had more the look of a hound on whom the fox had turned.

'If you've nothing for me, why the hell did you imply you had? This is just a waste of time. If you think you're going to persuade me to retract what I said in that article, you're a bigger—'

'I'm not asking you to retract anything.'

'Then what?'

'All I want to know is what you did with the information Nadine sold you.'

'Nothing. It wasn't worth anything.'

'Supposing that's the case, what led you to the Skein of Geese in the first place?'

'Intuition.' Minter tossed the word back like a dart.

'And what took you back there after your visit to Rhodes?'

'I liked the menu.' The young man glared at Harry with something close to resentment. The role of the biter bit was clearly not one he cared for. He leaned across the table and lowered his voice. 'Listen to me, Barnett. If you really are the Mr Persil in all this, that's fine by me. I took you for a bit of a rogue, but maybe you're just a fool. Either way, I buy information, but I don't sell it.'

'I'm not offering to pay you for it.'

'Or give it away.'

Harry was beginning to enjoy himself. There was genuine pleasure to be had from pinning Minter to the ropes. He too lowered his voice. 'An exchange is more what I had in mind. Your answers to a few questions – in exchange for my silence.'

'Your silence about what?'

'The relationship between you and Virginia Dysart.'

For a fraction of a second, Minter's eyes widened. Then he drew on his cigarette in an attempt to mask what Harry had already glimpsed: the shock of one who perceives a threat too late to evade it. 'You were the man she answered the door to,' he said glumly.

'Yes.'

'That doesn't prove a thing, of course.'

'It doesn't need to. Alan Dysart trusts me. If I told him what I suspect and why, do you think he'd ask for proof?'

'No. He probably wouldn't.' Minter smiled faintly, as if the irony of the situation had suddenly struck him. 'What do you want to know?'

'Everything you've found out.'

'If I tell you, what guarantee do I have you won't blow the gaff to Dysart anyway?'

238

'You have my word.'

The smile broadened. 'Is that meant to reassure me?' Minter leaned back in his chair for a moment, regarding Harry as if he were a specimen of endangered wildlife. Then his expression altered to something less decipherable. 'Well, maybe some home truths about Alan Dysart, public servant and national hero, will make you reckon he deserves the marriage he's got. I surrender. Ask away.'

'You and Clare Mallender were contemporaries at Oxford?'

'Yes. She was at Breakspear, I was at Queen's. We studied the same subject.'

'And became lovers?'

'I loved *her*. Clare, as I recall, was rather more indiscriminate with her affections.'

'But you did become engaged?'

'At my insistence, yes. But I knew it wouldn't last. She had her eyes set on a bigger catch than me.'

'Meaning?'

'A politician. Nobody specific, you understand. Anybody sufficiently powerful and influential would have done. She was a single-minded girl, our Clare. She thought an MP's bed was the quickest route into politics for a woman. She was probably right. Dysart just happened to be the one she chose. She already knew him, of course, as a friend of her father. It was he who recommended her to apply to Breakspear College when it started admitting women. When he left the Navy with a suitably heroic reputation, she must have reckoned he was her dream come true.'

'You're implying she became his mistress?'

'What do you think?'

'I think you're wrong.'

'Only a man who offers his word as a guarantee could be so naïve. All right, Clare never admitted it and I can't prove it, but it still seems a betting certainty.'

'Is that what prompted you to enquire into Dysart's past – jealousy?'

239

'No. If it had been, I'd have started digging for dirt before Clare died, wouldn't I?'

'Then what did?'

'Clare herself, strangely enough. Two days before she was killed, she phoned me out of the blue. We hadn't spoken in months. She asked if we could meet. I was surprised she could spare the time in the middle of an election campaign and concluded it was genuinely urgent. We met that evening and she asked me straight out if I'd be interested in an exclusive story: a scandal affecting a government minister. With the election less than a fortnight away, I could hardly believe my luck. Clare wouldn't name names there and then. She wanted me to clear her fee with my editor. She was asking a quarter of a million. It may seem a lot to you, but for a cast-iron story that might bring down a government, it's cheap at the price, believe me. We arranged to meet again three days later and agree terms. I don't deny I hoped it was Dysart she was planning to ruin – I wondered if there'd been a lovers' tiff – but she let nothing slip. Chapter and verse were to be forthcoming when the deal was settled. Well, I scurried off and did my bit, but, the day before we were to meet again, she was killed – and the story with her.'

Minter fell silent, letting his next, unspoken implication declare itself. 'You're not suggesting,' said Harry, 'that Clare was murdered to stop her selling you this story?'

'The possibility crossed my mind, yes.' He smiled at Harry's confusion. 'But the facts rule it out. The bombing of the yacht was definitely the work of the IRA. Dysart was an obvious target: ex-Navy, Ministry of Defence, outspoken in support of the Union. And the eve of the election was an obvious time to strike. Much as I was inclined to suspect otherwise, Clare was simply the victim of bad luck.' He leaned still further across the table, his shoulders hunched, his voice scarcely rising above a whisper. 'But I didn't leave it there, because Dysart had had one lucky escape too many for my liking. You could argue it wasn't his fault that Clare was killed – or that she didn't love me as much as I loved her – and I'd have to agree. What I'm not prepared to accept is that he's entitled to lead a charmed life while others struggle and falter and fail. Partly for Clare's sake, but mostly for my own satisfaction, I decided to do my level best to break that man. I reckoned he *was* the minister Clare was planning to denounce and I set about trying to discover his secret for myself.'

'But you've failed?'

'Only as far as proof goes. I'm on to him, take it from me.' Envy was written clearly on Minter's face: envy of another man's success. It was not a pleasant emotion, but it was a powerful enough one to have sustained him in the search when evidence was lacking. 'How much do you know about Alan Dysart, Harry?'

'As much as you, I expect.'

'That I doubt. I've made a special study of him, you see. I've assembled his biography brick by brick, just so I can have the pleasure of taking it apart. He was born in Birmingham forty-one years ago. His father had migrated from Scotland and set up business there. Dysart Engineering was one of the success stories of West Midlands industry after the Depression and, as Gordon Dysart's only son, young Alan was a dozen rungs above the likes of you and me on the ladder of life before he'd so much as lost his milk teeth. Off he went to Oundle, destined already for Oxford and probable greatness. By then the Dysarts had moved into the countryside. The old man had a house built for him in a pretty little Warwickshire village a few miles from Stratford, with the Avon flowing through the garden. Not a good move, as it turned out, because Mrs Dysart drowned in that stretch of river in 1963 and Gordon, never the same man again, died two years later, during Alan's first year at Oxford, making him a wealthy man overnight. Strangely enough, though, when he left Oxford he wound up the business and joined the Navy, despite the fact that he could have lived handsomely off his investments. Perhaps he thought a Naval commission was the right way to start his career. I've certainly always had the impression that he planned every detail of his life. It's like a glowing *curriculum vitae* was the first thing he produced when he learned how to write. Anyway, at Dartmouth he met Virginia—'

'I wondered when we'd come to her,' Harry put in. 'Was it she who told you all this?'

'No, as a matter of fact it wasn't. Dysart reveals little about himself, even to those close to him. What I've learned, I've learned the hard way.'

'Seducing the man's wife was the hard way, was it?'

Minter smiled. 'It was more a case of *her* seducing *me*. Dysart's no fun to be married to, you know. He's been looking elsewhere for years.'

'You know that for a fact, do you?'

'Virginia does. According to her it's not unusual in Naval marriages. The husbands become used to male company. They think of women in one light only. So, what's sauce for the goose . . . . You know how it is.'

'Do I?' The truth was that Harry understood Minter better than he cared to admit. But for the generosity Dysart had shown him over the years, he might even have approved of his actions. Yet he had no intention of revealing as much. What he most disliked in Minter – a suspicious temperament channelled into a grudge against the world – was what he most disliked in himself.

'Listen to me, Barnett,' said Minter, anger seeping into his voice. 'It's only because it might hamper my investigations that I don't invite you to tell Dysart about his wife's infidelity tomorrow. Don't think the morality of it troubles me for an instant. Now, have you heard all you want to hear?'

'Not quite. Why did you contact the Cunninghams last year?'

'Because Clare had mentioned dining at the Skein of Geese and Cunningham's an Old Breakspearean. He seemed a useful source where Dysart's Oxford days were concerned. But it was a waste of time. The man's too bowled over by Dysart's politics to be of the slightest—'

'Yet you went back there recently.'

'Yes, and got what he'd refused to tell me from his wife. Lurid nonsense about somebody being pushed out of a window twenty years ago. I only paid her five hundred in the hope she'd come up with something better.'

'But why *did* you go back?'

'Because, three months ago, Heather telephoned me and asked if I'd taken Clare to the Skein of Geese a couple of weeks before her death. I couldn't work out why she should be so interested, but the answer was no: I'd never taken her there. According to the pneumatic Nadine, Dysart was Clare's escort on that occasion, which was no surprise to me. When Heather disappeared, I thought it was a lead worth following, but it led nowhere. The Tyrrell Society and all that pining after defunct Oxford cabals – it's irrelevant, Harry, don't you see? Dysart's secret – the chink in his armour – is rooted in the here and now, not the lost and gone. It was Virginia who gave me the clue. Naval husbands, she said, were loyal to their shipmates ahead of kith, kin or country. And Charlie Mallender is exactly that: an old shipmate. Dysart's commanding officer on his very first ship to be precise. So I started enquiring into Mallender's little business enterprise – and guess what I found?'

'Well?'

'Mallender Marine sailed into troubled waters in the early eighties: failure to win orders, bad debts, profits turning into losses. Their recovery since then stems from winning several lucrative long-term Defence contracts. And it coincides almost exactly with Dysart's appointment to the Ministry of Defence three years ago. I'll tell you what I think, shall I? I think Dysart is feeding commercial secrets to his old skipper, Charlie Mallender, and that Clare found out about it. As Dysart's employee and Mallender's daughter, who could be better placed to smell a rat?'

Harry leaned back from the table and considered Minter's theory. It seemed to him quite possible that Dysart should exploit his official position to save an old friend

243

from bankruptcy. All it confirmed was the value he placed on friendship, which Harry well knew already. The world would denounce him for it unmercifully. No mitigation would be allowed for the fact that loyalty, not financial gain, was his motive. But Harry could not bring himself to condemn him. He doubted if Dysart deserved to be ruined by the ruthless young woman Clare Mallender seemed to have been, any more than he deserved to be hounded by the unscrupulous journalist Jonathan Minter undoubtedly was. Besides, as Minter was in the process of admitting, he had so far assembled not a shred of evidence to support his claim.

'When I found out you'd been sacked by Mallender Marine, I thought you might be able to supply the proof I need. If you do know anything, my offer's still open, you know. I should think you could use some money just now. Am I right?'

Minter, had he but known it, was right as well as wrong: right that Harry was running short of cash, wrong if he believed that currently mattered to him a jot. 'I can't help you,' he replied. And it was true. Even if there was a case for Dysart to answer, it was not relevant to Heather's disappearance. She had been following a trail Minter had turned his back on, but Harry had the photographs to keep him on course.

'Please yourself.'

'I will. You see, I've no intention of helping you ruin a man I admire.'

'Then why all these questions?'

'I hoped you might tell me something that would lead me to Heather.'

Minter snorted derisively. 'My answer's the same as yours. I can't help you. I don't know where she is – if she's alive at all – and I don't much care. She was always just Clare's plain, timid little sister to me: inferior, inadequate and inconsequential. She means nothing to me and nothing to Dysart either. Neurotic enough to have vanished of her own accord – or even to have got herself murdered. What

244

difference does it make? After drawing a blank on Rhodes, I had to write something that justified my travelling expenses, so I made you the villain of the piece. Besides, I thought it might sting you into giving me something on the Mallenders. You did work for them, after all.'

'Ten years ago. Nothing from that period supports your theory.'

'Have it your own way.' Minter glanced at his watch. 'I've got to go. I take it you've heard enough?'

'Yes. I think I have.'

'Then hear one last thing. If you should decide to tell Dysart about me and Virginia, bear in mind *The Courier* could make your life here in England very unpleasant for you. Heather Mallender's murderer walks free – that sort of thing. You get my drift?'

Harry did not reply. When the door of the pub slammed shut behind Minter a few moments later, he sighed with relief and took a lengthy gulp at his beer. It was at least gratifying to know that his initial dislike of the young man had been justified. He doubted if his hatred of Dysart could even be honoured with the description of revenge. His claim to have loved Clare Mallender and to have had her stolen from him somehow lacked conviction and, anyway, his conquest of Virginia Dysart could be said to have evened the score. No, Minter was motivated more by the unreasoning malice which individual achievement seemed often to inspire in others. The irony was that, by dismissing as irrelevant all talk of the Tyrrell Society, he had closed his eyes to the vital clue Rex Cunningham could have given him: the identity of the man whose photograph Clare Mallender had carried about with her. Armed with that information, he might have re-directed his enquiries long ago.

As Harry squeezed through the ruck to order another pint, he could not suppress a private smile at Minter's expense. For all his zeal and determination, for all the trained wiles of the investigative journalist, he was wide of the mark. The truth lay elsewhere. And Harry knew where.

27

Confidence, that most fickle of emotions, had deserted Harry. He did not know why and, in the absence of an obvious explanation, attributed it to his first ever professional encounter with a psychiatrist. There was no archetypal couch in Dr Kingdom's consulting room, although a chair by the window looked as if it could be converted for the purpose. But for the titles of the books on the shelves, however, Harry felt it would have served for the conduct of almost any other business than that of healing troubled minds. Nevertheless, the chair he was sitting in was soft enough and the recorded harpsichord music sufficiently soporific to calm the anxieties and lower the defences of most people. But not of Harry.

Was Kingdom himself, perhaps, the source of his unease? This snappily dressed, half-smiling man with something of the looks of the young Cary Grant about him did not approximate to his vision of a psychiatrist. Glancing through a file (which Harry took to be Heather's) with the pursed lips and darting eyes of an auditor perusing an unsatisfactory set of accounts, he conveyed none of the warmth or insight which Harry supposed successful psychoanalysis to require. To make matters worse, there was a cast to his expression and a pitch to his voice which Harry found strangely familiar, as if, inconceivable though he knew it to be, they had met before.

A steadily worsening headache and a dry throat that was

rapidly becoming sore compounded Harry's discomfort. Perhaps he had drunk too much at the Grapes. Perhaps he was sickening for a cold. Either way, concentration seemed to require an enormous effort and forceful argument a better assembled set of thoughts than he currently possessed. He had intended to sweep aside any reservations Kingdom might have about revealing a patient's secrets by pointing out the overriding importance of finding Heather, but, instead, he had become meek and subdued, as if content to accept Kingdom's judgement unreservedly on how much or how little he could divulge.

'I'd like to help you, Mr Barnett,' Kingdom said after a lengthy silence, 'but I can't. Naturally, I hope Heather is alive, but, if she is, she has every right to expect that I will observe absolute confidentiality where her medical history is concerned. My hands are tied.'

'All I want to know—'

'All you want to know is what I cannot tell you: whether her recent illness might in some way explain her disappearance. To bare one's soul to a member of my profession, Mr Barnett, is no small hurdle to surmount. If there was the slightest risk of what one revealed in the process becoming known to others . . . . Well, I trust you appreciate my position.'

'Could I at least ask a few questions?'

'Ask by all means, so long as you understand how limited my freedom may be to answer.'

Harry took a deep breath and struggled to shape some propositions that would not offend the doctor's code of ethics. 'Heather had a breakdown last year, didn't she, following the death of her sister?'

This at least seemed to pass the test. 'Yes,' Kingdom replied cautiously.

'And spent some time in an institution?'

'She was a voluntary resident at one of the hospitals where I act as a consultant.'

'She's been your patient since then?'

'Yes.'

247

'The circumstances of her sister's death must have been very upsetting, but was there anything else which—'

Kingdom held up his hand. 'No good, Mr Barnett. Facts I can supply. Clinical details I cannot.'

Harry leaned back in the chair. His headache was perceptibly worse. 'There wasn't much point agreeing to see me, was there?' he said wearily.

'I wouldn't say that. I was grateful for the information you conveyed regarding Heather's reading matter on Rhodes. I wanted to thank you. It may be highly significant.'

'But you can't tell me how?'

'I'm afraid not.'

'Nor whether it might indicate she'd met somebody on Rhodes she was frightened of?'

'The same objection applies.'

'Then I'm wasting my breath.'

'Not necessarily.' The tone of Kingdom's voice had altered. Harry was no longer looking at him, but felt sure he had leaned forward across his desk, as if their discussion were only now taking the desired direction. 'After all, I am very worried about Heather. And you were the last person to see her. The Hippocratic oath doesn't apply to you, Mr Barnett. You could be as frank as you wanted with me.'

'Frank? What about?'

'Oh, your feelings about Heather. Your assessment of her character. What you hoped for from your friendship with her.'

'Would that help?'

'It might.' When you did not see the scrupulous, disinterested face of Dr Peter Kingdom, his words had a soothing, almost seductive quality. Was this, Harry wondered, the key to psychoanalysis: not so much interrogation as mental massage?

'It was obvious Heather had been unwell, but she seemed almost completely better. Perhaps that was the effect of Rhodes as much as anything else. I liked her from the start.'

'In what way did you like her?'

How to answer? Harry stared up at the ceiling and followed with his eye the pattern of the coving.

'We just hit it off together,' he replied lamely. 'Allowing for the generation gap, we found we had a surprising amount in common. Both of us are misfits, really, aren't we?'

'Are you?'

'Oh yes. Coming home's taught me that. I've no family apart from my mother, no job, no money, no property, no prospects. As far as I can see, England doesn't welcome a prodigal son like me.'

'That sounds rather like self-pity.'

'It is, I suppose. But when nobody else feels sorry for you, you tend to feel sorry for yourself, don't you?'

'Excluded from society, you mean? Passed over by change? Starved of sympathy?'

The diagnosis was all too succinct. 'Yes,' Harry murmured.

'Do you think Heather felt the same way?'

'You tell me.'

'You know I can't do that.'

The upper branches of a plane tree were visible through the window, swaying faintly in a gentle breeze. They looked proud and mournful to Harry's eye, burdened with too much memory. He wondered if Heather, sitting in the same chair and gazing at the same view, had somehow bequeathed to him this reaction, or if it were entirely his own, a product of the self-pity Kingdom had identified. In the end, however, the sensation that Heather had been and felt this way before him was overriding. When he spoke, it was almost as if she had put the words in his mouth. 'It seemed to me she'd been worn down by leading a life she wasn't fitted for. She'd been required to be beautiful and talented and independent, but she hadn't wanted to be any of those things. The result was a family who didn't understand her, a career that didn't satisfy her and a generation that didn't accept her.'

249

'But you did?'

'I think so, yes. At least, I tried to.'

'And did she let you?'

This was one question which Harry could not hope to answer truthfully. His insights into Heather's character had followed, not preceded, her disappearance. To admit as much would be to admit he had been as negligent of her difficulties as anyone else. Therefore he lied. 'I'm not sure what you mean.'

'Then let us approach the subject from a different direction. Heather was due to return to this country within days of your visit to Profitis Ilias, wasn't she?'

'Yes.'

'Was she looking forward to leaving Rhodes?'

'No, I don't think she was.'

'Then why was she going to leave?'

'All holidays have to end, don't they? Besides, it was expected of her.'

'By her unsympathetic family and friends in England, you mean?'

The drift of their exchanges had begun to disturb Harry. He did not know where they were heading, but already it was clear the destination would not be of his choosing. 'Er . . . yes,' he replied hesitantly.

'Did *you* want her to leave?'

'No, certainly not.'

'In fact, you wanted her to remain?'

'Well . . . yes, of course.'

'You both wanted her to stay on Rhodes, but neither of you felt able to admit it: is that what you're saying?'

It would have been more accurate to say he preferred that version of events to any other, but one lie had committed him now to several distortions. 'Yes, I suppose it is.'

'So, by preventing Heather from leaving, you would have been acting in her best interests as well as yours?'

'I'm sorry?'

'And the trip to Profitis Ilias was your last chance to make her see reason, wasn't it?'

Heather's receding figure, dwindling as it climbed the pine-bound slope, twitched once more on the invisible line that trailed between them. Harry felt stiflingly hot, choking almost, as he loosened his collar. He knew he had done nothing, knew beyond suggestion's reach that he had been innocent of action as well as intention. And yet, and yet . . . . Ever since his dream of Heather that last night in Lindos, ever since those images of Aphrodite and Silenus had been planted in his mind, knowledge, even certainty, had not been enough.

'What went wrong, Harry? Was there a misunderstanding? A struggle? A panic?'

Turn and look. You cannot run yet. Where she has fallen. Face averted, thank God, flaxen hair blown across the glimpse you might have had of her frozen expression. Her white, goose-pimpled body. Left leg straight, foot still braced against the ground, heel raised, toes gouged into the litter of leaves as if scrabbling for a hold. Right leg bent double, knee red from impact, a scatter of dark soil across her calf, as if she had been trying to run even as she fell. The image held, precise and petrified: the mound of her hip, the curve of her stomach, the arm resting, its unavailing fist closed around a handful of cold, cloying earth. Harry could not move, could not speak, could not judge for this suspended moment whether what he saw was recollected or imagined.

'What happened, Harry? You can tell me.'

Kingdom's words were like harsh daylight flooding into a photographer's dark-room. The picture that had so nearly secured its hold faded from the refracting blankness in the instant it took Harry to realize what it was that Kingdom wanted from him. Something most of his patients gave willingly: a confession. But, in this case, a confession to murder. 'You think I killed her?' he said numbly.

'Well, if you did—'

'It won't go any further, is that it?' Suddenly, Harry was angry. How dare this wheedling, simpering doctor set out to trap him? 'If you think I came here to ease my conscience, you're wrong.'

'Am I? Why did you come, then?'

'I told you: I'm trying to find Heather. And all everybody else seems to be doing is trying to stop me.'

'I'm not trying to stop you.'

'Aren't you? Your professional reticence is a pretty effective obstacle, isn't it?'

'I've explained to you—'

'Or is it *your* conscience that needs easing?' Stung by his susceptibility to Kingdom's line of questioning, Harry fought back with the only weapon at his disposal: knowledge the other man could not be aware he possessed. 'You took Heather to dinner at the Skein of Geese in Haslemere on the tenth of September, didn't you, Doctor?'

'How did you—'

'Were there any other candlelit evenings? Any other discreet little out-of-town excursions? You asked me in what way I liked her. Well in what way did *you* like her, Doctor?'

'I won't be spoken to like this.' Kingdom jumped to his feet. The mask of professional reserve was down now, revealing the average short-tempered human beneath.

'Or is that another question you think Heather might not want you to answer?' Harry too rose from his chair, determined to allow Kingdom no further advantage.

'I won't be interrogated by you, Mr Barnett.' Kingdom brought the flat of his hand down heavily on the desktop. 'I won't have it, do you hear?'

That was it. The exact phrase, tied to the same blustering expression, the same explosion of unnecessary anger. It sought and found in Harry's memory the niggling familiarity he had already sensed. He dragged it to the surface of his thoughts. And brought with it a precise and sharply-etched recollection that required no effort of the imagination to build or bolster. For this was reality, as durable as it was crucial, as incontrovertible as it was incomprehensible.

*

Lindos: Sunday the sixth of November. High blue skies above a fragment of one of Harry's last carefree days, when Profitis Ilias and Heather's disappearance lay in wait but unforeseen, nearly a week in the future. It had been a day of rare pleasure for Harry, climaxed by lunch with Heather at the villa. Now, having passed the late afternoon imbibing gently at the *Taverna Silenou*, and feeling unusually tolerant of the rash of visitors the sabbath always brought to Lindos, he was picking a dawdling path back along one of the town's winding cobbled alleys, squinting against the strength of the sun. As he ambled past Papaioannou's trinket shop, he was amused to hear an English tourist resisting the proprietor's notoriously persistent sales technique. Glancing in, he saw a tall, flustered figure turning away in disgust from the counter. He was, perhaps, a little too smartly dressed for a holidaymaker, but the point he was making was clear enough.

'I won't have it, do you hear?'

He brushed against Harry as he emerged from the shop, but uttered no apology, as if he was too irritated to have noticed. Then he hurried away towards the main square. Harry, for his part, exchanged a knowing smile with Papaioannou, then went on in the direction of the village. Within twenty yards, he had forgotten the incident. Nor would he ever have remembered it, had he not met the man again, a long way from Lindos.

'I won't have it, do you hear?' Kingdom had said much else besides that, and had concluded by asking Harry to leave the premises at once, but the echoes of one repeated phrase were all that filled Harry's head as he moved distractedly towards the door. Dr Peter Kingdom was the man who had stormed past Harry out of Papaioannou's shop in Lindos five days before Heather's disappearance. Five short days. 'A meeting at a particular place, which has been expected beforehand, amounts in fact to a rendezvous.' It was a phrase from the very page she had been reading. A meeting misinterpreted, a warning ignored, a danger defied. He had thought it might be so and now he had the proof. Kingdom on Rhodes, where he had no reason to be, where he had no cause to fear he would be recognized, far less remembered. But Harry had seen him. He had been looking for the omen Heather might have nerved herself to disregard. And now he had found it.

28

Two trains had come and gone on the northbound platform of the Bakerloo line at Marylebone tube station, but Harry had boarded neither. The rush-hour crowds had thinned and he was alone now on the bench, but in no hurry to depart. The black tunnel mouths, the stale warm air, the distant wail of a saxophone: these had become sensations that scarcely penetrated the borders of his awareness. His mind was fixed elsewhere, struggling to piece together the fragments of an event he had participated in but not understood. He knew it was a hopeless task – like assembling a jig-saw puzzle without the picture to serve as a guide – but still he could not abandon it.

The Heather he had known on Rhodes was an uncomplicated and instantly likeable young woman: a little gauche perhaps, a little unsure of herself, but essentially only what she might be expected to be. Now he saw it had all been a sham. Either he had been pitifully unobservant or she had been expertly deceitful. There had been secrets, fears, dangers and delusions filling her every thought. Her dead sister. Her family. Her psychiatrist. The Tyrrell Society. The bombing of Dysart's yacht. The past. The present. The future. And the ninth photograph she had taken was of a school. Harry drew the wallet from his pocket and leafed through the pictures until he found it. It was where Jack Cornelius taught. Of that there could be no doubt. It was where she had gone after visiting the Skein of Geese. It was where he would have gone in her shoes. It was the logical next step. But the next step along a road leading where? Profitis Ilias. That was all he knew. If only he had paid more attention when he had had the chance. If only his head did not ache so badly that thought seemed driven out by the throbbing. If only—

'Mr Barnett!' trilled a voice next to him. 'What are you doing here?'

He thrust the photographs back into his pocket and jerked round. Beside him on the bench sat Kingdom's secretary, clad in raincoat and headscarf. She was smiling brightly, but her eyes retained a solemnity that was strangely intimidating. In the instant before his failure to reply became conspicuous, it occurred to him that he had never met anybody whose natural gaze was so wide-eyed and unblinking, so direct yet unrevealing.

'You left the surgery nearly an hour ago. I'm surprised you're not well on your way. Didn't you say you live in Swindon?'

'Did I? Well yes, I do, but—'

'So you're making for Paddington?'

'Er . . . yes.'

'Then we'll be travelling together for a couple of stops. Here's the train.'

A train had indeed arrived. It burst out of the tunnel in a gale of hot air and shuddered to a halt. Harry obediently followed Miss Labrooy aboard and sat down opposite her. A glance at some of their fellow-passengers suggested to his mind several reasons why she should be glad of a companion. Every day, presumably, she journeyed through this worm-hole of noise and filth from one of the unlovely suburbs listed on the route plan above her head to type letters and answer the telephone for Dr Peter Kingdom. She must know as much of his patients' secrets as he did himself.

'I couldn't help noticing,' said Miss Labrooy as the train lurched into motion, 'that Dr Kingdom seemed rather upset after you left. I do hope there wasn't a disagreement.'

256

Harry forced a smile. 'Let's say a difference of emphasis. I think finding Heather is more important than observing confidentiality. Your boss doesn't.'

'I thought that might be the problem. Dr Kingdom really is in a difficult position, you know.'

'So am I, as it happens. I'm being accused of things I didn't do – and I'm missing a friend.'

'You mean Heather?'

'Yes, Miss Labrooy, I mean Heather.'

The train vibrated to a standstill at Edgware Road. During the curious lull that followed, in which nobody seemed to get on or off, Miss Labrooy leaned forward in her seat and said: 'Do you know why I decided to help you when you came to the surgery last week, Mr Barnett? Because you spoke about Heather in the present tense, as if you genuinely believe she's still alive.'

'I do.'

The train started. 'I hope you're right. Heather was – is – a friend of mine too.'

'Really?'

'She gave me some help when I badly needed it. I'm not likely to forget her kindness to me, so if there's any way I can help her now . . . . '

Hope flared in Harry. The gratitude Miss Labrooy owed Heather might outweigh her loyalty to Kingdom. 'Anything you can tell me might be helpful,' he said cautiously. 'For instance, how did Dr Kingdom react to the news of her disappearance?'

'He was very concerned. Of course, I didn't see him until some days afterwards, so I can't really—'

'What do you mean – "some days afterwards"?'

'Well, he was in Switzerland at the time. He didn't get back until . . . on, it must have been Tuesday of the following week.'

'Switzerland?'

'He's a special consultant at the Versorelli Institute in Geneva, which specializes in cases others have given up as hopeless. His work often takes him there.'

257

'How long did he spend there on that occasion?'

'I'm not sure I can—'

'You said you wanted to help.'

The train had stopped again. They were at Paddington. But Harry made no move. 'This is your station, Mr Barnett.'

'It doesn't matter. I'll overrun.'

She leaned still further forward and lowered her voice. 'I'm not sure Dr Kingdom would want me to discuss his work with you. You must see how delicate my position is.'

'What about Heather, Miss Labrooy?' Harry sensed that very little pressure would be required to overcome her scruples. 'Mightn't her position be even more delicate?'

The doors hissed shut and the train began to move. 'It might be, yes.' Miss Labrooy's struggle with her conscience was visible in her face. 'What do you want to know?'

'The duration of Dr Kingdom's visit to Geneva.'

There was a further moment of hesitation, then she said: 'He flew to Geneva on Friday the fourth of November and returned on Monday the fourteenth.'

Harry could scarcely suppress a smile. It was the confirmation he needed. 'Is that the normal length of time he goes for?'

'It's usually less.'

'And how do you know he went to Geneva?'

'I booked the tickets for him.' Miss Labrooy frowned in puzzlement. 'And he telephoned me a couple of times that week from the Institute.'

It did not matter, of course. Harry had never really expected to be told anything different. Geneva on the fourth. Rhodes on the sixth. It was a demanding itinerary, but by no means an impossible one. The crucial question was: where had he been on the eleventh? 'Any idea as to the days on which he telephoned?'

'Monday, I think . . . and Wednesday.'

So: there had been no contact on the day of their visit

to Profitis Ilias. Not that it would have proved anything if there had been. A man could say he was telephoning from a clinic in Geneva and actually be in a hotel on Rhodes. It was all feasible enough. Only the purpose remained obscure. They rattled to a halt and Miss Labrooy's brown, far-seeing eyes engaged Harry's in earnest scrutiny.

'Why are you questioning me about Dr Kingdom's movements, Mr Barnett?'

'Because my impression is that he's using the privacy of the consulting room to hide something. And what's more' – he decided to risk a wild guess as the train started again – 'I think you know he is.'

Her stare would not release him. It held him in an interval of assessment more potent than the silence that accompanied it. What he was asking her to do required a degree of trust that he had too little time to earn. The train pulled into Maida Vale. And pulled out again. And then she spoke.

'Heather's problem was that she didn't feel she belonged, Mr Barnett. Belonged, that is, in the family she was born to and the world she moved in.'

'I see you really do know her.'

Miss Labrooy smiled. 'Always that stubborn present tense. Your optimism is admirable, Mr Barnett, the more so since pessimism is, I suspect, your natural mood. An Englishman exiled in his homeland. Is that not your condition?'

'I suppose it is, yes.'

'It is mine also, in a sense. I am Sri Lankan by birth, but English by upbringing. My mother was the daughter of an English officer in the Indian police, who fell in love with a humble clerk in Jaffna and had the temerity to marry him. The offspring of such a union are never quite accepted – on either side of the racial divide. So, you see, neither of us feels at home here – but it is our home nonetheless. Perhaps that is why Heather felt more at ease with the likes of you and I than with her family and the friends they chose for her.'

259

The train stopped at Kilburn Park and the last passenger within earshot disembarked. Harry wondered what it was Heather had done for Miss Labrooy, but felt glad, on the whole, that he did not know. It was enough to have discovered one true mutual friend whose testimony could be relied upon. As the train accelerated out of the station, she said what he wanted to hear.

'You are right, Mr Barnett. Dr Kingdom *is* hiding something, though I am not sure he is aware that he is. Certainly Heather did not realize what it was. Only to me, who knew them both, was it obvious. Heather entered Challenbrooke Hospital near Maidenhead as a voluntary patient in November of last year. Dr Kingdom was the consultant who took charge of her case. When she was discharged in March of this year, he continued to see her regularly, in order to monitor her recovery. As the months passed, it became clear to me, however, that he was doing something else as well.'

'Which was?'

The train was running in the open now, the blackness beyond its windows relieved by distant amber lights which seemed to track their progress like the eyes of forest-dwelling creatures fixed on a lonely wayfarer. 'He was falling in love with her, Mr Barnett. Slowly but surely, he was becoming obsessed with her. It is always a danger for doctors, I suppose. Their relations with patients must be intimate yet impersonal, trusting yet guarded. The balance is a difficult one to strike, the more so when a thorough knowledge of the patient's mind as well as her body is required. I cannot say what it was in Heather that Dr Kingdom found so enthralling. The mystery of what one person finds fascinating in another has, after all, defeated the finest philosophers. But there is no doubt in my mind that his attitude to her became increasingly unprofessional in the course of the spring and summer.'

'Is Dr Kingdom married?'

'No. He lives alone. Many would regard him, I think, as an eligible bachelor. Highly eligible, if it comes to that.

There would have been nothing improper in his paying court to Heather, had she not been his patient. Indeed, the fact that he did not refer her to a different psychiatrist convinced me for a long time that I had misconstrued the situation. I have worked for him for more than three years and have come to admire him both as a doctor and a man. Ethically, he had always been above reproach. That is why his conduct with regard to Heather was so difficult to understand and why, in the end, I concluded that he was in the grip of an obsession he was powerless to resist.'

Another stop. Queen's Park. A gangling youth with personal stereo and the thickest-soled baseball boots Harry had ever seen fell into the adjacent seat and began slapping his knee in time to the music only he could hear. The train doors lingered open to the musty night air, encouraging Harry to sink his voice to a whisper as he said: 'Do you have any real evidence for this, Miss Labrooy?'

'I have the evidence of my own senses. Dr Kingdom became increasingly preoccupied and distracted, brooding, I imagine, on the conflict between heart and duty. Heather did not realize what was happening, but I did, and it saddened me to see it.'

'It's only your opinion though, isn't it – only your subjective assessment?'

'Not quite.' The doors closed, re-opened, then closed again. 'There is rather more to it than that.' With a plunging lurch, the train started. 'My suspicions were confirmed when Dr Kingdom stopped giving me material for Heather's file. I generally type all his notes, reports and correspondence, but, during the summer, he took to typing such items which related to Heather himself.'

'What explanation did he give?'

'None. Nor did I feel able to ask for one. Heather and I were on friendly terms by then. We often lunched together after her weekly consultation. Dr Kingdom could have cited that as justification for keeping the material back. All the patients' files are kept under lock and key in his office, so I only see what I am asked to type.'

261

'But I don't understand. What would have been the point of keeping the contents of Heather's file secret?'

'You should know the answer to that, Mr Barnett. You had a month to become acquainted with her on Rhodes. Isn't it obvious?' She glanced out of the window as they drew into Kensal Green station. 'We've come to the parting of the ways. This is my stop.'

'But we can't leave it there.'

Miss Labrooy did not reply. Instead, she rose smartly from her seat and stepped out through the doors as they opened. Harry hurried out behind her, heard her shoes clicking with angry swiftness on the platform, wondered what he had done to annoy her – was he too obtuse, too inquisitive? – and was about to call after her when she pulled up abruptly and turned to face him. In the dim light, he could see her lower lip trembling slightly, as if resolution had suddenly failed her.

'What's wrong?'

'I may have said too much. I may have abused the trust Dr Kingdom placed in me.'

'I didn't force you to say anything.'

'No. You didn't.'

'But now you have . . . .'

'I can't just stop: is that it? You're right, of course, but it all depends . . . .'

'On what?'

'On what really happened at Profitis Ilias on the eleventh of November. I know what the newspapers say – and I don't believe them. But what do you say, Mr Barnett? What's your version of events?'

'I don't know what happened. If I did—'

'But you were there. You were with her in the days and weeks that led up to it. Only you can tell me what I need to know. Only you can help me to be sure. Will you?'

At last Harry understood what she wanted of him. Since returning to England, he had searched in vain for somebody who was, like him, a true friend of Heather Mallender. Little had he thought to find one where now

262

he had. Suspicion had been his watchword and perhaps Miss Labrooy's as well. Now they were obliged to abandon that in favour of something far riskier but potentially more rewarding. For Heather's sake, they had to trust each other.

'Tell me every detail, Harry. Re-live every moment of those last days you spent with Heather. Then maybe I'll know whether my fears have any substance.'

They walked slowly away from the station through a maze of dingy terraced streets. Pounding music in thin-curtained rooms. Cars propped up on bricks. Cats and who knew what else scrabbling through piled rubbish in overgrown front gardens. Boarded windows. Blocked-up doorways. Dereliction. Decrepitude. Decay. Halfway along improbably named Foxglove Road, where darkness seemed a mercy and nobody, felt Harry, deserved to live, Zohra Labrooy turned a key in a wobbly lock and welcomed Harry to her home.

A narrow passage, flickeringly lit. Dodgy wiring, thought Harry: typical of the neighbourhood, no doubt. To their left, a door stood open by about six inches, revealing a cluttered sitting room. In a vast and threadbare armchair, surrounded by brass and ivory knick-knacks, draped in a voluminous shawl, three-bar electric fire trained on her feet, sat an old woman, breathing wheezily and staring with obvious relief at Zohra. She had the sad and deflated appearance of somebody who had once lived life to the full but now had only the memories of such times to sustain her – like a galleon whose sails sag limply round the masts where once they have billowed majestically.

'It's me, Mrs Tandy,' said Zohra, leaning into the room. 'With a friend.'

'So I see.' The old lady smiled at Harry like a dowager duchess greeting her granddaughter's suitor.

After a few seconds of awkward introductions, Zohra excused herself with a promise to be down for cocoa at the usual time, then led Harry upstairs. 'Mrs Tandy remembers Kensal Green when it was a desirable area,' she explained as they reached her flat. 'Apart from an occasional tendency to treat me like the ayah she had in India as a child, she's the perfect landlady.'

Harry was taken aback by Miss Labrooy's flat. His prejudiced expectations of orientalism were confounded by restrained furnishings which could have been chosen by any Home Counties newly-wed and an offer not of tea but of gin. Seated beneath a standard lamp, glass in hand, impressionist art on the wall and thick floor-length curtains closed against the night, he found it possible to believe he was almost anywhere but where he really was.

Profitis Ilias, for instance. Zohra Labrooy was the ideal audience for reminiscence or confession. Neither impatient nor inattentive, she had a positive gift for remaining still and alert, her large brown eyes fixed upon him as he reconstructed those distant events, willing him to remember and recall every incident, however minor, every remark, however trivial.

He kept nothing back. Nothing, that is, of what he could definitely state. Only his sighting of Kingdom in Lindos five days before Heather's disappearance did he withhold: he did not yet want to test Zohra's loyalty too severely.

When he had finished, she said nothing for more than a minute, but continued to stare at him, as if still seeking the assurance she had hoped his account would supply.

'Well?' he said at last.

She sighed heavily. 'It is as I feared. Not so simple. Not so simple at all.'

'Did you think it would be?'

'When I last saw Heather, anybody less in need of psychiatric treatment it would have been hard to imagine. Calm, purposeful and entirely self-possessed: so she seemed to me.'

'Yet she was still seeing Dr Kingdom.'

'Yes. I thought that was why he began to type his own notes, you see. I even hinted at it to Heather. Because she had recovered completely, I mean, so completely that she no longer required Dr Kingdom's services as a counsellor. His part in her life was over, but I don't think he could accept that it was. I believe he continued to treat her long after he needed to, that he misled her into believing such treatment was necessary and that he faked his file notes accordingly.'

Harry let out a long breath. It could be true, of course, and there was more to support the idea than Zohra knew. But if it was, and if Kingdom had come to Rhodes with some sinister intent – to lure Heather away, to abduct her, to seduce her – what of the photographs? They became a wild goose chase after an obsession of Heather's very own, which, all else apart, cast doubt on Zohra's confidence in her mental stability. Moreover, where – aside from Harry's unsubstantiated sighting – was the hard evidence to support such a contention? And where, assuming it to be well-founded, was Heather?

'I have said nothing because nobody would believe me if I did, because a doctor's word would always be taken against his secretary's, and because . . . . '

'Yes?'

'Because I may be wrong. Even if Dr Kingdom did feel more for Heather than a doctor should for his patient, it doesn't mean that had anything to do with her disappearance.'

'But he *was* out of the country at the time.'

'In Switzerland – a long way from Rhodes.'

Now was the time to tell her. He would need her help if they were to take the matter further. She had to know. 'Not so very far. He left for Geneva, you said, on Friday the fourth of November. I saw him in Lindos on Sunday the sixth.' He read in her face the surprise and shock that a suspicion confirmed can sometimes bring. 'A chance encounter, that's all. Not one he'd remember. Not one I'd have remembered, but for his losing his temper with me this afternoon. He was angry that day, too, you see. It was his anger I recognized.'

Zohra Labrooy sat quite still, her face a mask of frozen

reaction. She might be frightened, Harry supposed, by the discovery that her frail and hesitant theory had substance after all. She reached out for her glass and swallowed most of the contents at a gulp.

'If he told you he was in Geneva throughout his absence, he was lying.'

'He did tell me that.' Her voice sounded numb, as if she had only now abandoned the hope that her employer was more misjudged than misguided.

'His phone calls to you may not even have been made from Geneva.'

'They may not.'

'He could have remained on Rhodes until the eleventh. He could have met Heather on Profitis Ilias – by agreement or by surprise.'

'He could have, yes.'

'That could have been the meeting she foresaw – or expected. The meeting whose dangers she tried to reason away by recourse to Freud.'

'As you say, Harry – it could well have been.' She nodded faintly, passed a nervous tongue along her lips, then looked at him intently. 'But there's not a shred of proof, is there?'

'None,' he responded bleakly.

Another heavy sigh, this time of courage being summoned. 'I may be able to obtain some proof. What then?'

'What proof did you have in mind?'

'I know several members of staff at the Versorelli Institute quite well. My opposite numbers, you understand. I could ask them for details of Dr Kingdom's visit in November. I could say he had lost some documents, needed the dates and times of his attendance – patients visited, doctors consulted and so forth – to complete his records. There's no reason why they should think such a request odd – or even unusual.' She frowned in anticipation of what would be entailed. 'They wouldn't check with him, I'm sure. They'd treat my questions as entirely innocent and provide the answers without the slightest difficulty.'

'You'd be prepared to do that?'

'If there's no other way, yes.'

And there was no other way. The glance they exchanged acknowledged as much. 'How long do you think it would take?'

'I don't know. A few days. It's a question of the right opportunity presenting itself.'

A small silence was filled by mutual contemplation of the step they were about to take. Both knew it would not end with tricking information out of the Versorelli Institute. 'It'll be risky,' said Harry, noticing as he did so how his choice of tense had changed from the conditional to the future. 'If Kingdom finds out—'

There was nobility as well as determination in the gaze with which she cut him short. 'What choice do I have, Harry? Heather is my friend as well as yours. If Dr Kingdom *has* done anything to harm her . . . what choice do I really have?'

29

Harry woke with a violent start. His sleep, he knew at once, must have been unusually deep, for he had no clear idea how long it had lasted nor where for that matter he was. For several seconds, his brain refused to function, resisting all his efforts to impose the reassuring certainties of time and place. He felt cold to the point of shivering, weak enough for standing to be out of the question. He raised his trembling hand to his forehead and felt the dampness of sweat against his skin. He tried to swallow, but there was pain waiting deep in his throat to defeat him. And there was noise and motion as well, some rattling, juddering momentum of onward travel. He raised his head cautiously and looked around.

He was in a tube train. Of course he was in a tube train. How could he have forgotten – even momentarily? He was on his way back from Kensal Green to Paddington, on his way back from discovering in Zohra Labrooy at least one friend of Heather's who was prepared to be an ally of his. As if to convince himself he had not imagined their encounter, he forced his mind to concentrate on what she had agreed to do.

She would elicit from her colleagues at the Versorelli Institute the exact itinerary Kingdom had followed there in November. When he arrived. When he left. When he was absent for as long as a day. And when she had gleaned every detail . . . why then they would have him, wouldn't they? All Harry had to do was return to Swindon and await

268

her word. She had undertaken to contact him by the end of next week to report what progress she had made and he did not doubt she would do so, for she was a woman of her word. Or so he thought. But, then, what did he really know of her? Heather had never spoken of her friend Zohra Labrooy, or of any other friend come to that. Yet friendship remained the only star to steer by. Dysart was a friend. So was Heather. Maybe Zohra could become one as well.

The train was beginning to slow for the next station. Suddenly, the hideous possibility occurred to Harry that he had slept past his stop and would have to retrace his route from some remote reach of the Bakerloo line. His weariness rebelled against the prospect and he glanced across at the opposite window in search of some clue as to his whereabouts. But what he saw was something altogether different.

The man in the seat opposite was thin, sallow-faced and raincoated. His black hair, streaked with grey, was plastered across a bald scalp. He was so ordinary as to be extraordinary, so obscure that only stealth could be his calling. And his two small eyes, twinkling like a rodent's, were fixed on Harry. Surely he could not be, but surely he was . . . . The man on the train at Reading. In his hand, as final confirmation, was the same paperback book, on its cover a girl in black underwear, slumped dead across a couch, strangled with a scarf.

The train was braking hard now, but Harry could not think fast enough. What was the probability – the unvarnished statistical likelihood – of such a coincidence? Next to nothing, surely. Surely to God. With a sudden pang of remorse, he reproached himself for not telling Zohra about the warnings he had received, if warnings they were, about the messages he had decided to ignore, on her behalf as well as his own.

They were in the station now, reaching and passing the moment when deceleration made the blurred nameboards legible. It was Warwick Avenue, the last stop before Paddington. At least, thank God, they had not overshot.

What should he do? Get off here? Or remain to stare down the reflection of his own fear? Even as he sensed his incapacity to make such a choice, it was made for him. Incredibly, the man was leaving. As Harry watched, he slipped the book into his pocket, rose and moved towards the door.

The speed at which the station lights flashed by was diminishing fast, like some faltering heliograph whose meaning Harry could not discern. The man was standing by his left shoulder, waiting for the train to stop. Harry had only to reach out his hand to restrain him, but movement seemed suddenly to have deserted him. He remembered a newspaper article he had read about people waking on the operating table, paralysed by the anaesthetic, but aware of everything that was happening, conscious of pain but incapable of protest. The train had nearly stopped, but only one thought filled his mind: how many warnings was he to be allowed? How many chances did he have left?

The train squealed to halt. The doors slid open. But the man did not move. It was as if he were timing something, judging to a nicety some effect he wished to produce. He looked down at Harry. And spoke.

'*Kalinichta, kirie Barnett.*'

Then he was gone. Through the doors even as they began to close. A lithe step out onto the platform, a turn of the heel and away. Harry, galvanized by the words, sprang from his seat and lunged towards the door, but too late: an impenetrable barrier of glass and metal separated him from his quarry. The train jolted into motion, throwing him against a steel upright. He clung to it for support, crouched for a view, glimpsed a retreating figure on the dwindling platform, then was swallowed in the soot-plumed tunnel.

'Goodnight, Mr Barnett.'

30

'Influenza, Mrs Barnett. Classic case. Lot of it about.'
Doc Allsop's professional grin, broad and crumpled as
a crushed melon, was much the same whether he were
offering congratulations or consolations. That much Harry
remembered. 'It's the mild weather, you know. Makes the
viruses breed like rabbits. And vice versa, no doubt.' The
cheese-grater laugh was also dolefully familiar. 'Resistance
probably undermined by this hot climate you tell me he's
been living in. And the over-indulgence that generally goes
with it.' Over-indulgence? If he did not feel so dreadful,
Harry would tell the fellow just what he could do with his
bedside wit. What on earth, come to that, was the old fool
still doing in general practice? It was he who had inflicted
an appendectomy of doubtful necessity on Harry forty-two
years ago. Good God, the man must be seventy if he was
a day. 'Rest. Aspirin. Whisky. Lots of all three. Should
do the trick, eh?' Doc Allsop lumbered towards the door,
with Harry's mother close behind.

Good riddance, thought Harry. Illnesses did not require
names in his scheme of things: they were merely misfortunes to be endured. Like irony, if it came to the point, of
which there seemed at present a good deal to be borne. His
old bedroom, preserved as in a museum. The wallpaper,
the chair, the tiny desk, the narrow bed: all were exactly
as they had always been. Even the Commonweal School
group photograph on the wall: September 1948, with
Harry featured twice, having sprinted along the back

while the camera tracked round, thus appearing with smile and combed hair at the extreme left and with smile and tousled hair at the extreme right. Not very funny, then or now. Strange to think, though, that time had passed even while the moving lens recorded that carefully assembled multitude. Photographs usually sustained the illusion that time could briefly be halted, but in this case . . .

The front door slammed. Allsop was gone, taking his tired homilies and pink placebos with him. Harry propped himself up on one elbow and pulled open the top drawer of the bedside cabinet. They were still there: the wallet of photographs and the envelope containing three postcards. They, at least, he had not imagined. And his pocket diary. He picked it up and turned to the address section at the back. Zohra Labrooy, 78 Foxglove Road, Kensal Green. 01-986-4316. After 6 p.m. Some things, then, were more reliable than his own twin likenesses in the school photograph. He dropped the diary into the drawer, closed it and fell back on the pillows. She would be in touch. She would prove him right. But the man on the train? Would he be in touch? Perhaps he *had* been an illusion. Perhaps Doc Allsop would have confirmed as much if Harry had asked him. 'Hallucinations? Entirely consistent with influenza, old chap. Only to be expected. Take two or three of these before meals and let me know if the symptoms don't clear up.'

Plodding footsteps on the stairs. His mother was about to reappear. He suspected she could have wished for nothing better than to have him confined to bed and reliant on her care. It would only be for a few days, of course. Then he would be up and about, able to apply himself to unfinished business. He tugged at the sheet and closed his eyes, hoping she might think he was asleep. But he hoped in vain.

'Well, Harold? You heard what Dr Allsop said.'

'Yes, Mother. Rest, aspirin, whisky. Sounds like a good idea – apart from the aspirin.'

'Rubbish. The old fool doesn't know what he's talking about.'

'Then why did you call him in?'

'To confirm my diagnosis. There's only one way to treat influenza – and strong drink isn't it.'

Her father had been a strict Baptist. Harry thought he had a good deal to answer for. 'What is?'

'Why, beef-tea, of course. I shall go down to Mr Sturch's straightaway.' Sturch had been in butchery about as long as Allsop had been in medicine, insofar, it occurred to Harry's mind, as there was any real difference between the trades.

'But Mother—'

'It's for your own good, Harold!'

He was too tired to argue. 'Yes, Mother.' At least he could sleep while she was away.

On the third day of his illness, Harry received his first visitor: Alan Dysart. Harry's mother reacted to his arrival as if the Prince of Wales had called by unexpectedly. If she remembered he was the same man whom her son had once employed, there was no way of telling from the awed reception she gave him. Harry decided that the embarrassment this caused him was a sign he was getting better. As for Dysart, he simply pretended not to notice.

'Laid up again, Harry? You seem to be making a habit of it.' He looked exactly as he had on the day of their last meeting, the day of his departure to the United States: calm yet concerned, sensitive yet restrained, the perfect model of the thinking politician. Why Harry felt sorry for him he did not know. It could have been the comfortless chair he was sitting in. More likely it was the knowledge that, for all Dysart's manifest charm and proven ability, he had a wife who was at best an adultress, at worst a traitor; either Minter's dupe or his co-conspirator.

'How did you hear I was ill?'

'I didn't. I got back from Washington on Friday. This was my first opportunity to find out what progress you'd made.'

'In looking for Heather, you mean?

'Unless you've given it up.'

'No. I haven't given it up.'

How much to tell? Dysart had been, over the years, as loyal a friend as any man could ask for. The least he deserved in return was that Harry should tell him all he knew. Besides, if he had been to Tyler's Hard, he would doubtless have recognized Harry from Morpurgo's account of a strange visitor the previous Saturday.

'I've tried to retrace some of her movements. She went to Tyler's Hard with Nigel Mossop, a colleague at Mallender Marine, on the twenty-eighth of August. I went there myself last Sunday. I hope you don't mind.'

'Not at all.' Dysart smiled. 'Willy did mention it. I was puzzled, I'll admit, but now I understand. How did you know Heather had been there?'

The photographs were one secret Harry would not share. 'She spoke of Mossop as a friend. I knew him as well, of course, so I contacted him and he told me about the trip.'

'I see.' Dysart nodded, but how much he saw was not clear. Nor did he ask the obvious questions which Harry would have found so difficult to answer. Why had Mossop been so cooperative? Why had Heather chosen him as a companion? 'Did you speak to Mrs Diamond, Harry?'

'Yes.'

'Tell me what you made of her.'

Harry had largely forgotten the woman as soon as he had concluded that her complaint about Morpurgo smiling on the day of Clare Mallender's death was of no significance. Yet Dysart's expression reminded him of something else she had said: that Dysart and Clare had been arguing immediately before the explosion; that there had been friction between them for some time. 'Good-hearted, I suppose, but a terrible gossip.'

'Reliable?'

'As a witness – not very.'

Dysart smiled. It was what he had wanted to hear. They both knew what Mrs Diamond had said, but neither proposed to give it the status open discussion would confer.

274

After all, if Dysart *had* fallen out with Clare, he was not likely to have broadcast the fact after her death. 'Mrs Diamond never liked Willy, I'm afraid,' he said. 'Some people simply cannot conquer their horror of disability.'

'Cyril Ockleton told me how Morpurgo came to be disabled.'

'Did he?'

'Heather went to see him in Oxford on the third of September. He drove her to Burford and showed her the site of the car crash.'

Dysart frowned. 'Why should she be interested in that?'

'I don't know. I'm still trying to find out.' Suddenly, Harry was gripped by a sneezing fit which dissolved into painful coughing. At his signal, Dysart poured out a spoonful of linctus (obtained courtesy of the pharmacist, in the teeth of Doc Allsop's advice) and stood by while he swallowed it. Slowly, the power of speech returned. 'I really am sorry about this, Alan. You'd better keep your distance.'

'Don't worry. Politicians have total immunity. I just hope I'm not tiring you. Your mother would never forgive me if I caused a relapse. Where did you pick up this bug?'

'I don't know. I began to feel under the weather on Thursday morning after leaving Haslemere. Heather went there on the tenth of September, you know, to see Rex Cunningham.'

'What did she want with him?'

'As far as I can see, she attached some significance to the fact that you, Morpurgo, Ockleton and Cunningham are all former members of the Tyrrell Society. She'd obtained a Skein of Geese matchbook from somewhere. Perhaps from her sister, because she knew you and Clare had dined there last year, shortly before . . . . '

'Shortly before Clare was killed in mistake for me.' Dysart's voice sounded unusually grim as he finished Harry's sentence. 'I took her there for a last relaxing evening before we threw ourselves into the election campaign. As a matter of fact' – he frowned in concentration – 'I do recall her putting a matchbook in her handbag at one point and saying she would pass it on to Heather because she collected the things. She made a joke of it, saying she had given Heather all the most exclusive matchbooks in her collection, that it was ironic how she'd become a slave to her sister's hobby.' A flicker of recollected pleasure that swiftly turned to the pain of regret crossed his face. 'But what of it? I see Cyril Ockleton whenever I go back to Breakspear College. He told me Willy was destitute. I was in a position to give the poor fellow employment and accommodation. As for Rex Cunningham, he runs a decent restaurant: where better to take Clare, since she was an Old Breakspearean as well?' Something seemed suddenly to catch his eye: the Commonweal School group photograph on the wall above the desk. Springing up, he took two steps across to it and peered at the glazed array of schoolboy faces. 'You're in this, of course, Harry. How old would you have been in – what does the caption say? – 1948?'

'Thirteen.'

'Aha. Thirteen. Let me see.' A minute or so of scrutiny passed, then he said: 'Got you. Far end. Third row back. Standing.'

'What does my hair look like?'

'Your hair? All over the place. Why?'

'Well, look at the other end.'

A second later, Dysart chuckled in understanding of a forty-year-old schoolboy prank. 'Very good, Harry. Very good. I recall some of the chaps doing the same at Oundle.'

'But you didn't join in?'

'No.' He turned away from the photograph. 'I don't think I'd have cared to be represented by two images in the same picture. It would have seemed . . . eerie. Like being tracked by your own ghost. Like being . . . . ' He laughed off the solemnity of the thought and returned to the chair. 'Anyway, that photograph has as much bearing on our present difficulties as the Tyrrell Society. I can't understand why Heather should have wanted to dig up such stuff. The car crash. The death of Ramsey Everett. Old tragedies best forgotten.'

'I can't understand it either, but she did.'

'You say she went to the Skein of Geese on the tenth of September. Did she dine there?'

'Yes.'

'Alone?'

'No. Dr Kingdom accompanied her.'

'Did he? Have you met Dr Kingdom yet, Harry?'

'Yes.'

'What's your opinion of him?'

'Professionally cool and aloof, but surprisingly easy to rile.'

'You think he's hiding something?'

'I know he is. You see, I recognized him. From Rhodes. He was in Lindos five days before Heather's disappearance.'

Whilst Harry recounted the circumstances of his brush with Kingdom at Papaioannou's trinket shop, Dysart listened attentively. Then his gaze moved again to the Commonweal School group photograph. 'You know, Harry, when I met Dr Kingdom, it seemed to me he was altogether too self-possessed to be true. This proves the point. He presents himself neatly combed to the world. But you've caught him out – in a tousle-haired moment.' A smile of grim satisfaction. 'What are you going to do?'

'He's supposed to have been at the Versorelli Institute in Geneva from the fourth to the fourteenth of November. I'm in touch with someone who should be able to tell me exactly when he was at the Institute – and when he wasn't.'

'You think they'll find he was absent on the eleventh as well as the sixth?'

'It's a possibility.'

'One visit to Heather on the spur of the moment could be innocent enough,' Dysart said musingly. 'Psychiatrist

277

concerned for his ex-patient, that kind of thing. There's nothing sinister in her not having mentioned it to you. But if he was away from the Institute the day she disappeared . . . . That would be different. If you do find that's the case, I'd like to know straightaway.' His expression was unmistakeably serious. 'Will you contact me in that event, Harry? Wherever I am, I mean. It could have very serious implications.'

'Yes. I will.'

Dysart had left the chair again, this time to stand by the window, gazing out at the view which had met Harry's bleary eyes every morning of his childhood. The backyards and rear walls of the houses fronting on Bristol Street, with the distant roofs of the railway workshops looming behind them: a domestic vista of brick, slate, chimneypot and curling smoke, as irksomely familiar as it was strangely precious. 'Have you found out anything else?' said Dysart, without looking round.

'One other thing, yes.' One other thing he could admit to, at any rate. What he felt most inclined to do – warn this man who was his best and oldest friend that his wife was not to be trusted – he had given his word he would not. 'Have you been to the Skein of Geese since you took Clare there last year?'

'No.'

'Or spoken to Rex Cunningham?'

'No.'

'Then he won't have told you what he told Heather about the evening you dined there.'

Dysart turned round and stared enquiringly at Harry. 'Which was?'

'It seems he surprised Clare gazing lovingly at a photograph of a man whilst you were away from the table. A man he recognized as a fellow member of the Tyrrell Society: Jack Cornelius.'

An upward twitch of the eyebrows was the only signal of surprise Dysart permitted himself. 'Jack Cornelius?'

'Yes. I wondered if you'd introduced them.'

'Well, they may have met through me, yes. I've invited Jack to a few receptions which Clare would have attended, but even so . . . . '

'Heather seems to have taken it as a confirmation of her belief in the significance of the Tyrrell Society.'

Dysart frowned in puzzlement. 'That's beyond me. The Tyrrell Society was just one of a dozen drinking and dining clubs at Breakspear College twenty years ago. It attracted people of similar views and backgrounds and it's no surprise – or shouldn't be – that such people still mix in the same circles now. I suppose it's remotely possible Clare was romantically involved with Jack Cornelius, although it doesn't say much for my powers of observation that I was unaware of it, but it's equally possible Rex Cunningham has simply jumped to the wrong conclusion: he was ever one to do that. Either way, what of it? Clare was a free agent. And if Heather thought there was something sinister about her relationship with Jack Cornelius – assuming there was a relationship – why did she never ask me if I knew anything about it?'

'Because you were a member of the Tyrrell Society as well.'

'Ah yes, of course.' Dysart sat down on the end of the bed. 'How do you account for Heather's obsession with a long forgotten student club, Harry?'

'I don't, unless she thought the Tyrrell Society was somehow an unlucky influence. Ramsey Everett. The car crash. Then her own sister.'

Dysart nodded, considered the point for a moment then said: 'Some might say it was a sign she hadn't recovered as well as we'd hoped.'

'Yes. Some might say that.'

'A more unlikely candidate for Clare's affections than Jack Cornelius . . . . ' Dysart shook his head. 'He's always struck me as something of a misogynist. But perhaps even misogynists can kick over the traces. That steely Irish charm of his would appeal to some women, I don't doubt. Perhaps Clare was one of them. It *is* possible. Just possible.

279

I can't deny that.' He looked up at Harry. 'What do you think Heather did after Cunningham put this idea into her head?'

'I imagine she confronted Jack Cornelius.'

'And you propose to do the same?'

'Yes. Once I find out where he teaches.'

Dysart smiled. 'Hurstdown Abbey, near Taunton. It's a Roman Catholic boarding school attached to a Benedictine Monastery. Very exclusive and very expensive. Not quite Eton or Harrow with incense thrown in, but close to it. Jack must have been there, oh, ten years or more. He teaches history and coaches rugger: his two great passions.'

'You know him well?'

'I did do, certainly. After leaving Oxford, he went back to Ireland to teach. He was in Belfast when the Troubles began, then I heard he'd gone to Italy. Next he cropped up at Hurstdown. He lured me there a couple of years ago to talk to his sixth form group about the Irish Problem. He seemed completely in his element, though all those monks flitting round the place rather gave me the creeps. I thought it odd at the time that he should feel so at home there.'

'Why?'

'Because he'd been a novice monk himself once, in Ireland, before he went to Oxford. He was older than the rest of us at Breakspear, you see, having tried for some years to make a go of a religious vocation before abandoning it in favour of teaching. He always used to speak so bitterly about his experiences as a monk that it seemed bizarre to think of him working alongside them at Hurstdown. But, then, time is a great healer, isn't it?' In this case, Harry was far from sure that it was. 'Yes. Go and see him, Harry. If Heather did track him down, we need to know what he told her. I'd speak to him myself, but—'

Harry was convulsed by a second bout of sneezing. This time, it did not dissolve into a coughing fit. Dysart smiled at him sympathetically as he hurled a bundle of damp tissues into the bin by the bed and plucked a handful of replacements from their box.

'I think it's time I let you get some rest.'

'I'm all right, really.' But Harry could tell by the blocked and croaking sound of his own voice that he was not.

'When you *are*, see Jack Cornelius – and let me know what you learn about Dr Kingdom. Meanwhile . . . .' Dysart moved across to the desk and stooped over it. He had taken something from his jacket pocket and Harry could see that he was writing on it.

'What are you doing?'

'I know you insisted you didn't need any money, but I'm sure that isn't really the case. I'm as interested in what you can discover about Heather's state of mind as you are yourself, so it's only fair I should contribute to your expenses. The Skein of Geese doesn't come cheap, for a start . . . .'

'No, but—'

'You have the time and I have the money, Harry.' Dysart turned back from the desk smiling broadly. 'So don't argue.' He slipped a cheque under the base of the bedside lamp. 'Besides, it comes with a condition attached, so don't think of it as a gift.'

'What condition?'

'As soon as you find out anything that suggests Heather is still alive, as soon as you learn where she might be or whether she's in any danger, contact me at once. Is it a deal?'

It seemed the least Harry could promise. 'Yes,' he said wearily. 'It's a deal.'

'She may be relying on our efforts, you know, so we must be sure we don't let her down.'

'I don't intend to.' Harry looked for the first time at the cheque where it lay beside him, flattened by the base of the lamp. A thousand pounds. It was more than he needed, but not less than he could use. What, it occurred to him, was the difference between accepting this contribution to his expenses and taking the kind of bribe Jonathan Minter had offered him? Some would say none at all, but he knew it was not so. A gift from Dysart was a gesture of friendship, from Minter an act of corruption.

'As a parting thought, Harry.'

'Yes?'

'This photograph Rex Cunningham supposedly saw in Clare's possession: the one of Jack Cornelius. Don't place too much store by such evidence.' Dysart was standing, had he but known it, within inches of the pictures Heather had taken, the pictures on which Harry would rely if all else failed. 'As you should know from your own experiences' – he glanced up at the framed portrait of Commonweal School staff and pupils, September 1948 – 'the notion that the camera never lies is a fallacy. It doesn't set out to lie, of course, but it sometimes succeeds. It sees everything – and understands nothing.' He looked back at Harry and smiled. 'So take my advice: don't believe everything it tells you.'

The day after Dysart's visit, Harry began to feel distinctly better. By Tuesday, he was able to venture out of doors for the first time since arriving home, late and ailing, on Thursday night. An expedition to the bar of the Glue Pot convinced him that, apart from a hacking cough and a tendency to tire easily, he was very much his old self.

On Wednesday, he swallowed his pride, banked Dysart's cheque and purchased a car with most of what remained from the cash he had brought back from Rhodes. His experiences at Barnchase Motors meant he was well aware how seriously to treat the sales patter at the Sapphire Garage, 'Wiltshire's premier value-for-money used car outlet'. A Vauxhall Viva resprayed in unspeakable tangerine to conceal a multitude of rusty sins and described as 'a sound and reliable workhorse' looked to his eye more like a duck very near death's door. Still, for two hundred and fifty pounds he had no room for complaint. He reckoned it would take him where he wanted to go – at least for a few weeks.

Returning to Falmouth Street in his new acquisition – and already encountering some resistance to engaging first gear – Harry listed in his mind the excellent reasons for buying a car. Mobility. Convenience. Flexibility. The following day he would underline all three by driving it to Hurstdown Abbey. There was another reason, of course, but he was not prepared to admit even to himself that it had played any part in his decision. In a car he would be safe from the man on the train and the messages he carried. He would be rid of him at last. But that, he was determined to believe, had nothing to do with the matter. Nothing whatsoever.

31

Harry turned off the car engine and wound down the window. Then he took the wallet of photographs from his pocket and leafed through them to the ninth picture in Heather's collection. The match was perfect. In miniature gloss-printed image and sparse grey winter-lit reality, Hurstdown Abbey lay before him. He climbed from the car, slammed the door and leaned back against it, giving his imagination as well as his vision time to absorb the place and its setting.

The village of Hurstdown was a straggle of drab cottages either side of the main Taunton to Williton road. A pub, a post office, a garage, a war memorial, a litter-choked horse trough and an Anglican parish church whose size and proportions were more suited to a Nonconformist chapel. As a settlement, it was nothing. And the reason was not far to seek. Hurstdown Abbey, an arched and buttressed temple to Victorian Gothic, soared above the village in grand and lofty superiority, leaving all else to huddle at its feet in subjugation. Around it were gathered the cloisters, quadrangles, halls, dormitories and playing fields of the school, stretching away up a gently sloping flank of the Quantock Hills. Here, its high walls and castellations seemed somehow to declare, the temporal power of the Church was not a distant memory but a present-day reality.

Harry crossed the road, passed through an ancient arched gateway and started up the drive towards the school. What he had judged from the photograph to be red-brick he saw now was deep red Quantock stone, used in the construction of the Abbey and all its surrounding buildings. Its colouring, combined with the dismal weather, the heavy-handed architecture and the beech trees dotting the grounds, created an atmosphere by which he felt instantly oppressed. It was as if the whole weight of the Abbey's sombre traditions were bearing down upon his shoulders and he was shrinking beneath the load.

After a hundred yards or so, the drive divided, leading in one direction towards a classroom block, in the other fanning out into a courtyard where cars were parked either side of the main entrance. Harry's original intention had been to approach Cornelius via a secretary or administrator. He had timed his arrival for shortly after midday in the hope that lunchtime would find the staff free of commitments. Now it came to the point, however, he sensed a reluctance within himself to confront any member of this self-important establishment on his own ground, far less his own terms. He crossed the courtyard hesitantly, unsure what his next move should be.

Then he saw – or rather heard, for the clip of their boot-studs on the flagstones was what first caught his attention – a file of boys in football kit making their way along a covered path linking the courtyard to the playing fields that lay behind the school buildings. As his route and theirs converged, Harry remembered that Dysart had said rugby was one of Cornelius's 'two great passions'. He doubted if these boys had been playing soccer – Hurstdown's sporting young gentlemen would surely scorn such a plebeian game – and, sure enough, the boy bringing up the rear, older and taller than the rest and evidently in charge, was clutching a rugby ball to his chest. Stepping into his path, Harry enquired as innocently as he could if Mr Cornelius was anywhere to be found.

'Yes, sir. You'll find him on the practice pitch.' Catching Harry's uncertain look, he added: 'Wynne-Thomas will be happy to take you there. Wynne-Thomas!'

Harry's guide was a small fair-haired lad whose purple-and-orange hooped shirt reached nearly to his knees. He led the way along a series of paths, up assorted flights of steps and out across a seemingly limitless expanse of finely mown rugby and hockey pitches that climbed the hillside in stepped succession.

'There's Mr Cornelius.' Wynne-Thomas pointed towards two men standing together on the next pitch. One was tall and grey-haired, thin but broad-shouldered, wearing a voluminous cricket sweater over baggy grey trousers. The other was an overalled attendant of a line-marking machine, whose accuracy the pair seemed to be debating. Wynne-Thomas presumably thought it unnecessary to say which of them was Jack Cornelius. 'Will that be all, sir?'

'Oh, yes.' Harry could not help smiling at the boy's excessive politeness. 'Thanks.' He was tempted to add, but did not, 'You can cut along now.' Not that it mattered. Wynne-Thomas cut along anyway.

As he moved towards the two men, Harry savoured the moments of secret observation that preceded their awareness of his presence. Dysart had said Cornelius was older than his contemporaries at Breakspear and this man did indeed look nearer fifty than forty, unruly iron-grey hair framing a gaunt high-boned face, the brow hooded enough and the nose sufficiently hooked to add a sinewy hint of predacity to his relaxed and smiling features. Physically strong, Harry judged, and mentally agile: the Corinthian sportsman and the patrician academic, with some diabolical ingredient thrown in that curdled the mixture.

It was, in testimony to his alertness, Cornelius who saw him coming first. He turned away from the other man and grinned crookedly in greeting. Then, before Harry had even rehearsed an opening remark, he said: 'You must be Harry Barnett.'

Instantly, the tables were turned. Harry was suddenly the victim of the surprise he had hoped to exploit. 'Yes, I am,' he stumbled, 'but—'

'Alan Dysart phoned me a few days ago.' Cornelius shook Harry by the hand. His grip was firm and self-assured. 'He warned me you'd be paying me a visit.' The warmth and perfection of his enunciation were marred only by his faint Irish accent and the artificiality which it seemed to impose on his genial tone. Harry sensed a harshness, an edge, a flinty ruthlessness buried beneath the practised charm. 'I have an undeserved reputation for brusqueness, Mr Barnett. I think Alan was hoping to ease your passage.'

Surely Dysart had never suggested he might do such a thing? For the moment Harry could not be certain. Perhaps illness had dulled his recollection. 'Did he tell you why I'd be coming?'

'You want to speak to me about Heather Mallender.' No prevarication, then, and no evasion either. 'I can spare you half an hour before my presence is called for in the refectory. Why don't you come to my room?' Without further ado, he started off towards the school buildings. Harry fell in beside him, struggling to keep pace with his rapid strides. 'I read about her disappearance, of course, and your part in it. The episode has placed Alan in a difficult position. The papers can't find anything in it to use against him, but, all the same, it leaves his career in something of a vacuum.'

Suddenly, Harry's increasing breathlessness sparked off a coughing bout. He had the impression whilst he paused to recover himself that Cornelius was watching him intently, that his piercing gaze was sweeping over him in search of every weakness, every strength, every facet of his character that an opponent might need to know.

'It sounds bad,' Cornelius said drily, when the coughing had subsided.

'I'm getting over flu,' Harry panted.

'Perhaps you should have given yourself longer.' Harry looked at him then and thought he saw what it was that glimmered beneath the affable surface of his remarks. Contempt, coursing like some seam of metal through his words and their meaning, the contempt felt by one who knew his own powers for one who clearly did not. 'It's always a mistake to overdo things, Mr Barnett, don't you agree? To reach beyond one's grasp.' Now, Harry was certain, Cornelius meant more than the length of time a middle-aged man should give himself to recover from influenza. 'If you're ready, we'll carry on.'

They descended a flight of steps, entered a classroom block by a side-door and began to thread a route through corridors and passages busy with bustling knots of purple-blazered schoolboys. Harry noticed in their faces, as they glanced at Cornelius, neither affection nor hostility, but something he would never have associated with the juvenile mind: awe. To every humble last one of these boys, Jack Cornelius was either a devil or a god. The realization bit into Harry's confidence that he could outwit such a man: who was he really fooling?

A broad staircase led down into a hushed and panelled hallway. Here, it seemed, pupils were not permitted to stray. The only faces that greeted them belonged to sundry dead abbots glaring down from dusky oil paintings. Cornelius's striding progress carried them to a heavy oak door with the sign HEAD OF CAREERS fixed to it. He opened it and stood back to let Harry enter '"Head of Careers" is an absurd title, isn't it?' he said. 'As if I could in some way decide for those leaving us what they will go on to do.'

Harry remembered the expressions of the boys they had passed. 'Perhaps they think you can.' But Cornelius's only answer was a gnomic smile. He was not to be drawn.

The room was large, furnished like the private study of a rich and cultured man: desk, chairs and bookcases in what looked like hand-tooled mahogany, a tapestry covering one wall, several ornately framed paintings, a *chaise-longue*, a couple of wingbacked armchairs. The windows were tall and mullioned, looking out onto the courtyard Harry had crossed earlier, with the top panels stained purple and gold to match the colours of the school.

'I generally have a glass of sherry before lunch,' said Cornelius. 'Will you join me?'

For all his loathing of sherry, Harry heard himself agreeing. A drink was pressed into his hand, a chair held back and he found himself seated opposite Cornelius by the window, for all the world like some sixth-former seeking advice on whether to go for Oxbridge or the Guards.

'Let me save you some time, Mr Barnett. Heather Mallender visited me here on Sunday the eighteenth of September. She wanted to know – as I suspect you do – what my relationship had been with her late sister. I told her – as I am happy to tell you – that I had met Clare Mallender on three of four occasions, all of them in the company of other people. Receptions to which Alan had invited me – and an educational conference which we both attended. We were the vaguest of acquaintances, nothing more.' There was no false note in Cornelius's voice, but, all the same, Harry doubted every word. 'Heather was as sceptical as you yourself appear. Rex Cunningham had told her that he had seen Clare in possession of a photograph of me which had convinced him we were intimate friends. Well, dear Rex was either lying or labouring under a misapprehension. No such friendship existed. I cannot say with absolute certainty that Clare Mallender did not possess a photograph of me, but I can say that there was no reason why she should have done.'

It was as simple as only a barefaced lie could be. Yet it was also unchallengeable. Cornelius was too accomplished a performer to let his smugness show, but it was palpable all the same: he could not be caught out. Heather had made no headway and nor, Harry felt sure, would he. 'You reject Rex Cunningham's claim?' he said lamely.

'No,' Cornelius replied with a smile. 'Rex is as capable of making an honest mistake as he is of lying. I would not venture to say which he is doing in this case.'

'Haven't you taken it up with him?'

'Why should I? He wouldn't change his mind, whatever I said.

289

'But if it isn't true—'

'It isn't, believe me, Mr Barnett. Besides . . . . ' He cast a sidelong glance through the window, as if ruminating on a philosophical problem. 'Besides, it occurred to me that Rex might be deliberately misleading Heather in order to prevent her discovering some connection between Clare and himself.'

The suggestion was preposterously unlikely, but that, Harry suspected, was just the point. It declared as openly as Cornelius dared that he could invent a dozen different theories if he was obliged to, behind which the truth, whatever it was, could be concealed forever. 'Is that all Heather wanted to know?' Harry said, detecting as he spoke the strain of exasperation in his voice.

'No.' Cornelius signalled by a flicker of one eyebrow that he knew Harry had expected him to say the exact reverse. 'She also asked me to recount for her the circumstances leading up to the car crash in May 1968 in which poor Willy Morpurgo suffered brain damage.' Honesty, it seemed, was also a string in the expert liar's bow. 'Are you familiar with that sad tale, Mr Barnett?'

'Yes. I am.' Cornelius, the man who had suggested the ill-fated drive to Burford, the man who had stayed behind when the others started back to Oxford, sat before Harry, twenty years on, with a smile on his face that mixed candid reminiscence and flagrant duplicity. According to Ockleton, he had become 'as maudlin as only an Irishman in liquor can.' But now, looking at the lined, self-knowing expression of this consummate dissembler, Harry found it easier to believe he had merely staged a performance, an expert and convincing charade that had achieved the desired result. 'You were very lucky that day, weren't you?' Harry said hesitantly. 'To miss the return journey, I mean.'

'I was also drunk, Mr Barnett. We Irish are renowned for both qualities.'

Drunk? Harry had the impression this was one man who had never been drunk in his entire life. He guarded

290

his tongue and his thoughts too well to let alchohol betray them. 'Why do you suppose Heather wanted to know about such distant events?'

'She claimed they might have some bearing on Clare's death. Why such a bizarre notion should have entered her head I cannot imagine, but I did not like to disillusion her, so I told her what I could. She thanked me for the information – and then she left.'

Had Heather really gone that quietly? Cornelius's smile, reaching Harry across the grey pool of light that spread between them, glistened like the fly on a fisherman's line. Harry would learn nothing, it implied, unless or until it was too late for him to profit by it. Far too late. 'You're an historian, I believe, Mr Cornelius. Can't you conjecture why Heather should be so interested in this piece of ancient history?'

The smile broadened. 'Which piece do you mean, Mr Barnett? Walter Tyrrell? The Burford Mutiny? Or a simple car accident on the seventeenth of May 1968?'

Betrayal, the theme that had first entered Harry's head in Burford, recurred to his mind now as the link between all the widely spaced events that had borne down on Heather Mallender. An arrow in the forest. A lie on hallowed ground. A push in the dark. The laughter of drunken fools. And of one who was wiser than the rest. A country lane, wet after rain. The squeal of rubber tyre and human terror. But no skid marks. No clue or sign or token. Unless Heather had found one. 'Actually,' he said, commencing slowly what every contrary sense told him was a venture into dangerous territory, 'the piece of history I had in mind was a defenestration. Not the famous one at Prague, but another, closer to our own time.'

A mirthless chuckle was Cornelius's admission that Harry had displayed more subtlety than expected. 'Your grasp of history impresses me, Mr Barnett. Perhaps you understand – as many do not – that the past is not only always with us, but *is* us, the cause and context of our every action. What we do is prompted by what we believed a minute or a year or a century ago. Wouldn't you agree?'

Anthony Sedley. Prisoner. Prisoner of the past. Was he the reason Cornelius had lured them to Burford that day? To point a moral? Or betray a trust? 'Yes. I'd agree.'

'Then perhaps you can assist me on a minor point of methodology?'

'I'm sorry?'

'What enabled you to be so certain Heather Mallender visited me here?'

'It seemed likely—'

'Not likelihood, certainty!' Cornelius's voice was suddenly harsh, as if a pupil's essay had revealed a deficiency of logic. 'You did not deduce that Heather Mallender came here. You knew it for a fact. That is obvious to me. The question is: how did you know?'

Harry did not know what to say. No lie would aid him in a contest with a master of the craft, but the truth, his only hope of gaining the upper hand, had to remain hidden. He felt confused beneath Cornelius's unwavering stare, unsure whether he had not betrayed himself by patting his pocket to check if the photographs were still there. Cornelius had no cause to suspect their existence, of course, yet – Suddenly, there was a tap at the door. With a rush of relief, Harry looked round to see a boy – senior, to judge by his appearance – peering nervously into the room.

'Oh, excuse me, sir. I thought you'd be alone.'

'What is it, Appleby?'

'Well, I was hoping to have a word with you about this week's Greek tutorial.'

'Hmm.' Cornelius's expression mellowed. 'All right. Wait outside. I'll be with you in a few minutes. Mr Barnett and I have nearly concluded our business.'

'Thank you, sir.' Appleby withdrew.

'I trust I'm correct,' said Cornelius, as the door clicked shut. 'There's really no more to be said, is there?' A moment ago, he had seemed to have Harry at his mercy.

Now he was content to release him, to toss him back in the water like a catch unworthy of the landing.

'Er, no, I suppose there isn't.' Harry rose from his chair, eager not to let the opportunity of escape slip from his grasp. He wanted nothing so much at the moment as to be out of this man's piercing sight and withering scrutiny. It was only when he had followed Cornelius most of the way across the room that the significance of what had just happened dawned on him. 'Hold on! I thought you taught history here?'

'I do,' Cornelius replied, pulling up and turning round to face him.

'And Greek as well?'

'Ancient Greek. To those few students of Latin who express a particular interest. There are not many. Hurst-down's Benedictine origins encourage us to emphasize the language of Catholicism at the expense of that of Orthodoxy. But one or two boys every year venture into Greek in preparation for a Classics degree.'

'And you're able to help them?'

'As it happens, yes.'

The writing on the wall. The name on the envelope. The phrase learned and spoken by the man on the train. At last they began to make sense. At last the warning pointed to its source. 'You find a knowledge of Greek useful, then?'

'Occasionally.' Cornelius smiled and stretched out his hand to open the door. 'As you'll appreciate, Mr Barnett, it does have its applications.'

293

32

The Rose and Crown, Hurstdown, extended an icy welcome to strangers. The fireplace was monopolized by a garrulous half dozen whom Harry identified as a fair sample of the school's lay teaching staff: lots of leather-patched tweed, regimental ties and braying accents. At the other end of the bar two or three farm labourers muttered glumly to each other. Somewhere in the glacial no-man's-land between, Harry ordered a pint and drew the ninth photograph from his pocket.

'My hobby's ecclesiastical architecture. A friend recommended this church to me.' He held the picture out for the barman to see. 'Do you happen to know if it's near here?'

The barman's expression suggested he found it as easy to believe Harry was a student of ecclesiastical architecture as that he was an undercover weights and measures inspector. He glanced at the picture for about half a second, then said: 'Could be.'

'Any idea where?'

Another glance, this time a lingering affair of about three seconds. Then an ostentatious sniff. 'Looks like Flaxford. Next village north of 'ere. 'Bout three mile. Turning to the left. You can't miss the sign.'

Silence lunged from every briar-riddled field and stark-boughed tree as Harry climbed from the car outside Flaxford church. It lay half a mile or so short of the village itself and as far again from the turning off the main road, its sombre red stone darkened still further by the damp and chilly hollow in which it had been built. The setting rendered its vast and soaring tower – tier upon traceried tier of lights, buttresses, pinnacles and battlements – so absurdly ill-proportioned that Harry could almost have believed it was an optical illusion. But the photograph in his hand proved it was not.

He went through the lych-gate and walked up the short gravel path to the porch. Rank grass between crooked gravestones. Lichen-choked inscriptions. Celtic crosses worn smooth by time and weather. There was nothing unique here, it seemed. All was much as it might have been in a hundred other neglected country churchyards: winter closing on the dead and disregarded. He turned the handle of the heavy iron-strapped door and pushed it open.

Inside, dampness contended with beeswax polish, darkness with columns of light shaped by lancet windows. Belfry, font, aisle. Pews, pulpit, screen. Choir, organ, altar. Where was the clue, where was the key? Dust. And Harry's footfalls echoing on uneven flagstones. Heavy velvet. Warm wood. Glittering plate. Nowhere did Heather seem close at hand. And yet, and yet . . . . Anthony Sedley. Prisoner. Was that a mouse scratching in the rood-loft? Or another prisoner, carving his name for perpetuity's sake? His name – or hers.

On a table just inside the door were arranged missionary leaflets, guidebooks on the church's history, a card requesting donations to the tower restoration fund and a visitors' book, held open by a rubber band, ballpoint pen tied to a length of string beside it. With sudden eagerness, Harry snapped off the band and turned back through the pages. Heather had been here on September 18th. He knew because Cornelius had told him so. He knew because Heather had given him a way to be certain. Each page was ruled in four columns, headed 'Date,' 'Name', 'Address' and 'Comments'. He ran his finger down the dates on the right-hand sheet. 15th September. 16th. There it was, in Heather's recognizable hand. '18th September 1988. Heather Mallender. Sabre Rise, Portesham, Dorset. I found no ghosts here, not even the one who left her name.' The one who left her name. Some instinct had drawn Heather here from Hurstdown, some instinct that told her this was where Cornelius's denials would be refuted. If he had only known Clare as 'the vaguest of acquaintances', she would never have been to Hurstdown, far less Flaxford. She would have had no reason to come here. Or to leave her name.

Flaxford Church did not attract many visitors, it seemed, for eighteen months took Harry back only half a dozen pages. Why he looked first for 16th May 1987 he did not know, except that Clare and Dysart had dined at the Skein of Geese that day, which made it as good a starting point as any. This time he ran his finger down the column of names rather than dates. And, at the bottom of the first sheet, found what Heather had discovered before him.

'22nd May 1987. Clare Mallender. London.' That was all. No comment. No praise for the stained glass. No message from beyond the grave. Just a date, a name, a place – and a lie nailed.

33

Some amalgam of guesswork, inspiration and logic uncannily like an assurance from Heather's own mouth told Harry that the site of the eleventh photograph lay close at hand. Heather would surely not have left Flaxford without seeking further evidence of Clare's presence there and the gloomy stone house at the end of a tree-arched drive she had captured on film had all the makings to his eye of a run-down country parsonage. A card in the church porch referred enquiries to the Reverend F. J. Waghorne, BD, at Flaxford Rectory, an address which did not prove difficult to find. Overgrown and over-sized, the rectory stood in its own grounds just the other side of the village. And was instantly recognizable.

The door was answered by a tiny blonde-haired girl in white tee-shirt and bright yellow trousers, feet lost in a pair of her mother's high-heeled shoes. She stared up at Harry through breakfast-saucer eyes and solemnly announced, 'You're not Mr Clatworthy.'

'No.' Harry attempted an appealing smile. 'Is your father in?'

'Mummy thought you were Mr Clatworthy.'

'Well, as you see, I'm not. Is your father . . . . ' But it was useless. Turning away, the girl began an awkward, shoe-shovelling retreat along the hall.

'Mummy! It's not Mr Clatworthy!'

Harry could see the entrance to the kitchen at the far end of the hall. As he watched, a flustered figure in apron and jeans, hair held back by a bandeau, appeared in the distant doorway. 'What? Victoria, why on earth are you wearing– Oh!' She noticed Harry and grinned nervously. 'Sorry. We were expecting the plumber. To be honest' – she glanced apprehensively towards the sound of running water – 'we were praying for the plumber.' She began wiping her hands in a towel. 'What can I do for you?'

'I was hoping for a word with the rector.'

'He's rather busy at the moment.'

'It's a matter of some urgency.'

She frowned with irritation, then seemed to decide against contesting the point. 'You'd better come through, then.'

Harry ventured along the hall. Through an open door to his right he made brief eye-contact with a sullen little boy who was lying on the floor staring at a comic, surrounded by model racing cars. By the time Harry reached the kitchen, the girl had taken the place of her mother in rapt contemplation of whatever was gushing so ferociously on the other side of the room. Mrs Waghorne, meanwhile, had gone ahead of him down a side-passage and was peering round the edge of a door, whispering explanations to someone on the other side.

'You've got a visitor.'

'Who is it?' a tired voice responded.

'I don't know.'

'Didn't you ask?'

'No,' snapped Mrs Waghorne. 'Do you realize what state the kitchen's in?'

'Hasn't Clatworthy been yet?'

'Of course he hasn't. When did he ever – Oh!' She suddenly became aware of Harry close behind her. 'There you are!'

'Sorry if I made you jump. The name's Barnett. Harry Barnett.'

'Don't know the name,' came the languid reply, floating over Mrs Waghorne's shoulder. 'Not a parishioner. Probably better off seeing one of the churchwardens.'

Mrs Waghorne smiled tightly. 'Could you explain the nature of your business, Mr Barnett?'

Shock tactics seemed the only hope. 'I'd like to speak to your husband about the Mallender sisters. Clare and Heather.'

At this, Mrs Waghorne's self-control dissolved. The dark cloud of some unstilled suspicion crossed her face. She threw the door wide open and stalked past Harry towards the kitchen, muttering 'He's all yours' as she went.

'Good afternoon,' said Harry, confronting the rector across the thickly rugged width of his study. As he spoke, he became aware of funereal music seeping from unseen loudspeakers, the high and mournful voices of a disembodied choir. Near the stereophonic eye of this plangent dirge sat the Rector of Flaxford, wreathed in cigarette smoke behind a broad and paper-scattered desk, one eyelid flickering faintly as he stared unsmilingly at Harry, curly grey-shot hair falling across his forehead, sagging jaw dark with stubble, a voluminous mohair cardigan draped over clerical shirt and collar. 'Reverend Waghorne?'

'Yes.'

'May I come in?'

'You better had, I think.'

Once he had closed the door behind him, Harry joined the rector in his sealed world of tobacco and burial anthems, cut off from the mayhem of plumbing and parenthood. He moved to a chair indicated by his host's cigarette-waving hand and heard his own voice sink to a respectful murmur. 'I saw your name at the church. I was hoping to speak to you about—'

'Clare and Heather Mallender.' The rector nodded. 'So I heard.'

'You're acquainted with them, then?'

'Not as closely as my wife seems to think.' A weary smile. 'But, yes, you could say I was acquainted with them.'

'You read of Heather's disappearance last month?'

'I did.'

'I'm contacting anybody who might know something that could explain what's become of her.'

'You think I know something?'

299

'Possibly. Heather visited you here on Sunday the eighteenth of September, didn't she?'

The rector's eyebrows shot up in surprise. 'Yes, she did, but how—'

'She wanted to know if you'd met her late sister here in Flaxford on the twenty-second of May last year and, if so, whether you could explain her visit to the parish.'

The rector's eyebrows remained on high. His lower lip slid out slowly to join them in a signal of amazement. 'Are you a policeman?' he said after a moment's deliberation.

'No.'

'A private detective then, hired by the Mallender family?'

'No. Just a friend of Heather's who's trying to find her.'

The rector's features relaxed. 'And what did you say your name was?'

'Barnett.'

'Should I know it?'

'I was the last person to see Heather prior to her disappearance.'

'That's it, of course.' The rector tossed back an encroaching strand of hair. 'The depraved villain of the piece, according to the tabloid press. You don't look your part, Mr Barnett.'

'That's because it's not my part.'

'Whose is?' The rector leaned forward to stub out his cigarette in an ashtray. Then he scrabbled through the papers in front of him, found the cigarette packet and matchbox, waved them at Harry, took his shake of the head for a refusal and set to lighting one for himself. Meanwhile, Harry's eye was drawn to the sheet of paper nearest him, headed in handwritten capitals 'FOURTH SUNDAY IN ADVENT'. Beneath this were several lines of script heavily crossed through, then the same single word, also in capitals, on the next five lines. 'SHEEP'. 'Just as well you're not from the bishop,' said the rector, catching the direction of his gaze. 'What exactly do you want of me, Mr Barnett?'

'Information, that's all.'

'Not a perpetual smile? Not a shoulder to cry on? Not a consoling text?' A blue haze of smoke was spreading round the Reverend Waghorne as he spoke, adding its acrid scent to the bitterness of his words. 'Maybe I *can* oblige you, then.'

'I'd like to know what you told Heather when she came here on the eighteenth of September.'

'It was certainly a Sunday in September. As to the date, I'll have to take your word for it.' The rector took a reminiscent puff at his cigarette; his gaze seemed to drift out of focus. 'It was during the few hours of peace I enjoy between morning service and evensong. If you can call it peace. Not that I minded speaking to her, since she was a lamb from somebody else's flock.' He smiled. 'A lamb, not a sheep. I entertained her to tea in this very room. As you appear to know, she wanted confirmation that her late sister had been in Flaxford on the twenty-second of May last year and thought I might be able to supply it. She had gleaned the date from the visitors' book in the church. As did you, I take it?'

'Yes.'

'Perhaps I ought to take a razor to the relevant page.' Another rueful smile. 'Or to something else. It was all guesswork on Heather's part, so she told me. She had reason to believe Clare had visited Hurstdown shortly before her death and had left in some form of distress. She thought she might have gone to a nearby church and prayed for guidance. Flaxford fitted the bill and there was Clare's signature in the visitors' book to confirm it. Then it occurred to her that Clare might have turned to a priest for help with what was troubling her. Hence the visit here.'

An interval followed, filled only by the doleful voices of recorded choristers. Suddenly, a violent thumping started somewhere deep in the fabric of the house. This protest from the recalcitrant piping seemed to revive the Reverend Waghorne's powers of recollection. He resumed, in a sadder vein than before.

'Heather guessed right, Mr Barnett. Sisterly instinct, I suppose. One Friday afternoon in the spring of last year – the twenty-second of May – I encountered a young woman at the church. She said her name was Clare Mallender and asked if I could offer her some confidential advice over a moral dilemma which she faced. She did not want me to hear her confession, you understand, or to absolve her of her sins, merely to listen to her problem and suggest a solution. Naturally, I agreed to her request. We went into the vestry and she explained her difficulty. I responded with what I thought a happy combination of the constructive and the sympathetic. Then she left. Nine days later I heard on the radio that she was dead.'

'You told Heather this?'

'Yes. She pressed me to say what Clare's problem was. I resisted on the grounds that neither Clare's death nor the fact that Heather was her sister entitled me to abuse the trust she'd placed in me. But Heather swiftly persuaded me to change my mind.'

'How?'

'By pointing out that Clare had misled me. She had given me to understand, you see, that she was a total stranger in the locality and knew nobody hereabouts. That was what enabled me to offer her completely disinterested advice. I never thought, not for a single moment—'

'That she was intimately acquainted with a member of the teaching staff at Hurstdown Abbey?'

The Reverend Waghorne blanched visibly. 'You know?'

'Yes. Jack Cornelius. History master. Rugby coach. Tutor in Ancient Greek.'

'I have never met Mr Cornelius. I do not wish to. It's simply not fair. Clare should have warned me.' The rector rose abruptly, strode to the window, leaned one elbow on the sash-rail and glared back at Harry. 'For all the efforts made over the centuries to destroy them, Mr Barnett, the monastic orders continue to thrive, proof, it seems, against the frailties that rack us lesser mortals. Up there' – he gestured vaguely in the direction of Hurstdown Abbey – 'they

302

offer smug confirmation that nothing, absolutely nothing, will ever loosen their . . . . ' He broke off. 'Excuse me. This is irrelevant. Jack Cornelius is no monk. That, you might say, is just the problem.'

'What was it Clare Mallender wanted your advice about?'

'Telling Heather the answer to that question was a mistake, Mr Barnett. A burden shared was, in this case, a burden doubled. Believe you me, I've no intention of trebling it.'

'All I'm trying to do is find Heather. To help her.'

'Meaning I'm not?'

'I didn't say so.'

'Do you really think any of this has any connection with her disappearance?'

'As a matter of fact, yes.'

The Reverend Waghorne did not reply at once. He looked out through the grimey window into the dank garden on which dusk seemed already to be settling. '*In the midst of life we are in death*', the choristers intoned. '*Of whom may we seek for succour?*' He pressed two fingers to his left eyelid to still its fluttering, then sighed deeply. 'Have it your own way,' he murmured. 'Clare Mallender was the last straw so far as my camel's back of a priestly vocation was concerned. The very last.' He lumbered back to the desk and slumped down in his chair. 'Her problem was commonplace enough, Mr Barnett. She was pregnant.'

Of course. Clare pregnant. Not by her employer, her former fiancé or any of her no doubt numerous admirers in London, but by the man whose photograph she carried with her and had been seen staring at six days before she sought the Rector of Flaxford's unbiased advice. She had driven away from Hurstdown Abbey on 22 May 1987 – perhaps after some quarrel with Cornelius, perhaps after telling him for the first time that she was carrying his child – and called in desperation at Flaxford Church, there to bare her soul and her secret to the wavering Reverend Waghorne. But why? Had Cornelius refused to do the decent thing, urged abortion on her, denied responsibility? What had he done that could only be whispered in a clerical stranger's ear?

'She told me she was pregnant and I assumed the usual things. That the father was a married man. That she was agonizing over whether to have an abortion. That she could not face her parents with the news. None of which was the problem, as it turned out. The father was willing to stand by her, she was determined to go through with the pregnancy and she had already told her parents how she was placed.'

Already told. So Charlie and Marjorie Mallender knew. Probably Roy as well. And Heather? If so, she would surely not have needed Waghorne to confirm it. 'What *was* the problem, then?'

The rector let out a long, slow breath. 'Clare had just discovered that the man by whom she was pregnant was irredeemably homosexual. He was prepared to marry her but was incapable of loving her. As she was incapable of loving him, now his true nature was apparent to her.'

That was it, of course. Jack Cornelius, attractive to women but attracted to men, surrounded by monks and schoolboys, prepared to marry Clare if she insisted but repellant to her once she knew what she should have known all along. 'What advice did you offer?'

'The usual. Pious claptrap about the growing bond of parental love. Solve the problem together. Make a go of it for the sake of the unborn child. Trust in God.' The Reverend Waghorne smiled. 'What did you expect? What did she expect? When I'd finished my recital of predictable platitudes, she looked at me as if she'd turned to an old and respected teacher for guidance and found he'd descended into senility since last they'd met. She left without another word. And nine days later was dead.'

The wheel turns. The wheel of chance. Or of something else. A push in the dark. A severed cable. A bomb on the water. A mountaintop meeting. There was more to it, surely, more to it than Waghorne could guess – but not than he could tell.

'I had no idea, Mr Barnett, not the least notion, that the

man Clare was referring to taught at Hurstdown Abbey. Not till Heather came here and told me did I realize that Jack Cornelius was responsible for Clare's dilemma.' He stabbed out his cigarette with excessive force. 'I did try to meet him. Just once. The day I heard of Heather's disappearance. It seemed to make the knowledge of what she'd told me insupportable. I wanted to shrug off my troubles onto his shoulders, I supposed, to make him suffer for the inadequacy of the advice I'd given. My wife tried to stop me, but to no avail: I was determined to confront him. I stormed up to the school that morning and demanded to see him. But he wasn't there. Away, they told me, on compassionate leave or somesuch. Away, at any rate. Had been for a week. Due back the following day. But by then—'

'What did you say?' There it was. The final chink in the armour. And the light flooding through was as clear and cold as on the summit of Profitis Ilias. 'He'd been away for a week?'

'Apparently so. I can't remember—'

'Think, man, think! How long had he been absent? Precisely how long?'

Shock at Harry's vehemence was written on the Reverend Waghorne's face. 'Well, let me see,' he said slowly. 'I spoke to a secretary. She said, as I recall, that he'd been away for a week. No. That he'd been given a week's leave. Some personal emergency or other. And that he was expected to be back in school next day. Tuesday, that is. I went there on the Monday morning, when the press first reported Heather's disappearance.'

A week's special leave, expiring on Tuesday 15 November. Commencing, therefore, on Tuesday 8 November. And certainly embracing Friday 11 November. The evidence was clinching. Jack Cornelius had been absent from Hurstdown Abbey, whereabouts unknown, on the day of Heather's disappearance.

'Is that what you wanted to know, Mr Barnett?'

'Yes. That's what I wanted to know.'

305

34

There was no doubt in Harry's mind as he nursed the car back to Swindon that he had at last seized truth by the tail. Jack Cornelius was in some way implicated in Heather's disappearance; she had learned too much for her own good about his relationship with her sister; his were the threats she had detected on Rhodes and fatefully ignored. As for Dr Kingdom, his presence in Lindos on 6 November was a red herring. Perhaps, as Dysart had surmised, he had merely been satisfying himself as to Heather's well-being. At all events, Harry was certain Zohra's enquiries would prove Kingdom had been dutifully occupied elsewhere on the day of their visit to Profitis Ilias – unlike Jack Cornelius.

He reached Swindon still wrestling with the conundrum of what to do next. Logic suggested he should confront Charlie Mallender with what he knew, but a carload of grim-faced policemen were still fresh enough in his memory to deter him. Perhaps the time had come for Dysart to raise matters on an official level. Either way, Harry had little attention to spare for his mother's account of a troubled day.

'At my age, I should be ex-directory.'

'Why's that, Mother?'

'Well, it'd stop these weirdoes getting my number, wouldn't it?'

'Heavy breathers, you mean?'

'Oh, nothing so straightforward. Six times that dratted

phone's rung today if it's rung once. I've picked it up, said hello, there's been a pause, I've repeated myself, then they've just hung up.'

'Annoying for you.'

'All I can say, Harold, is that you might look a little more concerned about it.'

'What can I do?'

'Phone the one person who did speak.' She thrust a note into his hand. 'A very well-mannered gentleman named Kingdom. He wants you to call him back.'

Harry gaped at the note. Why Kingdom should have telephoned him he could not imagine. It was almost as if he knew what Harry had discovered. To make matters more impenetrable still, the number he had given was not the number of his Marylebone consulting rooms. Harry felt absurdly nervous as he began dialling.

'940 2406.'

'Dr Kingdom?'

'Ah, Mr Barnett. Thanks for calling. How are you?'

'All right, but—'

'I wanted to apologize for what happened last week. I've thought about it since and really I can find no excuse for such unprofessional conduct. You were fully justified in becoming angry with me.'

'Well, that's—'

'The fact is, I think our misunderstanding may have prevented a very useful exchange of information and opinion. As you pointed out, Heather's safety should be our first concern. We should be cooperating, not bickering.'

'Yes, I suppose we—'

'Could we meet and discuss the situation? You may be assured there'll be no repetition of last week's unpleasantness.'

'Well, all right.'

'I'm working at home at the moment. Perhaps we could meet here rather than at my consulting rooms. A change of scene might be beneficial, don't you think?'

'Well, I suppose it might be.'

'Would tomorrow suit you?'

'Er, yes.'

'Good. Tell you what. I live just round the corner from Kew Gardens. Heather often used to meet me there rather than travel to Marylebone. Why don't we meet at the main gate at eleven o'clock tomorrow morning?'

Before Harry could do more than utter a bare agreement, Kingdom was gone. As he slowly put the telephone down, puzzling over what the man's motives might be, it instantly rang. As he picked it up his first thought was of his mother's anonymous callers. 'Yes?' he said cautiously.

'Hi, Harry. It's your old friend Jackie here.'

Jackie? Of course: Jackie Oliver. What could the wretched woman want?

'Harry?'

'Yes, Jackie?'

'You might sound more pleased to hear from me.'

'What can I do for you?'

'Since we bumped into each other, I've been thinking it might be nice to have a longer chat about old times, that's all.'

'Really?'

'Yeh. Why don't you let me cook you lunch this Sunday? I'm a wow in the kitchen and we could swap life stories. You looked a bit down in the mouth when we met. I could try and cheer you up.'

Sunday lunch with Jackie and her latest husband was the very last thing Harry judged capable of lifting his spirits, but somehow he could not find the energy to argue.

'What do you say, then?'

'All right. I'll come.'

'We're at seven, Chelsea Drive. Quite a way for you to travel. Do you want me to pick you up?'

'No. I've got my own transport.'

'Great. See you about midday, then.'

Suddenly, Harry's company was in demand and he could not for the life of him understand why. To compound his bemusement, the telephone rang again before he had taken

308

three steps along the passage. He snatched it up irritably, only to find that this time the caller was somebody he had been anxious to hear from.

'Harry? It's Zohra Labrooy here. I've got the information we need.'

'You have?'

'Yes. And now that I have, I'm at a loss to know what we should do.' She sounded worried, which was odd, since Harry had expected to hear that her enquiries had put her mind at rest. 'Could you come to Kensal Green on Saturday morning? We need to talk this through.'

'Well, yes, but—'

'I'll expect you about eleven o'clock, then.'

'All right, but Zohra—'

'Yes?'

'It's clear to me that I was making more of my suspicions about Dr Kingdom than I should have done. The Versorelli Institute have confirmed he was with them on the eleventh, haven't they?' There was no reply. 'Zohra?'

'You're mistaken, Harry.' She sounded calmer now. 'That's what I want to talk to you about. He was absent from the Versorelli Institute from midday on Thursday the tenth until midday on Saturday the twelfth. His movements on Friday the eleventh are completely unaccounted for.'

It made no sense. Jack Cornelius and Peter Kingdom, both absent from their posts, whereabouts unknown, on the day of Heather's disappearance. Surely to God, surely to calm sweet reason, they could not be in this together.

'Harry?'

'Yes?'

'There's something else you ought to know. I can't think what's caused it, but I'm almost certain it's the case. He knows I'm spying on him, Harry. He knows we're on to him.'

35

By reaching Kew Gardens with a quarter of an hour to
spare, Harry hoped to win himself a much-needed interval
of planning and preparation, a chance to assess Kingdom's
choice of venue and to rehearse what he would say. As soon
as he turned away from the entrance booth with his ticket,
however, he realized the folly of imagining he could outwit
somebody as familiar as a psychiatrist was bound to be
with the wiles and strategems of humanity. For there was
Kingdom, waiting for him on a nearby bench and smiling
in greeting. Harry had been forestalled.

'Glad you could make it, Mr Barnett,' Kingdom said, as
he rose from the bench and extended a welcoming hand.
'You're early, I think.'

'A little, yes.' But not early enough: that was clear.

'Do you know the Gardens?'

'Not at all.'

'I'll lead the way, then.'

They set off down a broad driveway, with glasshouses to
right and left and tree-dotted acres stretching away beyond.
The day was still, grey and mild, the gardens solemn and
wintry, reserved and silent as if made over for their private
use. Kingdom was immaculately dressed in crombie, tailored trousers and polished shoes, their steel caps clicking
self-importantly as he walked. He was breathing deeply, as
if sampling the air, and gazing about as some squire might
in his personal domain. Trailing beside him in his ill-fitting
clothes, the thinning sole of one of his shoes admitting the

dampness of the path, Harry felt as overawed and inferior as he suspected he was meant to.

'Heather adored the Gardens at every season,' said Kingdom. 'Since I live nearby, she often preferred to meet me here rather than in Marylebone. One advantage psychiatry has over other branches of medicine is that it can be practised in a variety of surroundings. Shall we aim for the river?'

'By all means.' What direction they took was of no consequence to Harry. Kingdom's presence and all the immanent uncertainties it gave rise to were more than enough for his senses to cope with.

'I hope your agreement to meet me signifies that we may forget our misunderstanding of last week, Mr Barnett. There was no call for me to question you so aggressively, nor for me to react as I did when you responded in kind.'

'I agreed because you said you were concerned for Heather's safety.'

'So I am. That is why I thought it necessary to examine the possibility that you knew more of what had occurred on the day of her disappearance than you were yourself aware of knowing.'

'How could that be?'

'The suppression of a traumatic experience by the conscious mind is a commonplace of psychology, Mr Barnett. It can be overcome by a variety of methods: hypnosis, analysis, therapy. But all require time and trust. I regret to say that I rushed the fence.' He shot Harry a smile of transparent reassurance. 'For Heather's sake, I'd like to try and mend the fence.'

'You're suggesting I become your patient?'

'I'm suggesting we pool our resources – your memory and my expertise – in the hope of discovering what has befallen our mutual friend, Heather Mallender.'

'That's how you think of her, is it? As a friend?'

Kingdom chuckled. 'You're referring now, I suspect, to my outburst when you implied our relationship might have been unprofessional. Well, I did and do regard Heather as a friend, yes, as I do all my long-term patients. And I did take her to the Skein of Geese on the tenth of September, but not as part of some campaign of seduction. Heather asked me to escort her there and I agreed.'

'If not seduction, what was the purpose?'

'To establish the validity or invalidity of a conviction which she felt unable to accept was merely a delusory symptom of her illness.'

'You can't tell me what that conviction was, of course,' said Harry sarcastically.

'On the contrary.' A smile of mild reproof. 'I came here today specifically in order to do just that. On condition that you agree to help me in any way you can.'

Harry had no intention of helping a man he knew to be a liar and suspected of being something worse. Yet the promise seemed cheap in view of what it might yield, so he gave it eagerly. 'All right. I agree.'

'Good. What do you know of Heather's illness, Mr Barnett?'

'Not much. She hardly spoke of it. Depression sparked off by her sister's death, I assumed.'

'It was rather more than that, I fear. Heather suffered a severe breakdown in November of last year: sudden and substantial personality dysfunction with many of the characteristics of clinical schizophrenia. She was admitted to a hospital where I am retained as a consultant and her case was referred to me. Once her condition had been brought under control, it became clear that her sister's death, though pre-dating her breakdown by five months, was the cause of her mental disintegration. This was not delayed grief, you understand, but an inability to sustain normal life without the counterpoint of her sister's example, compounded by a belief that her family and friends would secretly have preferred her – the less beautiful and talented of the two – to have been the one to die. It was a difficult case, because there was some justification for how she felt. Her family, so far as I could judge, were crassly unsympathetic. Nevertheless, after some initial

312

problems, excellent progress began to be made. She was able to leave hospital in March of this year and to resume a relatively normal existence. I had hoped a few months of regular consultation would see her recovery complete, but one' delusion proved particularly stubborn and it was in the hope of ridding her of it by shock tactics that I agreed to take her to the Skein of Geese on the tenth of September.'

Harry could not deny that Kingdom was master of a persuasive tone. It would have been wonderfully and utterly convincing, but for all the good reasons Harry had to disbelieve every word: Zohra's belief that he was a man obsessed; Harry's sighting of him in Lindos; his absence from Geneva on the day of Heather's disappearance. They were traversing a rhododendron glade now, and, after pausing to allow a gardener with a wheelbarrow to pass, Kingdom resumed.

'Heather's deepest rooted delusion was that her sister's death had not been the terrorist mishap everybody supposed. She could frame no specific allegation as to what had occurred, yet she persisted in the belief that Clare had been deliberately murdered, rather than merely killed in mistake for her employer. She had tried to suppress the notion in the immediate aftermath of the event, but this had only added to the severity of her breakdown when it came. It was therefore no surprise to me that it proved the most durable feature of her disorder. I presented her with its obvious interpretation: that to invest the incident with a deep and sinister significance was to give it some meaning which might lessen the horror of its impact, in other words that the belief was a subconscious device for keeping at bay the sense of inferiority to her sister which was the true origin of her illness. She accepted this interpretation, but still could not bring herself to abandon the belief. I hoped the visit to the Skein of Geese would finally lay it to rest.'

They emerged from the tree-lined path onto an open lawn, with a broad sweep of the Thames coming suddenly into view beyond a boundary fence. On the farther shore the empty acres of Syon Park stretched towards the distant bulk of Syon House. Drawn up on the lawn and commanding this vista were several benches. Kingdom walked casually across to one of them and sat down, waiting for Harry to join him before continuing.

'The last time Heather and I met here was on the sixth of September. That was when she challenged me to take her to the Skein of Geese and prove or disprove her point for good and all. She knew Clare had dined there shortly before her death and was convinced that if she could discover what had happened on that occasion, her suspicions of foul play would be vindicated.'

'Clare dined there with Alan Dysart.'

'Quite so. An innocent enough event, it would seem, and that is what I hoped Heather would be able to accept. I think she might have done, but for the proprietor, Rex Cunningham, feeding her a cock-and-bull story about seeing Clare in possession of a photograph which he was sure only a lover would carry. Like Cunningham and Dysart, the man in the photograph was an Old Breakspearean and that was enough for Heather: he immediately became the villain of the piece so far as she was concerned. As soon as Cunningham delivered his fanciful recollection, I knew she would fall for it and I knew why.'

'Well?' said Harry, once Kingdom's failure to continue could no longer be ignored.

Kingdom turned to face him: he smiled faintly. 'I have your assurance you'll hold nothing back yourself?'

'Yes.'

'Very well. Heather believed Clare was pregnant when she was killed. I was unable to decide whether this belief preceded or arose from her breakdown. Her contention was that Clare had admitted the fact to her around the middle of May last year – no more than a couple of weeks, that is, before her death – in the strictest confidence. She had not named the father. She had further told Heather only three days before her death that she proposed to have an abortion. After Clare's death, Heather had tried

314

to elicit from members of her family some evidence that they knew of the pregnancy, but it seemed they did not. When the subject arose during my treatment of Heather, I approached Clare's general practitioner and he assured me that, so far as he knew, she had not been pregnant. Of course, it is not uncommon for a single woman to keep such a fact from her GP, so his statement was scarcely conclusive, but, taken together with Heather's predisposition to believe Clare was murdered, it suggested that she had invented the episode in order to lend weight to her theory. The disturbed mind is surprisingly cunning, Mr Barnett. It is capable of many subterfuges.'

'You dismissed Heather's version of events, then?'

'To my own satisfaction, yes. But her disappearance casts a new light on affairs. It could prove she had not recovered as well as I'd hoped, or it could prove she genuinely had something to be afraid of. What I want to ask you is whether anything she ever told you or anything you've subsequently discovered could suggest that Clare Mallender really was pregnant when she was killed.'

More warnings than Harry could absorb sounded in his mind at that moment. For more than a year, Heather had struggled to persuade herself that Kingdom was right: her memories were delusions. Then, at Flaxford Rectory on 18 September, she had learned the truth: that only her memories were to be trusted. She had confided no more in Dr Kingdom. Harry had the man's own word for that. Therefore, he must follow her example. 'I've absolutely no reason to believe Clare was pregnant.'

Kingdom sighed with disappointment. 'I'd hoped you might have turned something up.'

'I'm afraid not. Cunningham told me about the photograph he'd seen in Clare's possession, but I'm not sure I believe him. The man in the photograph is a schoolteacher named Cornelius. As far as I can establish, he had no connection whatsoever with Clare Mallender.'

Kingdom nodded glumly. 'My enquiries had the same result.' He pressed a gloved hand to his forehead. 'Let me

315

ask you something else, Mr Barnett. When Heather met me here on the sixth of September, what she said made me fear that a relapse in her condition was imminent. Aside from insisting that we should visit the Skein of Geese, she claimed to have been given evidence that her father's firm, Mallender Marine, for which she'd been working part-time since April, was guilty of large-scale bribery and corruption. Have you found anything that might suggest that was true?'

'No. Nothing at all.'

'Then I must assume I was correct in my interpretation of her claim. Wild allegations of this kind can be a by-product of schizophrenia. Within a few weeks, Heather was herself prepared to admit she might have been wrong. She seemed happy to accept Dysart's offer of a holiday on Rhodes in the hope that there she could put all her delusions behind her.'

A name had suddenly lurched to the front of Harry's mind: Nigel Mossop. He had been unable to understand Heather's choice of Mossop as a companion on her visit to Tyler's Hard. Now it began to make sense. They had worked in the same office. They had drunk and talked together on Friday evenings. They had travelled with each other to the New Forest on 28 August. And eight days later Heather had told Kingdom she had evidence of financial irregularities at Mallender Marine. The connection was irresistible: Mossop was the source of her evidence. 'What would it mean,' Harry said, trying to sound calmly speculative, 'if we could prove Clare had been pregnant and that Mallender Marine had been resorting to bribery?'

Kingdom looked back towards Syon House. 'Why then, Mr Barnett, we would know those beliefs were not delusions on Heather's part. In that event, it would become conceivable that her belief her sister was murdered was likewise not a delusion. And it would become distinctly possible that whoever had murdered Clare had also been instrumental in Heather's disappearance.'

Kingdom was right. All of that did flow from what he

316

had presented as a remote hypothesis but which Harry sensed was the absolute truth. But why had he volunteered as much as he had? Anxious to staunch the sudden desire to trust the man, Harry said: 'When did you last see Heather, Dr Kingdom?'

'Mmm?' Kingdom's manner suggested the point was an inconsequential one, but to Harry it could be scarcely more significant. Kingdom had been in Lindos on 6 November, as Harry knew from the evidence of his own eyes and ears. He could only have been there to see Heather. It was possible, just possible, that the visit had an innocent explanation. If so, he would make no secret of it. If not, it followed as night followed day that he had only staged this expert pretence of seeking Harry's help in order to gauge how much he knew and how great a threat he posed. 'When did I last see her?' he repeated quizzically.

'Yes. I wondered what her state of mind was when you last met.'

'But I've already told you, Mr Barnett. She was beginning to believe she'd been mistaken all along in detecting some sinister conspiracy behind her sister's death. That was at our last consultation, in Marylebone, on the eleventh of October, two days before her departure for Greece. That was the very last time we met.'

Kingdom was condemned from his own mouth. A chill ran through Harry as he realized that this well-dressed, well-spoken, well-mannered man seated beside him on a bench amidst Kew Gardens' manicured charms was more than just a proven liar. It was also quite possible that he was Heather's murderer.

'The real question is this, Mr Barnett: are you willing for me to probe the sub-conscious areas of your mind in the hope that we may find there the clue your conscious mind has not so far uncovered? You may have seen or heard something, glimpsed or gleaned some sight or impression that would tell us what's become of Heather.'

Harry knew that if he had not recognized Kingdom from

their encounter in Lindos – if he had not learned from Zohra to distrust him – he would probably have succumbed to his ploy. And in agreeing to Kingdom's proposal for Heather's sake, he would probably have betrayed himself. 'What would be involved?' he said, struggling to sound no more than understandably cautious.

'In this case, I think only hypnosis would answer the requirement. It frees the mind of all stresses and inhibitions. It liberates the totality of recollection.'

'Hypnosis?'

'I don't wonder at your reluctance, but it has a history of success in such applications. You are the only known witness to the circumstances of Heather's disappearance. You may have forgotten or suppressed some feature of them which is crucial to an understanding of what occurred.'

Or crucial to an understanding of whether Kingdom had anything to fear from Harry. That, Harry felt certain, was really the object of the exercise. 'I don't know,' he said hesitantly. 'It seems a good idea on the face of it, but . . . .'

'Why don't you think it over?' Kingdom smiled at Harry as Harry did not doubt he smiled at all his patients before winkling their secrets from them. 'You could perhaps come to my consulting rooms next week. Speed is obviously of the essence, but I appreciate it's not the sort of step you'd wish to take without considering the implications.'

'No, it isn't. But I *will* think about it.' And Harry silently vowed that while he was thinking about it, he would turn the tables on the subtle, self-confident Dr Kingdom. But how? And why, if Zohra was right in thinking Kingdom already suspected her, was the fellow prepared to be patient?

'Do that, Mr Barnett.' Kingdom's broadening smile gave Harry no answers to his unspoken questions. 'I really think you'll see the wisdom of it. Let me know just as soon as you reach your decision.'

36

It was already dark when Harry reached Weymouth. He parked the car thirty yards or so from the entrance to Mallender Marine, waited till his wristwatch showed a quarter to six, by which time he judged most of the staff would have dispersed, then walked boldly in. He passed nobody but an oblivious cleaner on his way through the dimly lit corridors. Mossop's office was empty, but with the lad's jacket still over his chairback and his briefcase stowed beneath the desk, it was certain he could not be far away. Harry settled himself at the desk facing Mossop's, eyed the furnishings that had once formed the environment of his own working day – decrepit filing cabinets, overloaded cupboards, chart-posted noticeboards, memo-strewn tabletops – and waited.

Ten years had passed since Harry's sudden and ignoble exit from Mallender Marine, ten years that had drained its premises of familiarity but not contempt. That had merely lain dormant, sustained by an unsettled grudge, awaiting the moment of its revival. And now, with the thought Kingdom had sown in his mind, the moment had come. Roy Mallender had been the accuser eleven years ago and Harry the accused. Now the roles were about to be reversed.

'Harry!' Mossop started so violently as he walked through the door that most of the contents of his watering can – which he had evidently been away to fill – slopped onto the floor. 'Wh-wh-wh—'

'Close the door, Nige, and sit down. I want a word.'

Mossop contrived to slam the door and strike a ringing blow against a filing cabinet with the watering can before he subsided into his chair. 'I didn't,' he began, 'didn't . . . expect to s-see you . . . again—'

'So soon?' Harry lapsed into his old habit of finishing Mossop's sentences for him. 'You hoped you wouldn't, more like.'

'N-No . . . . Not . . . not at all.'

'Come off it, Nige. You thought you'd pulled the wool over my eyes, didn't you?'

'W-Wool? . . . I d- . . . I don't . . . . '

'You thought you'd got away with just driving me to the New Forest and back. You thought you'd persuaded me Heather only went with you that day for the pleasure of your company.'

'N-No. I never s-said—'

'Where's the evidence, Nige?'

'Wh-What evidence?' With a quivering finger, Mossop pushed his glasses back up his nose. There were beads of sweat on his forehead, liquid proof that he of all people would never make a good liar.

'You got to like Heather, didn't you? Don't look so bashful. It's understandable enough. You wanted to impress her, didn't you? You wanted to show her you were more than just a pen-pushing nonentity, more than just the butt of her brother's jokes. So you showed her something – some record stowed away and forgotten in the files – that proved her family's commercial ethics weren't as lily-white as she'd supposed.' Harry leaned across the desk and fixed Mossop with a stare. 'You may as well tell me all about it, Nige. I'm going to find out anyway.'

'Find out what?' The voice was harsh and booming and instantly recognizable. When Harry looked up, it was to see Roy Mallender standing in the doorway, dressed like the respected business man he would want to be thought but revealing by his cold-eyed stare and pouter pigeon stance all the bluster and belligerence he had once been famed for.

'Hello, Roy.' Harry injected as much false amiability as he could into his tone, knowing it would cut deeper than any insult. 'Working late?'

A single twitch in Roy's expression revealed that fury was simmering only just beneath the surface. He took three swift strides to the desk and raised Mossop bodily from his chair by a choking grip on his collar. 'Go home, Nigel,' he barked. 'See me first thing Monday morning.'

In a sudden scuttling rush, Mossop gathered up his jacket and briefcase and fled from the room. Pity swept over Harry as he watched him go. Perhaps he had been unfair to the lad. Perhaps he should have broached matters more gently. Either way, it would be some days now before Mossop was even coherent, let alone forthcoming.

Roy walked to the door and kicked it shut, then rounded on Harry. 'You must be a bigger fool than I thought to come here like this, Barnett.'

In some ways, Harry conceded, Roy was right, for this was one confrontation he was not ready for. He rose from his chair and began to walk calmly towards the door, but Roy stepped into his path.

'Christ, I'd have been doing everybody a favour to have finished you off in Rhodes, wouldn't I?'

At close quarters, Roy's loathed and swollen features were pitted with memories: memories of raging disputes won and lost, of injustices inflicted and grievances instilled. Looking at him, Harry found it difficult to believe that ten years separated him from the worst this man had done to him.

'What did you want with Nigel?'

'It was a private matter.'

'Nothing that happens *here* is private.' Roy's blunt forefinger jabbed sharply into Harry's chest. 'Not from me.'

'Don't try to intimidate me, Roy. I'm not in your pay or your pocket anymore.' Harry took a deep breath. There would be a time to avenge all the humiliations he had suffered at this man's hands. There would be a time, but this was not it. 'If you don't mind, I'd like to leave.'

At first, Roy did not move. For a moment, Harry thought he really did mean to finish what he had started on Rhodes. But no: he was lingering because, like all bullies, he never wanted his opponent to have the last word. 'You had your warning, Barnett. Coming here tonight means you've ignored it. So go, by all means.' With that, he cleared Harry's path. 'But don't think there won't be any consequences, because there will. Very serious consequences, believe me.'

Harry did believe him. But strangely, at this moment, he did not care. Whatever the consequences, he was sure they would come too late to stop him. As he strode from the building, he was aware only of a bewildering self-confidence. Against the odds and his own expectations, he had teased out the tangled strands of Heather's fate and was too close now to their source to be turned aside. A little more time was all he needed. A little more time and a meagre ration of understanding: then he would hold the truth in his hand.

37

Harry and Zohra were sitting on a bench in the overgrown heart of Kensal Green Cemetery as a grey midday came and went. Around them the crooked tombstones and gap-roofed mausolea of a Victorian necropolis stretched away along the rank and moss-fringed avenues. About thirty yards in front of them, the tiny bobbing figure of Mrs Tandy could be seen tending the marbled plot where her father, mother, several aunts and uncles and a founding pair of grandparents had been committed in succession since the century began. But no other living soul was visible or detectable in the acreage of neglected graves. It was, therefore, the ideal place to choose for the discussion they were obliged to hold, innocent yet secure, above board yet out of prying earshot.

Whilst Mrs Tandy, who had been profusely grateful to be driven to the cemetery, had bustled about filling vases for the flowers she had bought on the way, Zohra had calmly relayed to Harry all she had learned from her covert enquiries of the Versorelli Institute. Dr Kingdom, it transpired, had arrived in Geneva on Friday 4 November and had dined with the Director of the Institute that evening. He had attended a meeting at the Institute the following morning but had then been absent until the afternoon of Monday 7 November. So far, then, so good, since clearly he could have paid a flying visit to Rhodes on Sunday 6 November without being missed. Zohra had even contacted the airlines and confirmed that it was feasible.

There had followed a full round of commitments at the Institute until the morning of Thursday 10 November. He had then once more absented himself, reappearing for the monthly senior consultants' lunch on Saturday 12 November. None of this had struck Zohra's informants as even remotely odd – Dr Kingdom was entitled to a portion of leisure like everybody else – but Harry and Zohra were compelled to take a different view. They knew where he had been during the first forty-eight-hour gap in his itinerary and they as good as knew where he had been during the second. As to why, or what he had done there, they had no evidence worthy of the name, but they had suspicions aplenty. They had proved he could have been on Rhodes, even on the very slopes of Profitis Ilias, at the time of Heather's disappearance and, in their own minds, they had come to believe he must have been.

A measure of justification for their certainty had already been supplied by Kingdom himself. Zohra had found him increasingly secretive of late, given to working at home and telling her less than he would normally have done. The past week had seen an uneasy watchfulness added to these developments, as if he had sensed or detected the enquiries she had been making. Yet she was sure her approaches to the Versorelli Institute had not been reported to him; she had given those she had spoken to not the least cause to suspect her motives. As for Harry, his meeting with Kingdom at Kew Gardens had left him in awe of the man's subtlety but in no doubt of his duplicity. The suggestion of hypnosis had been a testament to both characteristics. If Harry refused, he would reveal his distrust of Kingdom. If he agreed, he might reveal far worse. Whichever his answer was to be, one would soon have to be given. And somehow, before then, he and Zohra had to gain the measure of their opponent, for Heather's sake if not their own. They had reached the limits of conjecture. Now they needed something more.

'There may be a way of making Dr Kingdom give us what we need,' Zohra said quietly, after they had sat in silence for some time contemplating the difficulty of their position. 'I've been thinking about it for several days. Ever since I learned the dates of his absences from Geneva, in fact.'

'What is it?'

'Well, as I told you, he keeps all his patients' files in a locked cabinet in his office. I have no access to it in the normal course of events, but I've noticed he often leaves it unlocked during the day if he's in, even when he pops out for a few minutes. It might be possible . . . .'

'To examine the contents of Heather's file?'

'Or to photocopy them.' Zohra grew suddenly sombre. 'It would be risky. Telephoning the Versorelli Institute was one thing. Rifling through a cabinet I've absolutely no business opening is another. If he came back unexpectedly and caught me in the act . . . .'

The outcome did not need to be defined. At the very least, Zohra would lose her job. At the worst, Dr Kingdom could prove to be as dangerous as they feared. Harry felt instinctively that it was a risk he could not allow her to run. 'Are you sure what we'd find would justify taking such a chance?'

'No. But the fact that he's stopped preparing material for Heather's file through me makes me think it must contain something he wants to hide. If so—'

'If so, I should be the one to play thief.'

'How could you do that?'

'Go there at night, perhaps. I daresay the cabinet could be forced.'

Zohra frowned. 'But then he'd know what had happened. What I'm suggesting would mean we had his notes on Heather in our possession without him being any the wiser.'

Zohra was right. Her method had every advantage over a clumsy piece of cat-burglary. Yet Harry could not suppress some rebellion within him against the fact that she would be courting disaster while he sat back and awaited the results. 'I'm not sure I can let you do this. It's too much to ask of you.'

'But you're not asking it of me. Heather is.' Her dark eyes swept across him, leaving him in no doubt of her sincerity. 'Besides, I know Dr Kingdom's habits better than anyone. There's no reason why anything should go wrong.'

'When would you make the attempt?'

'As soon as the circumstances seemed favourable.'

'And you wouldn't take any unnecessary risks?'

'No. I *won't* take any unnecessary risks.' So: the decision was made. 'Don't worry, please.'

'I can't help it.'

There came to Zohra's face the radiance of a sudden smile. 'Well, it's not so bad to have somebody worrying about me. In fact, it's rather a pleasant novelty.' She looked away. 'I think Mrs Tandy has finished. Shall we join her?'

Without further protest, Harry followed Zohra down a narrow path between the jumbled gravestones towards Mrs Tandy's family plot, where the old lady could be seen bundling together discarded flower stalks. As they went, it occurred to him that Heather, whatever her other misfortunes, had been luckier in several friendships than he had ever been in one; he doubted if anybody would have done as much for him in similar circumstances as Zohra was prepared to do for her.

'I'll be in touch as soon as I have some news,' she said, as they passed between two towering monuments to the respected dead of another generation.

'I don't mind admitting I'll be anxious to hear from you,' Harry replied. 'I wish you'd—'

In a split-second of realization, he was struck dumb. From somewhere to his left had come a faint click that could have been a squirrel cracking a nut but which conveyed to his ears a hint of the mechanical, a slight but unmistakeable suggestion of a closing camera shutter. He whirled round and there, not twenty yards away, was a

326

figure in a raincoat standing amongst the crowded tombs, lowering a camera to his side. Harry was clutched by the horror of instant recognition. It was the man from the train at Reading, the man who had wished him goodnight in Greek at Warwick Avenue station.

'What's wrong?' said Zohra, noticing his alarm.

But he could not reply. This shabby, innocuous stranger whose vapid grin would have persuaded most people of his utter harmlessness possessed the power to strike him rigid with fear. It was beyond logic but beyond denial. And every time it was worse.

'What's wrong?' repeated Zohra, with great emphasis.

'Good afternoon,' piped the stranger in a voice Harry could have predicted he would use: that of a simpleton whom nobody would pay much heed. 'The funerary monuments are quite delightful, are they not? And eminently photogenic.'

'Yes,' Zohra replied. 'They are, aren't they?' It was obvious to Harry that she had been taken in completely. 'Do you come here often?'

'As often as I feel the need. You might say I haunt the place.' It sounded so like the joke an eccentric grave-spotter would crack that Harry was sure only he would see through it. 'Do excuse me. I must go a-snapping before the light starts to fail.' With that he turned and hurried away, his grey raincoated figure dwindling rapidly amidst the forest of raised crosses and broken pillars.

Zohra touched Harry's elbow, as if trying to wake him from a trance. 'Are you all right?' she said, clearly bemused by his behaviour.

'Yes. I'm all right.' He took a deep breath, forcing his tensed muscles to relax. 'I'm sorry. It's just that . . . . I could have sworn I'd seen that man before.'

'Where?'

'On the train, when I left here last week.'

'Maybe you did. He probably lives locally. What of it?'

'Do you think he was really photographing the monuments – or us?'

'He seemed genuine to me. The cemetery *does* attract photographers.'

Harry did not try to argue. He knew how innocent the event was bound to seem to anybody denied his glimpses of the grand deception in which it played a part. Reading. Oxford. Haslemere. Kensal Green. Every step he took was traced, every move he made forestalled. He should have told her before now, he should have warned her of the snares that lay in wait for them. But if he did, would she believe him? And if she did believe him, would she still take the chance that might hand them Kingdom's guilt on a plate? In the face of such uncertainties, he could only stifle his fear and hold his tongue.

'Besides,' Zohra continued, 'what would be the point? What would a photograph of us together prove?'

'I don't know.' He turned towards her and smiled reassuringly. 'Nothing, I suppose. You're right. Let's forget it.' But his brain told him to do the exact reverse. Print this moment on your memory, it commanded. Record it faithfully so that later, when all these incidents have conspired to produce the climactic event you crave as much as you dread, you will be able to name the time and place when fear was finally conquered. The self-control that had returned to him now might count for nothing in the end. But at least it would sustain him until the end, whatever that was and wherever it was to be found.

38

'Let's face it, Harry,' said Jackie with a mischievous grin as she handed him his coffee cup and let her knee brush briefly against his thigh, 'you and I are both too old for fresh starts in life.'

'I thought that's what your return to Swindon represented,' Harry replied, accepting the cup and recoiling to the corner of the sofa.

'Hardly.' The smile stiffened and dissolved. She lit a cigarette, exhaled the first lungful of smoke towards the spot-lit ceiling, then reclined against the cushions. 'Hardly that at all.'

'I'm sorry to have missed your husband.' Harry was uncertain why he was troubling to proclaim such regret. To judge by the tastelessly expensive home he had bought in Swindon's south-eastern suburbs and the charmlessly pugnacious expression he wore in his wedding photographs, Tony Oliver, entrepreneur and athlete, was someone Harry had no wish to encounter. On the other hand, his unexpected business trip to Frankfurt had clearly left Jackie with an empty weekend on her easily bored hands and Harry had the disquieting impression he was intended to enliven it. Lunch and politely reminiscent conversation seemed increasingly unlikely to be all she had in mind. 'Does he have to go away often?'

'At least once a month.'

'That must be a nuisance.'

Jackie ignored the remark and cast Harry a weary

look that suggested she had expected better of him than faltering platitudes. 'You never thought of matrimony yourself, then?'

'Thought of it, yes. And thought better of it.'

Jackie laughed. 'Sometimes I wish I'd done the same myself.'

'Matrimony doesn't seem to have treated you too badly.' Harry nodded at the costly expanse of cream-carpeted lounge. 'This is all a far cry from your father's ironmongery shop in Wood Street.'

'Trust you to remember that.'

'Well, we go back a long way, Jackie. You said so yourself.' It must have been in the spring of 1968, Harry reflected, around the time Ramsey Everett had plunged to his death from a window in Oxford, that nineteen-year-old Jaqueline Fleetwood of the long blonde hair and criminally short skirts had first deployed her non-existent secretarial skills and super-abundant alternative charms at Barnchase Motors. Harry had interviewed her for the post himself and so, in a sense, was as responsible as his philandering partner for what had ultimately come of her appointment. 'Do you ever hear from Barry these days?' he said, before the indelicacy of the question had occurred to him.

'No.' Jackie smiled and an ambiguous look of nostalgia crossed her face. 'We've lost touch completely. When the divorce came through, he had some kind of time-share business going in the Canary Islands. But that was five years ago. Since then, I wouldn't know.' And her expression implied she did not care. Harry admitted to himself that at rising forty she was still as physically attractive as she had been at nineteen. The hugging cashmere sweater, the short skirt and the long, prominently displayed legs left him in no doubt of that. 'What about you, Harry? What have you been up to since you got back?'

'Nothing much. I'm still trying to find my feet.'

'Seen anything of Alan Dysart?'

The question surprised him into an admission. 'Well, yes, I have.'

'You two keep in touch, then?'

'Yes.'

'I thought so.' Jackie bent forward to sip her coffee, ran a crimson-nailed forefinger pensively round the rim of the saucer, then leaned back and drew deeply on her cigarette. 'You're lucky to have such an influential friend.'

'Yes, I suppose I am.'

'Do you think he'd remember me?'

'I'm sure he would.'

Jackie's gaze shifted from the plate-glass tabletop to Harry's face and rested there for several moments of concentrated assessment. 'Perhaps,' she said at last, 'you could re-introduce us.'

'Sorry?'

'Arrange for Alan and me to meet up again after all these years.'

What exactly did Jackie have in mind? Harry could scarcely believe, even of her, that the answer was what he was tempted to conclude. Had her second husband outlasted his usefulness? Had Harry been invited to lunch in his absence in order to be recruited as intermediary between Jackie and a glamorous future as wife or mistress to a famous man?

'Barry didn't like Alan, you know,' she continued. 'Didn't trust him, anyway. I don't know why. I had the impression something had happened between them, but I never found out what. Still, that's Barry's problem, isn't it? It needn't affect you and me.'

'No.' Harry said doubtfully. 'I suppose it needn't.'

'So you *could* arrange for us to meet?'

'I . . . I don't know.'

'It wouldn't be difficult, would it?' She transferred the cigarette to her right hand and let her left snake across the sofa cushions towards him. 'I'd be very grateful.' There was, in her slowly broadening smile and carmine-clawed proximity, a hint that her gratitude might know no bounds. 'Really I would.'

Before lunch, she had shown Harry round all the

331

rooms in the house, glorying in a sequence of domestic extravagances. Now the mirror-lined and thickly rugged interior of the master bedroom recurred to his mind. For an instant, but no more, a vision of Jackie filled the scene, draped wantonly across the bed, naked and stretching out her hand in invitation. Then, much as an alarm clock will splinter a dream, the telephone rang.

'Oh, damn. Excuse me. It might be important.' Jackie rose and hurried across the deep-piled vastness of the room. As she went, long legs brushing faintly together, shapely rump working beneath the clinging material of her skirt, Harry felt more relief than regret at the interruption. 'Hello? . . . Who? . . . Oh, I see . . . . Hold on . . . . ' She headed back towards the sofa, telephone in hand. 'It's for you, Harry.' There was a scornful curl to her lip. 'It's your mother.' Jackie's proposition, it seemed, was not to be the day's last surprise.

'Hello, Mother?'

'Is that you, Harold?'

'Yes, of course it is.'

'Could you come home straightaway?'

'Well, I—'

'There's a young man here who's anxious to speak to you. He says it's a matter of *extreme* urgency.' She lowered her voice to a whisper. 'He seems positively distraught, Harold. *Refuses* to leave without seeing you. Says there's something he absolutely *has* to tell you.'

'What's his name?'

'Quite honestly, he stutters so badly it's hard to be sure.'

'I'll be there in ten minutes.' Harry was already rising to his feet. 'Don't let him leave before I arrive.'

'It *is* important, then?'

'Yes, Mother. I think it probably is.'

39

A pot of strong tea reinforced by a sly addition of whisky appeared to have a calming effect on Nigel Mossop. At length, perspiration ceased to flow down his face, his stammer declined and his limbs grew less tremulous. Harry sat opposite him in the soothing gloom of his mother's front parlour, waiting as patiently as he could for the lad to become master of himself if not of his destiny. Eventually, his forbearance was rewarded.

'S-Sorry to b-barge in on you . . . like this, H-Harry.' It was Mossop's first coherent remark since Harry had returned.

'I'm the one who should apologize, Nige, for landing you in hot water with Roy.'

'N-No. I should have . . . should have st-stood up to him.'

A less likely proposition Harry could scarcely imagine, but now was not the time to remind Mossop of his frailties. 'Perhaps you're doing just that by coming here.'

'I h-h-hope so. You see . . . if I g-go back in tomorrow . . . I'll be on the car-car-carpet g-good and proper. . . . You know that. . . . If R-Roy threatens me with all the f-fires of hell – and he will – I'll never . . . never . . . have the c-courage to tell you.'

Courage, oddly enough, was just what Mossop was displaying, courage of the highest order when set against a lifetime of abject timidity. 'Don't worry about Roy. I'll deal with him.'

'I w-w-wish . . . I could believe that.'

'If you don't, why are you here?'

'Well, I've been . . . been th-thinking . . . about it . . . since R-Roy threw me out of the office on F-Friday . . . . The f-fact is, Harry . . . I've got to tell you.' Every muscle in Mossop's body was rigid with tension. His eyes were blinking madly in a semaphore of barely controlled panic. Yet there was also a strange and admirable determination locked within him, a degree of resolution which Harry had never expected to find there. 'I've g-got to bring the truth . . . out into the open . . . . I owe it to H-Heather, Harry . . . . D-Do you understand?'

'Yes, Nige, I understand. Why not just start from the beginning?'

'Like . . . . Like all g-good stories . . . you mean?' Mossop tried to grin. 'Well. . . . Well, you w-were . . . r-right . . . about Heather. . . . I did like her . . . a lot. You don't . . . don't meet . . . many p-people who are good . . . through and through . . . but Heather was one of them . . . *is* one of them. She j-joined the c-company in April . . . and we w-worked together from then . . . then on. I got to like her . . . like her awfully . . . but I knew . . . knew she was just being f-friendly . . . knew she didn't see anything in me . . . except somebody to p-p . . . somebody to pity.' He bowed his head briefly, then resumed with a greater measure of self-control. 'Don't worry, Harry. This isn't g-going to be . . . a sob story. Had we l-leased Cambridge Road . . . in your day?'

By Cambridge Road Mossop meant a small warehouse on the Granby Industrial Estate just outside Weymouth, which Mallender Marine had acquired, largely on Roy's initiative, to provide extra storage capacity. Harry had poured scorn on its viability at the time and had not been thanked for doing so. 'Yes, Nige. I remember it well.'

'Well, we've hung onto it . . . even though, as far as I can see, we don't need it.' Harry could guess why that was: admitting mistakes had never been Roy's strong suit. 'It's used . . . used as a dump now . . . for broken machinery and . . . old paperwork nobody's bothered to sort into what needs keeping . . . and what doesn't. A real . . . real glory-hole.'

'I can imagine.'

'Hardly . . . . Hardly anybody ever goes there. But last summer . . . well, you know how slack we get then . . . . Around the end of July, Pickard had this g-good idea.' Mossop frowned. 'You remember Pickard, don't you?'

Pickard was a worthless toady of Roy Mallender, introduced as office manager shortly before Harry's dismissal. 'How could I forget?'

'Well, he decided the records at Cambridge Road . . . needed going through at last. A thorough . . . sorting out. And he chose . . . Heather and me for the job. So. . . off we went. It was quite a cushy number . . . actually. Just the two of us, sifting through old paperwork . . . without anybody breathing down our necks. Most of the stuff was w-worthless rubbish. Some of it went back . . . years. I even came across notes in your handwriting, Harry. That prompted me . . . prompted me to tell Heather about how you'd been dismissed . . . set up just because Roy didn't like you. The idea that her b-brother could behave . . . like that . . . s-seemed to shock her. But, as it turned out, she had . . . had a much bigger shock in store. Amongst the newer stuff . . . was a whole load of files from last year r-relating to the Phormio contract. Phormio is some . . . some new development the Navy's been working on at P-Portland. Strictly top-secret. Not . . . not that there was anything secret in the file. It just contained details . . . of Mallender Marine's tender to s-supply some of the . . . electronics. Nothing. . . .nothing odd about it at all. We got the contract, too. One of our . . . most lucrative in years . . . actually. But that was just the point. Amongst the documents . . . I found the original exchange of memos between Roy and Charlie fixing the p-price to be offered . . . . And on one of them, added in Roy's own handwriting, a n-note. . . clearly sh-showing . . . sh-showing that . . . .'

'There was bribery involved?'

'Yes. That is. . . . N-No. . . . Not b-bribery, as far as I could tell. But c-certainly . . . c-c-c- . . . .'

'Corruption?'

Mossop's face reddened with the effort of expressing himself. 'Yes. Corruption. It had to be. It couldn't be . . . couldn't be read any other way. The memo was d-dated the t-twenty-s-second of June . . . and the tender had to be in by the end of the month. It showed the p-prices we were qu-quoting for each s-section . . . of the contract. We were awarded every s-single one in the end and there was the memo, in my hands, setting them all out. At the t-top, Roy had written a note to his father, dated the t-twenty-third of June, just before sending the memo on its way . . . I suppose.'

'What did the note say?'

Mossop managed a smile. 'It was short enough for me . . . for me to remember every word. 'These prices,' it said, 'will put us five per cent ahead of the competition in most of the categories according to . . . to . . . to . . . .'

'According to who, Nige?'

'It was just . . . just a pair of initials, Harry, that's all. . . . They didn't mean anything to me . . . at the time . . . except they didn't b-belong to anybody in the c-company. Some kind of informant, that *was* c-clear to me . . . . I showed it to Heather, well, because I wanted to blacken Roy's name as m-much as I could. . . . As s-simple as that . . . . And that's all . . . all I wanted to do. . . . I hate Roy . . . and I wanted to make Heather hate him as well. . . . But she recognized the initials, Harry . . . . She realized who they belonged to . . . and how s-serious my d-discovery was . . . . I'd never have sh-shown her . . . if I'd understood . . . what it meant.'

'What were the initials, Nige?'

For answer, Mossop launched himself on a flawless recital of the note Roy Mallender had written to his father. '"These prices will put us five per cent ahead of the competition in most of the categories, according to A.D."'

Harry flinched physically as well as mentally. A.D. could only be Alan Dysart, Member of Parliament, Under-Secretary of State at the Ministry of Defence, decorated war hero, man of the people, terrorist target, friend in need . . . and stooge of the Mallenders. Twenty-three days after Charlie Mallender's daughter had been killed aboard his yacht, Dysart had evidently passed commercial secrets to Charlie Mallender's son. Who better to ensure that Mallender Marine would win the contract than the man in charge of those awarding it? But why? Why should he have risked his reputation in such a way? A vague sense of responsibility for Clare Mallender's death could not be the reason. There had to be more to it.

'I see you recognize the initials as well,' Mossop went on. 'Alan Dysart, the p-p-politician. Heather told me at once . . . they had to be his. The man her s-sister had worked for. I was ama-amazed. I knew . . . knew Dysart had s-served with Ch-Charlie in the Navy and might have done the company one or two f-favours, but . . . but not this kind of thing. It was m-mad . . . . It made no . . . no sense.'

'What did Heather make of it?'

'That was the s-strangest part of all. She treated it like . . . like confirmation of something else. I don't know what exactly, but something to do with her illness. She reckoned it p-proved she'd been right all along about her sister. She wouldn't say more than that . . . . She r-reckoned I'd be safer not knowing what it proved.'

What would Heather have deduced from such a document? The answer had to lie in her belief that Clare had been pregnant, a belief others had been keen to interpret merely as a symptom of her illness. Suddenly, chanced upon in the archives, she had obtained evidence that Dysart had bought her family's silence within a month of Clare's death. What else but Clare's pregnancy by him would Dysart have needed them to be silent about? Heather could not have known at that stage how much less straightforward the circumstances really were. She could not have guessed one fraction of all she was subsequently to discover. 'What did you do with the information, Nige?'

'I wish . . . wish to God . . . we'd destroyed it. But Heather decided to confront Roy with it. To prove to him, I suppose, that she hadn't been mad to believe whatever she had believed about her sister. Anyway, the next thing I knew she was off sick. Then Roy called me in and told me I was being . . . pr-promoted. I couldn't . . . couldn't understand it. There was no . . . no mention of what we'd found . . . then or later. According to Roy, I was being r-rewarded for l-long and l-loyal service. I was being shut up . . . of course. . . . I knew that . . . well enough. But what . . . what c-could I do? Without Heather . . . and the evidence . . . what could I do?'

'Nothing, Nige. Go on: what happened next?'

'Well, Heather came back after about . . . about ten days. She seemed very . . . subdued . . . and didn't say anything about what had occurred. She hardly spoke a word to me . . . in fact. I took it . . . took it she didn't want to d-discuss it, so I didn't . . . didn't press her to. I th-thought we'd just pretend it had never . . . never happened. But then, the Friday before August b-bank holiday . . . she asked me to have a drink with her after work. It was the first time we'd been alone together . . . since working at Cambridge Road. Well, that was when she t-told me . . . what Roy had done when she'd shown him the memo. He'd taken her st-straight in to see the old man, it seems, and they'd persuaded her to hand it . . . over to them, saying she'd misconstrued the situation, didn't understand business affairs and should put it out of her mind completely, otherwise . . . well, if she went round making wild allegations, p-people might think she needed to be re-committed to h-hospital. She'd gone along with them . . . because she'd been f-frightened by what they'd said . . . but she'd also decided to m-make some enquiries on her own account . . . after the d-dust had settled. Not repeat the mistake of telling her family what she was doing, just see what she could dig up. She asked me to d-drive her to Tyler's Hard that w-weekend . . . to make a start. Apparently, she'd met Dysart's c-cleaning lady at Clare's funeral and wanted to f-follow up something the woman had said. Roy and Ch-Charlie probably thought they'd frightened her out of doing anything, but . . . they were wrong, Harry, so . . . so wrong. She'd acquired this . . . this determination . . . to go on with her personal crusade . . . and I could see . . . see there was no stopping her. So I drove her to Tyler's Hard on the Sunday, like I told you before. She didn't involve me after that. She said . . . said it was better if I had no p-part in what she was doing, said that way I could p-pretend I knew nothing about it.'

'That was good advice, Nige.'

'But you . . . you've found out, haven't you, Harry? You've f-found . . . what she was really after.'

'Yes, I have.' Truly, the sequence was complete. They had told Heather she was deluded to believe Clare had been pregnant and mad to suggest she had been murdered. But Roy and Charlie's reaction to the evidence Mossop had turned up had suddenly given her confidence in her own suspicions. At first, she must have thought she was following Dysart's trail. From Mrs Diamond through Willy Morpurgo and Cyril Ockleton to Rex Cunningham. Then the target had shifted to Jack Cornelius: corruption at Mallender Marine must have seemed a red herring at that point. Next, the Reverend Waghorne – and proof positive that Clare had been carrying Cornelius's child. But Heather had spoken to Waghorne on 18 September. By 11 October, according to Kingdom, she had been willing to accept that she was mistaken: a rest cure on Rhodes was the order of the day. How could such a change have come about? 'Tell me, Nige, when did you last see Heather?'

'Well, she left . . . left Mallender Marine . . . early in October. I can't remember . . . the exact date, but that . . . that m-must have been the last time I saw her. The f-first week in October.'

Suddenly, Harry remembered what Marjorie Mallender

had said about her daughter's departure from the family firm. 'The relapse she suffered in October. . . . It's why she left Mallender Marine.' But what relapse? Kingdom had never mentioned one. It was a strange kind of relapse that the patient's own doctor did not know about. And then again . . . the next photograph after Flaxford Rectory was of some kind of institution. Signposts. Parked cars. Driveways. Harry should have thought of it before. Hastily, he grabbed the wallet of photographs from his pocket and scrabbled through them to the one he wanted, then snapped on the lamp beside his chair and peered closer. Yes. There they were: the tell-tale signs he should not have missed. It was not just some kind of institution. It had bars at the windows.

Less than an hour later, they were there. The Vauxhall had lapsed into a dream of its super-charged youth and propelled them along the M4 at chassis-splitting speed. Challenbrooke Hospital stood red-bricked and austerely wooded on sloping ground above the Thames just east of Maidenhead. Admittance by appointment only, according to the board at the end of the drive. But Harry did not require admittance. Even at a range of several hundred yards he could see that Challenbrooke Hospital was the subject of the twelfth photograph.

'Why . . . why have we come here?' said Mossop.

'Because this was how they finally suborned her. This was what they threatened her with. Confinement here for as long as it would take her to accept that what she knew was a delusion. Once mad, always mad, if your family says so. That's what they must have told her. And she was right to believe them.'

'I don't . . . don't understand.'

'Never mind, Nige. Like Heather told you, it's better if you don't.' The greyness of the weather made the prospect more dismal still. It was grey in the photograph as well, the day Heather had come here to confront the consequences of persisting in her pursuit of the truth. 'I'll have them for this,' Harry murmured. 'I promise.'

'What?'

'Never mind, Nige.'

'But what . . . what are we g-going to d-do now?'

Harry patted Mossop's shoulder by way of comfort. '*We* are doing nothing. *You* are returning home, and if you'll take my advice, reporting sick tomorrow. That'll give us a few days to play with. Go fishing. Read a book. See a film. Do anything you like, but don't go back to Mallender Marine until you hear from me.'

'Wh-When will that be?'

'As soon as I've heard Dysart's version of events. I owe him a lot. But this time he owes me something.'

40

Forty-eight hours had passed before Harry could be accommodated in Alan Dysart's hectic round of meetings and speeches. Yet, as he trailed behind a pin-striped myrmidon along the arrow-straight corridors of the Ministry of Defence, he still felt a sense of acceleration growing within him, as if neither delays nor obstacles could slow his progress. Here, where he should have felt least at home, where swishing doors and subtle undertones were symbols of a rarely used but crushing power that could be turned against him, he was aware of nothing but a light-headed certainty of purpose, an intoxicating strength of mind and will. This, discovered so late in life, was what he supposed it must be like to be a man with a mission.

A waiting room and an archly mannered secretary, then another room and a coolly reticent official, finally 'Mr Dysart's inner office': panelled in dark wood, carpeted in sombre hues, papers piled on plateaux of teak, books towering to the ceiling behind leaded glass, the heavy note of antique clockwork, and beyond the three tall windows, dusk settling over London, distant clusters of light moving behind a deepening veil of drizzle.

'Hello, Harry.' The handshake was as firm as usual, the smile as warm. Only perhaps the smudges of grey beneath his eyes revealed Dysart's fatigue, only the faint irresolution of his gaze suggested he knew what Harry had to say. 'I'm sorry I couldn't see you yesterday. I was tied up in an emergency debate all afternoon.'

'It doesn't matter.'

'But I gathered it was very urgent.' An upward twitch of Dysart's eyebrows invited Harry to prove the point. 'Take a seat. A drink, perhaps?'

'No thanks.' Harry wanted to remain completely sober for a little longer yet. He subsided into an armchair and felt the richness of its buttoned leather enfold him. 'You asked me to contact you at once if I found out anything,' he began uncertainly.

'About the good Dr Kingdom?'

'No. Not about Kingdom. Not yet, anyway. I've come across . . . something else.'

'If it concerns Jack Cornelius—'

'It doesn't. It concerns . . . . ' Harry switched his gaze to the end of the room, where most of the wall was filled by an ornately framed oil painting so huge and dark it could have been the mouth of a cave. 'It concerns you, Alan.'

Dysart said nothing. He had been standing by a wooden filing cabinet near the window and now he leaned back slowly against it, raising his head slightly and folding his arms. There was to be neither encouragement nor intervention, it seemed. Harry was to be left to proceed at his own pace and on his own initiative.

He recited as dispassionately as he could the factual record of his discoveries: the testimony of the Reverend Waghorne that proved Clare Mallender had been pregnant by Jack Cornelius and the testimony of Nigel Mossop that proved Dysart had passed commercial secrets to Mallender Marine. He exaggerated nothing. He omitted nothing. And when he had finished, and looked up to judge Dysart's reaction, he found that his host was smiling at one corner of his mouth, as if in appreciation of a private joke. What Harry had said constituted potential ruin for this tall, handsome, elegantly clad man of wealth and probity, and all he could do in response was essay a weary grin.

'You realize what I'm saying?'

'Naturally.' Dysart turned towards the window and

beckoned for Harry to join him. 'Sample the view for a moment, won't you?'

Dusk was fusing imperceptibly with night over the neon and amber of London. The Thames had become no more than a gulf of blackness beyond the mobile lights of Embankment traffic, while to the south Big Ben loomed familiar and floodlit above the Mother of Parliaments.

'You don't need me to tell you, Harry,' Dysart said softly, 'that corruption has always held a seat in that gemmed palace of democracy. Peculation, malversation: it goes by many names. And more are guilty of it than are ever exposed.'

'I understand that. I'm not a fool. I'm not suggesting you took a bribe. Nor was Heather suggesting it, was she?'

'No. She wasn't.' Dysart took a deep breath. 'Do have that drink, Harry. We both need one.'

'All right.'

The drinks poured, Harry returned to his armchair, while Dysart, glass cradled to his chest, walked back and forth in front of him, talking quietly and unhurriedly. 'Heather came to me much as you've come now and asked me to explain what seemed to her so inexplicable. I'd thought I could avoid telling her the truth about her sister and I suppose I thought I could keep it from you as well. In both cases, I was wrong. Perhaps I should have told you sooner. If so, I apologise.'

'Clare *was* pregnant?'

'Yes. By Jack Cornelius, it would appear. I had no idea they were on such intimate terms. Ironically, I introduced them, at a conference about four years ago. Until Heather discovered the truth of the matter, however, I'd have said they were nothing more than acquaintances. Certainly Jack's name never occurred to my mind when Clare told me of her condition.'

'When did she tell you?'

'At the Skein of Geese, the last time we went there. It was a surprise, but nothing more: her private life was no

344

concern of mine. Or so I thought. But it rapidly transpired she had more in mind than booking maternity leave. Much more. I ought to explain that there was a time a few years back when our relationship as employer and employee might have developed into something more. Virginia and I were going through a difficult patch. Pressure of work meant Clare was seeing more of me than Virginia was. And Clare, well, Clare was one of the most ambitious people of either sex I've ever met. Becoming my mistress would have suited her purposes rather well. But it didn't happen, then or later. We never . . . . We never even once made love. I emphasize the point because it will help you appreciate how astonished I was when Clare told me, not only that she was pregnant, but that unless I cooperated she would tell the world the child she was carrying was mine. It was, to do her justice, a very cleverly thought-out ultimatum. The general election was less than a month away. Through Minter she could ensure her claim was given front page treatment in the Sunday press immediately beforehand. I could deny it, of course, and blood tests might subsequently cast doubt on her story, but not before I'd paid the electoral penalty, not before my chances of a Cabinet post had been well and truly blasted. As to the alternative, she wanted a negotiable but substantial sum of money and, following a discreet abortion, my energetic assistance in obtaining a candidature for a winnable seat in Parliament. And there you have it. I did say she was ambitious, didn't I?'

'What did you do?'

'The Duke of Wellington would have been proud of me, Harry. I told her to publish and be damned. In some ways, I felt sorry for her. I was sure Minter had put her up to it and almost sure Minter was the father of her child. I could have afforded the money, God knows, and I wouldn't have had any qualms about putting her forward for a vacant seat, but I wasn't going to submit to blackmail under any circumstances. Where would it have ended? No, I told her to do her worst. An anxious couple of weeks followed, I don't mind admitting, while I waited for her to make a move.

345

I tried several times to make her see reason. Even that last morning at Tyler's Hard. Strangely enough, she *did* seem to be having second thoughts then. Within a matter of minutes, of course, it was all supremely irrelevant. The bomb went off, she was dead – along with the child she was carrying – and I had far more to occupy my mind than how to resist attempted blackmail.'

'Where does Mallender Marine come into all this?'

'There's the rub, Harry. Once Clare was dead, she became public property: a martyr, a heroine, even something of a saint. The dedicated secretary who laid down her life to save her employer: above criticism and beyond reproach. I went along with it: what else could I do? I was genuinely appalled by what had happened. I certainly hadn't wanted it to happen. I tried to put our recent dispute out of my mind. I attended her funeral in Weymouth, I even addressed the congregation. I did what was expected of me. I paid her the homage she was due. Then, straight after the funeral, Roy took me to one side and applied his own brand of pressure. It seems Clare had written to her mother only a few days before her death confessing she was pregnant, naming me as the father and saying I was urging her to have an abortion. She must have been preparing the way for her grand exposé. Well, you know Roy: as ruthless as his sister was ambitious. He's always resented me because I've done most of the things Charlie would have wanted him to do – if he'd been capable of them. It was his chance to even the score. He would hand the letter to the press unless I handed Mallender Marine the Phormio contract on a plate. This was much more serious than what Clare had been threatening. Now she was dead, any suggestion that I'd refused to stand by her would seem doubly bad. Nothing could be proved or disproved. Any denials from me would sound like treachery in view of the sacrifice she'd inadvertently made for me. And the election was less than a week away. I'd been prepared to defy Clare when she was alive, but I knew I stood no chance in a contest with her memory.'

346

'So you agreed to Roy's demands?'

'Ultimately, yes. But first I appealed to Charlie. I beseeched him to call Roy off, for Clare's sake as well as my own. But he couldn't help blaming me for Clare's death, whatever he said to the contrary in public, and, besides, Mallender Marine was in deep water financially. Winning the Phormio contract was about the only way to keep their creditors at bay. So, even if he'd wanted to, he couldn't afford to be merciful. That left me no choice as I saw it. I could abandon public life and all the things I hoped to achieve in it, or I could do Mallender Marine this one favour. It was a small enough favour, God knows, in view of all the pocket-lining that goes on in Defence contracting. Roy and Charlie both knew Phormio was in my gift. They both knew how easily I could make sure they won the business. So I agreed. A few weeks later, they were awarded the contract and I received Clare's letter to her mother in return. I destroyed it and tried to erase the whole ghastly episode from my mind. I genuinely believed then that I would hear no more of it.'

'But you reckoned without Heather?'

'Yes. As did her family. Only after her breakdown did it emerge that Clare had told her she was pregnant. By then, of course, the pretence that she had not been had to be maintained at all costs, otherwise the question would arise: why had it been hushed up? Not that I knew anything about the conspiracy of silence they indulged in. I knew Heather was ill, but that's all I knew. The first I heard of her enquiries was when she confronted me with their result. She'd evidently followed the trail you've since retraced, though at the time she was prepared to say nothing about how she'd arrived at her conclusions. She'd established Clare's pregnancy as a fact, she'd learned·of the part I'd played in Mallender Marine winning the Phormio contract and she'd identified Jack Cornelius as Clare's lover. What she hadn't found was what I suspect she most wanted to find: evidence that Clare had been murdered. But her discoveries were bad enough from her family's point of view without that. Accordingly, they threatened to have her re-committed unless she forgot everything she knew. She came to me with rather more than an accusation, you see. She came to me for help.'

'And did you help her?'

'As far as it lay within my power. I told her the truth about her sister. I told her why I'd helped Mallender Marine. I took her to Tyler's Hard so she could meet Willy Morpurgo and satisfy herself he wouldn't hurt a fly. I even arranged for her to speak to the police officer who'd led the investigations into Clare's death so she could weigh the evidence of IRA responsibility for herself. I invited her to spend a weekend with Virginia and me in Devon so she could appreciate that ours was a happy marriage I wouldn't have put at risk for the sake of a fling with Clare. I undertook to intervene if her family tried to have her re-committed. I suggested that, in her own interests as well as everybody else's, she should drop the matter. And I offered her the use of the *Villa ton Navarkhon* to think it over. I last saw her a few days before she left for Rhodes, at which time she seemed disposed to take my advice.'

'And then?'

'Then? Why then, Harry, the wheel comes full circle. She travelled to Rhodes. She met you. On the eleventh of November, she vanished. And we are still none the wiser so far as I can see, still a thousand miles from the truth of what took place that day.'

348

41

Harry walked slowly north along Victoria Embankment, the chill of deepening night seeping into his bones along with the thickening drizzle. To his left the traffic surged on mindlessly. To his right the Thames lapped in vast and unseen motion. Behind him, had he cared to turn and look, a light could still be seen at a lofty window in the Ministry of Defence. And ahead? Ahead lay an uncharted realm of darkness and indecision.

Alan Dysart was not a bad man. That was clear. But neither was he as virtuous and far-sighted as Harry had previously supposed. In one sense, Harry was relieved to discover that Dysart, like everyone else, could be frightened into doing things of which he was later ashamed. In another sense, however, he was disappointed: disappointed to learn that the one man he had thought infallible was nothing of the kind.

Not that Harry blamed Dysart for succumbing to Roy Mallender's demands. In the circumstances, he would probably have done the same himself. The lapse was a modest one. It did not even involve a loss to the taxpayer. Nobody's life was on the line, nobody's future at stake. And Dysart had done his best to make amends: by the help he had given Heather, by the offers he had made to Harry in the wake of his admission, by demonstrating that his reputation for generosity was not ill-founded.

'I'll have a word with my opposite number at the Home

Office, Harry. That will ensure you receive no more unwelcome attention from the police. As for young Mossop, I can put his name forward for recruitment to the Civil Service. A change of career is just what he needs. Meanwhile, I'll make sure Roy understands that leaning on him – or you – is strictly out of order.'

This, then, was how such matters were settled. Whisky and soda, soft armchairs, a warmly lit room where bargains had been struck for decades past, influence, patronage, compromise, favouritism: was this the only way? If Harry had not been able to boast Dysart as a friend, how could he have set about learning what Dysart had proposed to glean with no greater effort than a suitable request whispered in an appropriate ear?

'If Kingdom's whereabouts on the eleventh of November are unaccounted for, Harry, it's time they received closer attention. Suffice it to say that we have the resources here to establish whether he was in Rhodes at the time – assuming he travelled by plane and did so under his own name. As for Jack Cornelius, discreet enquiries can be made of Hurstdown Abbey and the reason for his absence that week verified. I think this represents the limit of what I can do on a semi-official level, but it will suffice, won't it?'

Oh, it would suffice. There was no doubt of that. Indeed, information-gathering of the sophistication Dysart had at his disposal made Harry's self-sufficient blunderings seem hopelessly redundant. Perhaps that was what he resented: the suggestion that now he had come so far it was best for matters to be taken out of his hands into altogether more sensitive ones, the implication that he had done enough to warrant being withdrawn from the firing line and rewarded with a little hospitality.

'Why not come down to Devon after Christmas, Harry? You've never stayed at Strete Barton, have you? Virginia would love to meet you again after all these years.'

Virginia's enthusiasm for Harry's company existed, of course, only in Dysart's imagination. Nevertheless, Harry had accepted the invitation, because he saw in it a way of remaining faithful to his original purpose. To retrace Heather's movements as far as he was able meant to follow wherever the photographs led. And they led next to Dysart's Devon home. Therefore the invitation could not have been more timely.

Besides, Harry consoled himself as he crossed the road and headed up the side street where he had left the car, he was on the track of a more conclusive insight into Dr Kingdom's motives than a mere record of whether he had flown from Geneva to Rhodes on 10 November. If Zohra could copy the contents of Kingdom's file on Heather, if they could thereby obtain clear evidence that Kingdom was, as Zohra believed, a man obsessed, why then . . . .

The instant Harry saw the car in its parking space ahead of him, he saw also the white shape behind the nearside windscreen wiper. Why he did not assume it was a parking ticket or some worthless piece of advertising he could not have explained. Perhaps thinking about Zohra had planted a fear in his mind that this pale and insignificant object seemed somehow to fulfil. Whatever the cause, his hand was trembling as he reached out to touch it.

It was a blank envelope, barely damp, as if it had only been there a matter of minutes. And there was something inside. Harry pulled it free of the wiper blade, stepped back into the light cast by a nearby street-lamp and tore it open.

A photograph. Black and white, tinged amber by the lamplight. A footpath in a cemetery, viewed through a thicket of gravestones. A sideways view of two people walking along the path, one behind the other. A young dark-haired woman in a duffle coat. And a greying middle-aged man in an anorak. It was Kensal Green Cemetery three days before. The woman was Zohra Labrooy. And the man was Harry, captured on film one split-second before he heard the shutter close.

42

'Hello?'

'Zohra! Thank you God you're all right.'

'Harry? What on earth's the matter?'

'I thought . . . Well, it seemed as if . . . . Never mind. Let's just say the waiting got to me.'

'I'm afraid it'll have to go on for a little longer yet. I haven't had even the ghost of a chance. He's been very careful.'

'I hope you're being careful too.'

'Of course I am. Now, don't worry, I'll let you know as soon as I make any progress.'

The shortest day of the year was in many ways the longest for Harry as he paced the house in Swindon, not daring to go out in case Zohra rang in his absence, not succeeding for a single moment in forgetting the risks she was running on his behalf. His mother could not understand his behaviour, but derived some wry satisfaction from his insistence on being the first to answer the telephone. As he discovered, she had not exaggerated the number of anonymous calls, greater surely than any amount of misconnections could explain.

'Hello?'

'Harry? This is Zohra.' It was the afternoon of the following day. Her voice sounded different: guarded, uneasy, disturbed. 'I have what we need.' He could scarcely believe it: she had copied the file. 'Can you meet me in London in a few hours' time?'

'Where and when?'

'The Victoria and Albert bar, Marylebone station, six o'clock. Don't speak to me when I come in. Don't even look at me. I'll have the papers in a carrier bag, which I'll put down beside you. I'll have one fruit juice, then go, leaving the bag behind. We can talk later.'

'Why the precautions? Has something gone wrong?'

'No. It went without a hitch. I'm nervous, that's all, probably for no good reason. Now I *must* get back. See you at six.'

The Victoria and Albert was crowded, but not crammed. Groups of office workers swapped jokes and gossip before bolting their drinks to be sure of catching the 17.57 to High Wycombe. Others sat alone, reading evening papers and sipping halves, reluctant, it seemed, to be on their way. Harry chose a bar-stool next to a pillar, ordered a pint and checked that he could see the door in the mirror behind the bar.

Zohra arrived at three minutes past six. Harry saw her pause just inside the door and scan the row of backs confronting her before recognizing his, but he was sure nobody else would have thought she was doing anything more than taking in her surroundings. She wore a raincoat and flat-soled shoes, held the promised carrier bag in her left hand and looked exactly what it was best for her to look: simply one forgettable face in the stream of commuting humanity. She walked to the bar, eased herself into a space beside Harry and lowered the bag to the floor. Harry raised his glass to his lips and kept his eyes on the mirror. There was no-one, behind or around them, who was paying them the slightest attention.

'St Clement's, please.' Zohra's voice sounded calm and controlled.

'That'll be ninety-eight pence, love.'

'Thank you.' Zohra drew up a stool, started her drink,

unfolded an evening paper and studied the horoscopes, finished her drink, put the paper away and left. Harry looked at the clock. It was ten past six. Then he glanced down at the carrier. A large brown envelope was visible inside. He was on the point of draining his glass and going when he remembered the need for caution. He took his time. It was seventeen minutes past six when he walked from the bar, swinging the carrier casually in his right hand. And three hours later, in the privacy of his bedroom in Swindon, when he opened the envelope.

Dr Kingdom's involvement with Heather Mallender commenced with a letter from a senior member of staff at Challenbrooke Hospital thanking him for agreeing to take her case. The letter was dated 23 November 1987 and referred to Heather's admission a fortnight earlier. A note from her GP was enclosed, a Dr Lisle of Wellingborough. Heather had taught at Hollisdane Primary School, Wellingborough, and it was there that she had suffered an hysterical collapse at the children's firework display on Guy Fawkes' Night. Kingdom wrote back on 26 November confirming his acceptance of the case. Detailed clinical notes followed, listing the incidence of certain symptoms and the dosages of various drugs, all impenetrable to Harry admidst the jargon of psychotherapy and the milligrammage of pharmacy. There was a chilling reference in early December to 'ECT not yielding positive results'; he had at least some inkling of what that meant. Dr Lisle had written in mid-December seeking a progress report and Kingdom's reply exhibited nothing but an energetic professional concern for his patient's welfare.

> The original suggestions of a stress-related disorder have not been borne out. Heather's condition appears to me to be related less to feelings of inadequacy in the teaching environment than to feelings of inferiority towards her late sister. These are so deep-rooted and

354

have been so completely suppressed until the recent crisis that drawing them out may prove a long and difficult process.

By early January, in another letter to Lisle, Kingdom was expressing qualified optimism:

Heather has displayed remarkable strength of character in confronting the series of neuroses leading to her illness. Certain convictions of a quasi-hysterical nature remain, but on the behavioural level there is no doubt that she is making excellent progress.

And by late January he seemed certain that she would soon be ready to face the outside world:

I have discussed with her family the importance of providing a secure and supportive post-discharge environment. A return to teaching is out of the question and I would also be unhappy about her living on her own. Her parents seem willing for her to live with them, however, and in due course there is the prospect of undemanding part-time employment with her father's company. I am therefore approving a series of weekend home visits during February and March and will review her progress in the light of how successful those visits prove.

All seemed to have gone well, because on 10 March Kingdom had written to Charlie and Marjorie Mallender, with a copy to Lisle, saying that Heather was now ready to leave Challenbrooke Hospital on a permanent basis. 'This', he had stipulated,' is on the strict understanding that she will sustain a regular series of consultations with me for six months so that her recovery can continue to be monitored.' Was this, Harry wondered, suspiciously stringent of him? Was this the first hint that he was reluctant to let Heather go?

A note from the registrar at Challenbrooke Hospital followed dated 18 March 1988: 'Miss Mallender was formally discharged at ten o'clock this morning into her parents' care.' And so began the phase of Kingdom's relationship with Heather in which Harry was most interested. Every week, she travelled to London to see him. And every week he recorded his remarks on her progress. At the base of each sheet appeared the initials PRK/ZL which told Harry that Zohra had typed them. Predictably, therefore, they remained correct and dispassionate in every particular. 'Heather is adapting well to living with her parents.' 'Heather is enjoying the modest challenge of returning to the world of work.' 'Heather is becoming noticeably more relaxed and self-confident.' Suddenly, on 12 July, Zohra's initials vanished from the photocopied pages. Immediately, Harry's concentration tightened. If the real Peter Kingdom was ever to emerge into the open, this was the moment.

At first, the only obvious change was in the quality of typing. If the content became less cautious and more revealing, it was only marginally so. Yet one comment of Kingdom's did seize Harry's attention. 'I have decided to re-examine Heather's claim that her sister was murdered. It has become for her an intellectual premise, but I intend to demonstrate that it retains a schizo-hysterical root.' Why, Harry wondered, had Kingdom reverted to this painful subject? Could it be because it offered him a vehicle for sustaining a relationship which was no longer medically necessary?

Two weeks later, describing a meeting at Kew Gardens, Kingdom had written: 'Heather remarked on how like a courting couple we must seem to others, strolling amongst the blooms. That she felt able to say such a thing illustrates the beneficial sense of equality that now obtains between us.' Beneficial to whom? Harry would have liked to ask. A brief note on 9 August recorded that Heather had broken her appointment. When she returned a week later, the relief detectable in Kingdom's prose could almost have been that of a lover discovering that he had not been jilted after all.

> My fears were groundless: a family dispute is the explanation for Heather's absence last week. It revolved around evidence she claims to have uncovered of corrupt business practices at Mallender Marine. She is clearly convinced that it supports her notion that her sister was murdered, a notion which is in danger of assuming obsessive proportions.

There was not one hint Harry could detect that Kingdom blamed himself for having focused Heather's thoughts on what he had now dubbed an obsession.

August 23:

> We discussed the advisability of Heather pursuing enquiries into her sister's death against her family's wishes. I recommended that she start cultivating friendships and interests unconnected with Weymouth and Mallender Marine. She has had, it seems, no close friend outside the family circle since a colleague at Hollisdane School with whom she was on excellent terms left to teach abroad last summer. Perhaps such a friendship would have averted her breakdown. Perhaps, she agreed, it would help her shed her preoccupation with the events of last year.

A purpose behind Kingdom's observations began to hover at the margins of his words. To assist her in abandoning her obsession with Clare's death – an obsession which Kingdom had gone some way to encouraging – Heather needed a good and reliable friend. Had Kingdom been grooming himself for this role? Harry wondered. Had he hoped to become her friend? Or something more?

Kew Gardens was the venue once again on 6 September. 'Heather asked me to escort her to a restaurant in Surrey,'

Kingdom had written, 'where she hopes to learn something crucial to an understanding of what happened to her sister.' The next sentence was underlined. 'In view of the exceptional nature of the circumstances, I agreed.' Curiously, given the significance Kingdom had evidently attached to Heather's request, there was no subsequent note describing their visit to Haslemere, no reference to it at all in the pages that followed. A bland and solitary sentence recorded that Heather had broken her next appointment and the following consultation, on 20 September, was described in sparse and grudging tones, as if Kingdom were still recovering from some setback, some loss of confidence or blow to his pride. Harry knew, of course, that Heather's reason for going to the Skein of Geese had been precisely the one she had given Kingdom. But perhaps he had thought it a mere pretext. Perhaps he had fondly believed Heather wanted to cultivate him as a friend. If so, the discovery of his error must have been a profound disappointment, an intolerable assault on his self-esteem. And there was worse to follow.

October 11:

> Heather announced that she had accepted an invitation from Alan Dysart to spend a few weeks in his villa on Rhodes. She seemed deflated, even depressed, all her former confidence that she was right to doubt the accounts she had been given of her sister's death drained out of her. She seems very tired and as much in need of a rest as a change of air. Rhodes offers both, but, technically, she needs my permission to suspend our consultations. I expressed certain reservations, based on the fact that she knows nobody on the island and may therefore fall prey to loneliness and hence further depression. She responded by pointing out that the six-month consultancy I had laid down as a condition of her discharge from hospital had now expired and that she knew of no grounds for it to be extended.

Nor, evidently, did Kingdom, since he had lamely noted: 'In the circumstances, I felt obliged to grant her request.' What ravening sense of rejection may have lain behind his agreement? Harry wondered. Nine months before, Heather had been wholly dependent on this man's care and sensitivity. Now she had made it clear she was determined to cut free of him. How had that made him feel? Whatever the answer, no more than the faintest hint of resentment had crept into his concluding remark.

I remain very concerned about Heather's state of mind, for all her insistence that she is now self-sufficient. Obviously, I cannot accept her judgement in such a matter as final. The possibility therefore exists that further intervention on my part will be necessary.

It was the last comment on the last page. Nothing was resolved, nothing defined, nothing excluded. On 11 October, all Kingdom had been prepared to say was that further intervention on his part might be necessary. What form that intervention might take was not explained. All Harry knew was that one month later Heather had disappeared.

'Hello?'
   'Zohra, this is Harry.'
   There was a pause, then she said: 'Have you read what I gave you?'
   'Yes. And you?'
   'No. There wasn't time. I just copied what was there.'
   'Then we must meet. Soon.'
   'Come here Saturday morning, as early as you like.'
   'All right. But Zohra—'
   'Yes?'
   'Until we meet, be careful, will you?'
   'You sound worried.'
   'That's because I am. Very worried.'

43

Harry drove back to Swindon from Kensal Green on Christmas Eve with the knowledge that at least forty-eight hours of irksome inactivity separated him from any further progress towards his goal. After reading Kingdom's notes on Heather, Zohra had agreed with him that it was no longer possible to believe that Kingdom's presence on Lindos on 6 November had an innocent explanation. Proof that he had returned to Rhodes and played some sinister part in Heather's disappearance on 11 November was still lacking, however. The man best placed to obtain such proof was Alan Dysart and Harry was due to be a guest at his Devon retreat from Boxing Day onwards. Since Harry did not know where he would be in the interim, the only sensible course was to wait until then. Certainly it seemed so to Zohra, who did not have to return to work and uneasy proximity with Kingdom until the Wednesday after Christmas.

What Zohra did not know – because Harry had not told her – was that somebody was aware of their association, somebody who had commissioned the man in the raincoat to dog Harry's footsteps and to take a photograph of them walking together in Kensal Green Cemetery. Harry had meant to tell her, but, when it had come to it, had somehow lacked the heart to inflict the knowledge upon her. And throughout his return journey to Swindon he reckoned he had made the right decision: a trouble shared was in this case more likely to be doubled than halved. Not until he walked into the house and met his mother in the passage, indeed, did he doubt that he had acted for the best. Her eyes were wide with alarm and her finger was pressed at right angles against her lips.

'There's somebody here to see you, Harold,' she whispered, gesturing towards the closed door of the front parlour.

'Who is it?' Harry's first thought was that Dysart's promise to call off the police had not been fulfilled.

'That fellow who telephoned you last week. Dr Kingdom.' The name was like a clutch at Harry's throat. 'You know, there's something about him I don't quite like.'

Peter Kingdom looked even taller and more elegant than usual in the humble front parlour, the tangy scent of his after-shave blending oddly with the indefinable aroma Harry always recognized as home. He was standing by the corner cabinet, leafing idly through a photograph album, the old dog-eared leather-covered album on whose thick black pages Harry's mother had meticulously gummed every family snapshot, whether good or bad, since the inaugural church door portrait of Mr and Mrs Stanley Barnett, Whitsun 1932.

As Harry closed the door behind him, Kingdom turned and smiled in greeting. 'Mr Barnett! Good to see you again.' He held up the album. 'Just admiring these vignettes of your childhood. Tell me, what's "Trip"?'

Harry was too taken aback to reply. He had read Kingdom's secret notes on Heather and the knowledge they had left him with was incompatible with the relaxed and charming exterior this man chose to show to the world. He moved unsteadily across the room and found himself at Kingdom's elbow, staring down at a page of photographs of his own barely recognizable eleven-year-old face, frowning on a pier, grinning on a beach, pouting at a boarding-house window, with a caption beneath in white ink recording Trip, Weston-super-Mare, July 1946. 'It was the annual summer holiday for GWR employees and their families,' he heard himself say. 'I hated them.'

'Really? Why?'

The answer was that, even as a child, Harry had distrusted the herd mentality. Every July, the Railway Village emptied as the population boarded excursion trains for the coast. And every July young Harry wished he did not have to go. The sheer compulsory jollity of the whole communal extravaganza repelled him. But to Dr Peter Kingdom, forty years on, he was not about to admit any of that. 'I'm sure you didn't come here to listen to my reminiscences of a deprived childhood,' he snapped.

Kingdom raised his eyebrows. 'Was it deprived?' Then he seemed to have second thoughts about pursuing the point. 'Excuse me,' he said with a smile. 'It's my training getting the better of me.' He closed the album and slipped it back into its place. 'Actually, of course, I came here to ask if you'd decided yet whether to take up my suggestion of hypnosis.'

'No. I'm still thinking about it. I was going to contact you after Christmas.'

Kingdom nodded. 'I thought you probably were.'

Every second Harry spent under this man's scrutiny was, in present circumstances, a torment. He tried to cut it short. 'In that case, I don't understand the purpose of your visit.'

'It was prompted by something else, I must admit. If you don't mind my asking, how long have you known my secretary, Miss Labrooy?'

Harry's heart seemed to miss a beat. He felt sure his mouth had sagged open before he could shape a reply. 'Why . . . why do you ask?'

'You'd be within your rights to tell me to mind my own business, of course.' The smile that accompanied the remark gave it an unmistakeable weight of sarcasm.

'What is there . . . . What makes you think I know Miss Labrooy?'

'A photograph, Mr Barnett. A rather puzzling photograph. I received it through the post yesterday morning. See for yourself.' Kingdom drew an envelope from an inner pocket and slid the contents into Harry's hand. It was the photograph taken of Zohra and him in Kensal Green Cemetery. 'There was no note with it and the address was typed,' Kingdom went on. 'Posted in London EC1 on the twentieth.' The twentieth: the day Harry had found a copy of the self-same photograph wedged under the windscreen wiper of his car. 'Odd, isn't it?'

One glance at Kingdom's face was enough to convince Harry: this was Kingdom's devious way of announcing he was on to them. The man in the raincoat was working for him. And therefore he knew Harry and Zohra had joined forces against him. But, if so, surely he would not have been so careless as to give Zohra the chance to copy his file on Heather. Unless, thought Harry with a sudden lurch of fear, he no longer cared how much they learned.

'I wondered if you could suggest an explanation, Mr Barnett. The incident left me at a loss.'

'No. That is . . . . No, I can't.'

'But you do know Miss Labrooy? Socially, I mean.'

'No. We're just . . . . ' Every lie he could contrive would be transparent, he sensed, yet anything was preferable to the truth. 'We met by chance . . . in Kensal Green Cemetery . . . last Saturday.'

'Really? Who took this photograph, then?'

'I don't know. But . . . I've received a copy as well.'

'Have you? That strikes me as odder still. What does Miss Labrooy make of it?'

'I haven't told her.'

'Has she been sent a copy?'

'No.' Too late his brain overhauled his voice. 'I mean I don't think so.'

Kingdom slid the photograph back into the envelope and replaced it in his pocket. He was frowning now, his keen eyes scanning Harry's face in search of clues. 'When did you receive your copy, Mr Barnett?'

'Tuesday.'

'Through the post?'

'No. Actually . . . it was left under the windscreen wiper of my car, in a blank envelope.' Kingdom knows this already, thought Harry: this charade of question and answer is merely a test of nerve.

'Here in Swindon?'

'No. I was in London at the time.'

'Meeting Miss Labrooy, perhaps?'

'No. I told you: we met by chance last Saturday. We've not met since.' There had been nobody watching them at the Victoria and Albert, Harry felt certain. And Kingdom could not know that he had just returned from Kensal Green. In this lie at least he was secure.

'So what makes you think she hasn't received a copy as well?'

'I've spoken to her on the telephone. She'd have been bound to mention it if she'd been sent one.'

'But you didn't feel bound to mention it to her?'

'I didn't want to worry her.'

'Very considerate of you.' Kingdom's frown faded into an ironical stare. 'Well, I suppose there *is* no point bothering Miss Labrooy. She's on holiday until Wednesday. But when she returns, I shall certainly inform her.'

'That's up to you.'

'What really puzzles me, Mr Barnett, is that being sent a photograph of yourself, taken anonymously and without your knowledge, doesn't seem to have surprised you at all. Why is that, may I ask?'

'I've had a few days to get over the shock.'

'It *was* a shock, then?'

'Well . . . yes.'

'Yet you've done nothing about it.'

'What can I do?'

Kingdom did not reply. In the silent interval during which his eyes remained fixed on Harry, all the bluffs and double bluffs that were the substance of their encounter seemed to refine themselves into the piercing intensity of his gaze. Then, as if satisfied that he had learned all he could hope to learn, he broke away and strode to the door. 'You'll let me have your decision before the end of next week, I trust?' he said, pausing with the door half open and smiling back at Harry as if they were discussing a business proposition of small moment.

'Yes.'

'Good. I'll wish you the compliments of the season then, Mr Barnett, and I'll look forward to hearing from you.'

As the door closed behind him Harry suddenly noticed how tense every muscle in his body had become. Unclenching the fists his hands had formed, he found every crease in his palms lined with sweat. His first inclination was to rush to the telephone and alert Zohra to what had happened. But that was surely what Kingdom wanted him to do. That was what his visit had been intended to provoke. Therefore Harry must do what was most difficult in such circumstances: he must do nothing. He moved to the window and twitched back the net curtain. There was Kingdom, climbing into his car a little way down the street. 'You'll be hearing from me all right, Doctor,' he heard himself murmur. 'Perhaps sooner than you think.'

44

Harry had not spent Christmas Day in England for ten years and had forgotten just how gruelling the experience could be. Why people considered annual torture by turkey and television to be in any way desirable was to him an impenetrable mystery. For his mother's sake, however, he tried to pretend that three pairs of green woollen socks were just what he needed and that the Queen's speech was something he could not bear to miss. Only when darkness fell and his mother began looking for her double-set of Salvation Army carols to put on the gramophone did he sense that his tolerance was ebbing; it was time to beat a retreat. But the streets of Swindon were empty, the pubs were closed and the scenes of his childhood had vanished; there was nothing in all the silent night to give him either comfort or courage, nothing, that is, except the knowledge that tomorrow he would be on Heather's trail once more.

Trip 1949 – Harry's last before school leaving age rescued him from its annual excruciation – was to Paignton. That, and Alan Dysart's wedding day, constituted all he knew of South Devon. The consequence was, as he drove down through the West Country on Boxing Day, that the two events coalesced in his mind. It was as if a sherbet-stained schoolboy had blundered into the wedding reception and elbowed his way through the champagne-sipping guests. None of his memories seemed willing to obey orders: they jostled and hid and appeared in disguise.

366

The car too was playing up, producing enough rebellious symptoms to force Harry off the motorway and on to slower routes through empty market towns slumbering in a Christmas trance. An enforced halt to let the radiator cool finally turned the journey into an ordeal and it was not until the afternoon had taken its first turn towards dusk that he reached Strete Barton through a switchback of high-hedged lanes halfway between Dartmouth and Kingsbridge.

A tarmacadammed drive between bare-branched trees, sleek Jersey cattle chewing nettles in softly sloping fields: Harry remembered none of this. It had been early summer last time, of course, with the trees in leaf and the birds in song: perhaps that was the only difference. He drove over a cattle-grid, then through a gateway into a wide and empty yard, with a Dutch barn to one side and an older stone barn doing service as a garage on his left. Ahead, beyond a low hedge, stood the house itself, slate-roofed and cob-walled, with mullioned windows and a porched entrance, smoke curling from the chimneys. Beside the house, a lane led off past a double-fenced paddock towards a stable-block where Harry could see a figure at work with a bucket and broom. In the garage stood Dysart's Daimler, a mud-spattered Range Rover and a gleaming red sports car. Here, the scene left Harry in no doubt, landed wealth was at its most tangible. And here, one glance at the picture propped on the dashboard reminded him, Heather had taken her thirteenth photograph.

As Harry climbed from the car, Dysart appeared in the porch, his arm raised in greeting. He was wearing an old Navy sweater over twill trousers, his hair was swept casually back, he was smiling broadly. Before he could even wonder why the thought had come into his head, Harry pondered the mystery of this man's easy transition from tie-pinned mandarin to glad-handed man of leisure: there was no occasion, it seemed, no setting or context for which Alan Dysart could not devise and present the ideal persona.

'Good journey, Harry?' the firm handshake, the touch on the shoulder, the flashing smile: the warmth of Dysart's welcome, the admission it always implied to the charmed circle of his friendship, was undiminished. 'Come on in. I'm afraid Virginia's not here at the moment.' He led the way and Harry followed, glimpsing as they moved along the hall towards the rear of the house a large and richly furnished lounge, where a huge and splendidly decked Christmas tree stood beside a crackling fire. 'I was in the study when I heard your car. A politician's work, you know . . . . ' The study was darkly panelled and lit by one broad window that looked out over rolling pasture and wooded coombes towards the church tower and clustered cottage roofs of the nearest village. 'I expect you could use a drink.'

'Please.' Harry glanced round at the sporting prints and well-stocked bookshelves, at the broad and paper-strewn desk with its ever-present, ever-changing view of the Devon countryside. Was this, he wondered, the real Alan Dysart – the man of tweed and tradition, of shooting rights and rural values? Or was this just one more expert pose, one more approximation of what others expected of him? A glass was pressed into his hand. 'Cheers,' he said, sipping the contents; Dysart's taste in malt whisky was as impeccable as ever.

'What's in the envelope?' said Dysart, nodding at the parcel Harry held by his side.

'Something rather significant.'

'Concerning friend Kingdom?'

'Yes.'

'Then let me tell you what I've learned about him since we last met.' He waved Harry to a chair. 'It's amazing what you can find out when you have the resources of Interpol unofficially at your disposal.'

'Where was he on the eleventh of November?'

Dysart leaned back against the edge of the desk. 'Bear with me for a moment, Harry. I should first explain that it seems Jack Cornelius is in the clear. He was given ten days' compassionate leave by Hurstdown Abbey because his father had died. Well, I had the point checked: he wasn't making it up. On the eleventh of November, he was at his father's funeral in Dundalk.'

'And Kingdom?'

'A different story. Airline records confirm your sighting of him in Lindos on the sixth. He flew from Geneva to Rhodes on the fifth and returned on the seventh.'

'But the eleventh?'

'Still a blank. There's no airline record of him paying a second visit to Rhodes. But in looking for one, Interpol came across something rather interesting.' Dysart plucked a paper from his desk and began to read from it. 'A Briton named King, initial P, travelled with Olympic Airways from Geneva to Rhodes via Athens on Thursday the tenth of November. He left Rhodes again the following day on the 17.50 flight to Athens, stopped there overnight, then caught the 8.20 Swissair flight to Geneva on Saturday the twelfth.'

The dates and times were right but the name was tantalizingly wrong, unless P. King and P. Kingdom were one and the same. 'You're not suggesting—' Harry began.

'It's possible. Passports and tickets tend to be checked separately at airports. Customs officers are more interested in whether your passport is genuine than in what name's on your ticket. Besides, you know the Greeks as well as I do. Administration's hardly their strong point. But there's something else as well. According to the passenger lists, the mysterious Mr King travelled to Rhodes alone. Yet he returned with his wife.'

'His wife?'

'Or a female companion using that name.'

Recited by Dysart, the facts sounded bland and inconsequential, but if King was Kingdom's *nom de guerre*, then he had neither excuse nor alibi. He had been on Rhodes at the time – at the very hour – of Heather's disappearance. And he had not left alone. His threatened intervention had found its form.

'Now,' said Dysart, 'do you want to tell me what's in the envelope?'

Harry reckoned it would take Dysart at least an hour to read and appraise Kingdom's file notes. He filled the time by taking his bag up to his room, unpacking and bathing away some of the strain of the journey. It was nearly dark when he returned to the yard for a breath of air. He lit a cigarette and decided to take a stroll down the drive, relishing the stillness and silence that was everywhere about him, the dampness that clung to his breath, the scent of woodsmoke that enveloped the barns and hedgerows. If England, his England, had been more often like this, he would not have been so eager to leave.

Suddenly, looming through the thickening dusk, a horse and rider appeared, coming slowly up the drive towards him, seeming somehow ghost-like until the leisurely clop of the horse's hooves caught up with the vision. A tall chestnut mare, clotted with mud to the hocks and blowing hard, ridden by a woman in full hunting kit. With a shock, Harry realized she was Virginia Dysart. He stepped back towards the hedge and thought for a moment she meant to ride by without acknowledging him. But no: she reined the horse in as they drew alongside.

'Hello, Harry.' The mare was even taller than he had supposed. From its saddle Virginia gazed down imperiously, unsmiling and unabashed. Her hair was drawn up in a snood beneath her hat, exaggerating the severity of her features. 'Alan told me you were coming,' she said. 'I hope he's looking after you.' She was going to pretend they had not met at Minter's flat. She was going to defy him even to imply as much. And already, gazing up at her, Harry found himself questioning how this proud and perfectly attired huntswoman could be mistress to an unscrupulous scandalmonger. 'It's good to see you again,' she continued, 'after all these years.'

Now was the moment, if there ever would be a moment, to throw the evidence of his own eyes back in her face

370

But he could not. Shamelessness on this scale seemed to demand respect. 'It's a pleasure to be here,' he heard himself say.

'Good.' Her eyes narrowed, her lips compressed in a smile tight as a drum-skin. 'See you at dinner, then.' And with that she twitched at the reins and the mare trotted on up the drive.

Dysart had grown sombre in Harry's absence. He poured them both a drink and paced the room in silence for fully a minute before subsiding into the chair behind his desk and sliding the photocopied file notes back into their envelope.

'What do you think?' said Harry.

'I think I'd like to know how you obtained these.'

'Through Kingdom's secretary. She knew Heather quite well and she doesn't trust Kingdom. She thinks he may have prolonged Heather's treatment unnecessarily.'

'Her initials are Z.L.?'

'Yes. Zohra Labrooy.'

Dysart leaned back in his chair and stroked his chin thoughtfully. 'And it was she who discovered Kingdom was absent from the Versorelli Institute on the eleventh of November?'

'Yes.'

'I made some enquiries about the establishment, you know. It's a private psychiatric clinic. Judging by its fees, it caters only for the wealthiest of clients. Foreign patients are a speciality, discretion a byword. As far as I can establish, the Versorelli Institute is the sort of place where an embarrassingly disturbed relative can be securely if expensively maintained and, in time, forgotten.'

A vision came to Harry's mind of a large gabled house set among snow-covered pine trees, with alsatians patrolling the grounds and Heather's frightened face glimpsed at an upper window. 'Do you think Heather's being held there?' he said.

'I don't know, Harry.' Dysart pulled himself upright

and a gleam of concentration came to his eyes. 'You said Miss Labrooy suspected Kingdom of being reluctant to admit Heather had made a complete recovery. Why should that be?'

'Because he wanted her to remain dependent on him.'

'All right. Let's agree there's a hint of that in his notes. When she went away, what did he do?'

'He bided his time. Then he followed her to Rhodes and persuaded her to accompany him to Geneva.'

'She went voluntarily, you think?'

'For some reason, she agreed to meet him on Profitis Ilias in secret. Presumably for the same reason she agreed to travel incognito to Switzerland.'

'Where she's been ever since?'

'At the Versorelli Institute, yes.'

Dysart frowned and let out a slow sigh. 'The same thought came into my mind, Harry. The man's personality; his absence from the Institute on the day in question; these notes; the King coincidence. They all point to the conclusion you've drawn. But as far as proof goes I'm afraid they also amount to absolutely nothing.'

'Then what do we do?'

Dysart swung his chair round and gazed through the window at the darkening skyline. 'What indeed?' He reached back across the desk and snapped on a lamp. 'First, I think we need to satisfy ourselves that the Mallenders genuinely don't know where Heather is.'

'You mean Kingdom might have been acting on their behalf?'

'It's a remote possibility, but a real one. I thought I knew Charlie Mallender and what he was capable of, but the pressure he and Roy put on me over the Phormio contract proves I was wrong. We know they threatened Heather with re-committal to Challenbrooke Hospital unless she cooperated with them. Well, they may have gone a step further and recruited Kingdom to do their bidding. For some reason, they may have preferred people to believe

Heather had disappeared rather than been confined in a Swiss asylum against her will.'

'If so, they're not likely to admit it, are they?'

'No, they're not.' Dysart smiled faintly. 'But I shall be able to tell if they're lying. I telephoned Roy last week and made clear your friend Mossop wasn't to be hounded. I thought then I might have to see them face to face in order to reinforce the message. Well, I think the time's come to pay them a visit.'

'When will you go?'

'Tomorrow.'

'Do you want me to come too?'

'No, Harry. Your differences with Roy would only complicate matters. I'd prefer you to wait here. I should be back within the day.'

'And then?'

Dysart's expression grew stern. 'Then the time for standing idly by will be over, Harry. The time to act will have come.'

45

Dysart set off for Weymouth at dawn the following morning. Harry heard the Daimler growling away down the drive as he lay half-awake in bed and Nancy, the housekeeper who served him breakfast an hour later, confirmed that her employer had made 'an uncommon early start'. It was also Nancy who gave Harry directions into the nearby village of Blackawton. With several cupfuls of strong coffee, three rashers of crispy bacon and two of the neighbouring farm's free-range eggs inside him, he set off to walk the route on a morning whose brightness and warmth seemed more suitable for spring than the depth of winter. There was genuine pleasure to be had from a tramp along damp and deserted lanes in such conditions, but Harry was set on something more purposeful: the scene of Heather's fourteenth photograph.

Half an hour brought him to the fringes of the village and there, rather than at the church whose tower he had been aiming at, he found what he was looking for: an overspill graveyard set in a small field – a cluster of no more than fifty graves beyond which the ground fell away steeply, opening up a limitless vista of patchwork farmland and wooded valleys. He stood amongst the stones for several minutes, letting the breeze ruffle his hair and the details of the view seep into his mind. It was, he reckoned, just about the nearest mankind could come to a perfect place. A humble field, exposed to wind and sun and rain, on the edge of a peaceful village. Who could crave Westminster Abbey after seeing this?

FRANCIS DESMOND HOLLINRAKE. As Harry looked at the gold letters carved in the black marble stone, he wondered what had prompted Heather to photograph it. The other pictures she had taken had followed a pattern in which Virginia Dysart's father seemed to play no part.

'You're an early riser,' said a female voice from behind him. When he turned round, it was to see Virginia Dysart striding towards him. She wore jeans, a guernsey, a red silk scarf and a sheepskin jacket and was smiling broadly. In all of this was scarcely recognizable the stern horsewoman or the silent dinner-table companion of the previous night.

'Not as early as some.'

'You mean Dysart?' It was a strange way to refer to her husband. It declared a distance between them that excused her from explanation. 'He hardly sleeps, it seems to me. Politically a great asset, I believe.'

'You know where he's gone?'

'Yes.' The smile tightened. She glanced down at the grave. 'What brings you here, Harry? My father died fifteen years ago.'

'So I see. Do you visit his grave often?'

She would not be shamed into pretence, her expression declared. 'Hardly ever.'

'Then I could ask you the same question. Why this morning?'

'I thought I might find you here. Nancy told me which way you'd come.'

'And you guessed this was my destination?'

'Oh no. It was no guess.' She timed a pause to perfection. 'The last time I was here was with Heather.'

The last time was with Heather. Harry glanced back at the panorama of miniature folded fields and could almost believe for an instant that it was autumn as well as winter, that Heather was between and beside them, that that day and this had become simultaneous. For the last time was with Heather.

'How did you know she came here, Harry?'

'I didn't.'

She ignored his denial and in so doing declared its futility. 'She wanted to hear all about my father, you know. But you *do* know, of course, don't you?'

When Harry looked at her, he could not be sure what piece of knowledge she meant: Heather's intentions or her infidelity. 'Did you bring her here?'

'Yes. She asked me to. She took a photograph. I thought that odd. Macabre, I suppose. Look in any family album and you'll see weddings and baptisms galore. But never funerals. Love and birth. But never death. Heather, on the other hand . . . . Death was all that concerned her. Don't you agree?'

'No. As a matter of fact, I don't.'

She smiled. 'Will you come for a ride with me, Harry? In the car, I mean. I left it in the lane.'

'A ride where?'

Another smile. 'Where I took Heather, of course. Where else?'

Virginia drove fast but expertly, the scarlet Mercedes hugging the rutted bends as they surged east from Blackawton. Harry had glimpsed a sign in the village stating four miles as the distance to Dartmouth and it seemed scarcely as many minutes before they were speeding down a long straight hill towards the mast-stippled blue of the harbour, with the manicured grounds of Britannia Royal Naval College climbing away to their left.

'Heather stayed at Strete Barton the weekend before she went to Rhodes,' Virginia explained, slowing as they neared the foot of the hill. 'I had to come into Dartmouth on the Saturday morning and I invited her along. Little did I know what she had in mind for the journey. First the stop at the graveyard, then the endless questions. Mildly curious to start with, then almost obsessive, as if she wanted to glean every scrap of information she could.'

They pulled up by the harbourside and climbed from the

car. Dog-walkers and out-of-season tourists were patrolling the broad pavement, moored dinghies knocking gently against each other in the swell of the estuary. On the opposite shore, cottage roofs were dotted along the thickly wooded slopes. Virginia leaned back against the waterside railings and gazed towards the College standing four-square and red-bricked on its landscaped summit above the town.

'Has Dysart ever told you how we met, Harry?'

'No, I don't think he has.'

'Up there.' She nodded towards the College. 'Because of that. Divisional cocktail party, September 1968. He was a cadet then, just down from Oxford. I was one of the eligible local girls invited along for the budding officers to practise their social skills on. Nineteen, that's all. So very very young.' She sighed. 'Three months later, we were engaged.

'You knew Dysart when he was at Oxford, Harry. That should give you some idea why I was so taken with him. He had the looks and brains of a god. I was tongue-tied and nervous, shivering in some silly summer frock. I just couldn't believe it when he chose to talk to me. And as for asking me out . . . . Well, it seemed like a dream come true. The parties. The late nights. The wild rides through the lanes in his MG. Taking him home to meet my father. Dancing with him at the end-of-term ball. The gown I wore. The things he said. A glass of champagne by one of those tall windows. The lights of Dartmouth below us. My heart thumping so hard I was afraid it might burst out of me. The whispered proposal. The tremulous acceptance. I was so proud at his passing-out parade a couple of days later. So proud that he was mine.' She shook her head. 'You must think I'm mad to be talking like this. You must think I never was the vulnerable young girl I'm describing.'

A tall, remote and finely boned beauty in her wedding dress. A gloved handshake and a meaningless smile at the reception. Then, years later, a fleeting visit to Lindos: he had seen her walking along the beach one spring morning in a white bikini and could remember thinking how majestic she was, how haughty she seemed with her head tossed back and her wet hair falling across her shoulders. She had never come again. This, it suddenly occurred to him, was all he knew of her, this and a testy encounter at Minter's door. 'Why are you telling me all this?'

'Because it's what I told Heather.'

'But why me?'

'Because Dysart asked me to. Last night he asked me to tell you everything I'd told Heather when she was here. And I agreed. I agreed, while he was in Weymouth, to put you in the picture.' She smiled. 'There's just one tiny little irony.'

'Which is?'

'He doesn't know what I told Heather. He doesn't know what I'm telling you.'

The Green Dragon, Stoke Fleming, had just opened its doors when Harry and Virginia arrived. It was a cold, ill-aired and unpopulated inn tucked away down a side-turning in the first village south of Dartmouth. Why they had called there Harry did not know. Nor did he even try to object when Virginia ordered and paid for the drinks. They took them to a window table. She lit a cigarette and inhaled deeply, with obvious relish, tossed her hair back and gazed around the bar, chin raised and eyes narrowed, disdain bordering on contempt ingrained in her expression.

'The cadet divisions all had adopted pubs,' she said after a first swallow of vodka. 'This was Dysart's divisional watering hole. I met him here quite often and would sit at this very table, watching him and the others cavorting and carousing, waiting patiently for him to buy me another g and t or spare me a few words. God, I was submissive then, so very much what I was expected to be. Just like we all were.'

'But not anymore?'

She smiled. 'Do you know why I stay with Dysart, Harry?'

'It's none of my business.'

'Because he owns Strete Barton. Christ, of all the ironies: that man owns my family home. My father, you see, had been in financial difficulties for years without my knowing. Paying for my education – not to mention my wedding – can't have helped. I suppose he looked upon Dysart as the son he'd never had, the man who might take over the running of the farm when he couldn't cope any longer. So he began confiding in him, seeking his advice and following it. Then he started borrowing money from him – big money. He ended up mortgaging the whole place to him. And neither of them told me. My father must have been too ashamed to face me with it. Besides, I suppose he thought he could pay Dysart off without me ever knowing. Instead of which, he died and willing me the property signified nothing. It was Dysart's in all but name and has been ever since. It was his decision to rent out the farmland to neighbours and keep just the house, for instance. Always his decision.'

'Surely you could have farmed it yourself.'

She laughed. 'Don't be silly, Harry. You know what I am – a pampered bitch. Dysart made sure of that. He's always known what I wanted more than freedom from him: fine clothes, jewellery, thoroughbred horses, fast cars, a generous allowance.'

'Even so—'

'I could leave him?' A smile of self-reproach. 'No. Then I'd lose everything.' Her eyes drifted out of focus. 'I didn't tell Heather any of this. I was on my best behaviour with her. Besides, she didn't know about Jon.' The name was out: the pretence was over. 'He's one of my interim revenges, you see.'

'Interim?'

'He'll do, until I find a better way.'

'A better way of what?'

'Of making Dysart pay for the life he's made me lead.'

The speed of Virginia's driving turned the high-hedged

lanes to a blur. Staring out at them, Harry wondered why, wherever he went in Heather's footsteps, he found bitterness and disappointment, sad and sterile lives led against bankrupt pasts and mortgaged futures. A need for fresh air came suddenly upon him. He lowered the window and breathed in deeply.

'Where's Heather, Harry?' said Virginia. When he looked across at her, he saw that she was smiling. 'It's not such a stupid question as it sounds. What I mean is: do you think she is somewhere?'

'Of course.'

'Really? Somewhere specific, living and breathing, eating and sleeping? You think that? Because I'm not sure I do. Heather seemed to me almost, well, almost ethereal. As if her grasp on the real world was weaker than most. As if she could easily have lost touch with it one day for no apparent reason.'

'Is that a serious suggestion?'

'At least it fits the facts. A mountaintop is where you'd expect such a person to vanish.'

Harry was reminded of a conversation he had had with Miltiades. 'You mean death without a corpse?' he murmured.

Virginia nodded. 'It's a good phrase for it.'

'It's not original.'

'Never mind. One thing's certain: Heather was the diametric opposite of her sister, as unworldly as Clare was—'

'You knew Clare?'

'Of course. And before you ask, yes, I knew she was trying to blackmail Dysart. She came down here last year, a few weeks before her death, and informed me, in that precise, hard-faced way of hers, that she was carrying his child.'

There was a sharp deceleration and a jolt as they turned in to the Strete Barton drive. 'Did you believe her?' said Harry.

'No. I didn't. There was something about her story that wasn't quite right. It was too pat, too simple, too obvious a trap for Dysart to have fallen into. That's why I said nothing to Jon about it. If I ever do give him something to use against Dysart, I want to be sure it'll stick.'

'But if you had been sure?'

'Then I wouldn't have hesitated.' So there it was, calmly and shamelessly stated. In Virginia, Dysart had what no man deserved in a wife: a potential enemy. 'Shocked?' she disingenuously enquired.

Before Harry could answer, an inconsistency strayed across his mind. Clare had come to Strete Barton a few weeks before her death? Surely that could not be right, not if – 'When exactly did Clare visit you?'

'Mmm? Oh, it was the May Day bank holiday. Dysart was opening a fête or something in his constituency. That's how she must have known she'd find me alone here.'

'May Day?'

'Yes. You know: the first Monday in the month. Surely they'd made that a holiday before you moved to Rhodes.'

Harry frowned. This did not make sense. According to Dysart, Clare had unveiled her threat to him at the Skein of Geese on 16 May. It was inconceivable that she had first shown her hand to Virginia. Therefore Virginia must be mistaken. It was easy enough, after all. There were two bank holidays in May. She must simply have confused them. As the car drilled over the cattle-grid, he was about to press her on the point when the thought was banished from his mind by a sudden braking and the sight of Nancy hurrying towards them across the yard with an anxious look on her face.

'What's wrong?' said Virginia as they climbed from the car.

'Am I glad to see you back, Mrs Dysart.' Nancy was out of breath. She had to take several gulps of air before she could continue. 'I bin proper spooked, I can tell 'ee.'

'Spooked?' Virginia sounded more irritated than concerned. 'By what, girl?'

'Well, I were in the kitchen doin' the washin'-up when it 'appened. I looked up from the sink and I sees this bloke

381

standin' in the yard, lookin' in at me like 'e'd bin there a long time, just starin' in. 'E weren't a delivery man or nothin'. 'E weren't dressed right for that. And 'e weren't doin' nothin' either, just starin'. Made me shiver all over. Anyway, I looked away just long enough to put down the pot that I were 'oldin' and when I looked back – no more 'n 'alf a second later – 'e were gone. Vanished into thin air. I rushed outside, but 'e were nowhere to be seen.'

'Perhaps he'd driven away,' said Virginia testily.

'No. There weren't time. Nor the noise of an engine either. I came out 'ere and looked down the drive and there were nothin'. Not a sign. I walked down to the stable-block and there were nothin' there either.'

'A hiker, then.'

''E were no 'iker. Weren't dressed for walkin'. Looked more of a townie.'

'Whatever, he's gone now?'

'Must 'ave. But I dunno where or 'ow. I looked everywhere abouts. There weren't a trace. That's when I thought 'e might be 'idin' somewhere. Back o' one o' the barns or somethin'. And that got me well and truly worried.'

'When was this?'

' 'bout quarter of an hour ago, I s'pose.'

'I expect he's gone now, but I'll check the horses anyway.' With that, Virginia strode away towards the stables.

'She won't find nothin',' Nancy said to Harry with a dismal shake of her head.

'Can you describe the fellow?' Harry asked, trying to sound sympathetic.

'Thin. Middle-aged. Somewhere in 'is fifties, I s'pose. Bald. Well, black 'air going' grey scraped across 'is 'ead that is. Yellowy skin. Sickly-lookin'. With these two little rat-like eyes. Wearin' a raincoat 'e was, though—' She broke off. 'Are you all right, Mr Barnett? You've gone proper pale all of a sudden.'

46

Silence and solitude enveloped the house. It was two hours
since Nancy had been sent home to calm down, one since
Virginia had set off on her regular afternoon ride. Resisting
a powerful desire to leap into his car and drive away, Harry
had searched the stables and barns one last time and had
found, as expected, nothing. Returning to the house and
starting violently at every creak in its elderly beams, he
had concluded that Dysart's malt whisky was probably the
best hope of avoiding outright panic. Now, as its reassuring
warmth seeped into him between anxious sips, he scanned
the fields through the study window, seeing nothing but
cattle, sheep, trees, grass, hedges and a vague reflection
of his own face.

Who was he, this silent observer, glimpsed only when
he chose? How had he been able to follow Harry to Strete
Barton? How had he been able to anticipate his every move?
Whose bidding was he doing – Kingdom's or his own?
Another gulp of whisky. And still nothing moved.

Harry turned away from the window. Dysart's study,
comfortably yet clinically furnished, was a strangely empty
place, the desk cleared, the books neatly aligned. No half-
finished letter lay on the blotter, no note or scrap or jotting
to betray its owner's character.

Side by side on the wall facing the desk hung three group
photographs of Naval personnel. Harry walked across and
inspected each in turn.

Dartmouth cadets, September 1968, Seaman Class.

There was Dysart, third row back, composed and unsmiling, neither arrogant nor humble but what he had always seemed to Harry: supremely self-possessed. Next came the crew of HMS *Atropos*, April 1971, with Commander C.V. Mallender seated centre front, shoulders braced and jaw jutting. Lieutenant A.J. Dysart was an anonymous figure four to the left. Nothing in the pose or expression of either man hinted at what they would later mean to each other – and to Harry. Finally, HMS *Electra*, July 1982, the frigate Dysart had captained in the Falklands War. Scarcely any older, it seemed, or outwardly changed in any particular, the perfect blend of daring and discipline, Commander Dysart sat at ease amongst his men.

Harry moved slowly back towards the window, running his eye along a row of books on the nearest shelf as he went. Politics, literature, the sea: the themes one might expect of such a man. Then he stopped and re-examined one leather-cased spine, reciting under his breath the gold-blocked title. *The Reign of William Rufus*. He pulled it down and opened it at the title page. *The Reign of William Rufus and the Accession of Henry the First*, by Edward A. Freeman, Honorary Fellow of Trinity College, Oxford. Published 1882. Its condition was excellent, without so much as a frayed page to reveal its age. Harry turned back to the fly leaf and started with surprise at the inscription. 'To Dysart, in commemoration of his inception of the Tyrrell Society, Breakspear College, Oxford, 23rd April 1968.' Five surnames were appended, each in a different handwriting. Cornelius. Cunningham. Everett. Morpurgo. Ockleton. So St George's Day 1968 had seen a presentation as well as a defenestration, an act of recognition as well as an act of betrayal. But whose recognition? And whose betrayal? Six men had known the answers. One was dead, another as good as. And the other four were not telling.

The telephone on the desk went off like a claxon. Harry slammed the book down beside it and snatched up the receiver.

'B-Blackawton 753?'

'Harry! It's Alan Dysart. Virginia not there?'

'No. She's gone riding. Where are you ?'

'Weymouth.'

'With . . . with the M-Mallenders?'

'Are you all right, Harry? You sound upset. And no, I'm not with the Mallenders.'

'It's nothing. I'm quite all right.'

'Are you sure?'

'Yes.'

'Very well.' A pause, then: 'The Mallenders are as much in the dark as we are, Harry. Whatever their other misdeeds, it's clear to me they aren't conspiring with Kingdom to have Heather confined anonymously in Switzerland.'

Heather and Dr Kingdom. Of course. Why could Harry not concentrate on what was important? 'You're certain?' he said numbly.

'Absolutely.'

'So where does that leave us?'

'Charlie and I have agreed we should meet Kingdom as soon as possible. Not to accuse him, just to try and get his measure. It's vital we know what sort of a man we're dealing with.'

'How will that be arranged?'

'It already has been. Charlie telephoned Kingdom and asked him to meet us here tomorrow. He agreed. He's due at Sabre Rise at eleven o'clock.'

'Tomorrow?' Harry wanted to protest at the speed with which events were moving. He wanted to call a halt, a truce, a breathing space. But all he could say was: 'It's settled?'

'Yes. You'll join us, of course?'

'Well . . . . Yes.'

'Good. I'll stay here overnight. Tell Virginia I'm detained on business. She won't query it.'

'All right.'

'Until tomorrow then, Harry.'

Until tomorrow. As Dysart replaced the receiver and a burr of disconnection intruded, Harry sensed the doubt as well as the silence waiting in the room around him. He put down the telephone. It rang again instantly.

'Blackawaton 753.' No answer. 'Hello?' Still no answer. 'Is there anyone there?'

A click, a faint change of tone, then an answer, of a kind. '*Parakalo?*'

A Greek voice, on a telephone line in Devon. Harry could not speak.

'*Parakalo?*'

Had the same voice wished him goodnight on a tube train in London? He could not say. He could not be certain.

'*Parakalo?*'

Who was behind this? Who of all the men and women he had met was doing this to him?

'*Parakalo?*'

There could be no reaction, no response, no rising to the bait. He would not give them so much satisfaction.

'*Parakalo?*'

He put the telephone down. And silence followed, like a soothing hand on his forehead. Silence that spared him an answer. Until tomorrow.

47

They made a curious tableau, Harry would have been the first to concede. The lounge at Sabre Rise, though expensively furnished, was as comfortless as a station waiting-room. Amidst its carpeted wilderness, the interrogation of Peter Kingdom proceeded with the courtesy and restraint of a charity board meeting. Charlie Mallender, blunt of speech yet cautious of meaning, posed gruff questions about his daughter's state of mind from an armchair by the fire. In the chair opposite him, Dr Kingdom assumed an expression of stifled impatience and reiterated his diagnosis. By the window, Alan Dysart walked back and forth, frowning in concentration, requesting clarifications here and speculations there in a tone of polite but probing enquiry. Beside Harry on the settee, Marjorie Mallender trembled perpetually and said nothing. And at the very centre of their uneasy gathering, the coffee-table photograph of Marjorie with Clare, Heather, Roy and Jonathan Minter on Clare's twenty-first birthday stared silently back at every glance.

'None of this differs from what I told you when Heather left Challenbrooke. I'm surprised you need me to go over it again.' There was a strain of irritated protest in Kingdom's voice. He spoke like a learned tutor exasperated by his pupils' obtuseness. 'A complete recovery from mental illness can never be guaranteed. Many months of normality may precede a sudden relapse. For that reason, my assessment of Heather's state of mind on the eleventh of October is next to useless in terms of establishing her motivations on the eleventh of November. Surely that's clear to you?'

'Of course,' said Charlie. 'But we thought there might have been some contact after the eleventh of October. A letter, perhaps, or a phone call. Anything that could—'

'There was no contact of any kind.' Kingdom had been and remained inflexible on the point. But what did his lie conceal? What purpose did it serve? 'Her disappearance came as a total surprise to me.' So he said, yet he allowed a cynical curl to remain too long on his lips. Harry knew he could trust this man in nothing.

'If you will forgive such a question,' Dysart put in, 'might I ask what limit you would apply to your obligation of confidentiality towards a patient?'

'What exactly do you mean?'

'Simply this. Let us suppose – purely suppose – that you had agreed to a patient's request that certain aspects of his or her illness, and details of its treatment, should be withheld from their next of kin, whatever the circumstances—'

'It would be highly irregular!'

'But not inconceivable?'

'Perhaps not, but—'

'Then the question remains: what would release you from such a commitment?'

'How can I possibly say?' Kingdom glared at Charlie. 'Mr Mallender, I came here to offer any help and advice I could in attempting to discover what's become of Heather. Shouldn't that be your prime consideration?'

'It is.' Charlie reddened. His voice had a strangled quality, as if he were playing a part alien to his character. Which indeed he was, as Harry could testify. 'We're grateful for your cooperation, Dr Kingdom.'

'What significance is there in your son's absence today, may I ask?'

The significance, as Harry well knew, was that Roy could not have been relied upon to maintain the pretence to which they were all party: the pretence that Kingdom was merely being asked to assist in the search for Heather rather than tested for signs of his guilt. 'My son could not be with us,' Charlie said slowly. 'The fact has no significance whatsoever.'

'I wondered if it might be related to Mr Barnett's presence.' Kingdom nodded in Harry's direction and smiled faintly.

'Not at all,' said Charlie. 'Roy accepts like the rest of us that Mr Barnett had nothing to do with Heather's disappearance.' Only years of conditioning could have given him the talent for sham, Harry suspected. He would be proclaiming him next as a family friend.

'In that case,' said Kingdom, 'I suggest you persuade him to take up my recommendation of hypnosis. It's the only hope I can hold out of making progress in this case.'

'Harry's aware of that,' said Dysart. 'He wants to be satisfied that we've exhausted every alternative before pursuing what he considers a desperate course. His attitude seems very reasonable to me.'

'We *have* exhausted every alternative.'

'Well, perhaps you're right.' Dysart turned towards Harry, no flicker of his gaze revealing their complicity. 'What do you say, Harry?'

It was time to speak his lines. 'I suppose I'm bound to agree,' he said, with a sigh of assumed reluctance.

'Really?' Kingdom was evidently surprised. 'You'll undertake a trial session?'

'Yes.'

Kingdom stared at him intently. 'I'm delighted you've seen reason,' he said in a tone devoid of all delight. 'When would be convenient?'

'Next week?'

'No sooner?'

'I'd rather not.'

'Very well.' Kingdom pulled out a pocket diary. 'Shall we say Tuesday?'

'Yes. Let's say that. The afternoon.'

'All right. Two-thirty, at my consulting rooms in Marylebone?'

'Suits me.'

Kingdom pencilled the time in the diary, then slipped it back into his jacket. 'The exercise may yield nothing, of course,' he said. 'That is clearly understood, isn't it?'

'Yes,' said Dysart. 'Clearly understood.'

'It's kind of you to take it on at all,' Charlie added, still in his script-reading monotone. 'Not your usual line of country, I imagine.'

'No,' Kingdom replied. 'Not exactly. But if there's any chance it might give us a clue to what happened, it's worth trying.' His gaze moved round the room and came to rest on Harry. 'I'm relieved you've been converted to my point of view, Mr Barnett.' His eyes seemed to scan Harry's face in search of clues as to what lay behind his change of heart. 'Let's hope the exercise proves worthwhile.'

'Yes,' said Harry. 'Let's hope so.' To open his mind to Dr Kingdom would be, he knew, an act of folly. But it was easy to imply he was prepared to commit such an act, easy when he knew, as did everyone in the room except Kingdom, that two-thirty next Tuesday would find him a very long way from Marylebone.

Ten minutes had passed. Dr Kingdom had taken his leave, assuring the Mallenders that he would inform them promptly of anything material gleaned from Harry's 'trial session'. Marjorie had escorted him to his car, with Dysart watching through the window. At the sound of an engine starting, he turned back to Charlie and Harry.

'Do we agree?' he said quietly.

'The fellow's hiding *something*,' Charlie muttered. 'That's plain.'

It occurred to Harry that they were all hiding something, concealing past differences behind a pretence of united action, appeasing their consciences with an overdue pursuit of the truth. Less than a month ago, Charlie had thrown him out of the house and set the police on him. Now, cowed and compromised by the record of his own misconduct, he had glumly conferred upon Harry something which previously would have been inconceivable: his trust.

'If what he's hiding is Heather's presence at the Versorelli Institute,' said Dysart, 'we need to prove she's there beyond question as soon as possible.'

'Agreed,' growled Charlie.

'And you think Miss Labrooy would be willing to help you do so, Harry?'

'Yes.'

'So she could produce a plausible version of what we've drafted?'

Harry took the folded sheet of paper from his pocket and looked at it again. Beneath the heading 'To the Director of the Versorelli Institute' was the rough wording of a letter in Dysart's handwriting. 'This is to introduce Mr Harold Barnett, who has reason to believe a missing relative of his may be among my patients at the Institute. I should be most obliged if you would afford him every assistance. Yours etc. P.R.K.' 'Yes,' said Harry. 'She could do it.'

'And I rather think that if you presented yourself there, armed with such a letter, they'd feel obliged to let you see Kingdom's patients. Don't you?'

'They might check with him first.'

'That's the beauty of it. Miss Labrooy takes all his calls. She could tell them he was unobtainable. On holiday. Gone away. It doesn't really matter what.'

There was a certain beauty in it, Harry had to admit. Whilst Kingdom was sitting in Marylebone, eagerly awaiting his opportunity to learn just how much Harry knew, he would be in Geneva, running his secret to earth. 'Yes,' he said. 'It might work.'

'It *will* work,' said Dysart with sudden enthusiasm. 'I can't believe the Versorelli Institute are party to any malpractice. They'll have believed whatever explanation Kingdom's given them. Therefore they'll also believe that letter – and do as it asks.'

'I suppose they will.'

'We can't force you to try this, Harry. We wouldn't attempt to. But what alternative is there? If we went through official channels, Kingdom would be forewarned.'

'Do you want me to crawl?' put in Charlie. 'Is that it, Barnett?' His colour was altering, his reserve of self-control dwindling fast. 'Do you want me to beg you to help us? I've done a lot of things in my life I'm not proud of, including threatening Heather with return to that bloody hospital. But I never meant her any harm. I never meant anything like this to happen.' The door clicked shut behind Marjorie as she returned to the room. Charlie's tone instantly softened. 'I'm loyal to those close to me, Barnett, whatever their faults. I don't happen to think it's such a bad trait.'

Marjorie moved to her husband's side and laid her hand on his shoulder. Harry could see her fingers trembling, could see a tic working in Charlie's flushed cheek. 'We've no right to ask this of you, Mr Barnett,' she said softly. 'You certainly owe us nothing.'

'I dare . . . . ' Charlie's voice faltered. His pride would not admit what his conscience acknowledged. 'I daresay we owe you . . . . '

An apology? Harry knew better than to expect one. Dysart caught his eye and seemed to smile, as if he had foreseen and exactly concurred with Harry's every thought. This was an alliance of necessity, nothing more. But necessity could not be gainsaid. Harry's gaze shifted to the photograph on the coffee-table and saw there Heather's young, earnest, trusting face. '*I can't turn back now, can I?*' She at least would have understood.

'Well, Harry?'

'I'll phone Miss Labrooy tonight.'

'And if she agrees?'

'I'll go.'

Harry and Dysart parted shortly afterwards in the driveway of Sabre Rise. A grey curtain of cloud was slowly closing across the clear sky of morning, a breath of genuine winter rising from the hills and fields about them. Harry could see Marjorie watching him from the lounge window as he opened the car door. He could feel the weight of her tremulous hope bearing down upon him even as his conscience reminded him that it was not for her sake but his own that he was taking this course of action.

'Thanks, Harry,' said Dysart, laying a hand of gratitude as well as detention on his shoulder.

'For what?'

'For not throwing Charlie's lies back in his face. For not evening the score. For not taking revenge.'

'What would have been the point?'

'Revenge seldom has a point. The fact remains, however, that Charlie's treated you shabbily enough over the years to deserve nothing but your contempt. Even now, even when he knows you could as easily tell him to do his own dirty work, he can't bring himself to apologize.'

'I didn't expect him to.'

'Nor did I.' Dysart smiled. 'By his lights, Charlie's not a bad man. As captain of a ship, he earned my respect and admiration. He virtually admitted his fault to you today: loyalty. It's loyalty to a corrupt son that's led him astray.'

'Does Roy know what we're doing?'

'No. Even Charlie agrees that this time he must be kept out of it.' What had Dysart said to Charlie Mallender? Harry wondered. Had he employed scorn or reason? Whatever the method, he had clearly gained his complete subservience. 'You'll let me know if there's any difficulty with Miss Labrooy?'

'There won't be.'

'And you'll make contact as soon as you've established that Heather's at the Institute?'

'Immediately.'

'Then it only remains for me to wish you good luck.' Dysart shook him firmly by the hand and turned back towards the house.

As Harry watched him go, he felt his mental defences begin to slip. In a moment, he would be on the road to Swindon, alone at the wheel of a car. It was a long drive, too long for him to blot from his mind throughout it the memory of why now he must do Dysart's bidding. He could tell himself he would have done so anyway: out of affection for Heather or perhaps out of pity for her mother. He could even have cited a wish to clear his own name, if such a thing were any longer possible. And maybe, all along, this would have sufficed. But now it did not need to. Now there was something else.

He climbed into the car and started the engine, eased it down the slope into the lane and turned north towards Dorchester. By the look of the sky, he would be lucky to reach Swindon before dusk. He winced at the thought, knowing that only daylight could hold at arm's length his memory of the previous night. Whilst daylight lasted, he could pretend those events had not occurred. But when it failed, as fail it must, they would return to taunt him. He had uncovered betrayals at every turn. And now he had added his own.

What woke Harry in the small hours that morning at Strete Barton he did not know. Undismayed by Dysart's absence, Virginia had taken him to the village pub for supper and there, aided by convivial company and innumerable rounds of drinks, had succeeded in persuading him that Nancy could well have imagined the man in the yard and that crossed lines were only to be expected of rural switchboards. She amused the locals with her account of the incident, talked Harry into playing darts and somehow ensured that he passed his most carefree evening since returning from Rhodes.

But all that was undone by five minutes' wide-eyed confrontation of the absolute, inky-black silence that comprised a moonless, windless night. The luminous dial of his watch showed two-forty, bleakest and deadest of times, and by his own alertness he knew sleep lay several anxious hours away. He rose, slipped on a bathrobe and crossed to the window. It was so intensely dark outside he could scarcely distinguish the outline of the stable-block against the sky, so black and empty it was almost possible to believe the world beyond Strete Barton had ceased to exist. He turned back towards the bed. And heard it.

What was it? A movement? An impact? A stirring within the fabric of the house? Whatever it was, it could not be ignored. Somewhere below him, something had made a noise. Urging himself to act before fear had a chance to blossom, he eased open the door and looked out along the landing. There was nothing. No light to suggest Virginia was awake. No second noise to confirm the first. He headed for the stairs.

His eyes had adjusted to the darkness now and as he prowled each of the downstairs rooms in turn he began to suspect that his senses had deceived him. Every old house had its share of creaks and groans. It was to be expected. He should pull himself together. Concluding his tour in the study, he reckoned a healthy slug of Dysart's malt might settle his nerves and enable him to sleep. He turned on a lamp to guide him, but before he saw the whisky bottle, saw something else instead.

The Reign of William Rufus still lay by the telephone. Cursing his carelessness for leaving it there, he carried it quickly back to the bookcase. As he slid it into the waiting gap, the familiarity of the act struck home. Surely he had replaced it before leaving the study that afternoon. A flush of alarm engulfed him. Surely he had. Surely to God.

The room was hot. At all events, he felt hot, his limbs prickling, his breath quickening. And there was someone in the room behind him, someone close at hand. Someone he knew. The door must be open, for there was a draught where previously all had been still and stifling. And brought to him on it was the faint but recognizable scent of gardenias. Did he mean scent? Or perfume?

He whirled round. Virginia Dysart was standing no more than six feet away, her eyes fixed intently upon him. She wore a silken dressing gown of some pastel shade. Her hair fell freely about her shoulders. She was breathing rapidly, panting almost as she stared at him, as if she too had been disturbed and had feared an intruder.

Why could he not speak? Why could he not break the spell that seemed abruptly to have been cast between them? There was a tension, a charge almost of the air about them, a sensation of imminent passion, like heat rushing from a sudden blaze. She stepped towards him. He struggled to find some words with which to fend off the impulse of the moment. But she pressed her fingers to his mouth to silence him.

'You were Heather's Silenus, weren't you, Harry?' Her voice was thick with something. Desire or deliberation. He could not say which. Her hand traced a line down to the point of his chin, then fell to his chest. 'What will you be for me?'

She had to stop. In a moment – a second it seemed – it would be too late. He had never known, never experienced, such intensity before. The phrase was like a trigger. 'You were Heather's Silenus, weren't you?' No. He had not been. The image was a travesty. It had never been like that at all. Yet why could he not put Heather's likeness out of his mind? Heather as he had never seen her. Heather as he could not now refrain from imagining her.

Virginia's hand ran down to the cord of his bathrobe and released it. He squeezed his eyes shut as the robe fell open, knowing what she would see, knowing the lie it would give to any attempt by him to deny what he felt. She touched him, caressed him, moved her hand once, twice, then drew away.

'Did she do this for you, Harry?' She pushed the bath-robe from his shoulders. He heard it fall at his feet. There was silence for an instant. Then he opened his eyes. She was three feet away, waiting with her calm and arrogant expression to meet his gaze, waiting with eyebrows faintly raised, head tossed back, one corner of her broad mouth curling, waiting with one hand raised on the knot that fastened the sash about her waist. 'You were Heather's Silenus, Harry. Won't you be mine?'

With one tug, the sash fell away. Then she shook the gown from her shoulders. Harry heard it slither to the floor. She held his eyes with her own for one further moment, then looked down. Tall, taller than he was, more muscular than he would have expected even from that one glimpse in Minter's bath-towel, there was something of the Amazon about her, something of the warrior as well as the wanton.

She fell to her knees, glanced up at him once, then reached between his legs, cradling his testicles in her hand as she lowered her mouth towards the jutting head of his penis. Her hair slid forward across her face as she did so. He could feel it brushing against his thighs as her lips moved back and forth. For no more than an instant, his gaze moved to the uncurtained window and saw there, reflected against its blackness, the lamplit reality of what he could not believe was happening. Virginia kneeling naked before him, her flowing hair and raised arm barely concealing her purpose, the horror at what he glimpsed eclipsed only by the arousal he could not halt.

She drew away, falling back on her haunches and gazing up at what she had made of him. He stooped towards her. She touched him again and pulled his hand down onto her breast. Into his mind flooded a chaos of sensations: her cool, faintly goose-pimpled flesh; the warm, impatient smell of her; the shortness of her breath; the stiffness of her nipple between his fingers; the preposterous beauty of her hair in the lamplight; the accelerating certainty of what was bound to occur.

They fell onto the floor. A smile formed on her lips as he drew back to survey her pale body turned gold by the lamplight, her hair fanned out across the rug beneath her. He thrust violently into her, his penis swollen in his mind to impossible proportions. Her breath was racing faster than his own, her head arched back, her face flushed with a secret joy. They rolled over. For an instant she was astride him, lunging back and forth as she impaled herself upon him, eyes closed, mouth open, strands of

397

hair falling across her face. He ran his hands down her back and over the twin humps of her parted buttocks, felt with a shock even his own crescendo of sensations could not obsure the furnace-like heat of her body, then heard, between her panting breaths, a cry of triumph that told him at last why he had been chosen, why this place had been selected, how this time had been determined.

'Damn . . . . Damn you . . . . Damn you . . . . Damn you Dysart!'

They rolled over again. It was too late for the betrayal she had led him into to be averted. In a moment, he knew, he would feel a stab of remorse. But not now. Now they were beyond recall, bodies joined and squirming, the gasping breaths shooting out of Virginia as he pounded into her, the frenzied sawing motions of their limbs: every muscle taut, every sense alive. It was too late, far too late; they were a long way past the point of no return.

A few seconds, no more. A few paltry seconds as muscles slackened, breaths slowed, limbs unravelled. Detumescence. Then disgust, coursing into his mind, a vile scorching influx of self-loathing. Even as he slid back out of her, the knowledge of what she had made him do closed around him like a noose.

He rolled onto his back, pulled his discarded bath-robe across his midriff and stared up at the ceiling. 'Why . . . why did you do it?' he murmured.

'You know why.' Her voice was low, husky with a dreadful satisfaction.

'I can't believe it.'

'You're his best and oldest friend, Harry. You're his good-luck charm. That's why. Because doing it here, with you, in this room where he writes his impeccable speeches, is like doing it to his face. Imagine if he'd been sitting there, behind his desk, watching all the time, watching and hearing everything we did.'

'You can't—'

'Imagine it, Harry! Just imagine. Because that's what I did. That's what made it so wonderful.'

'Who told you? Who told you about Silenus?'

She did not answer. Instead, she sprang to her feet. He saw her above him, stooping to retrieve her gown, saw for the last time the thighs he had lain between, the breasts he had kissed, the buttocks he had clasped, the flesh he had touched. Then the gown was firmly wrapped about her and she was striding towards the door. 'I'm cold,' she said. 'I'm going back to bed.' She paused in the doorway and glanced at him over her shoulder. 'Join me if you like. Or not. As you please.' Then she was gone.

48

Peter R. Kingdom, MA, PhD, AFBPsS, MNAHP
7 Lictor Place
Crawford Street
LONDON
W1M 6QU

30th December 1988

My Dear Konrad
   This letter is to introduce Mr Harold Barnett, a fellow-countryman who has reason to believe he may be related to one of my patients at the Institute. I would be very grateful if you could give him all the assistance he may need in ascertaining whether this is the case.
With best wishes,
Yours as ever
Peter

Professor K.V. Bichler
Director
Versorelli Institute
Route Chersoix
12295 Geneva
SWITZERLAND

'It's perfect,' said Harry, folding the letter away into its envelope.

'As near perfect as I can manage,' Zohra replied with a smile. 'I never knew I had such a gift for forgery.'

Harry tried to smile back, but his lips resisted the order. Instead, his face set in anxious immobility. 'The ends justify the means,' he muttered solemnly.

'Of course. I only meant . . . . ' Zohra looked crestfallen and Harry felt instantly sorry for her; she too, after all, was taking a risk. 'When's your flight?'

'Three-thirty tomorrow. I want Monday to see how the land lies. Then I'll call at the Institute mid-morning on Tuesday.'

'I'll be ready if they phone Dr Kingdom. There shouldn't be any problem: he's fully booked all morning.'

'Good. I'm relying on you.'

'And I on you. Be careful.'

'I will be.' He rose to leave. Her hand on his elbow detained him for an instant.

'Are you all right, Harry?' Her eyes were wide with genuine concern. 'You seem strained, withdrawn, weighed down in some way.'

He attempted a grin. 'Just nerves, I expect. I'm not used to subterfuge.'

'Neither am I.' She smiled again. It transformed her more than a smile did most people, Harry noticed, as if a gold-shaded lamp had shed its light into a dark recess where beauty hid, as if . . . . But no. Such thoughts were foolishness.

'I must go.'

Suddenly, she leaned up and kissed him lightly on the cheek. 'Remember what I said,' she murmured, her lips still close to him. 'Be careful. Be very careful.'

Poor Zohra. Harry saw her watching him from Mrs Tandy's narrow and dimly lit passage as he started the car. Unsmiling now, those large eyes seeming to reach out to him across the darkness, she was of all Heather's friends he had met the one for whom he preserved an undiminished respect. A young Asian woman, alone in

401

a city that begrudged her, she was prepared to endanger her very livelihood for Heather's sake. The others, himself included, had been compelled to act, prodded by guilty conscience, goaded by force of circumstance. Only Zohra had been free to stay her hand – and yet had not. He wished he had waved goodbye. He wished . . . . But what was the use of wishing?

He aimed the car towards Acton and the M4, driving slowly through strangely empty streets. London's amber-leeched blackness closed about him, as if the ailing Vauxhall had become a capsule isolated from the future he was travelling towards as well as the past he was fleeing from. Wishing and regretting: what was the use of either? But how else could one live? He thought of Zohra's good-luck kiss and wondered if she had noticed him flinch as her lips touched his cheek. Even if she had, she could not have guessed the reason. He raised a hand to his face and ran it round the rough, unshaven jaw. Poor Zohra. In all this she was still what he had ceased to be: an innocent.

He had not seen Virginia again during the few hours he had remained at Strete Barton. Whisky. And water. Hot, healing water. These had seen him through till dawn. Then he had packed his bag, taken it to the car and driven away without daring to look back in case she should be watching from an upper window, watching to remind him of what he could not forget.

Breakfast in a Happy Eater near Exeter. Strong coffee, poached eggs, steamed-up glass, a steady buzz of traffic on a perversely spring-like morning. Regret, corroding his will like acid. Remorse, burning in his throat like bile. It had not mattered then where he went or what he did. Time and distance were all he could put between himself and a welter of vivid recollections. White bodies, his and hers, writhing in the darkness. Sights and sounds he could not bear. He had headed on. He had convinced himself he could outrun them.

*

He was driving faster now, south past the dark and empty reaches of Gunnersbury Park. Ahead, the lights of the M4 threw up their amber halo. In a few hours, the old year would fade imperceptibly into the new. A few hours after that, his journey to Geneva would begin. And he would be glad when it did, for Geneva, after all, might just be far enough to outpace whatever was following him. His conscience, for one thing. And for another?

This morning, lying on the kerb beside his car in Falmouth Street, lying by the driver's door where it could not be overlooked: a crushed and empty cigarette packet, the red white and gold design at once familiar to his eye, The Greek brand-name instantly legible. ΚΑΡΕΛΙΑ ΣΕΡΤΙΚΑ. The brand he had smoked on Profitis Ilias but never since. *Kerelia Sertika*. The brand he had favoured on Rhodes but had never seen for sale in England. *Karelia Sertika*. The final warning.

49

Geneva, Tuesday. A small station on the line to Lausanne, at a point where affluent city suburbs gave way to a tamed landscape of vineyards and lakeside villages. Weather dry, cold, still, grey to the very marrow. Harry, the only passenger to disembark, listened to the subsiding rattle of the trains as he plodded up the sloping road that led north-west between shuttered, tree-screened residences, listened to it until it had faded into silence and then to his own footfalls as they carried him towards his goal.

Thirty-six hours in Geneva had confirmed all his lifelong suspicions of the Swiss. Manically tidy. Infuriatingly polite. Intolerably efficient. He had grudged and growled his way around their manicured city of international understanding and had detested everything he had seen. He would be glad to leave it.

He reached a cross-roads and turned right. Not far now, as he remembered from yesterday's reconnaissance. Not far till he had a long-craved chance to lay this matter to rest. The boundary wall of the Versorelli Institute appeared to his left, high and implacable, with only pine trees visible within. It had a *cheval-de-frise* to deter entry – or prevent escape. The sight of it made him shudder. He quickened his pace.

A broad, stone-pillared entrance, the gates standing open, an automatic barrier blocking the drive beyond. One of the pillars bore a large and freshly painted sign. L'INSTITUT VERSORELLI. Then a stream of French he could not follow. *Hôpital mental*. That at least was clear. *Les recherches psychiatriques*. He had a glimmering of what that meant. *Directeur: Prof. K.V. Bichler, Université de Genève*. The name on the letter: he checked its presence in his pocket. All was well. He stepped between the pillars and moved towards the gatehouse.

'I wish to see the Director. I have this letter of authorization.'

The gatekeeper stared at him blankly for a moment. There is nothing to fear, Harry reassured himself, nothing at all. (He was wearing a new raincoat, a clean collar and tie, a jacket and trousers similar enough to be taken for a suit. He had shaved and combed his hair. He was sober and he was smiling. He had never looked more respectable.) The gatekeeper snatched the letter and peered at it, but written English seemed to be beyond him. He made a phone call, held a brief conversation, put the phone down, then nodded glumly. '*Entrez, monsieur*.' He handed back the letter and pressed a button. The barrier rose.

The grounds were extensive, paths threading away through the woods, lawns and flower borders leading the eye up the driveway towards a cream-stone château, vast and austere in its parkland setting. Other buildings, lower-roofed and modern, could be seen amongst the trees behind it. Several dozen vehicles were drawn up in a car park to one side of the château, but of their occupants there was no sign. No patients were wandering the lawns, no doctors hurrying about their business, no gardeners pushing leaf-laden barrows: all was still and empty.

When Harry was about ten yards from the main entrance, the door opened. A young man, no more than thirty, pencil-thin and alert, with wiry hair and a bright-eyed smile that gave him a quirky, vulpine look, stepped out and stood at the top of the short flight of steps to greet him. 'Mr Barnett?' His English accent was almost perfect, his lack of a white coat almost reassuring.

'Yes ' They shook hands. 'Professor Bichler?'

'Professor Bichler is on holiday. My name is Junod. I am Professor Bichler's assistant. Follow me, please.'

The interior of the château was cheerier than Harry had expected, bright and airy, with light cascading down a monumental staircase. But here again nobody was to be seen or heard. There was not even a smell of disinfectant to prove it was a hospital. Junod led the way down a wide, marbled corridor, opened the third door along and ushered Harry in.

The room was large and well-furnished, the trappings of administration artfully concealed behind lavish couches, thick rugs and giant Oriental urns. Junod took Harry's coat, showed him to one of the couches and arranged himself primly on a stiff-backed chair. He sat for several seconds in expectant silence, then, just as Harry was about to speak, said: 'You have a letter, I gather?'

'From Dr Kingdom, yes.'

'Of course: Dr Kingdom. I know him well. We have worked together. May I?' Harry handed the letter over and Junod read it, frowning as he did so. But as soon as he had finished, the smile was restored. 'Thank you.' He handed it back, paused for a moment, then said: 'I am surprised Dr Kingdom did not forewarn us of your visit.'

Harry endeavoured to look surprised as well. 'Oh. I understood he was to write to you separately. Perhaps the letter's not yet reached you.'

'Perhaps. Well, no matter. We are always anxious to oblige. How may we help you, Mr Barnett?'

'I'd like to meet each of Dr Kingdom's patients here, if I may.'

Junod deliberated. 'It is an unusual request. Most unusual.'

'As are the circumstances.'

'Yes. Perhaps you could enlarge on the . . . circumstances, Mr Barnett.'

Harry had expected the question. He launched himself on the answer he had prepared. 'My niece vanished seven years ago. Her father died shortly afterwards and her

406

mother, my sister, has never recovered from the dual loss. For my sister's sake, I've done all I can to discover if her daughter is still alive, but without success. Three weeks ago, my sister received a telephone call which she is convinced was from her daughter. The call was brief and garbled, but my niece evidently referred to being in Switzerland under the care of Dr Kingdom. Since I did not take the call and since my sister is quite capable of imagining such things, I was sceptical at first. But in view of the fact that Dr Kingdom is a practising psychiatrist who has links with an institution in Switzerland, I felt obliged to check the point with him. He was naturally surprised and thought, as I still do, that my sister must be mistaken. Nevertheless . . . . '

'You decided that only by visiting us could you settle the matter once and for all?'

'Exactly.'

Junod's brow furrowed. He plucked thoughtfully at his right ear-lobe. 'What age would your niece be now, Mr Barnett?'

'Twenty-seven.'

'Her name?'

'Heather King.'

'King?'

'Yes. It could explain my sister's misunderstanding, of course. King and Kingdom.'

'Quite. You have a photograph of her?'

'Yes.' Harry pulled out the snap Marjorie Mallender had loaned him: Heather in a sheepskin coat, Christmas 1980. 'It was taken the year before she disappeared. Obviously she could look completely different now. Thinner perhaps, with dyed hair. Who knows?'

'Who indeed?' Junod handed back the photograph. 'I do not recognize her, Mr Barnett. But as you say, that means nothing. As to the likelihood of her being here, I should say it was nil. Did Dr Kingdom explain the circumstances and origins of our patients?'

'No. He said he could tell me nothing without breaching

confidentiality. He said that only if I had good reason to think one of his patients might be Heather could the matter be taken any further. Hence this visit.'

'Hmm.' The ear-lobe was being waggled now, quite violently. 'I see his point. It is inconceivable, of course. Apart from anything else, our patients have no unmonitored access to the telephone. But even so . . . . ' He seemed suddenly to reach a decision. 'Wait here, Mr Barnett, if you will. I shall not detain you long.' With that, he bustled from the room.

Harry tried to relax, tried not to imagine where the fellow had gone or why. He glanced at the clock. Eleven twenty. Therefore ten twenty in London. Coffee-time in Marylebone, with Zohra Labrooy sitting expectantly by the telephone. Would they check? He could not be sure. Five minutes passed. Then ten. God, this was agony. Sheer, unmitigated agony. He was too old for such play-acting, too damned old altogether. And he was sweating. It was cold in the room, yet the sweat was pouring off him. Why was Junod away so long? Why had he not returned? Perhaps he should have had a drink beforehand after all. Perhaps he should have had several.

The door opened. Junod was back, smiling as before, eyes twinkling, a folder under his arm. 'I'm sorry to have kept you, Mr Barnett.'

'That's all right.'

Junod resumed his seat and opened the folder. 'One or two formalities, you understand.' The smile became a grin. Harry did not understand. Neither did he care. 'Dr Kingdom has an interest in twelve of our patients, whose details I have here.' Relief flooded over Harry: the delay was explained. 'Of those twelve, five are male. Of the seven females, only three are in the same age group as your niece and none, according to our records, is twenty-seven. The nearest is . . . twenty-nine.'

'The others?'

'Twenty-four . . . and thirty-three.'

'May I see them?'

408

'Certainly. Come with me, please.'

They rose and left the room. As they stepped into the corridor, the enormity of what might be about to happen swept over Harry. Heather might be within yards of him, might be waiting in one of the château's innumerable rooms for his recognition to pluck her from Kingdom's shadow.

'You will appreciate, Mr Barnett, that I can tell you nothing of these patients. You may see them. You may address them. That is all.'

'It's all I ask.'

They headed up the wide baronial stairs, grey light descending from high windows. 'Also, you will appreciate that they are highly disturbed individuals. I must ask you to do nothing that might alarm them. Do not touch. Do not shout. Do not expect too much.'

'I won't.'

The top of the stairs had been partitioned off, the path blocked by a stout door in new, white-painted wood. Junod produced a key and unlocked it. They stepped through into a dark corridor. Pools of light from open doors. Institutional paint. And a smell somewhat worse than the one he had anticipated. 'Lucy is normally to be found in the day-room. This way, please.'

'Lucy?'

'Twenty-four. Schizophrenic. Highly suggestible. But warm-hearted and generous. Perhaps too much so.'

There were two nurses in the day-room. The one by the door nodded to Junod as they entered and spoke to him in French. Apart from Lucy's name, Harry could catch nothing of what was said. The nurse pointed towards a window-seat, where a girl in a stained pinafore dress was crouched over a jigsaw-puzzle. She looked much younger than twenty-four, long blonde hair falling to her waist. She glanced up as they approached, wide-eyed with apprehensiveness. Then she giggled nervously. She was not Heather. Harry shook his head at Junod. A few desultory words about the jigsaw, then a cheery farewell. They left.

'Juliet, Mr Barnett, is thirty-three. Also schizophrenic. But reclusive, with none of Lucy's sweetness of character. We shall find her in her room. We never find her anywhere else.'

They climbed a flight of stairs to a silent corridor of closed doors. At the far end, they knocked and a subdued voice replied: 'Come in.' She spoke in English. Harry's hopes rose.

It could have been a nun's cell, but for the absence of a crucifix. A tiny cot-bed, a wardrobe, a table, a chair, a basin in the corner, a narrow window propped open for all that it was numbingly cold. Juliet, an angular creature with a swan-like neck and long brown hair, regarded them disdainfully from the head of the bed. She was clad in ill-fitting pyjamas, broadly striped in pink and white.

'Not cold, Juliet?' said Junod.

'Only when I see you.' The answer was like icy water thrown in the face. Her expression was calm and ordered, hostile yet strangely peaceful. There was nothing in her of Heather. Not a trace. Not even a faint resemblance.

'Do you know this man, Juliet?'

She fixed Harry with an imperious stare. 'You are English?'

'Yes.'

'I thought so. The eyes have it, of course.' She chuckled. 'Have we met somewhere?'

'You tell me.'

Another chuckle. 'I knew you once: but in Paradise.'

'Have you heard enough, Mr Barnett?' said Junod.

'Yes.'

'If we meet,' said Juliet as they left, 'I will pass or turn my face.'

Junod closed the door. They set off along the corridor. 'You are positive neither could be your niece?' he said neutrally.

'Absolutely certain.'

'Then that only leaves Maureen, the twenty-nine-year-old.'

410

'The nearest to Heather's age. Why didn't we see her first?'

'Because I assumed she could not be your niece.'

'Why?'

They paused at the head of the stairs. 'Let us say I hoped rather than assumed, Mr Barnett. I hoped, for your sake, that you did not know her.'

'What do you mean?'

Junod's face grew suddenly solemn. 'As to that, Mr Barnett, you will soon understand.'

They left the château by a rear door and followed a narrow path between pine trees and a tennis court compound. Several single-storey whitewashed buildings lay ahead, flat-roofed and of a vaguely military character, with bars at all the windows. *Les Malades violents* warned a sign. *Entrée interdite*. An uncontrollable tremor ran through Harry. Could this be where Heather was? So far, so very far, from all she had loved and known.

They turned down a side-path leading to the second building. At the door, they stopped, Junod sorting through a bunch of keys, clicking his tongue as he did so, whilst Harry glanced about him. The weather was closing in, a freezing mist creeping towards them through the silent conifers. He could feel the weight of the inmates' collective sadnesses bearing down upon him. What a place. What a truly awful place.

Junod unlocked the door. They entered a scrubbed and spartan lobby. A man in a small office nodded to Junod, who marched ahead and knocked on a set of double doors. A grim female face glared out through a panel of barred and wired glass, then unlocked one of the doors and opened it just wide enough for them to pass through.

A dozen or so beds, six either side of a central aisle, separated by head-high partitions, occupied a room that could have been a second-rate public school dormitory but for the bars at the windows and the keys clanking at the hip of the nurse who had admitted them. There were

411

rugs by some of the beds, a few sickly potplants on one of the windowsills and a couple of armchairs visible beyond a curtain at the far end. Otherwise there was nothing that could comfort or console: no pictures, no books, no entertainment of any kind.

Not that Harry had much chance to assess his surroundings, because his senses were invaded simultaneously by two overwhelming forces: noise and smell. Somebody in the room was laughing hysterically, yet without an ounce of joy. The sound was frenzied, piercingly pitched and hopelessly permanent. This, and the acrid stench of stale urine that gagged in his throat, struck Harry like a club. He reeled back before it.

'Are you all right, Mr Barnett?' said Junod.

'Yes . . . . Yes . . . . Fine.'

Junod broke off to speak to the nurse, their conversation drowned beneath the hyena laugh. Harry scanned the cubicles for its source without success. A red-haired woman lying on one of the beds caught his eye and smiled. He smiled nervously back, at which, to his horror, she dragged down the front of her gown and exposed one of her breasts.

'We are in luck, Mr Barnett,' said Junod. 'Maureen is in one of her more tractable moods. This way, please.'

They set off along the aisle between the beds. Harry kept his eyes trained on Junod's back, aware even so of the redhead mouthing and gesturing at him as he walked by. When they had nearly reached the end, Junod stopped and smiled at the occupant of one of the lefthand beds. '*Bonjour*, Maureen,' he said in his brightest tone. 'I have a visitor for you.'

Harry turned and looked. Maureen was propped up on several pillows, the blankets gathered about her, her hands splayed out on the counterpane, each finger stretched and spaced to the maximum. Her face was gaunt, the mouth compressed, with deep shadows beneath the eyes, her hair shoulder-length, an unkempt brown; perhaps, Harry could not deny, perhaps it had once been flaxen. He stepped

412

closer. There were spots of blood on the front of her gown. Her jaw was trembling faintly, as if she were about to cry.

'Do you know this man, Maureen?' said Junod.

Her eyes moved to focus on Harry. Large, mournful, far-seeing eyes. In that instant he was certain. She could not be Heather. Yet when she raised one hand and beckoned for him to draw nearer, he did not resist. She opened her mouth and tried to speak. He had to stoop to hear her words.

'Please,' she said falteringly, 'please take me away from here.'

'I'm sorry,' he replied. 'I can't do that.'

A final rake of her sorrowful eyes, then she turned her face to the pillow. He stepped back. 'Well?' said Junod.

'No. It's not her.'

'You're sure?'

'Yes. Can we leave now, please?'

The open air. The fresh, free, open air. Harry stood gulping it into his lungs as the mist rolled down across the tennis courts. He wondered why he could not hear the hyena laugh out here, why that dormitory full of the addled and abandoned could seem so many miles away when it was only twenty yards behind him. He tried to think of anything that would keep a dreadful conclusion at bay. But Junod would not let him.

'She is not here, Mr Barnett, is she?'

'I'm not sure.'

'What do you mean? You personally assured me none of the three bore any resemblance to your niece.'

It was true. But to accept it was true meant more than Junod could possibly imagine. It meant the trip to Geneva had been a wild goose chase. It meant Kingdom was innocent after all. It meant the mystery of Heather's disappearance was as impenetrable as ever. Against this, in the teeth of logic, Harry rebelled. 'What about Dr Kingdom's other patients?'

'They are too old, Mr Barnett. All of them are over fifty, one in her eighties.'

'There could have been a mistake about their age.'

'That is preposterous and I think you know it.' Junod's tolerance was wearing thin. His smile had given place to a tight-lipped frown.

'Perhaps she was registered as somebody else's patient.'

'Mr Barnett! I have done my best to assist you, but you are now becoming unreasonable. You must accept that your niece is not here.'

'She'll have arrived on the twelfth of November. All you have to do is check who you admitted that day.'

'You specified no date before.' A tone of suspicion had now been added to the frown.

'It didn't seem necessary.'

'Had you done so, I could have saved us both a good deal of time. Lucy, Juliet and Maureen have all been here several years.'

'I'm sorry. You're right. I should have mentioned it. But now I have, couldn't you check the point?' Harry had no need to simulate the desperation in his voice. 'I appeal to you: what harm can it do?'

Junod's expression grew stern. 'I have done all that Dr Kingdom asked. Your niece is not here.'

'If there's just a chance—'

'There is no chance!'

'Then why not prove it?'

Junod seemed to engage in a brief inner debate. Then impatience turned to exasperation. 'Very well. If you insist, Mr Barnett, so be it. Come with me.'

They returned to the château and walked swiftly along a sequence of corridors, Junod's shoes clicking angrily on the marble floor. He said nothing and nor did Harry. They entered a room occupied by four middle-aged women, each tapping busily at word processors. One of the women looked up and smiled, but Junod paid her no heed. He headed straight for a door on the farther side of the room, paused long enough to rap once with his knuckle, then went straight in. Harry followed.

A tall grey-suited man with short-cropped silver hair and steel-rimmed spectacles looked up from an orderly desk. He and Junod exchanged a few words. The man frowned, shrugged, unlocked a drawer beside him, took out a large leather-bound book and handed it to Junod.

'Our day-book, Mr Barnett,' said Junod testily. 'It represents an independent record of all admissions.' He laid it open on the desk and turned to the current page. 'November, you said? Last November?'

'Yes. The twelfth.'

Junod's finger ran down the margin to the date. 3 November. 7 November. 15 November. He looked up at Harry. 'There was no admission on the twelfth, Mr Barnett.'

'None at all?'

'This is not a hotel. Patients do not arrive and depart daily. I tell you: there was no admission on the twelfth.'

'Later, then. What about the fifteenth?'

Junod glanced back at the book. 'A male patient.'

'The next female, whenever it was.'

'November twenty-fourth. Ah yes. She is forty-eight years old, Mr Barnett: a widow from Munich.'

'The next, then.'

Junod took a deep breath, then slammed the book shut. 'Enough.' He glared at Harry. 'I know for a fact, Mr Barnett, that no female patient of your niece's age has been admitted to this hospital on or since the twelfth of November. I think your enquiries have come to an end, don't you?'

'No. There has to be some mistake. You —'

'There is no mistake! Your niece is not here. Your niece has never been here. I must ask you to leave.'

'I can't. Not without—'

'If you refuse I shall summon the police.' Junod's expression left no doubt of his seriousness. 'Do you want me to do that?'

'No. Of course not. But—'

'Then, please Mr Barnett, go. You must, you know, you really must.'

Harry looked from Junod – set and inflexible – to his companion – blank and impervious – to the day book – closed and uncompromising – and back to Junod. He was right. Harry had no choice. He had played his trump and won the hand, but the hand was empty. Heather was not there. Perhaps, the bleaker trend of his thoughts suggested, she was nowhere. Perhaps she was lost forever. Perhaps she always had been. Without a word, he turned towards the door.

'I am sorry we could not help you, Mr Barnett,' said Junod.

Harry did not reply. He was dimly aware of the women in the outer office pausing from their work to stare at him as he passed, then he was in the corridor, hurrying towards the exit. It was the end, he suddenly realized. There were no other clues to follow, no other hopes to cling to. The forged letter, the faked story, the fraudulent visit: they had all been for nothing. He was as far from Heather as when he had run up the slope of Profitis Ilias in search of her. And she was as far from him.

50

'Alan Dysart is not in,' said Alan Dysart's recorded voice. 'If you wish to leave a message, please speak after the tone.'

'Alan, this is Harry Barnett. Heather isn't at the Versorelli Institute. I don't think she ever has been. We've been wrong all along. I don't know how or why, but there it is. There's no point staying here now, so I'll be returning to England straightaway. I'll be in touch when I get home.'

Harry put the phone down, raised his feet onto the bed and leaned slowly back against the pillows. His brain felt as weary and drained as his body. He could neither accept his fate nor resist it. He emptied the whisky miniature on the bedside cabinet into a glass and took a sip, toasting as he did so the futility and failure of his search for Heather. This, he assumed, was how it ended: talking to a machine from a hotel-room in Geneva. He swallowed some more whisky and gazed up at the ceiling, watching the darkness compete with the spokes and circle of light cast by the bedside lamp.

'Goodbye, Heather,' he muttered to himself.

He put the glass down and picked up the two items that lay beside it: the envelope of postcards and the wallet of photographs. He slid the postcards out into his lap and stared down at them. Aphrodite, soft and pliant, face averted. Silenus, erect and shameless, hand raised. And Anthony Sedley, Prisoner, a last plea scratched in stone. The goddess, the satyr and the betrayed: they made a pattern he did not understand.

'Goodbye,' he murmured.

He slipped the photographs from their wallet and began leafing through them. Mallender Marine. Clare's memorial. Nigel Mossop. Tyler's Hard. Breakspear College. The Lamb Inn. The Cotswold lane. The Skein of Geese. Hurstdown Abbey. Flaxford Church. Flaxford Rectory. Challenbrooke Hospital. Strete Barton. Frank Hollinrake's grave. He had followed the sequence faithfully, clinging to the thread that led from one to the other. And now it was over, the sequence ended, the thread broken. All that remained was what he already knew. Athens. Rhodes. Profitis Ilias. Lindos. The *Villa ton Navarkhon*. Himself drunk. Heather laughing. The end of the film. The end of the search.

Wait though. Wait one moment. What if he had abandoned the photographs too soon? He did not know all the rest, not every one. He leafed through them again, came, as he had before, to the full stop of the fourteenth photograph, then turned slowly to the next, ridding his mind as he did so of all the suspicions that had formed in it since leaving Rhodes. Back in Lindos he had believed in the photographs and nothing but the photographs. They were the only trail that Heather had left.

'Trust them,' he said aloud. 'Trust them and nothing else.'

Athens: the fifteenth photograph. Not Geneva. Not England. Not Rhodes. Of course. It was so obvious, so simple he could have cried. He had not yet reached the end. He had not yet reached the limit of hope. All he had to do was what he had done before: follow in Heather's footsteps.

He sprang from the bed, grabbed the telephone directory, scrabbled through it for the number he wanted, then snatched up the receiver and dialled.

'*Bonsoir. Swissair.*'

'*Bonsoir. Parlez-vous Anglais?*'

'Yes sir, of course. How may I help you?'

'I want to book a flight.'

'To go where, sir?'

'Athens. As soon as possible.'

418

51

It was cold on the summit of Lycabettos. Not as cold as on
Profitis Ilias, Harry would readily have agreed, but still a
distant travesty of the shimmering heat in which the Greek
capital was supposed to bathe. He had no grounds for
complaint, of course: nobody had asked him to come to
Athens in early January. He followed the steps up from the
funicular platform, turned up his raincoat collar and squinted
out across a panorama of endless grey suburbs. Nobody had
asked him, it was true, and now, alone on Lycabettos's island
of barren rock amidst the poisoned ocean of modern Athens,
he was far from sure why he had come.

His doubts had set in the previous evening. Arriving
from Geneva in mid-afternoon, he had accepted the taxi-
driver's recommendation of his uncle's Hotel Ekonomical
near Omonia Square without quibble. One run-down
cheapskate out-of-season hotel would do, he had reckoned, as well as another. With night falling rapidly, he
had passed what remained of the day in ill-lit local bars,
growing even more morbid than *ouzo* normally made him
and concluding in the end that his journey to Athens had
been a mistake.

Daylight had helped a little. But not much, Harry
thought, as he followed the path round the small hilltop
chapel to a paved viewing platform and gazed out across
the serried concrete and congested tarmac of contemporary
thrown-together Athens. The Acropolis looked forlorn and
isolated, rather, it struck him, as Stonehenge might in the

middle of New York. The sky was clear but the sun weak, too weak to burn away the yellow haze of pollution that hung over the city like a perpetual atmospheric reproach. 'The birthplace of democracy, boys,' Cameron-Hyde had called it; 'the cradle of civilization.' And Cameron-Hyde had lost an eye in the Battle of Crete to prove his devotion. But Cameron-Hyde had never been to Lycabettos.

There was work to be done, Harry reminded himself: delay would not make its futility more bearable. He drew the wallet of photographs from his pocket and leafed through them to the one he wanted. Number fifteen: Lycabettos, snapped during Heather's stop-over in Athens, therefore some time over the weekend of 14/15 October. He held it up, took six paces back, checked again, then settled on the spot. He was standing exactly where Heather had stood all those weeks ago, looking at exactly the same view on which she had trained her camera.

What made him suddenly glance over his shoulder he did not know. He cursed his own nervousness and heard his heart pounding in his chest. There was nobody there, nobody at all. He wished at least a few other visitors were on hand to stave off his solitude. He remembered that Heather had certainly not had the summit to herself and looked at the photograph to confirm the point. In it, the blurred cityscape was framed by people sitting on the low stone wall of the viewing platform: a woman in a green dress at the left, a mother and fretful child at the right. Stare at them as long and hard as he liked, Harry could find nothing significant in their poses or expressions: the child grimacing, the mother frowning, the woman gazing out across the city. He turned instinctively to the sixteenth photograph and found there more of the same. The Parthenon at close quarters, sunlight falling starkly on its crumbling pillars and rocky surrounds. The Parthenon on a Sunday afternoon, aswarm with tourists, and Heather one of them. In her picture there were three Japanese weighed down by video recorders, a group of baseball-capped Americans, a Teutonic husband and wife, a stray youth, a pair of nondescript women and a glum Greek labourer. They, like the trio on Lycabettos, had just happened to be there when Heather pressed the shutter.

Harry subsided onto a bench and held the photographs before him, one in either hand. Antique sites, chance groupings: they told him nothing, absolutely nothing. Looking at them on Lycabettos, with the Acropolis visible in the background, made no difference. Why he had ever thought it might he could not imagine. Lycabettos; the Parthenon; the places; the faces; the dates; the details. As his eyes switched from one photograph to the other, then back again, his mind scanned their contents, searching and sifting for the clue he could only pray was there. A woman in a green dress; a mother and child; three Japanese; four Americans; two Germans (probably); an Australian (possibly); two women, nationality indeterminate; one Greek looking . . . .

Suddenly, the components stirred fractionally and for long enough to reveal their camouflage. Suddenly, for no more than the instant it took Harry to see it, the answer showed itself, then made to withdraw once more, but too late: he had it and he would not let go.

The two women walking away from the Parthenon towards the camera were not together. At least, there was nothing to prove they were together. And one of them had about her something which was unmistakeably familiar. The tee-shirt and jeans were different, it was true, but the build, the hairstyle, the sandals and the sunglasses, they were all the same. There was no doubt about it. Indeed, he could not think why he had not seen it before: she was the woman in the green dress on Lycabettos.

The same woman, in both photographs. Harry stared at her dual representation, letting the scale of its significance disclose itself to his mind. It could not be a coincidence: that was too preposterous to believe. Therefore Heather must have known her. A chance acquaintance? Surely not. A friend, then? Yes. That had to be it. She was a friend of Heather's, a friend perhaps of long standing and some

421

intimacy. But who was she? He could not recall anybody mentioning her existence. All had implied, indeed, that Heather had no friends. That was one of her problems. According to Kingdom, it had—

According to Kingdom. Of course. A phrase from his secret file notes. Something about the lack of a close friend. Something about a colleague at Hollisdane School. What was it? Precision eluded him. But that did not matter. He had left the notes at the hotel. He had only to return there to discover what Kingdom had said. He had only to read the good doctor's words to grasp what they and the photographs meant. Out of the blue had come his answer.

23 August . . . 'She has had, it seems, no close friend outside the family circle since a colleague at Hollisdane School with whom she was on excellent terms left to teach abroad last summer.'

Kingdom's phrase was more than Harry could have hoped for. He could have shouted with joy when he read it. 'Left to teach abroad last summer.' He did not doubt that her destination had been Athens. He did not doubt that to see her had been the real purpose of Heather's visit to the city.

He picked up the telephone, cajoled the hotel operator into giving him an outside line, then dialled England. The reply came clear and crisp, as if from the next room.

'Directory Enquiries. Which town please?'

'Wellingborough.'

'And the name of the person?'

'Hollisdane Primary School.'

'Hold on, please . . . . Hollisdane, did you say?'

'Yes.'

'The number is 0933 – the code for Wellingborough – 28765.'

'Thank you.'

Another curt exchange with the hotel operator, then a telephone was ringing in a distant English school. Harry closed his eyes and prayed when he realized the

Christmas holiday might still be in progress. Then somebody answered.

'Hollisdane Primary School. Can I help you?' A male voice, measured and authoritative.

'Ah, hello. Could I— Who is that please?'

'I'm the Headmaster. How can I help you?' Thank God for a conscientious headmaster, thought Harry: he must be working during his holiday.

'Ah, good. You don't know me, of course, but I was— Well, the fact is, I'm trying to trace somebody who used to teach at your school. She left in the summer of 1987 to teach abroad.'

'Oh yes. I remember her. You mean Sheila Cox.'

'Yes. That's her.'

'Well, you're right, Mr . . . ?'

'Barnes. Horace Barnes.'

'Well, Mr Barnes, Miss Cox did leave us to teach abroad, but I'm afraid I've not heard from her since. At least . . . . Remind me: which country did she go to?'

Was this a trap? If so, it was also a risk Harry had to take. 'Greece,' he said, crossing his fingers.

'No, surely not. I think you're mistaken. Spain or Portugal: I'm almost certain.'

'Isn't there any way you could check?'

'I don't believe there is. My secretary's on holiday, you see, and— Oh, hold on. There might be a way. Can you hang on for a minute?'

'Yes. No problem.'

There was a clunk, a rustle of papers, what sounded like a drawer slamming, more rustling, then: 'We're in luck, Mr Barnes. As I thought, she left us to teach in Lisbon.' Harry swore under his breath. 'Sorry?'

'Nothing.'

'Oh, right. Well, you had the correct date – July 1987 – but not the destination. It seems— Wait a minute: what's this? Oh, I see.'

'What is it?'

'I owe you an apology, Mr Barnes. It seems we're both

423

right. Miss Cox only stayed in Portugal for a year. Then she moved on to Greece. Athens, to be precise. I'm sorry?'

'Nothing. It's a bad line.'

'I see. Well, her new school wrote asking for a reference last spring when she applied to them. I've a copy of it here in front of me.'

'A school in Athens?'

'Yes, Athens, that's right.'

'Could you give me the name and address?'

'Certainly. Nothing simpler, Mr Barnes. Nothing simpler in the world.'

Shelley College was set discreetly amidst the walled and gated villas of Kifissia, one of Athens' most exclusive suburbs. Harry took the metro north to its terminus at Kifissia, then begged directions from a newsvendor. The college, it transpired, was not far away, along a quiet tree-lined avenue. Harry found himself hurrying needlessly, rushing breathlessly towards his destination. He was torn between a wish to know the truth and a fear of learning it, a desire to end his search and a dread of having nothing left to search for.

Only the sign on the gates distinguished the college from its residential neighbours. It was a large stone-faced terracotta-tiled house with Byzantine conceits to its architecture: arched windows, dog-toothed crenellations. Around it fir and palm trees swayed demurely. There was a glimpse of a more modern structure to the rear, an empty car park, a flagstaff, a cycle-shed, a brushed and scrubbed air of expensive education. Harry traversed the forecourt cautiously, listening for the sounds of children's voices but hearing none.

He climbed a flight of stone steps and entered a high-roofed hall. Ahead, a woman was laboriously polishing the parquet floor. To his left he could hear a raised female voice, apparently engaged in a telephone conversation. She was speaking English in a clipped and hectoring tone.

'That is not acceptable . . . . No . . . . Absolutely not . . . . The choice is yours . . . . It was almost certainly explained to you at the time . . . . '

424

He followed the voice to its source: a brightly-lit room furnished like the centre-spread in an office equipment catalogue. The only occupant, the woman on the telephone, was as sleek and hard as her voice, clad in shimmering purple, with rings on every finger and a face like a hungry eagle.

'As you please . . . . No, the deposit will be forfeited . . . . Very well . . . . Goodbye, then.' She cast a cold appraising eye over Harry. 'Can I help you?'

'Ah, I hope so. I believe Miss Cox is a teacher here. Miss Sheila Cox.'

'Yes.'

'Well, would it be possible to see her?'

'The college is not in session at present. Miss Cox is not here.'

'Ah, I see. Would it be possible, then, for you to let me have her address?'

'That would be contrary to our policy. I can disclose no personal details of our staff. If you care to leave a message, however, I will see that Miss Cox receives it.'

'Oh, right. When, er, when would that be?'

'The spring term commences next week.'

'Next week? I can't, um, can't really wait that long. Is there any chance . . . of getting in touch with her sooner?'

'No.' Her expression assured Harry that none of the obvious devices – persistence, flattery, ingratiation, bribery – would advance his case. 'There's nothing—' She broke off as the telephone rang. 'Excuse me . . . . Shelley College . . . . Ah, Mr Rossi . . . . Yes, of course . . . . You too . . . . Did you not? . . . No, it's a full pre-term staff meeting . . . . The Principal's office, ten o'clock tomorrow . . . . You're welcome . . . . Goodbye, Mr Rossi.' She looked back at Harry. 'As I said, I'm afraid there's nothing I can do for you. Do you wish to leave a message?'

'No thanks,' said Harry, exerting himself to suppress a smile. 'On reflection, I don't think I want to leave any message at all.'

52

Athens, Friday. Harry sat at the wheel of an anonymous grey hire-car, parked in the shade of a bedraggled pepper tree opposite the entrance to Shelley College. Around him the villas and avenues of Kifissia had slipped into a silent midday languor and the wintry sun falling on the windscreen compounded the effect: Harry was barely holding sleep at bay. He had lain awake most of last night rehearsing the varied uncertainties of the day ahead and now, sluggish from too much *metaxa* and too little rest, felt ill-equipped to cope with what he had so carefully planned. In an office in that large building on the other side of the road, Sheila Cox sat debating timetable clashes and examination dates with fellow-teachers. He had seen her go in, had scanned her features and compared them with those of the woman in the photographs, had concluded beyond reasonable doubt that she was the same person. All he had to do now was keep his eyes trained on her car and wait for her to reappear.

But waiting was not easy. Harry looked at his watch. It was gone half past eleven: he had been at his post for two numbingly inactive hours. He looked at the photographs again and Sheila Cox's face gazed back, her expression familiar to him in every much-studied detail. Was she really sheltering Heather? Could it really be that simple? Another glance at his watch. Eleven thirty-five. Therefore nine thirty-five in London. What was Zohra thinking at this moment? he wondered. What had Dysart made of his failure to return promptly from Geneva? He should have explained, he supposed, he should have told them what was in his mind. But the clue had seemed so flimsy, the hope so frail. How could he have justified to them a journey he had scarcely been able to justify to himself?

And yet it was no fool's errand. Of that he was certain. As he replaced the photographs in his pocket and massaged his forehead into alertness, he suddenly became aware that the moment had come. From the front door of Shelley College a straggling group of men and women had appeared, ambling towards the car park. The pre-term staff meeting was at an end.

Harry sat up and looked anxiously from one member of the group to another. At first he could not see her; panic threatened. Then he relaxed: there she was, lingering with a colleague at the top of the steps. Her hair was shorter than in the photographs. This, combined with the leather coat and slender valise, gave her a groomed and efficient look in stark contrast to her companion: a shambling, chaotically clad man with a briefcase so crammed and bulging he could not close it. The forgetful Mr Rossi, Harry surmised.

Most of the others had driven or walked away by the time Sheila Cox reached her car, but Rossi showed no inclination to emulate them. He was still gabbling away excitedly, still struggling to fasten his briefcase. She unlocked her car and opened the door, but did not climb in. Harry supposed she was too polite to cut the conversation short. Then Rossi grew more animated still, smiling and gesticulating. In gratitude, it transpired, for the lift that had been offered to him. He galumphed round to the other side of the car and they started off.

Sheila Cox was a sedate driver; her car was a distinctive yellow; the roads were quiet. At first, therefore, Harry had no difficulty in following at a discreet distance as they headed south from Shelley College. The route was familiar to him and remained so all the way to the metro station. There, amidst much hand-waving and briefcase-grappling, Rossi was set down. Fortunately, with taxis and buses backing and blaring around them, she was unlikely to have noticed Harry waiting for her to continue.

She drove faster without a passenger and there was more traffic to contend with as they left Kifissia and headed south-west along less exclusive residential streets. Harry was compelled to abandon the map by which he had hoped to trace their progress and concentrate on keeping the little yellow car within sight. What with motorbikes forever cutting in and his unfamiliarity with left-hand drive, it was as much as he could do not to slip disastrously behind.

They joined what seemed a major route. There were more lorries and vans, more vehicles of every size and kind. Roadworks, dust, traffic lights, congestion, confusion: Harry found himself cursing the city and its crazy transport system. So flustered was he becoming that his grasp of the Greek alphabet deserted him. ΛΥΚΟΒΡΥΣΗ, one destination board declared. ΜΕΤΑΜΟΡΦΩΣΙΣ, ΗΡΑΚΛΕΙΟ. It might as well have listed Venus, Mars and Jupiter for all the help it gave him. But whether he was lost or not made in the end no difference. For all the panicky manoeuvres and heart-stopping separations, he still clung to Sheila Cox's tail.

They must have covered four or five kilometres before leaving the major route. They were in a good-class suburb now, less affluent than Kifissia but still prosperous enough for a well paid teacher. Three- and four-storey apartment blocks were commoner here than villas, but they were generously spaced and shaded. The parked cars looked new, the shopfronts smart. Sheila Cox, driving from memory along ever narrower streets, was surely nearing her destination.

She turned into a side-street and slowed noticeably. Harry did the same. Then a dead stop, right-hand indicator winking. Harry dropped to a crawl. She began reversing into a parking space just as Harry spotted another space three cars behind her and steered uncertainly into it. With no time for delicate positioning, he settled for an acute angle against the kerb, turned off the engine, grabbed the map and peered cautiously over it.

428

Sheila Cox climbed from her car, then leaned back in for her valise. On the other side of the road was a three-storey apartment block with stepped and whitewashed balconies, decorative railings and smoked-glass picture windows, pine trees flanking the communal entrance. If this was her home, it was clearly a comfortable one. She slammed the car door, locked it and began to cross the road, then stopped halfway and looked back past Harry as if something had just caught her attention. She shaded her eyes, peered uncertainly for a moment, then raised her hand and waved. Harry looked in the wing-mirror but was met only by a reflection of the petrol-cap. He was about to risk a glance over his shoulder when a cycle-bell sounded from close behind. Then a figure on a bicycle swept past the car window, braked to a halt and dismounted. It was Heather.

'Take the keys,' she had said, 'in case you want to go back to the car.' Harry could not breathe, could not think, could not react to what he saw. 'Don't worry.' The rising panic of being unable to find her, the sheer blind headlong terror of losing her, washed back across his memory. 'I'll keep to the path.' And with it came the recollection of every hard and winding trail he had followed in search of her. 'And I won't be long.' Every week of her absence was a scar: the interrogations, the questions, the accusations, the doubts, the suspicions. 'It's just that I can't turn back now, can I?' Turn back? How could he not? To Profitis Ilias in cold, clear, silent air, November's dusk threatening, her loss gouging at his self-control. She had smiled back at him once and then gone on. From that day to this. From a mountaintop in Rhodes to a street in Athens. From her departure to her return. Heather stood before him.

She dismounted alongside Sheila Cox and leaned against the handlebars, smiling breathlessly. She was wearing jeans and training shoes, her sweater was white rather then red, but the black corduroy jacket and the dark woollen gloves were the same. Her hair was shorter, cropped and bobbed in a way that made her look younger, her flaxen hair that he remembered brushing against her shoulders. And she was laughing, laughing so easily and thoughtlessly that he could scarcely bear to hear it. How dare she be so relaxed and carefree? How dare she be so normal? He had never expected it to be like this. He had never hoped or feared to find her as now he did.

They were crossing the road, joking with each other as Sheila sifted through the shopping in Heather's cycle-basket, squeezing a loaf of bread here and prodding a cauliflower there. And Harry, paralysed by the humiliation their every casual gesture deepened, could only watch as they went. To leap from the car, to make himself known, to accuse, to protest, to demand, was as unthinkable as the conclusion he could no longer keep at bay. She had not been murdered or abducted. She had not been set upon or spirited away. She had not lost her memory or her hold on reason. On the contrary, she had been calm and methodical throughout. She had planned and prepared the whole charade from start to finish. And he was merely a witless stooge she had accommodated in her calculations, an obliging fall-guy to distract enquiries, an honest witness who would not know he was telling a lie. She had used him and discarded him. She had made of him an utter fool.

Heather propped the bicycle against a post and locked it, then took the shopping from the basket and followed Sheila to the door of the apartment block. A key was flourished, another laugh exchanged. They entered. And the last Harry saw of her, as the door closed, was a smile of girlish mirth at the anecdote of a friend.

A friend, as Harry had fondly believed himself to be. A friend, as now he knew he had never been. They must have found it easy, he supposed. A pre-arranged signal – perhaps the whistle he had heard – a lonely road on the other side of Profitis Ilias, then a fast drive to the airport. They could have been in Athens before the alarm was even raised. They could have read and laughed at every newspaper article, could have hugged themselves with glee at the success of their plan. And the best joke, the biggest laugh, the greatest dupe of all? Why that was Harry of course. That was the man who sat alone on an Athens street and stared bleakly at the closed door of his own folly. That was the man whom Heather had deceived – but not eluded.

'Dysart.'

Alan, this is Harry Barnett.'

'Harry! Where are you? I've been wondering when I'd hear from you. I got your message.'

'I'm in Athens.'

'Athens? What took you there?'

'Heather. I've found her.'

'You've found her? In Athens?'

'Yes. Alive and well. She's staying with a woman called Sheila Cox, a friend from Hollisdane School who teaches here.'

'But . . . this is incredible. You've spoken to her?'

'No. But I have seen her. There's no doubt about it. She's here, in hiding. I don't know why and I don't know for how long. All I know is the search is over.'

'Does she know you've found her?'

'No. When I realized she was lying low here of her own accord, I couldn't face speaking to her. She looked so contented, so pleased with herself. I've been a fool, Alan, a gullible fool. I thought she needed help. I thought she wanted to be found. I thought I'd be rescuing a damsel in distress. Instead . . . . We were wrong. Kingdom can't have had anything to do with it. The disappearance was all her own idea. She staged it with this Cox woman and left you and me to pick up the pieces.'

'You sound angry.'

'I am. Aren't you?'

'I'm relieved, certainly. Do you want me to tell her parents?'

'Why not? They've a right to know. Her address is—'

'Hold on. I'll need a pen. Right: go ahead.'

'Flat three, twenty-four Odos Farnakos, Iraklio, Athens. The flat belongs to Sheila Cox, who teaches at Shelley College, Kifissia.'

'I'll let Charlie know straightaway. What will you do now?'

'I'm not sure. Come home, I suppose. I may stay here a few days yet.'

'To see Heather?'

'No. I never want to see her again. If I did . . . . Well, the best thing I can do is forget the whole rotten business.'

'Do you think you can?'

'Probably not. But I intend to try.'

53

This excellently preserved bronze statuette of Silenus, a demon in Dionysus's thiasos combining the features of man and horse, comes from Dodona. The ithyphallic attendant of Dionysus leaps with enthusiasm, his left arm high in the air, his right resting on his buttock. His pointed ears, long tail and hoofed legs are equine traits, while his demonic nature is emphasised by the distorted features of his face, the bulbous nose and bestial eyes. The curls on his long hair and beard are indicated by incised lines. An excellent work of Archaic miniature art fashioned with technical expertise. Height 0.192m. Circa 530/520 B.C.

Harry closed the guidebook and confronted through a thin sheet of glass the infamous original of the satyr whose likeness he had been carrying with him since leaving Rhodes. It was smaller than he had expected, and more finely wrought, this proudly preserved piece of antique vulgarity. For two and a half thousand years it had been grinning and flaunting itself at all who cared to look. Harry did not suppose he was the first to find reflected in it the shame of a personal memory. But he could scarcely have left Athens without paying the lusty old devil a visit, so it was with a faint but genuine smile that he turned away and headed towards the exit.

The National Archaeological Museum was crowded with

guided tour groups for whom Silenus was no more than an amusing postscript to the glories of Mycenaean sculpture. Harry threaded between them, oblivious to what they were admiring, remembering as he went what Miltiades had told him about Silenus. 'According to Euripides, he was incapable of distinguishing between truth and falsehood.' If that had been the point Heather was trying to make by leaving a postcard of Silenus for him to find, then he had abundantly proved it for her.

Emerging at the top of the steps leading down from the museum entrance, Harry paused and took several breaths of what passed in Athens for fresh air. What a fool he had been. What a purblind nose-led fool. He wondered if Heather had anticipated the lengths he would go to in order to find her and reckoned on balance that she had not. After all, she could not have expected him to obtain the photographs and without them there would have been no false trail to follow. To do her justice – which was not his inclination – she could never have intended him to discover how she had deceived him. In that sense, his humiliation was of his own making.

He descended the steps and sat down on one of the benches ringing the circular lawn in front of the museum. From his pocket he took the envelope containing the post-cards of Silenus and Aphrodite. He slid them out into his hand, carefully tore them into four pieces and dropped the fragments one by one into the bin beside the bench. Miltiades might have called it destruction of evidence, but Harry preferred to think of it as an act of resignation. His role in Heather's life, and hers in his, was at an end. His fantasy of friendship was over. This morning he had very nearly succumbed to temptation, travelled to Iraklio and confronted her, but in the end he had settled for a visit to his ancient *alter ego* at the museum and now he was sure he had made the right decision. He must either face her or forget her. And by ridding himself of the postcards she had left him he could hope to do the latter.

There were still the photographs, of course. Rightfully

434

they were Heather's, though she must have given them up as lost long since. He took them out and looked through them once more, one last valedictory time. Twenty-four photographs, from Mallender Marine to Heather at the *Villa ton Navarkhon*, two dozen deceptive images which he had faithfully followed. He smiled grimly. Since they belonged to Heather, she should have them back. He replaced the photographs in their wallet along with the strip of negatives, slipped the wallet into the empty envelope, gummed down the flap and wrote Heather's name and address on the front. He would post it the day he left Athens, he decided. She would recognize his handwriting and realize what the gesture meant. By then, her parents would probably already be in touch with her. If so, she would know from them that he had led them to her and the photographs would tell her how. It was a petty revenge, perhaps, but it was the only one available to him: to bring to her attention the one mistake she had made.

As he slid the envelope into his pocket, he noticed for the first time, lying beside him on the bench, the postcard he had bought at Burford Church. It must have fallen out as he removed the postcards of Silenus and Aphrodite. *Anthony Sedley. Prisoner.* He chuckled ruefully. Well, perhaps that was the only fitting memento he could have of his part in Heather's plans. *Harry Barnett. Prisoner.* Of his own gullibility, of his own inability to believe that she might have misled him. He could not blame her for wanting to escape from her past and present. But neither could he forgive her for using him to achieve that escape. He could not blame her for the many failures strewn through his life. But neither could he forgive her for this last and most bitter failure of all. With a heavy sigh, he rose from the bench and trudged wearily away.

Harry had only been in Athens three days, but already he had established with the barman at the Hotel Ekonomical a close if scarcely warm understanding. Tacky coasters and greasy bowls of salted almonds did not accompany

435

his drinks, as they did for other patrons. Nor was the barman's stock of saturnine pleasantries raided for his benefit. Harry was left in fact very much to his own devices. Following his return from the National Archaeological Museum, these amounted to nothing more than emptying successive bottles of extra-strong imported lager whilst staring at a reflection of his increasingly flushed face in the mirror behind the bar.

Harry began by applying his mind to the question of when he should leave Athens. This led him to confront the problem of where he should go when he left. And this forced him to admit that he neither knew nor cared. Lindos and Swindon seemed equally unthinkable. Alternatives were quite simply non-existent. The only choice he found remotely palatable was to drink away the remainder of his money in Athens and hope for inspiration along the way.

Noticing that a recently departed customer had left a copy of *Athens News* – the city's only English language daily – lying on the next stool, Harry leaned across and appropriated it, reckoning its contents might slow his lager intake even if they did not entertain and enlighten him. Perusal of the first pages, however, failed to fulfil his hopes and he was about to toss it back when his eye was taken by an advertisement in the classified columns sandwiched between 'Attractive young lady seeks foreign gentleman for good company' and 'Luxury Glyfada apartment to let.' He could not say what had seized his attention. A word had seemed, for a fraction of an instant, familiar, but what that word was he did not know. Certainly the heading – 'WANTED: friendly, efficient staff to work on Aegean islands April to October' – did not explain it. Out of little more than idle curiosity, he read on. And then he understood.

WANTED: friendly, efficient staff to work on Aegean islands April to October. Must be fluent in English and either French or German. Selected individuals will be trained by an expert for a career in time-share promotion. Those seriously interested should attend the recruitment sessions being held at the Athens Hilton on Saturday 7 and Sunday 8 January, 3pm to 5pm each day or phone 722 0201 and ask for Barry Chipchase.'

It was nearly five o'clock when Harry reached the Hilton Hotel, thirteen storeys of white-slabbed opulence at the traffic-snarled junction of Sofias and Konstantinou. Gazing up at its fluttering pennants and gushing fountains, he wondered whether he should not simply turn on his heel and walk away from the very idea of meeting Barry Chipchase again, more than sixteen years after their strained friendship had been shattered by a final betrayal.

En route from the Ekonomical, Harry had lingered on a bench in the National Garden considering the same point. He had recalled to his mind the draughty barrack-room where he and Chipchase had first met in 1953, Harry overwhelmed and confused by every aspect of life in uniform whilst Chipchase had shown himself the instant master of a dozen ploys designed to spare himself hard work. He had spirited Harry away on illicit expeditions to far-flung pubs and village dance-halls where local girls could be pursued. He had recruited Harry as his assistant in the covert acquisition and disposal of assorted RAF property. He had, in short, provided Harry with a thorough education in the ways of the world. Why Harry had not therefore anticipated just what kind of business partner Chipchase would be he was at a loss to explain. Barry's fast tongue and quick wits had several times been the salvation of Barnchase Motors, but there had always been in him a tendency to overreach that had created as many problems as he could solve.

Dysart had warned Harry that Chipchase's greed would be their undoing and, subconsciously, Harry had known he was right. Not that greed was, in his view, the real flaw in Barry's character. Rather was it a juvenile delight in pulling off a stunt that he had never outgrown, a boredom with steadiness and sobriety, a craving to test his luck and judgement to the limit – and sometimes beyond.

And Harry's own indolence had been, in its way, equally to blame. He could still remember, as if it were yesterday, the shale-faced receiver eyeing him across his desk and asking for the umpteenth time: 'Do you really mean to say, Mr Barnett, that you had no inkling of what Mr Chipchase was planning?' Yes. That really was what he had meant to say. Barry, after all, had encouraged him to slip away to the Railway Inn if there was an irate customer to be faced or an unpaid supplier to be pacified. Only when it was too late had Harry understood why. Only when it was far too late had he appreciated the price to be paid for wilful ignorance.

Harry had emerged from the National Garden opposite the Presidential Palace and watched for half an hour or more the balletic manoeuvres of the two sentries, backing and scraping in their pompommed clogs. The sight had recalled to his mind Chipchase's characteristic observation on the rigours of drill and dress. 'Do you know what I think every time that bastard Trench' (a much-loathed warrant officer) 'marches us down to the airfield barking out his instructions? I think: enjoy this while you can, Trench, because soon you'll feel my boot on your shoulder passing you on the ladder of life. Bloody soon.'

Crossing the foyer of the Hilton, feeling suddenly down-at-heel amidst the sharp-suited businessmen and the glamorous women reading fashion magazines over afternoon tea, Harry could not help remembering Chipchase's promise to force his way up the rungs of material success. If the Hilton was where he could afford to recruit staff, Harry could only suppose he had succeeded.

Barry's name was known to the Charybdis-eyed receptionist. She directed Harry to a seminar room on the first floor and, within minutes, he was standing at the door, wondering if he should not take this last opportunity to turn back. Seeing the door was ajar, however, he pushed it open wider and peered in.

The room was large, spreading out across acres of carpet and leather furniture towards a window that soared higher than a cinema screen. The gathering darkness beyond was broken by the snaking headlamp trails of the city traffic and, couched remotely above them, the floodlit ramparts of the Acropolis. To one side of the window a porter was stacking chairs whilst, at a side-table, a small dapper-looking man sat arranging slides in different boxes. There was a projector on the table beside him and a pile of leaflets. Between each placement of a slide, he glanced nervously towards another man, who was patrolling the space in front of the window, declaiming in loud and confident tones.

'Stick to my coat-tails, Niko, and you're on the gravy train to Paradise. I made a pile out of time-share in Spain and I intend to do the same here. It'll come to the Aegean. It's bound to. The trick is to be in at the ground floor. Know what I mean?'

Harry knew, even if Niko did not, for Barry Chipchase had not varied his formula, merely juggled the ingredients. RAF surplus, used cars, jerry-built haciendas: it was all the same to him. Nor physically had he changed as much as Harry had expected. Fatter yes, but only marginally, and greyer or balder not at all. The wavy black hair did not look as if it still broke combs, but many a fifty-three-year-old would have been proud of such a thatch. The voice had dropped an octave or two and developed a croak that suggested forty cigarettes still reached his lips each day. And as for the clothes – lightweight suit, coordinated shirt and tie, flamboyantly draped pocket handkerchief, alligator shoes, a flash of gold about the wrists and fingers – they all suggested what Harry found it hardest to forgive: that the intervening years had treated Barry Chipchase uncommonly well.

'This is only the start, Niko, mark my words. Turkey. The Adriatic. North Africa. The sky's the limit. I smelt profit in this room this afternoon. Big profit. Do you know what they used to say about me in Spain? That opportunity was my middle name.'

It was too late to turn back now. Harry was striding across the room and preparing to speak. 'Opportunity's a new one on me, Barry,' he said aloud. 'I thought your middle name was Herbert.'

The hand with which Chipchase was raising his cigarette to his mouth froze in mid-movement. He turned slowly round and stared at Harry in wide-eyed amazement. For once his pliant features were legible. For once he had been taken unawares. 'Harry,' he murmured. 'Bloody hell.'

'Hello, Barry. Good to see you're keeping well. I'm sorry this isn't a Monday.'

'A Monday?'

'Well, that's when I expected to see you again: a Monday morning. I remember you saying as you left the garage: "See you Monday." But you never showed up. You sent the bailiff instead.' Chipchase tried to summon a smile; Harry pressed on. 'Why don't you introduce me to your chum?'

'Er . . . . '

'The name's Barnett, Niko: Harry Barnett. I'm one of those who fell off the gravy train to Paradise – shortly after it left the station.'

54

'You should be grateful to me, Harry. Bloody grateful. But for me, you'd have had no excuse. You'd have had to face up to the fact that, as far as business went, you were a babe in arms. I made it easy for you. I'll bet you told everybody that you had no idea how bad things were, that I'd kept the truth from you, that I'd run off and left you to face the music. As sob stories go, it must have been a gold medal weepy. So don't give me the old long-nosed resentful treatment, because I won't let you get away with it.'

Two hours had passed since Harry's arrival at the Hilton. He and Chipchase were in a dimly lit corner of the Pan Bar, the low table beside them scattered with empty bottles, paper coasters, cigarette ash and pistachio husks. Chipchase's initial embarrassment had changed to ingratiation; he had plied Harry with brimming drinks and grinning regrets. Now, with their respective post-Barnchase careers paraded for inspection in an excess of drunken candour, Harry could only admire the skilful manner in which his companion had made embezzling company funds and fleeing the country with Jackie seem an act of generosity.

'You see, Harry, your problem's always been the same. You don't like life at the bottom of the heap, but you don't know how to make it to the top. Too many scruples. Too little talent. It's a fatal combination. It gives you more pleasure to gripe and growl at failure than revel in success.

So leaving you in the lurch at Barnchase was really the best turn I ever did you.'

'It didn't seem like it at the time.'

'Maybe not, but you have to see it from my point of view. What good would it have done for me to carry the can along with you? My running out on you meant you could play the innocent and get away with it.'

'I *was* innocent.'

'Pull the other one. Better still, drink it and we'll order another. After all, this *is* a celebration. The old firm back together. Who'd have thought it, eh? Who'd have bloody thought it?'

'I had to sell my house.'

'Oh, stop complaining, for God's sake. At least you weren't stuck with Jackie. Taking her along was a big mistake, I can tell you, probably the biggest I ever made. I thought she loved me, you know. I thought she'd be loyal to me. Christ, can you believe old Chipchase would be so bloody naïve? As soon as she got to Spain, she started giving the eye to those tall dark beanpole Latins. Wobbling her charms up and down the beaches waiting for them to snap her up. Well, she didn't have to wait long, take it from me.'

'She tells it differently.'

'She would, wouldn't she? She was always quick with a cover story, our Jackie. What line did she say she was in now?'

'Hairdressing.'

'And married to money?'

'Apparently. Big house. Fast car. All the trappings.'

'Proves my point, then doesn't it? A cunning little bitch from the first, our Miss Fleetwood. I blame you for taking her on. And what about you, Harry, eh? Seems to me you didn't exactly end up in jankers. Rhodes: the island of roses and all that crap. The Villa ton bloody something. Sounds like just about the cushiest number a bloke could land.'

'Alan was very generous, it's true.'

'Huh!' Chipchase swayed back in his chair and signalled

to the waiter for refills, then shaped a sarcastic sneer. 'As for Alan Dysart, I wish you well of him. I wouldn't trust him further than I could toss a ballot-box.'

'Got it in for politicians, Barry? This is a new side to your character.'

'Nothing of the bloody kind.' A brief silence intruded whilst the waiter fussed around the table, then Chipchase resumed. 'Politicians are on the make just like the rest of us. But that's not why I distrust our former car cleaner turned darling of the people.'

'Why, then?'

Chipchase took a gulp from his recharged glass. 'It's a long story,' he muttered. 'And an old one. Let's change the subject.'

'If it's that old, why haven't I heard it before?'

Chipchase let out a sudden breath that set his cheeks vibrating and puffed on his cigarette. 'You really want to know?'

'Yes. I really want to know.'

'Well, it's no secret. I didn't like him from the start. Too many airs and graces for stripping down car engines. Too many brain cells not to notice what was what in the used car business. And too many easier ways to earn a holiday crust. Why did he latch on to us, Harry, eh? Why did he come all the way to Swindon to cool his heels in the vacations?'

'A girlfriend originally, wasn't it? In Wootton Bassett.'

'Girlfriend in Wootton Bassett my left buttock. She was pure bloody fantasy, I'm sure of it.'

'What makes you say that?'

'Since you ask, Harry old cock, I'll tell you.' Chipchase leaned forward across the table, his eyes alight with enthusiasm. 'I'd probably have told you at the time, but it was just before I left in a hurry. You and I weren't exactly on gossiping terms then, were we? July '72, it must have been. Do you remember I went up to Birmingham to re-schedule our credit with Cosway Tyres?'

'Vaguely.'

443

'Wonderful phrase, that: re-schedule our credit. Anyway, the point is I got lost on the way back. Birmingham's roads are more of a maze than Hampton Court. I ended up stopping somewhere in the Solihull area to ask directions. It was a long straight road with houses one side and a cemetery the other.'

'I don't quite—'

'Don't be so bloody impatient, Harry: I'm coming to it. I'd been given a route to the A34 by some long-winded poodle-trotter and was on the point of setting off when, about a hundred yards away on the other side of the road, who should I see but Alan Dysart climbing out of his car? You know, that white Spitfire he used to run. He was dressed in black and carrying a wreath in his hand. Just like he was going to a funeral. Except there was no funeral. No hearse, no coffin, no eye-piping mourners. Nothing except an empty cemetery sloping away up this bit of a hill beside the road. I'd have beeped the horn or called out, but there was something, well, odd about him. He walked in through the cemetery gate, headed up the main drive, then turned off and I lost him amongst the tombstones.'

'I'd have thought—'

'Will you hold your bloody horses, Harry! What you'd have thought or done makes no difference. What I thought was that it was all a bit fishy. And what I did was wait. I lit a fag and smoked it through. And I was about to light another when he reappeared, minus wreath, climbed into his car and roared off.'

'For God's sake, Barry—'

'This is it!' Chipchase's voice hissed with emphasis. 'This is the bloody point! I was in no hurry. And I was suspicious. Always had been, if it comes to it. So I got out of the car and took a stroll in the cemetery. Headed for the part I'd seen him in. Wandered about looking for the wreath he'd been carrying. Well, there weren't many fresh wreaths, so it didn't take me long. There it was, white lilies, no card, on one of the graves. And guess whose grave it was?'

'How should I know? His aunt Doris?'

'Oh no. Not an aunt or uncle. Not a brother or a sister. Not a father or a mother.' Chipchase's face was split by a vast grin of delight at the secret he was about to share.

'Whose, then?'

'His own, Harry boy. His own bloody grave.'

Less than half an hour later, Harry was in a taxi speeding north through Athens' suburbs, destination Iraklio. Watching the lights of other cars flash by the window, listening to the blaring horns and whining sirens, Harry seemed to see and hear them through a screen of displaced awareness. Barry Chipchase's eager, twitching face and the strange, malicious story he had told were still to the fore of his perceptions, the sights he had conjured and the words he had chosen still holding all else at bay.

'His own bloody grave, Harry. Alan Dysart. Died April the something, 1952, aged five. Your ears have pricked up now, haven't they? Your eyes have widened. Well, it's God's own truth I'm telling you. Dead as mutton, thirty-seven years ago, aged five. Which would make him now?'

It would make him Dysart's age. Exactly. Harry had not needed to say it. He had not needed to say anything. Chipchase had read the incredulity in his face.

'You can't believe it can you? It doesn't make an ounce of bloody sense, does it? If Alan Dysart is dead, who's the Alan Dysart we know, Harry, eh? Who the bloody hell is he? I wish I could tell you. Funny thing is, you'll have to take my word even for the little I do know. I went home to Swindon that day rattling my brains for an answer and I came up with nothing. In the end, I began to think I'd imagined the whole bloody thing. So I went back. About a fortnight later, I took a day off. To play golf with the bank manager, I told you. In fact, I went up to Solihull, found the cemetery and looked for the grave. But the stone wasn't there anymore. You could see the base where it had

445

been hacked off, but the stone had gone. And with it the inscription.'

Harry shrank back against the car seat, recoiling physically from all that Chipchase's story implied. Dysart not Dysart at all. Then who? And why?

'He must have spotted me, Harry. That's all I can think. A fly customer, our so-called Alan Dysart. He must have guessed I'd find the stone and be intrigued by it. But he was too clever to let me see he'd rumbled me. He just made sure the next time I came – or anyone came – there'd be nothing to find. He had the stone removed. And that's not all. I was dumbstruck to find it gone, but I wasn't about to convince myself I'd been mistaken. Oh no. That's asking too much of old Chipchase. I went to the cemetery office, dug out the attendant, got referred to some superintendent of the dead in a bigger cemetery the other side of Birmingham, went there, demanded to see the relevant register, was shown it and . . . guess what?'

Like a boulder accelerating down a slope, like floodwater rising about him, Harry saw and felt the certainty of deception. Dysart's deception. Not just of Harry. Not just of all those who had supported and admired him. But of the whole world he had moved and lived in. '*I was slick, I was witty. I was word-perfect.*' He had said so himself and he had meant it. He had played a part and never been caught out. Till now.

'The page was missing, Harry. The bloody page was missing. Sliced out so close to the spine you'd not have noticed till you looked for its contents. Well, the superintendent went into a bureaucratic bloody spin about it, I don't mind telling you, but there was nothing either of us could do. The stone was gone. The page was gone. And every shred of evidence with them. Dysart had made sure, you see, made sure it could only be my word against his. There was nothing. Not a trace.'

Oh, but there was. Harry knew that even if Chipchase did not. Like a dove returning to its cote, truth had fluttered into his mind, pale and silent as an unmarked

446

grave. This was the secret. Of course. Not corruption. Not murder. Not any other fantasy of an unavenged sister. But Dysart's own secret. The secret of his life. It came to him without the need for proof or evidence. It came to him with a flood of guilt for doubting Heather. This was what she knew. This was why she had fled. Because to know the truth about Alan Dysart was to be in danger. Like Ramsey Everett. Like Willy Morpurgo. Like Clare Mallender. No wonder Heather had sought refuge in Iraklio if this was the connection she had made. Like the scattered shards of a broken stone reassembling themselves before him. With a name inscribed upon it. Alan Dysart. They were all his prisoners now.

'Well, I dropped it there and then, Harry. What else could I do? I had gristlier joints than Dysart's past to chew on around that time. Arranging a moonlight flit with Jackie and her wardrobe, to be precise. I forgot all about it as soon as we left the country. And I'd never have remembered but for Dysart playing Lord Nelson in the Falklands. That was a bad time to be an Englishman in Spain, I can tell you. It brought it all back to me. All that charm, all that casual dazzling bloody brilliance. I hear he's in Parliament now – a minister in the government. I hear he's so important those Irish headcases keep lobbing bombs at him. Well, maybe they've got it right. For the rest, they're welcome to him. And so are you, Harry boy. I shouldn't care to have Alan Dysart for a landlord. I shouldn't care to have anything to do with him. As far as fraud goes, I'm not even in the same league as him. What's flogging a time-shared shack on Mykonos compared with peddling a dreamed-up life? I don't know who or what Dysart is, but this I do know. I wouldn't trust him an inch. Not a bloody inch.'

The warning had come too late. For Harry *had* trusted Dysart. And with far more than friendship or loyalty. He had trusted him with the secret of Heather's hiding-place. *'Hold on. I'll need a pen. Right: go ahead.'* Harry had been duped all along, it was true, but not by Heather. He saw that now. He understood at last. *'Flat three, twenty-four*

Odos Farnakos, Iraklio, Athens.' So simple. So precise. Heather's secret was out. Courtesy of Harry, Dysart's prisoner had been returned to him.

Harry leaned forward across the back of the front seat, touched the taxi-driver's shoulder and pushed a five thousand drachma note into his hand. *'Pio grigora, parakalo.'*

The taxi-driver glanced round at him, then down at the note. *'Endaksi,'* he muttered. Then he swerved into the outside lane and pushed the accelerator towards the floor.

55

Odos Farnakos was dark and still, moist and chilly air suspended grainily in half a dozen porch lights. Harry made his way cautiously along the narrow pavement, pitted with shadows, until he reached number twenty-four. Then he gazed about him, straining his eyes to penetrate the gulfs of blackness that loomed between the pallid walls. Nothing stirred. Nothing moved. All was drab and silent normality. Only his tautened senses suggested otherwise. There was nothing to see, nothing to fear. Except what he had already imagined.

He moved up the path between the pine trees, caught their scent on the air, and reached the door. Six buttons, each lit by a tiny bulb. Six names typed on perspex-covered card. Six grilles in which to plead a case for admission. On the third card, in capitals, ΚΟΞ. No initial, no marital status, no Anglicized version: a strange conceit. Harry noticed his finger shaking as he pressed the button. Thirty seconds that seemed as many hours passed, then there was a crackle through the grille and a voice said: '*Pios eenekei, parakalo?*' It was Heather's. He leaned closer to the grille and tried to speak, but managed only a nerve-dried croak. '*Ya soo?*' She had heard something and sounded anxious.

'It's me. Harry.' The words were out at last.

'Harry?'

'Can I come in, please? It's vital I speak to you.'

'Harry?' She seemed unable to believe the evidence of her own ears.

'Will you let me in? We must talk.'

The crackle ceased. Communication was suspended. But the door did not open. Instead, there was the sound of something heavy rolling back above him, a fluttering movement, a deepening of the shadows about him. He stepped back and squinted up at the first-floor balcony. A figure was standing by the parapet, looking straight down at him. He shaded his eyes against the light.

'Heather?'

'How did you find me?' She spoke quietly and much as he remembered, yet a tone of softness had vanished from her voice.

'I could explain. But that doesn't matter. Not now.'

'What do you want?' Her face was nothing more than a silhouette against the sky. He could distinguish nothing of her expression.

'To talk. That's all.'

'What about?'

'I need to know if I've done wrong. I need to know if I've endangered you.'

'How could you have done that?'

'By telling somebody else I'd found your hiding-place.'

'Who?'

'Dysart.'

She drew back as if struck. He thought he heard her gasp, thought he saw her grip on the parapet tighten.

'Heather?'

She seemed to sway above him, seemed almost about to fall, then recovered herself. He heard her take a deep breath. 'Wait there,' she said decisively. 'I'll let you in.'

She was waiting in the doorway of the flat when he reached the first-floor landing, still in silhouette, the light behind her. As he approached, she turned away and he followed her down a short corridor into a spacious lounge. Thick rugs on a parquet floor. Dark curtains across the balcony window. Minimalist, clean-limbed furniture. Subdued lighting. A kitchen visible beyond an archway at the end of the room. Music playing somewhere: a folk singer he did not recognize. And Heather, facing him at last across no more than a yard of space.

She was as he had seen her on Friday, somehow younger than on Rhodes, her flaxen hair cropped, her expression more elfin than he could ever remember. She was wearing an apron over jeans and a sweater and embroidered on the apron were row upon row of contented pandas chewing bamboo shoots. The cosiness of the image was like a blow to his ribs. And then he noticed how violently she was trembling.

'How did you find me?' she said unsteadily.

He took the photographs from his pocket and handed them back to her. 'These were waiting for you in Rhodes. I found the receipt and collected them. The two shots you took here in Athens led me to Sheila Cox. I followed her here from Shelley College yesterday morning and saw you come in together. Where is she now?'

'Out. When did you tell Dysart you'd found me?'

'Yesterday afternoon.'

'Why?'

'So he could pass the information on to your parents. I didn't want to speak to them in person. They've suspected me of God knows what since you disappeared. Have you heard from them?'

'No. And I should have done by now, shouldn't I, Harry?' She turned abruptly away and seized a chairback as if for support. 'I don't have time to express any regrets, Harry. You're owed quite a few, I know, but the trouble is you don't understand what you've done by telling Dysart.'

'What have I done?'

She looked back at him, her face distorted by rising panic. When she spoke, it was almost in a scream. 'If he finds me, he'll kill me.'

'That can't be true.' But it could be. He knew so in his heart. 'He's been as anxious as me to . . . to . . . . '

Heather looked down at the photographs in her hand.

451

'To what, Harry? The answer was here all along, if you'd only known. The secret he's trying to hide. The secret he killed Clare to keep.'

'Clare? That's impossible.'

'Don't you realize what these are about?' She turned and waved the photographs in front of him. 'Don't you have any idea?'

'Of course.' A childish wish to prove his intelligence came upon him. 'The Tyrrell Society. The Defenestration of Ramsey Everett. The car crash. Willy Morpurgo. Cyril Ockleton. Rex Cunningham. I traced them all, you see. I know Clare was pregnant. I know your brother black-mailed Dysart into giving Mallender Marine the Phormio contract. But none of that proves Dysart murdered Clare. Or that he could even think of murdering you.'

'I thought the same myself at first.' She seemed almost inclined to smile. 'I spilled out my wild theory to Dr Kingdom and he poured polite scorn all over it. I went to Rhodes to try to forget it.'

'But he followed you there. Why?'

'Dr Kingdom? Oh, merely to confirm I was all right. To reassure himself my recovery was proceeding well. How did you—'

'What about his visit – a few days later?'

'What other visit? I've not seen him since he came to Lindos on my last Sunday there.'

'That can't be true. He was on Rhodes the day you disappeared.'

'No he wasn't.' Heather frowned. 'He can't have been.'

'But he was. He returned. And he didn't leave alone. And according to his file notes . . . there's every reason . . . to think . . . . ' His words died where under-standing was born. Had he ever seen the file notes in Kingdom's possession? Had he ever seen the airline records of Kingdom's journeys to Rhodes?

'I didn't run away because of Dr Kingdom, Harry. He was the one who convinced me I had nothing to fear, the one who finally persuaded me my theory about

452

Clare being murdered was a delusion, a symptom of my illness. It wasn't because he came to Lindos that I changed my mind.'

'Why did you, then?'

'Because of what happened three days later. I went into Rhodes Town on the bus. Remember?'

'The day you hired the car?'

'Yes. I saw Jack Cornelius there. I saw him, but he didn't see me. And then I knew Dr Kingdom was wrong. There could only be one reason for Cornelius to be on Rhodes. Me, Harry. He'd come to arrange my death. It would have been another terrorist attack gone tragically wrong. That's why Dysart offered me the use of the villa: to make me a sitting duck. They're in this together, you see, he and Cornelius. They killed Everett. They as good as killed Morpurgo. They murdered Clare. And they mean to murder me. And now you've led them to me.'

Dysart had assured Harry that Cornelius was attending a funeral in Ireland on 11 November. And had also convinced him Kingdom had been on Rhodes the same day. But not so. Dysart had lied to him every inch of the way. And why? Because he must have thought Kingdom suspected him. He must have guessed the Versorelli Institute was where Heather was hiding. He must have employed Zohra Labrooy to lend credibility to the false schedules and faked notes which had sent Harry scurrying off there to do his bidding, only for a dreadful miscalculation to become apparent: Heather was not there at all. Then where was she? In the nick of time, obliging old Harry had rung from Athens with the answer. And that was already more than twenty-four hours ago. 'I'm sorry,' he murmured bleakly.

'I must leave here at once,' said Heather, ignoring the futile apology. 'God knows what they're planning, but I must—' There was a sound from the hallway behind them. Harry saw Heather's face twitch with fright, then relax at the jangle of a bunch of keys. It was a noise she seemed to recognize. 'Sheila?' she called, smiling in relief.

When Harry turned round, Sheila Cox was standing in

453

the room, gaping at him in amazement. 'Who's this?' she demanded.

'Harry Barnett,' said Heather. 'Don't worry. We've nothing to fear from him.'

The look in Sheila's eyes suggested she was not convinced. 'But he's a friend of Dysart's. You told me so yourself.'

'He is yes, and he's told Dysart where I am. Nevertheless—'

'Let's keep calm,' Harry interjected. 'There's no sense—'

'You've given Dysart this address?' Anger was being added to surprise in Sheila's expression.

'Yes, but—'

'How long? How long has he known?'

It was Heather who replied. 'Since yesterday afternoon, I'm afraid.'

'My God! Do you realize what this means, Heather?'

'Yes, I realize. It means we've got to get out of here. Immediately.'

'It can't be as bad as that,' Harry protested. He could hear the pleading note in his voice and knew Heather would be able to as well. But she could not supply the reassurance he craved and he could not make good the damage he had done.

Sheila fixed Harry with a hostile glare. 'If you're not working for Dysart, why did you tell him Heather was here?'

'Because I thought he was trying to help her. Because I thought Dr Kingdom posed the real threat to her safety.'

'Dr Kingdom?'

'Yes. According to Zohra Labrooy—'

'Zohra?' said Heather. 'What has she to do with this?'

'She persuaded me Kingdom was obsessed with you, that he was determined not to let you become independent of him.'

'That's absurd.'

'Maybe, but it's what I believed. I thought she was your friend, for God's sake. What was I supposed to —'

454

'Zohra!' exclaimed Heather. 'Of course. She *was* a friend, Harry, but she's also a Sri Lankan national fighting a deportation order. I introduced her to Dysart six months ago because I thought he might be able to help her win a reprieve. She told me later he'd taken up her case personally. If she's deliberately misled you, it can only be because—'

'Otherwise Dysart will let her be deported.' The reality of betrayal closed around Harry as he finished Heather's sentence. Every friend was false, it seemed, every ally a deceiver. Those he had believed he should have doubted. Those he had doubted he should have trusted. Those he had trusted he should have accused. 'You're right,' he murmured. 'We must leave here at once.' Yet still he seemed unable to summon the urgency he knew he should feel. 'We can't stay here a moment longer.'

'Where should we go?' Heather's voice was bitterly reproachful. 'You've already closed off my last escape route, Harry. So where do you suggest we go next? Nobody will believe us. Nobody will even listen to us. Above all, nobody will protect us.'

Suddenly, the realization hit Harry that he was the biggest traitor of all. He had not been blackmailed. He had not been threatened. He had acted out of pride and spite. He had betrayed Heather for no better reason than to avenge a petty humiliation. And this – the unattainability of safety, the impossibility of escape – was the result. Heather was right. There was nowhere they could flee to and nobody they could turn to. For all their sakes it would have been better if Heather had never been found, the mystery of her disappearance never solved. Death without a corpse, as Miltiades had called it, seemed at this moment a merciful oblivion. And then, as Harry thought of the phrase and its inventor, the answer came to him. 'Miltiades,' he said abruptly. 'We must go to Miltiades.'

'Who?'

'He's a senior police officer in Rhodes. He handled your case. I got to know him quite well. Even to like him.

He's met Dysart – and your brother. He's intelligent and imaginative. He'd give us a fair hearing – and I think he might believe us.'

'Go back to Rhodes, you mean?'

'He's the only man with the power to help us who might be prepared to do so. He's the only potential ally I know. So yes: I think we should go back to Rhodes.'

Heather neither moved nor spoke. Harry saw her lick her lips nervously and exchange a glance with Sheila. 'I'm not sure,' she began. 'It might—'

'How can we trust you?' Sheila interrupted. 'You've admitted acting as Dysart's informant.'

'Not deliberately!'

'How do we know you're not just leading us into a trap?'

Harry looked from Heather to Sheila and back again. He had no proof of his sincerity, no way of persuading them to trust him with anything, least of all their very lives. 'It's no trap,' he murmured.

'But how can we be sure?' said Heather.

'You can't,' he replied.

'Exactly,' said Sheila.

'But if you don't come with me,' Harry continued, 'what will you do? Stay here and wait for whatever's going to happen?'

'We could go to the police here in Athens,' said Sheila.

Heather shook her head. 'They wouldn't believe us. Not for a moment.' She looked at Harry intently. 'You really think Miltiades might take us seriously?'

'Yes. I do.'

For a few silent moments, she hesitated. Then she strode across the room and snatched up the telephone.

'Who are you calling?'

'Olympic Airways. To book three seats on the next flight to Rhodes.'

'Don't!' Harry shouted. Into his mind had come a host of crossed lines and anonymous calls and with them an awareness that already they might not be proof against

456

prying eyes or ears. 'Our only advantage is that nobody will guess Rhodes is our destination. We must keep it that way. Phone nobody. We'll drive to the airport, buy the tickets, then wait. It'll be safer there anyway.' He turned to Sheila. 'Is your car outside?'

'Yes. It's been there all day.'

'In that case—' His words were cut short by a sudden upsurge of fear. Her car had been outside all day, obligingly parked opposite the entrance to the address he had given Dysart. Sabotage. Booby-traps. Expertly arranged accidents. There was no reason why the list might not yet be extended.

'What's wrong?'

Harry swallowed hard. 'Have you used the car since you drove to Shelley College yesterday?'

'No. I went into Athens this morning on the metro.'

'You're afraid of a bomb, aren't you, Harry?' said Heather. 'A bomb like the one he used to kill Clare.' Her voice was flat, her expression a mask, but behind them terror was beginning to stir.

'Not afraid. Just cautious.' Even as he lied, Harry knew he was doing so as much for Heather's benefit as his own.

'We could take a cab.'

'Phone for one, you mean? Or start walking? Through the streets, at night?' Harry shook his head. 'No.' He scoured his mind for whatever courage he could find there. 'Give me the keys. I'll go down and start the car. Join me when I sound the horn. Not before. There's nothing to worry about. Nobody could know which car is yours. But just in case . . . .'

'You really think he might . . . .' Sheila began.

'I don't know,' said Harry grimly. 'I don't know anything. Except this. For what it's worth, I'll do my best to get you both safely out of here.'

'Your *best*?'

'It's all I have to offer.'

*

Nothing had changed outside. Odos Farnakos was still a residential cul-de-sac consumed in darkness and domesticity. Harry stood beneath the pine trees, letting his eyes adjust to the lack of light, aware his heart was racing, the blood pounding in his head, conscious with heightened sense of every small sound that reached him. A baby was crying somewhere nearby, its wailing merging oddly with a distant siren. A dog was barking several blocks away. He could hear the needles stirring faintly in the tree above his head, could detect the clip of what sounded like a woman's high-heeled shoes in the next street. All, by any rational analysis, was normal and secure.

He took a deep breath and marched swiftly across the road, taking a diagonal route that led him to the driver's side of the car. He slipped Sheila's torch from his pocket and shone it at each of the windows in turn. All the lock buttons were depressed: so far so good. He glanced along the street in each direction: not a soul to be seen. He moved to the front of the car and prised gingerly at the bonnet: it was firmly fastened. Then he lowered himself to the ground, rolled onto his side and trained the torch on the underside of the car. Everything looked as uniformly caked in grime as he could have hoped: no tell-tale pool of brake fluid, no sign of any tampering. The engine was the same. For the first time he could remember, he felt glad of the experience Barnchase Motors had given him. He rose to his feet and returned to the driver's door.

Allowing himself no opportunity for a loss of nerve, he took the key from his trouser pocket, slid it into the lock and turned it to the right. The button rose. He withdrew the key and reached for the handle, pausing halfway to command his hand to stop shaking. To his amazement, it obeyed. He lifted the handle. The door clicked open, creaking like some dungeon entrance as he swung it back He flashed the torch around the interior. There were some dog-eared papers and a couple of folders on the back seat, a screwed-up peppermint packet on the dashboard: the normal car driver's detritus. He reached out, found the lever Sheila had told him about and slid the seat forward till it hit the stop. Then he clambered in behind it, crouched to the floor and shone the torch beneath each of the front seats. Again, there was nothing. He climbed back out and switched off the torch.

The air was cold, but he was sweating. The barrel of the torch was clammy. He could taste the salt on his upper lip. This is laughable, he thought, this is madness: there is nothing to fear. He smiled to himself. 'I can't turn back now, can I?' he whispered to the night.

He slid the driver's seat back into position and lowered himself into it, his arms shaking with the intensity of his grip on the door-frame. He could have done with a cigarette. Or a drink. He wondered if Heather was watching or if she could not bear to. He let go of the door-frame and shifted in the seat, then groped for the ignition, found it and pushed the key in. A couple of reassuring grates of metal on metal: that was all. The notches and grooves of a simple mechanical function: how could anything be wrong? How indeed? Perhaps nothing was wrong. Perhaps this was all a grotesque misunderstanding. He had known Dysart for more than twenty years. He owed him more than he could ever repay. How could the nearest he had ever had to a friend be a murderer several times over?

He turned the key, felt the steering wheel loosen and moved his foot to the accelerator. One more turn was all it took. One more simple turn and it was done. Or he was. He could still stop now, of course. He could still climb out and walk away, wash his hands of Heather and Sheila as they had washed theirs of him. Or could he? Did he really any longer have a choice? A window in Oxford. A country lane near Burford. A river estuary in Hampshire. This act might or might not be one further link in the chain, but, either way, it had become inevitable. The moment held him prisoner.

He twitched at the key. The engine coughed and died. He turned the key again, more firmly. The engine fired. When he touched the accelerator, it roared absurdly. But that did not matter. Relief – a ludicrous desire to sing – was all he could feel. He jerked the car into gear, reversed out down the road, then drove across to the opposite pavement, pumping the brakes several times before he came to a halt. He sensed he was smiling, though what about he could not have explained. There was, he supposed, a childish pride at what he had done, a pathetic delight that not all his judgements had been wrong. When he thumped the horn, it sounded almost triumphant to his ears.

56

'There were times when I wanted to trust you,' said Heather. 'But Dysart was your best and oldest friend. You said so yourself. So how could I tell you what was in my mind, Harry? How could I trust you with anything?'

Harry did not reply. He stared ahead at the darkness beyond the car windscreen, scanning it as he had a dozen times before. They were in the middle of the airport car park, safely distant from other vehicles, with a clear view on all sides, waiting as patiently as they could for the slug-gardly night to pass. The flight to Rhodes was not due to depart until 5.40 a.m. Until then there was nothing to do but wait. Sheila had fallen asleep on the back seat, but for Harry and Heather sleep was out of reach.

'Not that I ever really suspected you,' Heather went on. 'You seemed the nearest to an innocent bystander I'd met since becoming caught up in all this.'

'Is that why you chose me as your witness?'

'Yes. I'm sorry they gave you such a hard time, Harry, truly I am. You should have told me about the trouble with the Danish girl. Then I'd have found somebody else. But I can't think my family genuinely believed you'd murdered me. Not that I have much idea what they genuinely believe about anything. I hardly feel I know them anymore.'

'Because of Clare?'

'Because of what they did to convince me I'd imagined her pregnancy, yes. That's what set me on the road to a breakdown: the brick wall they erected around her

461

memory. And then to discover, as I did, what it was really all about . . . . ' She fell silent for a few moments, then resumed. 'I wasn't so much horrified as gratified when I learned that Roy and my father had used undue influence to win the Phormio contract. It gave me a way to get back at them, you see, a way to prove I wasn't the brainless child they seemed to think. But what was their reaction? Shame? Repentance? Oh no. All they were interested in was how they could shut me up. They didn't care what the knowledge might do to me or what it told me about the kind of people they were. All they were concerned about was how to keep me quiet.'

'It's to your credit that they failed.'

'Oh but they didn't, Harry. The fear of going back to hospital stopped me talking more effectively than any gag. It's just that it couldn't stop me listening. It couldn't prevent me asking questions and hearing the answers.'

'Starting with Molly Diamond?'

'Yes. I'd always half wanted to believe Clare was the victim of a conspiracy. According to Dr Kingdom, it was my way of coping with grief: to give it a purpose which the anguish and emptiness left by an indiscriminate terrorist killing doesn't have. And I tried to accept that, God knows. But once I'd spoken to Mrs Diamond, it just wasn't possible. The clues kept coming, the loose ends insisted on being followed. And I began to realize the scale of what Alan Dysart was trying to hide.'

'You think he murdered Ramsey Everett?'

'I'm sure of it. And I think Willy Morpurgo was as well. He either saw what happened or saw enough to know Everett's death was no accident. He said nothing at first presumably out of loyalty to a fellow Tyrrellian. But he couldn't remain silent. His conscience wouldn't let him. He must have decided to speak out at the inquest. Perhaps he warned Dysart of what he would say. Perhaps Dysart guessed. Either way, the visit to Burford was arranged simply and solely to stop him, arranged, that is, between Dysart and Jack Cornelius. They were accomplices even then, you see. Cornelius suggested the trip when Dysart's car was conveniently out of action and Dysart volunteered to stay behind. But did he really stay behind? I don't think so. I think he followed the party to Burford and sabotaged Morpurgo's car while they were in the pub. Then Cornelius dropped out of the return trip and the trap was sprung. They knew Morpurgo was a reckless driver. By then he was drunk as well. Somewhere on the way back to Oxford, they could rely on him coming to grief.'

'But what about Cunningham and Ockleton?'

'It's the callousness of the whole thing that's so breathtaking. They were simply regarded as expendable. So much for loyalty. Of course, it didn't quite work, did it? Instead of speeding back along the A40, Morpurgo took a wrong turning, crashed on a minor road and survived. But not to tell his tale. And that was good enough for Dysart's purposes.'

'Why should Dysart have involved Cornelius? Why should Cornelius have agreed to help him?'

'For a long time, I couldn't understand that. Nothing I learned about Jack Cornelius made sense. Least of all the idea that he and Clare were lovers. It seemed incredible. She'd never even mentioned his name in my hearing. And nobody I spoke to thought they were more than vague acquaintances. Yet Cunningham had seen Cornelius's photograph in her possession. "The sort of snap a lover might carry", he called it. And Clare's visit to the Reverend Waghorne seemed to provide the final confirmation. And yet . . . . ' Another pause. 'The answer came to me during the weekend I spent at Strete Barton. It was the way Virginia talked about Dysart, the way she used his surname all the time, the way she resented his owning the farm. She didn't simply hate him: that would have been understandable. She despised him, Harry, felt for him nothing but an inexhaustible contempt. Why? That's what I wondered. What had Dysart done to earn his wife's contempt? And why did they have no children? You'd expect Dysart to want a son and heir: he's that sort of man. Or seems to be. Well, the answer began as no more than a guess, but it's a guess I know to be right. It explains why Cornelius should have risked his neck to help Dysart evade justice. It explains why Clare told the Reverend Waghorne she'd just realized the father of the child she was carrying was homosexual. Not because Cornelius was the father, but because, as she'd originally claimed, Dysart was.'

'You mean . . . . '

'There were things I always disliked about Clare, things I preferred to forget in the grief of losing her. Her ruthlessness was one, her cool, dispassionate, far-seeing way of planning to reach some goal in life, then following her plan to its conclusion, whatever had to be done in the process, whoever had to be hurt. Only in this case it was Clare herself who got hurt. I suppose she calculated that if she could force Dysart to marry her, she would have access to the money and influence she needed to pursue a career in politics on her own account. But she must have misread Virginia's character, must have assumed she'd be outraged by an accusation of paternity levelled against her husband. I suspect Virginia enlightened her about Dysart's homosexuality. Revelled in doing so, in fact. Hence Clare's visit to the Reverend Waghorne. She'd been to Hurstdown to confront Cornelius all right, but not because he was the father of her unborn child. She'd been there to confirm that Cornelius and Dysart were lovers.'

Now Heather had said it, Harry could only wonder he had not guessed the same himself long before. All those intangible hints of complicity; all those echoes of something more than friendship: they pointed unwaveringly in the direction Heather's thoughts had taken. It was the truth. It was the answer. 'You think they've been lovers since Oxford?'

'Yes. It must have begun at Breakspear College. A close and secret love they shared with nobody. It endured through long separations and diverging careers. It left them cold to others, seemingly devoid of emotion. It ensured they would help each other in any emergency. And the exposure of their relationship was just such an emergency. Quite apart from political ruin for Dysart, it would have given Cunningham the answer he'd sought for twenty years: who'd betrayed whom that day at Burford. Cunningham was right to call the photograph of Cornelius the sort of snap a lover might carry, but wrong to think it belonged to Clare. I think she found it in something Dysart owned: a wallet, a jacket, a secret place. I think she stole it, intending to use it as proof of his relationship with Cornelius. Once her intentions were clear to them, however, her fate was sealed. Camouflaging her murder as a terrorist attack on Dysart was a master-stroke. And it was cleverly done. According to the police, it had all the hallmarks of the IRA. They even phoned later to claim responsibility. Or somebody did. But who better than a government minister to know the code words an IRA spokesman would use? It left them completely in the clear.'

'Except for you.'

'Not really. As long as any suspicions of mine could be dismissed as symptoms of mental illness, I posed no threat. Besides, I really believed I *was* imagining it all. Dr Kingdom persuaded me of that. So did Dysart. He was so kind, so calm, so unlike what a murderer should be. He admitted Clare had been blackmailing him, but he deceived me about the reason and convinced me her death had been a pure coincidence. I tried hard to go on believing that. I accepted his invitation to stay in the villa. I went to Rhodes. I met you. And every day I told myself: forget it all; enjoy yourself; relax; recover; prove your sanity. You helped, Harry. You knew nothing about any of it. You were my touchstone of normality: genial, reassuring and fallible.'

Little better than an aged and disreputable labrador: that, Harry thought but did not say, was the role he had briefly filled in Heather's life. It was not enough. It was not what he had aspired to. But it was all he had been allotted. And now he was glad of the darkness inside the car to cloak his disappointment.

'When Dr Kingdom came to see me, he must have been reassured to find I no longer believed there was anything suspicious about Clare's death. What he can't have realized, though, was that it was the environment, not logic or reason, that had changed the way I thought. On Rhodes, everything seemed long ago and far away, disproportionate, irrational, simply not worth worrying about.'

'But that changed when you saw Cornelius?'

'Yes. Utterly and completely. He was sitting on a bench outside the post office, reading a newspaper. My heart nearly stopped when I recognized him. Until then I'd been able to believe that my theories, however plausible, were baseless: they just couldn't be true. But Dysart had phoned the day before to say he was coming to Rhodes on official business and would be in Lindos the following Monday. With that in mind, the sight of Jack Cornelius on the island could mean only one thing: they were planning to kill me. My only advantage – my only hope – was that they didn't know I was on to them. Assuming they meant to use the same ploy as before – a faked terrorist attempt on Dysart's life claiming an innocent victim – I had until Monday to make my escape. But simply running away was no good. It would only have postponed the day of reckoning. An unexplained disappearance seemed the only answer. I'd confided in Sheila during the weekend I spent with her on my way out to Rhodes and she'd offered to shelter me in an emergency. She'd been the one person to take my suspicions seriously, you see. And Dysart didn't even know of her existence, so I reckoned there was a good chance he'd never trace me. When I contacted her, she agreed to help straightaway. She's been a good friend to me, Harry: a very good friend.'

'What made you use Profitis Ilias?'

'I'd been there before. I knew the area quite well. It was relatively close to the airport, with several routes to choose

466

from. And it had a special, rather disturbing atmosphere. You must have sensed it yourself.'

'Oh yes. I sensed it.'

'I hoped it would encourage speculation that I'd been murdered or abducted. I left my scarf at the summit for the same reason.'

'After you'd gone, I heard a whistle. Was that Sheila?'

'Yes. It was her signal to help me find her. She was waiting in a hire-car on the trail the other side of the mountain. She'd driven the long way round to get there, through Embona, and we took another indirect route back to the airport, through Apollona, to make sure nobody saw her both going and coming. Even so, we were in plenty of time for the six o'clock flight to Athens. Since it was internal, I didn't have to show my passport or give my name.'

'So you were off the island before I'd even raised the alarm.'

'I'm sorry, Harry, really I am. It wasn't fair to leave you in the lurch like that. But what else could I do? I couldn't let you know what I was planning. I couldn't leave any kind of trail for Dysart to follow.'

'But you did leave a trail.'

'The photographs? Yes, that was stupid of me. I'd used them to record the places I'd been. They were my secret symbols of all I'd discovered. Then, in the rush to get away, I forgot them. Later, I gave them up as lost. Instead of which, they were already in your hands.'

'And what about the postcards you left in the car? Of Silenus and Aphrodite.'

'What about them? I just grabbed two off a stall in Rhodes. They could have been of anything. I hoped they would support the idea that I'd been intending to return to the car.'

Harry did not know whether to laugh or cry. The postcards had meant nothing. They had concealed no message. They had held no secret. They were simply two minor components of the charade in which he had played the part of an obliging fool. And now this last hope that he had played some worthier role in Heather's life was shattered, he scarcely had the heart to listen to what more she had to say.

'Do you know what really frightens me, Harry? Not the thought that he'll kill me if he gets the chance, but the thought of every one of those other deaths strung over the decades. Clare was only the latest. Before her there was Willy Morpurgo. He wasn't killed, I know, but he might as well have been. Then Ramsey Everett. What did he do to provoke Dysart, do you suppose? According to Ockleton, he was something of a misfit in the Tyrrell Society: an amateur criminologist who dug up his fellow students' guilty secrets for a pastime. So was that the mistake he made? Did he find a guilty secret that Dysart was hiding? If so, what was it? His relationship with Cornelius? Or something else?'

A wry and unseen smile came to Harry's lips. Heather, he was forced to conclude, did not realize Dysart's very identity was in question. Chipchase's recollections had convinced him Heather knew the secret of Dysart's life buried in a Birmingham cemetery. But not so. After all her probing of the mystery, she was further from the truth than he was himself.

'I've thought often of the kind of mind a person would need to plan and commit such murders: cold; calculating; ruthless; resourceful; devoid of mercy and conscience; free of doubt and uncertainty. But is that what Dysart's really like? Is that what's inside him? You know him better than I do, Harry, so what do you think? Is that the true and total measure of Alan Dysart?'

'I don't know.' Harry heard his voice continuing to speak, but at a distance, as if it were not quite his own anymore. 'You tell me these things about Dysart and they seem to be true, but as far as I'm concerned you might as well be talking about a different person. A stranger. Somebody I'm not acquainted with. Somebody I've never even met.'

*

Ten minutes had passed. The car still stood in its patch of isolated night, but Harry was no longer inside. Muttering assorted platitudes about the need to stretch his legs and take the air, he had left Heather to her own devices and now sat thirty yards away on a low wall, sipping the whisky he had bought earlier at the airport shop. He had promised Heather he would not go far or let the car out of his sight, so his word was intact, even if Heather's faith in him might not have been, had she realized how fragile his confidence had become.

Ramsey Everett. Willy Morpurgo. Clare Mallender. Their names had formed in his mind a mantra of incomprehension. He thought of Alan Dysart, perpetually young, golden-haired and smiling in his memory. He thought of all the kindnesses he had been done by this man he had now to believe was a murderer. And still the very idea remained absurd and remote. It could not be. It could never have been. And yet, and yet. Save for Morpurgo, they were dead. As to that there could be no question. Nor were *they* all. There was another in the sequence whom Heather did not know about: Alan Dysart himself, the Alan Dysart whose grave Barry Chipchase had seen.

He took a last sip from the whisky bottle and slid it back into his pocket. Whatever else he was to do, he could not afford to become drunk, delicious though its promise of oblivion seemed. In a few hours they would be on Rhodes. Refuge of a kind would have been found. But what then? Even if Miltiades took them seriously and agreed to protect Heather, what was Harry to do? Stay on Rhodes? Return to England and confront Dysart? He did not know. However long and hard he thought, he could find no answer.

He sighed and rubbed his eyes. The *psarotaverna* where he and Heather had lunched before driving up to Profitis Ilias came to his mind. That, he supposed was the last time he had felt contented. Since then, doubt and suspicion had conquered all the ways in which he had sought to isolate himself from the world; doubt, suspicion and the crazy self-flattering notion that he could find Heather and so refute his accusers. Well, he had done it. And now he wished he had not.

He shivered. It was cold out here, alone in the dark, with a chill breeze blowing in off the sea. Yet he had no wish to return to the car. He had nothing to say to Heather and she, if the truth be told, had nothing to say to him. Fear and necessity bound them together. As for friendship and loyalty, he had only ever imagined their existence. He reached into his jacket pocket for the cigarettes he had bought with the whisky: *Karelia Sertika*, naturally. He pulled one out of the packet with his lips and chuckled ruefully. Heather could rely on him. Even if she did not know it, she could rely on him. He would do his best by her. He would do it to spite her. He slapped his pockets in search of the matches, found them and plucked out the box.

Suddenly, there was flame and heat close to his face. Not the matches. The box still lay unopened in his hand. It was the blue and yellow flare of a lighter. As he made to turn, he was at once aware of a tall, darkly clad figure standing immediately behind him, leaning forward over his shoulder, lighter held before him.

'A light, Harry?' He towered above him, his gaunt and shadow-shrouded face gazing down at him like some bird of prey hesitating in the instant before a kill. 'I may call you Harry, may I not?' He was Jack Cornelius. And in the wake of his name came a flood of fear, rising with hideous speed round every thought in Harry's head.

57

Cornelius extinquished the lighter. Resting a hand on Harry's shoulder, he climbed over the wall and sat down beside him. 'I would be grateful,' he said, 'if you did not move or call out.' There was a softness in his voice, a sibilance that held within it a certainty of command. 'I do not think Heather will miss you for a little while yet, do you?'

Harry swallowed hard. It crossed his mind that he might claim Heather was expecting him back at any moment, that unless he returned shortly she had instructions to drive away. But Cornelius's very manner assured him that lies would be useless. Just as his sinewy hold on Harry's shoulder implied that any attempt at flight would be in vain.

'It may have occurred to you to wonder how long I have been here. The answer is as long as you have. I followed you from Iraklio, after witnessing your somewhat comic precautions against sabotage. I was there when you arrived, hotfoot on your rescue mission. I was waiting for you, Harry, and you did not disappoint me.'

Speech and movement seemed beyond Harry. The hand on his shoulder, the serpentine pitch of Cornelius's voice, the knowledge of what had happened to Clare Mallender and the others: all held him in their paralysing grip.

'I haven't long, Harry. You must excuse me if I dispense with preliminaries. How much has Heather told you – how much have you deduced yourself – about Alan and me?'

Harry struggled to compose an answer. 'She thinks . . . I think . . . that you've been . . . that you are . . . . '

'How coy we are, how prudish. Well, let me spare you an attempt to describe our relationship. It has been a secret for so long that it is difficult to find appropriate words. Suffice it to say that Alan means more to me than any other living soul. I have been prepared to go to great lengths to protect him.'

'Such as murder?'

'Yes. Such as murder. I shall not seek to excuse the inexcusable, but let me ask you this: have you ever loved anyone? Perhaps not. Perhaps you have never known what it is to be willing to die for the one you love. Well, it is a short step from that state to being willing to kill for them as well. A very short step. And one I confess I have taken. You know the occasions to which I refer. You know them but you do not clearly understand them. Am I not right? I would like you to understand, Harry. Really I would.'

Whilst Cornelius went on talking there was hope of rescue or reprieve. To that hope Harry clung. 'Why don't you explain the circumstances?' he said, as calmly as he could contrive.

'Oh I intend to, Harry, I do indeed. Where shall we begin? Oxford, of course. Breakspear College. Where Alan and I first met. At once our salvation and our ruin. I arrived there as a lapsed monk whose nature had wrecked his vocation, Alan as a young man whose material wealth was only equalled by his emotional poverty. For a very long time we sought to resist the attraction each of us felt to the other, but not for ever. And once we had ceased to resist, we realized how perfectly we were matched. From the first, however, we observed a pact of total secrecy. Though we roomed together and spent a great deal of time in each other's company, nobody was given any hint that we were lovers. Strictly speaking, our relationship was illegal, at least until Alan was twenty-one, but that was not the reason for secrecy. The reason was Alan's ambition to become a naval officer and in due course a politician, careers which would have been closed to a known homosexual. I confess that as our time at Oxford drew towards its end, I came to dread our separation. I began to suspect Alan would abandon me, that he would feel it necessary to deny the love he felt for me. I began to crave some way of binding us together, of committing us to each other irrevocably, so that the future, whatever it brought, could not divide us. That, I suppose, is why I agreed to help Alan when he told me he had killed Ramsey Everett.'

'Why did he kill him?'

'Why? Because Ramsey Everett was a vile and greedy individual. Because he deserved to be killed. He was jealous of Alan's popularity in the Tyrrell Society, jealous also of his wealth. He burrowed into Alan's past like the weevil he was and tried to blackmail him with what he learned. For money, you understand. For nothing grander than a grubby handful of cash. Alan refused. Everett set a deadline: the St George's Night dinner. And while we ate and drank in one room, Everett had his answer in another. An argument by an open window, a struggle, a push, a fall: if that was murder, I could blame no man for committing it, least of all the man I loved. Alas, Willy Morpurgo witnessed the event. And he thought it *was* murder. He threatened to denounce Alan at the inquest. Alan appealed to me for help. We agreed that if Willy could be sufficiently frightened, he would hold his tongue. Hence the visit to Burford. Sabotaging his car was intended to result in an alarming experience, nothing more. Alan planned to leave him in no doubt that a more serious accident could be arranged if he insisted on speaking out. As you know, things went rather further than that. Poor Willy. Happy enough with his lot now, I gather. Which is more than most of us can claim.'

'If this is meant to justify—'

'No! Not justify. *Explain.* A blackmailer dead. An honest fool crippled. I felt my conscience could bear such offences. I still do. Clare Mallender likewise. She was no less a blackmailer than Ramsey Everett. And what she threatened to reveal was far more serious, though I admit she can have had no inkling of what it really was.'

'You had a hand in her murder?'

'I condoned it. I made it possible. So yes, I was an accessory. To be frank, I had very little choice. It was her life – or mine.'

'Surely not. It was only your reputation—'

'More than that. Far more. It is time you knew how much more. Twenty years have passed since Oxford, Harry, twenty years during which Alan and I have grown apart in the eyes of the world, yet have stayed loyal to each other, loyal to our love if to nothing else. Alan is a hero of his country, a minister in its government, a spokesman for all that government does and believes. And I? What am I? A middle-aged schoolteacher? Something else as well, Harry, something else altogether. I am a patriot. An Irish patriot.'

'So?'

'It means I recruit; I pass information; I gather intelligence; I cultivate young minds; I strengthen the cause of Irish unity; I participate in the struggle to free my country from British occupation. Do you think the IRA is sustained by nothing more than bloodlust and mania? Do you imagine it has survived and thrived all these years without the support of well-placed and educated sympathizers? Dozens of young Irish Catholics come before me every year at Hurstdown. I pay close attention to those with imagination and perception, I monitor their intellectual progress and to a select few, before they leave, I explain how they can give practical aid to those who fight and die on their behalf. You would, I think, be surprised to learn how many of them now, in their widely differing careers and professions, continue to help us. Some are wealthy, some eminent, some influential. All play their part. And all do so at my instigation.'

There was pride in Cornelius's voice, a vibrant sense of glory at the secret role he had played. But for Harry there was only the mounting horror of an insistent question: why was he prepared to reveal so much? 'Does . . . . Does Alan know this?'

474

'Of course. How could it be otherwise? He knew before I took the post at Hurstdown. You might even say he has always known, always known, that is, where my heart lay on matters touching Ireland.'

'But . . . . But he's a minister in . . . . '

'The British Government. Precisely, Harry, precisely. We stand on opposite sides of the armed struggle. We owe allegiance to two different and conflicting traditions. Yet we also owe allegiance to each other. Intellectually, he agrees the British have no place or right in Ireland, no place they have not stained with Irish blood, no right they have not stolen from Irish hands. But publicly he must be seen to avow a different version of history. I shall not debate the matter with you. I shall not lecture or proselytize for the cause. Like most of your fellow-countrymen, I imagine you know as much of Ireland as you do of Madagascar or Mars. So let us leave it there. Its relevance is this. One of the few things I would not do for my country is betray my love for Alan. I have never tried to extract information from him. I have never sought to exploit our relationship for the benefit of the organization which I serve so assiduously in other ways. Alas, my fellow patriots would not understand my reasons. They would regard my conduct as treacherous. They would assume that if I had not corrupted Alan, then he must have corrupted me. That is why I could not allow Clare Mallender to expose us. Not because it would have meant political ruin for Alan – although it would – but because it would have marked me down as a traitor, a traitor for whom only one punishment would have been deemed appropriate.'

'Death?' said Harry hoarsely.

'Yes.' Cornelius sounded almost wistful as he confirmed the point. 'Death. In such cases, neither swift nor painless. And now I have compounded the offence, every sinew of the organization will be strained to ensure the sentence is carried out.'

'Compounded? How?'

'I supplied Alan with the kind of explosive and the

475

type of device the IRA regularly employ. I provided the code-words which we used to persuade the police that the IRA had planted the bomb which killed Clare. I betrayed the operational secrets of the IRA for my own benefit. In short, Harry, I mixed the two worlds which I had striven for seventeen years to keep separate. And I fondly believed I could escape the consequences of such an act. Alas for folly. Alas for Jack Cornelius.'

The grasp on Harry's shoulder tightened. All about him stretched darkness and isolation. His very future seemed restricted to the scant diameter of his sight, limited to whatever the man beside him would say or allow. He forced himself to speak. 'What do you mean to do?'

Cornelius chuckled. 'Nothing, Harry. Nothing at all. I have already done what needed to be done. I have put matters right.'

'I don't understand.'

'No. But shortly you will. You have learned much about Alan in your search for Heather, have you not? Well, so have I. And what I have learned has led me to consider the possibility that the killing of Ramsey Everett was premeditated and that Willy Morpurgo's accident was always intended to be fatal. Do you follow, Harry? Do you see where such possibilities lead?'

'I . . . . I'm not sure.'

'He has deceived me, Harry. He is not what I thought. He has gone too far. The man I love has betrayed me. Ramsey Everett and Clare Mallender were blackmailers. In a sense, they deserved their punishment. But Heather's is a different case. She has done nothing. She has committed no offence. She has threatened nobody.' Cornelius fell silent for a moment, then resumed, his tone more disciplined than before. 'I am as guilty of Clare's murder as Alan is. That I do not deny. But I was determined to ensure it ended there. There could be no more. That was the last for me, the very last. When Alan decided Heather was too close to the truth, he thought we could repeat the trick. I did not try to dissuade him. I could see he was beyond dissuasion.

476

It would have been another bomb, at the villa, during his visit to Rhodes, another sister claimed by accident. But I forestalled him. I agreed to help. I volunteered to travel to Rhodes ahead of him and plan the operation in detail. Instead of doing that, however, I made sure Heather would see me and take fright.'

'You *let* her see you?'

'Of course. Did you suppose I could have been so negligent as to allow her to realize I was on her trail unless it suited my purpose to do so? I knew what her response would be, though I confess the theatricality of it surprised me. My visit to Rhodes was a warning. It was my way of alerting her to the peril she was in.' Cornelius permitted himself a dry and mirthless snigger. 'I know what you are thinking, Harry. Why should somebody who aids and abets assassination and arson in Northern Ireland quibble over the execution of one irksomely inquisitive Englishwoman in Rhodes? Why should blood and bombs rest easily on my conscience in Belfast but not in Lindos? Admit it. You had wondered, had you not?'

'Suppose I had.'

'Well, there is an answer, though I do not expect you to subscribe to it. The organization I serve is engaged in a morally justified war. But the murder of Heather Mallender could not be defended on moral grounds – or any other. I have my credo and shall be my own confessor. I seek neither your approval nor your comfort. But be assured: she is in no danger from me.'

'Then what . . . . If that's so, why are you here now?'

'To call off the chase. To cut short your unnecessary retreat. Perhaps I should have acted sooner, but I did not imagine you would ever find her. To be frank, you seemed ill-equipped for the task. Clearly, Alan was a better judge of your capabilities than I. Not that he told me the full extent of the enquiries you were making on his behalf. I think he began to have doubts about my loyalty from the moment Heather fled. I think he identified you as both more reliable and more malleable. Had he taken me into his confidence sooner, of course, I could have told him Dr Kingdom was not sheltering Heather and that deceiving you into believing he was would achieve nothing. As it was, he did not apprise me of the full extent of your activities until yesterday, shortly after you had given him the location of Heather's hiding-place. Suspicious or not, he needed my help, you see, to travel incognito, to act as his eyes and ears, to spy on Heather and plan her demise.'

'But you refused?'

'No. Refusal would have availed me little. That at least was clear to me. If you are not with Alan you are against him. If you are not his friend you are his enemy. I could see my status was in the balance, so I agreed with as great a show of enthusiasm as I could contrive. I volunteered to come here at once and monitor Heather's movements until we were ready to proceed against her. At this moment, he must still—' There was a catch in Cornelius's voice. He broke off. When he resumed, Harry could almost have believed he was close to tears. 'I promised him that this time nothing would go wrong. I assured him that there would be no mistakes. And nor will there. No mistakes at all.' He released his hold on Harry's shoulder. 'I have taken certain actions which will ensure Heather's safety. I have done what I should have done when Clare first came to me last year. But she was all her sister is not: arrogant, spoilt and contemptuous. She threatened me. She offended my pride. That is my excuse for succumbing to the course Alan proposed, the course for which I must now suffer. I thought frightening Heather into hiding might avert a desperate remedy, but thanks to you, Harry – thanks to what Alan inveigled you into doing – I have been left with no alternative but to pull down the curtain on the lie we have lived. You are acquainted, I believe, with an unsavoury journalist named Jonathan Minter?'

'Er . . . . Yes. Why?'

'In tomorrow's – I should say today's – edition of *The Courier*, there will appear a front-page article credited to Minter exposing a long-standing homosexual relationship

478

between a junior minister in the British government and a member of the IRA, between Alan Dysart, that is, and myself.'

A few minutes before, Harry had cowered in fear of the man beside him. Now, suddenly, everything was altered. And where fear ended, wonder began. 'You've admitted everything to Minter?'

'I have admitted enough to ruin Alan, yes. I have supplied Minter with certain letters which leave no doubt as to the nature of our relationship and which make it clear Alan has long known of my activities in the Republican cause. He will be hounded from public life as a consequence. He will be the subject of universal scorn and vituperation. He will be an outcast from his party and his society, a pariah, a leper, a man disowned. As to murder, both past and present, I have made no mention. Nor have I needed to. Alan thrives on the admiration of his peers. That has always been for him the greatest spur to achievement. That has always been what he most wanted to preserve. To lose it, as now he must, will be a more serious blow than any legal sanction. And once it is lost, Heather will no longer pose any kind of threat. Thus she will have nothing to fear. And nor will you.'

'But you said . . . . You said that if the IRA ever came to know . . . . '

'They would kill me.' Cornelius took a deep breath and exhaled slowly. 'They *will* kill me, Harry, if they ever find me.'

'You're not going back to England?'

'Hardly. That would be tantamount to suicide. You see me at the outset of a nomadic existence, flitting from one city to another, from one continent to another, always on the move, always glancing anxiously over my shoulder.'

'How long will you have to stay on the run?'

'Forever. For as long as I can. For as long as it takes them to catch me.'

'You think they will catch you?'

'Oh yes. Eventually. When I grow tired or careless.

479

When I can no longer summon the energy needed for continual flight. Then they will find me.'

The night seemed to grow darker still. In it Harry felt he could sense the certainty of Cornelius's fate, the certainty which Cornelius would live and breathe every day, for as many days as remained to him. 'By doing this, you've ruined Alan. But you've also cut your own throat.'

'In a manner of speaking, yes.'

'How could you? When you knew the consequences?'

'I had no choice. I could not permit Alan to continue and this was the only sure way to stop him. When he told me you had found Heather, I realized there was no alternative. I had to act. Minter has long harboured an animus against Alan. His reaction to the material I supplied was that of a greedy young boy for whom Christmas and a brace of birthdays have arrived simultaneously. He will do a good job. Of that I am confident. But he will not understand its purpose, for its purpose is mine.'

Cornelius was right. His was very likely the only way to halt the murderous trend of Dysart's life. And so, in spite of all the other reasons to hold him in contempt, Harry could not but admire him. What he had done required a special brand of resolution. What he had done Harry feared he himself could never have done.

'Do you think me brave, Harry? Do you think me courageous to the point of foolhardiness?'

'I suppose I do, yes.'

'You are wrong. Courage is easy to find when you have no choice. Remember Anthony Sedley, the man who carved his name on the font at Burford Church? He was frightened because he knew that if he renounced the principles for which the Levellers stood his life might be spared. He was not held prisoner by a locked door but by his own fear. Only when there is no hope of escape does fear evaporate. And I lost that hope when I understood that the planned and premeditated murder of Clare Mallender was far from the first such crime Alan had carried out – and would not be the last. I confess that part of what drew me to him in the first place was the hint of infinite daring that surrounded him like an aura. But I never guessed the full extent of that daring. I never realized – until it was too late – that Clare had only followed in the footsteps of Ramsey Everett. Do you know what Alan told me the last time we met, late on Friday night? That the pleasure of committing an undetected murder surpassed any other pleasure he had ever known. Do you appreciate what that means? Its worst implication came to me only later. The motive for pushing Everett from a window, for sabotaging Morpurgo's car, for blowing up the *Artemis* with Clare aboard, was purely secondary. The satisfaction of bringing off such deceptions mattered far more than whatever provoked them.'

'What did provoke them?' The need to know lurched to the fore of Harry's senses like a sudden thirst. So far, he had gained only hints and glimpses. Now he craved the answer whole, the truth complete.

'As to Clare and Morpurgo, you already know. As to Everett, the information he tried to blackmail Alan with was provocation in itself.'

'What was the information?'

'I cannot tell you.'

'Cannot?'

'I am bound by the promise I made Alan twenty years ago: the promise that I would never reveal what he had killed Everett to keep secret.'

'But surely—'

'No!' Cornelius's voice was stern and commanding, all suggestion of weakness sucked out of it. 'The act of treachery Alan has forced me to commit is enough. Ask him yourself and he may tell you the whole truth. But you will not hear it from me.'

Cornelius's code of honour, flawed and distorted though it might be, was evidently inflexible. Harry's only hope of

481

learning more from him was to reveal the little he had himself learned from Chipchase. As he pondered the wisdom of such a disclosure, Cornelius peered at the luminous dial of his wristwatch and clicked his tongue.

'Time is marching on, Harry. The printing presses of *The Courier* have ceased rolling. Trains are rumbling out from the termini of London, radiating like splinters in a stone-pierced sheet of ice, bearing their grubby bundles of scandal to the several corners of Britain. Soon the wholesalers' vans will be speeding along deserted streets in every town from Penzance to Inverness, depositing their cargo beside the milk crates on countless newagents' doorsteps. Within a few hours, the early risers amongst Alan's constituents will be collecting their newspapers from the porch and those who take *The Courier*, as they yawn over their first cup of tea and cast their blurred gaze across the front page, will see what they least expect to see, and gulp, and start, and rub their eyes, and look again, and realize that they are not dreaming. Alan Dysart's day is done. And so is mine.' He sighed and rose to his feet. 'It is time I was on my way, Harry, time I was on the move.'

'Where will you go?'

'Many places. It is better you should not know, better that nobody should know. But I would ask of you one favour.'

'What is it?'

'You will see Alan, I have no doubt. You must see him – as he must see you. It is why I chose to confide in you.' How Cornelius could be certain such a meeting would take place Harry did not knew, but there was a force and confidence in his tone that brooked no contradiction. 'I would like you to convey a message to him from me. Will you do that?'

'If I can. What is the message?'

'Simply this: he left me no choice.'

'Nothing else?'

'Nothing.' Cornelius took a deep breath, threw back his shoulders and began to walk away. Then, when he had covered no more than six paces, he stopped and looked back. 'Perhaps one other thing.'

'Yes?'

'Tell him I forgive him.' And before Harry could respond with any word or gesture, Cornelius had hurried on into the night.

58

An Under Secretary of State at the Ministry of Defence has sustained for many years a homosexual relationship with an active supporter of terrorism in Northern Ireland. That is the only conclusion to be drawn from evidence recently and exclusively made available to *The Courier* and set out in detail on pages 2 and 3. It is a shocking and scandalous indictment of government vetting procedures and raises a host of disturbing questions about lapses in security stretching back over several years. The minister concerned – Alan Dysart, a former naval officer decorated for his conduct in the Falklands War –

Larissa railway station in Athens was a tumult of mass departure. It seemed to Harry that half the city was decamping aboard the Venice Express, taking most of their worldly goods with them. Heavily strapped cases were being hauled aboard by Thessalonian *grandes dames* with fractious children and yapping dogs in attendance. Whistles, shouts, roars and petulant gestures were being exchanged by a rag-bag of guards and porters doing battle with the timetable and their own lethargy. Whilst Harry, as short of luggage as he was of energy, stood by an open door of the train shouting his farewells to Heather above the cacophany around them.

'I have your word you'll contact your parents?'

'Yes, Harry, I'll contact them. But I don't promise to

see them. I'll let them know I'm alive and well, but for the moment that may have to be all.'

'It's all I ask.'

'I still don't understand why you're travelling back by train.'

'Money.' Harry smiled. 'All this air travel's left me short.' Though that, he acknowledged to himself, was only an incidental advantage of favouring the two and a half day rail route to England.

'When will you arrive?'

'Wednesday afternoon.' It sounded all too soon to Harry's ears. By then he would have to decide what to say to Alan Dysart, or to whatever the whirlwind of public disgrace had left of his sometime friend.

'You feel sorry for him, don't you?'

'What?'

Heather's gaze was sharp-eyed and perceptive. 'Despite everything he's done – despite everything you've learned about him – you pity him, don't you? You don't think he deserved all the harsh things Jonathan wrote about him.' She held up her copy of *The Courier*.

'Oh he deserved them all right.' But Harry knew, even as he said it, that Heather was correct. He had never met Ramsey Everett. He had never spoken to Clare Mallender. They were remote and insubstantial. Even the extent to which he had himself been misled and manipulated seemed of small moment compared with what bulked so large in his thoughts: Cornelius embarked on his hopeless flight and Dysart besieged by the heralds of public ruin.

'It'll be all over by now, I should think,' said Heather. 'He'll have been forced to admit it's true. He'll have been compelled to resign.'

'Yes. He probably will.'

'I'm glad. Glad he'll have been made to suffer.'

'So would I be, in your shoes.'

'But you're not, are you?'

No; Harry was not. He remembered Dysart taking him home drunk one night from Barnchase Motors; rescuing him from penury and bankruptcy; salvaging him from unemployment and self-pity. What he owed Alan Dysart could only be measured by what he would have become without his help, so for him there could be no pleasure or satisfaction in Minter's double-page spread of gleeful condemnation. 'I'm glad it's over,' was all he could bring himself to say.

'That's really why you're going by train, isn't it? To avoid the worst of it.'

A fusillade of whistles and slamming doors excused Harry from answering. 'I must go,' he said, climbing aboard. He closed the door behind him and leaned out through the open window. 'Goodbye, then,' he announced, smiling stiffly.

'Goodbye, Harry.' Heather craned up to kiss him and for a self-deceptive instant he believed he could see tears glistening in her eyes. 'And good luck.'

'You too.' Harry felt relieved that the moment for recriminations had passed with none exchanged. The train lurched into motion.

'I'll write, I promise.'

'Do that.'

'And Harry—'

'Yes?'

'I'm sorry, you know.' Now there could be no doubt: she really was crying.

'What for?'

'Everything, I suppose.'

That was the last Harry's straining ears could detect as the train gathered speed and the shrieked farewells of others buffeted around him. He stepped back from the window, realizing as he did so that he would probably never see Heather again. A dwindling figure on a mountain path; a vanishing face on a crowded platform: at least this time he understood the moment for what it was. He stumbled down the corridor and began to look for a seat.

Harry followed the immediate repercussions of *The Courier*

article at several removes, for which he was grateful. The effect was numbing. It lessened the enormity of what had overtaken Dysart. It made it possible to pretend that the man involved was just a disgraced politician with whose fate Harry had no more to do than had any other passenger on the Venice Express.

According to the selection of Monday morning's London newspapers which Harry bought that evening during an hour's lay-up at Belgrade, Dysart's resignation from the government had been swiftly tendered. A letter to the Prime Minister expressing his 'deep regret at the embarrassment and consternation the article must have caused' and insisting that 'at no time has the security of civil or military operations in Northern Ireland been compromised' was widely quoted. Dysart's whereabouts were evidently a mystery, however. There were no photographs in fuzzy long-shot of a strained and fugitive figure, only well-lit portraits from the file, accompanied by uninformative pictures of his locked and empty London flat and some pensive studies of Virginia offering a stern 'no comment' on the doorstep at Strete Barton. Emergency meetings of the Cabinet and of Dysart's constituency party were widely anticipated, a host of political analysts and security experts extensively consulted. Editorially, the press was of one mind: Dysart deserved nothing but vitriolic contempt. He had betrayed his party and his country in a way that was little short of criminal. If he was not technically guilty of treason, then he was morally guilty. As for the revelation of his homosexuality, that, it was pruriently implied, only deepened the dye of his treachery.

The Venice Express reached its destination on Tuesday afternoon. There Harry boarded a train to Paris. During a lengthy wait at Milan, he was able to obtain a selection of that morning's English newspapers and gain his second insight into the progress of what they had now dubbed *The Dysart Scandal*. The Cabinet had met and commissioned an urgent inquiry into the security implications of the affair. Meanwhile, Dysart had announced through his constituency party chairman that he would be taking immediate steps to vacate his seat and withdraw from public life. 'Many loyal party workers feel betrayed by Mr Dysart,' the chairman had said at a press conference. 'He has accepted that this is the only course open to him.' Of Dysart in person there was still no sign. A blank had been drawn at Tyler's Hard, whilst at Strete Barton Virginia remained tight-lipped, although she had confirmed that she had neither seen nor heard from her husband since the story had broken. On the future of their marriage she had declined to be drawn.

With Dysart in hiding, most newspapers had devoted considerable attention to the instigator of his fall from grace. Photographs of Hurstdown Abbey and its beset headmaster were therefore much in evidence. 'Privileged and prestigious educational institution confronts its shameful secret' was among the more memorable judgements. Cornelius had vanished, bound who knew where, and the school he had betrayed was clearly intent on expunging him from its memory and conscience before a trickle of pupil withdrawals turned into a flood. Nobody knew him; nobody liked him; nobody could be found to defend him.

By noon on Wednesday, Harry was aboard a Boulogne to Folkestone ferry. Seated on deck, where freezing conditions assured him of privacy, he sifted through a third tranche of newspapers and noticed a hardening of attitudes as well as an ebbing of interest. *The Dysart Scandal* had now retreated to inside pages and with both of its protagonists still proving elusive, the cameramen had been called off. The government inquiry had commenced its work with a statement of its confidence that it would find no evidence of damage to security, whilst from Downing Street had come confirmation of Dysart's vacation of his parliamentary seat; a writ for a by-election would be moved as soon as the House of Commons returned from its Christmas recess. Considerable huffing and puffing had emanated from Northern Ireland's Protestant politicians, accompanied by demands for Dysart to be deprived of his DSC. In the letter columns this idea found much favour with those who would have preferred a public flogging for such an individual and wished to draw more general lessons about declining morality and tarnished honour. Meanwhile, a clutch of ex-pupils of Jack Cornelius had been tracked down; all wished to emphasize that he had never tried to recruit them for the Republican cause, that he would have been wasting his time had he done so and that they had never much liked him anyway. As for the IRA, their reaction had been neither sought nor offered.

On the train from Folkestone to London, Harry reached a decision he had been agonizing over since leaving Athens: he must find Dysart. There could be no evading such a confrontation, no scuttling back to Swindon and forgetting all he had suffered because of him, no dissociating himself from the man simply because he had brought about his own ruin and deserved no sympathy: they had to meet.

But such a decision was easier reached than implemented. An army of journalists had failed to track Dysart down and Harry had none of their resources. He did possess, however, one advantage: a knowledge of who, besides himself, Dysart had employed to further his objectives. Zohra Labrooy had deceived him at Dysart's bidding: she would therefore be his first recourse. She would answer for her conduct and aid him in his search. From Victoria station he headed straight for Marylebone.

The woman seated at the reception desk in Dr Kingdom's consulting rooms was not Zohra Labrooy. She waited till Harry had finished his explanations, then said: 'Miss Labrooy no longer works here.'

'When did she leave?'

'Last week, I think. At any rate, I started this week.'

'But . . . why did she leave?'

'I really couldn't say.'

'Surely—' A sidelong flicker of the receptionist's gaze

cut Harry short. When he turned round, it was to see Kingdom standing in the doorway of his office, staring straight at him.

'Would you mind stepping in here, Mr Barnett?'

'Well, I . . . . '

'I won't keep you long.'

Meekly, Harry obeyed. He could think of no good reason to refuse; Kingdom seemed as softly spoken and self-controlled as ever. But as soon as they were alone, the doctor's tone altered.

'You have a damned nerve to come here like this.'

'I was only—'

'Only looking for your confederate, I know. Your visit to the Versorelli Institute was reported to me, Mr Barnett. I'm amazed you could have thought it wouldn't be. As for Miss Labrooy, I'm equally amazed she could have thought the forgery of my signature on that letter wouldn't be traced to her. I dismissed her as soon as I heard of it.'

'Ah. I see.'

'Do you? Do you really? You've caused me a great deal of embarrassment and inconvenience. You've been party to theft, fraud and the most appalling misrepresentations. I'd be within my rights to press criminal charges against you, Mr Barnett. Do you realize that?'

'Why don't you, then?'

'Because – and only because – Heather's mother telephoned me this morning. It appears Heather is alive and well – in Athens.'

'I know. I was the one who found her.'

'So Mrs Mallender said. Which leaves me wondering why you thought it necessary to make a nuisance of yourself at the Versorelli Institute.'

'If you'd admitted visiting Heather in Lindos five days before her disappearance, maybe I wouldn't have.'

'Oh for God's sake—' Kingdom broke off and stalked away to the window, where he stared out at the street, back pointedly turned. 'How did you know I'd been there?'

'I saw you.'

490

'And because I never mentioned it, you thought I'd played some part in Heather's disappearance? You thought I'd spirited her away to Geneva?'

'Yes.'

'No doubt you'd say I only had myself to blame for—' Kingdom turned back from the window, an irritated frown on his face. 'I suppose it *is* possible you thought you were acting for the best. How did you persuade Miss Labrooy to help you?'

So Zohra, it seemed, had not disclosed Dysart's role in events. Perhaps, thought Harry, that was just as well. 'If she didn't tell you, I'm not about to.'

Kingdom stared at Harry with a mixture of bafflement and distaste. 'What are you two hiding? With Heather found, safe and sound, what purpose does all this secrecy serve?'

Harry said nothing. In one sense, he and Kingdom owed each other an apology. But in present circumstances that was the sentiment least likely to be exchanged between them.

'Do you know what I think, Mr Barnett? I think there's a great deal more to this than I've ever appreciated. Perhaps Heather's safety was never the real issue. Perhaps it was merely a smokescreen for something else.'

'Such as?'

'I don't know. But I think you do. And I think Heather's reappearance coinciding with Alan Dysart's public disgrace somehow holds the key.'

Kingdom was close to the truth but Harry sensed he would never draw any closer.

'But you're not going to tell me what it's really all about, are you? You're not going to tell me anything at all.'

Harry smiled, enjoying for an instant the other man's frustration. 'No,' he said. 'As a matter of fact, I'm not.'

All the way to Paddington station, Harry debated whether to travel to Kensal Green and confront Zohra straightaway, but in the end fatigue deterred him. With forty minutes to wait for the Swindon train and the rush hour in swirling progress around him, he queued for the use of the telephone and dialled her number. There was no answer. He re-dialled, with the same result. Then he tried Mrs Tandy instead.

'Hello?'

'Mrs Tandy? This is Harry Barnett. Remember me?'

'Of course, Mr Barnett. How are you?'

'Er, fine. I've been trying to contact Zohra.'

'She's away. Didn't you know?'

'Er, no. No, I didn't. Where's she gone?'

'A cousin in Newcastle, I think. To be honest, I'm not really sure.'

'When will she be back?'

'There again, I'm not sure. She left in rather a hurry. A few days, I suppose. I wouldn't think she'd be gone longer, would you?'

'I don't know, Mrs Tandy. I really don't know.'

So Zohra was in some form of hiding. And finding Dysart was to be less straightforward than Harry had hoped.

'Do you mean to tell me, Harold, that this Mallender girl's been sitting pretty in Athens these past two months while her parents have been worrying themselves sick?'

'Yes, Mother.'

'Letting papers like that Korea suggest you knew more than you were telling? Letting half the busybodies in this street imply you had something to do with her disappearance?'

'Well, she can't be blamed for other people's maliciousness, but—'

'I don't understand it, I really don't. What way is that for a well brought up young girl to behave?'

'I'm not sure her upbringing has anything—'

'And Alan Dysart! I'd always thought him so nice, so well spoken. What I've been reading about him these three days past would have turned my hair grey if old age hadn't done the job already. Mixed up with these Fenians. And

492

other such goings-on as I don't like to speak of. To think he was standing in this very room not a month ago, smiling and bobbing fit to charm the birds off the trees. I don't know what the world's coming to, I really don't.'

'Neither do I, Mother.'

'It can't go on. That I *will* say. It simply cannot go on.'

'No, Mother. It probably can't.'

59

A lengthy lay-up had not mellowed the temperament of Harry's car, which grated and growled its way along the road when he left Swindon the following morning. If the newspapers were to be believed – which on this point they were – nothing had been seen of Dysart at his London flat, or at Tyler's Hard, or at Strete Barton, following the appearance of *The Courier* article on Sunday. Since the flat would therefore be empty and only Morpurgo was likely to be on hand at Tyler's Hard, Strete Barton was the one destination which might yield some information as to his whereabouts.

It was midday when Harry drove into the yard. The Range Rover stood alone in the garage. Of Dysart's Daimler and Virginia's Mercedes there was no sign. As he climbed from the car, a silence suggestive of emptiness closed about him. But there was a window open at the front of the the house, so it was not without some hope that he approached the door. To his surprise, it opened before he had reached it.

'Mr Barnett!' It was Nancy, aproned and headscarfed, a duster clutched in one hand. 'Well, well. Fancy you turnin' up 'ere.'

'Hello.' Harry stopped and smiled at her awkwardly. The realization came to him that he had no pretext for his visit. 'I . . . er . . . heard about everything.'

'Reckon you'd need to 'ave bin down a mineshaft all week not to. It's bin terrible, real terrible.' And there was indeed a strained look on her face that suggested she had been badly affected.

'Is . . . er . . . Mrs Dysart at home?'

'Not 'er. Got so fed up with these journalists pokin' an' a-prying' that she took 'erself off on a 'oliday. Ski'in', I think she said. Only went yesterday.'

'Ah-ah.' It was not, Harry reflected, quite the action of the concerned wife determined to stand by her beleaguered husband. But for her absence he was duly grateful. 'Left you to hold the fort, then?'

'That's right. I was just doin' a bit o' cleanin'. My dad, well, 'e said as I shouldn't work up 'ere no more, not after what's come out. But I said: they've always bin good to me, so why should I let 'em down?'

'Very laudable. Have you . . . er . . . seen anything of Mr Dysart?'

'Well . . . . ' Her voice dropped and Harry had to step closer to hear. 'Matter o'fact, 'e showed up yesterday, couple of hours after Mrs Dysart left. Breezed straight in and straight out again.'

'How did he seem?'

'You'd not 'ave known anythin' 'ad 'appened, Mr Barnett. You'd not 'ave known, I swear. Looked an' sounded just the same. Like 'e 'adn't a care in the world. 'Ow 'e kept up such a front I dunno, not considerin' some o' the things I've read an' 'eard about 'im these past few days, but there 'tis. Mind . . . . '

'Yes?'

'I couldn't 'elp thinkin' 'e might've bin waitin' for Mrs Dysart to leave. Waitin' till the coast was clear, like.'

'To do what?'

'Oh, I dunno. 'E was 'ardly 'ere five minutes. Went to 'is study, came back with a few things in a bag; an' drove away. All smiles, 'e was. Jus' like always.'

'Would it be all right if I . . . looked in the study?'

'Well . . . . ' Nancy's brow furrowed. 'S'pose so. Why not? Can't do no 'arm, can it? You won't . . . take nothin', will you?'

'No, Nancy. Not a thing.'

The study was exactly as Harry remembered. Nothing was out of place, nothing disturbed. The photographs of Dysart's class at Dartmouth and the crews of the *Atropos* and *Electra* still adorned the walls, the books on the shelves were still neatly arrayed and dusted. What had he taken, then? What had he carried away?

Suddenly, as Harry surveyed the room, the memory of what had occurred there – the recollection of what he and Virginia had done – intruded so sharply on the present that for a second he could almost see and hear . . . . He gripped the corner of the desk to steady himself. Then he remembered – as if it was still there to be seen – the book he had found lying by the telephone that night: *The Reign of William Rufus*. He crossed to the bookshelves and looked along them in search of it. Strangely, it was not there, although there was a gap of about the right width where he would have expected it to be. Perhaps . . . . Then it came to him. *The Reign of William Rufus*, inscribed with the signatures of Cornelius, Cunningham, Everett, Morpurgo and Ockleton. Their gift to Dysart on St George's Day, 1968, the day Ramsey Everett had died and what was now unfolding had been set in train: that was the possession Dysart had come to retrieve; that and nothing else.

At the pub in Blackawton, the Dysart scandal appeared not to concern those who joked and gossiped at the bar. Either it had ceased to interest them some days since, Harry supposed, or he was recognized from his visit with Virginia a fortnight ago and was viewed therefore with suspicion. He took himself off to a settle by the fire, drank his beer in sorrowful gulps and cast about his weary thoughts in search of inspiration as to his next move. Where was Dysart? What was he thinking? His life had been founded on easy success and expert concealment. How did such a man confront total ruin and the exposure of a damning secret? How did he propose to carry on?

496

Harry's gaze drifted to the wall beside the fireplace, decorated with a wartime poster concerning evacuation of the locality for D-day preparations. *IMPORTANT MEETINGS. The area described below is to be REQUISITIONED for military purposes and must be cleared by 20 December 1943. Arrangements have been made to . . . .* 1943: all so long ago. Ramsey Everett, Willy Morpurgo, Clare Mallender and Alan Dysart were all then unborn. And Harry? He was just a short-trousered schoolboy who spent his days wondering if a bomb would ever drop on his classrooom. If he had foreseen then what his life would hold, he would have—

'Evacuations are in season again, I understand,' said a voice behind him, a voice that was immediately though imprecisely familiar.

Harry looked round and found himself staring up at a tall, thin, raincoated figure with a sharp, weasely face, greasy grey-streaked hair dragged over a bald head and a complexion the colour of the poster he had just been studying. The man from the train; the man from the cemetery; the man Nancy had glimpsed from the kitchen window at Strete Barton: he must have heard Harry's shocked intake of breath, must have seen the flinching realization in his eyes.

'Mind if I join you?' He lowered himself onto the stool beside Harry, put his glass on the table and gave a thin-lipped smile. 'Nice drop of ale here, don't you think?' He nodded up at the poster. 'Saw you looking at it. A bit ironic, isn't it?'

'What?'

'Well, like I said, evacuations are suddenly the order of the day again. At Strete Barton, that is.'

'Who . . . . Who the hell are you?'

'Vigeon. Albert Vigeon. Certificated bailiff. Also available for a wide variety of confidential assignments. Matrimonial. Process serving. Missing persons. Covert surveillance and photography. Currently concerned with what you might call a bad debt.'

'You've been following me, haven't you?'

'Yes, but not for the past couple of weeks. This is strictly a chance meeting, though not much of a chance considering we're both here for the same reason.'

'What reason?'

'To find Dysart. Isn't that so, Mr Barnett?'

All the nameless fear this man had instilled in Harry was suddenly gone. He sat across the corner of the table from him, a drab and ferret-eyed figure in a grubby-collared raincoat. He was no phantom, no herald of the unimaginable; he was sallow flesh and watery blood; he was Albert Vigeon, enquiry agent. 'Who are you working for, Mr Vigeon?'

'I *was* working for Dysart.'

'But not anymore?'

'Hardly.' The same taut, mirthless smile. 'Actually, I'm concerned he might have overlooked my account in view of all that's happened to him.'

'Your account?'

'For services rendered.'

'What services?'

'Unorthodox ones, I grant you, but chargeable on a strict scale. You'll be familiar with some of them, I think, since you were the subject and a certain amount of visibility was called for by my client. Monitoring your movements. Making a few anonymous telephone calls. Taking some photographs. Learning a little Greek. Daubing some words on a wall. Reading a book on a train. Wishing you goodnight. Leaving a calling card in your hotel room. Slipping a snapshot under the windscreen wiper of your car. Discarding a Greek cigarette packet outside your home. That sort of thing, Mr Barnett. All that sort of thing.'

Every mirage dissolved at Vigeon's words, every deception turned to confront itself. There had been no warnings he had not supplied, no interventions he had not arranged. And all – every single one – had been done at his client's bidding. 'Dysart hired you to follow me? He employed you to carry on this . . . this campaign?'

'Call it a campaign if you want. I'd call it a commission.'

'To break and enter? To harass by telephone? To dog my footsteps? Good God, I've a mind to—'

Vigeon's hand clasped Harry's forearm. 'Moderation, Mr Barnett, please. Nothing you can prove I've done is illegal and anything illegal I may have done you can't prove, so may I commend a little restraint? I'd hoped we could help each other.'

'You? Help *me*?'

'To find Dysart. He owes me money. As to what he owes you, I'll not enquire.'

'Don't give me that. You must have some idea what all this was for.'

Vigeon's expression suggested Harry had impugned his professionalism. 'Certainly not. I make a point of knowing only what I need to know. And what I need to know at the moment is where my former client is hiding. He owes me a substantial amount of money.'

'That's your problem.'

'He's not in London. I've tried every one of his bolt-holes. He isn't at Tyler's Hard. I spent yesterday there and all I had for my trouble was a mouthful of gibberish from his gardener.'

'Well he's not here either.' It afforded Harry some slight satisfaction to know that Vigeon the arch-surveillant had been wasting his time at Tyler's Hard during Dysart's visit to Strete Barton.

'So it appears. Where is he, then?'

'I've no idea. Abroad, perhaps?'

'I don't think so.'

'Then your guess is as good as mine.'

'Listen, Mr Barnett.' Vigeon's voice dropped. 'It's vital I find Dysart. I reckon he'll be in touch with you sooner or later, so—'

'Why's it vital? If it's just a question of being paid—'

'There are other . . . considerations.'

Suddenly Vigeon's true motive unveiled itself in Harry's head. 'Another client, you mean. You're working for somebody else now, aren't you, Mr Vigeon? Somebody who wants Dysart found.'

'Well, it's possible—'

'Who is it? Who's your new client?'

'As to that, I couldn't possibly say. Absolute confidentiality is the watchword of someone in my line of work.'

The subterfuge was not over. Maybe it never would be. But for Harry the limits of his tolerance were fast approaching. 'You're going to offer me money for putting you on to Dysart, aren't you?'

'Perhaps.'

'Save your breath. I'm not interested.'

'I'm sure we could—'

'No we couldn't.' Harry leaned across the table to ensure Vigeon understood him clearly. 'Go to hell, Mr Vigeon. And leave me alone. That's all I ask of you. I don't want your money – or your client's.'

'Oh dear.' Vigeon pursed his lips. 'Your uncompromising stance obliges me to broach a painful subject, Mr Barnett. My photographic activities were not confined to Kensal Green Cemetery, I'm afraid. They also included Strete Barton on the night of the twenty-seventh of December last.'

'What?'

'An uncurtained ground-floor window, with internal lighting, posed few technical problems, it must be said. I was able to obtain several arresting studies of events inside.'

'You? You photographed—'

'Mrs Dysart and your good self, explicitly juxtaposed. Yes, Mr Barnett, I fear so.' Vigeon lowered his voice still further. 'Now I'm no longer working for Dysart, the film I took is available on the open market, so to speak, and could be traded for cash or kind – money you don't have, that is, or Dysart's whereabouts, which you may yet establish. You take my meaning?'

'Oh yes. I take it.'

'Excellent. We can do business, then.' Vigeon grinned.

'I must say, Mr Barnett, that in all my years of matrimonial enquiries I don't recall anything quite as entertaining as the display you and Mrs Dysart—'

The rest of the beer in Harry's glass hit Vigeon's face and drowned his words in spluttering dismay. He stumbled to his feet and scrabbled for a handkerchief, coughing and swearing as he did so. But before he could see clearly Harry too had risen. Charged with rage at all the man had said and implied, he swung back his fist and struck him somewhere under the right eye with a force he did not know he possessed. Vigeon was sent sprawling in a scatter of toppled furniture and smashing glass and Harry, not waiting to see what damage he had inflicted, blundered towards the door.

Outside, in the cold grey air, voices raised in alarm behind him, Harry was aware of a sharp pain in his right hand and a breathless sense of release. Hitting Vigeon proved nothing, of course, but striking back at all he represented held its own reward. Laughing at his folly, he hurried across the road to his car.

60

Chesil Beach was empty beneath a tenebrous sky, the wind-stirred surf crashing and roaring up the shore. At the top of the shingle bank, gazing out at the tumult of the ocean, Harry Barnett and Nigel Mossop stood side by side, pitting their voices against the gale that lashed their faces and tugged at their clothes.

'Heather ph-phoned me t-two days ago, actually. It was a bit . . . a bit of a sh-shock, naturally. And a relief, of course. As for Dysart, well, I've no m-more idea where he might be than . . . than you have, Harry.'

'I'm glad at least that he helped you out of the hole I dropped you in.'

'It wasn't really your f-fault, Harry, but . . . yes, Dysart p-put in a word for me. The Ministry of Agriculture, in Dorchester. I st-start next week. Looking forward to it. G-Glad to have left . . . . '

'Mallender Marine? You would be. I went to Sabre Rise this morning, you know.'

'Oh . . . yes?'

'I didn't see Charlie, of course. According to Marjorie, he's taken the revelations about Dysart badly. Feels betrayed, let down by somebody whose loyalty he thought was beyond question. It's amazing really.'

'What . . . . What is?'

'That a man who treated his daughter as badly as Charlie did – a man who was happy to bludgeon and bribe and defraud his way out of financial problems if he could – has the gall to feel *betrayed* by anyone.'

'Well, it was a bit . . . a bit of a shock.'

'Yes, I know, but even so . . . . ' Harry looked at Mossop and smiled. 'We'd better go back to the car, Nige. I think you're shivering more than you're stammering.'

They started back down the path towards the car park, Harry reflecting as they went that a second day of fruitless enquiry was fast drawing to a close. After leaving Blackawton the previous afternoon, he had driven straight to Tyler's Hard, found only a dark and clearly unoccupied house, thought better of knocking up Morpurgo in the garage flat, returned as far as Weymouth, sought hospitality with Ernie Love and spent the evening becoming morbidly drunk whilst Ernie treated him to his assessment of the Dysart scandal at the bar of the Globe Inn. The following morning, he had struck out for Sabre Rise. Marjorie Mallender, evidently embarrassed to see him, had gritted out an unconvincing apology on behalf of her family for all the false accusations they had levelled against him; she was herself shortly to visit Heather in Athens; Charlie would not be accompanying her. As for Dysart, she had neither sympathy nor contempt; her daughter's welfare was now her sole concern. Hoping for her sake that Heather never told her the full story, Harry had left on a note neither of rapprochement nor of resentment, rather of new-found indifference. It was a sentiment confirmed by his reaction to sighting Roy Mallender driving out of Mallender Marine a couple of hours later; he could no longer summon his former loathing for the man; he was finished with Roy; he was finished with the pack of them.

'What . . . . What will you do now?' said Mossop, as Harry started the car and headed back towards Weymouth.

'I'm not sure, Nige. Go on looking for Dysart until I find him, I suppose.

'But he could . . . could be anywhere.'

'I know, but I can't give up now.'

'Why not?'

Harry did not reply. He had many motives for tracking Dysart down – the explanations he was owed, the promise he had made Cornelius, the tangled knot of Dysart's deceptions that he was determined to unravel – but strangely, hovering beyond and behind them all, he sensed there was one that surpassed and preceded the rest, a purpose he could neither name nor know till it had attained its objective, a purpose only Dysart could make him understand.

61

Harry arrived back in Swindon early that evening to find his mother in a state of wide-eyed perturbation. A Mr Ellison, full of softly-spoken politeness and flourishing some kind of official identification, had called to see him more than an hour ago and had insisted on waiting for him to return; he was currently installed in the front parlour with a pot of tea, as patient and inflexible as when he had first rung the doorbell.

'Mr Ellison?'

'Indeed. Mr Barnett?'

They shook hands. Ellison had the firm grip and square shoulders of a military man, the languid gaze and drawling tone of the upper classes. His suit was as black as his hair; all about him was trimmed and regulated severity leavened only by a crooked hint of irony about the mouth. Beside his chair was a black briefcase with a coat of arms embossed on the flap in gold. Of colour the only trace lay in the stripes of his tie: old school, Harry suspected, though which he could not say.

'Sorry to lie in wait for you like this, my dear fellow. Certain amount of urgency, you know.'

'About what?'

'Your friend, Alan Dysart.'

Take care, Harry instructed himself. 'I'm not sure I follow.'

'Come, come.' A vexed frown. 'I'm attached to the

Ministry of Defence, Mr Barnett. I've been assigned to the inquiry into the Dysart scandal of which the newspapers have made so much in recent days.'

'What's that to do with me?'

'In itself, nothing, but there is official concern over how Dysart's . . . compromising associations, shall we call them? . . . escaped notice for so long. This has necessitated a thoroughgoing investigation of all his activities and acquaintances. I am one of those charged with conducting that investigation and you, Mr Barnett, represent one of its most puzzling strands.'

'Really?'

Ellison described a striding circuit of the room, twitching his eyebrows and nostrils at the fusty furnishings, the bric-à-brac cabinet, the *To Thine Own Self Be True* sampler, the plastic bag full of knitting stowed beside the armchair. Then he treated Harry to a one-eyed smile which stated all he did not need to say: thirty-seven, Falmouth Street, Swindon was as far from Dysart's normal territory as Harry was from his normal society.

'He worked for me once. He's done me several favours. We've stayed in touch. Where's the puzzle in that?'

Ellison moved closer. 'I've been obliged to become a close student of Alan Dysart, Mr Barnett, closer than I'd like. I've explored his marriage, his finances and his friendships in detail: great and sometimes distasteful detail.'

'What have you been looking for?'

'The key, my dear fellow. The key to unlock what could create and then destroy such a man. Not for his sake, you understand, not for our general enlightenment, but in the interests of avoiding – or at least anticipating – any further such . . . embarrassments, shall we call them? . . . as Dysart has inflicted on his political masters. They do not like this kind of thing. Poovery and Popery: a nasty combination; very nasty indeed.'

'Why don't you come to the point?'

'But I have. *You* are the point, Mr Barnett, you and what you mean to Alan Dysart. You did not go to Oundle

506

or Oxford with him. You did not serve with him. You have not done business with him. You are not consonant with the life he has led. You are a discrepancy, an inconsistency, and therefore a puzzle.'

'Sorry, I'm sure.'

'And there is more. I understand you've recently been instrumental in the restoration of Miss Heather Mallender to the bosom of her family, the family whose other daughter was killed in an IRA attempt on Dysart's life in June 1987.'

'Yes.'

'Well now, two thoughts have occurred to me, Mr Barnett. Firstly, why did Dysart's . . . chum, shall we call him? . . . who was by his own admission privy to the IRA's innermost secrets, not forewarn Dysart of his pending assassination? And why, when the said chum left this country so abruptly last Saturday, did he choose as his destination the very city where you were even then engaged in seeking out Miss Mallender?'

Harry tried to look and sound surprised. 'Cornelius fled to Athens?'

'Quite so. You saw nothing of him there, of course?'

'Nothing.'

'Nor do you have any idea where he is now?'

'Still in Athens?'

'No, my dear fellow, not, we think, still in Athens. Cornelius has dropped out of sight, as has his . . . chum. Of course, you would also be ignorant of Dysart's whereabouts, wouldn't you?'

'Er . . . yes.'

'Then let's try something you're bound to know. Why did Dysart write you a cheque for a thousand pounds on the eleventh of December?'

Harry's brain refused to supply him with a swift or plausible answer. He stared at Ellison blankly, he made to speak, he hesitated . . . .

'Where is he, Mr Barnett?'

'I don't know.'

507

'I think you do.'

'No.'

'We're very anxious to find him, very anxious indeed.'

'Why?'

'Matters can't be left as they are. You must see that. Too many loose ends, too many . . . incongruities, shall we say? Where is he, my dear fellow? You must tell me, you really must.'

'I don't know.'

'I've spoken to Dysart's old college friends, Ockleton and Cunningham: a treacherous pair. Also to Dysart's wife, currently seeking solace with a ski instructor in Kitzbühel: a hard woman. On one point they all agreed. If there is somebody Dysart trusts – aside from Cornelius of course – it is you. Nobody else. Just you.'

'They're mistaken.'

'What is it, Mr Barnett? What is it here or in you that Dysart clings to? A terraced house in an anonymous town. An old woman and her scapegrace son. Nothing that he knows or needs. Nobody that he should care a fig or give a damn for. And yet he does. A wife he hates. Friends he despises. Acquaintances he exploits. A lover he hides. And you.' Ellison's dark eyes roamed around the room before returning to Harry. 'What binds him to you, Mr Barnett?'

'Nothing.'

Ellison clicked his tongue and sighed. 'It is better that *we* should find him, my dear fellow, than the others who may be looking, better by far.'

'What others?'

'My card—' Ellison plucked one from his pocket and pressed it into Harry's hand. 'If you should have second thoughts . . . if you should wish to unburden yourself, shall we say? . . . I can be found on that number at any time.' He turned aside abruptly and retrieved his briefcase. 'Now I must away. Remember—' He held Harry's gaze with his own. 'He needs help. He needs *our* help. Soon. In his own best interests. If you care anything for his welfare, call me.'

508

And then he was gone, swiftly and silently, leaving Harry to lower himself into the armchair and stare at the blank television screen on which he had seen Dysart the first night of his return from Rhodes. '*I was slick. I was witty. I was word-perfect.*' But not just, it seemed, for the benefit of the camera. All his life had been the same: a slick, witty, word-perfect performance. And now it was over. The game was up, the disguise seen through, the mask ripped aside. Only the object of concealment remained unknown. Only the purpose of the pretence had not been found.

'Has he left?' Harry's mother asked as she entered the room.

'No, Mother. He's hiding behind the television set.'

'I suppose you think that's funny.'

'Not really.'

'What did he want?'

'Something I couldn't give him. Something I don't possess.' Harry smiled. 'Yet.'

62

Ten o'clock on Saturday morning found Jonathan Minter gravel-throated, unshaven and clad only in mules and a towelling bathrobe. Harry followed him down the short hallway of his flat to the large and antiseptically furnished lounge with its view of Tower Bridge, watched him slump into a low armchair, saw him reach for the cigarette left smoking in a saucer and felt contempt for this man's youth and arrogance rise in his throat like phlegm.

'Christ knows why I let you in,' said Minter. 'Curiosity, I suppose. What do you want?'

'I'm looking for Dysart.'

'Join the queue. We're all looking for him. It's the new national sport.'

'I thought you might have some idea where he is.'

'If I did have, I wouldn't tell you, would I? I'd save it for tomorrow's front page.'

'Isn't one front page story enough?'

Minter smiled. 'One's never enough. Why? Come to give me another? Come to sell me your slice of dismembered Dysart?'

Harry took a deep breath. Anger was useless. He looked at the blue sky beyond the window, at the absurd and dazzling majesty of the Thames, found there a measure of proportion if not of consolation and sat slowly down on the edge of the couch opposite Minter. 'If you have any clue as to Dysart's whereabouts, I'd be prepared to give you some of the information you offered to buy a few weeks ago.'

510

'No deal, Harry. Don't need you now. I've done it all on my own. Besides, I can't trade what I don't have and I don't have any idea where Dysart is.'

'What about Virginia? Does she know?'

'Ask her yourself. She and I have . . . fallen out. Seems she thinks she should've been forewarned of the story Cornelius gave me. Didn't enjoy being written up as the wife of a closet queer. Wanted Dysart ruined, of course – always has – but on her terms, not mine.'

'*Your* terms?'

'Well, Cornelius's then. God knows why he decided to put the knife in. Lovers' tiff, perhaps. Whatever the reason, he gave me what I wanted: the hammer to drive a nail through Dysart's life.'

'Satisfying, is it, to have destroyed him?'

Minter took a long drag on his cigarette. 'Not as satisfying as I'd anticipated. Too easy, I suppose. A phone call out of the blue. A meeting last Saturday at Paddington station.' He glanced at his watch. 'Yeh, just around this time. And there's Cornelius handing me the full story. A signed statement. A taped confession. Compromising letters. The whole shooting-match. Well, I didn't have to do a lot of work for it, did I?' He sprang from the chair and ambled across to the window. 'I've spent years wondering what it would feel like to ruin that man and now I know.'

'What does it feel like?'

'Like I've been cheated, if you must know. Like I've fought hard to beat an opponent, only to realize he's thrown the game away; let me win; handed me victory on a plate – for reasons of his own.'

'What reasons?'

'I don't know. That's what sucks all the pleasure out of it. What's the point of winning if you know you've been allowed to? Ever play a card-game called solo whist, Harry?'

'Yes.'

'Well, I feel as if Dysart's called *misère ouvert* and won the hand. He's shown me every card he holds. He's defied

511

me to stop him losing every single trick. And he's got away with it. God rot him, he's got away with it.'

'Where do you think he is now?'

Minter gestured towards the sky and the city, towards the river and the sea beyond. 'Somewhere out there.'

'Hiding?'

'If he isn't, he ought to be. Some of the people who are looking for him aren't doing so just for the pleasure of offering him their sympathy.'

'Who do you mean?'

'I imagine the intelligence services would like a lengthy chat with him. As would the IRA. They probably think he could point them in Cornelius's direction. Then there are members of my own august profession, followed by a ragbag of freelancers and grudge-bearers. Rex Cunningham for one. He's been on to me lately for the same reason you're here now – where's Dysart? He seems determined to dredge up that old story about a defenestration at Oxford in the wake of my article, though God knows why.' Minter grinned. 'Behind that lot, Harry, you finish a pretty distant last.'

'You don't think I'll find him?'

'I don't think anybody will find him.' Minter drew on his cigarette. 'Unless he wants them to.'

63

Just as Harry was beginning to think his detour to Kensal Green was completely in vain, Mrs Tandy opened her front door, frowned towards the reggae music billowing from a neighbouring first-floor window, then fixed her attention on him with the sweetest of smiles, as if he were a schoolboy paying his respects to a great aunt.

'Mr Barnett! What brings you here?'

'I was just . . . er . . . passing. Wondered if you had any news of Zohra.'

'You're in luck. She came back last night.'

'Is she in?'

'No. She went to do some shopping for me about half an hour ago. Such a kind and helpful girl, Zohra, don't you agree, Mr Barnett?'

'Well . . . . I . . . . '

'But here she is now!' Mrs Tandy's smile grew radiant. 'She must have known she was wanted.'

Zohra was standing no more than six feet away when Harry swung round, the collar of a winter coat turned well up about her face. She neither flinched nor blinked. In her expression it was impossible to detect the slightest reaction to his presence. But in her right hand, where it clasped the strap of her shoulder-bag, there was the faintest of tremors.

'I didn't expect to see you again,' she said neutrally.

'I found her, you know,' Harry replied. 'In Athens.' He timed a pause. 'Small thanks to you.'

513

Still there was no sign of discomposure. Zohra glanced at Mrs Tandy, then back at Harry. 'Why don't you come upstairs? We can talk there.'

But Zohra did not talk. She led the way to her flat, opened the door and closed it behind them, took off her coat and carefully put it away, lit the gas fire and began preparing coffee for one. And throughout she said nothing.

'Heather thought Dysart must have been blackmailing you,' said Harry with stubborn emphasis, following her into the kitchenette. 'Blackmailing you, that is, into deceiving me.' There was no response; she stared intractably at the blue flame playing around the kettle on the stove in front of her. 'I don't know what to think, of course.' Still no response. 'But you *did* deceive me, didn't you?' Another few moments passed; the water in the kettle began to sizzle. '*Didn't you?*'

Zohra reached slowly forward and extinguished the gas. 'Yes,' she said, turning slowly round to face him. 'I deceived you!'

'The suspicions you claimed to have about Dr Kingdom's attitude towards Heather?'

'False.'

'The discrepancies in his itinerary at the Versorelli Institute?'

'Imagined.'

'And the file notes on Heather?'

'Faked.'

'In fact, the whole story, from start to finish, was a pack of lies?'

'Entirely.'

'And you did all this at Dysart's bidding?'

'Yes.'

'Did he tell you why? Did he explain the purpose?'

'No. But I guessed. He was convinced Dr Kingdom was sheltering Heather at the Versorelli Institute. He needed you to flush her out. And he needed evidence to persuade you to do so.'

'And you helped him, knowing what he meant to do to Heather if he ever found her?'

'Yes. But I was sure all along he was mistaken. I was confident you'd fail to find Heather – at the Versorelli Institute or anywhere else.'

'Is that your excuse for what you did? Is that supposed to justify the lies you told me, the distortions, the falsehoods, the misrepresentations?'

'No. Nothing could do that.'

'All right. Forget excuses. What about explanations? Why did you do it?'

'I had no choice.'

'Was Heather right? Was Dysart blackmailing you?'

'In a sense.'

'Threatening to have you deported?'

'Yes.'

'So, to avoid being sent back to Sri Lanka, you were prepared to put Heather in danger – and make a fool of me.'

At last her gaze fell, her chin dropped. Harry felt sympathy surge perversely within him. Then Zohra recovered herself, tossed back her head and confronted him anew. 'Everything you have said is true, Harry. Everything you could say I richly deserve. I betrayed Heather. I deceived you. I abused a position of trust. And I regret it all. I am ashamed of what I have done, bitterly ashamed. I said I had no choice, but of course I did. I could have refused his terms. I could have defied him.'

'Why didn't you?'

'Because I was frightened. There: I have said it. Fear took precedence over loyalty and friendship. Do you think it always must, Harry?'

'No.'

'Neither do I. Which makes it doubly sad, doesn't it?' She shivered. 'It's cold in here. Come and sit by the fire.'

Harry followed her back into the lounge; she lowered herself wearily into an armchair in front of the gas fire. But

515

Harry remained standing, keeping his distance, waiting for her to continue.

'My work permit was due to expire at the end of June last year. I'd already been told it wouldn't be renewed: the Home Office wanted me to leave the country. I said nothing to Dr Kingdom because I was afraid he would dismiss me straightaway if he knew I might have to resign at short notice. Instead, I confided in Heather. Knowing her sister had worked for an MP, I thought she might be able to influence the authorities. She was very sympathetic and arranged an introduction to Alan Dysart. He seemed equally sympathetic and promised to do what he could. That turned out to be quite a lot, because I was immediately granted a three-month extension. Naturally, I asked him what the chances were of a longer-term extension and that's when he began to apply pressure. The chances were good, he said, if I helped him.'

'To do what?'

'Spy on Dr Kingdom. He wanted to know every detail of Heather's case. He wanted copies of every note Dr Kingdom kept and every letter he sent pertaining to her. He wanted me to report anything he said about her and everything he said to me. He wanted it all.'

'And you agreed to give it to him?'

'Yes. It seemed harmless enough at first. And, sure enough, another three-month extension was my reward. Then Heather disappeared. I tried to persuade myself that the information I was passing to Dysart had nothing to do with it. By then he'd begun to suspect Heather and Dr Kingdom were in league. That changed to a firm conviction when you told him you'd seen Dr Kingdom in Lindos a few days before Heather's disappearance. My instructions were to plant the idea in your mind that Dr Kingdom was holding her against her will at the Versorelli Institute. I never asked them for the dates and times of his appointments there. I merely relayed to you the dates and times which Dysart calculated would arouse your suspicion. As for the file notes, they were a mixture of genuine

516

material and Dysart's own concoctions, slanted to support his theory. Our nervous conferences and secret rendezvous were simply designed to compound the effect.'

Harry remembered the double of Heather Miltiades had sent after him in Rhodes. Then and ever since, it seemed, he had been grasping at shadows and pursuing impostors. 'When we took Mrs Tandy to the cemetery,' he said, not troubling to disguise the bitterness of his tone, 'a man photographed us. Were you expecting that?'

'Yes. Dysart had warned me. But I didn't know why it was done.'

Zohra did not know, but Harry could guess. He had believed Kingdom was behind it: that was what he had been intended to believe, that and all the rest. 'What was your reward this time?' he asked.

'Permanent residential rights.'

'And they made it all worthwhile?'

'They seemed to, yes.'

'So you're satisfied – even if nobody else is?'

'Not exactly.' For the first time since sitting down, she looked directly at him. 'You could say I'd had my reward all right, Harry, but it isn't the one I'd hoped for. Even if Dysart intended to honour his promise, his fall from power means he's in no position to. It leaves my case tainted by association, linked with his name in the eyes of the Home Office. As a result, I go down with him. See that letter on the mantelpiece?'

There was a crumpled manila envelope propped behind a china crocodile. 'Yes,' said Harry. 'I see it.'

'Take a look at it.'

He picked the envelope up and slid out the single sheet inside.

'It's a deportation order,' said Zohra. 'I'm to be gone by the end of the month. And believe me, it's no forgery.'

Harry glanced down at the piece of paper in his hand and let his eye wander for a moment across the bureaucratic prose. 'You are required to leave the United Kingdom

517

by the thirty-first day of January . . . . No right of further appeal against this ruling . . . . In the event of non-compliance, forcible deportation to your country of origin will ensue . . . .' Then he replaced the letter in its envelope and met her gaze with neither sympathy nor condemnation. 'Is it really so bad?'

'Oh yes, Harry, it's very bad. I have a distant cousin on my mother's side who's a solicitor. I've been to see him this week in the hope that I could contest the ruling or at least go somewhere other than Sri Lanka. But the case is hopeless and he doubts any other country would admit me.'

'So you'll go back to Sri Lanka?'

'I must. There's no alternative.'

'Well, I'm sure you'll soon settle—'

'You don't understand. My brother Arjuna is a prominent member of the Tamil separatist movement. The government regards him as a dangerous terrorist. There's not much they wouldn't be prepared to do to force him to surrender to the army. By returning I would become their hostage. Ever since Arjuna went underground three years ago, I've been trying to avoid a return to Sri Lanka – for my sake and for his. That's why I was prepared to do as Dysart asked. Had the need not been so pressing—' She looked away. 'Never mind. Never mind what I might have done or should have done. That letter is the consequence of what I did do. That letter is my just reward.'

Now it was Harry who averted his gaze. What Zohra had said could not excuse her conduct, but it had succeeded in planting in his mind a disturbing thought: what would he have done in her position? He returned the letter to its place on the mantelpiece and stared down into the mischievous eyes of the china crocodile. She had tried to warn him, had she not? In her own way, she had urged caution upon him. 'Be careful,' she had said to him as he prepared to leave for Geneva. 'Be very careful.'

The telephone was ringing. Seemingly from a great distance, but actually from just the other side of the room, its insistent note forced its way into Harry's thoughts. He heard Zohra rise from the chair and walk slowly across to answer it, so slowly that he half expected it to stop before she reached it. But it did not stop.

'Hello? . . . What? . . . ' Something in her tone made Harry turn and look towards her. She was pale and trembling. 'Yes, but . . . . Very well.' She looked at Harry. 'It's Dysart. He wants to speak to you.'

How Harry crossed the room, how he took the telephone from Zohra's hand, what glance passed between them as he did so, he could not afterwards have said. As soon as he heard Dysart speak, his world shrank to the dark realm of that distant voice. All else lay beyond his perception.

'Harry?'

'How did you know I was here?'

'I saw you go in. I followed you from Minter's flat. From Swindon, as a matter of fact.'

'Where are you now?'

'Nearby. It doesn't matter where. You couldn't find me if you tried.'

'What do you want?'

'To meet, that's all. To talk. To understand each other.'

'Where and when?'

'Tyler's Hard. Four o'clock this afternoon. Can you be there?'

'Yes, but—'

'No more until we meet. I'm trusting you, Harry. Come alone and come on time.'

64

Four o'clock. A still and cloudless day that had known a few deceptive hours of mildness was releasing its feeble hold. Colour and warmth were fleeing as the light failed, draining all comfort from the motionless trees, the calm water, the winding lane, the empty fields. Harry heard his own footfalls and no other sound as he walked towards Tyler's Hard, the jetty casting out its shadowed finger across the estuary, the house unlit and silent, crouched and withdrawn, unwelcoming yet expectant.

The gate stood open. Harry looked about, noting the absence of a car, the lack of a bonfire, the chill breath of emptiness hovering at the blank windows and smokeless chimneys. He walked through the gate and on towards the front door of the cottage. Nothing moved. Nothing rustled or flickered or hinted at a presence. Yet the certainty of being observed was absolute and incontrovertible. *'Come alone and come on time.'* He had done both and was not, he knew, to be cheated now.

The door was ajar. It creaked as he pushed it open, then silence was reimposed. A short passage, stairs and a kitchen towards the rear, doors to either side of him, both ajar. Then, at last, independent sound. Wood on wood. Something closing, gently, like a desk-lid being slowly lowered, in the left-hand room. With little consciousness of movement, he headed towards it. And entered, as if waking far from where sleep had begun, as if re-discovering a place he had never visited before.

It was a small and conventionally furnished lounge dimly perceived in the twilight that lace curtains had filtered to a grey and shifting herald of total darkness. Harry saw Dysart standing in the corner one second before he snapped on the standard lamp beside him, an erect and unmoving figure lost in a sudden flood of brilliance.

'Hello, Harry.'

His voice was unaltered, assured and mellow of tone. His clothes were impeccable – shoes polished, trousers pressed, shirt an unblemished white. And he was smiling. Beneath the swept-back fair hair, he was smiling. Only in the eyes – only in their fractional loss of clarity and confidence – could any trace of change be detected.

'It was good of you to come as I asked.'

As Harry approached, he saw Dysart was standing by a low glass-topped cabinet, with medals displayed on a green baize bed within. The thought that the sound of its lid being closed was what he had heard from the passage caused his gaze to linger on the contents.

'Mostly my maternal grandfather's,' said Dysart. 'He commanded a cruiser at Jutland, you know. He died before I was born, but stories of his achievements made me want to follow him into the Royal Navy. I think he'd have been proud of my career, but I can't be sure. He might have held it against me that I wasn't really his grandson at all.'

It was said. It was admitted. It was conceded between them. Harry looked up from the colourful ribbons and their pendant medals to see that Dysart was still smiling, still enfolding him in the strange intimacy of a friendship he had betrayed but not renounced. 'I met Barry Chipchase in Athens,' Harry said slowly and deliberately, so that his meaning could not be mistaken. 'By chance.'

'And he told you about the grave in Solihull?'

'Yes.'

A dry chuckle. 'I might have known even chance would turn against me.'

'You weren't Gordon Dysart's son?'

'They adopted me, Harry, when their only child, Alan,

died of polio. They adopted me and gave me his name. They made of me a likeness of a little boy who had died. And they never told me that I was not their true issue, not their rightful heir, not their son at all. A month after I went up to Oxford my father died, bequeathing me his fortune, his house, his business empire . . . and a sealed letter courtesy of his solicitor informing me of the long ⸰overdue truth. I had built, I had planned, I had prepared every detail of what my generation of the Dysarts was to be and suddenly it was rendered pointless. I was not and never could be his son.'

'Whose son were you?'

'According to the letter, my father didn't know. A nameless orphan of unidentified parents. That was all the information he cared to impart. That, now he and my mother were both dead, was all he thought I was due. Except for my inheritance of course, my inexhaustible, inexpungeable inheritance. I was wealthy, able and much envied. Yet in my heart I was reduced to a beggar, a chance beneficiary of a rich man's charity.'

'Is this what Everett found out?'

'Yes. That I wasn't a Dysart. That I wasn't what I claimed to be.'

'And you killed him to stop him telling others?'

'Ramsey Everett was a swine, Harry, a cruel and vindictive swine. He reckoned I'd do a great deal to avoid the embarrassment his revelations would cause me. He was perpetually in debt through living beyond his means and wanted me to pay off his creditors in return for his silence. I didn't plan to murder him, I didn't plan to do anything. It happened in a flash, a burst of anger. And it was so easy. He was standing by the window – low-silled and fully open – reciting the squalid details of what he would make known if I rejected his demands, when I lunged at him and he hurtled backwards into the night with such a surprised look on his face that I don't think he could believe what had happened until he hit the flagstones.'

Dysart took several quick steps across the room, as if a

522

certain distance was suddenly necessary, a certain remoteness across which to admit all that he had kept hidden for so long. Yet still, as he faced Harry again, there were the overtures of a smile about the lines of his mouth.

'The rest – the other murders, real and attempted – followed from that one impulsive act. But I needn't tell you, need I Harry, since Jack already has. You met him in Athens, didn't you?'

'Yes.'

'I thought so. I thought he'd choose you to confide in. Tell me, did he ask you to pass on any kind of message for me?'

'Is that why you wanted to see me?'

'No. There were other more compelling reasons. But I'd still like to know if there was a message.'

'There was. He asked me to say you'd left him no choice.'

'No choice? Well, perhaps he's right. Anything else?'

'And he forgives you.'

Some spasm that might have been a stifled sob convulsed Dysart. Clapping his hand to his brow, he moved to the fireplace and leaned heavily against the mantelpiece. Then he seemed to regain control of himself. He squared his shoulders and looked back at Harry. 'I made a pact with Jack never to reveal what we mean to each other and I shan't break it now.' With that explanation, he shrugged off his sudden descent into frailty. 'He told you everything, I suppose: how we set about preventing Willy giving evidence at the inquest into Everett's death; what we did to frustrate Clare's attempts at blackmail; what I proposed to do to stop Heather discovering the truth about her sister's death.'

'Yes. All of it.'

'And how I manipulated you into finding Heather on my behalf?'

'That too.'

'Bad, isn't it, Harry? Beneath contempt. Beyond forgiveness. And what you're wondering is: why did I do it? how could I bring myself to? I killed Everett in the heat of the moment. But sabotaging Willy's car and booby-trapping the *Artemis* before tricking Clare into going aboard: they were planned; they were premeditated.' Dysart shook his head in rueful recollection. 'It's strange, isn't it, what you find out about yourself when you're forced into a corner? Turning round from the window through which I'd just pushed Everett to his death, confident that I'd got clean away with it, I suddenly saw Willy staring at me from the doorway with a look of genuine horror on his face. I knew then that, one way or another, I'd have to silence him. And I knew as well that I'd stop at nothing to do it. Of course, I believed then that it would end with Willy. Later, I even tried to square my conscience by giving him employment and accommodation here. And I wasted no time in taking steps to ensure there were no records for anyone else to follow where my origins were concerned. Since disposing of the last piece of such evidence – my namesake's gravestone in Solihull – I'd assumed my secret was completely safe. And so it would have been, if Clare hadn't tried to use me to realize her political ambitions.'

'Was she really pregnant by you?'

'Yes. A foolish lapse. I was tired and depressed at the time and not a little drunk. She chose her moment well, I can't deny that. But I don't care to be threatened, Harry. Those who have tried that game with me have lived to regret it.'

'Was Heather threatening you?'

'No.' Dysart sighed. 'She would have been the first completely innocent victim.'

'And I was to lead you to her?'

'Yes. I'm sorry, Harry, but there was no-one else I could trust.'

'Or use?'

'That too, perhaps. Fame is a handicap, you see. Once Heather had vanished, I had to assume the worst: that she'd realized what I was planning to do; that she'd gone into hiding, probably with Kingdom's help, and meant to

524

stay there until she'd gathered enough evidence to move against me. So I couldn't let her remain hidden. I had to find her before she had a chance to piece together a case. Yet I couldn't be the one to look for her. I was too well-known, too conspicuous. I needed somebody else to do the looking for me. You already had a good reason of your own to want to find her and you trusted me. What more effective camouflage could there be? You became my surrogate, Harry, my plenipotentiary, my sergeant-at-arms.'

'Then why set Vigeon on my tail?'

'Because I had to be sure you weren't holding anything back. I had to be certain you were telling me as much as you knew. At the same time, I couldn't risk you losing heart or coming to suspect there wasn't really anything sinister behind Heather's disappearance. I know you better than you do yourself, Harry. Nothing could drive you on more effectively than the conviction that somebody was trying to stop you. Hence the messages, the phone calls, the photographs. Hence Vigeon letting you realize he was following you. And hence the heavy-handed warning-off from the police. Not Charlie Mallender's doing at all – but mine.'

'What about Zohra Labrooy?'

'She was a mere auxiliary, useful for keeping you on what I judged to be the right course.'

'You realize she faces deportation?'

'Yes. It's unfortunate, but I can't do anything to prevent it now. The irony is that her labours on my behalf were in vain. Dr Kingdom turned out to know nothing about any of it. Which makes your achievement in finding Heather all the more remarkable. How *did* you manage it?'

'Do you really want to know?'

'Perhaps not. Perhaps it's better left unsaid. But tell me this, Harry: can you follow Jack's example; can you forgive me?'

'No. I don't think I can.'

'Why not? Because of the murders? Or because I made a fool of you?'

The point lanced home. It was difficult to summon wrath on behalf of dead strangers, easy to do so in search of revenge for injured pride. 'I can't forgive you for any of it.'

'You will. Very shortly, you will.'

'Why?'

'Patience, Harry. Patience for a little longer. There's something you must understand first. This isn't an excuse, this isn't special pleading, but it is something closer to the truth of why I did these things than I've ever admitted before, even to myself. My birth, my life, my family: they were all built on a lie; the lie that I was what people thought me. Well, I've gone on telling that lie ever since. Behaving as somebody in my position should behave. Believing what somebody of my social standing should believe. I've grinned and I've fawned my way through Oxford, the Royal Navy and Her Majesty's Government. I've succeeded in everything and failed in nothing. And do you know what I've learned from all these cheap victories and easy triumphs? That at the centre there's nothing: a vacuum, a void representing the lie that everybody else lives as well as me. Honour. Loyalty. Integrity. Patriotism. Morality. Merit. They mean nothing. Hypocrisy is our sovereign and pretence the heir apparent. That's why I've no regrets about betraying or disappointing the pack of fools and rogues who are baying for my blood now I've been found out. Because what my guilty secret says about their judgement enrages them far more than what it says about my honesty. All that admiration, all that promotion, all that respect I cheated out of them is gagging in their throats, gouging at their inflated opinion of themselves. What they resent more than anything is what my disgrace proves about the palm-greasing back-scratching sham of a society they run.'

'Is everything a sham then? Even friendship?'

'No.' In Dysart's eyes there was a depth of appeal his harsh words had lacked. 'Not friendship. Wouldn't you agree I'd been a good friend to you?'

'Yes, but—'

'And I'd have gone on being one.'

'What if I'd come to the same conclusion as Heather? What if I'd realized that you'd murdered her sister – as well as Everett?'

Dysart smiled. 'Even then.'

'Are you sure you wouldn't have arranged another fatal accident, this time for me?'

'Quite sure, Harry, quite sure.' A winsome, almost nostalgic look had come to his face. 'You see, in a curious sense, I did it all for you.'

'For *me*?'

'There's something I ought to explain to you. Ramsey Everett did rather more than discover I wasn't Gordon Dysart's son. He discovered whose son I really was. What I later went to such great lengths to conceal wasn't the fact that I'd been adopted, but the fact that I was in reality the son of a murderer.'

'A *murderer*?'

Again, the sad, reflective smile. 'Paul and Gwendolen Stobart. They're just names of course, but they happen to be the names of my real parents. What little I know about them I'll tell you. Paul Stobart was a London docker more often out of work than in, with a history of drunkenness and violence. Gwendolen, his wife, originated from South Wales. They lived in a terraced house in Bermondsey. My arrival probably strained their finances as well as their tolerance of each other. It seems clear that Paul Stobart often beat his wife and it's possible she feared for my safety as well as her own. Whatever the exact cause, matters came to a head only a matter of days after my birth. At the height of an argument overheard by neighbours, Gwendolen stabbed and battered her husband to death with a bread-knife and a poker. She then fled, taking me with her. For several months, there was no trace of her. Then a woman who'd recently gassed herself to death in a flat in Cardiff was identified as Gwendolen Stobart. The search was over.'

'What about the . . . . What about you?'

'By then I was in an orphanage, with no clue to whose child I was. But Gwendolen Stobart left a note, saying where and when she'd abandoned me, and so the mystery of my identity was resolved. There being no surviving relatives of either parent, it was decided I should stay where I was. And since the Stobarts hadn't even given me a name or registered my birth when the murder occurred, it was agreed that anonymity was the kindest state to leave me in. It was in that state that the Dysarts found me when seeking a child of the same age and sex as their dead son Alan. Nobody saw fit to tell them the truth about me. Perhaps, by then, there was nobody on hand who knew the truth. Certainly my parents lived and died in happy ignorance of who I really was. It took the tenacity and ingenuity of Ramsey Everett to winkle the facts about me out of the archives. Do you know one of the last things he said to me, Harry? Do you know how he tried to twist the knife? I can still hear his high, piping, sarcastic voice. "I might make your case the centre-piece of my thesis, old man." Can you imagine being forced to listen to such stuff? "Or perhaps we could put a motion up for debate in the Tyrrell Society on whether the murderous instinct is hereditary." God in heaven, can you blame me for what I did?' Twenty years on, the anger Everett had inspired still blazed in Dysart's face, the violent reaction still quivered beneath the surface of his speech.

'Perhaps not,' said Harry, shocked into mildness by Dysart's vehemence. 'But what about . . . what about . . . .'

'The others?' Dysart shook his head dismissively. 'I can't claim mitigation where they're concerned. Perhaps Everett had a point when he mentioned heredity. Perhaps it's something of a self-fulfilling prophecy. Or perhaps – as I've proved – the second murder is easier than the first and the third is easier than the second and the fourth . . . .' He looked straight at Harry, willing him, it seemed, to believe what he was saying. 'Jack was right to pull the rug from under me. I had to stop. It had to be ended. And the way he chose was the only way that would work. With Jack gone, there's nothing left I want or need, nothing I'd be prepared to kill or die for. The game is up. The chase is—' He broke off abruptly and signalled with his finger against his lips for silence, as if he had heard something Harry had not. He stood stock still for a moment, then moved swiftly to the standard lamp, switched it off, twitched back the lace curtain and peered out of the window.

'What's wrong?'

'I'm not sure. Something outside. A car in the lane, I think.'

'Is that so—'

'It's Willy!' There was an urgency in Dysart's voice, a sudden tightening of his grasp on the curtain. 'I've been wondering where he'd taken himself off to. He doesn't usually stray far.'

Harry craned over Dysart's shoulder and made out Morpurgo's crooked, shuffling figure approaching along the path from the gate. He was dressed, as before, in beret and boiler suit, and though the light was too bad to see if he still wore the Breakspear tie around his neck, Harry felt sure that he did. 'Surely Morpurgo can't drive,' he whispered.

'Just so, Harry, just so. Somebody must have dropped him off.'

'Won't he go back to the garage flat?' For some reason Harry found himself hoping he would do exactly that.

'It doesn't look like it. He seems to be coming this way.' Dysart stepped back from the window. 'Wait here. I'll go and speak to him. Don't come out. Seeing you might alarm him.'

Dysart strode swiftly from the room, leaving Harry alone in the half-light. When he glanced back through the window, Morpurgo was no longer visible. At the same instant, Dysart's voice carried through the half-open doorway from the hall.

'Hello, Willy. Where have you been?'

No answer.

529

'I was getting worried about you.'

Still no answer.

'Have you had a visitor?'

At last Morpurgo spoke, in his familiar, lisping, faltering monotone. 'Rex-came-to-see-me.'

'Rex Cunningham?' Dysart's amiability was beginning to ring hollow. 'What did he want?'

'He-told-me-things.'

'What things?'

'About-the-car-crash.'

'What car crash?'

Silence fell, though to Harry's straining ears it seemed that he could detect amidst it the actual breathing of the two men: Dysart's shallow and alert, Morpurgo's nasal and distorted. What looks or signals, what hints or meanings, might be passing between them he could not guess. Instead, his mind ranged desperately over all he had learned since arriving at Tyler's Hard less than half an hour ago. *'I did it all for you.'* What could Dysart mean? What part had Harry played in the sad and twisted record of his life? Suddenly, Morpurgo spoke again and Harry's attention was wrenched back to the present.

'It's-true-isn't-it?'

'What is, Willy?'

'What-Rex-said.'

'What did he say?'

'About-the-car-crash.'

'I don't know what you mean.'

'Yes-you-do.-I-can-see-you-do.-I-can-see-it-in-your-eyes.'

Another chasm of silence opened, this time unmistakably filled by the panting breaths of two frightened men. Harry moved towards the door, then stopped. He had, after all, no right to intervene. Dysart must be left to answer the accusation as best he could.

'It's-true-isn't-it?'

'You've always been well looked after here, Willy.'

But Morpurgo was not to be deflected. 'It's-true-isn't-it?' came back the stubborn staccato.

530

There was a moment of deliberation, then Dysart's patience seemed to snap. 'What if it is?' he sneered. 'What are you going to do about it, Willy, eh? What in the wide world are you going to do?'

'You—' Morpurgo's voice disintegrated in a choking cry. Suddenly, the front door slammed with a force that shook the house. Through the window Harry could hear Morpurgo crying – great wrenching, heaving sobs that died abruptly in a whimper. Then there was a scatter of gravel and the sound of heavy, lurching footfalls on the path, fading rapidly into silence. He had fled.

'Sorry about that,' said Dysart, slipping back into the room with a whimsical smile hovering on his lips.

'What did Cunningham tell him?'

'What do you think? At a guess, I'd say a close approximation to the truth. Now Rex knows about Jack and me, he's quite capable of deducing what happened on the drive to Burford. And capable, it seems, of burdening poor Willy with the knowledge as well.'

'What will Morpurgo do?'

'Do?' Dysart's eyes seemed to focus on some object far beyond the confines of the room. 'I can't imagine. I really can't imagine.' His gaze returned to Harry. 'Now, where were we?'

'But you virtually admitted responsibility for crippling him.'

Dysart ignored the point. 'Have you put the pieces together yet?'

'What?'

'Have you seen the pattern? Have you re-assembled the jigsaw?'

'What pattern? What jigsaw?'

The smile broadened. 'Our life, Harry, yours and mine.'

'I don't know what you mean.'

'Really? You disappoint me. Perhaps a clue would be in order. Paul Stobart was murdered on the night of Thursday the twentieth of March, 1947. Gwendolen Stobart ran away

531

with her son the same night and vanished. Her son was not with her when she committed suicide in Cardiff four months later. He'd been lost along the way.'

'Along the way?'

'Perhaps I should say . . . along the railway.'

Forty years were swept aside like a curtain at Dysart's words. Harry was no longer standing in a cottage in Hampshire, no longer bound by the fatigue and self-pity of his middle age. Suddenly he was eleven years old, school cap askew, hair tousled, blazer button lost on a paling, knees chafed beneath the short serge trousers, shoes scuffed, satchel strapped to his back, tie tucked into his shirt. He was blowing between his mittened hands for warmth, wetting his pencil with his tongue and folding open his book of train numbers as he crouched by the gap in the fence between St Mark's Churchyard and the railway line. He was in Swindon at dusk, on the first raw, snow-covered day of spring in the year of our Lord 1947, unaware of the murder committed in Bermondsey the previous night, unaware that time and chance were about to dictate that his path through life and that of a nameless child who would grow to be Alan Dysart were about to intersect.

No, it was not a pile of snow. It was a cardboard box, propped against the far rail of the down-line, along which the Cardiff express was about to pass. The Cardiff express, number not yet legible but King class, if his luck was really in. Of course, it would squash a cardboard box flat without the driver even noticing. Not that – Hold on. That could not be right. There was something in the box, moving and flexing and, yes, crying, a tiny red-faced white-swaddled bundle that could only be – The train was moving faster, gathering its mighty strength as it left the station, smoke belching from the stack like a storm cloud, steam rolling like seaspray round the thrusting pistons and half-hidden drive-wheels as the whole unstoppable leviathan bore down on one fragile carton and its oblivious occupant. In a minute it would all be over. In less than a minute an infant life would be ended.

There was no time to think, no time to judge or calculate. An impulse of schoolboy derring-do carried Harry through the gap in the fence and across the narrow strip of snow-patched grass. Without hesitation – for he sensed hesitation would be fatal – he started across the three tracks separating him from the box, jumping swiftly from one rail to the next, each one vibrating more strongly than the last, his ears filled with the roar of the train but his eyes fixed only on his objective, his thoughts refined to a fervent prayer that he would neither slip nor stumble. Then he was there, stooping as he leapt, snatching up the box and its contents, clearing two more rails and turning as he came to a halt to see the driver's white and angry face glaring at him from the cab, too shocked to shout what he was doubtless thinking, too surprised to understand what had occurred.

Harry sank slowly to his haunches and set the box down gently in a safe haven between the rails whilst the carriages of the train swept by in a blur. The baby was staring up at him, blue with cold about the fingers and cheeks but apparently unperturbed by its brush with death. Indeed, as Harry peered closer, it seemed to him that the baby was smiling, a slow but genuine smile of unexpected beauty.

A dramatic rescue act yesterday by a Swindon schoolboy saved the life of an abandoned baby. When Harry looked at Dysart, he saw that he was smiling still across the interval of years. *The police have appealed for the mother to come forward as soon as possible.* 'It was you,' he murmured. *They praised young Harold's conduct and described him as a 'brave, quick-witted and resourceful lad'.* 'You were the baby in the box.'

'Yes, Harry. That was me.'

'*What is it, Mr Barnett? What is it here or in you that Dysart clings to? What binds him to you?*' Ellison's words chimed in Harry's mind as he stared in slowly deepening understanding at Dysart's smiling face. The murderer's son who survived to emulate his mother. Alan Dysart and Harry Barnett. One man and his saviour.

'It's why I came to Barnchase Motors and gave you all the help I could. It's why I persuaded Charlie Mallender to take you on. It's why I chose you as caretaker of the *Villa ton Navarkhon*. I've never forgotten what I owe you, Harry. I've never stopped trying to repay you. But how can you repay the gift of life itself?'

'Why did you never say?'

'Because I thought you'd value friendship more highly than gratitude. Because I thought you'd prefer generosity to recompense.'

'But . . . all these years . . . . '

'I've known what you haven't: that but for you I'd be dead.'

The corollary of Dysart's proposition struck Harry with hideous force. 'And your victims . . . would still be alive.'

'Yes.' Dysart nodded in solemn confirmation. 'That too, of course. That too. It's ironic, don't you—'

The door flew open as if hit by a battering ram and crashed against the wall in a scatter of plaster. On the threshold stood Morpurgo, flushed, trembling and breathing heavily, his one eye staring wildly at Dysart. And before him, raised as if to strike, he held a rake.

For a frozen instant, nobody moved. Then Dysart, signalling with his hand behind his back for Harry to retreat across the room, took a single step forward, smiling gently. 'Hello, Willy. What do you —'

A scything blur of the rake caught him on the head and sent him reeling against the wall. There was blood on his forehead and on the prongs of the rake: dark droplets of it spattered across the carpet. Harry gaped at the scene, unable for a moment to believe that it was happening, unable to accept the reality of what he saw: Dysart stooping forward, left hand steadying himself against the wall, right clutching at his brow; and Morpurgo, his breath hissing through his teeth like a piston, his one eye red and unblinking, the rake swinging back in his hands. *A thing, armed with a rake, that seems to strike at me.* The remembered phrase prised its way to the front of Harry's mind and capered there for a ghastly, mocking instant, as if to say: 'Didn't you foresee this? Didn't you realize it was bound to end like this?'

Morpurgo struck again, this time with a savage upward swing that jolted Dysart away from the wall with a blow to the left side of his face. There was blood now on Harry's shirt, blood and something worse blotting and merging across his chest and shoulders as Dysart staggered sideways into the centre of the room, moaning gently with arms spread wide and head uplifted, as if no longer seeking to shield himself or staunch his wounds. Through the gauze of his own disbelief, filtered but not obscured, Harry saw, where Dysart's left eye and cheek should have been, a raw crater of mangled flesh and bone. He and Morpurgo were suddenly equals. And with his other, barely focusing eye, Dysart was staring at Harry, acknowledging the irony of the moment, accepting the justice of what he was suffering.

A third blow, descending from somewhere above Morpurgo's head, a flashing arc of fanged metal that bit and sliced into its victim. A squelching, grinding composition of sound. A splatter of blood and tissue. A hideous, gurgling moan. And Dysart, tumbling slowly backwards into a tall bookcase set against the far wall, books and vases sliding and crashing about him, a shattered, twitching subsidence to the floor, shards of china and torn pages pattering down about him like the last tumbling pebbles of an avalanche.

Morpurgo advanced across the room, rake raised high. Dysart rolled onto his back, blinking up with his right eye from what had been, only a few seconds before, a handsome unmarked face. The torn edges of his mouth rippled, as if trying to speak or smile. His left hand quivered and flexed. And Harry, his limbs at last obeying his orders, lunged forward to block Morpurgo's path. But Morpurgo's strength was that of a man possessed. A single lash of his left arm felled Harry to the floor. And all he could see above him as he looked up was Morpurgo's crouching shape and the slender, saw-headed shadow of the rake stretching itself across the wall behind him, stretching and vanishing as it slashed down into its target, then recoiling to strike again and again and again, the sound of its impact worse than the sight of it could ever have been.

Then the frenzy was over. Less than two minutes after it had begun, it was complete. Dysart was dead. And Morpurgo, with a cry of grief as much as of triumph, flung the rake clattering into a corner, cast one panting glance at his victim, then turned and rushed headlong from the room.

Harry rose to his knees and confronted the butchered remains of Alan Dysart. Twenty years' worth of incoherent rage had found its quietus. What the train had spared the rake had claimed. What Harry had saved Morpurgo had slain. Alan Dysart's day was done.

And there, beside him on the floor, its covers spread flat, its pages creased and torn, was the book he had gone to Strete Barton to retrieve three days before: *The Reign of William Rufus*. Harry pulled it towards him and flipped it open at the fly leaf. Across the inscription and the signature of the book's five donors, visible now where it had always been implicit, lay an indelible circle of Dysart's blood.

65

Halfway through the service it occurred to Harry that this was the first funeral he had attended since Uncle Len's more than forty years ago. Two more contrasting occasions it would have been hard to imagine. For Uncle Len there had been several hymns, a lengthy address by the vicar, a snail's pace cortège to the cemetery, a graveside ululation by one of Harry's great aunts and a boiled ham tea at Falmouth Street. For Alan Dysart three mourners and a mumbling priest had gathered in the antiseptic ambience of Southampton Crematorium, attended by electronic music and a pervading impression of distasteful business being discreetly done.

Before it had seemed properly to begin, it was over. The coffin had slid silently away through the curtain, the music had reached the end of its tape, the last prayer had stuttered to its close and the sparse congregation had begun shuffling towards the exit. Ellison had led the way at the regulation pace, whilst Cyril Ockleton twittered along beside Harry at the rear.

'Extraordinarily poor turn-out, I must say. It was far from convenient for me to leave Oxford at such short notice with term but lately commenced. Nevertheless, I made the effort. Despite the dreadful scandal which Alan inflicted upon the college and the fact that I had to cancel three tutorials, I came. Purely out of a sense of duty, you understand. That and nothing more. And what do I find upon arrival? Well, with all due respect to you and this . . . this . . . . ' He flapped his hand towards the figure now leaving the chapel.

'Ellison. Ministry of Defence.'

'Quite. Well where, I should like to know, is Mrs Dysart?'

'Kitzbühel. Declined to break her holiday.'

'And other members of his family?'

'He had none.'

'What about people he served with in the Navy, then?'

'They sent a floral anchor. You'll see it outside.'

'And his political associates?'

'Washed their hands of him completely.'

'Good God.'

They were beyond the chapel doors now, passing but not pausing to inspect the paltry pair of wreaths that had been received. Ahead, Ellison was thanking the priest, whilst his driver was joking under his breath with the undertaker's men.

'And Rex. I really did expect to find Rex here. Did he send any kind of message?'

'Not that I know of.'

'It is perplexing, Mr Barnett, not to say distressing. This whole business has shaken me, really it has. Alan dead, Willy under arrest and Jack . . . . Tell me, was the newspaper report accurate? Was there really nothing to suggest why Willy set upon Alan in that brutal fashion?'

'Nothing at all.'

Ockleton shook his head. 'It is so uncharacteristic, so completely unlike anything . . . . I do wish Rex had come today, I really do.' He glanced about him. 'Well, I ought to pay my respects to the padre, ought I not? Excuse me, Mr Barnett. Charming to meet you again, quite charming.' With that, and a fleeting handshake, Ockleton bustled off.

Relieved to find himself alone, Harry took a deep breath of the damp grey air and walked slowly away from the crematorium concourse until he had reached a point offering a clear view up the drive. There he stopped and gazed

538

towards the main road for several minutes, so intently that he was unaware of Ellison approaching from behind him until his soft, insistent voice sounded in his ear.

'Looks rather as if we've got away with it, Mr Barnett.'

'Got away with what?'

'A quiet cremation. No press. No television. No curiosity-seekers. Hardly any mourners to speak of.'

'Would you rather there had been none at all?'

'None at all might have been conspicuous in its own right. As it is . . . . ' Ellison sighed. 'From an official viewpoint, Dysart's death is a positive godsend, of course, the more so since the man who killed him is clearly mad as a hatter, thus sparing us all the embarrassment of a trial. I cannot pretend, however, that this conclusion to my investigations does not leave me feeling slightly . . . cheated, shall we say?'

'Why should you feel cheated?'

'Because you still puzzle me, Mr Barnett, you and your late but excellent friend, Alan Dysart.'

Harry said nothing. He continued to stare straight ahead.

'Oh, don't worry. The case is closed. Your secret is safe, safe as . . . the grave, shall we say?' Harry looked round at him. 'The undertaker tells me you've asked for his ashes. Might I ask what you intend to do with them?'

'I intend to scatter them on a railway line.'

Ellison frowned. Clearly he suspected Harry of sarcasm and, equally clearly, he did not relish being its butt. 'I see,' he said slowly. 'Well, I'll bid you good day, Mr Barnett. I don't suppose we'll meet again.' Without offering to shake hands, he turned and walked away.

Five minutes later Harry was still standing in the same place, watching as three vehicles drove away up the crematorium drive. Ellison's official car was in the lead, followed by Ockleton's bedraggled specimen, with the hearse bringing up the rear. As the last of these turned onto the main road and vanished from sight, another vehicle turned in, almost as if it had been awaiting this triple departure as a signal for it to appear. It was a taxi and it came to a halt about halfway down the drive. As soon as he recognized the person who climbed out and began walking towards him, Harry raised his hand in greeting.

'I thought you weren't going to show up,' he said when she was within earshot.

'I nearly didn't,' Zohra replied. 'It seemed to me we'd said all there was to be said.'

'We had.'

'So what's changed?'

'Take a walk in the garden with me and I'll tell you.'

Around the crematorium gravel paths had been laid, winding through wooded glades where faded wreaths propped against tree trunks were a constant reminder of the common cause which brought people to such a place. For a little way, Harry walked in silence, listening to the crunch of his feet on the gravel and the hum of traffic from the nearby motorway. It crossed his mind that to any onlooker studying their appearance – Harry was wearing something that passed for a black suit, Zohra a dark raincoat and beret – it would seem obvious that they were discussing the loss of a mutual friend or relative. The true purpose of their meeting could never be guessed and, even if explained, would probably never be believed.

At the top of a hillock looking down on the chapel, Harry stopped and turned to Zohra. 'I've had an idea,' he said cautiously.

'About what?'

'Your predicament.'

Zohra flushed. 'If you've brought me here so you can have the pleasure of gloating—'

'I don't want to gloat. I want to help.'

She frowned. 'Why?'

Harry gestured vaguely towards the smoke drifting from the crematorium chimney. 'Because everybody's lost: Heather, Dysart, Cornelius, Morpurgo, you, me. We've all stooped or been lured to some form of treachery and none

540

of us has profited by it. You were right. We've all had our just reward.'

'So?'

'So I want to repair some small part of the damage that's been done, salvage something from the wreckage.'

'By helping me?'

'Yes.'

'But you can't help me, Harry. That's just the point. I'm beyond help.'

'I don't think so. If you could obtain immediate entitlement to British citizenship, they'd have to allow you to stay, wouldn't they?'

'What's the point of discussing it? I've exhausted every possibility there is.'

'Not quite. There's one way you haven't tried.'

'What way?'

'Well . . . . ' He smiled uncertainly. 'You could marry me.'

She stared at him in silent incredulity.

'I realize I'm not much of a catch. Twice your age, unemployed, penniless, all that and worse. On the other hand—'

'Stop it!'

'Today's the twentieth, Zohra. You don't have to leave for another eleven days. Ample time to arrange a register office wedding, I should have thought. This cousin of yours, the solicitor in Newcastle: he could confirm it would let you off the hook.'

'You're proposing a marriage of convenience – a legal fiction – to save me from deportation?'

'Not so fictitious if the authorities are to be persuaded it isn't just a ploy. We'd have to live together, at least for a while. After that . . . . Well, I don't know. But yes, it is what I'm proposing.'

'Why should you be prepared to do this for somebody you owe absolutely nothing?'

'I told you.'

'But what's the real reason?'

541

The real reason lay forty-two years in the past on a railway line in Swindon: Harry's finest hour, tainted forever by every one of the consequences it had scattered across the future. If he had known what rescuing the baby in the box was to lead to, he would never have intervened. If he had understood what his action was bound to mean for himself and others, he would have walked away across the churchyard and let fate take its course. Zohra's plight was just one fruit, by no means the most bitter, of the seed sown that day, but it offered Harry his only meagre chance of redemption. And this time the decision was not his to take. 'I just don't see why *everyone* has to lose,' he said. 'That's all.'

'I'm to be the lucky exception?'

'You can be. Perhaps we can be. It's up to you now.'

THE END

OUT OF THE SUN
by Robert Goddard

Harry Barnett is shocked to learn that he has a son – David Venning, a brilliant mathematician, now languishing in hospital in a diabetic coma. And this is only the first and smallest of the mysteries he is about to encounter.

David's condition is attributed to an accident or suicide attempt. But Harry discovers that his mathematical notebooks are missing from the hotel room where he was found and two other scientists employed by the same American forecasting institute have died in suspicious circumstances. Driven on by the slim hope of saving the son he never knew he had, Harry goes in search of the truth and finds himself entangled in several different kinds of conspiracy – none of which he ought to stand the slightest chance of defeating.

Harry Barnett was the flawed hero of Robert Goddard's earlier novel, the award-winning *Into The Blue*. But nothing in that experience prepared him – or the reader – for the baffling conundrums and heart-stopping suspense of *Out Of The Sun*.

0 552 14224 7

A LIST OF OTHER ROBERT GODDARD TITLES AVAILABLE FROM CORGI BOOKS AND BANTAM PRESS

THE PRICES SHOWN BELOW WERE CORRECT AT THE TIME OF GOING TO PRESS. HOWEVER TRANSWORLD PUBLISHERS RESERVE THE RIGHT TO SHOW NEW PRICES ON COVERS WHICH MAY DIFFER FROM THOSE PREVIOUSLY ADVERTISED IN THE TEXT OR ELSEWHERE.

All Transworld titles are available by post from:

Book Service By Post, P.O. Box 29, Douglas, Isle of Man IM99 1BQ

Credit cards accepted. Please telephone 01624 675137, fax 01624 670923, Internet http://www.bookpost.co.uk or e-mail: bookshop@enterprise.net for details.

Free postage and packing in the UK. Overseas customers allow £1 per book (paperbacks) and £3 per book (hardbacks).